DREAM OF REASON

DREAM OF REASON

Rosa Chacel

Translated by Carol Maier

University of

Nebraska Press

Lincoln

Publication of this
book was assisted
by a grant from the
NATIONAL
ENDOWMENT
FOR THE ARTS
National Endowment
A great nation
deserves great art.
for the Arts.

Publication of this book was assisted by a grant
from the Program for Cultural Cooperation
between Spain's Ministry of Culture and the
United States' Universities.

Library of Congress
Cataloging-in-Publication Data

Chacel, Rosa, 1898–1994.
[Sinrazón. English]
Dream of reason / Rosa Chacel ; translated by
Carol Maier.
p. cm. — (European women writers series)
Includes bibliographical references.
ISBN 978-0-8032-1473-6 (cloth : alk. paper) —
ISBN 978-0-8032-6364-2 (pbk. : alk. paper)
I. Maier, Carol, 1943–. II. Title.
PQ7797.C412S513 2009
863'.64—dc22
2009010022

Set in Carter & Cone Galliard by
Kimberly Essman.
Designed by A. Shahan.

FOR TIMO

O Timothy, keep that
which is committed
to thy trust.

SAINT PAUL

Contents

Where we pursue happiness, always belated.
ROSMARIE WALDROP, "At the Sea"

Translator's Introduction

CAROL MAIER

Rosa Chacel and *La sinrazón*

Were Rosa Chacel alive to write some prefatory words for *Dream of Reason*, she might well begin by recalling the introduction she wrote in 1977 for the book's third edition in Spanish (also included in the present volume).[1] She might remark too that both moments in the life of *La sinrazón*, which many readers and critics consider her most significant work, occur after a long absence. In the case of *La sinrazón*'s translation into English, the novel's first into any other language, she would not surprise us if she noted that almost fifty years had passed since the book's initial publication in 1960 and that the book was written during a period when she had little access to contemporary literature and philosophy. As Chacel commented in 1964, upon reading Sartre's *Being and Nothingness*, she realized that her own work, even her most recent, was "out of date" or worse, since it was filled with "things" that could seem rooted in the thinking of the French philosopher. The "coincidences of thought and even, at times, of words," she wrote in her diary, "would terrify me . . . if it weren't for the fact that those coincidences aren't only in *La sinrazón* and a few stories, whose publication dates I can't recall, but also in *Estación. Ida y vuelta* [Station. Departure and Return], written between 1925 and 1926" (*Alcancía. Ida* [Coin Bank. Departure] 358–59). The knowledge that *Estación*, her first novel, had been written and published (1930) well before Sartre published *Being and Nothingness* and that it had indeed been original reassured her, but she was also reminded of the unfortunate circumstances that had prevented the novel from reaching the readership she knew it deserved. As if to explain those circumstances and the close relationship between *Estación* and *La sinrazón*, Chacel wrote the dense but informative essay that accompanied the third edition of *La sinrazón* and its subsequent publication in 1989 as the first volume of her *Obra completa* [Complete Works]. Work that appears late may only appear belated, she seemed to remind her readers, and she would likely do the same with respect to its insertion into a language and literature in which it has previously enjoyed no presence.

Rosa Chacel was seventy-eight years old when she signed that introduction to *La sinrazón*. Much of her major work had been written; however, only recently had it become truly accessible to readers in her native country.[2] The same could be said about Chacel herself. She had left Spain in 1937 during the Civil War and spent two and a half decades abroad, much of that time in South America, where she had published most of her work. After making the first of several visits to Madrid in 1962, she had resettled there permanently in 1974. New editions of several titles had been published in the early 1970s, and she had begun to receive significant notice from the press. Despite that recognition and her close friendships with not a few Spanish writers and intellectuals, including several much younger writers who had played an important role in disseminating her work in Spain,[3] it was not until the late 1970s and early 1980s that Chacel became well known as a writer and garnered numerous honors and awards. For example, *Barrio de Maravillas* (*The Maravillas District*), the first volume of her autobiographical trilogy, received the Premio de la Crítica prize in 1976.

In view of her long absence and relative lack of contact with Spanish readers, Chacel availed herself of opportunities to present and discuss her work in essays, interviews, and lectures and by providing substantial introductions to new editions of the two novels she considered her most "personal" and "authentic." Those novels were *La sinrazón* and *Estación. Ida y vuelta*, the book she referred to as the "embryo" of *La sinrazón*. In the introductions she explained the circumstances in which she wrote the two books, the motive that informed them, and, in the case of *La sinrazón*, the integral relation between them. Almost invariably, in her commentaries she emphasized the continuity of her work over the years, affirming her participation in and stressing her fidelity to the artistic experimentation that had occurred in Spain during its "Silver Age" of the 1920s and early 1930s. Those years saw Spanish writers and artists born in the last decade of the nineteenth century and the first decade of the twentieth participating, as Roberta Johnson has explained, in "all the major vanguard currents—cubism, futurism, surrealism, expressionism, and dada" ("Context" 217).[4]

The writers in that group, known collectively as the Generation of '27, had achieved international attention as a generation of poets. One thinks, for example, of Federico García Lorca, Rafael Alberti, and Luis Cernuda, the youngest members, or of Jorge Guillén, Pedro Salinas, or even the Nobel Prize winner Juan Ramón Jiménez, all born several years earlier but often included as well. The very name of the generation refers to the outpouring of poetry associated with the celebration of the three hundredth anniversary of the Spanish poet Luis de Góngora and his extraordinarily complex work with metaphor. Not all members of the Generation of '27 were poets, however. As Chacel explains in her essay "Sendas perdidas de la generación del '27" (Lost Paths of the Generation of '27), her contemporaries also included such distinguished figures as philosopher María Zambrano and various writers of avant-garde prose. Their names, with the exception of Francisco Ayala, are less than familiar today, even to most Spanish readers, but during the 1920s and early 1930s they too produced highly experimental work, much of it marked, like the work of the poets, by intricate use of metaphor. Unlike the poets, though, they had neither the rallying point of the Góngora celebration nor a group of slightly older and established writers whose innovations and persons they admired and with whom they felt an affinity. Indeed, Chacel refers to the "abyss" that separated nineteenth-century realist prose (in which "not a single line . . . signifies a step forward" with respect to form) from that of the new century ("Sendas" 241), noting as well the absence of adhesion among the prose writers and the unfortunate circumstances that led to ill health and early death in the case of several. Only Ayala became, despite the years he spent in exile, a major presence in Spain and Spanish letters, and as Chacel herself lamented ("Sendas" 251–52), and he has explained, his later work veered from the avant-garde writing he associated with a well-defined period of his youth (94–97).

The prose writers, however, did have the example and inspiration of Spanish philosopher and aesthetician José Ortega y Gasset, who, according to Chacel, prompted the energy and confidence that gave rise to the innovations of an entire generation. Over the years, Chacel would take issue with some of Ortega's ideas and actions, but she consistently credited his prose with awakening in her and others a receptivity to the innovations in thought and writing occurring in Europe as well as a sense of possibility—"algo que puede ser" (something that can be) ("Sendas" 233). She never studied with Ortega, and she had not yet met him when, in 1924, she began to plan her first novel. But she was familiar with his work, which she had recently begun to read, in particular, *Meditaciones del Quijote* (*Meditations on Quixote*) and *El Espectador* (The Spectator). To meditate on the former, as she explained in the introduction to *Estación* written in 1974, "was to follow our path . . . , our eyes open to everything that passed and everything that remained" (11). Just this exercise in itself held the potential for "saving" not only "things" but also one's world and one's existence as an individual being; for, to quote Ortega as quoted by Chacel, "I am my self and my circumstances and, if I fail to save my circumstance, I fail to save my self" (*Estación* 11).

Chacel's circumstances were rich and complex during the years she wrote *Estación*. She was living in Rome, where her husband, painter Timoteo Pérez Rubio, had a grant to study at the Academia de España. The couple had recently married, having met in Madrid in 1915, when Chacel enrolled in the Escuela de Bellas Artes de San Fernando, where she briefly studied sculpture before withdrawing for health-related reasons and lack of vocation. She had begun to study art when she was quite young, but she had also written at an early age. Although she received little formal schooling, as she recounts in *Desde el amanecer* (Since Daybreak), the autobiography of her first ten years, her parents had strong artistic interests and talents and were excellent teachers. Since she was a voracious reader of philosophy, poetry, and prose—of Kant, Kierkegaard, and Schopenhauer, for example, or Heidegger, Nietzsche, and Rilke, to whom she referred as her "continual phantasms" (*Alcancía. Vuelta* [Coin Bank. Return] 110)—by the time she went to Rome she knew that she wanted to be a writer and that she would work in the novelistic form. She had written poetry and would continue to do so, but as she explained late in life in an introduction to a collection of poems whose publication she had previously forbidden, the passion for classical form she acquired in her childhood was at odds with the flexibility and risk taking that characterized the poetry of her generation (*Poesía* 257). In Rome, reading the work of Ortega, she thought deeply about Spain and intensified her commitment to the innovation of Spanish prose. She also read Spanish translations of writers such as Freud and Joyce, which introduced her to current developments in psychology and fiction; she often credited *Portrait of the Artist as a Young Man* for awakening her to the full range of possibilities available to the novel, in particular to the possibility of writing poetry in prose ("Poesía y prosa" 9). Proust she would also read, but in the original, once she arrived in Rome; like the wealth of other readings, contacts, and travels afforded by her stay there, it would influence the writing of her novels.

Ortega's influence remained paramount with respect to Chacel's ambition to write. In her 1977 introduction to *La sinrazón* she describes that ambition, making explicit, although metaphorically, her conviction (which she shared with Ortega) that "to explore the full range of possibilities of the novel" is an organic, biological endeavor that implies altering the formation of human thought. Such an endeavor, she explains in "Respuesta a Ortega" (Response to Ortega), an essay about Ortega written in 1956, is based on the "intimate relations with ideas" prompted by Ortega's writing (376). Or, in less metaphorical terms, her goal in writing *Estación* was to situate the plot of her plotless novel precisely in the place where the effort to invent a new Spain, now open to the experimentation happening in the rest of Europe, was occurring.[5] That place, she explained, was "the Spanish mind" or, perhaps in this context, more accurately "Spanish thought" ("Respuesta" 17). This effort, however, she quickly clarifies, is not a struggle to change values or ideas in the way efforts to influence minds are usually conceived. Rather, her goal was to "novelize" the very course of an individual's thinking, the act (of thought) that precedes thought in action.

Consequently, to narrate would not be to recount a series of ordinary events but rather, as Ana Rodríguez has explained, to use those events as "pretext" for exploring human consciousness and literary creation by inventing a chain of image-driven sequences in the mind of an unnamed protagonist who travels through three stages of his relationship with his wife: a "station" that serves as his point of departure; a trip away from that point; and a return to it (Rodríguez in Mangini, Introducción 27). That protagonist, as he thinks and writes, struggles to articulate—from within—the complex nature of his circumstances and the nature of human interrelationship in general. Indeed, at time these thoughts are not his but those of his wife. Hints of various incidents from his life flicker obliquely in the narrative, but they are never narrated in any conventional mode. Instead, they give rise to or are embedded in meditation and introspection as the protagonist considers the impossibility of seeing himself from without and realizes that true life ("verdadera vida"), life at its most intense, is inevitably life shared—collaborative, "communistic" life (*Estación* 59). Even the affirmation of an incipient new life at the end of the novel owes not so much to an event as to his having followed an experiment through to its conclusion and thereby achieving the freedom to embark on a new project.

As Chacel explained in 1977, she experienced a similar sense of beginning when she returned to Spain with *Estación*, eager to see the novel's publication and develop fully the narrative experiment it represented. More than twenty years would pass before she actively picked up the thread of *Estación* again, but not because she no longer wrote or because her ambition and concerns as a writer had changed. On the contrary, once back in Madrid from Rome, she and her husband resumed their previous life and creative pursuits. Chacel published in respected journals such as Ortega's *Revista de Occidente*, in which the first chapter of *Estación* had appeared while she was still in Rome; *Estación* was published in 1930; and, at Ortega's suggestion, she began to work on a novel about Teresa Mancha, the lover of Spanish romantic poet José de Espronceda. The early 1930s also brought the birth of the couple's son, Carlos; Pérez Rubio's appointment as assistant director of the Museo de Arte Moderno in Madrid; and, for Chacel, an extended stay in Berlin in 1933. In addition, those years found Chacel experiencing a period of intense cultural and political activity that marked the years preceding the outbreak of the Civil War in the summer of 1936—the years of the Second Spanish Republic (1931–36).

The achievements, struggle, and defeat of the Republic are well known and they altered the life of every Spaniard, regardless of political orientation. As Chacel explained years later (1983), "we all did things we hadn't done before" ("Ortega" 425). Those things, for her, involved engaging in politics by contributing to antifascist journals such as *Hora de España*, in which she continued to publish after she left Spain; signing letters and manifestos in support of the Republic; and, immediately after the war broke out, serving for several months as a volunteer in a Madrid hospital (*Timoteo Pérez Rubio* 336). However, she always referred to her participation in both the events leading up to the war and in the war itself as marginal, particularly with respect to those who fought in the war or those who directly suffered its consequences. Instead, as she explained in 1978, she preferred to describe her role with an adjective she believed was too infrequently used in such contexts but one that she associated with the task of the artist and intellectual: "meditative" (*Poesía* 251). At a time when "anguish, confusion, and failure" were becoming ever more "dense" and Chacel saw far too many people acting without stopping to think, she aligned herself with "those of us who still thought" (e.g., about the relation between "culture" and *pueblo* [people, nation], understood in radically different ways by Republicans and Francisco Franco's Nationalists). Her alignment with thought and the affirmation of change, risk, and an anarchism coupled with realism, all of which she associated with Republican values and morality, never wavered or ceased to figure prominently in her work (*Poesía* 251). Her meditative support, she believed, would issue in her words.

Concerned for the safety of her son, Chacel first moved with him from Madrid to Barcelona and then to Valencia, departing with him for Paris early in 1937. Pérez Rubio stayed in Madrid, where he presided over the Junta del Defenso del Tesoro Artístico (Committee for Artistic Treasures), which was responsible for protecting and saving Spain's artistic heritage, an effort that involved transporting many of Spain's most renowned paintings by truck, first from Madrid to Valencia in 1938 and then, in subsequent moves, to Geneva by way of Barcelona. During the remainder of the war, thanks to the kindness of other Spaniards already living outside of Spain, Chacel and Carlos spent time together in Paris, Greece, and Geneva. Pérez Rubio joined them there when the war ended in 1939, and he had the painful chore of signing over to a representative of Franco's government the treasure he and his colleagues had struggled to preserve.[6]

From Geneva, Chacel and her family traveled to Paris. They had received offers of support from various countries but decided to go to Brazil, for which they sailed from Bordeaux in April 1940. Rio de Janeiro would be Chacel's principal base until she returned definitively to Spain. She and Pérez Rubio were received warmly, but she adapted less easily than he to the culture and language. Before leaving Europe she had established contacts in Buenos Aires, for example, with Victoria Ocampo, in whose magazine *Sur* the first chapter of her novel *Memorias de Leticia Valle* (*Memoirs of Leticia Valle*) had been published in 1939. Those contacts and her desire that Carlos be educated in Spanish led Chacel to spend much of her time in Buenos Aires beginning in the early 1940s. At first she wrote little, but before long she was contributing literary essays to other publications such as *La Nación*, *Realidad*, and *Sur*, in which work by Chacel appeared twenty-seven times between 1939 and 1950.[7] She also wrote short stories, began to keep the allusive but informative diaries she would continue to maintain until her death,[8] and translated work by such writers as Racine, Camus, and

T. S. Eliot. In addition, *Memorias de Leticia Valle* saw publication as a finished work; her novel about Teresa Mancha was published; and she began work on *La sinrazón*, a project that would occupy her for most of the 1950s. Late in her life, when she looked back on the years spent in South America, Chacel would minimize their difficulties, referring to them in 1989, for example, as a journey rather than a period of exile (Glenn 16). Her diaries, however, offer a different perspective. Money, for example, was a constant concern: the family's financial resources were inadequate for maintaining two residences; essays and translations were often undertaken from necessity rather than inclination or inspiration; and payments for work were often slow to arrive. In addition, and even more importantly for Chacel's creative life, during the 1950s (precisely when she was conceptualizing and writing *La sinrazón*) she underwent a complex emotional, spiritual, and intellectual crisis (Rodríguez Fischer, "Estudio preliminar" 29).[9] Emotionally, the crisis was no doubt linked in part to troubled relations with her son, of which she often makes mention in *Alcancía. Ida*, and to other events to which she only alludes in her diary and in *Timoteo Pérez Rubio*. There was also a fear that the hormonal changes associated with menopause would result in the permanent loss of eros, which she discussed as appetite (*apetito*) for life in the widest sense, differentiating it explicitly in her diary from "erotic [sexual] emotion," about which she admittedly never felt comfortable writing, even in the diaries, where, as she noted, it "shines by virtue of its absence" (*Alcancía. Vuelta* 14). The loss of that appetite would mean, she imagined, the indefinite prolongation of what she described in spiritual terms as an aridity—the wavering or even lack of faith she was experiencing.[10] For, as Rodríguez Fischer has indicated, Chacel believed that creation and credence are inextricably bound—all forms of creation ("Estudio preliminar" 29), whether biological or artistic, owe to the conviction that it is humanly possible to accomplish something Chacel once described to Alberto Porlán as "superhuman" (Porlán 71). Consequently, Chacel needed to feel confident that when "the endocrine process" had fully stabilized she would still be able to experience (and not figuratively but literally, since she writes in her diary of "the inner clime that reaches to the limits our being") the violence of total—perhaps, more appropriately, ontological—emotion, in which every ounce of one's blood rushes toward an idea" (*Alcancía. Ida* 20).

There was also another preoccupation, which Chacel described in terms of her relationship with society. As she noted in 1956 (*Alcancía. Ida* 72), dividing herself between the intellectual and the social was "impossible": absorbed in the complex issues with which she wrestled in her writing, she also wrestled with worries about her physical appearance and with what she considered her crippling ineptitude for social situations. "Social life," she wrote, never much interested her, and the intense interest she did have in "the social" (the word with which she refers here to her "circumstances") as a whole was frustrated not only by the human inability to grasp that whole but also by the fact that, despite her many contacts and acquaintances and the affection expressed in the introduction to *La sinrazón* for the landscape of the pampa and the literary heritage of South America, Chacel never identified herself with either the Argentine literary world or the Spanish exile community (*Alcancía. Ida* 72). These feelings of distance and lack of ease are vividly recorded in her diary, in particular as she was working intensively on *La sinrazón*. Not only did she find it impossible to enter "the society of a country in which one lives ten years without being able to invite anyone to dinner," but her lack of an intimate familiarity with that country made it difficult for her to obtain the detailed information about places and customs she needed for her novel, which she had decided to situate in Argentina (*Alcancía. Ida* 27–28). Despite this impasse, however, and the extreme anxiety recorded in her diary, Chacel never lost the determination to salvage both her self and her circumstances—to "pull," as she wrote in 1952, "from my solitude *something* that will be of use to *someone*, anyone" (*Alcancía. Ida* 28).

That *something*, with respect to the crisis Chacel was experiencing at the time, was to be *La sinrazón*. The first-person account of a protagonist who agonizes deeply about the relation between self and circumstances, Chacel's novel is a fictional-philosophical exploration of the specific issues troubling her at the time of its composition and of the larger ontological and theological questions that concerned her throughout her life, in particular, the intimate relation between the individual and the collective. Although Santiago Hernández, her protagonist, fails to save his circumstances or, arguably, his self, the far-reaching scope of his ambition and his exceedingly detailed meditations exemplify the dynamic, multidimensional nature of "the social" about which Chacel had begun to write in *Estación* and to which she referred in her diary. Santiago's failure, then, is in fact Chacel's success as a novelist, since through him she dramatizes what years later she described to Ana María Moix as "the great conflict." "No matter how *ours* we are," she told Moix, "no matter how definitively I can say 'I know who I am,' we are exposed every minute to the possibility that within us might fall a word or an image that will modify us, divert us from our course, or plant itself before us, in some inaccessible sphere, making us prisoners of our desires" (*De mar a mar* 306). For Santiago, those desires—chief among them the desire to probe and, ultimately, surpass the limits of individual, human will and understanding—not only imprison him but lead to his death. His tale, however, and its telling are proof that Chacel had recorded (saved) her circumstances and her own struggle with and within them.

When *La sinrazón* was published in 1960, Chacel was no longer living in Buenos Aires. Thanks to a Guggenheim Fellowship, she was able to spend two years in New York City, where she wrote much of *Saturnal* (Saturnalia), a long essay about eros, aesthetics, and ethics closely related to many of the discussions in *La sinrazón*. During the next three decades—the first in Rio de Janeiro, the second and third in Spain—she would continue to produce outstanding work—one thinks, for example, of *Desde el amanecer*, the widely read and much praised *Barrio de Maravillas,* or *Timoteo Pérez Rubio y sus retratos del jardín* (Timoteo Pérez Rubio and His Garden Portraits), a biography of her husband, or of the penetrating essays about Sor Juana Inés de la Cruz, Simone de Beauvoir, and the role of women in history. Although Chacel never became a "popular" writer—she was far too much of an intellectual, far too opinionated and outspoken; her dense, tightly woven and at times frustratingly allusive sentences placed demands too heavy for some readers and her work resisted easy categorization—once she returned to Spain she gradually became one of the most respected and admired writers of her generation. The effort to save, simultaneously, self (intimacy) and circumstances (interaction) through the written word and to explore the dynamic between them resulted, as Susan Kirkpatrick comments, in a "search for meaning that she [Chacel] unleashes in every sentence" (xxii). If at times that search allowed Chacel's narrative to become overly essayistic or philosophical, it also allowed Chacel to probe human consciousness and conscience and write passages that Julián Marías has praised as unequaled in the literature of the twentieth century (52).

About *Dream of Reason*

Hooked from the first chapter, I knew that I wanted to translate *La sinrazón* even before I finished reading the novel. Far be it from me to explain the desire to translate, but at least three considerations come to mind. First, although I separate and order those considerations only for the purpose of discussion, was Santiago Hernández, a protagonist-narrator the reader cannot but find less than sympathetic but one whose tale is highly engaging nevertheless. Born in Argentina but raised in Spain, Santiago returns to Buenos Aires several years before the outbreak of the Spanish Civil War in 1936. A pair of coincidences makes him the manager and later the owner of a pharmaceutical factory and large hacienda outside the capital and enables him to enter into a highly desirable marriage with Quitina Suárez, the young woman with whom he has fallen in love. Although he is aware of the conflict brewing in Spain and the coming war, for some time his life is affected only minimally by suffering. He is tormented, however, by the thought that the turn of events that placed him in such felicitous circumstances—circumstances he had desired passionately but had neither deserved nor known how to effect with his own actions—owed to the sudden death of two individuals who prevented him from realizing his ambitions. Recalling a few words spoken to him years earlier by Elfriede Pabst, a German dancer with whom he had had an affair as a student, he is compelled to examine and test the power of his intention (his will). Could the "convulsion of an overwhelming force deep within me," he wonders, have been determinant in those deaths and in other, less momentous incidents when things had transpired exactly as he willed? The appearance in Buenos Aires of Herminia Lara, a distant relative from Spain, and her family, whose lives had been deeply affected by the war, and then the sudden reappearance of Elfriede, whom he has long forgotten, alter irrevocably the tranquillity of his comfortable bourgeois existence, obliging him to question his role in events with renewed intensity.

Santiago states repeatedly that his intent as a narrator is to present a straightforward, factual account of a series of events in his life, an intent that should, as he notes at the beginning of chapter 2, be easy enough to realize. However, from the beginning he meets with difficulties. Not only is it impossible, as he acknowledges, to begin at the beginning when one cannot accurately recall how one was at the beginning—before the events occurred—events are not discrete but integrally related occurrences; to recount them, inevitably one proceeds by lapping back. What is more, he notes, again in the first lines of chapter 2, events both define and are defined by a "subject" who is inextricable from them. A further narrative difficulty is inherent in Santiago's intent for his account, which he refers to as a "confession." However, his purpose, he says, is not to unburden himself of an action or actions he has committed but to lay out events in which he has been involved and, in doing so, come to understand them. In defining confession this way, he exemplifies the definition of it Chacel offered some years after writing *La sinrazón* as an endeavor to free oneself from a persistent conflict—a mystery one does not comprehend and perhaps makes confession only for the sake of hearing it recounted, in order to comprehend it (*La confesión* 49).

For Santiago, the mystery not understood is eros, not in the sense of sexual desire but as the "movement toward" that follows what Chacel described in *La confesión* many years after writing *La sinrazón* as "inspiration" (inspiración). "A passion, an action, a person . . . any one of those things sprouts, arises before one's imagination," she told Porlán in an interview, "and then comes the desire to accomplish it, capture it, grasp it. That's the movement" (Porlán 53). The linking of eros and possession here, however—and Chacel stresses this—is not one that involves ownership. Rather, it concerns the "identification with" that Santiago experiences immediately when he visits Las Murtas for the first time, or when he meets Quitina. It also concerns, for Santiago, an identification with God. As Rodríguez Fischer has noted, Santiago develops a theory of eros (his term is "love") that encompasses both the human and the divine. Both forms imply struggle for him—between the individual will and the force of circumstances; between the individual and God—since Santiago, like Chacel, believes that eros is a totalizing movement that ultimately and inevitably is the movement toward the divinity in hopes of gaining access to divine knowledge ("Estudio preliminar" 27). Explanation never accompanies eros, however, not in any context, above all the divine, identification with which involves not possession but surrender, faith. "To believe or to love," Chacel commented in *La confesión* about Cervantes and *Don Quixote*, "one must be mad" (23). Lacking explanations—reasons—one is driven to cry out, to confess, as Santiago does in his diaries, addressing the divinity but also, implicitly, as Ana Gómez-Pérez has explained, the reader—both the readers of his text within the novel (who will be Father Ugarte and, implicitly, Miguel) and the reader of *La sinrazón* (93–118, esp. 115–18).

Santiago Hernández and his confession, however, were not the only aspect of *La sinrazón* that drew me to the novel. Having translated Chacel's *Memorias de Leticia Valle*, a novel narrated in the first person by an eleven-year-old girl, I was intrigued to discover resemblances between Santiago's narrative and Leticia's. For in Santiago I found a convincing male narrator whose diaries included turns of phrase, even a passage or two lifted, one might say, from the narrative of his young predecessor (e.g., his description of his young son nursing at Quitina's breast duplicates almost word for word Leticia's hazy memory of herself as in infant). Even more importantly, Santiago and Leticia share a hunger for understanding, and they are similarly incensed by the absence of answers—reasons—that would explain their own role in events and the larger questions that trouble them. These were resemblances I wanted to explore from within, as it were, and translating *La sinrazón*, I suspected, would afford me the opportunity to do that. As it did, because translating the novel forced me to think continually about Santiago's relation to the female characters, the implications of their presence in the novel, and Chacel's comments in numerous essays and interviews about the women in *La sinrazón* and about women's role in society in general. A substantial body of insightful criticism has been written in the last two decades about Chacel as a woman writer and her position vis-à-vis both the feminism of her moment and that of ours. Here, I will neither summarize nor analyze that criticism but comment briefly on what I see as Chacel's meditation on gender and sexuality in *La sinrazón*.[11]

In that meditation, Chacel has created a male narrator who at times not only echoes a young female but, in the novel's final chapter, also interrogates his own masculinity—"I must define my masculinity as a whole"—leading the reader to speculate about both his "virility" in an age he describes in chapter 9 as "virile" and his relation, as a man, to the women about whom he writes. On the one hand, Santiago is the character who struggles to understand and articulate the philosophical and theological questions at the core of *La sinrazón*, and it is Santiago who is willing to gamble his soul, even his life, to obtain knowledge of the divine. In other words, it is he who takes—and accepts—risks, something that, throughout her life (from a 1931 ground-breaking essay about the brute force of eros and the siege to which it is constantly submitted, to provocative comments made shortly before her death about what she termed the "current feminization of society"), Chacel stressed women's lack of preparation and determination to do.[12] At the same time, however, Santiago gradually finds himself enmeshed in a sort of double life—a comfortable bourgeois existence and an increasingly anguished mental and spiritual exploration, the two spheres of which could not be reconciled, as Chacel noted in 1987 (García Valdés 32–33). Despite his profound experience and understanding of human appetite and his goal of defending and prompting life by awakening appetite in others, he fails to accomplish that goal, just as he fails to write the protective poem he envisioned after his haunting experience of beauty, vulnerability, and terror in the Buenos Aires zoo. At the end of the novel, as Chacel commented, again looking back at him in 1987 (García Valdés 31–32, 37–38), having pushed to the limit both his personal life and his sanity, he is alone, unable to resist any longer the disjuncture between the difficult, insignificant nature of his reason and the unknowable reason of a silent God.

Although the contrasts between Santiago and the three female protagonists in his narrative are striking, there are also notable similarities that may not be apparent at first glance. They may not have double existences as intense and compelling as his, for instance, but they too have complex—and courageous—inner lives. Those inner lives are not revealed to the same extent as his, however; the many conversations he sustains with each of them—conversations in which they reveal experiences and feelings unsuspected by Santiago—allow the reader to see strong, thoughtful women. In addition, and rather ironically, each of them is granted a stamina that Santiago lacks, and all three of them survive him.

Herminia, in particular, in her exchanges with Santiago and in her actions, proves herself to be the "admirable woman" Quitina claims she is, suffering a severe emotional crisis from which she emerges to involve herself actively in the lives of others and to work creatively. Chacel has granted that work and Herminia's life several lengthy conversations in Santiago's account, to the extent that Herminia's "story" constitutes what could be considered a counter-tale to his. Although, as Rodríguez Fischer has pointed out with respect to Herminia's involved explanation of her play (37), the sections in which that story is told may seem digressive (and probably could have been shorter without losing their effectiveness), but they are integrally related to the novel as a whole. For example, Herminia's preoccupation with the notion of masculine and feminine in relation to the lives not only of individuals but also historical moments, which drives her rewriting of the *Oresteia* and underlies her troubled relationship with Miguel, is as Fischer notes, the same preoccupation one finds dramatized through the life of Santiago and recorded in Chacel's diaries and commentaries ("Estudio preliminar" 37). Furthermore, Herminia's insistence that the true death of Clytemnestra occurs not when Orestes actually kills her, but when she realizes that he is *going* to kill her, suggests much about Santiago's experience (and the reader's) at the end of the novel.

Important as Herminia is to *La sinrazón*, however, the other female characters also have major roles in the novel. Elfriede's tale shows the reader a highly determined woman who survives not one but two breakdowns, and Quitina, as Santiago becomes increasingly aware, enters his life as a spoiled only daughter but develops into a mature individual who wrestles, albeit in different contexts, with some of the same issues he does and is able to articulate them clearly. In truth, especially if one bears in mind both the resemblances between Leticia and Santiago and the fact that Herminia, Elfriede, and Quitina narrate stories of their own, the contrast between Santiago and the three women becomes less clear. Moreover, Santiago's narrative itself begins to look less masculine (in the sense of having been written by a man) and far more complex: Santiago is at once a man created by a woman and a man whose narrative both echoes that of a woman and contains women who are narrators in their own right. This complexity makes it difficult to limit one's discussion of Santiago, for example, to an explanation of him as a male narrator created by a woman writer, or of uncomplicated narrative transvestism. It also calls to mind Chacel's comments about her close identification with Santiago and the similar bond she felt with Herminia. On numerous occasions she stated that she was or had been one or the other of them, and she repeatedly affirmed the autobiographical nature of all her work. In *La sinrazón*, for example, it would be possible to suggest that she shared an affinity with Quitina as well as with Herminia. The resemblances between her own experiences and her writing, however, were consistently more allusive than absolute, making it impossible to do more than speculate about her personal relationships or her sexuality on the basis of her fiction. This is particularly true with respect to the "strong underlying current of homoeroticism" throughout her writing that Elizabeth Scarlett has identified as one of Chacel's principal themes ("Rosa Chacel," *Twentieth-Century* 83).[13]

I have used "allusive" deliberately in the paragraph above, because the complex role of allusion in *La sinrazón* is the third aspect of the novel that attracted me most strongly. Aware that, for Chacel, there is an "intrinsic ambiguity or falsehood" not only in fiction but also in the genre that comprises diaries, memoirs, and confessions and thus ensures clarification for neither the one who confesses nor the one who receives the confession (*Alcancía. Vuelta* 83), I was not surprised that Santiago's diary, although kept in a safe named Factum, would prompt not a revelation but a "Who knows?" from its reader. Nevertheless, I found wondrous and challenging the richly allusive nature of the novel as a whole. Many of the allusions are sufficiently direct that one could consider them references—for example, the incorporation of phrases or even entire passages from classical literature and the European literary canon, to film, or to noir, both film and fiction; others (equally, if not more, numerous) are more subtle. Furthermore, in many cases, what seems to be a direct, self-contained reference is part of an intricate web of allusions that sometimes occur in widely separated passages; of those I will briefly discuss three examples: Argentina, which I came to think of at times as an intriguingly near-absent present, and the crucial, conflicted years in which *La sinrazón* is set; Racine's *Phèdre* (*Phaedra*), which Chacel translated into Spanish; and Rilke's first Duino Elegy.

Given the intense, almost documentary presence in *La sinrazón* of Buenos Aires as a city and of the landscape surrounding Las Murtas (the pampa), it might seem inappropriate to refer to Argentina as an absence. Chacel had what Paul Julian Smith has termed "an acute sensitivity to place" (25), and Santiago's narrative abounds with the names of actual streets and cafés and descriptions of identifiable locations, making it easy to think of Santiago as a *porteño*, or resident of Buenos Aires. To think of him in terms of a larger, Argentine context, however, is not as easy. For one thing, neither he nor the other characters in the novel speak like Argentines, who are not only known but frequently characterized (and caricatured) by their use of the pronoun *vos* (*voseo*) for "you" in both the singular and plural, rather than *tu* (singular, Spain and Spanish America) and *vosotros* (Spain) or *ustedes* (Spanish America). The absence of this usage in *La sinrazón* is significant, because it marks Santiago as a self-proclaimed Argentine who speaks like the Spaniard Elfriede insists he resembles and he declares himself not to be. It is also significant because it reflects Santiago's uneasy identification with both Spain and Argentina alike, his admitted lack of interest in politics as such, and the lifelong attachment he describes in chapter 2 to the "luminous region, Niza, Mallorca" associated with a freedom whose loss he mourns throughout his life.[14]

Consequently, a reader might struggle to place Santiago or the events in *La sinrazón* in the context of Argentina between 1932 and 1946, the years in which the novel is set. Those years included not only the Spanish Civil War (1936–39), the conflict described in most detail in Santiago's narrative and apparently the conflict that seems to affect most directly the everyday life of his family, but also what is known in Argentina as *la década infame*, the "infamous decade" that spanned 1932–1943 and received its name because of the "conservative corruption" by which it was characterized (Rock 214–61; Wilson 27); World War II, throughout most of which Argentina maintained a policy of neutrality, not siding with the Allies until nearly the end of the conflict; and the rise of Juan Domingo Perón, who became vice-president of the country's military government in 1944 and in 1946 was elected president. Santiago refers specifically to none of those events, simply noting at the beginning of chapter 16, for example, that "the war ended" without giving an indication of when or how; and it is not through him but Elfriede (or Damián or Quitina's father) that Chacel inserts the novel into a historical context. Here, however, it is important to point out that she does not neglect to create such a context and that she does so through a series of allusions to external "circumstances" that prevent Santiago's narrative from becoming exclusively a reflection of his inner world. His coincidental purchase of *Crítica* in the opening chapter (1932), for instance, even though he reads not the news but the culture page, links a decisive event in his life with a radical newspaper whose editor, in a few years, would provide strong support to Republican Spain and its exiles (Schwarzstein 123–38; Wilson 70–71).

Additional examples of similar insertions would include the conversations between Santiago and Miguel (which occur at widely separated points in the novel and consequently correspond to significantly different historical moments) about the nature of revolution and social change; or Santiago's description in chapter 9 of the "unclear" position he occupies in Buenos Aires by listing the things he is not—he does not belong to one of the nation's "old families," nor is he one of the small landowners originally from northern Europe who arrived more recently, and he is not "naive"; or, in the same chapter, the conversation at a cocktail party in which his reference to the exquisiteness of Japanese drawings prompts his interlocutor to suspect him of being a fascist; or Herminia's enthusiastic participation at the end of the war (chapter 14) in the young people's independent theater group. This last example brings to mind the intense cultural activity that flourished in Buenos Aires during the 1940s and whose "most novel aspect," as Luis Alberto Romero has explained, was possibly "the rise of 'independent' theater, . . . cultivated by non-professional actors, which provided a suitable terrain for a renewal in national production . . . and contrasted with the reproductive mediocrity of the big commercial state theaters" (117–18).

Santiago's recounting of Herminia's involvement in such an initiative provides a good segue into Chacel's use of allusions to literary works of literature and other art forms. In chapter 14, Santiago learns that Herminia has befriended a group of young men she met at the publishing house where she works as a translator; they interest her, she explains, because their assorted backgrounds allow her to study "the various combinations produced by this age"—implicitly, this postwar age. By the time she tells Santiago about this group, she has become part of their effort to establish a new, independent theater—so much a part that the inaugural production is to be a play the young men have prevailed upon her to write. Much of the lengthy discussion in this chapter centers on that play and Herminia's determination to write a modern tragedy not linked to the Oedipus myth, which she declares outdated (528). Instead, she has begun a retelling of Aeschylus's *Oresteia* that will turn on the transvaluation of masculine values, specifically heroism, which she believes is occurring in contemporary society, and on an altered understanding of the Apollonian. The conversation in this chapter is rich with allusions and specific references not only to Aeschylus's trilogy but also to other works—Baudelaire's *Fleurs du mal*, for example, and Goethe's *Iphigenie auf Tauris*. Perhaps the most arresting of those allusions, however, is the one Herminia makes to a conversation she had with Santiago and Quitina earlier in the novel—the "night of the fever," in chapter 10, when she suffered a severe emotional crisis after watching a performance of *Phaedra* and associating an allusion Theseus makes near the end of the play with a spiteful comment she had made to her son before leaving for the theater. That association prompted Herminia to reflect on what she describes as the "reverse" sort of love that operates irrevocably between mothers and sons, since the bond between them must gradually become attenuated, even severed, rather than deepened.

For Herminia, the crisis (the "Golgotha") prompted by Theseus's remarks is not only individual but also assumes larger, cultural implications: at a time when further devastating war has become unthinkable and conventional values related to "masculine" forms of heroism and risk have of necessity "ceded to a feminine world," heroism assumes a new form, as Herminia realizes while she watches *Phèdre*. The realization stays with her. Years later, it will give rise to the writing of the play she describes in chapter 14 and her desire to prompt a similar experience of recognition for her audience. When, in her conversation with Santiago and Quitina, she tells them of her struggle to complete the second act, her experience with Racine assumes an additional role, as it were, that of exemplifying both the way allusions accumulate and interact throughout the novel and the way a moment intensively lived can engender a literary work as the writer seizes a moment and creates from—and with—it.

Intent on exploring and refining the thesis of Herminia's play and finding a solution for the second act, neither Herminia nor Santiago pursues the allusion to the difficulties of literary creation in her explanation of the play's inspiration. It is interesting to note, however, that Chacel no doubt had precisely that allusion in mind. Writing about her translation of *Phèdre*, Chacel explained that the performance she attended in the Odeón theater in Buenos Aires compelled her to "adopt" the experience with its complex mix of emotions, and incorporate it into the work she designates as her most vital—the one with the greatest vitality ("Nota de la traductora" cliv–clv). I have placed "adopt" in quotes because, in addition to using the word Chacel used in her essay, I am alluding to her explanation in a conversation with Porlán that *La sinrazón* is the result of a series of "eternal instants" or "erotic [generative] moments" that she adopted, incorporated in her writing of the novel (Porlán 69–72). Although she does not refer in the conversation with Porlán to her experience in the Odeón, the "erotic moment" she experienced there also gave rise to a second desire—less immediate but, implicitly, not less intense, since her desire was for a greater closeness to Racine's play; that desire led her to translate *Phèdre* with an enthusiasm she did not usually feel when she translated, even when working with Racine's plays.

For Chacel, achieving greater intimacy with *Phèdre* involved an experiment in form: she wanted to know if the play's formal "omnipotence" could retain what she referred to as its "fragrance" in Castilian ("Nota de la traductora" clv). This omnipotence she also related to tone ("*Fedra* en español" 199), and her comment was in my thoughts often as I worked with *La sinrazón* and considered questions of form. Some of those questions involved syntax and punctuation—decisions, for example, about when Chacel's semicolons were best translated as colons, always with the aim, as Ronald Christ put it in an exchange about her use of stops, of "propelling the language forward with the fewest possible distractions" (29 March 2006). Achieving that forward motion, however, was frequently a challenge, seeing that, as Santiago remarks in numerous passages, his narrative cannot move toward the future without continual nods toward the past. In other words, not uncommonly the syntactic energy of a sentence propels the reader forward by ensuring the absence of any grammatical "distractions," but at the same time the burden of the sentence prompts a backward glance, almost invariably by way of allusion rather than exact repetition—a simultaneity crafted, as Chacel discussed with respect to her translation of Racine's theater, in response to the nature of Castilian as a language. Castilian, she noted, is hard and harsh, even granitic (*berroqueño*); to refine it—make it softer, more flexible—one eschews precise repetition as potentially grating, preferring instead a "discreet polychromy" ("*Fedra* en español" 200). That eschewal, she adds, holds true not only for poetry but also for prose: for both genres, allusion is a question of form as well as concept.

That Chacel would include prose in her discussion of translating poetry is not surprising, given her belief that for poetry verse is "a delightful but not absolutely necessary exercise" and that prose could also provide it with "an infinitely ample vehicle" ("Poesía y prosa" 9). A thorough study of Chacel's prose as precisely such a vehicle has yet to be written, but the complex allusions embedded in Santiago's narrative provide extensive evidence that her affirmation about poetry's potential can be sustained. An allusion to Rilke's first Duino Elegy offers a fine example of how prose can create the sort of refining polychromy Chacel refers to in the discussion of her work with *Phèdre*—and that she no doubt set as a goal for the translations of Rilke's work she was preparing during the years she wrote *La sinrazón*.[15] Consider the following phrase from chapter 12: "There where beauty begins begins horror"—a phrase Santiago quotes but without identifying its source, saying that it is the counterfigure of another ("danger is what beauty best produces"). Neither phrase, he says—-the first, dramatic; the second, frivolous—can express fully what he is thinking about at the moment. Together, though, as elements in his narrative, they participate in a web of allusively related allusions that spans the whole novel, and they evoke, especially the first, a third phrase that evokes the entire trajectory (not only is Elfriede, who appears in chapter 1, German, but when she reappears later in the novel she has become a devoted reader of Rilke) recalled and recorded in Santiago's attic room: "Denn des Schöne ist nichts al des Schrecklichen Anfang." In that third phrase, from lines three and four of the first Duino Elegy, beauty is identified not with an experience of pleasure and serenity but as the onset of terror, and the speaker in the poem realizes that a cry of alarm or despair will be met with silence. Indeed, the absence of not only an answer but any response at all from God is what Santiago defines as ultimate injustice, against which he rails night after night in the troubling, even tormenting presence of beauty incarnate—an exquisite blue butterfly associated repeatedly in his narrative with both beauty and horror and (thus implicitly) with both the emotions expressed in the elegy and with the words that express them.

The first mention of the blue butterfly occurs well before the allusion to Rilke's poem, in chapter 9, where it is listed as one of several items at which Santiago gazes as he tries to write a request for money to Quitina's father, the sound of Julieta and her son's voices a horrible murmur crowding his thoughts. On this night he first feels what, much later, on the last night of his life he will describe in retrospect as the butterfly's beauty tempting him, "with a wave of horrible voluptuousness," to will it to flutter its wings. By the time he dies, that temptation will have become an obsession, and the butterfly, in addition to the more common associations with beauty, fragility, and the human spirit or soul, will have acquired the association with horror suggested in Rilke's elegy, and also an association with death itself—the price, Santiago knows, of (possibly) seeing the creature's wings flutter. That association might seem questionable—in fact, even as careful a reader as Chacel's friend Pilar Gómez Bedate linked the butterfly exclusively with the soul (44)—if early in the novel Chacel had not begun to weave the fabric into which she inserted the allusion to the elegy by having Santiago pair it with the owl (frequently an ambivalent image of death and wisdom) in literature and mythology and if she had not written elsewhere about the butterfly as ominous, at times drawing on the potential ambivalence of the Spanish word *mariposa*, which includes both butterflies (diurnal *mariposas*) and moths (nocturnal creatures).[16]

In the autobiographical *Desde el amanecer*, for example, with respect to a childhood incident (in which a *mariposa*, after bursting from its cocoon during the night, had landed on her pillow while she was asleep), Chacel explains that the *mariposa* was the "only animal that inspired, and still inspires, horror in me" (309). Similarly, in her poem "Mariposa Nocturna" (Nocturnal Butterfly/Moth), the speaker addresses a creature that has come at night to the "confident, open window," bringing "terror" and prompting a reflection on the impossibility of embracing it without perishing (*Poesía* 71–72). Here, the creature is a "dark goddess" whose troublesome appearance at the window is reminiscent of Poe's raven. In addition, however, it is perhaps even more evocative of Athena and, consequently, of the owl Santiago sees when he first visits Las Murtas (in chapter 3) and will see again on subsequent visits. That first time, though, as he observes the owl, he likens its flight to the flight of a *mariposa*, thereby associating the two animals with his intense desire to possess the estancia and foreshadowing the significant role the blue *mariposa* will assume in his narrative and the charged emotions it will arouse in him. The foreshadowing is subtle, to be sure, yet as Herminia suggests in chapter 14 in the description of her play, sometimes the key to a work lies in a hint so subtle it can hardly even be called an allusion or an evocation.

In the case of Santiago's *mariposa*-like owl, one cannot know for certain what Chacel had in mind as she worked, but it is hard not to speculate that in her thoughts might well have been two instances in which the *mariposa* and the owl were closely associated, both of those instances works with she was very likely familiar. In the first, "Mariposas" (Butterflies), an essay, the highly influential Spanish avant-garde writer Ramón Gómez de la Serna (who also lived for many years in Buenos Aires, where the essay was published in 1943, and whom Chacel considered a poetic genius in prose) ("Sendas" 242) describes *mariposas* as "aesthetic insects par excellence" (167). His own *greguerías* (the name he gave to the clever humorous and aphoristic literary form he created), he says, are like *mariposas*, explaining that each night (again one thinks of Santiago) "in the solitude of my study," "deep down within" he tries to achieve a transformation as magnificent and daring as theirs (168). Unlike Chacel, however, who as a child was apparently disturbed by the worm's metamorphosis to *mariposa*, Gómez de la Serna admires both the worm's transformation and the butterfly's talent for self-protective disguise. Some *mariposas*, he notes—the most ingenious—are night creatures that disguise themselves as owls (175).

The concurrence of a writer in his study, nighttime reflection, a *mariposa*-like owl, and an owl-like *mariposa* evokes a second work that Chacel certainly knew well: Francisco Goya's *Capricho 43*, *El sueño de la razón produce monstruos* (The Dream/Sleep of Reason Produces Monsters). In that etching, a sleeping man, apparently in his study, head on his desk, is surrounded by a group of grotesque, menacing owls over which hover a hoard of bats. One of the owls seems to have alighted on his back, its wings spread wide, not unlike those of the bats or, a reader of *La sin-razón* might think, like those of a large butterfly. Whether the *sueño* in the title of the *Capricho* refers to dream or sleep is not clear; as Paul Ilie has explained, it can be read in four different ways: "Reason asleep . . . produces" (46); "sleep produces monsters" (46); "a dream produces monsters while Reason is asleep" (46); and Reason "has" a dream, "the visionary yearning, say, for social justice or utopia" (47)—a yearning not necessarily fulfilled (48). Each of those meanings, perhaps the fourth in particular, could be shown to have some relevance to Chacel's novel. However, in the case of Santiago, it is Santiago, not Reason, that sleeps, and it is Reason of which he dreams—for which he yearns. When that yearning is not fulfilled—when God does not respond by making the butterfly move its wings—he finds the lack of response and the ultimate limit inherent in his own reason so unreasonable (so unjust) that he loses his reason and (the reader is led to speculate) takes his life.

Although Santiago makes no direct reference to the *Caprichos*, the image and its many possible interpretations hover over his narrative, reminiscent of one of Goya's bats. Santiago and his circumstances are an allusion to the etching and, given the inherently allusive nature of *La sinrazón*, I decided that it would be fitting if, at least in part, the novel's title in English also alluded, at least in part, to the etching. The Spanish title too is an allusion, and a very rich one, but not one that would serve well as a title in English. Its strong power of allusion owes to the polysemy of the word *sinrazón* and to a Spanish reader's likely familiarity with its most immediate referent: ". . . la sinrazón que a mi razón se hace . . ." (". . . the unreason my reason is subject to . . ."). The phrase, which provides not only the title but also the epigraph to the second part of *La sinrazón*, is from the first chapter of *Don Quixote*. An excerpt from a quotation of a sentence by sixteenth-century Spanish author of novels of chivalry Francisco de Silva, it is cited tongue in cheek by the narrator as an example of the reading material whose "clear prose and intricate reasoning" was responsible for the hidalgo's loss of sanity. The play on *sinrazón* in which a would-be lover blames the unreason(ableness) or injustice (*sinrazón*) for his own loss of reason (*sinrazón*) reappears not only in Cervantes's novel[17] but throughout Spanish literature and philosophy, most notably in the writing of Miguel de Unamuno, which was influential in much of Chacel's work and thinking. By using it as her title and making it an integral element of Santiago's reasoning and what he considers the unjust limit God has placed on his (human) reason, Chacel ensured for her novel as a whole the complex resonance suggested in her title.

Aware that neither the allusive power nor the polysemy of *sinrazón* would be operative in English, and wanting an English title that would be allusive in a way appropriate to the novel, I worked alternately with "unreason" and "injustice" for a long time, knowing that both were provisional. When Ronald Christ suggested "El sueño de la razón" (26 November 2006), I hesitated at first, reluctant to relinquish resemblance to the Spanish. However, as I reread the novel with the choice of a title in mind, his suggestion seemed more and more fitting, especially when I considered it with respect to the epigraph for the first part of the book: "D'un monde oú l'action n'est pas la soeur de rêve." Like the words from *Don Quixote* quoted in the epigraph for the novel's second part, those words from Baudelaire's "Le reniement de Saint Pièrre" (*Les fleurs du mal*) express despair caused by the disjuncture between the world of the dream and the world in which the speaker finds himself; and, like the final pages of Santiago's narrative in chapter 16 of the novel, they form part of an invective against an unresponsive god—in Baudelaire's poem, a god who sleeps after sating himself on food and wine, despite the multitude of anathemas directed at him by his "chers Seraphins."

The words in the English title, then, differ from those in the novel's title in Spanish, as do the allusions they prompt. Santiago might speculate that the question of their difference is related to the question of the dog and the collars upon which he reflects in chapter 3 and to his conclusion that, given the many kinds of dogs, the clue to a definition of "dog" that comprises all dogs is found in the old saying about the same dog but different collars. Revising that saying as "the same dog with different furs and shapes," he muses that although those furs and shapes restrain the dogs, the dogs apparently neither find the restraint unwelcome nor chafe against the *obediential potency* he sees operative within them. Chacel, I believe, hinted at something not unrelated when, asked in an interview if she thought her work would have been different or almost identical (*igual*) if she had not spent so many years outside Spain, in exile, she responded that "[for the work to have been] identical is not possible, although of course it would have been the same, that's what counts" (Glenn 17). Consequently, although Chacel was adamant about her determination to follow what she considered the "lost paths" of her generation, she believed that the experimentation those paths implied could be carried out in similar ways in different places, even if not in identical terms. As she notes in her introduction to the third edition of *La sinrazón*, although she did not advocate carelessness or inattention, she was not preoccupied with precise details of a work's "atmosphere." Her goal in *La sinrazón* and throughout her life was to sustain and develop a "formula" (*Alcancía. Vuelta* 428), one characterized—and this cannot be emphasized too strongly—not by a prescribed form or set of instructions but by a capacity for the narrative experimentation that characterized the early, pre–Civil War work of her contemporaries.

Chacel and I never discussed the relation between that formula and specific formal features of a text with respect to translation, but both in choosing the English-language title of the novel and in preparing the translation itself, I have been guided continually by her comments about identity, dogs, and capacity for.

NOTES

1. *La sinrazón* was first published in 1960, in Buenos Aires, by Editorial Lozada. For the translation I have used the third edition as published in Chacel's *Obra completa*, volume 1, which includes the introduction she wrote for the third edition. Unless otherwise noted, all translations are mine.

2. As yet there is not a biography of Chacel in either Spanish or English. Nor is there a true critical edition of *La sinrazón*. However, Ana Rodríguez Fischer's "Estudio preliminar" in the *Obra completa* offers an excellent and extensive introduction to the novel. Both it and Rodríguez Fischer's numerous essays about Chacel and her work were of great help to me as I prepared this translation, as were the essays by Pilar Gómez Bedate, Clara Janés, Ana María Moix, and Shirley Mangini. Readers in Spanish will find useful the chapter on Chacel in Inmaculada de la Fuente's volume and the discussions by Pablo Gil Casado (301–6) and Ana Gómez-Pérez. In English, readers will find further information about Chacel in Mangini's work, in the essays by Meyers and Scarlett, in Susan Kirkpatrick's introduction to *The Maravillas District*, and in my afterword to *Memoirs of Leticia Valle*.

3. Chief among those writers was Ana María Moix, who wrote to Chacel from Barcelona in 1965, initiating a long correspondence and a close friendship. Their letters are collected in *De mar a mar*.

4. Although Johnson's essay focuses on the work of Spanish philosopher María Zambrano (1904–91), her comments will be useful to readers of *Dream of Reason*. In addition to coming of age in the same decade, the two women were acquainted with each other, corresponded with each other, and were both strongly influenced by Ortega y Gasset. See also Johnson's "'Self'-Consciousness."

5. Readers in English may be reminded of Van Wyck Brooks's "On Creating a Usable Past," published in 1918 in the *Dial*, which also published work by Ortega in English translation.

6. For information about the work of the Junta del Defenso see Daly's article, Argerich and Ara's *Arte protegido*, and Pizarro Gómez.

7. There was a close "parallelism" between *Sur* (noted by Ocampo herself) and José Ortega y Gasset's *Revista de Occidente*, to which Chacel had contributed before leaving Spain, as Ana Rodriguez Fischer has explained ("Introducción" 27).

8. The diaries were published in 1982 in two volumes as *Alcancía. Ida* (Coin Bank. Departure) and *Alcancía. Vuelta* (Coin Bank. Return). A third volume, *Alcancía. Estación Termini* (Coin Bank. Termini Station), was published posthumously in 1998.

9. Mangini also mentions the difficulties Chacel faced during the 1950s ("Exiles" 222).

10. Chacel writes of this in her diaries (*Alcancía. Ida* 20, 23), and Rodríguez

Fischer has related Chacel's crisis to the profound doubts Santiago experiences in *La sinrazón* ("Estudio preliminar" 29–30).

11. With respect to gender, see, e.g., Bellver, Fitch Lockhart, Gómez-Pérez, Johnson (*Gender and Nation*, esp. 210–23), Lázaro, Maier ("Siting *Leticia Valle*"; "Translator's Afterword"), Mangini (especially *Las modernas*, 144–58, although all of Mangini's work addresses gender-related issues in some way), and Scarlett ("Rosa Chacel," in *Under Construction*).

12. "Esquema de los problemas practices y actuales del amor" (An Outline of the Practical and Current Problems Concerning Love) (1931); Rodríguez Fischer, "Entrevista a Rosa Chacel"; and "La mujer y la creación" (Women and Creation) (1993).

13. Melissa Fitch Lockhart has noted the same impossibility, commenting that, despite Chacel's "calling attention to the entire notion of regulated sexuality and compulsory heterosexuality," the vagueness with which sexuality is presented in her work gives a reader "the freedom to read into the texts points of identification" (53). However, as Fitch Lockhart has observed, it is impossible to know if that freedom reflects Chacel's desire to grant the reader "a measure of autonomy in the interpretation" or if it is "merely the result of her realistic assessment of her potential for publication" (53). Chacel was undoubtedly "nonconformist" with respect to her life and her thought (Mangini, *Las modernas* 146), she was also unfailingly "discreet and reserved" about her personal life (de la Fuente 309), not only in her diaries and her fiction but even with her close friends.

14. Janés has written eloquently about this happiness (especially 155).

15. To my knowledge, these translations were never published, although Chacel refers to them several times in the first volume of her diary. She never mentions any titles, but on 17 June 1959 she notes (*Alcancía. Ida* 167) that she had finished with Rilke ("Acabé con Rilke").

16. There is not a word that denotes only diurnal *mariposas*. Moths are also known as *polillas*, but the word has almost exclusively negative connotations, since it refers to the sort of moth that destroys clothing. In *La sinrazón*, *polilla* appears only once, in a comment Herminia makes about a play she plans to write in the future; it will be titled *La polilla*, since "everything has *its* moth," she says (521). I have translated *mariposa* as "butterfly" throughout *Dream of Reason*, in order to maintain consistency of reference.

17. See, e.g., "Grisóstimo's Song," written by a shepherd whose death was attributed to the cruel "*sinrazones*" of the shepherdess Marcela (part 1, chapter 14).

Argerich, Isabel, and Judith Ara. *Arte protegido: Memorias de la Junta del Tesoro Artístico durante la Guerra Civil.* Madrid: Instituto de Patrimonio Histórico Español. Museo Nacional del Prado, 2003.

Ayala, Francisco. *Recuerdos y olvidos: 1. Del paraíso al destierro, 2. El exilio, 3. Retornos.* Biblioteca Ayala. Madrid: Alianza, 2001.

Bellver, Catherine G. "Literary Influence and Female Creativity: The Case of Two Women Poets of the Generation of 27." *Siglo xx/20th Century* 15.1–2 (1997): 7–32.

———. "Rosa Chacel: Masking the Feminine Voice." *Absence and Presence: Spanish Women Poets of the Twenties and Thirties.* Lewisburg PA: Bucknell University Press, 2001. 120–42.

Brooks, Van Wyck. "On Creating a Usable Past." 1918. *Van Wyck Brooks, the Early Years: A Selection of His Works, 1908–1925.* Ed. Claire Sprague. Rev. ed. Boston: Northeastern University Press. 21–28.

Chacel, Rosa. *Alcancía. Estación Termini.* Ed. Carlos Pérez Chacel y Antonio Piedra. Salamanca: Junta de Castilla y León. Consejería de Educación y Cultura, 1998.

———. *Alcancía. Ida.* Barcelona: Seix Barral, 1982.

———. *Alcancía. Vuelta.* Barcelona: Seix Barral, 1982.

———. *La confesión.* Barcelona: Edhasa, 1980.

———. *De mar a mar: Epistolario Rosa Chacel–Ana María Moix.* Ed. Ana Rodríguez Fischer. Barcelona: Ediciones Península, 1998.

———. *Desde el amanecer.* Madrid: Revista de Occidente, 1972.

———. "Esquema de los problemas prácticos y actuales del amor." 1931. *Artículos II.* Vol. 4 of *Obra completa.* Ed. Ana Rodríguez Fischer. Valladolid, Spain: Centro de Creación y Estudios Jorge Guillén: Excma. Diputación Provincial de Valladolid, 1993. 447–76.

———. *Estación. Ida y vuelta.* Madrid: CVS Ediciones, 1974.

———. "*Fedra* en español." 1959. *Artículos I.* Vol. 3 of *Obra completa.* Ed. Ana Rodríguez Fischer. Valladolid, Spain: Centro de Creación y Estudios Jorge Guillén: Excma. Diputación Provincial de Valladolid, 1993. 199–204.

———. Introducción. *La sinrazón.* 1960. Ed. Ana Rodríguez Fischer. Vol. 1 of *Obra completa.* Ed. Ana Rodríguez Fischer. Valladolid, Spain: Centro de Creación y Estudios Jorge Guillén: Excma. Diputación Provincial de Valladolid, 1989. 41–48.

———. "La mujer y la creación." Lecture presented at El Escorial Summer School, 1993.

———. "Nota de la traductora." Jean Racine. *Seis tragedias*. Trad. Rosa Chacel. Madrid: Alfaguara, 1983. cli–clvi.

———. "Ortega." 1983. *Artículos I*. Vol. 3 of *Obra completa*. Ed. Ana Rodríguez Fischer. Valladolid, Spain: Centro de Creación y Estudios Jorge Guillén: Excma. Diputación Provincial de Valladolid, 1993. 419–32.

———. *Poesía (1931–1991)*. Barcelona: Tusquets, 1992.

———. "Poesía y prosa." *Babelia. El País* 30 July 1994: 9–11.

———. "Respuesta a Ortega: La novela no escrita." 1956. *Artículos I*. Vol. 3 of *Obra completa*. Ed. Ana Rodríguez Fischer. Valladolid, Spain: Centro de Creación y Estudios Jorge Guillén: Excma. Diputación Provincial de Valladolid, 1993. 369–94.

———. "Sendas perdidas de la generación del 27." 1977. *Artículos I*. Vol. 3 of *Obra completa*. Ed. Ana Rodríguez Fischer. Valladolid, Spain: Centro de Creación y Estudios Jorge Guillén: Excma. Diputación Provincial de Valladolid, 1993. 231–66.

———. *La sinrazón*. 1960. Vol. 1 of *Obra completa*. Ed. Ana Rodríguez Fischer. Valladolid, Spain: Centro de Creación y Estudios Jorge Guillén: Excma. Diputación Provincial de Valladolid, 1989.

———. *Timoteo Pérez Rubio y sus retratos del jardín*. 1970. Vol. 8 of *Obra completa*. Ed. Carlos Pérez Chacel y Antonio Piedra. Valladolid, Spain: Centro de Creación y Estudios Jorge Guillén: Excma. Diputación Provincial de Valladolid, 2004. 267–431.

Christ, Ronald. E-mail to the author. 29 March, 26 November 2006.

Daly, Emma. "Defenders of Spain's Masterpieces." *New York Times* 17 July 2003: B1+.

De la Fuente, Inmaculada. *Mujeres de la posguerra: De Carmen Laforet a Rosa Chacel; Historia de una generación*. Barcelona: Planeta, 2002.

Fitch Lockhart, Melissa. "Chacel, Rosa." *Spanish Writers on Gay and Lesbian Themes: A Bio-Critical Sourcebook*. Ed. David William Foster. Westport CT: Greenwood Press, 1999. 49–54.

García Valdés, Olvido. "Conversación con Rosa Chacel." *Un Angel Más* (Valladolid) 3–4 (1988): 15–43.

Gil Casado, Pablo. *La novela deshumanizada española (1958–1988)*. Barcelona: Anthropos, 1990.

Glenn, Kathleen. "Conversación con Rosa Chacel." *Letras Peninsulares* 3.1 (1990): 11–26.

Gómez Bedate, Pilar. "¿El secreto de *La sinrazón*?" *Anthropos* 85 (1988): 39–44.

Gómez de la Serna, Ramón. "Las mariposas." *"Lo cursi" y otros ensayos*. Buenos Aires: Editorial Sudamericana. 167–89.

Gómez-Pérez, Ana. "Rosa Chacel y la confesión." *Las trampas de la memoria. Pensamiento apocalíptico en la literatura española moderna: Galdós, Baroja, Chacel y Torrente Ballester*. Newark DE: Juan de la Cuesta, 2005. 93–118.

Ilie, Paul. *Counter-Rational Reason in the Eighteenth Century*. University Park: Pennsylvania State University Press, 1995. Vol. 1 of *The Age of Minerva*. 2 vols. to date.

Janés, Clara. "Rosa Chacel y la libertad." *Salina* 14 (2000): 151–58.

Johnson, Roberta. "The Context and Achievement of *Delirium and Destiny*." *Delirium and Destiny*, trans. Carol Maier. Commentary by Roberta Johnson. Trans. of María Zambrano, *Delirio y destino*. 1989. Albany: SUNY Press, 1999. 215–35.

———. *Gender and Nation in the Spanish Modernist Novel*. Nashville: Vanderbilt University Press, 2003.

———. "'Self'-Consciousness in Rosa Chacel and María Zambrano." *Bucknell Review* 39.2 (1996): 52–70.

Kirkpatrick, Susan. Introduction. *The Maravillas District*. Trans. D. A. Démers. Lincoln: University of Nebraska Press, 1992. Trans. of Rosa Chacel, *Barrio de Maravillas*. v–xxiii.

Lázaro, Reyes. "Cartografía de la 'introversión': Rosa Chacel a la luz de Judith Butler." *Sexualidad y escritura (1850–2000)*. Ed. Raquel Medina and Barbara Zecchi. Barcelona: Anthropos, 2002. 181–92.

Maier, Carol. "Siting *Leticia Valle*: Questions of Gender and Generation." *Experimental Writing by Hispanic Women Writers, Monographic Review Revista Monográfica* 8 (1992): 79–98.

———. "Translator's Afterword: 13 Glosses." *Memoirs of Leticia Valle*. Trans. of Rosa Chacel, *Memorias de Leticia Valle*. 1945. Lincoln: University of Nebraska Press, 1994. 165–98.

Mangini, Shirley. Introducción. *Estación. Ida y vuelta* by Rosa Chacel. 1931. Madrid: Cátedra, 1989. 11–63.

———. "The Many Exiles of Rosa Chacel." *La Chispa '95: Selected Proceedings; The Sixteenth Louisiana Conference on Hispanic Languages and Literatures*. Ed. Claire J. Paolini. New Orleans: Tulane University, 1995. 221–29.

———. *Las modernistas de Madrid: Las grandes intelectuales españolas de la vanguardia*. Barcelona: Ediciones Peninsula, 2001.

———. "Women, Eros, and Culture: The Essays of Rosa Chacel." *Spanish Women Writers and the Essay: Gender, Politics, and the Self*. Ed. Kathleen

Glenn and Mercedes Mazquiarán de Rodríguez. Columbia: University of Missouri Press, 1998. 127–43.

Marías, Julián. "Prólogo a la segunda edición." 1969. *La sinrazón* by Rosa Chacel. 1960. Vol. 1 of *Obra completa*. Ed. Ana Rodríguez Fischer. Valladolid, Spain: Centro de Creación y Estudios Jorge Guillén: Excma. Diputación Provincial de Valladolid, 1989. 49–53.

Meyers, Eunice D. "Narcissism and the Quest for Identity in Rosa Chacel's *La sinrazón*." *Perspectives in Contemporary Literature* 8 (1982): 85–90.

Moix, Ana María. "La agonía de la razón." *Camp de l'arpa* 74 (April 1984): 74–76.

Pizarro Gómez, Francisco Javier. *Timoteo Pérez Rubio*. Badajoz, Spain: Departmento de Publicaciones de la Diputación Provincial de Badajoz, 1998.

Porlán, Alberto. *La sinrazón de Rosa Chacel*. Madrid: Anjana Ediciones, 1994.

Rock, David. *Argentina, 1516–1987: From Spanish Colonization to Alfonsín*. Rev. and exp. ed. Berkeley: University of California Press, 1987.

Rodríguez Fischer, Ana. "Entrevista a Rosa Chacel." *Insula* 537 (May 1993): 24–28.

———. "Introducción." *Artículos I* by Rosa Chacel. Vol. 3 of *Obra completa*. Ed. Ana Rodríguez Fischer. Valladolid, Spain: Centro de Creación y Estudios Jorge Guillén: Excma. Diputación Provincial de Valladolid, 1993. 9–30.

Romero, Luis Alberto. *A History of Argentina in the Twentieth Century*. Trans. James P. Brennan. University Park: Pennsylvania State University Press, 2002.

Scarlett, Elizabeth. "Rosa Chacel." *Twentieth-Century Fiction Writers*. Ed. Marta E. Altisent and Cristina Martín-Carazo. Farmington Hills MI: Gale, 2006. 80–86. Vol. 322 of *Dictionary of Literary Biography*.

———. "Rosa Chacel." *Under Construction: The Body in Spanish Novels*. Charlottesville: University Press of Virginia, 1994. 46–98.

Schwarzstein, Dora. *Entre Franco y Perón*. Barcelona: Crítica, 2001.

Smith, Paul Julian. *Laws of Desire: Questions of Homosexuality in Spanish Writing and Film from 1960–1990*. Oxford: Clarendon Press, 1992.

Waldrop, Rosmarie. "At the Sea." *Blindsight*. New York: New Directions, 2003.

Wilson, Jason. *Buenos Aires: A Cultural and Literary Companion*. New York: Interlink Books, 2000.

Acknowledgments

"Now I close myself up among these inert things and refuse to admit they have no life. It's obvious *for themselves* they don't, but they transmit the life of the people who created their lives. Someone made them and left them here like a written letter, to which I'm trying to respond."

These lines from chapter 12 of *La sinrazón*, written as Santiago Hernández contemplates a small "freakish" bronze frog dressed like a woman and muses that many years earlier someone had made it with the hope that one day someone else—namely he, Santiago—would truly look at it, were in my thoughts often as I wrote *Dream of Reason*. I knew that Rosa Chacel would not read it, but nevertheless I considered my work a response to a letter that had moved me deeply and one to which translation seemed the closest look I could give. Like Santiago, I worked in isolation; and I accept full responsibility for my work. At the same time, however, I knew that no translator works alone, since, by definition, translation is a collaborative endeavor. Ortega y Gasset's comment about the inseparability of one's self and one's circumstances comes to mind here, as does Roman Jakobson's observation—written during the years that Chacel was writing *La sinrazón* and first published in 1959—that words without their circumstances are in effect meaningless, seeing that "the meaning of a linguistic sign is its translation into some further sign." I was aware, then, that translating *La sinrazón* inevitably implied working with at least three "selves" and three sets of

xliii

circumstances—those of the novel as Chacel's letter, those of Chacel as a writer, and my own. To prepare a translation appropriate to my circumstances and those of *Dream of Reason* required a complex understanding of the novel's many signs and as a sign itself in multiple circumstances, in other words, frequent consultations with and help from numerous colleagues and friends.

Now, as I complete *Dream of Reason*, it is a pleasure and an honor to express heartfelt thanks, first to Rosa Chacel for the confidence in my work implied by the willingness she expressed before her death that I undertake the translation, and to her son, Carlos Pérez Chacel, for his patience and the kindness he and his wife, Jamilia, extended to me on various occasions over the years. I am also grateful to Ana Rodríguez Fischer, for her groundbreaking work on Chacel's oeuvre, her friendship, and her many responses to my queries; to Clara Janés, Ana María Moix, and Alberto Porlán, for their generous consultations; to Rolando Costa Picazo, for his help with Argentine expressions and for our correspondence about Rilke's beauty and terror; to the Argentine students, especially Micaela Novas, who answered many questions about places and terms; to Roberta Johnson, for her reading of and conversations about the first drafts of Chacel's introduction to the third edition of *La sinrazón*; and to Sarah Butler, for help with the preparation of the text of early versions of the manuscript. My sincere thanks to Kent State's Institute for Applied Linguistics and University Research Council for the support that made Sarah's work possible, to Kent State University for a sabbatical semester that gave me time to devote to the translation, and to the National Endowment for the Arts for a translation fellowship that also supported my work. To the editors at the University of Nebraska Press, with whom I have worked on both *Memoirs of Leticia Valle* and *Dream of Reason*, I can only say thank you for your encouragement and for allowing *Dream of Reason* to take far longer than any of us expected or wanted. For adequate thanks to friends such as Maryanne Bertram, Ronald Christ, Fred Maier, and Kathleen Ross, who offered assistance with interpretations, definitions, and at times "just" an ear, there are not words in any language. Fred and Ronald also read the entire manuscript. From Ronald, some passages received many readings, in each instance with the attention and interest one rarely finds anywhere except perhaps in the eye of a predatory bird. I can only hope that he has some inkling of how much I value each consultation and conversation as I honed my response to Chacel's novel, always bearing in mind the counsel in Rilke's ninth Duino Elegy: "Preise dem Engel die Welt . . . Sag ihm die Dinge."

Introduction to the Third Edition of *La sinrazón*

As *La sinrazón* begins a third sally into the world and I set out to write a few words of introduction, I'm thinking not about the book but about what Unamuno would call its embryo, *Estación. Ida y vuelta* (Station. Departure and Return), which began to stir in 1925, in Rome, in the garden of the Academia de España—a nook—, a bench in a grove of laurels, and time, idleness, distance. My being far away made it necessary to settle in among the things nearby, to become intimately acquainted with the things that are immune to distancing. The closest thing of course is oneself, with the self's own landscape, the only landscape that won't succumb to description, won't wither in the story—the foliage of that landscape, the varicolored clouds lend themselves to study, sparkle in analysis, expand gradually but, at the same time, withdraw into themselves, wall themselves up within a calcareous defense, like an egg inside the shell that gives it external form as an entity. Form was an ambition then, a longing—what you long for is what must be grasped. What longs is what's already yours, what desires form: the self, so as not to remain in itself, to become visible, to manifest itself as form, collects its aspects, enabling sight and imagination to grasp it. My goal there among the laurels was to find a man's unspoken discourse, unspoken not because it was ineffable but because it was free of any explanation or reference: I wanted to follow the process of a mind moving at the same pace as its vital concomitants—without controlling them, without assisting them as a guiding force. I did not, all those years ago, try to create a character who lacked direction or moral consistency—and who might seem quite modern today—I only tried to achieve the mental discourse of a man who sees himself, analyzes himself, and follows himself in his wandering—the subject's sole characteristic, the urge to wander—through three phases, *Estación. Ida y vuelta.*

An ambition or longing for form, then, became my supreme aesthetic motive, also, not separate from form, but also in the enumeration of appurtenances or conditions—also craft, the goal of doing something and doing it well, without taking into account what, at that time, was considered well done: to do this, confident that the work's veracity, which has nothing to do with its verisimilitude, was solid, a condition that is usually—or was usually—demanded of the novel. Because it was a question of creating a novel, of following a man—not following him as an observer capable of undertaking a story; it had to be the man's mind itself that followed after him, keeping at just the right distance for being able to judge him, not annexing him but joining him, that is, becoming imbued with the nuances of each phase. Of course, in each phase it was necessary at least to suggest its meaning, but without any sort of reflection, simply through the presence of the very elements that constituted the phase. The first phase had to contain the man's essential stability: that first phase is about things that are stable, it's the *estación*, the station, from which he can part, or flee, but it's also his point of departure. The second phase is the *ida*, the departure that leads to nothing consistent, that consists only in the urge to wander. The third phase is the *vuelta*, the return of the man who returns to his senses or to himself, to the place from which he departed.

That book finally sallied forth in Madrid in 1930, but you could say it never sallied at all—it traveled the streets, first in bookstores and soon thereafter in little carts that carried cheap books—cheap in price, a condition caused by their lack of cheapness. Books not everyone could afford—mentally, that is—and it was necessary to make them deceitfully cheap so that people would take a chance and buy them, although they would certainly never read them but, since the books were so cheap . . .

A few pleasant reviews and a warm reception by friends were all that the book accomplished with its sally, which is why it retreated, crouched in its burrow to await more propitious times. It happens that in the burrow or belly—in the mother, according to la Celestina—the embryo grows until it reaches its proper size, but in the mind's matrix dimensions are unlimited. I insist on that metaphor because I'm speaking not only about rational production—I've just spoken about the will to craft something well done, a will found in all who love form, in all who profess and confess that love, but as we all know, there's a vital will—will or tendency or appetite—that accumulates, collects, and combines substantive matter, that fuses out of affinity or, rather, composes into an organic, structural obedience, and this is what happens in the case of time—with the passing of time—whether pleasant or harsh. All times. May one pluralize? Where are the boundaries, the symphyses that articulate some with others? Are they *some* and *others* or are they rapids and poolings of their own current? All times leave their nutritive extracts in the egg. I must insist—people never insist enough: living is insisting—first comes the semi-liquid matter in which the genes sleep—without rest—I'm speaking about what happens without being noticed, without conscious noticing, and then the inner eye begins to see telltale signs of hands and feet—or of paws, plumes, hairs, numberless except to God, and when the plumage or pelt is visible, the time for contemplation begins—active, acting, artisanal contemplation—of the thing gradually coming into being. In this instance—I'm talking about the book as an instance, not as a work, which is what interests the critics—the unformed and evolving matter slept its accumulative sleep for twenty-five years; then, between the time it began to beg for specific features until when it finally broke out of its shell, another decade passed. What I can say about this second book, *La sinrazón*, is that I wrote it over a period of ten years, and I wrote it by hand. It was the time—the pooling, in a sense—when I had the opportunity to collect myself, in Argentina. For me, exile meant establishing myself in Buenos Aires, not with the conquering or productive, practical, enterprising security of those who are going to do something beneficial but with the depth, veracity, essential understanding of one who will know because he remembers . . . That's more accurate than it seems. For me, there was a memory in Buenos Aires. One of my short stories, "En la ciudad de las grandes pruebas" (In the City of Great Tests), begins as follows: "I had gone to that city because of love, not because I was led by some amorous adventure, but because of love for the city." In a way, the tango's invasion of the twenties had a lot to do with it—"I knew the songs," I added in my story— but not just the tango: it was something related especially to Spain, to my generation. The South American literature that interested us then was the quintessence of difficulty, refinement, and intellectualization of the genuine, the indigenous, land, landscape, homeland, fatherland, patria—I'll omit the hotbed of everything seething in that last word— condensed, consummately, in Ricardo Güiraldes's *Don Segundo Sombra*. At that time, Borges was beginning to exist—and to launch wise and fearsome (since they were so accurate) attacks, and Guillermo de Torre, who was very much a part of my group, my time—he was two years younger than I—was about to marry Norah Borges, of the angelic paintings. All this is what I recalled in Buenos Aires; what I saw for the first time came with those legendary bonds in tow, made the incredible love of Rubén Darío's "joyous knight who adores you unseen" come true—a love whose fulfillment was swollen with future but resplendent with memory and past.[1] In the pooling that was Buenos Aires I wrote *La sinrazón* by hand, pages and pages that no publisher would dare print—lack of paper (bakeries sold bread unwrapped)—but I did not forsake meticulousness, repetition, or the spiraling or shaving, taking form on its own, advancing but leaving nothing behind, imprisoning the reminiscences of its time, time (never lost) present in every present because it prompted no *recherche*, the advance of each swirl propelled by the preceding consonant, that is, each consonant rhymed with another, concealed or guided by pious oblivion, a coin bank full of memories, a cage whose open door permitted entrance and exit to anything that kept it swinging. My character, the imperturbable wanderer, poked out his snout—or beak or nose—to see what the weather was like, and he saw the time was right. A quick glance was enough for him to get a good idea of the climate; what he had yet to see was himself. Now there could not be—as there was in that little grove of laurels—an image of things close by, things known so intimately they're left mentioned because they're well known, wandering a Baroja-like Madrid, talking with oneself about "youth and egotism," about what one needed to enter the landscape, to be the man of that landscape laden with memories with which he must familiarize himself. His memories—all that was real—could resume only by his becoming enveloped in a common history of Argentinian-Spanish or Spanish-Argentinian on the pampa. Neither an evocation nor, even less, a story—simply the tone or ambience of the pampa—the only landscape from that side of the world that moved me as I looked at it. I was unconcerned about what people call "finding the right atmosphere" for the novel. Without meaning to, simply because of the elemental—and superficial—contagion implicit in years of coexistence, I erred in a few typical characteristics or expressions (apparently used in inappropriate contexts) whose misplaced imitation grated, but this did not trouble me unduly, because I believe that everything I lived in the province of Buenos Aires—from Güiraldes's pampa, with its owls and weasels, to the banks of the Quequén River, its meanders repeated like the ink stain on a folded sheet of paper, by the endless flock of seagulls—everything love entails, everything that was suitable for, kindred to, and homogeneous with a love drama and that could serve with utmost silence as background for it was, I believe, contained in the book, and I believe the small group of souls sufficiently close to me and the issues I addressed have been able to see this—those who were able to see a few lives and a concordant world far removed from any informing detail, harmonized solely by an inner diapason.

As for the love drama, it's a repetition—or a development—of the first book. The wanderer arrives in the pampa laden with things forgotten—cloistered, forgetting, crouched silently for a long time, circumspect in its arcane power, prowls throughout, haunts the three phases—also the season/*station* of the year—it's spring when stability settles in, he becomes accustomed to normality—normality is ostentatious, scandalous, provocative—, forgetfulness shatters the unpolluted glass, and this time the wanderer does not face *departure*: the forgotten path comes to lay itself at his feet. The *return* is equally faithful: the fugitive returns whole, but his steps have left irreversible tracks. The drama is his arrival at the edge of the ravine. The (embryonic) *return* ended with his youthful phase, with the smile of his virgin experience: "Everything has ended, now I can say *beginning*." On the second return, the drama stops at the edge of the abyss in which a struggle occurs—between two abysses, Life and Death, both inscrutable—, a struggle between what happened and what is going to happen. Death being more comfortable and, above all, easier—not Death adopted as a solution but Death reached by exasperating the life of the mind, from an attachment, a fidelity to life that consumes life itself. In the embryonic *return*, the danger of life was braved, discovering guilt—flaunting danger, *placing* within it—the passionate love of life: "I won't enter the company of honorable men with false merits . . . I won't take my life, since I want to live. What I will do is show life. I could hide it—in other words I could dissimilate my voracious pleasure in life, but I will expose it. My courage can reach that far. Neither tossing life with feigned generosity nor guarding it as something illicit. Going with it, loving it immensely, absorbed in it . . . And, if possible, may life be taken from me when it's most precious to me." I believe that these lines show clearly how much that anguished book needed to reach the full potential in its substantial notes. The character's amorality was similar to prenatal omnipotence, but his psychophysical organs, his preferential, project-planning gifts, expected laws empowered by the pleasing hope of imposition, resembling the irrepressible urge to bite down prompted by one's first teeth. In the second *return*, departure tries not to succumb to despair, it struggles—in war or death—to live to the last drop or moment without stopping when there's still time. "It's not yet one, I could take the car and drive into the city. At three, there are plenty of places to eat. If I ate and drank a lot, maybe I'd recover my common sense. Why not do it? Why not accept being the normal man I've always tried to be?" But he doesn't go, because what's urgent for him is risk, he needs to push his forces to the utmost or rational paroxysm; it's not enough that he expose them, as he did when he had the faith to move mountains. In the drama—in what is, in the end, a novel—his religious life and his love life run in perfect parallel. In the embryonic attempt this theme did not exist—or barely existed. There was a play on words between "communion" and "communism" that already revealed a sort of tingling, as when a limb that's fallen asleep starts to wake up. In the second sally—or sailing—the religious theme is conflictive from the onset. From the *station*, the theme is situated ostentatiously with normality, defined as the most natural, family-centered background and Catholic education, which little by little begins venturing into pragmatic superstitions, into animistic apprehensions that excite speculative activity and therefore create a dialogue, dealing, or commerce with God that is *too* quotidian—*too* quotidian because it's speculative: a mystical process of contemplation and surrender is susceptible to neither more nor less. The quotidian nature of that commerce, which is an unequal battle, converts the amorous struggle into a conjugal dispute or persistent contest. The soul—the wife—dissipates in trivial whims, continually demands proofs of love, becomes angry, irritated if not indulged at any hour of the day or night. The relationship cools from weariness, from the erosion or dulling of sensation until all that's left is the wrecked ship, in desolation and despair, and the only plank or handle in sight is prayer, provocative, defiant prayer: conclusive as a last risk, as a "let's see what happens," let's see how far entreaty can get.

It's a bit superfluous to talk about a book in the same volume in which the book appears in its entirety. But what book appears in its entirety? What book doesn't need continuation and news of its annunciation and slow incarnation? If I've gone into this at some length—almost to the point of recounting the plot—it's been to make clear the extent to which the book owed its rooting, rather, its existence, to my first novel, continued and preserved since then beneath other things—novels, short stories, and philosophizing in various genres on which I've spent my time and energy. I don't know which of my books might be the best, but these two are the truest and deepest—the most necessary. Unnecessary: for myself, I've written nothing, but this one—the two are one—is the most personal. To that, contemporary critics—authorized, intelligent, devoted and estimable no matter how you look at them—might say they find other books more authentic, but you shouldn't believe that what first leaps into view is what's most authentic. I can't put everything these two books lack into this introduction: I've tried to put that in all the other books; it's what everyone—everyone who writes—does in every book. I can't put it here, because space and time don't permit. I believe that the only thing worth stressing is what I've already pointed out: the formal effort for innovation, never detonation. Innovation on the basis of normality, which is neither conformism nor reformism but evolutionism of normality's own potencies toward their power. Be careful with that word! It means, *exclusively,* the *power to be*—an evolution that means reflection and a gauging of what's needed, what's lacking, what must be added. The innovation I pursued from the beginning was not, especially, in the prose—the rigor and simplicity already achieved or imposed by the school of my generation—; rather, it involved mental sequences in their inevitable natural linking. That's why, in my first book, I excluded even the names of the central characters in order to avoid anything concrete—within, there's no need to make things concrete. My theme was a man talking to himself, but *telling himself nothing*: he speaks about what he knows, and the references to one thing or another are presented in the images and sensations of their effects, in the emotions and passions of their causes. Was this a *novel* style? No, it was the search for an *image-driven* language, in other words, for kinetic images, linked by their fittings and connections, which enabled me to avoid (almost entirely) all morality, all convenience, all common sense. Automatism, surrealism . . . obviously. The only thing I tried to offer as my contribution was outrageous normality, the omission of any *oddity* or *extravagance.* Extravagance, vagrance, is eccentric, dispersive wandering, and my purpose was unfailingly concentric. Concentric vision need not be egotistic or narcissistic: it tries, solely and exclusively, to be essential. In the second book, because the scope was so much greater, I no longer continued to avoid names and concrete details, but I did maintain the supremacy of the image—my mental nourishment and instrument; I did not want to retain anything, such as forced rhyme, that could sap the naturalness of the development. My character embarks on his three phases and, with a certain ambiguity, the events and incidents of his story gradually become visible. To some extent, *imagine-driven* linking remains enslaved to logic, although it continues to be sovereign, always commanding in the present, but because it's fated to exist, not because of logic. The two books part company only in their endings. In the first, irresistible youth eagerly sets out, anticipating the pleasures of the journey; in the second, youth contemplates the footsteps along a path already traversed, contemplating, reflecting on, and considering not the irreversible but the current forks. The wanderer's past does not belong to him alone; other paths—the causes and effects of his particular route—led off in unexpected directions that described curves and angles, circling round and round, attracted, perhaps to the original path . . . The past causes neither discouragement nor terror, but you must immerse yourself in its explication until you understand or you die.

Anyone who reaches the end of this book will find more things than these: here, I've already told too much about too many.

Rosa Chacel
MARCH 1977

NOTE

1. [Trans. note] From "Sonatina," by Rubén Darío, *Selected Poems of Rubén Darío*, trans. Lysander Kemp (1965; Austin: University of Texas Press, 1988), 53.

DREAM OF REASON

PART ONE

*D'un monde où l'action n'est pas
la soeur du rêve*
CHARLES BAUDELAIRE

I

A few words, seemingly quite trivial when spoken, over time have become identified with one of the climactic moments in my life. What I'm
thinking about occurred during a period so frivolous I'm embarrassed
to describe it; nevertheless, I must describe it.

That whole period is very distant now, but I remember it well, well
enough to tell about it reliably, which is not at all unusual. People often remember past events in detail; the hard thing is to recall what you
were like then while you're recalling now, to summon, from experience,
knowledge, and disillusion, an exact remembrance of not knowing, of
innocence. That's very difficult and that's what I want to achieve, especially the recollection of innocence, because ignorance actually increases
with knowledge—experience and disillusion make it much easier for
us to ponder the extent of our ignorance. Innocence is not extensive,
though: innocence either is or is not.

Well, the fact is, my innocence definitely *is* no longer, but I remember
well the exact tone it gave my life when it *was*, and I must admit that its
tone can be tolerated only when you're quite young.

No. This path will definitely lead me in the wrong direction. One
more metaphor and I'll slip into irony, the very thing I want to keep out
of these pages entirely. Not one bit of irony: I must face up to the fact
that my story is very banal and be brave enough to confess that without
adopting the attitude of someone who's already on top of *everything*. I'm

3

not on top of anything; on the contrary, *everything* is on top of me. And my goal in starting this account is not to get out from under that weight, but to get what's on top of me in front of me. So I should go to my tale itself, without embroidering or paraphrasing with flowery profundities. To my tale of the most foolish, common things, in order to place on record—these pages are no more than a simple act of recording—that my life, what I experience inside as a seismic phenomenon, when seen as bare facts was in fact nothing more.

In the spring of 1932 about two years had passed since I returned from Europe. My absence had lasted almost as long as my entire life—when I left Buenos Aires I was only a few months old. Even so, even though that period was not clear in my mind, the idea that I had been here was always with me. The idea? Why not the memory? A memory is passed on, inherited, adopted. Yes, I always remembered having been here and always felt certain I would return. I knew I'd return to the city and the house where I'd been born, knew what the furniture was like in that house, and everything I did when I was very young—the trips and studies—was something I started so as to have it done with before I returned. Then once I was here, it was a question of recovering things, not of becoming acquainted with them.

I don't know if that initial premise has determined the way I am, because, the thing is, even in other, completely unfamiliar cities it's always seemed that I was searching for my own footsteps.

But this is already thoughts, reflections, and what I've proposed is to make that time, that naturalness, which was so comfortable, present now. I was a boy from Buenos Aires who studied and lived like any other boy, except I had a history. It was a history completely forgotten, not with the unfaithful kind of forgetting that tosses everything overboard, but with a forgetting that had come to be like a state of some body—mine: I had solidified in a body, but all the fluid things composing it were circulating within its tranquil mass, releasing their waves, their currents.

No, no, that's not it! I simply lived on Juncal and studied chemistry. I lived alone, and I had few friends; my only close friend was Javier Molina, a distant relative. I didn't have much family.

The first signs of spring had appeared, which had happened other years, but this is about that spring, the spring of 1932. It was late August, and I remember thinking about spring as I crossed the Plaza San Martín. It was beginning to get dark, and a wonderful light seemed to be walking across the grass. Dusk is so short here you can watch it go past. A warm breeze goes by, the sky, very clean and pearly, gives off a bleak light, which slips away toward the trees to hide in the branches, and suddenly, in the shadow of the trees, there's the glow of a newly lit streetlamp: dusk is gone. At that moment I bought *Crítica* and continued toward Santa Fe.

Why did I buy *Crítica* as I was contemplating the plaza? It's quite unusual for me to read a newspaper, but a kid came up to me, insistently waving a paper. It's highly unusual for me not to dispatch someone rudely if he happens to interrupt me at such a moment, because I was *truly contemplating* the plaza. I was standing on a corner, waiting to cross, but I'd hesitated there on the green slope, since I wasn't in a hurry, and the kid came up to me, shouting right beside me: "*Crítica! Crítica!*" His shouts didn't bother me or annoy me, which is how I usually react to any kind of shouting. I let it become part of my contemplation and looked at the boy. I think it was to apologize for my lingering gaze that I took out a few coins and bought the paper. Then, when I reached the La Santa Unión I went into the café, sat down, and started leafing through the paper.

On the cultural page there was a long article about the Ballet Montecarlo. I was skimming it quickly, when suddenly I saw one name: Elfriede Pabst. I read closely and learned that Elfriede Pabst was one of the secondary figures in the troupe, which would arrive that week in Montevideo.

From that moment on I can no longer recount the events step by step, nor is that necessary. The name Elfriede Pabst appeared in the August twilight, fifteen minutes after I stood on a corner thinking about spring. I kept myself very busy that whole week, since I could hardly set out right on the spot.

The ballet was to open on Saturday. Friday night, as the boat pulled away, I stood at the stern watching the varied lights of the port recede into the distance, followed by the river coastline, the Costanera, ablaze with lanterns. I recalled how at other times I'd leaned on the stone balustrade and watched the boat depart, imagining that it was probably filled with happy people, themselves filled with fantasy and adventure. Seeing the boat from the Costanera, I'd always thought it looked like a shining caterpillar advancing toward the darkness, and at that moment, as I leaned overboard, it pleased me to think that maybe there was someone watching this boat pull away, now that I was the traveler I'd imagined at other times.

But was I truly like those happy people in my imagination? No, I was not exactly the same, I was happier in a way, because I knew that I wanted to be happy. Or maybe you're happier if you're happy without knowing it? I wouldn't try to guess. The thing is, it was happiness I aspired to. Maybe happiness was my true city of origin, because I ached to return there. Since I was very healthy and my physical makeup was quite normal, I must have been richly blessed with happiness at birth; but in the first years of my life that wealth went astray, rather, it became buried as the result of unquestionably serious events, and all I had left of it was nostalgia. I said I aspired to happiness, but that's not what it was, because aspiration's a very lukewarm word: happiness was my missing amor, I desired it furiously, ached for it melancholically.

However, I don't mean to say I went through life feeling sad or pensive. I lived by making use of all my small everyday pleasures and, if I confess this did not satisfy me, someone will argue that I could have sought better incentives that would have brought me inner satisfaction. Obviously I didn't do that, but not because I looked at human problems indifferently; on the contrary, I often thought about the most dramatic of those problems, but such pondering was confined to the zone linked to effort. Separate, exempt from everything, untouched, was the pleasure zone—weightless as sleep, but real. For me, that was the supreme adjective: the *real* happiness, the *real* pleasure. As opposed to the gibberish about "Vanity of vanities" . . .

I'm straying too far from my story. This whole thing seems more and more like a theory, and I wasn't formulating a theory as the boat crossed the estuary: I was thinking about Elfriede, raising the entire structure of her memory so I could add another piece to it the next day.

There was a south wind blowing; I was leaning over the railing, looking at the water, the foam splattering my face with cold drops that helped me recall the rain in Berlin and Elfriede in the rain, the snow, or the forest fog. I recalled how she used to dress like a student—sweater, wool cap and scarf—which is exactly what she was wearing the day I met her beneath the sieved light of the museum. I recalled her skating on the neighborhood rinks in the January afternoons, dancing at night in the cabarets or at the fiestas held on Alexander Platz.

In the days I'd spent waiting for the moment of my trip, I'd imagined a thousand times how our meeting would be, imagining the things I would tell her and all the possible vicissitudes of our new adventure, but that night, as I was actually on my way to her, I made sure my memory of her was very current, as if I were going to take an exam. Not that I expected her to ask, "Did you think about me often?" No, ours hadn't been that kind of relationship. I hadn't thought about her at all, or very little. She wasn't going to ask for a flattering account of my thoughts, and I wasn't going to offer her one, but it seemed discourteous just to appear like that, without giving any notice, without knowing if she wanted to see me. I could have sent her a few lines—but I didn't—instead of carrying with me an intense memory that would legitimize my appearance to some extent. I was sure that I'd find noticeable differences in her—the climate, the season, her professional success would all have combined to make her look very different, and I didn't want to feel disconcerted by that difference. Did I feel uncertain about how well our meeting would turn out? Maybe that was it. Maybe I was bent on making the past current so I could impose on it whatever eventuality might arise in the present.

That was the cause of everything. If I'd spent the time on the boat sleeping peacefully, I would probably have behaved differently, but I didn't want to sleep, I wanted instead to awaken all the impressions I could still recall from those two months experienced four years earlier and now almost forgotten. I was delving into a very deserted zone and my memory had the same kind of power as an undegraded element. It was if I were telling myself a passionate story. I stood alone on the deck, all I could hear was the water lapping against the side of the boat, all I could see was the brilliant black of the moonless night, and I relived the serene light in the Altes Museum. I saw myself entering with two other boys who were studying chemistry, and Elfriede was sitting on a step beside the Altar of Pergamum; she smiled at one of my friends, we went over to say hello, and she joined our group.

I had to laugh as I recalled how brazenly I held forth in French, knowing I could get away with it since the others had only a relative understanding of what I said. Their scientific French was hardly good enough to follow my lively comments about artistic subjects, not delivered in an organized, academic way they would have found accessible but abrupt opinions, linked according to my own system. Elfriede's French was limited to a couple dozen words, and I assumed they included the adjectives commonly used to praise artists—when they'd introduced us they'd told me she was a ballerina—; in fact, those words were the only things she understood in my whole lecture. Like a snake charmer, I fascinated her, immobilized her, cornering her against that frieze, forcing her back into it until she seemed like one more figure in the poignant relief. If she tried to escape, I would say *"Superbe, grandiose!"* and she would be still. Besides, there were the other two boys, whose gazes were guarding her attentively, and I forced them to converge on her. We were talking about the barbarian physique copied by Hellenistic sculpture, and I had them compare Elfriede's head with that of the Nyx, as much like flesh, as human as any girls you see on the street in Berlin. Then I took her over to the large, sorrowful head of the mother of the Titans and had the boys note that Elfriede's forehead was identical. Using my index finger, I followed the line of the frontal bone that borders the deep sockets of the statue's eyes, and with the greatest self-assurance I stretched out my hand to Elfriede's head, drawing the same line on it with my finger. Elfriede started a little, but she got a grip on her nerves, and I realized that she was surrendering her hard-won serenity to me.

Impatiently, hastily, I seized the treasure I'd snared. We left the museum and my artistic harangue came to an end. She and I looked for a different atmosphere that would give us more privacy and let us express ourselves more openly: for two months we were inseparable.

Little by little, as I recalled her in other places we'd lived enthusiastically, I began to recall the music from that time: the waltzes flung by a loudspeaker onto the ice rink; the fox-trots and tangos from the cabarets at night. Elfriede danced with the rigor you find in professionals, and I would abandon my weight to her strong, lithe body until I felt the vertigo you feel when you're lying in a hammock being driven violently back and forth; if the source of that driving is in you yourself, it surrenders you to the power of an irresistible rhythm.

As I thought about this, I suddenly looked at my watch and was surprised that without realizing it I'd spent three hours leaning on the stern's railing. I'm sure my moment of absence had been the moment I recalled the rhythm of the dance, which may have been suggested by the rhythm of the water. One after the other I'd reviewed all the previous memories but on that memory I stopped, got lost. I might have spent two or three hours reliving the beat of a fox-trot, and I'm tempted to say reliving it without repeating it. Nothing but the time in which I thought of those notes that in one fast whirl had abandoned us to inertia. Nothing but those few notes making me press myself tightly against her so we could move totally within that drive—her hair was driven loose from her neck, sideward, like a heavy tassel, and there could have been a light laugh or a quick breath in response to our brief frenzy. Nothing but a violent levity in the semi-dark room, for a few notes. As I contemplated that moment in the solitude of the deck, three hours stopped or condensed into one unextended point; three hours turned into one fast whirl. Then I decided to go to bed.

I think that when I returned to my cabin I also recalled those nights in her room, when she prepared the cups for coffee and spread butter on the black bread, as the *bouilloire* spewed its torrent of steam toward the ceiling. Elfriede would be maneuvering around the room, moving in ways she moved only there, with the slow self-assurance of a woman at home. And I would be sunk in an armchair, watching her and thinking, nevertheless, she is a ballerina. Sometimes she'd be wearing heavy boots made specially to withstand the clips on her skates, and thick woolen socks, but none of it could hide the beauty of her athletic legs.

I recalled another thousand things, but finally I fell asleep and woke up when it was daylight.

On my way to the hotel I indulged in no further evocations, because I was clinging to something that was not an idea, it was a reality with one shore in the past and the other in the current moment, and I was immersed in it, even though at various times I thought I was paying attention to other matters. This was the important thing: the thousand incidents that arose in the outside world were not enough to wipe out the fixation responsible for my mood nor to replace the atmosphere created by my reverie. In other words, if I were to relate only the facts, I would have to say that the next day, in the morning, I seemed to be in that clear, wide-awake moment when one forgets the dreams of the night before, since I don't recall relating them consciously to any of the situations that followed—not even my meeting with Elfriede.

Our meeting was almost trivial, and somehow it seemed artificial: what was real remained deeply latent.

As soon as I arrived at the hotel—I'd found out from an agency where she was staying—I saw Elfriede appear in the hall, on her way out with three other girls. When she saw me, she made a gesture of exaggerated surprise. She came toward me, stammering, and began to say that she'd been so shocked to see me she'd been left speechless. Finally she decided to give me a very theatrical embrace. I tried hurriedly to formulate a plan, but her day was going to be exhausting. She had rehearsal in the afternoon; in addition, some problem or other had arisen with her wardrobe. We arranged to meet in the theater.

I was awake during the event. That is to say, I paid attention to the ballet and especially to Elfriede's performance, which I thought was excellent. At intermission I went to see her, in the midst of the human throng trying to get near the artists, but all she could do was extend a hand to me over a dozen heads. After the performance, the audience began to disappear, but several men remained, standing guard, more or less journalists or managers, who felt it was their right to monopolize the troupe until the dancers collapsed totally—they were taking them right from the theater to a party someone was holding in their honor. In the second that Elfriede and I had to speak, we decided to meet for lunch the next day.

Later, I've recalled that when I told Elfriede how happy I was to see her fulfill her ambitions, she answered me somewhat skeptically: "I don't know what to tell you; everything's hanging by a thread." I attributed this to tiredness or, rather, it didn't register on me. I went back to the hotel on foot, walked in circles around my room, and read a magazine before I went to bed, sitting in the middle of the floor under the one abominable light. The hotel was full, and I'd been given one of the worst rooms.

Did my dreams recur? I'd say instead that they continued until I fell asleep, while I slept, and when I got up, quite late, as I was getting dressed. The thing is, though, that's not exactly how it was. My thoughts changed. I had seen Elfriede in her new look: she was spring-like at the hotel, and classic, super perfect on stage, with a tutu so sheer it made you forget her serious head. But underneath my thoughts something remained unalterable: our fast whirl in the semi-dark room. That was what gave my mood the tone I couldn't change. No matter what my ideas were, what prevailed was the climate of that moment.

I woke up with just enough time to get ready before the time we'd agreed to meet, so I wouldn't have to wait—I'm always afraid other people won't be punctual. But almost before I was dressed, Elfriede's knuckles rapped on the door and she burst into the room. When I saw her walk in, I saw that reality was beginning; I saw Elfriede, finally, the way I was expecting her, although at the same time, as soon as I looked at her, I saw in her face how frustrating the whole situation was.

Elfriede began to speak. I can't say that I heard absolutely nothing of what she told me. It was something about a contract extremely important for her, something that had come up the night before, very late, and in the morning she hadn't wanted to phone from her room; she'd preferred to come in person and explain it to me.

On the dresser there was a nail file, a pipe, and a brush. Leaning against the dresser, I picked up the pipe and began to smack it against the palm of my hand. Even today it seems unbelievable to me that I would have fallen into that commonplace, that I would have committed such a stale action, reproduced the most worn out cliché imaginable. And conscious that I was doing something shameful.

Elfriede's words didn't penetrate into my ear. All I heard were the hollow smacks of my pipe in the palm of my hand; I was choked by annoyance and bewildered by embarrassment because I was doing that without being able to avoid it. My entire attention was monopolized by the repugnance I felt at the sound of those smacks; I don't know why, but it reminded me of those fish that puff up like bubbles in order to defend themselves. That hollow noise seemed to betray a bubble of anger puffing up larger and larger in my throat.

Nevertheless, I of course managed to smile and assure her that it made no difference, that any other day, whenever she wanted . . . I'm sure my tone of voice was not natural, because Elfriede's reaction certainly was not: she felt intimidated and also began to do false things. When she arrived, her bearing had been extremely open and unaffected; suddenly she started to maneuver around the room, trying to mime a doleful departure. She was attempting to trivialize the situation with comic poses, with poorly executed dance steps: I didn't see her. Just as a few minutes before I'd been unable to hear what she explained to me, I couldn't see what she was doing as she circled around in the hotel. I was aware only of hearing the smacks of my pipe and of my effort to smile.

I don't know how long that scene lasted, but I know my imagination ran through all the thoughts of the day before, and Elfriede's story came alive in my memory once again; except this time the dominant tone was not the warm half-light of the dance hall but the white light of the museum, one now crude, desolate, and beneath it, my emphatic voice, masked in a language almost inaccessible to my audience, kept repeating, "*Déjà chez Lysippe* . . ." That was the most embarrassing phrase, I don't

12   *Dream of Reason*

know why, it was like an accomplice or an accessory to the capricious adjectives she intuited—she now spoke French fluently—and it made a hollow sound that filled the entire expanse of the museum.

Suddenly, in one of her turns, Elfriede stopped sharply and raised a hand to her forehead. I remained impassive, believing it was part of her dance. But I saw that the lamp—a shade of counterweighted white glass hanging from a thick wire cable—was askew and swinging very low, and then it registered on me that I'd just heard a short, vibrant *smack*. I tore myself away from myself and ran toward Elfriede, who still had her hands on her forehead. There was a stream of blood running down her cheek and dripping onto her collar.

She had a cut a few inches long slightly above her left eyebrow, clean, like the cut made by an axe. I'd probably left the light in that low position the night before, when I was reading in the middle of the room. I tried to treat her with something I had in my overnight bag. As soon as I'd bandaged the cut she made an effort to leave, repeating and stressing her words: "I told you *I have to go*: I will go even if my head is split open."

Her hands were shaking and she was very pale. I begged her to rest for a minute, and she agreed to sit in the armchair.

In order to hold her there, I began trying to remove the blood spots from the collar of her white *tailleur*—something I knew was impossible—using a piece of white cotton dipped in alcohol, and I began making stupid comments. I wanted to distract her, to quiet her agitation, which had dissipated my own. At that moment I'd become completely calm and the only thing I wanted was to make her feel how much I regretted the mishap, how annoyed I felt about ending up in that situation. What bad luck, I said, all our plans were ruined! My intentions for today were so different . . . She looked at me as she never had and so truly, so deeply that she also seemed to be placing her entire history in that gaze. It's hard to find words for this, but she looked at me as she had never looked at me and as if that were how she always should have looked at me, as if she were looking at me from before, or *through* before. It seemed to me that her gaze and her silence were lasting a long time, but they weren't, because she responded to my exclamation immediately: "Your intentions! You'd better watch out for your intentions!"

Her answer made me shiver with something similar to fear: I thought it had made me feel uneasy because I didn't understand it completely. There was nothing at all mysterious about the sentence, but I noticed in it some incomprehensible dimension. What intentions was she referring to? She spoke as if she were wounded by my intentions, as if we'd just fought to the bitter end and she'd fallen, defeated by the force I'd felt turning agonistically inside. Because the fact was that a few moments before a boundless force had convulsed within me. It had been something disproportionate to its cause, a squall over a drama in which neither love nor hate played a role, something like a bull strangled by a silk cord. But some kind of black beast, some kind of hooves had indeed drawn sparks from the deepest part of my being. I felt as guilty as if I'd kicked her, and this made me feel an enormous respect for her.

Without moving away, I tried to look at her from a new distance, because at that moment, I don't know why, I realized for the first time that she was a foreigner. I invented a rather imploring smile so she would let me look deeply into her eyes. Their blue seemed more intense than ever and very distant, deep in those large sockets I admired so much. I realized that she saw me very well from that distant blue; maybe as I looked at her that way I dropped my usual cover, letting her see things even I myself could not discern but things that she, from her point of view, perceived with total clarity. Maybe she always knew them. A foreigner's gaze is sometimes blind to very obvious things, but it can also perceive things concealed from those with conventions in common, and from awareness, which itself acquiesces to common conventions.

I sustained Elfriede's intense gaze for a while, sitting on the arm of the armchair, holding her two hands in one of mine and, with my other hand, arranging the hair on her forehead, which had become damp. Freed now from the previous violence, I could caress her as always, and that contact reconciled me with her. I held her there only a few minutes. Then I accompanied her to her room so she could change her clothes, and I called a taxi but let her leave by herself. That night I took the boat and returned home.

When the ballet arrived in Buenos Aires, Elfriede was not listed in the cast.

This incident occurred many years ago, and I've neither seen her nor heard from her since. It's true that on my part I did nothing to make that happen, because I wasn't really in love with Elfriede. Elfriede never stood for anything important in my life. Never anything more than what's been told so far. Nothing more than that, but that's the beginning of everything.

2

It ought to be possible, I think, to relate only actions. But actions are one thing or yet another, depending on whether they're your doing or you're theirs, in which case you're automatically defined by actions.

I've just recounted an incident from my life, and something of my character may show through there, but my character isn't what's interesting—the incident *is*. Even so, I think I should go back, to my earliest years, although briefly, in order to show that in my history there was no precedent for the most important events that occurred later. There wasn't something in my character that caused them: that's what's important about the nature of those events.

As my point of departure I'll take the moment when my vocation was decided, by circumstantial impressions.

When I returned from Switzerland with my mother, in 1918, we went directly to Segovia. My mother wanted to rest alongside her brothers and sisters, and she knew her rest would come very soon. Me, they took immediately to Madrid, to the home of my uncle Andrés, who had to take charge of my education—of course I would do my undergraduate study with the Jesuits. But my uncle put off quite a while the moment for sending me to school. First, he enjoyed having me with him and spoiling me; second, since my mother had died suddenly and there hadn't been time for me to get to see her, my uncle said that he was afraid to shut me away at boarding school, where the dismal atmosphere might be harmful to me.

Those theories of my uncle Andrés helped me to formulate, for the first time in my life, my inclination toward and, I'm tempted to say, my adherence to happiness. My uncle would often say that a boy needs to live in a happy environment, that a boy must be happy by nature. I was deeply sad at the time, but when I heard my uncle speak that way, I would recall a cane fence covered with sun-scorched bellflowers casting a shadow on the sand, and from time to time there would be one exceptional open bellflower, whose color was dazzling. I never found out where the fence was, but I felt sure it was what my uncle was referring to, and I found out he was right: the best thing was to head toward that luminous zone, even though I saw clearly that it was in the distance.

But before casting my lot with happiness, I'd already decided what I would study. That happened during my first days in Madrid. My uncle had some large laboratories in Ciudad Lineal that provided medical supplies to the surrounding villages, and he took me to visit them. An enameled white door opened silently and we entered an enormous hallway, then we passed through corridors and rooms, walking on linoleum and seeing ourselves reflected on stucco walls. The people working there, men and women dressed in white, were wordlessly engrossed in their tasks, carefully operating sparkling equipment with precise movements or distilling liquids in glass containers with enchanting shapes. Everything was enveloped in an identical light that entered through the translucent panes of large windows, bouncing from one white wall to another, making shadows impossible.

They opened the movable pane of one of the lower windows, and a piece of the countryside toward Alcalá—some yellow poplars and a blue sky in furious opposition—blazed beneath the noonday sun as if they'd opened the window onto a world of fire. But the window was closed immediately and the cold light was again intact.

My uncle watched me admiring everything and told me in a suggestive, tempting voice: "If you were to study chemistry, all this would be yours when you finished."

I promised to study everything that might be necessary and I promised it to myself privately: I resolved, decisively, to enter whatever profession would give me that kind of care and clarity, that order, that silence of footsteps on linoleum.

For those memories to function as facts, I must make it clear that the decision taken then, when I was eight years old, and from which I have not deviated an iota, doesn't mean I found my image reflected there; on the contrary, it means I saw my antithesis in that whole situation. Because there was something feverish and gloomy in me; I wanted to settle in that immaculateness, as if between clean, soothing sheets.

When we were on our way home, my uncle suddenly said to me: "Don't tell anyone what happened at the laboratory."

"But why?" I protested, surprised, because it seemed impossible for me not to tell anyone how dazzled I'd been.

He immediately added that I could tell what I'd seen, but not what he'd promised me. And since he saw from my face that disappointment and doubt were rapidly sabotaging me, he hastened to assure me: "You think that once you've finished your studies I won't give you the lab? All right, then, we won't wait so long: I give it to you right on the spot. Be absolutely sure of it, the lab's yours now, but don't tell anyone, anyone at all. Later I'll tell you why."

I gave my word and kept it. I spoke with no one about the lab; not only did I refrain from telling that he'd given it to me, I never even mentioned the lab, not for a long time. Then, two years after the inevitable had occurred, my uncle decided to send me to school and that brought up the problem of whether or not I could refer to my future profession and my laboratory. When my uncle came to see me, I asked him how long I had to remain silent about it and, surprised by my discretion, he told me it was no longer necessary to keep the secret, that I could tell everyone. Then he looked at me, as if he were testing my stamina—I was almost twelve—and said: "Your mother was the only person you weren't to tell."

That day he refused to say more, but soon it came time for vacation, and one afternoon, as we were walking together in El Espinar, I plied him with questions until he wound up telling me. Then I learned my family history, which I will recount as a way of explaining how I am and am not Argentine.

A person never stammers as much when he's starting to tell a risqué, hair-raising, or complicated story as when he's starting to recount an unimportant event that will have to coincide in beginning and unfolding with very common tales that are well known to everyone. Putting aside my fear of seeming less than interesting, I will note as the origin of my family something that's similar in all respects to the beginning of an incalculable number of other family histories.

My great-great-grandfather, don Mariano Hernández, arrived in Buenos Aires at the end of the eighteenth century. He came with an official administrative post, which he'd procured for the purpose of leaving the Peninsula. He was very young, had studied law, and held advanced ideas. Naturally, he immediately aligned himself with the independence movement. He fought, bravely, on the side of the criollos, as proved by the numerous battle crosses I continue to hold on to, and later married a woman from his new land. That marriage probably also gave him a bit of land, which he soon learned how to increase. He had children. The eldest, Emilio, my great-grandfather, also studied law; he shared his father's deep love of the land and worked with him so capably that each year was more prosperous for them than the last.

My great-grandfather also married in Argentina and had only two sons. The elder, Santiago, my grandfather, studied traditional law, but this son did not strive meekly to increase his patrimony: he traveled throughout Europe and, when he reached France, he flatly refused to leave. He married a French woman who belonged to the society he wanted to enter—my grandfather had a taste for literature—, a woman of some culture and distinction who knew how to live in the great world of letters. For several years they lived in Paris, not allowing themselves to be uprooted, despite paternal entreaties. Finally, fearing that grandfather Mariano's last years were approaching, they decided to come back. Once they were here, in the patriarchal aura of their house, they produced an heir, whom the stagnant family fortune was awaiting in hopes of receiving a new impetus. My father was also named Santiago. As soon as don Mariano Hernández, who was in his nineties, had died, my grandparents returned to Paris and resumed their triumphant life. The younger son imitated them in everything and capably squandered his share of the inheritance.

My father studied literature, which was my grandfather's vocation, and it continued to interest him, but he didn't intend to make it his profession: he devoted himself to satisfying his curiosity about books, cities, and people. After traveling all over Europe and the neighboring countries, one day when he was in Paris it occurred to him that, Spain being so close, he could easily spare a couple of weeks and take a little trip to Madrid, which he still hadn't visited. There he met my mother, who wasn't even from Madrid; she was from the minuscule city of Segovia—a heap of yellow stones next to the dry sierra. My grandfather welcomed the marriage enthusiastically, because it seemed to him that it would draw the clan, which tended to scatter, back to the ancestral home. He served as best man by proxy, and my parents returned to Buenos Aires on their honeymoon.

But my grandfather had to content himself with a very short period of family life, because my father was more interested in books than in the land; a few months after I was born, my parents left with me for France, offering some pretext or other, or without any pretext.

Here my uncle's story starts to merge with a vague but powerful memory: the luminous region where I spent my earliest years, Niza, Mallorca. I had a Norman governess who looked after me while I played on the beach. I remember her well because I kept the same governess until I was eight years old, but I have one much earlier memory of her that's both partial and gigantic. I recall being on the beach one day, stark naked, and the waves were knocking me over on the sand. One hit full force and sent me rolling until I collided with two legs: Jeanne was standing there with her skirt hiked up to her knees and her feet buried in the sand. My head collided with her hard calf, which was covered with sand and firm as a post. I tried to grab hold, but the tide dragged me a couple of meters, and right away another new wave had me crashing into her again. That time, I managed to cling to her ankle; when the water receded, it couldn't pull me away, and I felt it pass, sweeping the sand from beneath my body. Up above, Jeanne was roaring with laughter.

That's one of the bright points I still have from the region where I experienced my natural happiness. There were only a few additional fragments I could insert into my uncle's tale.

In 1914 we were in Cassis when the war broke out. We went to Switzerland, settled in Geneva, and could have waited there until the disaster was over, but my father would not refrain from participating. He didn't go so far as to enlist in the Allied army, but he looked for every possible way to help France. He forged financial connections, carrying goods across the Pyrenees from Switzerland to Spain and procuring there, at a low price, everything that might be useful at the front. Primarily supplies for the Red Cross. That's how the laboratory got started, because my uncle, who was a pharmacist in Segovia at the time, also wanted to help France, and between the two of them they organized the comings and goings, of which my mother wanted to hear nothing. My father transported the things himself in his car, to medical posts nearest the front. From one of those outposts he did not return.

My mother didn't go to Spain. She would not be consoled. Not, however, because she feared the humiliation felt by weak souls when they realize that people feel sorry for them. No, she refused consolation because of an adherence to grief, as a way of maintaining her grief sealed off from anything that would vary it. She wandered throughout Switzerland, alone. Choosing the mountains, she would walk as long as her strength lasted. When she reached the highest peaks, she would rest, as if she were waiting for something. She was waiting for the illness then incipient in her to ripen completely.

All of this information comes from conjectures on the part of Jeanne and my uncle, who made several trips to pull her away from there. I can't say I was aware of any of it; they did everything possible to hide the disaster from me. Nevertheless, Geneva is no longer a luminous region in my memory. There was a period when I probably spent little time with my mother; they thought it better if Jeanne entertained me.

I don't know if a young child of four should be provided with a terrible blow. Ordinary children hear their mothers' heartrending cries, hear the prayers, see the candles and the coffin. Other times they witness quarrels caused by money or jealousy, listening to words that strip the bare wretchedness of some beloved being right before their eyes. All this enriches them greatly. But who would dare to make children suffer in order to enrich them?

Jeanne placed her full skirts between the spectacle of grief and my gaze; when my mother began to recover her reason I was allowed to go near her. Sometimes she would take me for a walk. I remember an atrocious winter in Geneva when they kept the snow piled on the railings in the parks, beside the water, where it formed huge balls like polar bears. We would be walking along and my mother would hardly speak, only if I would say: "When I grow up I'll do this thing that or that." "When you grow up you won't be here," she would answer. "You aren't from here. You're Argentine. Soon you'll go to Buenos Aires."

I remember all these sentences not because she said them often, but because she said them in a special way: she would emphasize them, as if to ensure that I would never forget them, that I would consider them unappealable on principle.

My mother's reason increased at the same rate as her illness. Sensing that her heart was weak from so much suffering, she'd egged it on the way people egg on wild animals, giving herself no rest. When she returned from her treks, if the tiredness she felt turned into insomnia, capricious doses of Veronal would work the desired effect; after four years of this regime she thought about returning to Spain.

Something else had also kept her in Switzerland: Jeanne flatly refused to follow us. She said categorically that she would never go to a country where they didn't speak her language, and doing without Jeanne was like being stranded without transportation, like carrying the burdens of our material life on our grief-stricken souls. But there came a moment when my mother realized that she had to return to Spain, even though she would be left without Jeanne. Besides, I'd gotten too big to sleep in Jeanne's lap and she was made to have a small child on her knee.

Once in Spain, I was under the guardianship of my uncle, who had promised—perhaps sworn—to follow my mother's wishes implicitly: first, I was to be educated by the Jesuits, and second, I was to be sent to Buenos Aires as soon as I was a little older, but two years passed without any decision being made. My uncle couldn't keep his promises without feeling keenly irritated. He didn't want to put me in Jesuit schools and he didn't want to be separated from me. Finally, a doctor intervened, more to justify my uncle to his siblings than to ease his conscience, and I was taken to the Augustinians: my nervous system was such that it would never withstand strict discipline, etc.

The five years at school passed quickly. Everything was good there— the priests, my companions. I experienced no difficulties on coming into contact with new people. I got along well with the other boys, made friends with one of them, who even went to the mountains with us, at Christmas. My uncle took us to Navacerrada and we spent the nights trying our hardest to see wolves. We thought we heard them howling, we wanted to take off into the hills without my uncle's finding out: we never managed it. One day, though, we did get to go with the goatherds to Peña Lara. If I don't remember that experience as a luminous region, it's because you can see the road to Segovia from any point in the mountains, and it seemed to me that there the light could kill.

After finishing high school I spent three years in Madrid, with my uncle, living a bachelor's life. His generosity, his unfailing approval of the stupidest things I did would have corrupted any human boy. That's how I understood it, and I accepted my responsibility with a certain arrogance. I didn't go so far as to belittle my uncle's weakness, because I knew it was only a secret plan devised by his heart: he wanted me to be the one who didn't want to go to Buenos Aires.

Continually, there were wordless comedies between the two of us. As we were on our way to the laboratory, he would ask suddenly: "What would you think about enlarging the right wing? Don't you think we should get more sterilizers?"

And that was how he consulted with me about the least little thing. I was no longer a child who could pretend he owned the laboratory, and my uncle didn't want to ask me in such a way that I would already have to answer as a man about whether I was going to stay or leave. He had confidence in that method of winning me over, and I'm sure he would never have been able to understand why his efforts were useless.

But my uncle was one of those people who live without thoroughly understanding their own lives. This is what made it impossible for me to communicate fully with him: I would never have been able to make him understand the inexplicable things about me. He wasn't capable of analyzing a feeling, an impulse, until getting at its indescribable cause. When I spoke with him sometimes about the hold America had on me because of my mother's words, he would cut me off: "Yes, of course, she had very fond memories from there."

And I couldn't say to him: That wasn't it, because, yes, she did have fond memories. But it wasn't that. It was because when she used to tell me, "You aren't from here" or "Soon you'll go to Buenos Aires," I would see her plan, my future projected in her mind, and I would accept it, preparing myself not to shatter it. However, what inspired a feeling of duty or obedience in me was not a command: it was a vital assent. How could I have explained such things at that age? Nevertheless, they were the things that commanded me from within. My uncle couldn't understand them, in the same way I couldn't understand some of his things. And if I don't understand someone—this is something I've felt certain about ever since I've gained consciousness—it's because not even he himself understands, in other words, he really has no explanation.

My uncle worked in the laboratory, which was his creation, a little reluctantly and as if to say: why did I get involved in this? As for family life, he'd let himself turn into a perfect bachelor and suddenly, finding he had a ready-made son, he was discovering his capacity for affection and his life was taking on meaning. But since what had been granted him was only a loan, he was doing his best to bribe fate, by erasing even the least trace of his authority. He gave me an all-encompassing freedom, trying to tie me down with it. But I wouldn't let myself be tied down, even though I found life in his home extremely pleasant. Nothing there rejected me, and nevertheless I related to things as if I were saying good-bye—and my good-byes were passionate. I enthusiastically embraced everything I knew I would soon leave, with the attentive enthusiasm that leaves an imprint so perfect it can prevail beneath forgetting.

For one of my many freedoms I was sincerely grateful: the freedom that had allowed me to know the night. At sixteen I had my own key and I could get home at whatever hour I wanted. I made use of it to wander the streets on those dramatically pure Madrid nights.

One afternoon in the autumn of 1928 we were going toward Ciudad Lineal. My uncle was driving and I was riding beside him as always, lost in thought, when suddenly, adopting the tone of a manager speaking to his boss, he said to me: "What would you think about making our purchases in Germany this year?"

I nodded my agreement and he continued. "But I believe it would be better if we made the purchases ourselves." At that point my ears pricked up.

"There must be a lot of new things," he went on. "Don't you think we should consider updating our equipment a bit?"

The conversation became quite animated; we began to plan the trip. As if in passing, and vaguely, my uncle said it would be good for me to travel around Europe before I entered the university: after that, I would be tied to books for several years. I agreed with everything. At times, deep down, he doubted that I would persevere with the idea of studying chemistry, because he'd seen me with nothing but literary books since I left high school. In addition, he knew I went to the museum often and I had friends who were students at San Fernando. But he felt reassured when I agreed with his plans, and from that day on we were totally involved in the trip. The following month found us heading straight to Berlin.

We took with us the addresses of several people involved in the same business and spent the first days visiting laboratories or the homes of their owners or directors. One of those people, a chemistry professor at the university, introduced me to two of his students so they could acquaint me with student life in Germany, where he assumed I would return later to complete my training. The two boys, a little older than

I, were two fonts of scientific knowledge. I dragged them to the Altes Museum and there I met Elfriede.

Since my perennial freedom had accompanied me to Berlin, it allowed me to become engrossed in Elfriede and to spend only short periods with my uncle. Some days those periods amounted to nothing more than a telephone conversation.

It was in Berlin that I began to give happiness a systematic form. With Elfriede I began to know a city where there are things for happiness. I won't say products, because it wasn't a question of drugs, which I would describe as everything from the daily beer to the wildest alcoholic drinks. No, in Berlin there were things and places, artificial factors for achieving happiness. Artificial? No, real. Artificially obtained, artificially incubated, but not for that reason less lively or less warm.

Probably the fact that I'd entered adolescence living in Madrid allowed me to notice how one happiness can differ from another. I knew only natural happiness—the one my uncle talked about—which, in fact, always derived from nature. Chestnuts and poplars in the spring, siestas with a hurdy-gurdy playing in the distance, and, in the summer, dancing at night in the Casa Juan or wandering all the way to the Cuesta de las Perdices. In all those places, happiness was like a climate, you inhaled it. Sometimes the atmosphere was overloaded with happiness, with a plenitude that was almost harmful, that put you in a state of not knowing what to do, and then happiness would turn into melancholy, because you couldn't see its depths, or because behind happiness you saw something more and didn't know what that more was.

In Berlin, everything was totally different. In Berlin there was also a more to happiness, but it was simply more happiness: it was a *crescendo*, a whirlwind. You skated, you danced, you went to cabarets, to Luna Park, either to restaurants filled with people or to the enormous stores where you could buy succulent things to put together a meal anywhere you wanted. In short, if you wanted to be happy you could do any number of things to achieve that; but in Madrid you were either happy or you weren't, and that was all. There were even times when, just from seeing that happiness in the air, tense like a bubble about to burst, you even grew sad.

I realized all this because I went to Berlin, that's evident. If I hadn't left Madrid, I wouldn't have made the comparison and I wouldn't have been able to understand it.

When we'd been there about a month, I began to notice that my uncle was worried and rather gloomy, and I suspected that my nearly total disappearance and my lack of interest in professional matters might be the cause. I asked him and he denied it. I tried to sound him out. From the beginning I'd explained my absence to him, with complete openness, as usual, and he seemed to have found it acceptable. He'd even smiled with a certain pride, as he always did when I told him about some manly action or gesture. Then I started to bring the subject up suddenly, abruptly, to see how he would react, and invariably his expression softened, he'd seem to forget his worries and say: "Good, good, you're not wasting your time."

I thought it might be the business affairs that had prompted our trip to Berlin, but I made some inquiries and found that everything had gone well. I suspected my uncle might have had an affair himself that had come to an unpleasant end, and I didn't want to ask him anything about that.

The two and a half months in Berlin flew by. On the way home we stopped in Paris, and since my grandparents lived in Fontainebleau, we didn't see how we could avoid a visit. Our relations with them had never gone beyond a few letters to mark some anniversary; when we were so close by, the situation was different.

We let them know we were coming and arrived a little before lunch. They lived in a tiny house set among chestnut trees, and they'd preserved a refinement more youthful than they were themselves. As we were having a glass of sherry, the conversation turned to my studies. My grandparents were very affectionate and interested in everything about me. We were talking about my future career and our trip to Berlin, which was closely related to my plans, when we went into the dining room. The table was long and not very large. I sat down facing my uncle, and once we were eating my grandmother picked up the conversation where we'd left off. She began by saying that the scientific world in Berlin was no doubt excellent but that there would always be time for me to broaden my studies. It seemed to her that until I completed my doctorate I should study in Paris.

At that moment my uncle was lifting a piece of paté to his mouth. Arresting the paté in mid-air, he said gently but decisively: "Santiago will study in Buenos Aires. Before long I'll be sending him there."

My grandparents gave their opinion about the pros and cons, but, as if the table had lengthened magically, at its ends my grandparents moved to immeasurable distances, and I saw nothing but my uncle sitting before his paté, which he ate slowly, carefully considering each tiny piece of bread. He had just admitted the cause of his grief.

Why? I asked myself. Why has he changed his mind, why has he decided to agree like this? Again, I felt afraid that he was unhappy with my behavior, but after all there wasn't the least indication of anything depraved about the things I'd been doing. Besides, I was sure that if my uncle had seen I was in some moral danger he would never even have thought of letting me leave his side. Something was going on, but I was totally incapable of guessing what because I was looking for its cause in him.

I racked my brains trying to figure out what was going on in his, and I couldn't, but suddenly something became evident to me: I noticed for the first time a strong resemblance between him and my mother. Of course they belonged to one of those families with a very characteristic physical appearance: they had those Castilian heads in which the skeleton, the bone is so predominant. But at that moment, rather than resembling my mother, it was as though he were being visited by her spirit. My mother was speaking through him.

The discussion lasted until the end of lunch, but it wasn't really a discussion: my grandparents expressed their opinions and my uncle agreed or disagreed in short sentences, almost with monosyllables. The whole time we'd been speaking in French. Suddenly, my grandfather spoke in Spanish, unearthing his Argentine accent with an archaeological effort that made his words seem like an imitation as he approved the decision for me to return to my home turf: "Bueno, muchacho, no me parece mal que te volvás al pago."

My grandmother rewarded her husband with a youthful laugh contemporary with the accent he'd resurrected and said that everything there was perfectly charming.

As we went back that night, on the train to Paris, I sat recalling the thicket of trees in Fontainebleau as a darkness that hid a problem. I'd seen the problem, in passing, but there hadn't been enough time for me to solve it. All I'd been able to do was glimpse its mystery: my grandfather, the Argentine, was commenting ironically on the decision to send me to Argentina again; my uncle, the Castilian—and through him, my mother—was decreeing laconically and irrevocably that I had to go back.

For the first time I found myself in a situation where I couldn't speak openly with my uncle, because I couldn't tell him I knew his decision was recent. He'd spoken as if, as my guardian, he were only carrying out my mother's wishes, which had never been threatened by noncompliance, and I was sure that two months earlier he'd been deeply inclined not to comply with them.

Before, I'd the lacked the courage to tell him that I wanted to go, that I knew it was my fate—I was hoping that some event or other would help me make that declaration. Now that he himself was stipulating it, I still didn't dare to speak because I was afraid that he was waiting for me to protest, that he was banking on my refusal to obey. And I was not about to refuse, I felt a great satisfaction in seeing that events were going to work out the way I wanted. It was impossible for me to admit my satisfaction to him.

But his thoughts were running along the same line as mine, because he also wanted to explain his change of plans to me yet didn't dare admit that his plans had changed. Then he took advantage of something I said about the things we'd seen, in order to make a comment: "Europe's in a bad way. No one knows what a bad way Europe's in."

I'd had a wonderful time in Berlin and the days in Paris had left me dazzled, so I couldn't understand what he thought was wrong, and I told him so.

"Politics," he answered; "the political situation is getting worse and worse."

"But what does politics matter?" I asked him. "As long as you don't get involved in politics. It doesn't interest me at all."

"Oh, it doesn't matter much to me. But if we don't get involved we don't solve anything."

There were a few more conversations similar to that one. We returned to Spain, where my uncle read one newspaper after the other, and I criticized him: "What a bad habit you've picked up." He did not break the habit.

By then it was 1929, and one day he said to me: "The monarchy's finished."

"I don't suppose that will worry you much," I said to him, "since you're a leftist."

"Well . . . ," he was thinking, "one never knows whether to be worried about the things that are coming to an end or the things that are getting started."

All that was impenetrable for me.

Here I can't help stressing something I said right at the beginning: it's very difficult, extremely difficult to speak, when *people know*, about a time when *people did not know* yet. It's very difficult to describe the ignorance that led us to make a mistake, knowing now that when we made it we were partly right. Sometimes an antithesis of this sort gets tangled up like a ball of string and you don't have either the energy or the ability to untangle it, but you're absolutely certain that the ball is a single unbroken piece of string, solely one, from beginning to end. When I observe it from here, my behavior during that time seems to be flecked with intelligence and stupidity, with disconcerting depth and triviality. Nevertheless, I'm sure it was neither egoism nor mental shortsightedness that made me so inept at some things. No, what I suffered from was the blindness of the specialist. From the time I began to exercise my ability to think, I was interested exclusively in human beings one at a time: mankind, things in general, did not exist for me, because each *one* grew so large in my interest, analysis, and contemplation, that it kept me from seeing the universe.

With this I'm merely trying to explain in some way my blindness with respect to the events, which at that time comprised the present, in the world all around me. I was not indifferent to that world during those twelve years I lived in Spain; on the contrary, I was intimately linked to everything that concerned me directly. My vision lacked distance, maybe because I always knew I was the one who would set off for a distant city.

My trip was arranged so that I would celebrate my twentieth birthday in Buenos Aires. The boat was to sail from Vigo on the seventh of January, and two days before that my uncle and I left Madrid by car, as if we were going to Ciudad Lineal—my baggage had been sent through an agency. The trip was marked by a dreadful silence. We traveled the longest radius you could stretch between Madrid and the coast, wishing that a tree would fall across the road so we could say: "A tree fell."

We parted bravely, and after an unimaginable length of time the boat set sail.

I stood watching the horizon until the coasts of the Peninsula were nothing but a gray line, and they finally disappeared. Then I said to myself, "This is the high sea." I walked from one side of the deck to the other, from stem to stern; I climbed up on the bridge until I was convinced there was no land visible from any spot. I was on the high sea; it was like finding a beloved face, long desired.

3

This stage of my first twenty years has been a necessary digression, but it's contained in itself. The events I want to recount are related to it only because they occurred in my life.

I won't even stop to connect this stage with what's going to follow. Since I described my departure, it would seem natural that now I would begin by speaking about my arrival, but I won't, because something culminated in my departure and this was not the case for my arrival. What I'd been awaiting as a momentous occurrence was only a daily task undertaken so simply, so naturally, that it almost turned into the imitation of that event: I arrived, lived, and studied like everyone else, like any other young man in Buenos Aires. Two years after my arrival, the first thing happened, the second occurred years later.

One day in what was by then 1935—I was finishing my doctorate—a fellow student introduced me to a British engineer who was about to return to Europe, and I learned in our conversation that for several years he'd been the technician for the company Puig y Zelaski. He'd just been offered a good position in England, and he planned to leave as soon as possible.

I recalled having met don Luis Puig, a very wealthy industrialist, in Madrid when I was a boy, and I thought the vacant position suited me perfectly. I'd been worried for several months as I looked for a solution to my financial situation, which was increasingly unstable—I won't say pressing, if the obvious state of things could be something other than pressing.

In order to make my situation clear, maybe I should say that what remained of my inheritance, which I received when I arrived, was extremely small and that my uncle frequently sent me money, not with the profuse generosity to which he'd been accustomed in Madrid. Was he determined to make me find life in Buenos Aires difficult and disagreeable? Perhaps. For my part, I decided to live as if life were agreeable and easy. In other words, I increased my financial instability considerably.

When the English engineer had spoken of his departure, he'd expressed a certain remorse for leaving his position so suddenly, and he praised Puig's behavior because Puig hadn't reproached him. I thought that Puig might need to replace him as quickly as possible, and it occurred to me that I might try for the job, without having to prove I could do it. A letter of introduction was unnecessary: I was sure that my family name would be enough for him.

I had the impression that I knew Puig well, because, soon after I arrived in Spain, I'd seen him once at my uncle's house, and I'd examined him the way you examine people at that age, with the same minute attention you pay to a watch mechanism or a music box. I'd studied the little hairs on his ears and the wrinkles on the nape of his neck, from which I believed I knew the whole man and he struck me as likable. The idea of seeing him again was pleasing, almost moving to me, as when you find a toy forgotten for years in the couch. It was wonderful that Puig would turn up now, at just the right moment, answering my summons.

All I needed to do was go to see him. I requested a long-distance telephone call, spoke with someone who seemed to be his secretary or personal attendant, said I wanted to see Mr. Puig, and was given an appointment. I was also told they would send the car to meet me at the station because there were no taxis. The estancia was a little beyond Las Flores, near the Quemado lagoon.

So I went. During the trip I didn't prepare a speech: I was sure everything would be spontaneous, and the road to the estancia corroborated my optimism. The landscape was so serene it seemed impossible that any contradiction could arise there. Everything I saw as we went along confirmed my thought that I'd been right to go and led me to hope that things would work out by themselves.

My memory of Puig was that of an arrogant, somewhat ordinary bachelor. When he appeared in his study, I had before me a man brimming with old age who had a tired look about him, as if it had cost him a huge effort to achieve a certain gentility in his bearing. He was no longer a robust man; he'd become a well-mannered, rather flabby gentleman. The first thing I noticed was that he seemed less hard, but he seemed more armored. His voice had gushed loudly with cordiality, of which only a few fatuous spirals remained, like barely elasticized bubbles.

The beginning was actually easy. I didn't have to help him remember, because my name was enough for him to know who was the person in question, nor did I have to make him adjust my present appearance to his image of me as a child, because at the outset he calculated the time that had elapsed, and he was used to the idea that I would have to be more or less how I was. But this doesn't mean he welcomed me coldly; on the contrary, he was even kind enough to scold me for not having come to visit him sooner.

The conversation was rising toward cordiality. Once a certain level had been reached there was a stationary period covered from beginning to end by a tacit persistence: "Let's stop here . . ."; "Let's move on from here . . ."; "Well all right, let's stop here."

I didn't keep him waiting long. I explained clearly what I had in mind, and Puig responded ambiguously: "But my boy, you don't know what all this entails!"

Immediately, he changed the subject, without giving any concrete answer.

Walking over to the window, he said: "Look, here I have another factory that makes less work for me."

Behind the house, situated in a copse of eucalyptus trees, there was a small community of hives.

From there, he went on to show me the books he'd followed in order to set up the hives according to the most modern advances in that secular science, and taking a luxuriously bound volume from one of the shelves, he held it out to me: "I have the best work that's been written about apiculture," he said. I opened the book and read, *Characteristics of Setter Breeds.*

"Oh no," he exclaimed with a huge guffaw, "that's not the book I meant to hand you; I don't have any setter bees. They'd be curious, really curious."

I laughed as though I were imagining exactly what a setter bee would look like. He took back the book; forgetting now about the one that dealt with bees, and explained: "This book is from when I spent my time on a hobby, which I've now given up completely. But if you like them, come with me: there are still a few left."

We went out. Behind the house, the garden was full of fruit trees and fragrant plants, food for the bees: large myrtle hedges, avenues of privets. We walked toward the left of the eucalyptus forest, where a rustic gate opened into a field with a wire fence, but even before we touched the gate we began to hear a chorus of trill-like barking. Voices of very diverse tones were mixing persistently in a clamor of cries and impatient barks.

A few geese splashing in the mud made way to let us past, protesting audibly as they hurried to hide in some scrubland. Puig explained to me that he'd always devoted that piece of land, less than two and a half acres, to farmyard animals, dogs, or even ostriches. But he'd grown tired of that too, and over time the chicken coops and everything he'd built had fallen apart.

He had to interrupt his explanation in order to calm the dogs, which were tied or penned in small enclosures where each one had a little house. The only setter left was a female with two pups; there was also a sheepdog, a mastiff, and a cinnamon-colored bulldog, as big as a calf. They were all purebreds that had won prizes in many contests.

An old man, the dog keeper, emerged from a small shed near the kennels. This was where he lived: his had his fire and kettle for making maté beside the door. He came over to greet Puig, and they talked about the dogs, the land, and the fall that was turning out overly humid.

I'd picked up one of the pups and was holding it in my arms, playing with it as I looked at the land. The afternoon was humid and gray, but there was no mist; the fields rippled very softly. In the lowest part of the field, about 200 meters away, a flat cement building with large windows sat silent; I couldn't see the least sign of life around it. It was the factory.

I hadn't known how to tell him I wanted to see the factory, but Puig saw me looking at it and read my mind. "The field's all muddy," he said, "some other day when you're here we'll walk over so you can see how it operates. Everything's all topsy-turvy. I don't know . . ."

I thought the moment had come for me to speak; it seemed he was alluding to Monington's departure, and when I heard him express his unhappiness over the condition of the factory I prepared a host of solutions to any predicament he might tell me about. But he didn't continue, he left the sentence unfinished, because the sheepdog caught his eye; it was tied to a tree and trying to break loose.

"Why, that animal's bleeding, José," he said. "Haven't you noticed?"

The dog had been struggling in every possible way since he'd seen his master arrive, and the buckle on his collar, which was old, had almost torn away from the leather, and it had become twisted so that the stem was cutting into him. It was nothing, barely a prick, but even one drop of blood on his white ruff caused an alarming spot. I left the puppy with its mother so I could attend to the sheepdog. They gave him a new collar and put some salve on the wound. He let me hold him down without any distrust, happy that our six hands had converged on his body.

While I held his head, I looked at the subtle coloration on his fur, mentally repeating the old saying about "Same dog, different collar." It seemed the best definition of a dog: same dog with different coats and different shapes. Because it's true that the makeup of dogs varies greatly, but it's still odd that the animal most capable of fidelity can appear in such a variety of guises. How to explain that within a greyhound and a Pekinese there are the same thing, which is a dog? How powerful fidelity must be in dogs for them not to get lost along a path with so many forks in it! How obedient they are to the original command to be dog!

I was thinking intently about all this—I believe I even went so far as to think about Ignatius's *obediential potency*. It would be impossible to imagine anything more foolish! I was thinking about how dogs are imprisoned in their shapes, about how those shapes are their collars and how, even so, they don't seem to feel burdened by obedience. When they try to break their chains, it's not to run away: if they break their chains, they stay right where they are, as if they were free.

I remained engrossed in those ideas until we were on our way back to the house. Then I realized I was so lost in thought that the matter at hand had been forgotten. I hadn't been able to steer our conversation toward the subject that interested me, and now there was very little time left to impose it. Maybe I'd let it slip my mind because I recognized my failure, but even so I couldn't give up without attempting an all-out attack.

When we got back, the tea table was already set in the study.

"I have some very good tea," Puig said. "It's left from the tea Monington bought, and the whiskey is his too. You'll taste it later."

I hurled myself at that allusion as if it were an eel.

"Monington made a huge impression on me," I said. "He thinks clearly, and he knows what he's about."

"Oh yes," Puig answered, "he's a good man. But he was homesick. He called it *spleen*, and I would say to him: 'morriña, homesickness. What you have is morriña.' Obviously, whiskey was his cure."

I could feel the down on my back bristle. Would I be able to continue? Would a duel with such banality, brandished like a foil, be bearable? I took a deep breath and slipped in a response: "A lot of people drink when they work. Monington's problem," I went on, "was that he never thought of settling here. And changes are harmful to any business: what's needed is continuity."

"Look," he cut me off, "drink is bad when you drink for some reason." There was a silence, each of us struggling, each pulling in a different direction, and he won: "If you drink to drink," he continued, unruffled, "you can give it up whenever you want, but if something is making you drink . . . then, as long as that something lasts . . ."

I saw it was useless to insist, although it was shameful to abandon the field without having exercised my faculties. But it was also stupid to persist in not seeing that I had no possible move left. Maybe right there was the only possibility of action left me: give up my plan as one that's over for and done with.

"Yes, of course," I said, "when you adopt it as a solution."

Then I added, sinking into my armchair: "I can understand that here, in the country, a person would drink, but the climate in Buenos Aires doesn't make you want alcohol; the proof is, people don't drink much. You almost never see a drunk on the street. The wines have a very low alcohol content. I don't know why it is, but Buenos Aires is not a city for drinking."

He was going to answer something, but I forestalled him: "The beer's not bad, but it's weak. And what you don't find is fresh cider. That's odd, since there's extensive apple production."

I gave him just enough time to corroborate my comment: "And such large communities of Galicians, Asturians, Basques."

I continued immediately: "I think it must be because the weather's so changeable. The overcast days don't last long enough for persevering in making cider or beer, and there aren't enough sunny days, although there are more of those, to invest in wine making. Because wine requires sun."

He understood, saw clearly that my game was a response to his own, and let me continue because he was comfortable with it. Maybe by giving in to comfort he let himself be captivated by my suggestions, since he was not expecting that kind of conversation, and he began to feel the need to talk about wines he knew and places where he'd drunk a lot when he was young.

"You know something?" he said. "I was raised on a masía. Business dealings have changed me, because you have to live with other people, but I'm a country man at heart, a real payés."

I wasn't sure if he expected me to answer him with an "obviously" or an "impossible," so I didn't answer at all, but I redoubled my attention, encouraging him to keep pursuing his evocations. And he did, although not completely without watching his words. He told what he'd decided to tell—why he'd left his provincial life in Catalonia and set out to see the world—, nothing more. I acted as interested as if I had made the trip just to hear that story, as if no other idea or intention could have been passing through my mind.

Meanwhile, the servant removed the teacups and brought a tray with bottles and glasses. I looked at my watch and said I needed to be on my way. Puig protested; I still had a quarter of an hour. The car would deposit me at the station in twenty minutes.

Puig picked up the bottle of whiskey quickly, trying to make that gesture go unnoticed. He didn't want to let me leave without tasting it, and he didn't want the subject of alcoholic beverages to come up again: he wanted to reward me for my good behavior. Besides, it seemed to him that now it was his turn to be decent: he had to give an answer. He held out a glass to me and poured less than a half a centimeter of whiskey in his own.

"That's all you take?" I began.

"I shouldn't even taste it," he said, settling the matter with a wave of his hand.

He avoided silence, tinkling the ice in his glass, the way one rings a small bell. Right after that call to attention, he said: "Look, I don't know what I'm going to do with all of this."

I raised my eyebrows and ran my eyes around all the nearby objects. He pretended not to notice my feigned incomprehension and continued: "The factory produces quite well; I'm not going to say it's useless. But for the last years of my life, to keep up that effort . . ."

As he was taking a breath, I threw myself into the ring: "Don't you think about going back to Barcelona? When I returned from France I entered through Port Bou and that section of the coast seemed wonderful to me."

"Yes, it is," he said seriously, but he didn't let himself be sidetracked.

"The thing is," he continued, "it's not easy for me to get rid of all this either, because then a whole heap of paperwork falls on top of me. While I'm here, everything seems to run on its own, but the slightest change means conflict."

Almost interrupting him, I asked: "Did you fix up the house yourself or is this how it was when you bought the estancia?"

"I fixed it up. How much of this section was here then? The walls. Making it habitable took a lot of work too."

We were talking about the house now; he wanted to return to the factory and he did: "These things, what they require is a good foreman, one who's very practical and experienced. The ones today, with far better academic training than foremen had twenty years ago . . ."

At that moment the chauffeur appeared at the door and I stood up. Puig asked him: "Does he need to leave now?"

"We have twenty minutes," the chauffeur said, "and that's just enough time, since we don't need to stop at the ticket office."

"Well," Puig said, "I'm very happy you thought of coming."

I didn't let him continue: "I'm sorry you didn't get to show me the hives," I said.

Flashes of very mixed emotions crossed his wide, passive face: a certain anger because he'd been defeated in our contest to see who could outsmart whom, a certain suspicion that he might be passing up a useful collaboration.

There were a few more words of farewell, the customary words, and the car set off.

Frustration, total failure. Why? Maybe there is no why, or at least no comprehensible why. But it hardly mattered why—the failure was visibly there. The frustration of everything that was going to be but now would not stood before me. It would have been more logical to think that it stood behind me, back at the door of his house, but it had not remained behind: something was crumbling before me, and it was something I was seeing.

The landscape of the pampa varies very little, but while I was thinking what follows below it did not vary at all.

We were driving along the road that crosses the estancia and leads to the local road; the sky was gray, so the light was the same—filtered: it was starting to get dark. On either side of the car all you could see were two strands of wire and the motionless pastures, since there was no wind. I saw that in front of us, some two or three posts ahead, there was a large owl perched on one of the posts, and I thought it would fly off when we got closer. Then I looked at that solitude, that gray light resting over the green of the pastures, and I felt myself choking with despair because now none of it would be. What would not be? That, me walking at dusk, beside the post with the owl perching on it.

How can I describe what I was feeling at that moment? I just wanted all that. But it's hard to explain how one can feel a violent desire for something that does not involve ownership.

What I felt was a sort of possessive fury I'd known at other times. The feeling wasn't entirely new to me and, I think I even remember entering it as if I were entering familiar territory. In other words, there was a certain density to my inebriation or alienation in which other similar moments were perceptible. I was there, totally, but a tiny branch of my consciousness sensed something that resembled "Once again this desire" . . . And now, from a distance: I see that the many occasions when I felt this sensation had nothing in common. I clearly recall one warm night when I walked along a tree-lined street and overheard the conversation of two lovers in a garage; one noon, in full sun, as I crossed through a commercial district amidst stevedores carrying bundles to shops from which emerged familiar but intensified aromas that poured freely into the air . . . At moments like those I'd stood motionless on one square of the sidewalk, as if the world were before me, as a whole and in all its details, as if at those vibrant moments beings and things passed into my possession by passing into my understanding, as if merely understanding them meant incorporating their life within me.

But those emotions had been momentary, whereas there was a fixedness to this one, a dialogue-like persistence that could not be interrupted. When I'd arrived, I'd let myself be permeated by the confidence inspired in me by my surroundings, and when I left, now lacking security, I found it impossible to detach my will from where it was entangled.

The posts were passing quickly beside the car, and I counted the ones left before reaching the owl—"five, four, three"—while my senses, which had become tentacles, clutched at everything that now would not be.

I'm very sure that I didn't think for even a moment about what could, in reality, be called my own affair. Certainly though, in my meeting with Puig, I hadn't been able to learn if what I was after was possible or not, was a good idea for me or not. My despair, my sense of being rent, were caused by something that a few hours before had suddenly become a deep-rooted certainty. When I went out there, I hadn't doubted for a moment that the entire venture was something incipient, something that would be.

When I thought of the move I'd made, all that stood out was its grotesqueness, but I couldn't laugh because my throat was blocked by a sort of strangling that made laughter impossible. At times, my stupid game of simple cleverness and everything I'd said ran through my thoughts, my agility beating a retreat and Puig's expectant face and impassive cheeks pushing me toward failure.

Lurching a bit in the potholes, the car reached the post, the owl flapped its wings, which were dark brown above and sand-colored underneath, and swooped over the car. Then it took off awhile at the same pace, a little ahead and to the right, flying low, as gently as a butterfly.

"Look how it's guiding us," the chauffeur said.

He accelerated in order to catch up with it. The owl hovered a bit in the air, beside us, looking at the car very attentively; then it tilted, let itself glide, and hung there for a moment before flapping its wings and flying off into the distance until it was lost from view.

We left the estancia and pulled onto the highway. Night had fallen quickly, and we were almost at the station when two small lights appeared on the road.

"Look at the viscacha," the chauffeur said. "And around here there aren't many of them."

He started to explain: "It's dazzled by the headlights. If we shine them right on it for awhile and then pick up speed, aiming to hit it with the fender . . ."

He put his strategy into action, driving very slowly in a straight line toward the animal, which sat there without moving; suddenly he stepped on the gas, and because the creature jumped quickly and went running off one side, he tried to swing into a curve so he could get it from the side as it ran, but what he hit was the edge of a paved crossing over the ditch. The front tire burst and the car cleared the ground, ready to go into a somersault, although it didn't; it landed on its wheels, and the chauffeur, who had remained calm, managed to bring it to a stop right in the middle of the road.

The man was terrified, but I reassured him because there were only four or five blocks left to the station, and I was certain I could get there in time, if I hurried. He insisted that the best thing would be for me to wait while he changed the tire since I could never get there in time on foot, but I didn't listen to him and I started walking.

When I'd been walking as fast as I could for three or four minutes, I began to hear the train, and I ran at a sprinter's pace. The train kept getting closer. I turned my head and saw it coming, but I guessed that it would not overtake me before I got to the station, which at that point was just a few meters away. I ran furiously, and the train passed me and came to a stop, but I got there right after it. My platform was the one on the other side. I thought I'd be able to get across before the train left, but it pulled away before I could catch it.

There wasn't a soul on the platform, and I collapsed on a bench, the blood pounding in my head, but the cold air brought me back to normal right away.

A few minutes later I saw the chauffeur coming up, and he was dismayed to find me there. I assured him that it made no difference, that it was all the same to me if I got back a little later.

"That will be a day later," he said.

"No," I said, "there must be some other train tonight."

He started arguing with me, saying it was impossible, and we went to look at the schedule. In fact, a train for both passengers and freight was to go by at 11:45.

"But the boss will have it in for me because it was my fault," he said.

"There's no reason to tell him about it; you go back home, and I'll stay here quite content."

He seemed to give in, asked my forgiveness a thousand times, and left.

Although it was only a little after eight, the whole place was deserted. Soiling the night's darkness, a turbid mist emanated from the town, which lay behind the station; but along the tracks, the red and green railroad lights stood out clearly.

Next to the road where I'd been running, not far ahead, there was a small house that stood by itself, and the light coming from it looked like the light from a grocery. I crossed the tracks again and walked in that direction because I wanted something to drink. I wanted to keep up the flush I'd gotten from the whiskey, which had brightened my spirits on the trip, and even if I couldn't find anything very good, I was willing to make do with an ordinary grappa.

The bar was very small—one corner of the store, set off by a screen. From the table where I sat down I could see both sections. I watched the storekeeper selling noodles and lentils and also tending the cash register on both sides, since there was only one waiter to serve drinks and clear away glasses in the bar. Conversation also moved back and forth between the two sides; a few men at the table next to mine struck up a spirited exchange of low-down remarks, full of the double entendres you find in the country, with a old woman who came in asking for vinegar, and two or three times I caught the men on both sides glancing at me for approval. They were aware of my presence because I was an outsider; but it was as if I were the outsider who had to be there, so their glances didn't seem strange to me. Once again I felt that the whole situation there was like something incipient, and the wave of anger swept over me again: none of that would be again, I never again would sit in that bar, because in order to get there I had to pass by the post where the owl sat, and, that I was sure—I saw this with complete clarity—would never be. Nevertheless, at the same time I saw it as something very enduring, something frequently repeated. I didn't see myself returning along the road in Puig's car, but alone, on foot or driving a small car: I would have to have a car, I told myself, I would have to have one so I could drive regularly, repeatedly on that road, where the owl would be waiting for me so it could flutter above my head on those evenings that will not be.

I drank a couple of glasses of grappa, and when I was about to ask for a third, there in front of me I saw the chauffeur, who had returned.

"There's nothing to be done; the boss wants you to come to Las Murtas."

"And if I won't go?"

"Fine," he said, "but you don't want to turn this into something unpleasant, and have me paying for it all year long."

"If you know your boss will make you pay for it, why did you tell him what happened?"

"Well . . . I didn't want you sitting here until midnight with this drizzle. Now, let's get going," he added, "he's waiting for you so he can sit down to dinner."

Will I go? Can I possibly be going? Will I go, really go? Mechanically, I put a few pesos on the table and started walking, repeating to myself: "But am I going to? Am I going to arrive at the estancia again? Am I going to see that chance repeated? Will the wheel of fortune turn again and I'll get to place another bet? Will revenge be possible? No, it won't; the game will be repeated and nothing else. Then why go? Can I really be going?" The car was speeding toward the estancia.

It seems that I'm spending too much time on details, deliberately prolonging my narration of that moment, but I'm not, in reality its dimension was incomparably greater.

We sped toward the estancia, and I was sunk in the backseat, in total darkness, still asking myself if it was true that I was going, because I was pulled by two opposing and equally powerful forces: one was a strange, light happiness, like a sliding, that urged abandon; the other, a braking, a contracting of my diaphragm like an alert, like the premonition of a collision. Because I knew for certain that I would collide and there was nothing I could do about it. But it would not be a collision that at least left me dashed to pieces in a reassuring failure; no, I was going to slam into an enormous round face, to blunt, or bounce against an elastic, deaf will that opposed me, without being able to understand why. It opposed me, that was all, because it was my opposite: it was the limit to my ambition. When, in fact, that face was just saturated ambition, sated with surplus and thirsting only for its former emptiness, its initial motivation. Yes, from the first moment I divined envy's snare in Puig's deaf hostility. And it seems absurd: I was the one with the petition, and he was the one with the possession. But he was sated, and lazy in his satiation, and he envied my desire, my ambition. As soon as he saw me, he envied the drive, the confidence that led me to express myself so directly, and he waylaid me with his rough, subtle aplomb, at once material and impalpable. For me, his neutral passivity was like the cork targets that darts strike soundlessly, but for him it may have been something else: the obstacle placed in the horse's path just for the pleasure of seeing the horse jump. He looked at me, almost contemplated me, from his distant comfort; perhaps he was remembering the unexpected hurdles that had sprung up from the ground in front of him when he was agile, and now he delighted in being a hurdle himself. Was I going to put myself on display again? Was I going to let him see that I returned in defeat? Anything but that. But since it was the truth, why go? Why not say, abruptly, "Stop, stop right now," and jump out? I was looking at the back of the chauffeur's neck—at first he'd tried to talk to me about his arrival at the estancia and Puig's reaction when he told him about the mishap, but now he was driving in silence, and it seemed to me that he too insisted that I be taken back against my will, so he could set me before the obstacle. It seemed to me that if I told him to stop he would refuse; I would have to grab him by the neck, hit him on the head, take hold of the steering wheel. I would have to do something, but I remained sunk in the backseat, looking passionately at the darkness of the road. At times the headlights revealed a whitewashed tree trunk along the shoulder: when the light dimmed nothing was visible.

Finally the car swerved to the left, the beam from the headlights fanned over the posts of the wire fence, and we turned into the road that led to the estancia. Timidly, blushing unnecessarily, I rolled down the window so I could see what the air was like around there now, so I could recognize the site from which I was on my way back to the estancia and the owl was fluttering overhead—where I would never be, where the owl would never flutter.

I don't know if all this is comprehensible or if it's more idiotic than what people in general are willing to put up with, but that's how it was. And I can't stop incomprehensible things that explain everything from always and forever being incomprehensible and never any different.

We got there. In order to give myself time to take a position, I decided to start by determining the topic of conversation, and I began to construct a defense for the chauffeur. I tried to persuade Puig that it had been my fault, because I'd engaged him in conversation throughout the entire trip, asking him questions about the countryside and the animals.

As if to say it didn't matter, Puig told me: "I know all about that guy; you can't shut him up."

We were still in the living room when the chauffeur returned to ask what time I would be leaving. I told him 11:45, but Puig assured me the train was out of the question, almost a freight train, and it made no sense for me to spend the night on it. He tried to dismiss the chauffeur, telling him I would decide the next day; at that moment, I decided definitively to leave on the seven o'clock train.

"Fine, however you like," Puig said, and immediately, before the chauffeur could reach the door, he added: "let's see if that viscacha's been prepared properly."

The chauffeur went out crestfallen, and I thought: he's relentless: that poor man's going to pay for the viscacha every day for God knows how long. My defense hasn't worked or it's been counterproductive. Who knows if the insinuation is meant for me, not for him, if it's the first obstacle, the first limit, rather, because there was no way to save the chauffeur. By hurling his ironic remark against what had been my purpose in making that speech, Puig showed me how inane the speech had been. I'd been trying to get in by hiding behind someone else's affair, and he'd immediately turned that affair into a defeat that was mine alone. Our battle had begun without my realizing it, and I was afraid the surprise might be making me seem dismayed. My hands were ice-cold and I know how my face looks when my hands are like that.

"I'm not quite presentable enough to sit down to dinner," I said.

"Go wash your hands if you like, but don't be long," Puig answered, "you're fine as you are."

Fortunately, a stream of boiling water poured out of the spigot. I washed my face, enduring the hot water on my eyelids until tears came to my eyes. By rubbing myself hard with the towel, I managed to regain a normal appearance. A cheerful appearance would have been preferable, but the vicissitudes of the evening would provide that.

I burst into the dining room. Puig was strolling from one side of the room to the other. The table was set with china and glassware worthy of the estancia. We sat down, were served pastel de choclo and exchanged a few sentences about our corn pie.

In a disproportionate voice, which I corrected immediately by clearing my throat and finding the right tone, I began: "It was very opportune . . . (tone corrected) very opportune that the viscacha ran in front of us."

Puig raised his head, waiting for me to continue. He did not have to wait long.

"If we hadn't crashed into the paving stone, I wouldn't have seen this dining room and I wouldn't have seen this side of you as the estanciero."

"There's nothing of the estanciero about me," he replied rather uncomfortably.

I saw he was beginning to feel afraid I'd set off on some strange path: I forged ahead.

"The estancia has seemed more lovely to me, returning at night. This will probably seem strange to you, since of course I couldn't see anything. But, you know, on the way here I was recalling the place as I saw it at three in the afternoon and realizing that it's truly magnificent. I like to see places that way, when there's no light, because then I think about them and I see them more clearly. You understand what I mean?"

He didn't raise his head, but I saw that his jowls were trembling, numerous vibrations he tried to restrain. In spite of himself, an ironic smile appeared, along with amazement, as if he'd suddenly heard me speak in Quechua.

I continued to ramble on about the estancia, and as I spoke I was asking myself: where am I going with this . . . I was talking about trivial things, giving them an incongruous importance. I didn't go so far as to tell him explicitly about my daydreams on the way back, but everything I was telling him had that aura. In other words, I was talking about things that were foolish, according to his reasoning, although he perceived in spite of himself that they were charged with mystery. Then I saw him reach the conclusion that he was not comprehending; basing his response on the one thing that was obvious, he said calmly and firmly: "No, no."

The last sentence was not to be either disputed or affirmed, but he was not disputing my last sentence; he was disputing all my potential sentences, the ones I'd uttered as well as the ones I hadn't. No, no, he'd said, as a conclusion to everything, because that was the only thing he saw clearly. After a perplexed moment, he was able to add: "You're one of those people for revolution from above."

"Me, for revolution!" I exclaimed.

My inquisitive expression led him to fear that his words had been inadequate.

"Well, that's not it entirely," he said. "What I mean is you're not one of those people who take things one step at a time and . . . not that, not that."

When he tried to clarify his first assertion, he immediately felt unsure and lacking in the strength necessary to give the explanations he saw were inevitable. I realized, however, that there was some sense to what he'd said, but I didn't let him see that I was so willing to be persuaded, and he had to recover his firm position by stressing his "not that."

He paused for a long time after saying it, like a person who's burst out with his last definite remark—all he needed to say was "not that" to whatever came up. *That* could be any one of my accusations whose lofty tone he found irritating. He'd used the trite phrase "revolution from above," even though I'd shown no signs of anything revolutionary, because what he saw was my unwillingness to climb the hill little by little, my unwillingness to snake along over the quicksand, my unwillingness to chip my nails scaling the smooth wall—my will to land at the top in one leap. And to *that* he had to say *no*.

The pause during which I realized all this lasted a second—the time it took me to swallow a sip of wine. Over the top of my glass I looked at his impassive face and Puig looked, automatically, at his glass, which had not been filled. He looked at the servant, pointing to the middle of his glass with his index finger. The servant did not pour the wine at once; on the contrary, he seemed reluctant, as if he were urging him not to have more. But Puig tapped the glass lightly with his finger and the servant gave him some more, although not as much as he'd indicated.

It then occurred to Puig that he should take advantage of the situation. He could have been unhappy about his "no, no," considering it too frank and thinking that now I wouldn't run the risk of being refused again.

Affecting a doleful tone, he said: "You see how my own people treat me. They won't even give me a drop of wine. And they let me see meat once a week."

"That shows you're surrounded by good people," I said, and the servant smiled, feeling flattered.

"If they're good to me," Puig added immediately, "it's probably because I'm not mean to them. They're all old-timers in the house: they've all had plenty of opportunity to know what I'm like."

He drank a little and sat with the glass in his hand, contemplating the wine.

"I've always tried to be a good person," he said, "always."

He was on the verge of feeling moved, and he wanted me to feel moved. I spoke at once: "That was the idea I had of you; I believed you were an excellent person."

My use of *believed* alarmed him a little, and I continued: "I was very young that summer you appeared in Madrid, with your raw silk suit and panama hat: I was left with the impression of you as someone triumphant, an indiano who'd gone to the New World and returned to Spain after all sorts of adventures."

Maybe because he was recalling that time, as I watched Puig's face his coloring suddenly seemed to become youthful. The enormous jowls looked less flabby, and he listened to me with an attention that reminded me of the vivaciousness that he'd once possessed.

I continued: "Besides, you seemed so exuberant and so verbal to me that I thought you could teach anyone to be a success. That's the idea I had in mind when it occurred to me to come see you."

At that moment also he wanted to say "Not that, not that," but he couldn't, because it would have meant denying one of his own qualities. Nevertheless, that was what he wanted to make me understand— he would not show me the way, he would not reveal the magic word to me. He adopted a modest pose, one so false it turned out to be comical and impossible to maintain; immediately he abandoned it. The wave of youthfulness that had rushed to his face demanded sincerity, but not so much sincerity that he would reveal his enigma to me; even if he'd told me, "Don't exert yourself, because you're not going to get anything from me," that at least would have worked to further my interests. But his momentary sincerity only unleashed his own interests, manifested itself as a sort of greed.

My evocation of his former personality, my confession of confidence, based on the image of him I'd preserved and that maybe he was seeing formulated for the first time, irritated him. Because that image was like an ideal that belonged to him, and when I expressed it he felt I was taking possession of it. In other words, although the image was *his*, he was seeing it as *my* property, and this made him feel once again that I had more than he did; consequently he rooted himself in the idea of not giving, of demanding.

"Now there aren't indianos anymore," I said; "people travel from one continent to another in a few hours and they no longer have adventurous spirits. Yours was the last generation capable of crossing the pond ten times in classic style."

"Did you come by air?" he asked me.

"No," I said, "I came by boat because I brought a phenomenal load of books. My father's library, which is the only part of our fortune left intact."

"Good heavens," he exclaimed, "you say that as if you find it amusing."

"Well almost, almost," I answered. "Or at least it doesn't worry me much."

He looked at me incredulously and I added: "If you think I have no ambitions, you're mistaken. It happens that my ambition is not the common one."

He cut me off. "Yes, yes, I know. I already told you that a while ago; you don't want to follow the beaten path, and it's hard to get where you want to go by following your method."

"That depends. If a person wants to go where only the beaten paths will take him, of course you're right. But it's not my ambition to go there."

He took a drink, swallowing the last drop of wine he had left.

"Where the devil do you want to go?" he said, giving a little shove to the plate of the dessert he'd just finished.

I burst out laughing in order to leave him waiting for an answer.

At that moment, the servant put a cup of coffee and a cup of peperina on a small table in front of the fire. Puig stood up, and when we were seated beside the fire, I saw his face take on a doleful expression because of the tea.

"That peperina makes the whole room smell wonderfully minty," I said.

He picked up the poker and struck the logs two or three times, until he had them crackling.

"If you like music," he said, "you can put on the Victrola. You'll find all kinds of records over there."

I put on a fox-trot that was popular just then.

When I returned to the fireplace, I stood looking at the fire; Puig pointed to some cracks in the wooden baseboard, next to the hearth.

"Look," he said, "that used to be Rudy's place. He was always there, and he liked to sharpen his teeth on that molding."

"And now, why don't you have him here?"

"How should I know?" he said.

He didn't know why he was giving up one hobby for another. I thought about the dog, who had half choked itself on its collar when he saw Puig appear, because he still bore the imprint of those winter nights when he dozed beside the hearth after he'd eaten the tip of an empanada under the table, after he'd pursued his vice of gnawing on the molding; and those impressions were blindly alive in him, amounting to something very similar to what we call love. Puig, on the other hand, was much poorer in conditioned reflexes, and he did not know why dogs as a hobby no longer interested him.

When the fox-trot ended, Puig said: "Don't you like serious music?"

"Yes," I answered, "of course, but sometimes music that isn't serious turns out to be serious to me."

I began to look through the records.

"I'm going to see if I find something that's really serious here," I continued.

After a lot of searching I put on a record—an old record that sounded at first like cardboard being scratched, but immediately there was a burst of some simple, rustic sounds, strummed on a guitar.

Puig hit the arm of his chair with his fist and let out a curse.

"Where the . . . ?" he started to say.

But he didn't finish his question, because the voice on the record predominated—a brash, uneducated, masculine voice not made for singing indoors. The voice of a worker, hurled into the wind in casual song, and it changed the light in the room: suddenly we were exactly at high noon.

Puig's eyes sparkled and a smile, recalled with difficulty, drew his cheeks, reddened from sitting so close to the fire, all the way to his cheekbones. Some raw nerve in him had been touched; the record had awakened the youthful beast writhing on its chain of boredom and disappointment.

When the record ended, I closed the record player, sat down in front of Puig, and said to him: "Well, did what I found seem serious enough to you?"

"You have a pact with the devil," he said, shaking his head.

"Nothing of the sort," I exclaimed. "I know very well which people it pays to associate with." Then immediately I asked him point-blank: "Why do you persist in believing that I'm too immature for any kind of business? Don't you think I'm practical minded enough?"

His expression quickly clouded over.

"Who's talking about that?" he said.

"I am," I answered.

For a minute, an eternal, silent minute he begged not to be taken to that ground; I pretended not to understand and added: "I put that record on to see if you remembered how it is at the beginning of one's life."

Then he made an effort trying to overcome his own resistance, trying to explain himself thoroughly.

"At the beginning of my life," he said, "I was not like you think. Well, in some respects I might have been, but so far as work goes, you don't have the slightest idea because you insist on going too fast."

Then after a pause: "What do you know about the beginning of life, if you're so full of books as to fill the hold of a boat? The beginning is when a person doesn't know where to start."

"And when he knows, but he can't?"

"That's where he starts. You have to spend a lot of time not being able, in order to know what counts."

He tried to put a certain cynicism in that sentence but added bitterness instead. Besides, he began to show signs of a particularly distressed tiredness, since he was also very agitated.

"We need to go to bed soon," he said. "They'll call you at six. As for me, I think I'll sleep poorly tonight."

We said good-bye. I assured him that I would leave in silence, without waking him, even though he slept on the first floor, near the hallway.

The servant accompanied me upstairs, and when he showed me my room, I asked if it had been Monington's room.

"No, this is the guest room."

I fell asleep straight off and slept deeply, without any dreams. I went to bed with an unpleasant feeling that I doubted I'd be able to shake off all night long, since it would be impossible to forget the sight of so much negation condensed in one opaque body. But before I knew it I was sleeping like a log, as if the guest bed, which lay fallow so much of the time, attracted dreams like a magnet and absorbed them like a sponge.

When they called me before dawn, I went down on tiptoe and left without making a sound. The car started silently.

There was a slight breeze, so the dreamlike atmosphere of the day before was disappearing from the road. It was the atmosphere that was missing, because, naturally, as I rode past I recalled everything, but I recalled it as something unimportant, as one of the thousands of fantasies a person can imagine.

I definitely had the feeling that I'd missed my mark, that deep in my heart lurked something troubled and unpleasant, but I tried to forget it.

When I reached Buenos Aires, I had to remedy the confusion caused by my absence. A broken appointment; I had to make my apologies. Another appointment, jotted on a scrap of paper; that one I had to keep.

This second appointment, with Javier Molina, on Martínez, made me feel uneasy. Of all the people I associated with, Javier was the one I found most agreeable; I could confide in him like a brother, and I was never bored when we were together because he was capable of remaining harmoniously silent for hours at a time. Even so, when I remembered our appointment I felt awkward because we'd arranged to meet on Martínez with a friend of his who was thinking about selling his car, which was almost new and very cheap. Javier told me about the opportunity on a day when I thought it was absolutely essential to buy the car—the day I met Monington. Now, not to go to Martínez meant having to explain that something had failed to work out. Of course I intended to tell Javier about everything, but I preferred to tell him en route. That way I could describe the failure as a change in circumstances: I would not let it assume dramatic proportions.

I went to Martínez and we took the car out for a drive, but we didn't come to an agreement—the owner was not entirely sure he wanted to sell. Probably his decision also depended on something that might fail to work out.

We sat talking in a café until late. About nine I took a train, which was nearly empty. At Olivos a man got in, sat down in the vacant seat in front of me, and unfolded the evening paper. I began to look at it over his shoulder, not wanting to believe what I saw. I got so close that he turned around indignant: I apologized, telling him that I'd seen something extremely interesting to me, and he let me have the paper. On the first page there was a photograph of Puig. I began to read: "The well known industrialist Luis Puig died this morning at his estancia Las Murtas." An obituary and a brief explanation of what had happened. At nine o'clock in the morning, after spending a somewhat restless night, he had suffered a stroke as he got out of bed.

I returned the paper, went to a corner of the car, and leaned my forehead against the window pane. The tennis courts, the racetrack, the stadium of some club, everything seemed so alone and so quiet, the lights looking so clear in the darkness, so vigilant, as if they were thinking something and would not say what.

4

Up to this point everything has been easy; I've written about the first two episodes and now I must tackle the third, but the third is linked closely with everything that's no longer episodic. I can't highlight it by narrating it from beginning to end, because I don't yet see the end clearly. One moment, though, stands out as completely autonomous, and I want to get there, I want to describe it exactly as it was, without adding a thing. Unattached, free, like an external force, that moment will explain why I still can't see myself freed from it.

There were some changes of scenery in my life and, although I was not entirely aware, some changes in my attitude as well.

I said that when I tried to make my move with Puig I was beginning to worry about my financial instability. In fact, I was very worried, and not without cause. When my uncle's prediction about the fall of the monarchy was confirmed, shortly after I arrived in Buenos Aires, no one here was alarmed; on the contrary, what happened in Spain seemed like a huge general fiesta to everyone: I viewed it with distrust. I won't pause to explain why; I tried doing that many times—in my department at the university, in some of the homes I visited often—and the wave of anathema rose against me. I was surrounded by scandalized voices: "Aesthetic reasons!" No, they were not aesthetic reasons—by this they meant rose-colored reasons—, they were not even reasons. It was an inner certainty that I could only have expressed by saying: "To me it smells like something that won't work." And that's how it was. Something that progressed at first as a felicitous occurrence was soon thrown into confusion and it began to die of consumption.

I wasn't really affected personally, but my thoughts, I couldn't avoid this, moved in the zone cast by the shadow. In the first years after I arrived, I was completely caught up in the life of Buenos Aires, because the spell of the city had an enormous power over me, and it seemed that unless I lived with complete abandon I would be ungenerous to the city. Then, when the horizon over there began to look very gloomy, when I began to see in the newspapers confirmation of my uncle's anxieties, which I'd considered obsessions, and when people like me, who didn't read the newspapers on principle but heard others talking and saw the headlines while riding the colectivo, ended up buying the paper when we got off the bus and reading what we wished we'd never read, then I began to understand that in some way I'd always felt anchored to the other shore, that until then my solitude, longed for, had been until that moment pure luxury, the greatest luxury that exists—living without precautions—and that if the mooring rope broke, living would turn into very hard work.

I even went so far as to think my uncle might need help and, before I knew how I could provide it, I wrote to him: "Leave all that and come." But he didn't answer in agreement or rather, he didn't answer. His letters continued to arrive frequently, and I told myself that everything was fine, that his situation hadn't changed, but there wasn't a word about my offer, even though I repeated it several times. I thought that as soon as I had something settled I'd be able to write to him with more authority. But what I hadn't even imagined was what I might settle. The thing is, fortunately I met Monington, and Puig's death the day after my visit caused affairs to take a most unexpected turn.

I reached the estancia on the seven o'clock train. There was no reason for me to go—no one called me, and my address did not appear among those of Puig's close friends, but I went. There I met his heirs—fortunate circumstance—, his associate, Zelaski—irritating happenstance—, and I spoke to all of them about our meeting the day before, which of course the chauffeur and the servant had already described. I also spoke about my relationship with Monington, turning the hour and a half we'd spent talking in a café into a longtime professional connection. In short, within a few days I went to Martínez ready to buy the car.

I'll go into all that later, since the details of how it actually occurred are important. I'm skipping ahead to my frequent trips to Martínez because alongside the importance of that fact, everything else pales.

As soon as I decided to buy the car, I called Javier and he said I should have lunch at his house, then we'd go and look. That's what happened; we looked during the afternoon, but nothing was definite. I went back day after day until I found a small, acceptable Chevrolet. One of those days I went to pick up Javier at the club and he urged me to start going there too, saying it was absurd for me never to get any exercise: I realized it was absurd.

Many afternoons, as I held my racket, Javier, a great tennis player, faced me patiently. I would be thinking: winter's almost over, it's pleasant to come here and, above all, to return after dark, when you can feel the river dampness, which I like so much. Soon the willows will start to bud . . . Besides, one of Javier's many good qualities is that he's very sociable. He has an enormous network of friends, there's no denying he's nice. Well, I never denied him his good qualities, but I like running him down a little—only in his presence—the way you run down people who have a lot of education, even though you often hit them up for some information. I'd get tired of telling him that he was frivolous and snobbish, that in his world nothing ever happened, nothing that was ever worth doing, and he would say to me: "In my world? And your world, which one is that?" I had to admit that my world was his world, the small part of his world that with effort he'd managed to foist on me. The truth is, without Javier I would have lived in the populous city of my dreams like an anchorite. Like a tramp, Javier would say, and he might have been right.

At the club, beside the tennis court, where we usually met up with some girls, a new girl appeared.

If I'd been asked to specify the point where frivolity and snobbery condensed—of course those categories are not condensable, it would be better to say where they flowed, teemed, bubbled—I would have named the corner of the tennis court where Javier and his cousins—Javier was a Hernández on his mother's side, and she was the daughter of one of my great uncles, a second cousin: the Molina sisters were Javier's first cousins, but from the very first they included me as one of their relatives—where Javier and his cousins had built—out of thin air—an intimate, childish world, a tiny world inhabited by rackets and sunburned calves. That was the world I saw in my mind's eye when I told Javier that nothing happened in his world. I saw it and even smelled it: the fragrance of recently cut grass and, behind the stone bench, the musk rose covering the garden wall. Pure colors, a light, gentle breeze. Very eighteenth-century, very ancient, and very modern, as Rubén Darío would say, which describes the spirit of that place exactly, that tender, charming snobbery. Well, next to that bench, one afternoon Quitina appeared.

When they introduced her to me I didn't understand her name, I could hardly utter a word. I can't recall how we decided to play a game and were soon out on the court, sending the ball back and forth, seldom through the air.

At that moment, nothing could have been more unsuitable, more foreign, or more contrary to my mood than gripping the racket and hitting with precision. I recall and will recall as long as I live everything I was thinking and feeling while I somnambulistically threatened the ball passing beside me, untouchable. The racket was in my right hand, tracing arbitrary curves from one side to the other, but my right hand was not on the racket: my hand was stretched out in front of me, clasping Quitina's hand.

Each time I picked the ball up from the ground and threw it to her she would say: all right, two or three more times and we'll be done. We don't need to keep doing this, we don't need to do anything: it's all been consummated.

I'm absolutely sure I'm not adding anything to what I remember, I'm sure my imagination never magnified that moment. As I circled crazily around the court, I was immediately fully aware of what had happened.

Finally, I'm not sure how, we decided to go to the bar and get something to drink because we noticed we were incredibly thirsty. I lifted the ball up from the ground for the hundredth time, and as she walked by the stone bench, Quitina grabbed a sweater she'd left there; at that moment I saw that one of her sneakers was untied and I nodded to her to put her foot on the bench. I tied the sneaker and since her sock had slipped down in the back, I pulled it out, smoothed it, and cuffed it around her ankle, so there wouldn't be wrinkles under her heel. Performing this task painstakingly took me several seconds during which Quitina blurred a little in front of me, and for an instant the emotion prompted by her proximity became perfect peace, as if with customary meticulousness I were carefully tying the sneaker that belonged to our son.

I've always liked to reflect on the strange relationship that exists between prophecy and memory, because there are occasions when the first time we do or think something it feels habitual from the very beginning. So that the first day I felt the entire building resting on the base formed by my trivial action. I remained there, absorbed, as if before a presence, absolutely sure that Quitina was perceiving it the same way. We stayed like that for a while, I'd have no way of measuring how long, without saying a word.

Our destiny was what had been born at that moment. Just as two kinds of matter, once they have been combined, are no longer two as they were before, our ecstasy—almost dismay—arose from the certainty of realizing that we would never go back to being the people we were moments before. That's why what resulted from our fusion was silence. If one of us had said something, the other would have been only a double; but by doggedly immersing ourselves in silence we were both saying the same thing at the same time.

Nothing could separate that silence—neither the chatter of the others nor the routine things we were forced to do individually, such as have a glass of wine or, afterward, walk to the car.

Javier agreed to take everyone who could fit into his car. We sank into quiet in the back, since quiet could also be one and the same in us both.

I rode sideways so that Quitina would have as much room as possible, because there were four of us in the seat; Quitina's shoulder was resting on my chest, I felt the warmth of her arm through my shirt, and the warmth of our bodies was a union so real it prevented us from feeling our boundaries. Her warmth flowed into a part of my chest that was like a breach in myself where I seeped out and became lost in her, where she emptied into me, invading me. If the car shook as it hit a pot hole or stopped suddenly, we felt ourselves jostled like inert objects separated or thrown into collision, we felt our point of contact tear, disintegrate temporarily, and then a tremor of happiness when we collided again, as if that caused our being to pour faster from one of us into the other. We looked at each other only every now and then, and only very quickly, because even a gaze could not have communicated the secret of what was happening in us. Trying to communicate something to each other would have seemed to indicate we weren't experiencing total communication.

I was riding in the left-hand corner and Quitina turned her head for a moment to look out. She didn't actually look at me, but I saw a green reflection in her eyes, a tiny snake of light mirrored in them like a flash of lightning, and I realized it was the neon light from one of the nightclubs along the shore. Those magic lights, lost among the willow groves, which held such an incredible power of fascination over me, stole Quitina's gaze for a moment, and in the gaze that hadn't reached me, I discerned the full extent of her rapture. It was an anxious gaze, in which she escaped toward the darkness of the woods, with me, because I ran with her too. When I saw the green spark shining in the black of her eyes I ran with her toward that shadow where I had wanted her so much, and this helped me recognize her.

What struck me about Quitina when I first saw her wasn't just her beauty; rather, I think I was so blinded that I stopped seeing her and everything around us. Quitina did not appear before me but within me. When I faced her, I didn't feel as though I were facing something unreachable but in front of something my own, specifically fated to be mine. That's what Quitina had, as opposed to all the other women I'd seen before, and it was not something new: it was an eternity. My love for Quitina was simply my faculty of loving, which had begun when my life did but was suddenly kicking into gear.

As I gradually understood all this—although "understood" is not the exact term: it was all bubbling in my head—my presentiment of Quitina was becoming fused with her image; all those totally indescribable moments when I'd been touched unexpectedly by a presentiment of her were becoming her credentials, attesting to her identity. Quitina was what I'd felt glued to my chest, the way at that moment I could feel her arm, each time that in some place or some atmosphere I laid eyes on something that made me brim with emotion. At such moments I'd always felt her as unique, as absolutely intimate, as on rare occasions one can only feel life itself.

That, more or less, is the whirlwind of sensations in which I was caught up—because only when they're written down the way they are here do they seem to be things I thought, which they weren't then—as the car left Palermo and the Plaza de Francia behind, turned into Alvear Avenue and then Rodríguez Peña, and stopped at the Molina sisters' door. There I held Quitina's hand in mine again for a moment, and when she disappeared with the other girls it got dark.

We probably went on to drop the others at their houses, and I suppose Javier left me at my house.

We saw each other again the next day and continued to see each other uninterruptedly during the month of October. None of what happened during that time is worth mentioning, because it would just be a repetition, more or less, of what I've already said. Between us, there was nothing but reciprocation and surrender from the beginning.

In our state of semi-absence, we trusted our friends to be compassionate as they devised the thousand schemes that were needed for us to spend as much time together as possible. Quitina had been close to the Molina sisters since she was a baby, and they made life easy for us by arranging for her to be with them morning, noon, and night. All they asked in return was that we serve as the butt of their endless jokes, but we could put up with that so everything went smoothly.

During the periods when we had to pay some attention to the group, pretend that we were taking part in the conversation, and, in short, tolerate the presence of other human beings, I'd been finding out who Quitina was. She wasn't Argentine but Cuban, her father was Spanish, she'd gone to school in the United States, that year—she was nineteen—she would graduate from high school. She was here with her mother, at the Alvear Palace—they came often, and at one time they had owned a house in Buenos Aires.

This information was more than enough, because the only thing that interested me no one had to tell me: I saw it for myself from the first moment. No sooner had I seen her appear than I knew who she was.

Of her I never asked questions, never talked with her about specific things; and I'm almost tempted to say I didn't talk with Quitina, but if I think about it carefully I see that would be impossible: I must have talked a lot, since nothing personal about either of us was unknown to the other. The thing is, I can't recall what I talked with Quitina about, because when I talked with her my ideas weren't dressed up if they were about to step out; the manner or getup in which people usually wrap their ideas in order to present them to others was something I never put on with respect to Quitina. With her I was exactly as I am with myself, and this explains why it seems to me as if that no words passed between us. Our abandonment, the way we forgot everything, meant that wherever we happened to be we were alone and naked.

What's curious is that the others noticed: they would tell us we weren't presentable, and they treated us like idiots, explaining to us whenever we arrived somewhere what kind of a party or human gathering we were about to witness, recommending that we at least try to seem normal.

One afternoon we found ourselves at the Yacht Club and the time passed quickly, as always. When the light began to fade, we all sat in a large group facing the water. Spring was already over and, what was more, we were having one of those warm spells that can appear in Buenos Aires at any time of year, with just as much right and without any more explanation than the really cold spells. The mood was one of perfect calm, and the two of us were sitting at the very edge of the group, just far enough away that we could exchange a few words by ourselves, but not enough to seem improper. Then . . .

What I'm proposing to do is impossible. I look at the whole and see the play of light and shadow, see the clear parts intensified by the dark ones, when what I wanted to record here is the innocent tone, the pure white of trust. If I'm rhapsodizing now as I recall how limpid that tone was, that's not because it stands out among so many dramatic traps, but because it was a limpid *innocence*, deleting from that word anything concomitant with the idea of guilt or sin. Strictly speaking, what I want to say is *youth*. I've paused in my story, preparing to describe a very mysterious moment, and what I see now is that it can be defined by a word less highly charged: a moment of youth.

Then I took a straw out of its paper wrapper, slowly flattened it with my fingernail until it was as pliant as a piece of ribbon, gave one end to Quitina, and, elbows on our knees, each of us holding one end of the straw, we traveled around the images of things nearby. We walked under the little tower at customs, followed a large transatlantic ship as it pulled away from the dock, and swayed down below with the yachts rocking like little plastic ducks when they were caught in the wake of a motorboat. We really looked at all that, resting our eyes by letting them roam over things, and it didn't seem to us that we were each looking with our own eyes, we weren't afraid that the diverseness of our focal points would distract or separate us: we were united by the straw-ribbon through a system of slight pulls that created a dialogue in which there were neither questions nor answers, only unanimous movements, turns, leaps, and glides.

Will such childishness seem unbearable? Perhaps, but I think it can be left as a paradigm of the kind of love a bride feels on her honeymoon— a foolish idyll that would be laughable if it weren't so serious. In that prison, as in a bell jar that fate had placed over us in order to culture us however it liked, I was thinking: "This is my fiancée." When I saw her the first day, I thought: "This is my wife," "this is my lover"; but there on the terrace, at the edge of the water, I was thinking, "This is my fiancée," because I was hoping for something from her that I could not obtain suddenly, in an ecstasy, in an embrace: something only life could give us when we stepped into the fire.

Suddenly, in the middle of the silence—simultaneously there came the sound of footsteps on the gravel—we heard a voice behind us.

"Pancha . . ."

Quitina stood up quickly. Her mother was waiting for her nearby, with two other women. Quitina ran toward her, and Laura Molina followed behind, like a bodyguard. All of us in the group stood up, but the women neither approached nor acknowledged us from a distance, so we sat down again. We saw how Quitina and Laura were arguing, laughing, pleading, and how they finally walked away from the women, saying: "All right, all right . . ." And the women left the way they'd come.

We had to take Quitina back to the hotel half an hour later; they were expecting someone for dinner that evening and her mother was afraid that she wouldn't get there on time.

She sat down beside me, and I took her hand but let go of it immediately, because I realized that if I'd kept holding it, she would have started to cry. Then I tried to direct her attention to what the others were talking about. Laura was telling how hard she'd worked to rescue Quitina.

"It was really a struggle!" she was saying. "When I heard that 'Pancha!' I said to myself: we're done for."

"Does your mother always call you Pancha?" someone asked Quitina.

"Yes, always," Quitina said.

Then, sitting on the edge of her chair, she leaned her elbows on the table and started to talk. It seemed to me that I was hearing her voice for the first time. She saw my look of surprise and looked back in a way that said: "Let me be, I have to talk." And she started to tell about the transformations her name had undergone in high school.

First they called her Francesca, because it's a literary name. Then, after they saw a letter from her mother, they made her explain how Pancha could be a diminutive of Francesca, and she'd filled a whole page for them with the thirty-six variations of her name in Spanish, a page that actually turned out to be a diagram, with brackets that held the derivatives and more brackets that branched off from those and enclosed the diminutives and augmentatives. Turning toward me, she said: "There are thirty-six at least, I assure you."

Quitina had never looked at me that way: I didn't think I could stand it. Neither did she, to such an extent she lost her train of thought, nearly strayed off course from the conventional aspects of her tale. She got hold of herself immediately, though, and went on to tell how her classmates had tried in vain to learn the whole thing, had unanimously chosen Quitina. They thought it was very funny that Quitina was a double diminutive. The triple diminutive bewildered them completely.

"You mean there's a triple?" Laura asked.

"Yes, of course," Quitina continued. "You can make Francisquitina from Francisquita and Francisquina. Since that's very long, when I was little I used to say only half of it. But you could make it even longer— Francisquirritina."

Everyone laughed and made amusing comments, but I saw that for Quitina her story was not so trivial. It was something she told with pleasure, dwelling on the details, as if she never wanted to finish telling it and, even more, as if she were thinking: "There's something in all this you can't understand." The others were bored by now with so much complexity, but since I was listening very attentively, Quitina kept on with her story and said that Francesca had been reserved for use only at serious moments, even though it wasn't Spanish. When she had to take an exam she'd get very pale and they used to say: Now you're looking like Francesca.

They'd just turned on a light, and I saw that she was dreadfully pale. She was still sitting on the edge of her chair and she hadn't stopped talking. Finally Laura said: "All right . . . the half hour's up."

I saw that she was thinking how stupid it was to have made such an effort to keep her there just so she could give that speech.

Once we were in the car—her hands were frozen—she began to sink into her usual withdrawal, and suddenly she said: "All that about the name are things from my father, things he used to tell me when I was very little. Tomorrow I'll show you a picture of him."

"Yes, yes," I said. "I want very much to see him. So you won't forget," I added, "put it in your pocket tonight."

"I can't put it my pocket," Quitina said, "because it's a meter and a half tall."

"Then where is it?"

"You'll see; tomorrow I'll take you to see it."

Just then we reached the hotel, and that's how everything was left.

The night was agonizing. It presented difficulties I was sure I could overcome, but there was something invincible in an immediate way in the difficulties themselves: a strange element was at work, thrusting itself like a wedge into our closeness. Suddenly I was consumed by horror to think that Quitina might be left alone, at the mercy of that strange element, although I realized that to her it was familiar: the same thing had happened every night, but I hadn't been aware of it. When we said good-bye at the door of the hotel, I thought I could follow her mentally. I would imagine all her movements, knew she didn't spend much time getting ready for bed and she got rouge on her pillowcase, even though her mother scolded her for it. That was all I knew about her nights at the hotel: how she would sit down at the table and say, as soon as she'd finished: "I'm dead tired."

She would run to her room, pull off her clothes haphazardly, and get into bed. There she was alone, so there she was with me. I could imagine the position of her body as she lay in bed, knowing that she would be imagining the position of my body beside her. That night, though, this intimacy could not exist. While I was tossing about without any chance of resting, I thought I could see her in the middle of a violent argument or, if the argument had been settled, pondering the crazy solutions that proliferate when a person can't sleep. But the night finally passed and at eight the phone rang.

"I'm calling from a bar," Quitina said, "because I don't want to talk from the hotel. I'm walking slowly down Callao toward El Aguila; bring the car. If you're not at the corner when I get there, I'll wait for you in the café. Hurry." And she hung up.

During the night there had been a change in the weather, and the morning was cool. I arrived two minutes before she did. She seemed rested; her cheeks were red and her hair disheveled by the southerly wind, which she'd put up with, walking leisurely so I'd have time to get there. The morning walk made her look as awake as if she'd come from the country, and she got into the car decisively, like a person setting out on a trip around the world. I asked her what had happened.

"Nothing in particular," she said. "I'll give you the details later, but now we head toward Anchorena and there you'll turn toward the Mercado de Abasto."

I wasn't relaxed; I wanted to know, but I looked at her and saw her smiling excitedly. She was impatient to show me what she'd promised and she'd forgotten everything else. I forgot all my worries too.

We'd gone out together only rarely, since someone else always had to make our meetings possible. That time was like an escape, or, rather, like a kidnapping. I felt as though Quitina was kidnapping me because she was leading, even though I was driving.

We drove along Anchorena like foreigners at that active hour, among the ordinary people of that neighborhood, seeing the windows and patios open to the life of morning as we passed, and a very brief, but very intense fantasy passed through my head. I felt that life's prose was moving alongside us, like a heartless fury, strong and tremendous. Quitina was a deity, solicitous, like a docent in a museum, who was showing us things so we would see them as they are: shabby, difficult, atrocious— but, what beauty!

Quitina reached into her pocket and took out a key ring with some little keys like suitcase keys on it.

"There," she said, "in the next block, on the right."

I stopped in front of a small house with a little garden in front. It was stuck out of sight next to a much taller house, whose side wall was covered with ivy. There were also vines growing on the front of the little house all around the door; in the middle of the vines you could see a sign with large letters: "FURNITURE STORAGE."

Quitina gave a brief explanation to the man who came to open the house—an old man who greeted her affectionately, as if he'd known her since she was a little girl. He led us to the room where her things were: an enormous drawing room crammed with furniture.

"I'm going to take a few books that are in one or another of the suitcases," Quitina said. "If you have things to do, don't worry; we'll manage by ourselves."

"However you like," the man said, and he left.

The objects were covered with canvas; they actually formed fortresses you had to circumvent, slipping between them. Quitina advanced quickly since she was on familiar ground, and immediately she found the portrait, which was against the wall, covered with a cloth and placed behind a chest of drawers so it wouldn't get bumped into. We lifted the portrait out from there and placed it in the only open space.

The room in fact was what had been the drawing room, and it had a very large balcony with iron shutters that were closed. But the embrasure was peaked in the middle, where there was a fan-shaped grate without a shutter, and at that moment the sun was shining directly on the grate. We stood the portrait in a suitable light. Quitina had me stand at the appropriate distance and she lifted the cloth.

It was one of those portraits from the Spanish school—prosaically realistic but very lifelike. As a painting, mediocre; as a document, excellent. I smiled as if the portrait had greeted me, although the portrait was not smiling but gazing straight ahead with a pair of intensely blue eyes and the vermilion on the mouth so authentic the mouth seemed about to move its lips.

The man in the portrait was not more than forty; he was a Celt with an aquiline nose and, at first, he seemed very different from what I was expecting. Immediately though, I began to discover things about Quitina she might have gotten from him, and I said to her: "You don't resemble your father, but it's clear that, because of him, you don't resemble your mother. He's why you don't look like a person from somewhere tropical."

"Yes," Quitina said, "they're so different!" And then, very sadly, "The situation's hopeless. At first I thought it was just a passing argument, but they haven't seen each other for ten years now and their attitudes haven't changed."

We sat down on a bundle of shapeless things, in front of the portrait, and Quitina told me how her life had been a question of seeing them only on vacations—this time with one, the next time with the other.

While we talked, I stroked her cheek, pinching it gently to watch how the blood rushed to the marks left by my fingers.

Our movements among the bundles had stirred up the dust a bit, and the light entering through the peak formed a shaft in which luminous particles spiraled upward in an apotheosis. Rather, it was a ray of annunciation falling in the room over the furniture's silence in which Quitina's story became lost.

As long as I live, life for me will have the smell of dust and mold, the feel of somber, closed-up places, a power of supreme voluptuousness. Within that humid, cold smell, Quitina's neck exuded a smell of warm amber. Contact with it transformed an attic into a magic palace.

Finally we put the portrait back in its place and left, laden with a few voluminous books and completely incapable of remembering that a car is something that must move forward in a straight line in the center of its lane. Nevertheless, we turned around several times without anything serious happening.

Suddenly, Quitina said: "We need to hurry; I have to be at Laura's house at eleven. My mother will be almost finished."

Then she explained to me how it was that she'd been able to escape. Her mother had an appointment with the kinesthesiologist, the dietitian, and another such person at some institute she went to often and never spent less than three or four hours. At eleven Quitina wanted to be at the Molinas', where she'd have lunch. She was determined not to be taken away from there. She hesitated, as if she were going to tell me something unpleasant, but she stopped.

"That way we avoid arguments," she said decisively.

I scolded her for never having mentioned those arguments to me, and she cut me off: "Why talk if things are going to stay the same no matter what?"

But she didn't say this either cynically or arrogantly; she said it naturally, as if it were obvious, and she added: "With my father I won't have to argue about anything."

I wanted to keep talking about him, but Quitina told me, with a pleading tone that sounded a lot like a command: "Not today! Not today!"

At that moment we saw Laura, walking very quickly toward the house. I braked right at the edge of the sidewalk, Quitina leaped from the car, grabbed her by the arm, and said: "What are you doing out walking around?"

Laura defended herself, laughing. "Don't get all worked up. Mecha and Rafaela are mounting guard."

From the car I could see them chattering away about something I could barely understand, and I waited until they'd finished so I'd be able to work my way into the conversation. But I couldn't; they'd forgotten me.

I got out and suggested we go into a bar right near there, on the corner of Arenales. Quitina didn't think we should, but Laura said: "All right, why not? We have time."

We sat down in a corner not easily seen from outside and Laura kept on telling about how well Rafaela spoke on the telephone like a little girl five years old: "Hello, hello . . . No ere, mummy no ere . . ." Quitina was laughing, looking very sad. I thought they'd gone crazy. Finally I realized it had to do with their efforts to tie up the phone: If Quitina's mother called they would answer by saying stupid things, in pretend voices so she would think there was some interference in the lines, or they would hang up after two words, as if the call had been disconnected on its own, in short doing everything necessary to make calls impossible and to be able to say later that Quitina had been there the whole morning.

They were sitting very close together on a small oilskin sofa that formed a right angle against the wall, and I was facing them, with my whole chair in a different light. Well, I was in the light and they were in the shadow; then I leaned back a little, resting against the back of the chair, holding my glass in my hand. I sat at a distance so I could observe them in their world, their girlish world made of small complicities, of innocent secrets.

When I looked at them that way, distanced from them so much, I remembered that minutes before, when I was trying to clarify some serious things, Quitina had said to me: "Not *today*, not *today*." When I remembered it, I noticed how she had stressed *today*. At that moment, speaking with Laura, Quitina had *yesterday's* expression on her face, I mean the expression she always had. Even more than that, an expression unknown to me. Now she was neither Quitina nor Francesca, maybe she was Pancha, something that for me was not entirely clear. But my thoughts must have been so piercing that Quitina turned her head for a moment and shot me a quick, pleading, anguished, and also imperious look. "No, no: correct that," her look said, and I corrected it. She was as much Quitina as Francesca and Pancha, there was no doubt, and the expression on her face was as much today's as yesterday's.

But that day, that today, was ending there. They stood up and told me it would be better if I didn't leave with them; they would walk to Laura's house—it was only three blocks away—, because we could meet up with someone.

"Well, good-bye," Quitina said to me. "Call me late this afternoon," and she took my hand in a very odd way. It was like those times when two hands that reach out to shake don't quite meet and their clasp misses or ends up being one-sided. I was going to take her hand, but she grabbed mine from on top, squeezed the back of it quickly and let it go right away, without allowing me to hold her hand. At the same time, just as quickly, she drew her face close to mine without looking at me, brushed her cheek across my mouth, raising herself a little on the tips of her toes and lowering herself immediately, so that I hardly had time to kiss her on the forehead.

"Ciao," Laura said. She tugged at Quitina's other hand and they left.

I didn't move until five in the afternoon; in other words, I was at home, unconscious . . . more unconscious than usual: deliberately unconscious. I recall very well that I opened the drawer of my desk and saw a letter. The letter was on top of the envelope, a habit of mine that's rather stupid. I never put a letter back in its envelope, because of some superstition. I hate superstition and especially commonly held superstitions. When I realize I've picked one up, I feel a loathing, as if superstitions were parasites; sometimes I do pick one up, though. That's one I haven't been able to get rid of. I take out the letter, read it and don't put it back in the envelope. Why don't I throw the envelope away? I don't know, but usually I put the envelope and the letter together in one of my desk drawers. That day, the letter and its envelope were in the drawer. I looked at them for a long time and pondered all these tangential details. I think I went so far as to reach out one of my hands, pull a little of the envelope out from underneath, and look at the stamp. My consciousness, not completely relaxed, suggested something like this to me: "Now would be a very appropriate time to answer that letter." Then I pulled my hand back quickly and closed the drawer. Clinging to its delicious dream, my consciousness brought me the memory of Quitina's words: "Not *today*, not *today*."

The only thing I could do and wanted to do, with my entire will, was relive the first hours of that day: to drive in the morning of eight o'clock light along those streets and see pink patios with flowerpots, streets that led to happiness and were filled with it. Driving along those streets I had no idea where I was going, but I felt that I was going toward paradise. Rather, I was already in paradise right there or, better yet, paradise was in everything I was seeing. There, where I'd seen life's prose, like a cruel deity, and had provoked her with flattery, telling her passionately: "What beauty! What beauty!" without stopping to see what it was she was showing me.

With those thoughts I made it to five o'clock. I telephoned Laura's house and Quitina wasn't there any longer.

Rafaela got on the phone and told me something unexpected had happened: some relatives had arrived from Chile. Quitina could not keep her mother from carrying her off.

My desolation must have been so obvious that Rafaela told me to come over; she was alone. The girls had gone to the movies and Quitina had said she would call last thing at night both Rafaela's house and mine so we could plan something for the next day.

I didn't feel like talking and I could tell that Rafaela really did. I hesitated, but ended up saying to myself: "All right, let her talk."

"I'll be over," I said.

Rafaela didn't come out for a few minutes. I sat down in an overly circumspect armchair in which no slouching was possible. Although the chair was not exactly hard, there was no give to the medallion that formed its back, and its arms, with their little cushions, demanded a bearing à la Louis XVI. The puma lay spread out on the floor in front of me, gazing at me; in a corner a display cabinet filled with ancient weapons, trophies and ribbons in the national colors.

I knew all those things down to their last detail, but the Molina house became a reality for me in the few minutes I spent waiting for Rafaela, alone, facing the puma. And that moment was not one of innocence, or of youth either. On the contrary; it was like the premonition of maturity or like a contact with something very old. The puma was speaking to me on behalf of all my grandparents, and it was warning me, reproaching me for something I couldn't understand. Well, I did understand that there, on the floor, was the puma's hide, with the animal's stuffed head and glass eyes, and that the weapons were in the display cabinet. Maybe the bullet that felled the puma had issued from one of those short, thick pistols: my grandparents certainly understood each other, and they regarded each other peacefully because they were history. Toward me, however, they exhaled a certain hostility. Of course that hostility was what made me feel the pressure of the bonds between us. Because I was no gringo: if I had been, they would have had nothing to reproach me for. Since I was not, they had . . . The puma, the puma's round toothy head, which stood up from the horizontal plane of the parquet floor as if it were swimming toward me, was reproaching me . . . For what? I wasn't the one who'd left it in its dry skin, gutted its insides, but it was reproaching me for that.

I don't know if my fantasy—and I recall this with complete certainty—

which consumed me during that whole time, arose from the fear that Rafaela was going to reproach me or, rather, accuse me of something, to show me some flaw in my behavior. In fact that was what she intended to do. But I never run from accusations: why would I be afraid of them on that occasion? The sad thing was that Rafaela's accusations turned out to be too gentle, too timid—less explicit than the puma's.

Once again I'm coming up against the difficulty of telling about *that moment*, without putting it into other words. Obviously, right there I didn't think clearly and concisely about what I've just expressed. I'm sure of that; it's not how I expressed it then, but what's even more serious is that then, at that precise moment, I entered this order of ideas, this climate, and of course I entered with the most total certainty that what was happening was an initial word, a theme, a ritornello.

I recall that I lit a cigarette, stood up and took a few steps as if I were going to walk from one side of the room to the other, but I remained motionless in the center, looking into space. At that moment I heard Rafaela's voice behind me: "What are you doing there like a fata morgana?"

Behind her the maid appeared with the teacart. Rafaela returned me to the Louis XVI chair, sat down on the sofa, and, with academic rigor, we entered the hour of truth-telling.

Rafaela was the aunt of Laura and of Mecha Molina. Old enough to be considered an old maid, besides, she was also the mistress of the house because the mother of her nieces had died some time before and their father only rarely put in an appearance. However, she liked to be among young people, to be the repository of their confidences, which she furthered or hindered according to her sympathies. Our affair she'd adopted as her own, because she'd been fond of Quitina since she was a little girl or, maybe, because she was not fond of Quitina's mother. When she spoke of her, she would say: "Hers is a *proud* beauty," laying the entire weight of her definition on the adjective.

"How did you manage to make such a bad impression on Hortensia?" Rafaela asked.

"I don't know," I answered. "I noticed it from the beginning and couldn't avoid it. What would I have to do for her to like me?"

"Well . . . nothing comes to mind. But in any case, she's not guided by what she does or does not like; she's a woman whose ideas are always formed in advance. You can't imagine how much I've worked on her about this."

"Yes, I can imagine," I said; "and I'm truly grateful to you."

"Oh, you don't need to thank me; it amuses me. Because she comes out with some really nasty *comments*, and you better believe it."

Rafaela told me about a great many of señora Hortensia Laso's *wise-cracks* . . . For instance, what Hortensia had answered the day that Rafaela had tried to impress her by saying: "But don't you think the love between those two young people is wonderful?" and Hortensia had made a skeptical face. Then, thinking that Quitina's mother doubted the sincerity of my feelings, that she might be taking me for a dowry hunter, Rafaela had expounded on the positive aspects of my character: I was a person interested only in higher things, completely unconcerned about practical life, and it made absolutely no difference to me that her daughter was rich.

There, Hortensia had cut her off: "That's precisely where I find him most opposed to my way of thinking; it makes no difference to him that my daughter is rich, and it makes a difference to me whether or not she continues to be."

Rafaela had not given up, though. "There are things more important than that," she'd told her. "The chief thing is that the boy is from a well-known family; you can't tell me you don't know who he is."

That's when Hortensia had exploded: "Because I do know who he is! Because I know who Santiago Hernández, son of Santiago Hernández, son of Santiago Hernández is . . ."

That's where the whole mystery lay; for Quitina's mother I was the third Hernández to follow a downward path. She had known my grandparents in Europe, where they were consuming in idle luxury what little their more or less alienated lands could produce for them. She knew that my father's life, which was very short, had been a game, and that he had lost his life by playing at war. And about me she knew nothing, but the day they introduced me to her at the Molinas' she looked at me with disbelief and fear, as if I were a ghost.

Rafaela told me a thousand things more in an attempt, if not to cheer me up, at least to give me some guidance. I saw very clearly that she was trying to tell me: "If you had a brilliant future, if you could give Hortensia the impression that you're not one of those people with their heads in the clouds." But she found no solution to the problem. I made some vague comment: that work didn't scare me, that precisely because I was certain I had the ability to do something, I could lead a rather carefree existence.

"I already know that, I already know that," Rafaela said. "I'm not the one you have to convince." Then she added, after a pause: "Now, when they go to Mar del Plata, you'll follow along behind, won't you?"

"Of course, right away."

"That's going to make things get nastier," Rafaela said in a very definite tone.

"Why? I don't understand what bearing that can have on this."

"Well . . . Look, last summer Quitina was with her father in . . . California, I think it was, but the thing is she didn't turn up here at all. The year before, she was, let's see, eighteen, seventeen; her mother could keep her on a very short rein. Now, on the other hand, girls have so much freedom, and it increases from day to day."

"But she has as much freedom or more in Buenos Aires," I said.

"Yes, in fact she does. She's free because she comes and goes whenever she feels like it, and because her friends help her; but her mother's watching at the hotel, because her mother has nothing else to do. In Mar del Plata it's different."

"In Mar del Plata, in the middle of the summer, there are things she has to do?"

"There are, there are . . . Well, and this is no secret to anyone, she spends hours in the casino. I don't know if Quitina knows this; maybe she doesn't. And I think that's the main reason they're postponing their departure for so long this year."

"Do you think she's afraid she'll lose her authority in Quitina's eyes if Quitina finds out how she spends her time? I don't think it's possible that Quitina wouldn't know about this, if it's already been going on for some while. She sees into people very deeply."

"No, it's not that," Rafaela said, "She's afraid of losing her own freedom, although she would never admit it, and that's what's bothering her. She knows people will be watching her. Now there will be two of you to become aware of everything, and she acts as if she were blind, when she's behaving that way she seems to be sleepwalking."

"Aha," I said, "I'm beginning to understand."

"Yes, it's possible you might understand her, but for her to understand you . . . Well, don't think I understand you much better. Not even Javier understands you, and he's truly fond of you; I've heard him say so many times."

"Then why do all of you like me?" I said, exaggeratedly feigning an anger that deep down was sincere.

"I don't know . . . a person can like people without understanding them."

"I can't, and it makes me furious that you like me and you don't understand me."

"That's all right, that's all right; we won't like you. We'll decide not to like you, because understanding you is going to be difficult."

"Where's the difficulty? Let's see, explain it to me; what is it you don't understand?"

"How am I going to explain to you something I don't understand? I don't understand you and that's enough; that's the explanation."

Rafaela was afraid that her categorical answer would be too harsh for me, and without trying to qualify it, she added: "You yourself have to realize that you're very different from our boys. Not physically; no, anyone could take you for a criollo, but in your manner . . . in your tastes . . ."

"Yes," I said, "that's because tastes are acquired when people are very young. Also their manner. It's obvious that my manner would be different if I'd sung 'Febo asoma' when I was eight years old and knew the national anthem . . ."

"Well, that might be it," Rafaela said, "but it's also what Javier says: you're an intellectual."

"Ah! Javier says I'm an intellectual? So much the better, because he tells me I'm an idiot."

At that moment we heard the voices of Laura, Mecha, and Javier in the hall.

"The girls told me you were sure to be here and I came, in case you found yourself among the unemployed," Javier said as he walked in.

"I still don't know."

"There hasn't been any news?" Laura asked me.

"Not a word."

"But it's not that bad. It's not so bad you have to look like you're at a wake."

"No, I'm not worried about that," I said. "The thing is, I was here, with Rafaela, talking about some serious things."

"Tell me."

"I can't tell you anything; actually what I'd like is for you to tell me."

"For me to tell you what you were talking to Rafaela about?"

"Something like that."

The girls had brought Rafaela something they'd heard recently, and the three of them went off down the hallway, talking in low voices. Javier preferred to pantomime his answer to me, and he made an ingenious, expectant face, like someone about to be interrogated. I drew him toward the balcony a little, and said, without any other explanation: "Sing the national anthem for me."

Javier paused for a few seconds, ran through the possibilities he could think of for coming up with something more comical than what I wanted and, not finding any, he decided to adopt the attitude of an obedient little boy and began to sing. But that's not all: with his hand raised as if he were carrying a flag, he started to circle around the room, marking time. Mecha and Laura appeared in the doorway, speechless.

Without stopping, Javier signaled to them that they should follow him, and they both fell into line behind him, singing with childish voices: "Febo asoma, ya sus rayos . . ."

The comedy didn't last long, but before it ended, I enhanced it with one more document. While they were parading and singing, I sat down on the puma skin, and in order to make what I thought to do playful, I leaned on my elbow, next to the animal's head, with my face on the palm of my hand. Then I perceived the smell of old skin, cardboard, glue, and dust emanating from the stuffed head, the smell that had probably accompanied all of Rafaela's nieces and nephews when they played. I signaled with my hand and the marchers fell silent.

"Have you noticed how bad this smells?" I asked.

"What?" all three of them answered, and they threw themselves to the floor, to smell.

"This creature has bad breath," Javier said.

"Oh, no," Laura protested. "It's a lovely smell. When I used to do bad things and Aunt Rafa scolded me, I would come here to the skin and cry. I would be down on it and cry like this, lying over its head."

"To me it smells like chocolates," Mecha said. "I've eaten so many of them sitting here."

"That's it, that's exactly what I wanted . . ." I started to say, but at that minute the telephone rang.

Quitina didn't stop to explain things to me because she assumed that Rafaela had brought me up to date. All she told me was that she'd needed to go and wait for her godparents who were coming from Chile and that, of course, they would eat with them that night. She wouldn't have even the faintest chance to escape for a while. But that wasn't the worst: she had the impression that they were planning an excursion to Luján for the next day.

She sounded very dejected.

"I'll call you early tomorrow, as soon as I can," she told me, "but I think it will be impossible to do anything all day. Bye."

From her voice, the way she was expressing herself and the scantiness of her words, I could tell she was speaking from someplace where she could be overheard. I said good-bye and prepared to deal with the snare.

When I finished talking they were all seated at the table, waiting for me. Laura asked me what was up and I told her. The girls burst out laughing: "To Luján in the morning, with this heat. What a scream."

"It doesn't surprise me," Rafaela said. "Paula, the little sister, is very devout."

This gave Rafaela the occasion to tell at length about Ambassador Laso's two Cuban daughters, who showed up in Buenos Aires before the war in 1914.

"Well, women dressed more elegantly then—none of the sweaters and things they wear now," Rafaela said.

"But Aunt Rafa," Mecha exploded, "what about those ladies with the *jupes entravées*? They were ridiculous."

"Don't believe it, they were not so ridiculous. In fact, those two were a little . . . tropical. But they caused a sensation. Hortensia all majestic and Paulina quite meek, like a timid violet . . . The thing is, they both made spectacular marriages right away. Suárez, the Galician, went completely nuts over Hortensia, and the little one caught an estanciero from the south . . . I don't remember what his name is. Well, he's from one of those English families that settled here many years ago; and I don't know what he does, but when they talk about him they always say: he's a great financier . . .

Rafaela was speaking to the whole group as she told this story, but she looked at me, as if to say: "You know what I'm referring to": "The brother-in-law is Hortensia's adviser. It's my understanding that he's the one who helps her keep her balance, financially. And there's Paulina crossing herself and saying: 'That sister!' But the three of them get along with each other."

Javier got me out of there—I wanted to go home, but he wouldn't let me; we went prowling around somewhere or other. We drank like pigs, and I wound up—I can't say drunk because I don't get drunk easily; on the contrary, when I drink, I experience a pathological lucidity—, I wound up making plans for the next day. I decided to spend it attending to all the affairs I'd neglected, determined to take on an incalculable number of hateful things, so that later, when I had to compare those twenty-four hours with the ones Quitina had spent they would be just as horrible as a tourist excursion on a December day or a family meal weighed down by a conversation about finances.

It was an infernally calm night: no breeze, humid heat stagnating between the trees, with not a single leaf stirring. We roamed around Olivos and along the Costanera. It was after three when Javier dropped me at my house, and my ability to plan was completely depleted. Sleep was the most urgent thing; I would have liked to stand under the shower, but I couldn't: I pulled off my clothes, which were so sweaty they stuck to my body, the way you skin a rabbit, and I fell into bed.

I'd been asleep for fifteen minutes when the phone rang. It rang in the distance, and I heard it ring three times before I could get myself moving. The telephone had been left in the hall, something that never happens at night. Bumping into the furniture rather than put on a light— the windows on both balconies were open and I was stark naked—I finally reached the hall, turned on a lamp, and dropped into an armchair next to the phone.

It was Quitina, I could not doubt that, but neither could I believe it was Quitina talking that way. "Calm down, please, and speak more clearly," I shouted at her, although I understood her perfectly: the fact that I understood her was what perturbed me. I understood the sense of her words, but I couldn't understand that what she was telling me could happen to us.

In short, there was no excursion to Luján being planned. That night her family had not exactly held a family council, but they'd closed themselves up in the Plaza hotel, where her aunt and uncle were staying, not on a tourist trip but passing through on their way to the United States. At ten o'clock at night, when Quitina could not understand why the four of them were still in that room, her mother had decided to show Quitina her passport and her ticket to New York; she would leave with her aunt and uncle at dawn.

It would be impossible to transcribe our conservation. I don't know how a person whose head was filled with curses could come out with intelligible words, much less loving words in the minimal dose required by a farewell. What matters is that I was able to ask Quitina what time they were leaving and to promise that I would manage to see her, even if only from a distance. I also tried to make her feel somewhat less agitated with vague resolves to fix everything, and she likewise managed to tell me that she expected her father to intervene, but her father was in Europe.

Finally that torture ended, because it could not continue. Ten times during the evening, she'd fought with her mother almost hand-to-hand to get hold of the phone: now that it was too late to do anything, they let her have it for a good while, but her voice and her energy were worn out from crying and shouting until her throat was raw.

When the telephone was silent, I began to repeat to myself the advice and resolutions I was not sure I'd actually formulated. You must keep calm! You must begin by seeing clearly what can be done! You must do something immediately!

I sat in the leather chair, totally crushed; the chair was sticking to my back and drops of sweat were running down my chest. There was not a bit of air, you could not breathe, and I continued to sit there in a state of collapse.

A fly was buzzing around me, a slow, fat one that kept trying to land on me. I tried swatting it with my hand a hundred times: useless, because it kept escaping, describing a few circles in the room, and at times I thought it had gone. I was holding my head with both hands, making an effort to see clearly, struggling to outline a quick, infallible plan. The fly would return and light on one of my shoulders, I would frighten it away, it would take a turn around the room and land on me again. The fly was like the first hurdle, and its flight had wound up weaving a sort of cage around me. I felt like a prisoner within its swoopings, its buzzing; it clouded my vision as it flew past, and it seemed to be intervening between my thoughts and the solution I was seeking. I kept sitting in that chair, sunk in it, crazed and lifeless, like someone who's been cornered.

The hall was lit by a fixture made of an iridescent glass disk held in place at the center by a metal bar about fifteen centimeters long, and attached to the bar there were four very bright bulbs. The corpses of several insects that had succumbed to the heat were visible through the glass. The fly went past, brushing my face, and I thought, thinking suddenly and specifically, almost in words and as clearly as if I'd spoken it aloud: "If that fly were to go in there and never come out again . . ." The fly went over my head, spiraled upward, and went in between the glass and the bulbs. It vibrated for a couple of seconds, sounding as if it had fallen into the skillet, and then was annihilated.

I'm very well aware that to the majority of people this means nothing. Nothing means anything except to the person for whom it means something. No answer is clear if you haven't asked a question. No event makes sense unless you sense its sense.

If I want to be precise, I can't say that I understood the sense of that occasion: the fair thing is to say that I saw and sensed what I'd occasioned. Without any reflection, and therefore, without any possible doubt. With a certainty as natural and immediate as the certainty that hits you in the instance of material acts because of the correspondence between touch and intention. If I want to hit, and I hit the table with my fist, as I hit it and encounter the table's resistance to my energy, as I hear my fist bang the table and see that the objects on the table teeter, I feel certain that I've hit. Well, that's how it was. I formulated my intention to destroy the fly and I destroyed it, using that intention as my instrument. I'd tried countless times to hit the fly with my hand, but I'd always failed. One time I doubted about whether I'd finally hit my mark, and I looked around me to see if I might find the fly lying there, but the last time I experienced no doubt. As I formulated my desire to see the fly annihilated, I did not try to hit it with the heavy instrument of my hand: I focused my intention on the fly and, and without breaking the spiral of its flight, I led it toward the glass. There the fly fell and my energy collided with it on the glass. I heard it fry, because that was neither a buzzing nor a vibrating. Through the translucent glass, I saw it kick for a moment, saw it toss around a very small area, and, then suddenly it was stopping, lying still and staying in one place, like a spot, denser than the others. In a single instant it fell and there it remained.

The blow reverberated throughout that uncommon limb of my will, shook its entire structure, and made all its branches tremble, awakening the echoes of former convulsions. Everything flashed across my mind. Everything, I mean, Elfriede and Puig, who became focused in poles or vertices of violence. I have no doubt that I thought clearly, something like: "Ah, this is that same thing." And more than thinking it on my own, it was as if I were responding to the ghost of Elfriede, who was repeating to me, her white jacket spotted with blood, her gaze intense and her voice confident, as in a prophecy fulfilled: "You have to watch your intentions!" . . . "Yes," I answered, "now I see that; it's true." And my reason accepted the evidence immediately, without dwelling on it too much, because my entire being was affected only by the impact of the force that had sprung from its most innermost core.

For a few minutes or, rather, for one of those spans of time that seem impossible to divide into minutes because they are so disproportionate they elude all measurement—parcels of time, which in ecstasy can be fickle and in terror monstrous, like small giants, like colossal dwarves— for a few minutes I thought about the power that was within me, which had lived off my own life, without my noticing it. Moments before, hearing Quitina talk, I felt so miserable, naked there as a frog, with no further evidence than my solitude and my vulnerability, and I saw myself sunk in my confusion as in the cottony darkness of a storm cloud and, suddenly, from myself, the spark had burst from my own faculties.

I extricated myself from the belly of the chair and went straight to the balcony. Above the houses the sky was growing light.

I finally turned on the shower. The water was the same temperature as the air. With my forehead I searched in vain for some cooler water, but there wasn't any or I didn't wait long enough to see. I got dressed, and a few minutes later I was flying along the highway toward Morón.

The speed helped me to concentrate. I continued to ponder my impulse, savoring my power and feeding it with my breath, inhaling oxygen for it, channeling all of my substance into it, because I considered my power to be my own, and consequently I never thought it was a supernatural power. If anything, it seemed supernatural to me, in other words something like an excellence in my nature—a sort of Herculean condition that also involved a bit of skill. I can't say I thought of it like this specifically; rather, my concentration was moving in those two directions: not to let my will discharge that energy; not to divert my attention from that perfect aim.

I got to the airport with half an hour to spare but, nevertheless, at that moment the airplane was taking off. Only two or three people were watching it leave; on the highway, two or three cars had already started back to the city. I refused to believe that it had been her plane, and I clung to the hope that another one would be leaving right away. I went to find out: that had been the plane. The second dirty trick had been deceiving Quitina about the departure time, so as to avoid any scenes and so she'd be forced to leave disappointed, stamped with the imprint of a deception.

In the time it took me to find out about the flight, the cars had already disappeared on the road. I flew along the highway, trying to overtake them, and I did catch up with a few, but the one that interested me did not appear. There was no way of knowing what shortcut it might have taken.

An idea began to obsess me: as I was leaving the house, when I was almost in the street, I had heard a phone ringing indistinctly; it sounded like mine, but I wasn't sure—at a moment like that all phones sound like yours. I hesitated a little, but I was afraid of wasting time if I went back up; besides, by the time I got there the phone would have stopped ringing. It didn't seem to ring very long. Now, though, I felt certain that it had been Quitina. What kind of kidnapping had she endured, that kept her from alerting me to the deception? In any case, if it was Quitina who called, she had to have been calling from the airport and I couldn't have gotten there in time. The plan must have been devised so it would turn out just the way it did.

The logical thing would have been to drive toward Las Heras, in order to go straight home. I didn't actually intend to go to the Alvear at that moment. I was thinking about when and how I would go, but I was already going. I was driving up Callao, and when I got as far as Guido I saw a car in front of me and in the car a head with a very tall nape. A small head on a long throat and perched on that head a hat I didn't recognize. I wasn't sure I recognized the back of that neck either, and I couldn't be sure it corresponded to the face I suspected it did, but I'd never seen the face as clearly as I was seeing it now, and I had a presentiment that it was hers. My premonition was so strong that I refused to confirm it: I preferred to follow behind.

When the car reached the Alvear Palace, it turned and I turned. It took the curve into the entranceway of the hotel and I quickly left my car in front, on the other side of the street. I bounded across the street in a single leap as she walked up the steps, slipping into the next compartment of the revolving door. She showed no sign of alarm when she sensed my steps behind her; maybe she was absorbed in her thoughts, although her head gave no indication of being weighed down by any sorrow. I situated myself to her right so I could cut her off if she walked toward the elevator, but I let her advance a few meters so we would not end up too close to the reception desk. I matched the rhythm of my steps to hers so exactly that I forced her to turn her head: she stopped short. I took one more step, placing myself between her and the elevator.

"You haven't taken the trouble to ask whether or not I'd be willing to see you," she said.

"Oh, no, I haven't, and you must excuse me. I didn't ask because I knew perfectly well you would say no."

I made my answer sufficiently composed that she had to tolerate it. My attitude was respectful and correct; nevertheless I saw that she was afraid it wouldn't remain that way, and she took a few steps toward the middle of the lobby, so that we wouldn't be too close to the elevator operator. Hemming her in with my steps, I forced her to continue to a sofa. At that moment, someone walking by greeted her familiarly and she had to respond with a sustained smile. The people behind me must have kept looking at her as they crossed the lobby, because I noticed that she felt herself being observed, gave in to the situation and, in order to seem more natural, sat down mechanically. She nodded to me so faintly that at any other moment I would have found her assent insufficient, but at that moment it was enough for me and I sat down in the chair, across from her.

She began by telling me sharply that we had nothing to talk about, and I told her that I hadn't gone there to talk; I wanted only to ask her a couple of questions. She wrinkled her forehead slightly, as if she were preparing herself to endure the onslaught, meanwhile thinking (her motionless face, with its pale features as delicate as an oriental mask, proved as easy for me to read as the clearest handwriting—black on white): "What impudence! I don't plan to answer anything."

I let her wait a few seconds for my questions, and finally I said: "Why . . . would you please tell me why you've adopted this attitude?"

She answered ambiguously: "No."

It was a "no" that tried to be total, and in fact was, because in it there was nothing but negation; however, it didn't carry the absolute firmness of a masculine "no." Hers wasn't the sharp answer that can provoke aggression: it was a malicious display of feminine impunity. "If I say *no*, we'll see what you do."

I didn't know what to do for a long while, but I began to speak before I knew. What I said, more or less, was: "Well, it seems to me I've expressed myself poorly, because . . . of course, what interests me is neither *your attitude* nor the causes of *your attitude*. Besides, I haven't the least right to ask you to explain *your attitude*. But the consequences . . . Do you understand? *Your attitude* has consequences that will turn my personal life completely upside down."

I was speaking slowly, something I don't normally do, and using long paragraphs, like a lecturer. I don't know why I adopted that tactic, but I saw immediately that it was the right one. Two or three times she took a breath in order to speak, without managing to; it seemed unimaginable that she was either too shy or too polite to interrupt me. I realized, rather, I suspected, that it was hard for her to use my language. She saw she was going to be attacked with words, and she had to weigh her own words well. She also saw—and this completely shocked her—that her *wisecracks* would have no effect on me. And she said with determination: "It won't surprise you that my daughter's personal life is more important to me than yours?"

The needle on the seismograph shook as she spoke those two words, *personal life*, as if she had never spoken them before or as if their meaning were untouchable.

"Oh no," I said, "it doesn't surprise me that it's important to you; what amazes me is that you're so determined to destroy it."

"That's your opinion, something that . . ."

"Something that for you doesn't count, of course."

"Of course."

"But señora, my relationship with Quitina is not a matter of opinions; it's the very reality of our lives."

Once again I felt her shudder. She was not a woman who blushed easily; she had the kind of skin often likened to gardenias—white, velvety, and thick—, which couldn't suddenly become flushed by a rush of blood, but even so, when something embarrassed her, her reactions were very visible: there was a sort of paralysis, annulment, absence. Suddenly, when a particular topic was mentioned—there was much more to our conversation than my memory will allow me to transcribe—, when I spoke certain words, she would withdraw into herself, and clam up with a "click!" . . . This seems like a contradiction, there's no other way to say it: her silence would burst. And her gaze, not overly candid but prodigal because of her beautiful eyes, was averted and it emptied like the gaze of the dead.

I sharpened my five senses as I studied her. I was set on finding her secret, and each time she went "click!" it startled me, because I thought I was getting close, but that absence would appear, leaving me speechless and confused.

She realized her refusal to answer my questions was getting her nowhere; and it meant I was the one speaking about things she preferred not to. Then she decided to speak, and skillfully, with the assurance of an expert tackling familiar topics, she made it clear that she was familiar with the insecurity of my financial situation. And how familiar! Much more so than I. In a few words she recounted for me everything the Hernández family had once had and everything they had no longer—almost everything. She knew, down to the last detail, how my father had squandered his fortune through idleness and travel, and she also knew how I was exhausting the very small remainder that had fallen into my hands. Assuring me that I could expect nothing from my grandparents, she said that in the years remaining to them they would use up their very last cent, or maybe even a bit more than their last cent. She did not hide from me the fact that she knew I did not stand to receive a peseta from my mother's side of the family and that I had an uncle in Spain, a pharmacist or something, whom I was sure to ruin by the time I was through.

I did not try to stop the avalanche, I let it fall. My silence was disconcerting to her, it seemed to her that a lack of protest indicated cynicism on my part. Then, in order to put me in the awkward position of having to say something, she paused. I decided to speak about the topic I was required to address, but I proposed to be brief and to begin at the beginning and go straight through to the end. I told her that her *rapport* seemed very thorough to me and that I did not plan to refute it, but in fact my pharmacist uncle had been responsible for my education, and he had taught me not to count on whatever my grandparents might have or might not have any longer. I'd taken my studies quite seriously, as boys in Europe do when they aren't wealthy, and I hadn't thought for a moment that my lack of wealth was an overwhelming misfortune. I'd gone to school because I liked the career I'd chosen, I'd studied spontaneously, because of a natural inclination. I was continually guided more by . . .

Click! She was not about to let me advance into that atmosphere, where she couldn't breathe. Not a word about likes or inclinations: numbers. But just plain numbers, unadorned in rational rigor, although exalted numbers, dignified this time with a certain responsibility or morality. The terms she used were outmoded, and I told myself: "She's too young to talk that way—all this is totally old-fashioned." *Position, comfort,* how ridiculous! She even talked about the importance of establishing oneself before starting a family, about security in life, about one's standard of living, about social hierarchy. I lacked the ammunition to refute such foolishness. Something even more serious was that it amused me to watch her, to see how the superficiality of her ideas flowed in the rhythm of her voice.

Since it was impossible for me to contradict her, I assented repeatedly and told her I understood very well, that everything she said seemed very sensible to me, but that I had a different direction in mind for my future and that I was completely certain of Quitina's willingness to follow that path with me.

"Oh, oh!" she said and her mouth widened in sort of a smile not seconded by the solemnity in her eyes. "Pancha?" she murmured, putting a very slight maliciousness in her interrogative tone.

I could not agree to repeat "Pancha," and I said: "Quitina accepts my future, because her feelings are on the same scale as mine." And I added: "I suppose that last night you had an opportunity to see that for yourself."

"Because of her tantrum, you mean? Bah! When Pancha was five years old she would throw such tantrums that you'd think she was about to die."

And then I had the impression that she was the one who felt amused and distant, as if she were under the sway of a memory. I refused to let her escape and said, in order to make her stick to the subject: "Yes, last night, it seemed as though she would either die or go crazy."

She answered my words, since she'd heard them, but her gaze remained fixed on something in the distance; her answer shot out, charged with whatever she was thinking about.

"Pancha is nothing but a willful little girl, who would still give her life to have pretty things, beautiful things, sumptuous things."

The unconscious compliment struck me as so comical that I had to invoke all the Furies in order to resist the temptation to laugh: "No, not the comical; laughter relaxes the will"—not irony, but definitely the laughter in "laugh 'til you cry." "No, anything but laughter," I repeated to myself, and I could hardly resist the urge to roll on the floor with laughter. But that urge lasted only an instant, because I could see that she had no idea how ridiculous her words were. She kept thinking about whatever she was thinking about before; and in order to stress her last sentence, she added: "She comes by it honestly."

Then I realized there was something serious in her words. I recalled the blue eyes in the photograph that I'd seen at the furniture storage, the vermilion of that vitality, which had probably burned for the pale beauty in front of me now, and I thought that Quitina, like her father, had fine skin that flushed easily. She did not resemble her mother at all except for the black eyes; there was a spirited blood in her, and a single glance could inflame it forever.

At that moment, as if in a truly magic mirror, I saw myself reflected in Quitina's eyes exactly as she saw me that afternoon. I saw my image and I saw her gaze, her first glance, with which she had created me— the raised eyelids, the motionless lashes, the quick, steady gaze, violent and pure; naked, total . . . I shouted again, mentally: "No, this even less! Not tenderness! Not voluptuousness, not desire, no! I can't think of Quitina now; now there is only one thing."

My opponent helped me return to her. She insisted that Quitina— Pancha—was a spoiled child, as young people in general are today. Their parents have no influence over them.

"I can understand," I said, "that parents would try to have influence over their children, but not that they would impose on them an irrevocable decision."

"It's the only safe thing to do," she said, "when you don't trust them." She paused briefly and her expression hardened to blindness. "When you see," she continued, "when you know they have a nature capable of bypassing all moral principles . . ."

This time the click! sounded inside my chest. My heart gave a tremendous leap and I'm sure I turned red as a beet, but from rage. She was talking about Quitina! She knew her nature . . . So did I! Could we possibly be thinking about the same thing? What did she know? Something that I'd forgotten during that embarrassing argument? I saw her move her lips, but I couldn't hear her. That being was speaking, was saying something infamous. I did my best to make out her words, allowing the syllables to register on me one by one, and from the whole chain I was able to isolate: "custom" . . . , "freedom" . . . , "opportunity" . . . , "avoid something irreparable" . . . No, she must not have known that nothing could possibly be avoided now.

How long did her lecture and my silence last? I don't know. Maybe a couple of minutes, but even so, it would be impossible for the normal mind to encompass everything that passed through my thoughts.

Maybe she was so accustomed to being looked at that she was not surprised to have my eyes fixed on her. I was scratching with those eyes in the lump of humanity I had facing me, searching, wondering what does she know? What's she alluding to? And, automatically, I put her in front of Quitina, I confronted them with each other. Undoubtedly she had presented her *ideas* more bluntly to Quitina than to me. I imagined the familiar terms, the crude creole words, the harsh Spanish sayings that must have crackled in the night of the same day Quitina had said "Not *today*."

I was also sure that Quitina would have sat there with her innocent expression, exactly as she'd done in the bar as she spoke with Laura. There, seated at some distance, I'd delighted in her innocence. Watching them exchange their girlish secrets, the phrase that defined the virginal Regina Olsen had passed through my head repeatedly: "a real *girl*." That hallmark was indestructible in Quitina, and it made me very happy to see that I would never be able to destroy it (perhaps nothing makes us happier than seeing what we believe to be true is true), for if this hadn't been the case, she and I would have succumbed to the vileness of the fate that decrees the inexorable laws of stupidity. But that's how the hallmark was, exactly as I'd observed it in the bar, and that's how it would have remained—inalterable—the fixed seat of her serenity, while the rest of her being struggled with fury.

Undoubtedly, she knew nothing. Quitina screamed at her from inside me: "You'll never know!" Of course to let her know would mean triumphing over her schemes, ruining her plans, but it would also mean a triumph for her—it would mean she was in the right, and to admit she was in the right was the last thing in the world. No, it was obvious that she knew nothing, that no information had ever made those sluggish eyelids suddenly twitch. Quitina had never spoken and I knew why very well. I felt her right there, clutching my hand, trembling with anger, with the look on her face familiar to me only from her convulsions on the telephone. Her voice was a pure disorder of sound, and the features of her face—Pancha's face, covered with tears, contorted with pain—would have been too. I felt her clutching my hand, with the terror repulsion causes, as she heard all those things about "custom" and "opportunity," and refusing to say, "Yes, it's happened like that," because to do so would mean falling into the swamp, admitting that it had happened like that, when it had not happened like *that*, although it had happened.

I couldn't possibly have been silent very long; from time to time I surely answered with some monosyllable. Nevertheless, something must have been written on my face. At first I'd tried to have an energetic but courteous attitude. By that point though, any purpose of mine had been reduced to merely automatic custom; in other words, I did nothing either violent or outlandish, but I passed to the plane of the definitive. Consciously? Yes, I was fully conscious, I surpassed consciousness; I was polarized as to intention.

I assume that she must have noted some change because she also changed, coming at her subject from a different direction and beginning to expound the situation in legal terms. She had custody, she had . . .

She stood up. Clenching her gloves into a ball in her right hand, she enumerated for me everything she had, and she seemed prepared to keep all of it indefinitely, or at least the whole time that, by law, no one could prevent her.

"No one, no one can interfere," she said, and that repeated "no one" became as concrete as a name.

I didn't become dispirited; neither pessimism nor fear disarmed me, but I did experience a huge fear, because until that moment I'd thought I would have to wrest Quitina from the power of a vain, ambitious mother, and suddenly I saw before me the real goal of a very deep hatred, of a battle between natures—something like the unavoidable war to the death between certain animal species. That *no one* who could not interfere was *someone* against whom her blows were aimed. She was clenching her gloves in her hand the way Medea clenched her dagger. And her rancor proved more terrifying because it was cold.

I don't know what tone of voice I used or what my expression was like; I don't even know what I was planning to say. I undertook a faltering sentence: "But . . . you won't be able to sacrifice . . ."

She interrupted me: "Yes, I will. For a year and a half no one can prevent me; so we'll see if all that passion lasts a year and a half. We'll see."

Those were her last words: "we'll see . . ." We stared at each other. An enormous, passive force was lying in wait within her, because her rancor was not a flash of impassioned vengeance but a craving, a challenge from patience to passion. Beneath that show of power there was an indignant anxiety and, as I saw into its void, I was placed for a second time before the infernal image of a powerful man dying from hunger, ripped apart by the teeth of a stomach cramp that will not let up until he satiates himself with the lives of others.

I left. I suppose I spoke some words of good-bye, but I don't recall, and as I stepped into the revolving door I repeated to myself, "Difficult, very difficult," pondering her thick, white skin and the neck that held her head so far from her body. "But not impossible," I said and walked to the other side of the street.

I drove slowly along the road toward home, but suddenly I thought of how the maid who was there in the mornings usually waited for me with the table set, how she was constantly offering me things, badgering me with questions about what I liked and didn't like. At that moment I could not have endured the presence of another human being; I telephoned and told her I wouldn't be home for lunch. I drove around for a while and had several cups of coffee; when I called again half an hour later, she'd left. Then I went home and lay down on the bed. The whole storm from that morning drifted away like a dream and before me remained the sole reality. Quitina was no longer in Buenos Aires.

My mind clung to that thought for a long time; beyond it nothing existed. I knew how urgently I needed to think about other things, but that was impossible. I was making a tremendous effort to get past my fixation, but it was like trying to get out of a well; one moment I would hoist myself up and then I would fall back down again. I felt terribly restless, and all the coffee I'd drunk made matters worse. I could not keep still, either lying down or sitting up. Finally, a dull pain in my stomach made me think I should eat something and I went to the kitchen. I took the lid off a pot on the stove; it was risotto, something I hate, although I had never told the maid this because she was from Genoa and considered it her specialty. I felt terribly disappointed, almost repulsed, but repulsed because I was annoyed; the smell wasn't repugnant; it was an honorable, persuasive smell. I picked up a nearby serving spoon and took a bite. The risotto was cold, but it tasted better to me that way. I ate another spoonful—the spoon was huge—and continued to eat right there, incapable of even shifting my position. Without realizing, I immediately experienced the required release, but it happened so violently I felt as if a dam were bursting inside, in my brain or my heart. Well, to put it bluntly, I started to cry. I cried as I hadn't cried for more than fifteen years, and I didn't feel bowled over by that rush, as I had when I was little; I was crying from rage, simultaneously relaxed by the tears and reassured by the risotto. The two things complemented each other well; now I wanted something more. In the refrigerator there was a raw steak . . . I limited myself to drinking a couple glasses of wine and thought I'd made myself sufficiently drowsy. I flopped onto the bed and fell asleep right away, but I was not asleep very long. After a few minutes, insomnia was at me, hitting and shaking me so hard I felt rigid again, riveted obsessively on my predicament.

I was lucid enough to realize that I needed to look for practical solutions immediately, but my emotions were too troubled for me to concentrate on anything but that predicament. I took off my watch, because the afternoon was still hot and humid, and I lay there looking at it. It was nearly four, twelve hours! At a quarter to four the phone had rung and the universe had shattered. The blow was so treacherous it had struck a sleeping man. And as I saw that happen, as I recalled the ringing that pierced my sleep and Quitina's voice hoarse, crazed, and ruined by tears, a new facet of anguish reflected an even more devastating ray in my direction. My fears could still keep growing, something could still be added to my host of apprehensions. As I recalled Quitina's voice I also recalled my own, and I verified that Quitina's desperate shouting had received harsh answers from me. Yes, there was no doubt about it. I reviewed my memory, replayed the tape over and over, explaining to myself: "What I wanted to do was contain her desperation, because hearing it made me afraid." Yes, that was it, but my voice sounded sharp, and my voice shouting at her, "Calm down, please calm down!" could not have been what she expected. Then, I'd repeated the habitual words of affection to her, as if I were unconscious—, those stupid, excessive, grandiloquent words that are trivial precisely because of those qualities, which make them good for playing games at times of intimacy, but useless for saying anything at singular moments, such as that one.

I leaped off the bed, wandered through the house from one end to the other until I paused in the hall; there I could hear better how my voice sounded, and its tone was undeserved, distasteful, dissonant. And that dissonance was what Quitina had carried in her ear as she set out on her infamous journey. It was after four; she'd been hearing my voice sound that way for over twelve hours.

Suddenly it occurred to me that the phone might ring and I would have to answer. Laura and Javier probably knew what had happened, and if they didn't know and they called I would have to tell them: impossible, the idea of hearing my voice on the phone again was unbearable. I disconnected it. If they hadn't learned about the disaster, they might think I'd gone ahead with the excursion to Luján, and if they wanted to know where I was, I'd show some signs of life the next day; before then, impossible.

I sat down at the table covered with books and papers and continued to look at the watch, which I'd not put down. It was still in my hand

and I'd look at it from time to time. If I looked at it, it would advance slowly, but other times, when I opened my hand I found that the watch had covered a good bit of distance. There was a direct ratio between its progress and the intensity of my thoughts. And each time I looked at it and heard its urgent beating, I thought how I couldn't lose a minute, but I was incapable of tearing my thoughts from the minutes that had passed. I needed to advance and quickly, but I couldn't advance without reviewing, down to the last shred of evidence, what remained behind. Because it was a fact that we'd been separated, it was a fact that the test to see how long passion lasts had begun, and it was also a fact that, at first, I hadn't fought appropriately against our actual separation. To the torrent of tenderness irrupting amidst Quitina's anguish, I'd responded with categoric energy, with assurance, as if my confidence in myself prevented me from becoming upset.

I saw all this clearly, and at the same time I thought: but Quitina has as much confidence in me as I have in myself. At this moment Quitina cannot be lamenting my harshness the way a person laments a payment that's too small. If by chance she's reproaching me in the same terms as I'm reproaching myself, she's correcting my mistake, overcoming the distance. She can't have fallen back from her position; she has to have come toward mine. Because if this weren't the case, our separation would have begun, and there can't be even a hair's breadth of separation between us.

It wasn't enough for me to go back over our phone conversation a hundred times in my memory. I went further, reconstructing the whole afternoon and evening that Quitina had been more or less kidnapped while I was talking with Rafaela and roaming the Bajo with Javier. I recalled all my actions and words, thinking with respect to each one: "All the while, she . . ." Does that mean there was separation then? Does that mean it had already begun? That being unaware of the other person's suffering, that struggling on their own: could that be the start of separation? Because the most important thing, most important by far, was not bringing separation to an end: the most important thing, the only important thing, was that it might never begin. I wrestled like that for hours.

The light was fading, night was falling. Its familiar sounds came through the balcony window, and then there was silence, equally familiar. Now it was late and all I could hear was a sound coming from the streetcars on Las Heras like a tide. Something similar to that sound of undiminished hardness was roaming around in my head; iron on iron. One thought and then another came from far away, growing larger, drawing closer, growing smaller, passing . . .

The clock struck 3:30. Twenty-four hours! Twenty-four hours since I fell into bed thinking about nothing more than getting a good night's sleep so that I would be ready for happiness in the morning. I undressed and lay down, without any hope of closing my eyes for the rest of the night. But I soon heard a gentle sound on the balcony like drops of water. During the whole day the sun had been relentless, without the announcement of either wind or lightning, and now huge drops of rain began to fall. The sound was becoming stronger and faster, and from my bed I saw a large curtain of water that, fortunately, was not falling toward the inside; a bit of wet, rain-scented breeze reached me, and I pulled up the sheet, covered my shoulders, and fell fast asleep.

The next day was entirely different; not even my despair was the same. The agitation caused by my tumultuous ideas had disappeared, and all that remained was a total devastation and an unequivocal, clear conviction that I didn't have a minute to waste.

I leaped out of bed thinking: today I'll have news, maybe I'll have an address, but by the time I can write, I will need to have taken some action.

Immediately I outlined my plan. Concentrating on it, I drank a cup of tea without sitting down; I didn't read the newspaper or do any of the usual things, so as not to delay my departure. The first thing was to go and see Zelaski, but before doing the first thing, I dialed the number of the Alvear and asked for señora Suárez, disguising my voice and using some name I made up. She answered the phone and said "Hello,

hello," in a clear, wide-awake, morning voice, and I hung up without asking anything else.

I left the house and walked toward the garage. I felt exactly the way you feel after you've played the lottery and confirmed that you lost. Also, as in that case, I had a lingering doubt: maybe they'd made some mistake in the list of winners? I had to confirm it again. Also, a little trick of my aspiration, as when you're hoping for the grand prize, sketched itself while I was dialing the number, but I would not have stopped dialing for anything in the world, and I knew that a few hours later I would dial it again.

I went to San Miguel to meet with Zelaski; I had to get my situation at Las Murtas arranged definitively. The meeting was anything but definitive.

I got back early in the afternoon; the telegram was on the table, but it was from Rio; still no address, nothing but more shouting, another outburst of anguish.

I dialed the number of the Alvear, asked my question; there was no answer in her room. I was connected with the concierge, who said: "The señora has gone out."

I couldn't ask the concierge of the hotel if he'd noticed how she looked, if he'd noticed whether she seemed sad or happy, but I was unwilling to end the conversation and, almost interrupting him, I asked: "She didn't leave a message at the door?"

"No, sir," the concierge said, "the señora has left for Mar del Plata."

He'd reviewed the guest list carefully; she was on her way to Mar del Plata, according to plan.

The fact that you can win the lottery does not disprove the fact that normally you don't. But even though you don't normally win, there's a feeling of loss every time that's confirmed, and it's not the loss of a particular amount of money but the loss of an energy, a current of will already affectively coursing, thanks to a certain number of pesos, and is in danger of being dissipated, annihilated, as that course sinks into nothingness.

If I insist on comparing my state of mind to a state of mind caused by the lottery, it's because, like that of a lottery player, my state at that moment was cold, predisposed to accept the negative results and even to consider the game absurd, but certain of having wagered and, therefore, possessing a probability.

Disappointment forced me to take better stock of my accounts. Up to that moment I'd made calculations on the basis of something that for me was as solid as capital. That base was me myself: my power. Of course, as I made concrete plans, as I dealt with Zelaski and tried to obtain a clear, advantageous situation for myself at Las Murtas, I wasn't thinking that my power would determine my success or failure; but I had confidence in something, I walked with a sure step, like a person with a base. I now saw clearly that I needed to start from scratch. With that conviction I had to begin by writing to Quitina. But how? Where could I find the words to keep her hope alive? At the very least, I'd have to make the effort to conceal from her just how low my spirits had sunk from the failure of an action, possibly unreal but in any case unconfessable.

Since I had nothing even moderately positive to lean upon to recover my balance, since I couldn't come up quickly with any reasons for feeling confident, I thought that maybe by going through the whole thing without omitting a single detail . . . by going back . . . In three hours I could be at Las Murtas; I could arrive before sunset.

I made the trip like a bat out of hell. I thought about nothing but getting there so I wouldn't think about anything else. It seemed best not to plan anything before I arrived. And I arrived as everyone was about to retire. I said I'd wanted to get there late that evening so I could have full use of the morning. They sent a few cold cuts to my room, and I made short work of them.

As if it were something I had to do, something habitual or necessary, I leaned out the window and listened a little while to the sound of the crickets and to all the noises of the warm night—the calls of toads answering each other in all that space and, far off, in some vague place, a barking, the only voice out there in the country that seemed to be calling to man. I didn't stay at the window more than a few minutes;

I withdrew almost right away, as if I couldn't do what I'd gone to do when I leaned out, as if I neither saw nor heard, as if nothing registered or I couldn't get something to work. I gave up; I went to bed and slept until dawn, like a log.

During the entire morning I expended the greatest amount of activity possible, and shortly after noon I was on my way home. I was thinking that the telegram's small white piece of paper would be on my table, maybe in the vestibule under the door, if it had arrived late. It was sure to bear an address, and even if it did not, I would spend the night writing.

I was no more unruffled than the day before, but I was definitely more awake; I'd begun to face up to reality, and even though reality was truly precipitous, I felt strong enough to bring it under control. How and to what extent, and my immediate prospects with respect to time and work—those were the first things that I had to explain to Quitina. But there was more. I had to speak to her about other things that, if this situation hadn't arisen, I would probably never have told her in the very dramatic way in which I saw them now. I had to tell her what the world had been for me before she had come to be my world.

In our relationship all we had done was devour the present; the whole time prior to that was still there, but it was not sufficiently blended, and it seemed to me then that such a time could contain seeds of infidelity. Not just between us; in general, the fact of infidelity could consist in a return to the prior state. If you feel yourself being born through love and feel yourself die when you're separated from the person you love, the most important thing is not to awaken the memory of a life before love, to keep that memory from becoming a proof that you can live, that you lived at another time, free from love's chains. Steadying myself with this idea, I saw that what I needed to do was implicate the past and invade all the chambers that had not been shut off by my contact with them.

I arrived home, and the telegram was under the door. There was no address; just one more lamentation.

I sat down to write, thinking that Quitina would be arriving now at the places where she'd spent her childhood, recovering the atmosphere, the landscapes of her earliest emotions, of the times she yielded to the freedom of presentiment. And most likely she would not react to all that, she would surely have the sensation I did when I opened the window at Las Murtas, the paralysis of your senses that can't repeat the wide-open attitude you have when you're waiting for love. That was what I had to prevent: I had to keep her from recovering the repose attained when you perceive the flavor of things, I had to keep her in her current state of refusal, of opposition to everything that was not part of our love's life inside her prison.

I bent over the blank page a long time, concentrating on all that. Even though my ideas were chaotic, I did not fill page after page with scribbles: I pondered, I wrote an occasional, seemingly cold sentence and continued to look for the way, the infallible system. Because I'd been served a summons and had to find a way of not succumbing in the time, according to law, everyone is expected to succumb.

The telephone rang, and I answered it although the untimeliness irritated me; it was Javier. In his first words I immediately noticed something strange. After I said hello, he asked: "Are you there?"

I could hear women's voices in the background, and I realized he was calling from the girls' house, because I thought I recognized the voices of Laura and Rafaela. Since Javier was just stammering, Rafaela grabbed the phone and said: "Look, Santiago, come over here right away. Something disastrous has happened to Hortensia. Hurry, as fast as you can, because we've been looking for you all day."

I didn't ask her anything, because I understood all that mattered. I was there in ten minutes.

Javier and the girls didn't know how to tell me. Mecha's eyes were red and each thing Laura said made the tears start up again. Only Rafaela seemed to realize what this meant to me; she gave me a cursory explanation of what had happened, getting right to the point.

"Not a scratch on the two Verasteguis," she said. "Just her."

There was a short dismayed silence and Rafaela added: "What's necessary now is to rush everything so Quitina doesn't see her."

"Quitina! What do you mean Quitina?"

"They'll be here the day after tomorrow, I assume."

"Who will be here?"

"Who do you think? Quitina and her father."

At that moment Mecha started sniveling again, imagining Quitina's arrival, and I would have liked to shout at her: Shut up and stop being such a baby, don't interrupt me, don't distract me! Quitina will be here at any moment and this is dreadful. The spell's broken, the threat that summoned us has totally dissipated and there's no rest in this. The roulette wheel has spun and pointed to the number we wanted, but by playing the lottery can you win at roulette? And if you aren't playing can you lose this much? She hadn't gotten to play, and she'd lost everything, and I . . . I could only grasp that it was not my game; the rules were different. The result was the same, but there had been something different, something unexpected that I could not understand: chance had intervened. And the curious thing about chance is that when it appears to us, we stop believing in it as chance.

We believe it's chance when the ball rolls past the other indifferent, indistinguishable numbers; then we think it's happened by chance. But when the ball comes dutifully and diligently to stop at the number we were calling it to, then it's not chance; then it's a response congruent with our request. And I'd thought of the lottery as the concierge at the hotel answered with that "The señora has gone out." Because you always believe the bullet goes astray by chance. If, however, at the exact moment when I had her face to face and was besieging her with my hate, wrapping her methodically in my carefully designed destruction, if at that moment she had dropped dead in front of me, to me it would simply have seemed the checkmate of a long, laborious game. But chance had intervened, in other words, it had been neither my skill nor my power—it had been something with a chancy, capricious blow that had showed me chance does not exist.

The Molinas could not understand why I sat there speechless. Since they weren't believers, they undoubtedly thought I remained silent in order to spare them the devout comments they supposed would be natural for me. Rafaela made an effort to salvage the situation.

"You're worried," she said, "because you're thinking about what this will mean for Quitina, but what do you expect? Children have to endure the disappearance of their parents; it's a law of nature."

I tried to make some gesture that neither denied nor affirmed anything.

"But there's been nothing natural about this situation," Javier said naively.

"No, this has been bad luck," Rafaela said. "A very sad coincidence."

Since I still gave no reaction, she could not restrain herself.

"Of course," she ventured, "all of you will say this happened because it was God's will, but it would seem like the devil's will instead."

I didn't nod assent, but I looked at her so intensely she thought she perceived my assent. Then, with some irritation, which she wrapped in irony, she fired the question at me specifically: "Because you believe in the devil also, don't you?"

"Yes," I answered, still looking at her, "I believe in the devil and also . . ." I was going to say "and Puig also believed in the devil . . . ," but I didn't. I ended the sentence by saying something like "and I could also believe the devil might not have been responsible." I phrased it that way because I couldn't say I wouldn't admit it, precisely because I believed in the devil and rejected his intervention with every ounce of my strength.

I don't know what they said about my response; undoubtedly they took into account how upset I was, and their comments were kind; it was no time for getting involved in an argument. They talked about going to the Verasteguis', where she was laid out; the funeral would be the next day, in the morning. I was not listening to them, I went on with my response to Puig: "Nothing of the sort, I know very well which people it pays to associate with." I went on contemptuously refusing his affirmation: "You have a pact with the devil."

No, not chance; chance does not exist. That's why she felt so attracted to it, because there's nothing you can love in chance. Time, attention, money, submitted to chance . . . submitted to a nothingness. Around the roulette wheel you always find several of those hearts that can only flutter or stop at the reversal of some nothingness. Chance is a dark alley. But now that the intervention was clear as daylight, could I admit it was the work of the devil? Not that either. Could I make a pact with the devil? Could I commit the blunder, the mistake that siding with the devil meant? It made no sense. Nevertheless, at that moment when I believed I possessed a certain power—and I had believed I possessed it, not that it possessed me—, I went from being depressed, overwhelmed, caught in a chain of adversities, to feeling I could do anything, I could do the impossible, and I hadn't stopped to think about where the power came from. I felt it, palpably, as mine; I knew only, I did know—that was never in doubt—Who I'd asked for it.

That statement might seem sacrilegious or stupid, depending on you how look at it, but it's neither one nor the other. "How long, Jehovah, will you forget me? How long will my enemy rise up against me?" the psalmist asks, because when a person is persecuted and insulted he invokes divine justice: when a person cries out in great pain, he cries out to heaven. When a person sees himself threatened with respect to what he considers his legitimate property, he calls upon God; the devil he invokes only in order to work some fraud, in order to trick the law of expiration, not to free himself from a real and fearsome enemy. "May those that rejoice in my misfortune blush and may others confuse them." "May they be like straw in the wind." "May ruin fall upon them without warning." Because it's not unlawful to ask for the destruction of one's enemy. "It's not Christian," say the God-fearing. Of course it's not, it's pre-Christian, something that belongs to an archaic stratum, and the roots of even the most Christian present always reach back to it. Because, in addition, for the total, absolute man, who is the Christian man, there is no present or past; each implies the other, like the Old and the New Testaments. One begins by crying out to heaven for the destruction of his enemies when pain wounds him at the original, germinal moment of life, and many centuries of pain must pass for that *one* himself before he ends up saying, "My God, why have you forsaken me?"

I think I was clinging to this idea or, rather, I was submerged in it, delving into every dimension of its abyss, when Javier took me by the arm, pulled me up out of the chair, put me in the elevator, and then into the car. I recall that we were going up Rodríguez Peña, and, as the car entered the shade of the rubber tree on Duhau, I was still repeating, "It's not unlawful to ask for the destruction of one's enemy." I know I said this mentally at the moment we entered the shadows spread by the rubber tree, and as the car emerged into the twilight still lingering on the street I felt a terrifying desolation: I felt that I was understanding something, a tremendous and inexorable truth. I understood that if it is not unlawful to ask for the destruction of your enemy, it is unlawful not to recognize that what you obtain is *granted*. It's not lawful to shout, I have a power! because no one has any power except the power to ask for one thing or another. And that power of being able to choose is enough. Evil begins when man confuses his selection with an action, when he believes he's alone with his power: that is the satanic moment. But what about the fly? Because when I'd heard the fly crackling under the lamp I'd exclaimed: "He fell and he died." It was the song of Deborah: "At her feet he bowed, he fell; where he bowed, there he fell down dead."

Then that shout of triumph is lawful too, otherwise it would not be in the Scriptures. But the shout of triumph aside, why had the fly appeared, and why had it let my intention lead it toward the glass? The fly must have appeared, at that moment, so I could exercise my power of deciding. Because the other times, although Elfriede might have described it as intention, it had been nothing more than a flare-up of anger. So could I believe that whatever had seconded my anger was not some satanic intervention? My anger, then, had it called on heaven or hell? Can anger call on heaven? Or maybe it wasn't anger?

We'd reached the Verasteguis', where we made our way through people speaking in low voices, greeted unidentifiable individuals, and reached the room where they had placed the coffin. There I kept thinking: "And the fly?"

In one group close to me a man was talking about a concussion. Hearing them chat about the accident in a meandering conversation that drifted from one detail to another, back and forth between the incident and the person, I thought how the people who had greeted her as she walked behind me in the hall at the hotel were probably among the many people there. I thought how they might be in another group saying: "Just yesterday we saw her in the Alvear, talking to a young man."

I don't know why I sensed that nearby were the people to whom she had beamed a long smile over my shoulder, at the exact moment when her brain, immune to any blow, was closing itself to my reasons—at the decisive instant when one of us had to fall. Because I could have lost and my defeat would have been very different. For that long-term defeat there is no mise-en-scène of wax candles and wreaths, there is nothing solemn; there is nothing but sordidness, just like in the slow cooking of a witch's kettle, where, in the end, human vileness floats on the surface like skin on a face. She was ready to spend a year and a half tending the kettle, and if she'd managed to dissolve whatever was purest and most substantial in us—using that slow fire of tedium, waiting, and thoughts fixed on a center, paralyzed by circumstances, and eaten away by strategic contingencies—one day she would have sung her hymn of triumph. Without dramatics, enjoying the way our drama was becoming degraded, as she listened to the comments in the banal chatter at teatime. In that case, she would be the one to tell the people who had walked behind me in the hall—the ones probably now evoking her sustained smile in hushed tones—, tell them, as if helping them recall a distant, insignificant fact: "He was the young man you saw me with once in the Alvear . . ." But she'd been the one who fell. Not in the way I sought, struck down like the fly; not in the way she'd intended for me, worn down by tedium. She'd been caught when it seemed she'd just about escaped the trap.

But caught by whom? What power had intervened when she was almost outside my grasp? Isn't it possible that no one had chased her and she'd fallen on her own in the immanent power of divine justice? Couldn't the scale's little pans have shifted because we were arguing so strenuously, and so, in the end, the weight of our truth was marked exactly?

At that moment, I understood, and very clearly, that man's relationship with the divinity is a mathematical or, rather, a geometrical, problem, because it is a problem of positions, of projections; that I walked
into the hall as if I were sleepwalking, took out my fountain pen, leaned
on a console table, and tried to write something down, although I don't
know what, because the formula can't be written down—much later I
was able to see clearly the idea that then I only intuited, and far from being foolish it turns out to be highly exact—, but I didn't write anything
down because there was a piece of French porcelain with cupids and
garlands on the table, and it interrupted my thinking for a long time.

Someone behind me mentioned Quitina, and I tried to listen but
didn't understand because it was as if I were inlaid in a wall. I'd walked
toward the table bearing the momentum of my thoughts, which had collided with the porcelain and been blunted. That light, fragile thing had
the effect on me of a lead barrier, an impenetrable antithesis, and when
I stood facing the wall, plastered to it, they were talking about Quitina
behind me, and Quitina was also something unthinkable. What was
Quitina for me at that moment? The memory of virginal life between
my hands. But they were talking about something else, which was also
Quitina: they were talking about telephone conversations with her father
and about how he'd arranged from Paris, through diplomatic channels,
to have her prevented from leaving Havana. He'd left immediately to
join her and from there they would already be on their way to Buenos
Aires. So Quitina at that moment was an agonized being who'd spent
days roaming around airports, seeing their inexorable early mornings
punctually usher in new days filled with horror. Those icy dawns in
waiting rooms—although she was in the tropics, the light at daybreak is
always the light of an icy world when it's seen through anguish—would
be making her pallor permanent, giving her the color of desolation, and
I wondered when and how it could be erased. Rafaela broke away from
the group behind me, put a hand on my shoulder, made me turn toward
the light, and looked at me.

"I think you have a fever," she said.

I said I didn't, but she touched my forehead and wasn't convinced.

"It seems not," she said, "but I'm sure you do."

She called Javier and made him take me home.

There were two envelopes under the door. One was a letter from Spain that I stuck in my pocket and the other was a telegram from Havana. I opened it fearfully, but all it said was: "We arrive Thursday at 6."

I didn't have a fever, but I'd been delirious for several hours, and since I had no fever the delirium was exhausting me, and I wanted to come out of it; above all, I wanted to get over the telegram. I drank a couple glasses of cognac and tried to sleep.

The funeral was the next day. The delirium didn't return, and I went through everything as if I were absent, but absent not because I absented myself and withdrew into my usual concentration. No, I was even more absent from my own thoughts, because underlying those thoughts was the telegram, and I didn't want to think about that. I didn't want to speculate or make unwarranted interpretations; I only wanted time to pass and six o'clock in the morning to arrive. Finally it did.

At five it was raining—a fine drizzle that wet the highway and clouded the windshield. When I reached the airport, they told me there would be no difficulty landing because the clouds were very high.

At the appointed time the plane appeared in the gray sky, it descended smoothly, and a horde of people wearing raincoats with turned-up collars emerged, Quitina and her father among them. Her father looked just like the portrait, but sad, truly sad. He embraced me as if he'd known me forever, and Quitina . . . Quitina threw herself at me, and I didn't see how she looked, nor did I look at her, and I don't think she looked at me; she buried her head in my chest and I hugged her insanely in my arms. The beret she was wearing slid from her head and I caught it before it fell; then I stroked her hair, which was wet where the beret hadn't covered it. I kissed her damp hair, she leaned her face against my raincoat, and we were together, locked in each other's arms, but I didn't dare to touch her skin. I stood there an incalculably long time, with my face hidden in her hair, hugging her fiercely. Close to her forever, but not with the former nakedness—with a modesty that was really terror.

5

One night in the dining room at Las Murtas, while Rudy slept next to the hearth—a night I stayed alone beside the fire until the last pieces of quebracho had burned completely and I felt the chill in the room falling on my shoulders as the ashes grew pale—I decided to write these confessions. I'm not calling them memoirs, because there's always something pleasant or appealing about the word "memoirs," and I haven't written these pages to recall something but to understand it. The following night I began recording in a notebook everything I've told so far.

Now, if I'm to continue, I must deal with the events closest to me, which aren't any more clear, even though they lack the cloudscapes created by distance. But first of all I want to explain how unexpected circumstances led to my spending so many nights at Las Murtas alone in the dining room with Rudy, beside the fire.

I've already stated that meeting Puig's heirs had been a decisive event, and I also said that I'd appeared at the estancia without being called by anyone. Well, even though I was a total stranger to everyone, there were two people who welcomed me with open arms: Puig's niece and her husband, the only, and the lawful heirs. Because I was a stranger to the people at Las Murtas that day, but Puig's niece and her husband were strangers to everyone in the Republic. They were a humble doorman at the Banco Español in Río de la Plata and a simple Catalan peasant woman who could not control her two children, a boy and a girl who were both very young.

When I went into the drawing room, I asked the servant to point out Puig's associate, and he indicated an ungenteel back and square nape that belonged to Zelaski; I went over to him immediately. Introducing myself as an old friend of Puig, I struck up a conversation concocted so perfectly that even if I'd pitched it to someone intelligent he wouldn't have considered it an impertinence. But the servant thought it his duty to go to tell Puig's niece and her husband, who had just become the owners of the house, who I was. Accustomed to looking after Puig's limited social life, the servant remembered my name, and as soon as they heard it, they exclaimed: "Don Andrés's nephew!"

In a corner, interrupting each other, they told me a story they maintained I should already know.

It had been in 1920, the summer when Puig visited my uncle's house often, when their fate had been decided. Puig would go there to talk about them; I had to recall it, but I didn't; I recalled only Puig's silk suit, his panama hat. They'd married very young, before the husband had a steady job; and the first time they ran into trouble they turned to Puig, who promised to pay for their trip to America, as long as Julieta's husband had lined up definite work—Puig was not willing to support them; he would give them a boost so they could try their luck, but they had to provide for themselves. Then someone suggested they apply for that position at the Banco Español, which was very difficult to get. They spent months taking steps that led nowhere, until one day, while Puig was speaking with my uncle, he learned that a member of the bank's board of directors was a friend of my uncle. All it took was a letter from my uncle for the position to be granted by return mail.

My arrival at Las Murtas seemed providential to them, because they found the abrupt change in their situation overwhelming; they didn't know how to act and they distrusted everyone. Julieta did nothing but mourn Puig's death and keep her children in tow. For her husband it was different: the change in their situation was so great for him that he was like a man experiencing some grave danger. He'd spent fifteen years as a doorman at the bank and he knew the importance of money but not its value; he knew that money is a powerful force, one to be respected, and he'd invested all his pride in the cult of that respect. He was a man without any talents, a man made to fail in every enterprise he undertook, but when he landed his job he discovered that among his passive attributes there was one virtue: honesty. In order to be an irreproachably honest man he didn't need to undertake anything; his mission consisted of wearing a jacket adorned with braid and of remaining at his station, preventing people from doing improper things, things that could alter the course of the activities going on inside the bank, behind the partitions, where he had never felt curious enough to look. Now everything had changed; now the money was going to leave that same bank to fall into his hands, to find its way into the pockets of his unadorned jacket, and this frightened him.

They'd always known they would come into an inheritance at some point, but Puig had never told them that he'd willed everything to Julieta, his only niece related by blood; he'd left them in that subordinate position for fifteen years. Gifts for the children on their birthdays and payment of the pharmacy bills when the children had whooping cough—that was all. Fifteen years of living in the Sur area, buying shoes and wool clothes at some department store on Rivadavia, with Julieta doing the cooking and taking her fake silk dresses to some tenement for mending so she could go to the parties held at Las Murtas on very special occasions.

That was the scenario I gradually put together as I combined the confidences from Julieta and García with my own observations. I recognized Puig's system: don't give, from the beginning, so they learn the value of things. But in this case, the system had been ineffective, because they'd learned nothing; they'd simply been held back, held down while the sum of money that would be theirs accumulated in the bank, while the life that was theirs went by, a life that, deprived of power—of money— had barely prospered, its horizons unable to expand. Of course things had happened this way because Tomás García was a man of passive virtues.

Once I'd formed my opinion of them I felt greatly relieved; I could drop my farce. With them, I didn't need to feign an enterprising spirit, as I had with Puig, or to pretend that I'd been involved in the running of the factory for a long time, as I had with Zelaski. On the contrary, I told them I knew nothing about all that, that I feared I'd be of absolutely no help to them, but they interrupted me, saying: "Yes, yes, we know who you are." What happened was that as soon as they found out who I was, they decided to ask something of me: they begged me to be present at the reading of the will; at the inventory at the factory, so they could check Zelaski's situation against their own; and, in short, at every transaction, every bit of paperwork where Julieta had to sign her name. That's what they implored me to help them with. García knew all about the endless papers where someone pencils in a little "x" and says, "Sign here." They wanted me to be close by so, when Julieta found herself in that situation, I could look over her shoulder and move my head to signal "sign" or "don't sign."

It was easy for me to oblige them, because their situation was completely legal and because no one was out to cheat them.

They also asked my advice when they moved to Las Murtas. I let them suit their own taste and only tried to make sure they didn't change a few things I was particularly fond of, specifically the dining room, which was so solemn and comfortable.

The servant who had been Puig's right-hand man and was the only person other than Julieta mentioned in the will, although he'd received a rather modest sum, left the service; besides, Julieta didn't like to have a man wait on her at the table. The driver stayed on; I fought for him and the kitchen help as well. They talked about getting rid of the dogs and I saved Rudy, telling them they couldn't be without a guard dog, and they kept him since this seemed evident to them; the other dogs they gave away. José, the old man, also stayed, to help with small chores, and I stayed too, although I traveled back and forth. Officially, I occupied neither Monington's room nor his job, because the survival of the factory was still in jeopardy. Zelaski and the Garcías did not get along. For the moment they didn't want to dissolve the business, because there were some important orders outstanding, but they spoke of trying to liquidate everything the following year. I made up for the lack of Monington and Puig by going there continually to keep an eye on the work.

The Garcías had another child who was older and was a boarding student at Don Bosco, where he was studying to be a mechanic; they brought him to Las Murtas. I strongly insisted that they bring him, leading them to hope he might become an engineer and give the whole enterprise a big boost. But the son, a boy of sixteen, took one very scornful look at the factory and said if that hulk weren't there in the middle, the slope would look like a golf course. Then he declared that he would not return to Don Bosco, because he wanted to be a lawyer.

No one had any interest in the factory; there was no one to firm up its existence, and I didn't give up, looking after it because giving up is against my nature.

Things went on that way for a while, until Quitina's departure, and the following day, during my turbulent meeting with Zelaski, I was at the point of throwing in the towel. But there was nothing definitive, and then events were so grim that everything else took second place.

I recovered Quitina, and I've already spoken about that. How did I? How I always did—I recovered her intact by means of her silence and her self-absorption. But a new separation awaited us; the period of mourning and a thousand other reasons had made her father decide to take her to Rio for a while. This time we didn't protest; Quitina's father was making the decisions and we had confidence in his decisions.

One day when I was having lunch with them, he said to me: "And you, where do you work?"

"Well, at something, to tell the truth, I don't know what it is."

"And you're sure it's worth the effort?" he asked, as if he found my response very natural.

"No," I said, "I'm not sure, but I'd like it to be."

"Why don't we go take a look at it?"

The three of us went. What a strange trip! I felt afraid to show them what I'd chosen, the spot that I persisted in frequenting, although I hadn't felt afraid to show them that my future was plenty unstable. I was only afraid they wouldn't see it as I saw it, afraid, even, I would see it just the way they saw it.

When we arrived in midafternoon, we had to accept an abundant spread at the Garcías'; then we took a detailed tour of the factory, and then I said I was going to show Quitina the garden, and we walked into the countryside by ourselves.

I took Quitina in that direction so I could talk to her about everything I'd planned to write to her about, and we went up the road a little way with our arms linked tightly. But I didn't actually talk to her about anything, because just as I was going to begin, a question arose for me: how much can I tell her? I refrained from speaking; all I did was press her against my chest until I could feel her where I was before I knew her.

When we got back, there was talk about the factory, which had done its best to look cheerful, and I truly regretted not having told Quitina about everything I'd put into it. But what need did I have to tell her?

Quitina's father took her to Rio, and in three days he was back. He called me as soon as he arrived, we got together for a while, and he told me that when he left she was well settled and that he'd come on some business that would tie him up completely for a few days. That alarmed me and had exactly the effect that he'd wanted to spare me. He saw I was alarmed and said: "It's something I have in the works; I think I'll have things resolved soon, and well."

There was no doubt of his telling the truth, but it was also clear that he was giving me to understand that I shouldn't ask any more questions.

Two days later, at Las Murtas, when I went to take the car out of the garage, I heard Julieta calling me from the window. She asked me to keep her company for a while before I left, and she spent the whole time talking about Quitina and her father. She said she'd been particularly taken with him. Just then García arrived and Julieta cut off the conversation; it seemed to me that I noticed him looking at her sternly.

Julieta went on to talk about things in the house, which gave her a lot of work, because, even though she had nothing to do, giving orders is also work. Suddenly she asked me if I thought the cook would know how to prepare a fine dinner.

"She's a fine cook, I know that already," she said, "but I mean would she know on her own what to serve and how things are presented at table."

Since the topic was trivial, while Julieta spoke I began to look out the window, but in order to answer her—I was going to tell her I thought she could manage very well on her own—I looked at her and saw she seemed confused and uncomfortable. Without waiting for my answer, she said: "You have to give me some advice about school for the children, although of course we still have time."

She cut off the conversation again and sat silent, looking at the floor. García's expression grew more annoyed by the moment.

Events of this kind are the ones that have the power to create an atmosphere of suspense around me—I perceive unconnected things, and I refuse to link them, not daring to interpret them because I'm too pessimistic. Maybe excessive precaution makes me hold my breath as if the least movement, the least thought on my part would prevent the connective that's about to be made. Nevertheless, even though I didn't look at them in the face, I saw how events were arranging themselves around a center.

Quitina's father gave no signs of life; I inquired about him several times and could never find him.

At Las Murtas, the strange atmosphere continued for three days. The third day, Julieta had me summoned when I was at the factory, and as soon as she saw me, she said: "Tomorrow you must stay and have dinner with us."

García came rushing over, and I didn't answer until I could see his expression. He still had his mysterious air, but he seconded the invitation insistently. I said, of course, I would stay and asked what they were celebrating.

"Nothing, nothing," Julieta said with such a false smile that her husband didn't dare to endorse it, and he interrupted her: "Well, we're involved in some business . . . But don't ask me anything about it, you know how muddled I get about these things. Tomorrow everything will be clear and then we'll tell you about it."

I was left feeling intrigued and insecure.

When I arrived the next day—it was Saturday, so I got there just at dinnertime—I saw that the office light was on. Julieta heard my car and went to meet me at the door, telling me she had to check on the table before she went into the office. Everything was fine. She consulted with me about the menu, which was excellent, and took me to the pantry where she showed me the dessert and the wines; the cook had certainly risen to the occasion. I'd seen four place settings at the table.

"Everything looks wonderful," I said, "but who's the other guest?"

"He's in the office, with Tomás," Julieta answered.

Finally we went into the office. It was Quitina's father, and he said to me: "But you really didn't suspect anything?"

I said I hadn't, although, as I said it, I realized I had.

The office clock began to strike nine, and they all looked at it and glanced at their watches, commenting on the small differences between them. They were waiting for a telephone call from Rio, which they had been promised at nine sharp, so Quitina would be on the line at any moment.

We waited in silence for a few minutes, and then the telephone rang. Quitina's father said: "We're going to report orders have been carried out."

García handed him the receiver. He began by asking her how she was and then he told her we were all at Las Murtas, that Julieta and García sent their regards, and that I would speak with her right away. Quitina must have asked him a question and he answered: "It's a fait accompli; the estancia belongs to the two of you. Are you happy?"

Then he told her a few other things I couldn't understand and handed me the receiver; Julieta had to keep me from dropping it. I opened my mouth, but no sound came out. Finally I could say, "Quitina!"

My memory of what happened next is confused. They tried to explain things to me, each of them attaching the greatest importance to whatever part most concerned them individually. Quitina's father said:

"I asked her 'What do you want most?' and she answered: 'Las Murtas, at any cost.'"

Julieta: "What makes me happiest is now the business will be Puig y Hernández." García: "What I'll never be able to thank you for enough is ridding us of that beast."

What had been acquired for us was the estancia; Julieta's capital remained in the firm, exactly the same as always. Quitina's father had managed to buy Zelaski's share, and both Monington's position and Puig's work fell to me, for the moment. I tried convincing García to look after a bit of the administrative part, and he protested, with an incorruptible modesty: "But how can you think I'd be any good . . ." His eyes were full of reproach for my ingratitude: he'd made everything easy for me, and I wanted to overwhelm him with that responsibility. I didn't insist and assured him that I would manage things on my own.

Everything had worked out so easily because the Garcías no longer had any interest in living at Las Murtas. Quitina's father had seen that at first glance. Ten months out in the middle of the country had proved to be an exile for them. They wanted a modern apartment in Buenos Aires that would not be far from the children's school; they had already spotted just what they had in mind. They dreamed of furnishing it with new things. The move would be a gradual one, made so as not to inconvenience anyone; as for us, it would be a while in any case before we could move in permanently out there.

After dinner when we went into the office, García was self-assured but not disrespectful as he opened the safe and took out a folder to show me the deed. He was already invested with the position to which he had been promoted, and I was the one who felt afraid at the thought of receiving so much. Thanks to the magic of a few signatures on a few papers, Julieta had gone from being a humble mother, worn out between the kitchen and the needle, to being a lady who could devote herself to watching her children grow up and, by the same sorcery, I could go from being a man delirious with desire for things to being a man who is master of things. Those things were a rainy evening, a fireplace with a dog lying beside it, a window open on the song of crickets. Of course for me the papers existed because there had been a command: "Las Murtas at any cost." A longing that had lived within me mutely for some time could come into being in Quitina's words.

That's how everything happened. The next day, I went into the office ready to organize things the way that I wanted them. Julieta tried to persuade me to live there, with them; they would fix up Puig's room for me, which no one had touched until then, but I refused and asked her to dispose of the furniture, because that large room, with its fireplace and doors into both the dining room and drawing room, would be perfect for the library.

Planning the reorganization of the factory, technical as well as financial, was a considerable task; but, on the side, I also wanted to take on the transformation of the house. In the margin of my formulas and budgets I jotted down things as they came to mind so when I brought Quitina everything would be in harmony, so that I could place her in the house as if in her case.

I must explain the apparent lack of connections a reader might notice in this narrative. The written word's single dimension forces us to place one thing after another. If we leave one of two simultaneous things in the background, it may seem that the first has been cut short, because sometimes we arrive at a third thing, as if there were nothing more to say about that first thing and, nevertheless, it too was linked to this third. I left hanging the commotion in my soul, the contact with the most turbulent part of my consciousness, and jumped to the story of Julieta Puig and Tomás García; following the flow of their simple and honest tale, I came to the point where Quitina's father intervened in our lives and the metamorphosis that turned Las Murtas, which for me was a vague, ill-founded longing, into our definitive home. I would have reached the same place by following the thread of the first, and the principal, events. Those events were joined with these others, just as night joins with day; rather, they were set, just as night is set between day and day; they were not erased, they were not refuted, they continued to shine in the darkness like the ruby, mounted in diurnal matter, forged from reason. And reason is something very broad in which it's not possible to proceed by leaps; one must move ahead step by step, telling how things were.

I wanted to transform Las Murtas in just a few months into an impeccable residence. With impeccable simplicity, of course, but I wanted everything to be fresh, the way things are when they've resulted from a design and an elegance all their own—something as genuine as one's handwriting. I had no money to finance this undertaking. I was sure I could have things at the factory pick up soon enough that I'd be able to do it, but I wanted it immediately and I had no money. I thought about selling my house on Juncal, and somehow Quitina's father suspected this right away.

"What are you going to do here?" he asked me.

"Something or other."

"And here?"

"Something different."

"And with what?"

I couldn't give him a very clear answer, and he told me: "Don't do anything so foolish. These four walls are all you have left from your family; keep them."

Then he continued: "When you move in you'll have all the basics and more; it happens that at the moment there's some checking that has to be done first. Besides, it's important for you not to have anything complicated still hanging. I'll be leaving for Rio immediately and who knows if I'll have to call you and hurry things along somehow. If I had to take a plane suddenly, Quitina can't be left alone any longer . . ."

This conversation had arisen as we were walking together down Calle Florida, two days after what had happened at Las Murtas; I'd stopped in front of the window at Comte's and let my imagination soar. We'd parked at the Plaza San Martín, next to a streetlight, and when we got to the corner, he asked me: "Have you heard anything from Spain?"

"No," I said, "not for days."

A cloud of anguish had me in darkness until we reached the car.

We turned into Santa Fe and, as if he were completing an unfinished sentence, he said vaguely: "A few pieces of old furniture, maybe some quite good ones . . ."

Then, decisively: "Keep going straight as far as Anchorena and then turn in the direction of El Abasto market."

I continued, although unconsciously, in something like a cloud of ir-reality that made me wonder not where am I? but when am I going? I stopped in front of the little house with plants.

Colonial furniture, and pieces as good as you could ever want, a baby grand piano, turn-of-the-century bronzes smiling beneath the canvases.

"Now it's my turn to show you something," I said.

I went to the chest of drawers that was shielding it and lifted out the portrait from in back. He found the story very moving, and I told it in a special way, but he said, in any event, the portrait was terrible and could not be hung anywhere. I assured him that Quitina would never want to be without it.

"But it's the work of some poor devil," he said, "a paisano from Gijón, who was wandering around over here without getting anywhere, and in order to help him, I . . . It belongs in the incinerator. Where are you going to put it?"

I refused to destroy it, and he insisted: "You're not going to put this in a house you intend to decorate properly."

I couldn't tell him I was, but I said: "I'll find a spot."

Very decisively, he reiterated: "No, I don't want a portrait of me hang-ing there . . ."

But he didn't finish the sentence, he looked around and went to sit on the heap of shapeless things where Quitina had sat. Once he was there, he said laxly: "Hortensia dreamed of having one of Zuloaga's portraits. The one of Ana Noailles is the one she liked; she wanted something like that, and now you see . . ."

At that moment everything rose to the surface, everything responded to the conspiracy: everything from the past, plus what from the past that was the present, which had just materialized, modifying the past, without changing it, of course; adding to it only a more complex irides-cence.

The ray of sun was not falling through the grate in the embrasure, but I sensed Quitina's perfume in the particles of dust, and there was a gray light in which a mutedly dramatic confidence was slowly unfolding, but I was reliving a moment of hurried passion stolen from the watchfulness of a hostile will. And that will, defeated by me in a merciless battle, was not gradually presenting itself in the ghost of its real memory. It was springing up like a memory completely unknown and autonomous—the memory of things never seen—and issuing from the furniture, the cupboards opened a hundred times, from oval backs of the chairs where she'd rested her hands, and, above all, from the bronze sylph, half-hidden in its corner, where it smiled as if caught in its moment of levity. The sylph was there, was her witness, guarding in its immortal bronze the smile that changed daily, along with her. Meanwhile, Quitina's father was struggling to explain to me how a person can be both irreproachable and unforgivable.

He recounted how the first ten years of their marriage had been a common story of love and jealousy. When they were married they'd known each other just a few months; in other words they hadn't known each other, and distrust had sprung up immediately. The only thing he knew about her with certainty was that she didn't belong to him, and this made him afraid she had another master.

After sitting quietly for a while, he said: "You see, jealousy is degrading, whether or not it's justified. It drives a person to do all sorts of vile things. I don't know if you can understand that."

He couldn't make up his mind whether to continue. I said I thought I understood quite well, but he moved his head as if he were thinking, that's not possible, not without having gone through it . . . Finally, by fits and starts, he resumed his confession with seeming incoherence, jumping from each sentence to the next.

"A person is conscious of everything he does," he said. "A person is blinded, up to a certain point; deep down he knows very well . . . He knows what he's doing is despicable and it might also be unjust. Well, so what? What does a person care if he's unjust? . . . And if he is just, he still doesn't care if he does something despicable. Right away he's getting ready to commit many more such acts. But the truth is, there's something worse: the worst thing is when a person is neither just nor unjust . . ."

I raised my eyebrows, admitting that I was starting not to understand.

"Have you read Cervantes's *Jealous Extremaduran*, his *Curious Impertinent*? I did it all, exhausted the classical repertoire. I set every kind of trap for her and she didn't fall into a single one. Of course this proved I was unjust . . . No, I was not unjust."

He fell silent again, as if it were hard for him to reveal how ashamed he felt for committing such terrible treachery, and finally he said: "Don't think that I found a letter or caught her on her way to some rendezvous. No, alone in my study, I finally understood the whole thing. I said to myself: I can test her one more time, I can devise some diabolical situation and once again have the satisfaction of seeing that she doesn't fall. I won't find the least satisfaction, because she won't fall, and of course that's something to be happy about, but I'll also see once again how she finds out about my cunning, how she realizes I've stayed awake devising the most perilous combinations possible and how she tells me for the hundredth time: 'You amuse yourself with such stupid things!'"

"So there was no bloody drama," I said, and he cut me off—

"Not even that. Because when a person discovers he has a rival, the first thing he thinks about is beating him to death, but what I discovered within her was no rival. If I could have said to myself: she's in love with herself, I don't think it would have occurred to me to kill her; more likely, I would have been moved by that, I would have fallen in love with that love, as something of hers, but no, it was something else. Something else, though I don't know what to call it; the only thing I knew as soon as I understood it was that I could do nothing."

He stopped, as if he found the imperfect nature of his explanation overwhelming. It was probably the first time he'd talked about all that for the purpose of explaining it, and the thread of logic that might have joined those events lay too hidden beneath so many years of bitterness.

He started to speak again: "I think what led me to make a decision was that suddenly my jealousy ended. And, you see, that was what I could not forgive. You understand? It made me ashamed, angry . . . I don't know . . . but I was sure that if I confessed to her that I no longer had my old worry, she would answer me, 'I always told you, you worried for nothing.' That was true, because for her it was nothing. And when I found myself free of jealousy—even that was gone!—I found myself without anything . . . One day I got on a boat and left, it was the only thing I could think of—to leave her alone so she would know what it's like to be indefinitely in the presence of something that's nothing. After some time, my lawyer formalized the situation, amicably."

I looked at the sylph, and she didn't refute him. I distinctly recalled the unbending head on the long neck, but not at the Alvear—that I could not recall—, I recalled it in the midst of her furniture, trying to understand, trying to know what something is like from its nothing-ness, from which it can't look out, can't break the prison of its void. But above all, I recalled her, in a way so real, so precisely detailed, it was as if I'd accompanied her every day while she leaned over the numbers on the roulette wheel. I could draw the line of her neck, the movement of her long hand gathering up the chips—every bit of her, even the slender-ness of her waist, which made her seem like a plant in its element, like a narcissus at the edge of the water, gazing at itself in the nothingness of chance.

Quitina's father stood up, kicked his foot against the bundle and said it probably contained drapes. There had been a lot of them in the house, heavy, green plush drapes, with fringe and tassels, which Quitina loved when she was little. Quitina knew the sylph's smile too; she too had probably copied it, watching from the shadow of the drapes, while she played with the tassels like a kitten.

We both thought about Quitina, and as we left her father said to me: "The only way she resembles her mother is in her stubbornness, you can't imagine how stubborn she is."

After we'd separated, I was left with the sensation that I'd left some-thing unsaid, and during the night I tried a thousand times to recall what I'd forgotten; but since there was so much I could not even allude to, I ended up believing that what had me feeling anxious deep inside was the pressure of all those silenced things. The next day we had lunch together; we talked for a long time, while my anxiety continued, underneath: "What was it that I had to ask him? What's the subject I'm forgetting?" I couldn't come up with that subject, and the following day he left for Rio early in the morning. In the afternoon, there was a letter from Spain. As I saw it slide under the door, I exclaimed: "That's what I wanted to talk to him about!"

My uncle's letters were changing: before he'd predicted all kinds of terrifying events, saying the world was going to pieces, there was going to be a cataclysm and then he'd immediately start speaking with his natural optimism, his serene spirit, about everyday things. No longer. Now he no longer talked about the state of the world but wrote instead about how he'd bought a pair of shoes or gone to the dentist. In those simple bits of news—those are actual examples, and some were even more trivial—his tone was like that of a person facing a lost cause. This letter, the first I decided to analyze, was frightening because it was so banal. It was like sending a blank piece of paper, like responding with a silence. On top of everything else, the letter wasn't even dated, but I could tell from the postmark that it was from early in January; he was answering my Christmas letter, in which I still hadn't explained anything to him very clearly, and his letter had crossed with another of mine, in which I'd told him how things were for me then. This led me not to pass judgment on this letter either, since I assumed the next one would be different. But two months passed and there was no letter.

I'll write later about what I did during those two months; that falls into the part that has to do with work.

The plan was for me to arrive in Rio at the end of May so we could be married there and spend some time in Brazil; but at the beginning of April they telephoned and told me to get everything in order so I could leave immediately. In a couple of days everything was ready and what surprised me the most was that García offered to lend a hand in the office. I hadn't really understood why there was this sudden urgency.

"We'll explain it to you later," they'd told me, "these aren't things to be discussed on the phone." But García understood everything; he'd spoken with people at the bank, and there they knew that something colossal was about to happen in Spain. García told me to go without feeling worried; he would be here.

I arrived in Rio at dusk; they were waiting for me at the airport and took me to a hotel. We talked for a long time about everything that was happening, about everything that could happen, and about everything that had to be done. At midnight they left me to myself and told me the consul would pick me up before seven. He came at six forty-five, and we drove up a strange hill inserted in the city, right in the middle of the houses.

As the car climbed, at times we could make out the silvery bay between two houses, with its patches of dark islands. The day looked as though it would be gray; the sky was leaded, which made the light resemble the light at dawn. For some reason, the idea of driving in a car, at dawn, with a man who was going to be my witness, made me think of a duel. At the top of the hill, at the door to the Temple of Glory, I would meet Quitina, who would also be with her witnesses, and on the field of honor we would take up the challenge implicit in decisions that bind forever.

As we reached the level, the other car caught up with us, and we both arrived at the same time.

The ceremony was very simple and very short; at least to me it seemed weightless, as if everything were happening at a great distance, as if nothing were real except the two of us being together, kneeling in the church, the holding Quitina's hand in mine, and losing myself in the form of prayer—I don't know to what extent it could be called prayer— that consists of looking at the flame of a candle trembling in a dark corner, or maybe at the pale light falling from the lantern in the cupola and coming to rest on the cornices. This can't be prayer for everyone, and it's not always prayer for me, but there are times when it is and to a very intense degree. There are times when, viewing something like that candle flame or that pale light becomes contemplation, when I experience transcendence in process, as if a window on the thing contemplated opened in the thing seen, although of course it's not a thing, and from there what I can reach is rarely within reach of human words. I say "rarely" because on some occasions the word itself can be a window or an arrow launched toward that window. In short, if I speak about this, it's because the most well known effect of such moments is the loss of one's sense of time. I had the impression that the ceremony had lasted five minutes, but in reality it must have lasted close to an hour.

When we left the church, the light had changed, the mist had lifted over the sea, and the sun was pushing on toward the chain of mountains that frames the bay—fleeing in that direction, wrapped in fleece. The royal palms, so steady the wind can't bend them, stood out in formation against the blue sky. There was no wedding march, but from the organ came something like a pastoral, eighteenth-century air; in the doorway of the church, pressing Quitina's arm, I replayed that air in my head.

There's no need for me to write anything about those days of abandon: they were like the calm at high tide.

When we were by ourselves, we'd take refuge in the Riviera to get away from the crowds of people that pour into the center of Copacabana, and we'd spend hours on the beach or walk all the way to Leblon to see the ocean where it's roughest. Wherever we were, we were waiting. We had so many things—bad and good—to wait for that sometimes we passed the time making an hourglass with our hands. I would let the very fine, white sand trickle in a thin, thread-like stream into Quitina's hands, and when every bit in my hands had fallen into hers, I would put my hands underneath and she would let the sand escape.

In the mornings there would always be a few transatlantic boats arriving from Europe on the horizon, and in the afternoons the sea filled with small fishing boats that sailed by, trailing their nets. Whether the day was calm or stormy, a single indescribable bird hung motionless in the sky.

Automatically, I said a *single* bird *hung* motionless, but there wasn't one bird, there were many and, of course, they would have been gliding.

I said it that way, because that bird can only be referred to as singular. We called it the scythe bird, but it's really the kind of seagull people call a frigate bird. Its enormous wings are very narrow, like scythes and, when it maneuvers, its long, split tail opens and closes like a scissors, making the bird's only visible movement: it glides rigidly and, being totally black, stands out against the sky as if it lacked depth, as if it were the object on a weather vane standing straight in the air, swaying almost perceptibly.

One afternoon when the sea was dark, leaden black clouds appeared everywhere, and gusts and waves began to pick up, creating the whole scenario of a violent storm, but the bird was in the sky, motionless— closer by and also farther off, the bird was motionless.

"That creature is sinister," Quitina said.

I understood that she meant "unlucky," but I avoided articulating the fear or premonition inspired by that afternoon with its overwhelming sky. I tried to caricature the bird, linking it to witches and macumbas, but Quitina said: "Don't worry; I'm well aware that for now I can't be afraid. God willing, nothing bad will happen, but whatever happens I'll do everything possible not to be afraid."

I didn't have the nerve to tell her with even a hint of certainty that nothing bad would happen, and I said: "Well, someday we'll remember him and then we'll know what he meant."

"Yes," Quitina said, "we're sure to think of him often."

I don't know why, but we both knew we would never forget him. And that's all I can say about the scythe bird.

Mid-July brought the first news about the conflict in Spain. Quitina's father telegraphed immediately, from Lisbon, to say he was safe. For the time being, there was no chance of hearing anything from my uncle.

Quitina was afraid, although she didn't want to be afraid. I tried to distract her, but in Rio that's difficult, unless you go dancing or gamble in the casinos. We traveled a little around the islands in the bay and to the nearby towns; and we kept waiting.

The efforts I made through the Argentine embassy led to the information that my uncle was alive, that he had refused asylum in the embassy, and that he was working for the Republicans. Quitina's father seemed to be on the other side. He didn't make anything clear in his letters, even though they came directly from Portugal, but this was not to prevent their being censored; it was because of Quitina. He tried to suggest that things didn't look very serious, that they would certainly end right away, but we knew from the newspapers and from the comments of people who were well informed that this was not the case.

Finally the thing that to us was the most important of all the things we'd been anticipating came to pass. A cycle of our life had been completed.

I think children are too little when they come into the world. I'm not talking about size, really, but about mental development: children aren't aware of the welcome people offer them. No matter how much enthusiasm you show toward them, they never act one bit differently. Women probably find this natural, but to a man the silence of newborn babies is disturbing; it gives him the feeling that you can't do anything with them yet, even though they've been born. That's what I thought, especially while I watched him as his nurse cared for him, handling him in the bathtub, diapering, or swaddling him in a precise, professional way he approved with his silence and docility. Later, when he was in Quitina's lap, his silence was more like the stillness of a beast in its lair, you could tell that he had absolute control of the situation. I was the only one who tried to talk to him, and of course he didn't answer me.

Sometimes I was afraid for Quitina, afraid to see her at the mercy of that strong, voracious little being feeding on her, but Quitina didn't seem to be frightened by anything. I spent long periods watching her asleep on the bed with the baby nestled in the hollow of her arm, the baby asleep as well, and it seemed that she'd gone with him to the depth of the mystery from which he came and that it would take the Creator's voice to rouse her, return her to me made anew.

Enough time had passed and I decided to go to Las Murtas for an inspection. I wanted to have at least a room ready for Quitina, at least a bed where she could amply unfold her regenerative sleep. I didn't want to take her to a hotel, and my house on Juncal was dreary; I would have needed to make radical alterations if I wanted to provide a home for her there.

I had the keys to the little house where the furniture was stored, and I went there for the third time. Once again I inhaled the smell of mildew and dust, and once again I recalled, but this time the porters kept me from fantasizing. When they'd lifted the canvases, I picked out a few things—pieces we'd need for the bedroom and dressing room. Only accessory pieces, though. I preferred to have the bed made to match all the other furnishings. I found fabric for curtains and bedspreads, everything exactly as I'd imagined it: I'd created a room that retained the character of the old colonial style, with nothing modern about it, except that it was brighter and less ornate.

It felt so strange to find the house at Las Murtas uninhabited. Julieta had left it in impeccable condition, and the empty rooms made it seem enormous. Only the dining room was untouched: the furniture was a present from the Garcías, who knew how much I liked those rather heavy, somewhat old-fashioned pieces that nevertheless seemed welcoming, because of the dark wood.

The office continued to run the way it always had. García appeared twice a week, checked over everything carefully, spent a good while just *being* there, as he'd promised, and then he left.

What I found finished was the bookcase in the library, which had already been started before I went away. I'd made the drawing for it myself, left things in the hands of a good carpenter, and wound up thoroughly pleased with the results. The shelves covered the wall up to a height of two and a half meters, except for one spot over the fireplace. I didn't plan to take my books there until everything was done but I did take the sylph: that empty space had been left for her.

Julieta found me the household help we'd need, and I flew back to get Quitina.

When I reached Rio I found that her father had arrived only a few hours before. He was on his way to Buenos Aires, where he'd been charged to conduct a commercial mission he was going to perform as a private transaction, even though he'd been commissioned to do it. I asked him why he'd picked that side.

"Because they're the ones who will win," he told me.

Neither cynical nor opportunistic, his answer was so simple it seemed to me that I should take it as a joke.

"But how can anyone know that?" I said. "Who made that prediction?"

"No one has predicted that they're the ones who will win," he answered. "What people know for certain is that the others are going to lose."

"They'll lose," I replied, "if there's no one to help them."

"No, it's the other way around: there's no one to help them because they're going to lose."

He stated it with such conviction that he didn't seem open to any reasoning at all, and when he saw I was becoming puzzled, he tried to make me understand his position.

"Look, it's not that I've picked either side," he said, "but what's clear is that Spain will be left in the hands of the side that wins. I'm not for one side or the other, I'm for Spain."

He was silent for a moment, and then he continued with great bitterness, in great disagreement with the inevitable: "As if we could tell one side from the other! The whole place is a madhouse!"

He saw that Quitina was looking at him worriedly, and he cut off the conversation.

"Well," he said. "We're wasting time here. We need to leave for Buenos Aires right away."

The baby was in his carriage, next to the balcony. Quitina's father picked him up and began to half run, half dance around the room, holding the baby in his arms and humming a tune from years ago. The nurse rushed over to him, horrified, but Quitina's father swaddled her in a glance that meant "Get the hell away," and he kept running with the baby, who seemed extremely happy.

The next day, as we flew over Brazil, I was thinking that when I returned to my affairs in Buenos Aires I would work more seriously than ever; I thought about my involvement at Las Murtas and also my life in the city, which I did not want to give up altogether. When I recalled my house on Juncal which was in urgent need of remodeling, the first thing I seemed to see was the hall: a couple of letters under the door, and it occurred to me that the news must not have arrived only at my house, but in the city as a whole, at every house. I would find the attention the entire world was paying to that very distant drama reflected in the newspapers and in people's conversations. And the few days I'd just spent in Buenos Aires had confirmed for me that, in general, sympathy lay with the ones who were going to lose. This was strange: were they really going to lose? . . . Then I remembered that once my uncle had told me, although I don't recall the context of his remark, that he was always on the side of the losers. At the time I must have been seventeen or eighteen, and I looked at him without indicating the agreement he expected. Then he said: "It seems to me that you're more inclined toward the winners. Of course! You're lured to the America of our sins."

My uncle didn't love America, my mother did. For my mother, America had represented love, well-being, and confidence; she hadn't spent the period of her sin—her despair—in America. Nevertheless, even though it had been my mother who instilled in me the lure of America, my secret truth lay in the words of my uncle: America, for me, was a land of sin, especially Buenos Aires. Now, seven years later, those feelings had been dulled by habit, but when I first came here, that was their true meaning.

I looked at Quitina's father—he loved America too—; he was sitting way back in his seat, but he had his head thrust forward, as if he felt too impatient to rest it on the back of the seat. I could see his aquiline profile against the light, and I thought to myself that for him too America was the land of his sins. And Quitina? Quitina was herself America, she didn't know what it is to go to America, and I don't think she knew what sin is either. Quitina was asleep beside me, with one hand between mine. Under her coat she was wearing a white batiste dress embroidered with tropical motifs that had a very low neckline, and where her breasts arose, the veins had begun to stand out, as if a tremendously powerful generator were running beneath her sleep and with more life flowing in it than her body could contain.

We reached Morón in the middle of the afternoon and by nine we were at Las Murtas. Quitina's father preferred to stay in the city.

Everything was ready and waiting for us. Miss Ray declared that the baby needed to be put to bed immediately, and she disappeared with him; at Las Murtas we had our first meal alone; after dinner I took Quitina to her room and laid her on the bed, between the curtains chosen to complement the shade of her skin and the color of her hair. Pressed close to her, I sensed that there was a still coldness in the air around us, a smell of wax and varnish, but I buried my face in her breasts, and I knew that the smell coming from her pores would gradually invade the house, warming everything and triumphing over the cold. I fell asleep thinking: "My God! I like things that can win."

We spent two days running from one end of Las Murtas to the other, checking every piece of equipment in the factory and every last blade of grass in the fields. We also went to Buenos Aires and started to move the books; we made two trips with the car loaded, and it seemed as if we'd not even begun. The third day, just as we were finishing lunch, we heard a car pull up and drive directly into the garage; right away Quitina's father appeared with a large rectangular package under his arm. He said he was leaving the next day—his business had been concluded, successfully, as always. He started to unwrap the package.

"I brought you this grotesque item," he said; "it looks a little better now."

It was his portrait. Quitina let out a shriek; he'd arranged for it to be cut down so that there were five inches on all four sides of the head, and then he had given it an antique frame that was very deep and wide, like a trough. The vermilion background had seemed trite before, but now, inside that frame, it was just the right match for the portrait to look serious and fresh. Quitina had to agree that it did.

We began to think about where we would hang it.

"It's not going to be hung anywhere," Quitina's father said, "it's going to be stood here."

He climbed up on a chair and simply placed the portrait against the wall, on one of the shelves in bookcase, in a half-light that was perfect for it, where it neither stood out nor suffered, and where it could pass almost unnoticed. We had to agree that he'd also chosen exactly the right spot for it.

Quitina vanished from the library and returned immediately, carrying something in her hands that she hugged against her chest. She hesitated a little before showing us what she had: it was a portrait of her mother in a small silver frame. The portrait was not even nine inches high; it was only a likeness of her head, on the antelope neck, and you could barely see her shoulders emerging from a décolletage of black tulle.

Quitina showed it to her father more than to me; clearly moved, he looked at the portrait for a minute and looked then at her. I felt the need to make some comment, in order to hide my emotion. "It's lovely," I said. Or something similar.

Quitina went right to the fireplace and placed the portrait beside the sylph. "She's putting it there because it's the most appropriate place for it," I thought. But Quitina tilted her head back a little and made a slight change in the way the portrait was leaning, then she also changed the position of the sylph and moved both things again several times, as if she wanted to balance them.

Just at that moment I saw García walk by in the hall, and I shouted: "García!"

I ran toward him and steadied myself on his shoulder, pretending that I'd forgotten to tell him something extremely important; I have no idea what it was and I might have made it up. But that wasn't necessary, because García really did have something he needed to tell me, something he said was very important.

He drew me into a corner and began to tell me that the day before, when we were in Buenos Aires, a really strange guy had come looking for me. He was some sort of Turk who couldn't speak even two words of Christian Spanish, and he'd been very determined to see me. García had told him he could leave any message he wanted, but the Turk had asked what was a good time for him to come back, because what he had to tell me was strictly personal. García had advised him to keep phoning until he reached me and to ask me for an appointment; that way I could avoid a meeting if I didn't want to talk to him.

I tried to calm García, who was particularly suspicious of anyone who looked foreign. I guessed what it was about right away, but I didn't say anything. I said I imagined it was someone who needed help. García had been very mysterious when he began to tell me about the incident, but he started to speak louder when he saw I wasn't alarmed; he tried to catch the attention of Quitina's father because he considered him intransigent about getting rid of intruders. But Quitina's father didn't seem to notice, so García closed himself up in the study, disappointed and worried.

Quitina's father, or rather, our father, because that's what we always called him, suggested that we have dinner in the city with him, since the plane was to leave early the next morning, and that way he could stay with us until midnight; he needed only four or five hours of sleep. Quitina hurried off to get ready.

In the garage we found that he'd come in a brand-new Packard. "You can drive this back with you," he said, "and I'll catch the airline bus out to the airport. The company gave me a very good price on it, because these days I've been driving nonstop all over the entire province. They wanted to loan me one, but I preferred to buy it, so I could leave it with you; you need something better than that old rattletrap."

Quitina was very happy with it, and of course I was too.

We got to the Hotel Plaza, and when we were eating he said to me suddenly: "Look, that guy probably comes from the side of the Reds."

That unexpected remark surprised me, and I listened carefully.

"Give him what he needs," he continued. "He's probably had a really hard time of it. But don't let him get involved in the factory. Understand?"

I nodded.

"That's the only thing you have to watch out for. Now if you want to help him any other way, why not?"

It was after three in the morning when we got back to Las Murtas.

A waning quarter moon hung high in the sky, and the night was marvelous, but Quitina could not get out of her mind the thought that her father was going back to a country at war. We'd tried in every possible way to convince him to stay in Buenos Aires, and everything failed. He said that he couldn't stay still anywhere, least of all in Buenos Aires. We could never get him to spend more than a couple of weeks here. Finally he promised to be in Portugal most of the time.

As I turned into the road at the edge of Las Murtas, I don't know why—maybe because the car was large, and different from mine, or because the beams from its headlights were unfamiliar to me—but I recalled my return to Las Murtas the first night. As the headlights fanned over the posts anchored alongside the road, I had the impression that the scenery was changing; it seemed to me that the curtain was rising on a set surprisingly full of memories. Quitina must have felt something similar, because she squeezed my arm.

"There's nothing special about this road," she said, "but it's so beautiful."

The next day the Turk called first thing, and I made an appointment to see him on Juncal.

He was a Jew, small, very Eastern looking, and inelegantly dressed; his clothing was not in bad condition, but it clashed with his overall appearance. His Spanish was better than García had said, except his pronunciation worked against his words, which he deformed systematically. I asked him if he preferred to speak French, but he said that wasn't necessary, and in that gibberish he gave me details about the Republican front.

I listened excitedly and paid attention religiously; but I noticed that as he spoke he stressed things that in my thinking were neither the most dramatic nor the most important, emphasizing them with a pause, speaking more harshly although no more correctly. He would emphasize the names of certain people or places, names that meant nothing at all to me. That's what he wanted to learn with his pauses; he was examining me.

I asked him specifically about my uncle's situation and he said: "Well, well . . . your uncle very responsible, very efficient."

He thought the most important thing was his opinion of my uncle. From his briefcase he took a piece of paper that was not in an envelope, just folded over twice.

"He gave me this for you," he told me.

The paper said: "I'm taking this opportunity to send you these words with a person I trust; there's no point in using the mail. For now I'm fine and we'll resist until the end. You two help however you can, and not only financially; public opinion is something we sorely need."

Under his signature he said: "I received several letters from you, very belatedly. I suppose that by now you're both at Las Murtas. Please tell me about Quitina, what she's like."

I said I was very grateful to him for bringing me the letter and that I would help however I could. He answered with a slightly ironic smile that personally he needed absolutely nothing, and that as far as those at the front, I could help by sending something: canned goods, woolen clothing . . . but what one person can send amounts to very little, and from Argentina itself you can expect nothing. He repeated this several times, always accompanying his words by moving his hand over the knee of his crossed leg, as if he were brushing some crumbs off a table.

"From here there's nothing to expect, nothing, nothing . . ."

"I'm Argentine and . . ." I was going to say I was very determined to help him, but he didn't let me finish the sentence and he cut me off.

"Yeah, yeah, you're Argentine, that's clear."

I tried to take a different tack and asked him if he'd had trouble getting into the country and if he planned to stay here. Then he laughed, openly this time, in other words, decidedly, with undisguised hypocrisy.

"No," he said, "not here. Why would I?"

He raised his shoulders all the way up to his ears and repeated: "Why? Why?"

He looked like a parrot or, rather, like Poe's raven, reincarnated and endlessly asking why? why?

Finally he contained his laughter and his question and said smugly, like someone who's right: "I'm going to Chile."

His gaze rested on a spot I'd seen it seek before. As we talked, I'd noticed that he would look at something above my head, something behind me. I thought he was employing the tactic often used by people who won't look you in the eye, one that consists of looking at some particular point very close to you; they think it's a way to make you believe they're looking at you. But he wasn't; he was really looking at something that had caught his attention right from very beginning.

I offered him a cigarette, which he refused; I got up and went to get an ashtray in another part of the room so that when I sat down again I could see what he kept looking at.

Right then, the appearance of an object that held no novelty for me surprised me too. My old study was starting to seem stripped; there were almost no books left on the shelves and on the wall there were marks from the two paintings I'd taken to Las Murtas; but in the corner behind where I'd been sitting, the light from the sunset was falling on a silver pitcher in which there had been a bunch of strawflowers since time immemorial.

I went back to my chair; now I knew what there was behind me—a silver pitcher brimming with gold flowers. As the sun set, it was making the strawflowers glow; they were the color of aged gold, so they seemed as metallic as the pitcher, and the little raven's eyes were riveted to that sight. He did not detect all the defeat that was in my house, all the bravely sustained poverty; he hadn't noticed that on the ground floor there was a tailor—I'll speak of him later—, that I had no help, that there was not a single piece of furniture less than sixty years old: he saw the silver pitcher. He'd also seen Las Murtas the day before, but it had impressed him less, and there he'd been received in the office. Here, though, in this very private room, I was revealing to him everything he might want to know about me. The pitcher was my homeland and my entire caste. I was different from my responsible uncle; I was from this city on the silver river, Río de la Plata, the city of the silver pitcher.

We spoke only a short while longer because we had nothing else to talk about, and he left. I thought how García could relax now, because he wouldn't turn up at the estancia again. I felt uneasy, though; the irony of that little raven, his insulting "why?" I could not erase from my mind, and I ended up deciding there was no reason to forget it, I would have to get used to having it around, because it was a reality.

"Why? . . . why, why? Why stay here?" Did he think I could give him a convincing reason why?

"Don't you have a crest?" the little raven asked.

"No," I said, and I looked around to see if there might be one—in all sincerity, because at first I didn't understand what he was alluding to, I only knew he was telling me I lacked something. It was precisely when I was repeating my offer of help, recommending that he hold onto my address.

"You don't have a crest?"

"No."

Three seconds; I check, watch in hand. In that minute fraction of time I experienced a centuries-old scenario—I stood before the old witch who walks by and says: "This garden is very beautiful, but you *don't have* the singing tree." I knew, of course, what a crest is, but of the five words that made up his sentence I didn't understand them all, I understood only three, *you don't have*. Why, if I'm a man who's not dying to have things? Well . . . the fact is that when he asked, since I didn't understand immediately crest, that was enough for me to desire one passionately, for me to feel miserable because I didn't have one. I'll make myself one, complete with acronym, for my own personal use, there's nothing else I can do. For example, *Ineffable thing, desirable thing*, ITDT. All those consonants together bother me; it would have to be *Ineffable thing, idiotically desirable thing*, ITIDT. That's a little better. What happens, though, is that as soon as the crest becomes tangible it's like all that other stuff industrialists have, and it doesn't interest me anymore.

That might seem like a lie. Tangible things interest me a lot, as much as they interest any other industrialist—although I'm a technician, I can't deny that I'm an industrialist—but they don't interest me the way they interest industrialists. I'm a very practical person, and not what people usually mean by practical. I *know about the actual practice* of things—the things I understand—and it's easy for me to get them to work, which is why I don't attach much importance to the professional side of my life. As I decided when I was a boy, my life has been devoted to painstaking, rigorous work, and my work is going well, quite simply, because I do it well; that's all.

But I need a crest, there's no doubt about it. Those witches and wizards that appear from time to time obviously perform a worthy mission, because they remind you that you *don't have* a crest, you don't have the thing you realize you need but can't name. It's true that I have many other things that keep me from living frivolously, but it's also true that I've always confined myself to the life of the mind and the emotions—inside, I can't tell them apart very well—; however, I feel detached from the systematized activity involved in my work. Consequently, I need a crest.

And the truth is, at the factory it is going very well. I can say it's going twice as well since I took over. Not because what they produced in Puig's time was bad. It wasn't, but what I'm producing is better. The proof is that our things are increasingly successful, because the presentation, the packaging, the delivery system, inspire more confidence, making it patently obvious that our quality control is unsurpassable.

The very next day after the famous interview with the little raven, I had an appointment in my office with the director of CICSA—those people have one!—who asked me if I knew of a commercial artist who might take over their advertising and, of course, I came up with more than one. I told him that would be very easy, because there are some young people here who draw very well and they'd be delighted to have the job.

Then he asked me: "And you, why don't you step up your advertising?"

I didn't know how to answer him, but I think he's right. Well, in terms of *his* sense of the practical. Although maybe he's wrong, since I know more about this than he does. The thing is, I would rather be the one who advertises the advertisers, the commercial artists—a few kids who want to have their own lifestyle, and it seems right that the industry pay for that life. So I promised Laurenz to have a few drawings for him and that way he could see their work.

I left very early. It was a rainy morning and not too cold; I wanted to be in Buenos Aires before noon and I was going over things in my mind to see if I'd forgotten anything and wondering if the drawings would really be in the office. I took out a cigarette and tried to light it without letting go of the wheel, but I'd forgotten my lighter. Since I was on the road that runs alongside the highway, I thought: "There's a grocery store here before the intersection," I stopped, went in, and asked for a box of matches.

"Be right there," the storekeeper called from the back room.

His voice came through a cold, early-morning light. At the corner of the bar, a small stream of water from the nickel-plated faucet was running onto the counter, and there were also drops of water zigzagged across the floor, as if to accomplish sweeping through irrigation—the store was breakfasting on water.

Behind me I heard a few steps, feet being dragged as they entered; a small human form appeared beside me and put something on the counter, an empty vinegar bottle. Then I recalled . . . and this is not a time when I can say "it came to mind." No, the memory came into my veins, I felt it in my hands and shoulders; it enveloped me, altered my body chemistry, and as I picked up the box of matches, I said: "Could I have a glass of grappa?"

I drank it in one gulp, the memory reached my legs, and I started to feel weak in the knees. Holding my glass, I walked to a table and sat down. A trapdoor in the floor opened and a boy emerged. He was coming up from the wine cellar, carrying a demijohn on his shoulder and, when he'd set it down, I asked for another glass of grappa.

This is what goes on here in the morning, I thought: the boy washes the floor, then he carries things up from the wine cellar. While he served me the grappa, I looked at him and asked: "And the others, what are they doing at this hour?"

Of course I only asked him with my eyes, and he answered me the same way: "At this hour people are at work."

When I'd drunk the second glass I thought: "It's time to ask for a third, but no, it's time to get going and leave a few pesos on the table."

As I started the car, I recalled that one day on the road leading to the estancia I'd seen small owls on the posts, some of those small early-morning owls that seem in no hurry to go to sleep even when it's well past midnight. I saw them often, but those slow-flying brown wings hadn't hovered over the car again.

The fact is, every bit of the presentiment I'd experienced that day had occurred, everything had been come true, totally. Las Murtas had started out as a place I went often, a habit associated with work and an almost daily drive, but it had become my home, my property.

For the first time, at that moment, I began to recall the association of property and possession. Possession occurred on my first trip, when I had turned back through opaque defeat, which had been rent suddenly, carrying me off in that trance. It was as if the poles of *always* and *never* had joined there, forming a spark of blinding light; as my reason was blinded, I saw being confirmed everything that had just been denied.

So this means that I was only a receiving device, that I managed to touch everything that would come about, but it's not that I'd done anything to cause it. I did not make things come into being, they happened. This did not diminish their value; nevertheless, it was one thing to suppose that I'd experienced a presentiment, a brilliant intuition of what would happen in the case of the Garcías' arrival, the systematization of work at the estancia, and even my acquisition of the estancia itself, but it was very different to suppose that what had occasioned the triumph was the superabundance of my will.

It was something very different, but which was better? Was it better for me to snatch all that away from Puig, breaking his neck in the blink of an eye, or for the Garcías to place their trust in me and make it easy for me to satisfy my whim by agreeing to sell the estancia? Of course the second of those was better, but surrounding the first there was that aura, that sort of anxiety. The stillness of the air, the way the green shone that day beneath the gray sky, was like an expectant limpidity. That's it exactly: the stillness there was not like a drowsy calm, it was a watchful tension.

If someone had said to me at that moment, "This estancia, with the house and factory, with the dogs, trees, and owls, all this will be yours," I would have answered, "That's ridiculous! I don't want any of that, what I want is to be the person for whom all that is waiting."

I don't know if this is clear. All that was an entire world that no one had seen, a paradise that still lacked man, its intact beauty awaiting a master. That the master of the estancia and everything else was Puig is something else again; in the world I'm talking about, Puig himself formed part of the paradise and I was the legitimate master of the world, with Puig in it. Not accepting it like that was the cause of everything. It would be logical to think that Puig could not accept something that for him was inconceivable, that as Puig awaited my attack he would suspect that I'd come filled with material ambitions, resolved to infiltrate there and get ahead at any cost. Nevertheless, that's not how it had been, and I knew what Puig wanted was to prevent me from possessing what at that time had no master.

He'd purchased those acres of land with the half-ruined house, he'd repaired the house, built the factory, divided the land into various parcels according to his hobby of the moment, and spent many years of his life doing it. All the energy he once displayed on the other continent was buried there at the estancia. The wire-fenced road had seen him arrive many times, his panama hat almost on the back of his neck, his forehead sweaty as he jumped from the car and began to give orders, make improvements—everything set in motion and inspected by him alone. What was it I was after when I came? To perform a modest, merely technical job, to occupy Monington's garret-like little room from time to time, and above all to come and go, to walk through the pastures at dusk. Puig knew that with just that I would be master of it all. Not because I would be shrewd enough or would earn enough to take possession, but from the first day I would be the master of the estancia and of him himself, his panama hat, his history. Of something obviously inconceivable to him.

Here lay the problem: none of that was conceivable for him, but he knew for certain it was what I wanted, what I would have. He knew that the men who took orders from him there got only what he gave them, that profits from the factory were parceled out between payments, expenditures, and savings, and that nothing leaked away. When he met me, he knew the accounts would not be quite accurate because there was something he could neither price nor put in the safe, and he knew I was after that something.

Now as I turned into Juncal, I realized that the things I'd been thinking about had thrown me into a state of agitation, as if the matter were still unresolved, as if it weren't something that had sunk into the past for good and, what's more, probably something imaginary. What had occurred for certain was the arrival of the Garcías, who happened to have that debt of gratitude with my uncle, and most important, there had also been the acquisition of the estancia, and my work as well. More than three years had passed, and the reasons for most of what I did during that time had been linked to those things.

I got to Juncal a little behind schedule. Laurenz was waiting for me; I apologized and we began to look over all the drawings and discuss them. It was two when we finished. Laurenz wanted me to have lunch with him, but I told him I had an appointment; we left together, he headed toward Santa Fe, and I started out for Las Heras. I went into one of those restaurants for chauffeurs and streetcar conductors, and while they were bringing my order I called Quitina. She hadn't been expecting me for lunch, but I knew she would not have been able to sleep well during the siesta unless she'd heard from me. I told her where I was and gave her a brief description of my table by the window, with its holey tablecloth and the aluminum cutlery, but I ended our conversation quickly because I could see steam rising from the buseca on its way to my bowl.

I ate with a mystical hunger, and the meal was simple but perfect. That tripe stew, hearty and thick, then an enormous steak, juicy but well done, grill marks on the fat, the pervasive smell of flesh meeting flame—the smell that rose from the holocaust. A tomato on the side, with olive oil, and afterward a bit of gorgonzola, quite strong. Creole bread and some sharp red wine. The spirit of the place made me spill two drops on the tablecloth, and they formed two violet stains.

I ate, forgetting everything, but with the forgetting that paralyzes only the surface of a person's consciousness—an intensely savored forgetting. I was one with what I was doing, eating each bite meticulously, down to the last crumb of cheese left on my plate, and watching the two cloudy purplish stains on the tablecloth. I saw them spread slowly and take over thread after thread of the thick fabric, which was becoming saturated but retaining a white cotton down not invaded by the dye. There were about two inches of wine in my glass and, looking all around me, as if I were about to do something illicit, I dipped a piece of bread in the wine and watched for a long time how the white crumb soaked up the red tint, transforming it and giving it the faded violet hue like what remains in some percales when they get old and very worn, in dresses washed hundreds of times that you seen on little girls from the country. I looked around again, ate the piece of dunked bread and drank the last drops of the fat, tannin-flavored wine, the anonymous wine one finds only in such places, where it must fall unfailingly on the tablecloth—that's the ritual.

The waiter took away the object I'd been contemplating and set my espresso in front of me. I missed my lighter again, and when I found the box of matches in my pocket, all the memories from the morning flooded back. Less lucid this time, less distinct, at less frequent intervals, more like a condensation of the anguish and anger I'd felt before I got to the post with the owl, when I was sure that none of that would exist again, like the pounding of your heart as you remember an unresolved argument, an issue still pending. In spite of feeling rather lethargic from drinking more than usual, I thought: "This is idiotic, since now it's all mine."

But the agitation I'd begun to experience did not diminish. I even thought it was as if I felt nostalgic for my hatred toward Puig, but how was that hate able to endure? I felt no hatred toward Puig, I did not wish he were watching my triumph from the other world, nor did I regret not having been able to defeat him while he was alive. The nostalgia I felt was for that moment, not, however, for any of the things surrounding me but for my own feeling about those things, for my faith in them.

I reflected again on how that day I'd intuited everything that had happened and how a person could not have given himself anything better than what had happened. Above all—the most, if not the only important thing—was my own personal story, my own personal triumph by making a perfect marriage early in life, one as perfect as the indestructible bonds found in the stories of history's great passions.

Those great passions can be identified by the ordeals undergone, and it's true that our passion had sidestepped such ordeals, but that was because they were unnecessary. We weren't living our passion with the thought of making it go down in history, but we knew beyond any doubt that it had the same caliber. And can't a person know this? Isn't it probably something all the great famous lovers knew? I find it hard to believe that in order to live through what they did they needed the collaboration of an adverse fate. The secret or the law of those passions is in the very being of the person who lives them, the important thing is to believe in them and to want to undertake that venture, to be capable of betting one's entire life on that card.

It's obvious that when fate stops goading us we forget that fire, we believe that only the things that happen in full view of everyone are real. And probably, only those things were real, or at least it's not necessary for any things other than those to be real. They were the things we anguished over, they were the ones we wanted to bring to life, even at the risk of losing life. But what inflamed our blood must not turn out to have been some frivolous argument with fate, let's not think we're longing for hand-to-hand combat with the enemy when we're one and the same body with our beloved.

It was starting to get dark when I reached home around seven—the time when I left Las Murtas the first day and, since that was a long while ago, I had obviously arrived at the same moment on other occasions, but I hadn't noticed. Now I noticed and I felt myself trying to do something the wrong way round: I wanted to relive the emotion I felt on the first occasion: but I couldn't because it could only be felt by leaving Las Murtas, not by entering.

I was arriving at the time I'd left; my return, when I went back after what had happened at the bar and the station, had been at night, and when I entered the house and found the drawing room just as it always was now that the house was mine, when I heard Quitina's voice, which showed me I myself was entering, I felt disconcerted; I can't say disappointed but, as if I'd tripped on the step at the front door, something was altering my rhythm, and precisely because of the urgent need I felt to overcome it, because of the discomfort it caused me, that something was making me arrive stuttering, like a person who's guilty.

As my cheek rested against Quitina's I was thinking: "Can I tell her I feel like an adulterer, that on my way home, instead of thinking solely about taking refuge in her aura, in her touch, as I did other days, I was reliving a conversation that had not occurred with her? No, I can't tell her that."

"What have you been doing"? Quitina asked.

"I've been far away."

"Where?"

I told her everything, the way a person tells something when he knows that the truth can deceive. I spoke about the warehouse, about a memory that had been suddenly evoked there, about my lunch at Las Heras, about the impossibility upon my return of reliving what I'd felt one day as I left. And all that, as the preamble to a real confession. While I was talking to her, I was thinking: "I'm going to get to the point, I'm going to describe something to her." But I didn't get to anything.

The agapanthus were in bloom, and through the window we could see the garden's central promenade bordered in blue, between the casuarinas there were patches of clear greenish sky next to the horizon and, inside, the semi-dark drawing room collected some of that sky in the shine on the furniture, in the yellow upholstery on two armchairs standing out in the dusk, as if the blue agapanthus had bloomed outside and the yellow armchairs inside, showing that here it was a different season, the season of reality.

I don't remember what happened day by day, but I do recall thinking insistently about all this. I also remember that at the same time I was thinking: "What am I thinking?" But right in the middle of those days there was a new development that at first seemed hardly even tangential to our life. Early, around three o'clock one morning when I was still half asleep, the telephone rang and I heard a woman's voice, one that was clear, brusque and sharp: a typically Spanish voice. "Is this Santiago? . . . This is Herminia."

"My God! Who could Herminia be?" I said to myself, but I answered: "Yes, go ahead."

"What," she continued, "didn't you get the letter?"

"No, nothing. What letter are you talking about?"

The voice became anguished; somehow I perceived that she was trying to hide her concern, not from me but from another person who was with her. I also realized the brusqueness in her voice at the beginning was a feigned naturalness.

"The letter from Andrés," she said, "well, more than one letter. But to be brief, we're here, at the port."

As soon as I heard "Andrés," I realized it was Herminia Lara, my mother's second or third cousin, although she had the same surname. I must have seen her sometime when I was a child, but I could not recall her. I recalled her name, because my uncle spoke often about Herminia; she was married to a soldier, who was stationed in the Balearics when I left Spain. Suddenly it all came back to me and I answered: "Oh, yes, Herminia. Forgive me, I was sound asleep. But when did you get here?"

"A while ago. And we can't disembark; we assumed that you would be at the port."

While I was explaining to her that I had received absolutely no notice, Quitina was behind me saying impatiently: "Come on, what are you waiting for? Tell her you'll be there right away and that's it."

She took the phone from me, gave me a shove so I would start getting dressed, sat down on the bed, and said: "Herminia, this is Quitina."

She started to ask about details, giving the same response to everything she was told: "Of course, why not? Everything will work out perfectly."

As Quitina spoke, the voice that answered from the other side was becoming less strident, withdrawing into the receiver like water calming.

Quitina told me again: "Dock number 3, don't forget."

Then she said good-bye to Herminia, advised her to be patient, hung up the receiver, and lay back on the bed, holding her head in her hands: "My God. What a voice, what a voice that woman had when she started to speak!"

She was deeply affected, but I didn't take time to calm her because that would have made her feel even more impatient. I left, putting on my tie as I ran down the stairs.

The road had never seemed longer to me; I looked at my watch fifty times, and as I passed the grocery store it was ten past six. I crossed the railroad tracks and pulled onto the highway at top speed, because I was thinking how dreadful it had to be for that poor woman, having to wait three hours after the disappointment of not finding anyone at the port and not even being recognized when she gave her name on the phone.

In spite of her agitation, she'd been able to outline the situation to me skillfully in a few words. She was on the dock, with her son, and I needed to introduce myself, saying that I was the person who had come for them, that they would be staying at my house. Herminia informed me of all this by telling me what my uncle Andrés had written to me in response to an imaginary letter I had sent him. When I asked about her husband, she insinuated that he was fighting on the Republican front.

I reached Dock number 3. The boat was there, tied to the wharf, with things in the state of abandonment and disorder found in houses on moving day; they had just about finished unloading. On the deck some people who looked like tourists were milling about but they weren't tourists, they were immigrants, caged in whatever difficulty prevented them from getting off the boat.

From the sharp voice that had crackled in my unpleasantly awakened ear, I guessed I would find a rather wild creature holding a little boy by the hand; things were entirely different. Less young than she seemed from her voice, she was extremely thin and serious—almost puritanical-looking, and beside her there was a young man much taller than she, well built, with very good features and an inalterably ingenuous expression. They recognized me as soon as they saw me and began walking toward me; I embraced them warmly.

I played my role as best I could; she was a perfect prompter, and I managed to get them out of there.

Once we were in the car, I tried to talk about ordinary things, asking her questions about the trip, but Herminia couldn't answer me. I looked at her and saw that her dark, almost amber-colored eyes were sparkling dryly, as if they could never cry again, but in her throat there was a knot ready to burst open at any minute. Finally she spoke; her voice was different from what it had been in the morning, but it was no less tragic: "I have to give you an explanation, I have to give you an explanation; don't think we're invading you."

I tried to stop her, but it was useless.

"Let me speak, you have to know what things have been like."

"But you'll have plenty of time to tell me later."

"Even if I tell you a hundred times, I'll never finish."

And she launched into a strange tale, which is impossible to transcribe, not because the events were strange but the whole thing, the labyrinthine way it was held together. Herminia expressed herself methodically, with professorial precision; she gave specific facts in short sentences, but there were so many of them and the events branched off in such incalculable ramifications, connecting with other events she only let one glimpse, as if they were connected at some other branching so distant that the story turned into a monstrous invertebrate, a madrepore, or rather, a reef of madrepores.

It had been necessary to work out all the details in just twenty-four hours. They'd needed to take advantage of two tickets provided by some Swiss journalists. The boy, Miguel, was fourteen, but looked older and he was already being pressured to bear arms. He was the son of a soldier, so his obligation to distinguish himself was even greater. Even though his father was at the front, fighting like a . . . She was going to say like an idiot, but she didn't. Andrés had arranged everything very cleverly. He convinced the Argentine consul that you'd called us and that it was an opportunity not to be missed. The hardest thing was securing safe-conducts so we could get to the front. We traveled in any truck willing to take us and we told all the drivers we were only going to the next town to carry out some assignment or other. Five days on the road . . .

Herminia talked all the way home, without taking a breath. It was half past two when I passed the grocery store again. Miguel had not opened his mouth even once.

"What about you," I asked him, "are you happy to have gotten out of there?"

"Of course."

He didn't say anything else. He did say that "of course," which was quite succinct in itself, as if he spoke without realizing it, as if he were responding automatically to one sound with another. We'd turned into the road that's now part of the estancia, and suddenly I saw him look at something, thrusting his head out the open car window; he was looking at the windmill, spinning at top speed.

"What a terrific windmill," he exclaimed with a kind of rapture.

Quitina was at the doorway of the house.

Above the door of a house you sometimes see a banner with gold letters that say "Welcome!" a garland of blossoms, a string of bell-shaped flowers, or one of those printed mottos that bless the guest and offer him the shelter of the home . . . Quitina was all this and more, standing on the threshold in a white dress.

Nothing worth writing down happened.

When we went into the dining room, I saw immediately that Quitina had been in charge of the table. In the center there was a large medallion of flowers, the colors grouped so they seemed to be inspiring each other, as if they were singing harmoniously in all their variety. There was more light in the dining room than most days; usually the blinds were half-closed while we ate lunch, but that day the window facing the plain was completely open, and the horizon was in full view, sending your eyes to your imagination for help; the wind fluttered the curtains.

At first the whole thing went exactly as Quitina wanted to keep everything—in an unalterable whole of unity, intimacy, and happiness. But Herminia began to speak.

I saw she was going to speak about the war, which would have been natural, and I tried to steer her thoughts in a different direction, just to make the moment last, since the story had to come out in the end. Imagining that she was a professor of something, I asked her if she had been working in Madrid, but she turned out to be an archivist.

"I trained to be an archivist," she said, "when we were sent to Madrid in 1930, in order to have something to do. Well . . ." She looked at the two of us inquisitively and decided to say: "You know how the Republicans are. Damián wanted Miguel to study for his high school diploma on his own, and I wanted him to study in a school. So I began then to prepare for some difficult competitive exams, in order to secure a permanent position and as a way of convincing him that it would be more convenient for me if the boy were at boarding school. I did very well on the exams, I got a wonderful job, and everything was going smoothly."

There was no way to stop her now; she kept on with her story. Gradually and systematically it filled with horror.

At first I set out to observe her curious voice, which was so clear, so distinct that its excessive vibration made it unbearable to listen to over the telephone. But it was actually a beautiful voice worthy of a podium. And the inflections in it were free of any rhetoric, the momentum was natural.

Precisely because I was listening to her very carefully, I sat for a long time with my head lowered, looking at the tablecloth. When I raised my eyes so I could see Herminia, I saw Quitina's gaze as well.

Quitina was beside herself—and therefore not fully beside me. Although I did not see that as concretely as I express it now, I did see it in a very intense way. I recalled Quitina's gaze at the club, her first gaze. Something had just become evident to her; in her gaze there was a new virginity. But not a new gaze, because then both would have been partial—her entire being, in her absolute virginity, was now opening its eyes to pity, just as before its eyes had opened to love.

This made me afraid that Quitina would discover that there's a world outside Las Murtas. But as always when I've felt afraid for Quitina, I saw that she had not been afraid, not at all; I saw that Quitina could not be afraid on that occasion or any other, and this frightened me. I felt ashamed, because compared to her I felt small. I'd kept on with my usual analysis, studying Herminia's voice. Then I thought: "What about Miguel?"

Miguel had picked up a fuchsia and was using his knife to dissect the flower on the edge of his plate.

At that moment Miss Ray appeared with Francisco, who had his arms held out to Quitina.

We went into the garden and Francisco passed immediately from Quitina's arms to Herminia's, because she was wearing a bracelet that fascinated him from the first moment. The baby played with the bracelet, and Quitina asked him: "Pretty! Don't you think so, Francisco? Pretty."

He couldn't repeat the word but he approved it with his gesture, his smile, and the enthusiastic way he looked at the bracelet. Quitina was already initiating him into her predilection for pretty things.

Miss Ray went back inside and Quitina told Herminia that she intended to let her go. She said Miss Ray was excellent, but she found her boring; to her, the child's life seemed too ordered and quiet. Then she explained that she had been cared for by a black woman who sang to her constantly.

"She knew an endless number of witch tales," Quitina said, "and when I misbehaved she would show me some little hole in the wall left by a nail and tell me the *Macaco* might come out of it."

Herminia looked at Quitina in great amazement and finally burst out laughing heartily. She laughed convulsively, with a laughter the connoisseur can classify immediately—a reckless, excessive laughter that swells gradually, straying from whatever occasioned it and eventually overflowing as a cataract of dammed up tears—the laughter of people who haven't laughed for a very long time.

Herminia dried her eyes with her handkerchief and took a deep breath.

"What a wonderful woman!" she said. Then she looked at Quitina tenderly: "You don't know how much good your *Macaco* has done me."

I had no time to mourn the loss of our solitude, as I feared at first. Within a week, without our being able to stop her in any way, Herminia had found a rooming house and some job or other that made living in Buenos Aires essential. They disappeared from Las Murtas.

I wanted to be sure that our solitude had remained intact, and it seemed necessary for me to draw Quitina further back toward the depths of my past. Every day I planned to tell her something, but I didn't really know what. Because it wasn't that I doubted what I should or should not tell her; when I went to tell her I would stop believing in what I'd been believing up to that moment. My secret was larger than the coffer that held it, but as soon as I opened the lid I discovered its empty depths. In order to calm myself, I repeated: "This is all nonsense."

Convinced of that, I was returning late one night with Quitina after we'd eaten dinner in the city. It was one of those nights with a full moon when there is nothing comparable to a road running across the plain. We got back and found the baby asleep, so we didn't dare touch him.

When we went into our room, Quitina began to take off her necklace, holding it in her hand as she walked toward the little table where she always put it. I don't know what gave me the idea of picking up the necklace, which dangled from two of her fingers as she went to place it as usual in the little basket, but I didn't put it down right away; I held it awhile in my hands and said: "Your warmth is still in the pearls."

Quitina leaned against the wall and remained there as if paralyzed. I ran toward her. She got hold of herself immediately.

"You know," she said to me, "that was Mama's necklace. And what you just said, the very same words, is what I used to say to her when I was a little girl and she would let me put the necklace on for a while when she came back from the theater."

I laid the necklace back in the jewel box.

"Since I was very little," Quitina continued, "she'd told me she would give the necklace to me when I grew up, and we'd agreed she would give it to me by taking it from her neck and placing it on mine, so the warmth would not be lost. When Verastegui gave it to me, it had been in a box for three days."

She told me many more things about the necklace, as she undressed, walked from one side of the room to the other, and finally got into bed.

I tucked her in a little.

"Don't you notice a change in the temperature?" I asked her.

"No."

"I do; it feels to me as though I've caught cold on the highway. I'm going to take something."

I pretended to be going to get an aspirin, went through a whole series of maneuvers, and left the room. Half an hour later, she seemed to be asleep, and I slid into bed stealthily. I moved my face toward hers, close enough to brush my lips against her hair—like that time!—hoping the darkness would make her presence disappear for me. In the course of a few seconds, I went from ecstasy to anguish countless times, until I moved away from her. Gently, decisively, I drew back and left a large space between us. Then I faced up to what I called my secret life; resolving in that darkness lit by my limitless insomnia, to gaze at the thing threatening to invalidate my real life. Immediately I sensed a conclusion: this nonsense must end.

Now there was no doubt, I could not establish the least communication between those two compartments. Quitina was in one of them. What choice did I have? Close up the other, act as if it had never existed. Fortunately I'd stopped myself in time. My ramblings had often taken us right up to the secret, along the edge, where I believed Quitina could follow, and that "how far?" had always stopped me. Now, she herself had told me how far I could go, and the only way never to reach that spot was not to set out, not to take any road that might lead to the point where the warmth had been interrupted.

While I was settling into that idea, there was a memory hounding me persistently; it was the memory of a single sensation, of once hitting my teeth against the pearls on Quitina's neck. I seemed to hear the gentle sound as they hit them and to feel a slight contact, but not as if it were with a polished surface, such as glass; it was a contact that let you think the edge of a tooth could chip pearls, when there are probably no teeth that would not break on a single pearl. Recalling that contact, I felt I should have broken the pearls and prevented the necklace from existing, which prompted me to utter those words.

The words came out almost without my realizing, while I was absorbed in the warmth between her hands. Actually, what the pearls inspired in me was a kind of tenderness, of childish ecstasy—some inert matter that seemed to live, as if Quitina's warmth had magnetized it. And that same ecstasy had dictated the same words to Quitina when she was handed the necklace. I seemed to see her—as I saw her when her father told me she used to like playing with the tassels on the curtains—, seemed to see her as a little girl, her whole being concentrated on savoring her mother's warmth with her hands; I imagined the two of them making their pact that the necklace would pass from one to the other, the waves of warmth would fuse in the pearly dust, and the vibration would never end.

Early in her childhood, Quitina had made that pact, had wanted to continue a living chain, and I had broken that chain.

No! I did not break anything. I screamed inside myself and swore to uphold the judgment I'd made about all such things being nonsense.

I reacted so abruptly some muscles jerked and that woke Quitina.

"What's the matter?" she said. "Can't you sleep?"

"No," I answered, "I told you before that I felt sick. Don't get any closer! I'm sure I've caught the flu."

"Do you think you have a fever?"

"Definitely."

Despite my warning, she moved closer and started to touch me.
"You're freezing!"

"Well, if I don't have a fever yet, I'll have one at any minute."

"What should I make for you?" Quitina asked, sitting up in bed. "You have to take something so you start responding." She wrapped her robe around her. "I'm going to fix you something, would you like that?"

"Yes, I'll take whatever you bring."

She went down to the kitchen. She must not have called anyone else, because I didn't hear her speak. All I heard were the small sounds made by dishes—a glass on a plate, a teaspoon in the glass. She was gone ten minutes and came back carrying a large glass filled with everything: hot milk, a beaten egg, rum, sugar, and cinnamon. I drank the boiling brew delightedly; it was a narcotic, exactly what I needed—a deep sleep until morning, until daylight made will-o'-the-wisps impossible.

I woke cured, everything forgotten. At each step I repeated to myself that I recalled nothing, and with Quitina I tried systematically to avoid saying even a single word that might take us into the past, hers as well as mine. No evocations: we had to pour our souls totally into the future.

And it turned out that the future imposed itself, once again, in the form of a new son. Quitina went back to dozing in her healthy suffering, vegetative life took hold of her, the veins in her breasts stood out again, and her whole body attended the future, with true devotion.

The process had an enormous influence on her nature, as if a force at once beneficent and overpowering simultaneously controlled and elated her. She seemed enslaved and more powerful than ever. Her body was in command, but it commanded chastity, rest; her nerves insisted on a truce, a laborious peace.

Her daily life did not really change, but she indulged herself in small ways, by having breakfast in bed, for example. The woman who had not lost her schoolgirl habits of taking a quick bath, running a comb through her hair, and fastening her dress as she walked downstairs began to stay in bed an extra hour, now that she'd decided to be mindful of her condition, beside her, a tray laden with jams, rolls, and crackers surrounding her tea. She would stretch, throwing over her shoulders a pink silk robe that inundated the bed; and I don't know if this was something I noticed then or if it was usually the case, but her lingerie became more evident. All around the bedroom, over the chairs, at the foot of the bed, there was always something made of pink silk: soft, heavy garments, grown almost marble-colored from use. It was as if Quitina's body were demanding outright all the attention and every bit of space.

On top of that, as soon as it was daylight you would begin to hear Francisco's voice calling from the next room. Miss Ray would try to quiet him, but he was demanding Quitina and she'd ask me to take him to her. I would go for him and he came in, clinging to my neck, until I let him fall into the sea of pink silk: Quitina's robe, Quitina's arms, and he himself, like one more garment cut from the same cloth. Intertwined in an endless game, they would let Miss Ray's authority knock at the door for the sixth time.

When the nurse took the baby, Quitina would begin to set herself in motion, with a certain slowness, which was not really slow; it was as if she were moving more reflectively.

There had also been a slight change in her expression. She was content and, above all, she was serene, but there was something serious in her gaze. The first day I noticed it I thought that she was letting her gaze fall with that particular seriousness of hers, of Francesca, but a doubt occurred to me: that seriousness, couldn't it be expressing denial of one part of her nature in favor of the other?

Immediately I saw it could not be explained this way; when speaking of Quitina it was not possible to speak of parts. Was it necessary to speak, then, of a second nature, a split personality? Even less so. Quitina was just one person, integral and identical to herself—the differences were only moments in her nature. In her gaze, when she looked serious, she was Francesca, and in her insomnias, her indulgences, and her whims she was Quitina. In any and all of them she was herself, in the same way her name remained constant in the thirty-six variants that comprised the complete picture. Perhaps those metamorphoses of the word, in which the root never succumbs but upholds them all in a cluster, like a sheer display of possibilities, are what best defined Quitina's diverse integrity.

Yes, that was it; I felt satisfied with the definition. But there was anguish in Quitina's serious gaze. There was also serenity, that was obvious, and the serenity corresponded to reality, to what actually was. The anguish wandered and seemed to prowl the zone of things that had not come into being.

Then I thought: "Could Quitina feel nostalgic for adversity? Could there prevail in her—as the fascinating memory of having to fight prevails in me—a yearning for greatness, which she used to attain when there was an opponent?"

If her mother had come out unscathed, Quitina would have fought for her passion and in that case her Francesca moment would not have been the one left beneath the light of irreality, beneath the apparent abdication. Everything would be completely different than it is now, and who knows if it would not also have been different than I imagined it. Who knows if instead of exhausting ourselves in tedium, we might have excelled ourselves in an invincible tension, who knows if her mother might have been forced to tell the people I saw that day in the Alvear: all of my efforts were useless, you can't fight a great passion.

Lost in thought, I considered that incident for a long time: I'm aware of some people walking behind me, looking at me; they wave and probably smile. I don't turn to look at them, I don't know what they look like, nor how many there are, nor whether they're men or women, or both. I hear their steps on the marble tiles, then I sense that they're fading, as if they're sinking into the carpet; this is simply unforgettable.

It's unforgettable because it's linked to another decisive and terrible event: that moment when the steps died away behind me was the exact instant when my triumph began, the moment when I dealt the blow that interrupted the warmth in the necklace. If I'd cut the string, the pearls would have scattered on the floor, but I only cut off the current threading them together as they vibrated.

That I had cut the current was undeniable, it was obvious that I had resorted to death, as obvious as it was that Quitina had resorted to life, had committed herself to, associated herself with life so she could triumph, although with life's implacable help she could only triumph as Quitina, as a being purely carnal, a being of pink silk.

When I had pondered all this to the point it was stifling, I cut my ruminations off at the root, saying: "I swore not to think about this nonsense any longer." Even so, I thought and re-thought for days and nights.

Herminia and Miguel came to spend the weekend with us several times, but they were never a burden; we always had to beg them repeatedly to come. One day I heard Quitina talking to Herminia on the phone; it was a Friday. Quitina was suggesting they meet me on Juncal so I could bring them to Las Murtas, but Herminia had something or other to do that afternoon and she was saying it would take so long she couldn't get to Juncal at a reasonable time. I interrupted to tell her not to worry on my account; I would wait for them as long as necessary. That day I had plenty of work on Juncal.

And I did have work, but by six o'clock it was finished. I went to lower the blind and, as I did that, I thought, as I had at other times: "It was a great idea my grandfather had to build this house facing the sunset! I need to put my mind to fixing it up. You can make a great study upstairs, with a picture window overlooking the distance.

Planning that idea for a study, I began to make calculations about the walls: it can come to here, have the doorway here . . .

In the hall there's a large window with a stained-glass pane. I peered out to look at the side rooms from there, thinking I could also make a small lab; the water and gas pipes run up that side of the building. My mental design was interrupted by the sound of a window opening on the ground floor, and at the same time I heard heels on the flag-stones outside. A masculine voice called out a modest reproach: "It was about time!" And the woman answered with a laugh that was also restrained.

In the garden it was getting dark now, and the woman who went inside began to turn on the lights. She was the wife of señor Filippo, the tailor.

She went in through the garden. Walking all the way to the back, she lit the kitchen light first—all I saw was the bright rectangle it cast onto the floor—, then she continued to walk toward the front, where she turned on the light in the bedroom. I saw how she tossed her purse onto the bed, how she untied a package and pulled out a piece of dark cloth that might have been velvet, because she caressed it as if it were something soft, and then, holding it on her shoulder, she looked in the mirror at the way it fell to her ankle. She tightened the cloth around her body, smoothing it over her hips; then she folded it and placed it in a wardrobe with mirrors on the doors.

She went into the next room and turned on the light, which revealed a little old man sitting in a chair. When the room was illuminated, the light fell on a table covered with a green felt cloth, on a rocking chair with a flowered cushion, on a three-legged stand with a flowerpot, on a sideboard, and on an old man. All those objects had been in the dark, motionless, and the light disclosed their presence.

The flowerpot and the sideboard remained motionless, as did the little old man, but without moving from his chair—his knees wrapped in a poncho—, he spoke to the woman in a high-pitched little voice and drew a handkerchief from his pocket, shook the handkerchief a little, and began to wipe his lips with it. He repeated this movement several times, as if he were in the habit of making it continually.

Señor Filippo entered the room, coming from the shop, which was located under the window where I was peering out. He was the one who'd reproached the woman for being late and he also came in now with a watch in his hand—a large watch, hanging from a chain. I saw him from the back. He was in his shirtsleeves; the watch hung from his vest, and he was pointing to the clock on the wall, which you couldn't see from where I was. I could understand him clearly: "I don't trust that one; you people control it."

The woman laughed again, removed the green felt cover from the table, and spread the tablecloth. Señor Filippo sat down in the rocking chair, and the little old man kept on talking with his high-pitched voice in some Italian dialect or other of which I could only make out the rhythm, as plates, glasses, and silverware for five people were laid on the table.

The pleasure some people derive from spying on lovers and the rigor others display when spying on criminals kept me at the window, not daring to breathe. I didn't move a finger for fear of making a slight sound that would give me away at my lookout. I wanted to get to the end, not to miss a detail of anything they were going to do, knowing they were going to do absolutely nothing. But the ecstasy that had taken hold of me was not about to be cut short; its tendency was to expand tirelessly into the insignificant nuances of the whole scene, which was not changing.

I recalled—being in the presence of the scene itself, I was trying to gloss it—some illustrations of French manners that I invariably find moving to look at: the kind of illustrations that open out and encompass an enormous area from an artificial perspective, letting you see first the *ferme*, then the *cottage*, the animals, the peasants, the kids on their way home from school. As prints they're mediocre, with their sincere realism and their totally didactic intention, but the rendition is so felicitous you can step into their world, run with the children or plow with the farmers. The attitudes of those figures are truth itself, precisely because they are entirely devoid of art. I had a very similar feeling as I observed that room lit up like a stage, where three people were moving artlessly with the simple truth their tasks required. In her movements as she measured the cloth against her body, the woman, and likewise the man as he drew the watch from the pocket of his vest, assumed generic attitudes you could imagine repeated by a million men and women in a million homes in the city. The whole thing made you think they were performing exemplary acts, dictated by a fourth, impersonal character. The table was set for two additional diners; no doubt señor Filippo's sons were going to arrive and, as they moved, their attitudes would also be artless and truthful.

Before there could be any more characters, Herminia and Miguel appeared, and we started our trip home.

Herminia did all the talking. I always answered her questions, though, because I didn't want her to think I found her conversation boring, and so I spent the whole trip lulled by her sparkling voice. Meanwhile, I was thinking: "Why would Quitina feel drawn to this woman so strongly? They're as different as night and day; nevertheless, Quitina has shunned the society of the female friends she's had since childhood and turned to this pedant for companionship. I have to ask her what she sees in Herminia; fortunately, there's no mystery around it."

Dinner was animated, as usual. The next day, before I could ask her anything, Quitina began to tell me that she was worried about Herminia and the boy; the rooming house where they stayed was a dump, and it was necessary to make them change their way of living. I told her we would do whatever she wanted, and I asked her: "Why do you like Herminia so much? How is it the two of you have become such close friends in such a short time?"

"Herminia's an admirable woman," Quitina answered.

As she answered my question she gave me a rather shocked look, as if she were telling me: Don't make me explain to you why half an apple and half an apple give you an apple . . . and I didn't demand further explanation. "Herminia's an admirable woman." Quitina has an axiomatic mentality; therefore Herminia's an admirable woman.

I lacked the courage to attack such a forceful, faith-filled sentence with my analysis; it was as impossible for me to assault her conviction as it would have been for me to hit a diamond with a hammer, even though I knew the diamond would resist the blow. I preferred to take it as a joke, and I said: "And her offspring, what do you think of him?"

The answer was not axiomatic, for Quitina was moved: "His mother thinks he's a genius."

"But I asked you what you think of him."

"To me he seems more like an angel."

Someone interrupted our conversation, but in any case, what followed was not important; what I have to point out is that the very same day I took advantage of their friendship, rather of the simple fact that Herminia was present, to leave the house even though it was Saturday; I said that I'd forgotten something at Juncal and I prepared to leave as soon as lunch was over.

When I went to get the car out, I heard a strange noise, a vibration that reminded me of the sound a handsaw makes when it's played, but this music was very faint and inconsistent. There would be one note, which was repeated, then another, which was repeated, and so on. The sound was coming from the garage, and I understood immediately who it might be—when we were having coffee, Miguel had disappeared from the dining room.

I walked stealthily as a wolf, trying to step on his footsteps, which led alongside the garage, and from the doorway I saw him in the back of the building, behind the two cars. Through the skylight a Rembrandt-like light fell on him, some mechanic's tools lay in the corner, and Miguel was holding a small sheet of steel in the vise, making the free end of the steel vibrate and shortening or lengthening that end from time to time.

What I've just recounted will probably not seem strange to anyone, but to me what I saw seemed very strange—not a boy playing with a piece of steel, but the quietude filling the garage. I guessed that he'd been there over thirty minutes and that if I hadn't bothered him he would have stayed for hours. He was beyond time. I thought he hadn't heard me come in, because not a muscle of his face moved, even though I was walking toward him; but he was perfectly aware of my presence, and asked me, without changing his position or raising his head: "Hear that wonderful little sound? You like it?"

"Yes, very much," I answered, startled, because I wasn't expecting that sleepwalker to speak.

I got the car out and drove toward the highway, wondering: "Is he a genius, an angel, or an idiot?" My own opinion—the last one—I found odious; the other two seemed implausible.

It was five when I reached Juncal, and I couldn't spend any more than two hours unless I wanted to stay in Buenos Aires for dinner. What I

166 *Dream of Reason*

needed to do could take a long time or no time at all; most probably I wouldn't do any of what I needed to do, and I was perfectly aware that I hadn't gone there to do it.

When I got to the house, I saw that señor Filippo's balcony was shuttered. I looked at the sign for his tailor shop; for seven years I'd been living upstairs and had never looked at it. It was one of those signs made of black glass that has deep-sunk gold letters with wide beveled edges. "Sastrería" it read, in English script written in elegant capitals, and underneath, in small letters, it read "Filippo Tobi."

In the house there was the silence you find on Saturdays, when it seems as if the city has been bled. "They've all gone out," I thought, but I couldn't help opening the window halfway and looking below. The window downstairs was closed. Although it was no later than five o'clock, there wasn't much light in the garden and the room was in the shadows, but through the glass I thought I could see the little old man in the same corner, in his armchair, his knees covered by his poncho. He was sitting so incredibly still I doubted what I saw, and I suspected that any object placed in that spot would have seemed like the old man to me; but as if he wanted to give me a sign of his existence, the little old man took his white handkerchief out of his pocket, wiped his lips, and placed it back in his pocket.

I left the window, glanced at my papers, and forced myself to work for about half an hour without managing to concentrate. After a little while the sun started to bother me, and as I lowered the blind I thought: "The study has to go upstairs." I opened the window and fixed my eyes on señor Filippo's apartment.

The room was completely dark now, and even if the old man had moved his white handkerchief I could not have discerned him; still, I was sure he was there and I couldn't stop looking. The window was a black hole, and as I looked I knew that in the dark room there was an old man and a clock.

For me, looking down from above, that room was a dungeon in which a live heart and a mechanical heart were locked up, facing each other, counting the drops of time. It seemed indescribably cruel to have the old man locked up that way, in the dark room, facing the clock; nevertheless, nothing about señor Filippo's family suggested they were cruel, since they seemed to be happy. More likely, the little old man felt that the clock kept him company; alone there, hearing nothing but the beat of his own pulse, maybe he seemed to get lost in time. Other times must have irrupted into his heart—times on other parts of earth, under other heavens—, he might even have felt terrified that sixty years were missing between the time he recalled and the actual date. On the other hand, with the clock right there on the wall, he always knew exactly what time it was. In the darkness, the clock told him every quarter hour that the moment when his children and grandchildren would return was getting closer—the moment when his daughter-in-law would come in, heels clicking, through the corridor, spread the tablecloth, and put the plates on the table.

I saw all this in the depths of the dark window, which for me was increasingly filled with light. For eight years, the same life had been going on, unchanging, beneath the floor I walked on, hearing my footsteps on the ceiling; now, because I had discovered that life, I abandoned my work so I could observe it. That life had irrupted into my life; I can't say I felt the impact of its irruption; rather, I felt my attention and my time were flowing irresistibly toward it, as toward a drain. But it discouraged me to think that the something leaving me would not arrive anywhere. A chance noise would alert him to my existence; if I were to walk along the hallway it would make him think: the upstairs neighbor is walking around. However, my complete attention alighting on the ledge of the window, my entire will on the watch could not make itself felt.

Night had fallen in the garden and the window below was a black rectangle, like a cistern with a glass surface. As my gaze examined it in depth, I had the feeling that in my hand I was holding the round paperweight that enclosed frozen flowers in its center; I thought I saw the sparkle and intense purple of the flowers and sensed the softness and weight of the crystalline hemisphere. I even felt that I was hurling it forcefully and precisely at the window; the panes toppled with a terrible crash, and in my fantasy the paperweight struck the center of the clock several times—the clock I could not manage to see from my window—ripping the clock open, making all of its unconnected innards jump out, and also striking the old man at times, giving him a sharp blow on the left side of the head the way you crack an egg, and the old man succumbed, opening his mouth, as if he were dying of surprise.

My delirium was very intense, and how long it lasted would be difficult to estimate. I would have thought it had been a flash of lightning if I hadn't heard señor Filippo and his family talking downstairs and realized it was past eight. I could no longer get to Las Murtas in time for dinner. I telephoned Quitina and lied, inventing an inopportune caller I hadn't been able to avoid. I told her they should not wait for me and she asked me: "Do you still have someone there?"

"Yes, still."

"All right," Quitina said, "I'll save you something for when you get back."

Why I told her that I still had someone with me I learned later, but at the time I said it, I didn't know.

That was the first night I stayed beside the fireplace with Rudy until the ashes were cold.

I got home very late, because I drove slowly, letting the car take over, to the point that whenever I reached a fork in the road I barely touched the wheel, waiting for the car to choose the route instead; and the car returned to its home.

In the garage Rudy ran around me in circles, whimpering with happiness. I petted him and said: "Ssh! Quiet."

I opened the door without making a sound, and Rudy slipped between my legs. I didn't put on a light when I went in, since I was planning to walk to the kitchen in darkness as I'd done other times so there would be only the light from the refrigerator as I opened it and took out a bit of roast beef or whatever I found; maybe there would be some chilled kakis—I'm very fond of those Japanese persimmons—, I recalled that Quitina had said "I'll save you something."

In the middle of the dining room I stopped; Rudy touched my hand with his snout and I patted his head.

"Quiet, Rudy," I told him again. I don't remember thinking anything specific; I kept hearing Quitina's voice: "I'll save you something."

When I went in, I noticed that the air in the dining room was warmer; the day had been cold, although we were barely into fall, and they'd built a fire in the fireplace. There were still a few faintly pink coals in the ashes. I put on a log that was leaning against the andiron and planned to go to the refrigerator while the log got hot enough to burn, but when I reached the door of the pantry, I stood paralyzed again. I was sure I'd find chilled kakis and again I heard "I'll save you something."

I didn't open the door, but walked back through the darkness until I reached the dining room cupboard, where I came upon a package of small cookies as soon as I stuck out my hand. I sat down in front the fire and put some Spanish broom under the log; it caught fire immediately. In the light of the flame I could see Rudy's impatience as he sat in front of me waiting for his cookie.

Even the noise of the cellophane, as I ripped open the package, annoyed me; at that moment I felt a decided aversion to everything audible. I tossed the cellophane into the fire and shared the cookies with Rudy; I wanted to continue sitting in the dark for a while, without hearing anything, but I could not stop hearing what continued to sound within my head.

It was the acquiescence to my lie, Quitina's swift, unhesitating trust that I could not forget. True, I had proudly told myself many times: "Quitina has as much faith in me as I have in myself." And it definitely still seemed right to me that she would, but no longer.

I had lied to her, inventing a visit that justified my lateness, and she not only believed there had been visitors in my office, she accepted what I said about them still being there. I had tossed her the lie wrapped in the vagueness things acquire when they *have happened*, and she believed I was speaking to her about something that was happening. Which is why I told her: "Yes, they're here." And her answer? "I'll save you something for when you get back."

I felt I would never forgive her for that, and I thought something even more monstrous. I thought: "If she allowed herself to be deceived, I would hate her."

Because when it must travel through a doubting atmosphere, the lie survives, thanks to its spirit of self-preservation, and it fights for its life; whereas if it falls into a trusting environment, if it splashes about in that acceptance without bumping into anything that counters it, the lie grows enormously large from such passivity. My lie was a vacuous mass that could continue to swell indefinitely. "They were here," when it fell into a benign environment, swelled until it became, "They're here." One day more in that breeding ground and "they" would turn into "So-and-so and What's-his-name," and there would be no way to keep it from reaching "They came for this or that reason," and so forth.

If I'd sensed a minimum of doubt in Quitina, I would not have found my lie so repugnant, I would have seen a positive side to it; because it would have conveyed to her soul the doubt that, I must confess, prevails in my soul right now. In other words, by making her doubt, the lie would have drawn her toward my truth. But Quitina had trusted, and that distanced her from me. Her faith and my doubt were as opposed as hot and cold, as sleep and wakefulness.

The wood was burning with a gentle flame; there was not the least crackling in the fireplace, and I listened to the silence as if I were listening to Quitina's sleep, not only hers, but the universe's as well. Everyone in the house was asleep: Herminia and Miguel in the guest room, Francisco in his crib with Miss Ray nearby, sure to count on eight hours of sleep, and Quitina alone in the large colonial-style bed. No one slept like Quitina; her sleep was immense, and I felt it above the house and the world. A firmament of limitless sleep radiated from her, and I thought: "Is the new life unfolding within her body awake or asleep?"

Life neither sleeps nor remains awake: it works effortlessly beneath sleep, so it's neither interrupted nor accelerated by contingencies of wakefulness. That's why Quitina submerged herself in sleep—it was one more form of her abdication. She would sleep so as not to see, because eyes are the most egoistic organs. Breathing, even eating, she let someone else control, but not seeing: impossible. When her eyes were open, she was at risk that life would run off after what she saw. That's why she closed them to everything, so that not even one of her powers would get away from her, so they would work inwards.

If Quitina had not been controlled by that sleep, would she have doubted, I asked myself. But can I want doubt to enter Quitina's soul? Can I want to bring her into my wakefulness? No, in this world of insomnia I have no right to any company but Rudy's; he stays awake with me without realizing that I can't help staying awake. If I sit motionless, he's still; if I get up, he follows without judging me. I could strike out into the country at midnight, wander through the fields or the city, and he would come behind me. He would accompany me with the same steadfastness if I walked for ten kilometers to help someone in need as if I covered those same kilometers robbing or murdering.

Rudy was stretched out very close to me and I nudged him a little on the back with my foot; he looked at me out of the corner of his eye and halfway picked up his ears, but nothing more. He completely understood that I planned to sit still there, in silence. The touch of my foot and the quivering of his ears were signs enough that we were in collusion.

Suddenly I recalled a mastiff that used to accompany me at El Espinar, when I was a child. He was a sheepdog, a huge, rough, mountain dog that was inseparable from me. We'd walk for hours together under the sun, through the banks of blackberry bushes, with me eating berries and him doing nothing; he was there because I was there. At any hour of the day or night, as soon as I went toward the door he was by my side. Even at that age I already had the same devotion for the night as I have now, so at times I would stay outside until very late. I would sit tirelessly on a stone wall that was half in ruins, listening to the cry of the stone curlew as it beat a retreat. The dog was always beside me; he'd climb up on some rocks, and whenever anyone passed with his dog, he'd make a little growling sound between a challenge and a greeting, and I understood that his growl in the darkness meant: "There's another man and his dog here too."

I relived those nights intensely. In the darkness, beside the fireplace, I felt above me for a long time the Guadarrama sky crossed by the Milky Way, and when I tried to return to reality, I thought how, logically, the dog probably didn't exist anymore, but how along the road there would always be men with dogs and little boys looking at the night. Suddenly, I recalled that at this moment in the Guadarrama Mountains there could be no men walking calmly along the roads. That May night I was here, with my feet next to the fire, but there, where the rockroses might already be in bloom, the spring night could not be contemplated. I thought how the guerrilla sentinels, the ones standing guard over the threatened towns hidden in the darkness, might have been gazing at the night's silent brilliance, but they were not contemplating it; they were probably scrutinizing it distrustfully, because at any moment they probably expected to see meteorites appear, ones that can't be called fleeting, that do not shatter into dust, producing a glorious fright, but go straight to their mark, mathematically aimed to cause destruction at a given point. Some of those vigilant men probably had dogs too, one of the men might be dying with his dog by his side, and another might be watching his dog die after being struck by the bullet intended for him.

Yes, that company, that mute, blind fidelity to man's actions is the fidelity that corresponds to those committed to the task of killing.

Once again the order demanded by the written word inhibits me, and it's hard for me to get the hang of rigorous succession, the conventionality that makes it necessary to baste ideas together, if a person wants to be understood.

I don't have all the thoughts that passed through my mind that night stored in my memory one beside the other: I express them here the same way I'd formulated them a thousand times before that moment and a thousand times afterward. Precisely because I was very familiar with those ideas, I can deduce now the order they probably followed, the way they were linked together, under which images they appeared, and why some of them persisted until they drew me to the secret they were hiding.

I recalled a stupid sentence from my student days, when I was in the habit of showing off how smart I was: "You have to examine the dog's whole process." This had occurred to me when I heard people in love with rebellion execrating the dog, calling his fidelity servility. But that night I formulated some reasoning or other about the topic: I definitely recalled the sentence and, above all, I saw and pondered for a long time my memory of the recumbent statue of a knight with a dog lying at his feet; it's an image of fidelity I find so satisfying: a stone dog sculpted in an era of faith. I also recalled, very visually, scenes in which the process was implicit: a conversation with some woman who was full of ideas, some information about Russia I'd read in a magazine from twenty years before, some North American movies about dogs that harbor the most tender love for a child or display lofty morals in defense of their countries. All the despicable, abortive topics of our murky age: "The dog is the defender of property," "The dog is the cop's henchman," or "The dog is heroic and self-sacrificing." This last one, the topic of various films, I pondered with respect to numerous moving scenes and, mixed with them, other very different scenes began to appear, the kind of scene where a woman in love gets involved with some guy concocted cinematically from a highly appealing mix of vices and crimes, loving him in the most obstinate, doglike way—one of those scenes everyone finds *very human*.

More concrete, harder than the statue itself, the faces of all the blondes I'd watched on the screen during that period began to pursue me intensely. Faces, mops of hair, waists, arms, and, above all, necks. I saw the windpipes on those necks stand out as the heads were thrown back, I saw the fine jaws that completed them, the protruding chins, the baroquely drawn mouths that offer themselves to criminals' kisses, and this made me feel infinitely nauseated.

Not the trivial nausea one feels walking out of the theater—which can be summed up by "how boring!"—but a nausea that felt like my reason failing, like a dizziness, caused by such insurmountable conflict.

To say that I nauseated myself would be easy, but it can't be expressed that way. I was truly the object of my nausea, but I was not the one who felt my nausea. It could be expressed this way, but no one would understand it. I have to proceed methodically.

A while back, when I said I would hate Quitina if she'd let herself be deceived by me, I said that in a fit of jealousy. The idea that Quitina would accept my lie infuriated me because the doubt that *she should have felt* suddenly sprang up in me. It was Quitina's jealousy that, since it could not awaken in her, flared up not in me but in what of her there was in me. The part of her that lives in me, insomniac and active as I am—once again I must reject the notion of part—, Quitina, with respect to whatever stands for the continuous act of our communion—the woman asleep was also Quitina, the one we abandon to the children we make, unknowingly—, Quitina, the woman who moves me, moves for me, who is joined to me fundamentally and indissolubly, was the one that swelled with anger over my falsehood. If I had not felt that wave of jealousy, it would have meant that Quitina was not alive in me.

So, much later, when the images of blonde women with their mops of hair and persistent mouths began to pursue me I felt a nausea and a dizziness that were nothing but the nausea Quitina felt in me. Because Quitina, in me, was face to face with my lie and with my truth; regarding the latter she had no choice but to feel dizzy, and regarding the former she had to feel nauseated. Women with doglike adherence to their men struck me as the opposite of Quitina, as what she could not be, as something I did not want her to be, and she was not.

I did not want the clinging sort of love that forgives everything. This might seem strange, but I've never wanted it. Which does not mean I don't want forgiveness. Forgiveness is godly love. If at some point I find it impossible to forgive myself, I will look for that forgiveness, I will ask Quitina to avert her eyes from me and look at me only in divine compassion. But I've not yet reached that point; I still can't stop wanting love for myself like any other creature.

I recall with complete certainty that, at the same time I was struggling feverishly with this obsession, I was thinking: "In this bourgeois house, filled with everything a person needs to be comfortable, I have, legally, a human world called family; by expending little effort, I get a good financial return from a job I like, and everyone's health is as good as that of irrational beings. Nevertheless, sleeplessness and anguish encircle me like a bramble patch with no way out."

I'm well aware that the vast majority of people in the present generation would get goose bumps if they heard a man construct a theory of absolute love based on his lawful wife: I could hardly care less. All this passed through my mind that night and it all culminated in the idea of *possession and surrender*. That would seem to be what love is and then would come the antithesis *communion* and *reserve*. But can that be?

If I live with the poison from my reserve dissolved in my blood, any act in which I try to communicate is false and, if the being who believes she's communicating with me fails to perceive the theft of my reserve, her communication is misguided.

Communion, then, can only be resumed on the basis of confession. The flow of my reserve, divergent for so long, would have to return to its normal course, and then . . . then there's the terror that communion won't be able to occur.

That was the issue; I knew the woman in me is different from what happens in me. And she's not different only because she's uninformed but because of her nature: such a thing could not happen in her. Then wouldn't confession, I asked myself, not reveal a point where concurrence between us would be impossible?

Because when I speak of possession and surrender, I'm not speaking about the same thing as when one alludes to copulation; I'm speaking about a surrender that involves a simple movement of one's being, an emitting of will similar to the act of assuming life, to the first breath of will in response to the command to be. And similar because of whatever life holds of eternity. The thing that life is, and that we know has a beginning, is life insofar as life seems endless and limitless. In the same way, love commences in a given instant, but while love is alive it imagines neither end nor borderlines. To identify a lump of finiteness would be like denouncing a tumor in the union's organism.

To refuse concrete similes and abstract definitions: love commences in common daily contact, stretching out on the grass, or maybe drinking from the same cup, or in those summer hours when one person moves mechanically to wipe away the sweat running down the chest of the other, as if it were one's own body. Also in the reaction to a taste or a smell experienced together, something like a harmony in their substance, which is neither adaptation nor habit, which is not at all mechanical, and is not an automaton because it has feeling, because it belongs to someone.

It's much more subtle and at the same time so simple! . . . It's woven from such basic threads that when I point them out I can't help saying: "But can something so straightforward be so unfathomable, so impossible to grasp?"

"Here I am with Rudy," I thought again. "I share any little treat with him and respond with a friendly gesture to his expressions of satisfaction: he licks his chops, pricks up his ears, he puts his head on my knees, and I pet him, then I point to his corner next to the fireplace, where he lies down and stays without moving as long as I continue to sit in my chair. We've had a dialogue of contacts, an understanding based on the material, through which his fidelity is bound to me. I could stab a man right before his eyes, and he would still put his head on my knees, he would still experience the same sense of well-being, the same trust at my side."

Once again back to where I started.

Well, it's impossible for the dog to make any mistakes in the dialogue of contacts that creates an attachment for him; it's the man who makes the mistake by interpreting the dialogue as if it held some sense of *truth* and *good*, which accounts for all those famous eulogistic or slanderous interpretations. Obviously other animals also gave rise to mythical representations based on their expressions or behaviors, but only the dog has lent its name to a school of philosophy, because the dog's expression, with its highly diverse nuances, is so close to us that its inner states amount to a way of thinking. The rooster or the goat is no less modest, but nevertheless only the dog's lack of modesty seems to make sense, only the dog's fidelity is sculpted in stone. What's been sculpted, of course, is not the mechanism of the dog's conditioned reflexes but the mystery inscribed in the dog's expression.

That's the dog. Now, about people . . . in people there is also the attachment referred to as a union of flesh—a bond that doesn't break even when one confronts the most repulsive things. In fact, sometimes it's even reinforced by repulsive things. In other words, sometimes it's a bond that's strong but superficial, other times it's a profound communion in infamy.

I must stress that all these machinations going on in my head, because of words I explain only halfway, were then just a procession of images. The qualifications and digressions I place here between commas and parentheses were there, in my thoughts, only irrupting gestures or human stances. Glimpsed in life? In the movies? I don't know, but I can confirm that they offered incontestable pieces of evidence, movements made by beings whose intentions and meanings were transparent to me, beings who unfolded and unraveled before me and to whom I said "no." Then the image of everything else appeared, the world to which I say "yes," the world I can confirm, the ground that's gripping me with its law of gravity. That world was union, the fulfillment brought by love, communion in joy.

How to describe the vision of that joy? I don't know. I contemplated it for a long time, and observing it—because the vision was before me— was hurtful.

I knew that a great, absolute, and pure passion—I mean an authentic passion—also withstands any disease that attacks one of its members. I did not believe that love would fade if whatever was loved proved not to be perfection itself, unblemished. No, I was well aware that the lover does not disentangle himself from the beloved, even though he sees the beloved fall into the deepest abyss; yet that very elasticity eats at love, dematerializes it, gradually making love as transparent as pity. Because that's what pity is, transparency. Pity is seeing the other through oneself and being the glass that does not see itself: self-denial. And that's what I don't want—which doesn't mean I disdain it—; what I want to feel against my frame is flesh full of will.

What process does a person undergo after confirming that there is something that he does not love in what he loves? Some transubstantiation must occur, come chemical change that turns blood, blood's spirit to tears. Anyone who follows his beloved to a place he does not want to go, goes without joy, because joy occurs only in will. Self-denial and pity are the highest forms of love, but the carnal possession found in pity terrifies me like violating a grave—the dead person is there, between the lovers.

If in the gaze exchanged by two people who love each other, in the daily possession that makes up the simple life of lovers, the only thing not loved is present like an opaque skin on a human face, their love is strangled, restricted in the unlimited reach it genuinely enjoyed when it arose as intention. And what's left of love if love loses its sense of the absolute?

Just as I recall with total clarity the visions that besieged me that night, I recall the shadowy voids that could darken my thoughts. I know that when I touched on certain ideas, sometimes a particular word would surface and become nailed between my eyebrows, I would sink into darkness, a darkness that drenched me gradually, as if it were about to dissolve me. Then, things I'd be thinking about when I returned to reality would seem to have no connection with what had gone before, but they did, a very intimate connection.

There was one moment in particular when I was thinking about what happens when the presence of God bursts into man's life. A human life touched by the supernatural does not recover from that contact; something inert, like coal, remains inside, something that can only be reanimated by an igneous life, but that no longer absorbs its sap from the earth, as it did before.

Immediately I saw that this state, too, is a question of surrender. A human life that as a whole leans toward the divine becomes a divine life, through immersion. Wrapped, bathed by grace, it is transported to a different plane and remains there; and whether or not it touches the earth is irrelevant, because its communication with earth has been severed. But when a human life becomes so delirious with grandeur it wants to attain categories that surpass the human, when it wants to make something absolute and eternal from the union of two finite beings and, surrendering itself to a child, believes that in the child there is the possibility of possessing the universe, it's possible for a human life to stumble upon God when least expecting it.

Such was my case, but I'd expected some sort of prologue. All my life, before I became a case, I'd always believed I was the creator of my own paradise—not a question of vanity here: vanity is incompatible with intelligence, with true intelligence—because I thought I could make better choices than anyone else. I was always sure of not erring, up until now I have never needed to correct myself. Did I think I was infallible? Yes, I always thought I was infallible.

Of course I was not taking evil into account. But not because I didn't believe in sin or was trying to abolish it: I did believe in sin, because I always accepted the doctrine that points to it in our origin, but I had not experienced sin. The formula "man is a sinner: I am a man, therefore I am a sinner" was in my mind by force of habit, but I had confidence in my exceptional qualities, in the healthy nature of my instincts, and in a sort of skill or sound judgment, a sense of orientation. Something like the tightrope walker's innermost feeling about his lightness and the boxer's about his strength. I was always sure of having one privilege— my will. Immune to the disease particular to every will, my will never enters into conflict. That's why I believed it was omnipotent, because any will runs down if it starts turning corners; with every veer, it loses a bit of energy, but I never walk zigzag: I go straight to my goal, like a bullet.

That's why my life is not divine but self-deified. I am not resigned, not resigned to repudiate my pride; I know what's inside it, an excessive love of perfection is driving my pride. Contemplating the perfect and wanting to possess it, conceiving of the infallible and wanting to be infallible were always the same thing to me. When the infallible impulse of my will collided with something impossible, it would snap, because it could not bend; and the fracture would affect my being at its core. What can I say in my own defense? That if in truth my will could not bend, neither could it rebel. I definitely did not find impossible things humiliating; they were deathly wounding to me, but my love for the power wounding me was so great that I could not try to evade it. Loving that power so much, I believed it was mine; I felt wounded to see it rise against me, although my love was not lessened.

But that last thing happened—in my consciousness—after the agony signified by the fracture had already occurred: that's where the lump was. The moment when a few words spoken over the telephone completely altered the universe for me. I was alone, naked—I remember that leather chair sticking to my skin like a womb from which I could not be born—facing the impossible.

If only I could know what happened at that moment! All I know is that it was precisely the moment before I realized that my will did not want to die and that its *wanting* to live was increasing to the point of *being able*, of power. It was then that I trapped the tiny life buzzing around me, annihilating it skillfully and speedily.

How to describe that event? Is there any dogma that would not reject it? Can I believe that I attained grace in the form of my ability to destroy? That's monstrous. Can I imagine that a satanic force came to my aid when I was crying for mercy from the depth of my anguish?

I remembered thinking, even at the time, that perhaps the event was only a concurrence in immanent Justice, and by this I mean that if the one who wished me harm succumbed, it was not because I asked for his destruction but because his own perversity had to be punished. But then why would I know that his perversity was going to be punished?

The day of my first visit to Las Murtas had been different, within me I carried no clearly adopted mission of destruction. There was, of course, that agonizing moment when I thought about my failure, when I contemptuously trampled the one who caused it, but I did not sentence him, I did not aim carefully so as to wound him in the skull; I only managed to see, against all reason, that what could not be would be. That was not how it was when I used my will to catch the fly as it circled and then to burn it in the globe, even less when I said, "As you fall so will she."

In a hundred thousand different forms, in innumerable images and echoes of words, I relived *everything*. I heard the smacks of my pipe in the palm of my hand, I saw the drops of blood running down Elfriede's cheek, I returned to the road that leads to the estancia and returned to the owl's wings, I returned to the lobby of the Alvear. Everything was immense, it was like a hundred lives, it was boiling in the veins of my temples and accelerating my breathing. Everything involved was a thousand times more true than the rest of the universe: it was Truth sealed.

After puzzling over those incidents for a long time, I could tell myself: "Everything happened in three sparks. How could the years of days and consistent hours go by, tranquilly adhering to logic and oblivious to all this delirium? How could things achieved, real life full of specific events, all of them clear and ordered, not give some hint of the dark origin from which they came?"

Finally, I wound up answering myself: "All those things were possible because of forgetting."

Man can tolerate only a limited dose of faith; rather, the dose of living faith compatible with life is not very great, or it's intermittent. If the life of faith becomes too powerful, it sweeps away one's personal life and its little pan on the scale wins out completely. Only the halfhearted can maintain a happy medium.

I asked myself again: "But what does all this have to do with faith?"

Nothing explicit, although it hovers quite close to faith. I hadn't arrived at that crossroads by following the path of faith but by following the path of love.

Faced with the threat of the impossible, of defeat, of deception, my will—will to love—had grown, had affirmed itself in its infinity, and that firmness had carried it to possibility, to power. But of course a return to reality was unavoidable, because the beloved object is there and it's an impossibility unless one is alive; so it was necessary to unbelieve, to erase contact.

By surpassing one's limits that way, one wanted to defend something on earth, but if the power to achieve this is bestowed from beyond the earth, it's impossible to live on earth again as an integral being; the seduction of the beyond demands that you free yourself from whatever inspired your drive, and that pressure on the part of the supernatural creates a feeling that's defensive—not rebellious, the rebel is merely a person who lacks salvation: the fallen one—, an attachment to earthly things and a centripetal movement of love, which reason assists by trying to calm the feverish itch with logic: "If this is what you wanted, now you have it, and all the rest is insanity."

But love can't linger for a long time folded over its object, because such constant closeness leads to atrophy; in order to feel what it loves, love must be felt as love, love must dilate again, must open its pores to the insatiable hunger that is its drive, and once again love will hear the call of the distance that it covered, that it knows it can cover.

Engrossed in a contemplation I could never put into words, I tried to understand the alternation of systole and diastole, repeating to myself: "It's the movement of love, love is movement, and that is the movement of love." Then in my head I heard Kierkegaard's lament: "I cannot make the leap of faith . . ."

A console table, a piece of porcelain with cupids and garlands of roses, a page from my notebook, and my halting hand trying to write down something like "Law of absolute relation . . ." All this arose out of those words.

Reconstructing what I glimpsed on that terrifying day, I had to acknowledge that it was not so foolish as it appeared. It was so concrete, so explicit that it seemed trivial, but using the number one to represent unity is not trivial.

This is what happened: The thing I wanted to understand from my terror that day was how what happened had been *able* to be, and the idea of *possibility* was what made me think about Kierkegaard. Then, as I recalled his desolate sentence, "I cannot make the leap of faith," I thought: "What leap would that be?" and right at that moment I heard a bell—it was probably the one from the church of Nuestra Señora de

Pilar; the note leaving the bronze vibrated free from any possible constraint or contention, and I felt it was drawing me closer to something: I intuited the existence of both another, somehow similar movement and of a clue, a possible comparison.

Groping like a blind man in the darkest part of my memory, I finally came upon what I was looking for.

The first thing I recalled was not the physical laws, formulated according to textbooks, but an incident from a sensationalist story in some source or other: "The note from a violin can demolish a bridge."

That phenomenon of resonance was the only thing comparable, in other words, the only thinkable thing that man has to lean on as he tries to imagine the law that governs his relation to God. I took out my notebook then and tried to write down what I'd intuited, but I was inhibited by the garland-laden cupids, the murmur of conversations, the smell from the candles, and the memory of Quitina. All of them, in their irreconcilable antagonism, stirred up a deafening noise that was hammering in my head as I concentrated on searching for my law, so I gave up searching.

That day in the Verasteguis' hall I got no further; when I recalled the phenomenon amidst so much solitude and silence, I threw myself into the pursuit of what was left to search out.

At first glance, the idea of searching for a law to explain such a *phenomenon* is repugnant—as is the need to call it a phenomenon, but that's what it must be called—because there seems to be no possible association with any kind of *force*, any determinative contingency; and that's how it is. There is nothing that determines grace; grace is given. But when the grace given is the one that was asked for—in this matter there is neither before nor after—, asking and granting form a harmony; they agree, and to such an extent that only in the textbook explanation of resonance can we find terms subtle enough to name what seems—and is—inexplicable.

"An acoustic vibration, of the necessary amplitude and frequency, emitted from a given point of a non-elastic structure, can produce the effect of enough resonance to unsettle that structure and make it sway." That sentence says it all.

That's saying it strictly, it's easier to understand if we imagine a man with a violin, underneath a bridge, searching for precisely the right spot for wresting the moving cry from one of the instrument's strings. He can spend days and nights, he can spend years without managing to do this; he can die of old age and be replaced by generations of unsuccessful violinists, but that will not disprove the law. The search, the approximate notes, are the prayer of thousands of men, few of whom hit on the right movement.

In short, man is placed beneath a structure that cannot be elastic because it's absolute—the *all* can neither grow longer nor shrink. That vault is the supreme goal of man's plea, and he vibrates beneath it to the point of exhaustion, in the same way the cicada releases its super-sharp note at noon, as if to make the stones cry out; why do the ashlars in the beyond quiver so seldom? Because there's a law.

If we were dealing with a real bridge, with a known arch, we could take a piece of paper and use a few rules of acoustics to determine the point, which might or might not be found under the bridge; but since we're dealing with an absolute arch, man has only to release his note at the point of his absolute. Only that, and if that doesn't work it's because he is not located at the true point of his absolute, so there are nullifying interferences. Because it's not easy to position oneself at that point's location. How to define that point? I think the only thing you can say is that it's a place where there is nothing but truth.

And here the comparison breaks down, because under the masonry bridge the interferences are equally true. But there's no reason to say any more about the masonry bridge.

There is a point of absolute truth where one's being is rooted, and it's very difficult to position oneself at the location of that point, to shout from there. Life is filled with mirages, which sparkle so intensely you're dazzled, and you can't reach the point of absolute truth by measuring and calculating, you reach it by abandoning everything else. Only when nothing matters but love's pure drift and you let go of everything else do you reach the nakedness of absolute truth, the place of absolute relation with God.

When I got this far, I turned back to search for connections.

The leap of faith is identical to or, rather the same as the movement of love, and what happens is this: when we put ourselves into loving one creature in the integral way that, rightly, we love only the Creator, the movement of our love resounds beyond creation, and the response perturbs us. We were calling, and the thing that responds calls us. We were asking for help here and they help us by transporting us.

To where, though? And why do I feel transported?

I veered toward reality. The intoxication I experience from so much analyzing leads me to subtilize things, and it seems I'm trying to sublimate them. Nothing could be further from the truth. Of everything I've said, the only thing certain is that something has cut into my life; what it might be, I don't know and, since I don't know, I don't dare communicate it.

This is where everything kept ending up.

If I were to make a long confession to Quitina, how would our relationship be left as a result? I can't even imagine that she would consider it as important as I do, and if she did, I don't think she'd be left waiting expectantly, asking me for news about progress in my department. No, I think—it could not be otherwise—that she would try to walk in my footsteps. And what would happen if she were to set out on that adventure? Besides, could I make any progress if I noticed it was impossible to breathe in that climate? Could I continue in the truth if I saw a repugnance in her toward all my past deeds?

At the same time, if Quitina were in the truth with me, why has something similar not happened in her private world? Can I be sure that it hasn't?

What's most serious about all this is that there's no way to conduct a test: when you're on grounds like that, whatever you uncover can't be covered up again later. Within myself, I can believe and unbelieve, because they both involve phenomena that alternate continuously, but if I were to mention them, I would seem to be destroying one with the other. I even believe it would be impossible for me to formulate either of the two completely; I would only need to start granting one of them validity, and the other would rise up from the depths and cut off my words. No, Quitina can never hear me utter those words, which one would want to take back as soon as he'd uttered them. I myself cannot conceive of them; what words could I find? Above all, what expression would I have on my face as I spoke them to her?

I thought about this for a long time and saw the expression she would have on her face: the expression of a crazy woman I met some time ago. When I saw her, I understood that she would never cease being a topic of horror when I recalled her. Recalling her then, I saw her from within, because her expression was my own, and I understood the mechanics of it because I felt her affect.

"I was the beauty of the world . . ." she was saying as she stood in the hospital corridor. The doctor who had taken me to witness this went up to her; she tightened her indigo-colored shawl over shoulders and began to tell her story. Since the doctor knew which spring activated her delirium and he wanted to me to see it, he gave her a push down the chute. She'd been impregnated by a supernatural being; this was the nucleus of her fantasy, and around it there was a whole plot of treacheries, of feminine jealousies, of torn flesh on her face, her neck, her breast . . . She opened her clothing a little so we could see her chest, and I, at least, saw that it was true, saw some claw marks on her neck and cheeks, which were not scarred. But she kept returning to the topic of what had caused her misfortunes, trying to describe to us her relationship with the being who had chosen her because she was the beauty of the world. Her cheeks, which moments before had seemed clawed by the outrage that had flayed them, trembled when she told this, as if they were contorted with an ironic grimace. Something under her parched skin was moving the muscles as if they were cords, turning her into a comic puppet, whose gestures had nothing to do with the drama it was reciting.

The double directive dividing her within frightened me more than her previous rage and I asked my friend surreptitiously, in a low voice: "But why is she laughing?"

With the usual lack of concern of a workman who knows every mechanism in that clockmaker's shop, he answered me loudly, without trying to keep her from hearing: "Don't you see? She knows it's all a lie."

That memory, so distant and so minimally related to my present condition, had never surfaced since then, but it invaded me now, and I became engrossed in thinking about the insanity that might be tied up with it, leaving mockery as the only freedom. Although not even mockery is truly free, because it doesn't try openly to break the spell; it's nothing but a convulsion that betrays the existence of something not caught completely in the net.

Fine, but that's insanity. I next thought, what's my condition? I don't know, but I feel there's also a net into which I've fallen. A net so subtle that if I tried to show it to someone, if I pointed to it and said "Here it is, this is its mesh," people would find me comical, like those illusionists who pretend they're being beaten up by ghosts.

If I tried to tell Quitina, it would all end up as a tragicomedy, because she would surely listen to me very seriously, but what if I laughed, if I threw things off-key with some frivolous gesture in the middle of the drama? Besides, in order to tell something in the first place, it's necessary to start at the beginning, and how could I tell her about what happened with Elfriede?

Of course Quitina knows she was not the first woman in my life, and I think I told her the story of Berlin, in great detail and very superficially. I had an affair with a girl and she was involved in dance. How could I tell her that Elfriede had also touched the ultimate truth of my being, that in my feeling for her there had also been something absolute? I don't know, I don't know how I could explain this to Quitina, because I've never completely explained it to myself.

A thousand times I've told myself, and with great conviction, that I was not really in love with Elfriede, but when I remember that moment and how I leaned against the chest of drawers, smacking my pipe in the palm of my hand, I know the drama blinding me was a universe. My will felt its fibers being torn apart on all four sides. Even so, my relationship with Elfriede was not what can be called love in every sense of the word. There was in me, it's true, a movement of love for something, and that something was a type of absolute value. It was, I repeat, a world: it was flesh. Yes, it was that; because I can't say that it was sex. No, it was not the mystic power, man's private, inner companion from the very beginning of his life, that sex is; it carried none of the generative drive, the flaming of eros that reaches from earth to heaven. It was flesh, specifically, contact as contemplation.

That's the exact word, because even though it was not at all subterranean like eros, neither was it a superficial sensuality. In it, there was something of knowledge. In the biblical sense? Yes, but not only that sense. It was the notion of body, the dazzle of contact. It was as though one body *saw* another body for the first time; it was the idea of a body, imprinted—but not on the skin, because it had thickness—, imprinted on the awareness of touch. An idea similar to the idea you have of the sea while you're swimming: the idea of an abyss beneath the abyss itself.

I could say it was the woman, but I prefer to say it was humanity—not Humanity—because it was knowledge, one humanity being contemplated by another humanity. And if this allowed me to approach absolute truth for a moment, that's because it was absolutely true.

Everyone has a right to believe his feelings are absolutely true, but what I mean when I say this is that only God and I know the agony experienced by my will, since it all happened within me. My external reaction was purely conventional and courteous, but right at the center, where there was no possibility of lying, was my indestructible desire. Without any mix of self-love or spite, without any calculations about the advantage of giving in or insisting; without conflict. Solely a force that could not be canceled out, like something that could not continue to be what it was so, in order to continue *being*, was suddenly something else.

But when that something else was a purely carnal desire, when it would have needed the body to be the instrument for possessing Elfriede's body, when it turned into *that something else*, in that fearful intention Elfriede suspected, which part of my anatomy did it use to push her toward the lamp?

That's what I need to know. If I doubt because my reason commands me to do so, if I admit that the event never really occurred, I feel I'm missing my amputated limb. And reflecting on whether it's a gift of divine mercy or an evil power acting as my second does not appease my obsession. Knowing whether such an action stemmed from good or evil is what's overwhelmingly important to me; what I absolutely must know is whether such an action occurred.

There's no doubt that I long to see it radiating from Providence and that I would hate to receive it from hell, but what I want more than anything else is to see it, to feel it spring up incontestably, to find that it's efficient, like a branch on my trunk. When I'm convinced, then I'll see what I do with my power. And yes, I have no fear of verifying it; once I know I have it, I'll be able to sacrifice it.

Then I asked myself: "What has all this investigating gotten me?" Nothing, knowing I want to know. Knowing I cannot confess because I don't know if it's virtue, or sin, or pure illusion. I cannot confess to Quitina, because confessing this way, confessing . . . I already tried it, without any success. One day when I was feeling very anguished, I turned to a poor Franciscan who was left speechless. He sat writhing in his box, containing his desire to tell me I was crazy and, finally, seeing that he couldn't convince me that it was all just my sickly apprehension, he told me: "Well, in any case, repent."

"How can I repent when I don't know if it's true?"

"Repent of your intention."

"But I don't know if I've been punished or rewarded."

"Repent just the same."

"I can't."

Naturally he did not absolve me, and that's how we left it.

One more thing Quitina doesn't know. How strange! This secret has been easy for me, I told myself; rather, until this moment, I hadn't realized that this secret has been here between us for a long time.

Actually, the only thing I was discovering was a silenced event, because the secret was really the cardinal one. I hid from her the fact that I was living in sin because the clarification of my sin was still in process.

Of course Quitina knows exactly what my beliefs are, she knows how I think, because she thinks exactly the same way. But it's one thing to think and quite another to live what you think. When thought must be carried out in an action and we feel reluctant to effect our thought, what appears is a shyness about revealing ourselves.

I'm definitely not talking about the shyness experienced by insecure minds frightened by someone else's opinion. No, when I have to present my ideas to other people or lay them out in opposition, I assert them as firmly as possible; what's hard is exhibiting the vicissitudes of your life, exposing the rise and fall of your power, saying: "Sometimes that power is imperious, sometimes it's flagging." And if that makes me blush, it's not because I think it *should be* in one particular way and not another; I blush because what's been said or expressed or carried out may already *not be* before one's finished saying it. It's terror that the crazy woman's grin might be able to pull my string at odds with my words.

The terror of that duplicity, that close-knit division!

I've said my will is not susceptible to conflict; it does not tolerate conflict, it vomits conflict, which is why I won't say anything until I know, and in order to know I will try myself in a decisive way. Trying myself like that might destroy me, but then the experiment will turn out to be an auto-da-fé. I'm definitely right at the edge of the bonfire, and I won't consider the trial settled until I know. It doesn't matter how close the fire gets, even if I'm breathing the flames themselves.

Breathing, the idea of breathing the unbreathable began to suffocate me, and automatically I took a deep breath that made me cough. The air hurt as it entered my lungs, the way it's painful when you suddenly move a part of your body that's gone numb. The cold made me shiver; it felt as though I had a frozen blanket thrown over my shoulders and the back of my neck, and through the cracks of the shutters I saw dawn already breaking.

Rudy was curled into a ball, his tail covering his nose, and from time to time he shuddered, which made me notice that he was starting to age. His tail was no longer magnificent; his whole body was shaggier, and he'd gradually left his long, fine hair behind in the thistle fields. As soon as he felt me move, he stood up; I opened the door and he went out into the garden. He looked at me for a minute to see if I was coming out too, but he soon realized I wasn't. It was his exercise time, and he forgot about me, pricked up his ears, and went running off to see what was moving behind some rhubarb plants.

I forgot about everything too. I stayed there for a while, looking at the garden through the half-open door, and what I saw—the avenue of agapanthus not yet in bloom, their shiny leaves full of moisture, receiving the first light—filled me with pleasure, with admiration as if to say "this is enough," letting me stand there contemplating such sufficient beauty, without profaning it.

Completely chilled, I walked upstairs as stealthily as a cat. I went into the bedroom without turning on a light; as I groped my way toward the bed, I tripped on something thrown over the bedrail, and it slipped under my hand. I picked it up from the floor and put it back, thinking: "Beauty is the veil of Beauty." Yes, but it's the veil *of* Beauty, and thanks to it we know Beauty: it's the veil that betrays her, even as it covers her. That soft warm silk is Quitina's robe, and Quitina herself is Quitina's tunic.

And so that night between Saturday and Sunday ended; I don't recall the date, but it must have been late May or early June. The next day fell on my blind spot, and I can't recall what Monday was like. I'm not even sure that Sunday was followed by Monday; I mean what had started might not have continued immediately. I know it got colder, winter made its presence felt in Las Murtas, and I followed along in a kind of cataleptic state, fixed rigidly where I'd fallen into position and blind to everything else.

Conscious purpose, none evident, but I recall well when my purpose became evident. I remember that I put the papers in their folder—I was on Juncal, of course—, stuck the fountain pen in my pocket and left the louvers on the shutters open, because the afternoon was so dark you couldn't tell where the sun was. I sat there for a while in front of the table, and maybe for a moment at first there was the start of an interior dialogue: "Why not?" "It's absolutely necessary." "Besides, it's possible." "It's absolutely possible."

If something like that was formulated within me, it faded immediately: all thought disappeared from my head. An inner process in which thought does not intervene is inconceivable; nevertheless, at that moment my mind was doing something similar to what a person does when he's trying to balance an object on one of its corners. By concentrating extremely hard, I was trying to tense up every one of my five senses, and there was one moment when I believed I'd done it; I felt the balance, the total harmony, but it lasted a very short while. In the middle of that silence, my consciousness said, "Something's lacking!" And of course, it was consciousness that was lacking. *Everything* had to enter into that experience; if it didn't, I was wasting my time. The most extraordinary thing was that I could feel the lack of consciousness, which was like a coldness. The result of it all was a cold, mechanical function, because the ingredient that represented *the why* was missing. Then I made my consciousness concentrate solely on *the why*, using a formula that read, more or less, "because, without this I cannot live." And very clearly, with a sudden presence, all the reasons began to ignite, throbbing, kindling, and inflaming the living motive that gives acts meaning.

I don't know if it took me a long or a short time to reach action. I know the first act required had me hesitating, as if my cumulative decision feared it would break down at the first movement. Rather, I hesitated as if I were afraid to be seen, which would mean that something of me had remained outside. But the first act required was simply to get up from the armchair and I could accomplish that without being seen.

I could also go over to the window and open it. There was light in the room below; they'd closed the windows and drawn the curtains, which were made of a sort of embroidered mesh, so that it was hard to see inside, although, by looking as hard as I could I managed to see, in spite of the mesh. The figures walking in front of the light cast their shadows on the curtain, and you could see them through the shadows, illuminated in their surroundings. Señor Filippo's wife was wearing a red sweater; a red eminence, when she walked in front of the light, the movements of her arms surrounded her with flashing liturgical red. But it was impossible to see what she was doing. She walked in front of the light again and again, always going toward the corner, where she would bend over as if to speak with someone or give them something. Fixed on the lighted window's rectangle, I was experiencing the sight of the window that I'd seen in the dark, exactly as it was at that moment when the old man in his corner, sunk in darkness, had waved his handkerchief and caused my brief delirium.

New reasons added fuel to the fire—for me there's nothing as combustible as reason—; like the fly, the tiny being who'd called to me with his white handkerchief represented a portion of discrete life that could *reasonably* be sacrificed to the verification of my power. The fly had to be a fly so I could make my *intention* clear without feeling any scruples. The little old man was a delicate victim who would succumb to the violence of my longing to know.

Once I dared to make up my mind, it was all a question of staying firmly on course and not letting my intention waver a single degree from my goal. Like the other times, exactly the same as the other times. Of course the effect could assume many different forms, but the result was always identical. It could be sudden and devastating, as with the fly; if this were the case, momentarily there would be a scream, the figures behind the curtains would become agitated, and the whole room would be thrown into turmoil. I held my breath, waiting for the tremor to rock everything in that drama on the illuminated stage; but all remained peaceful. This did not signify failure: things could play out in an entirely different way, they could take hours, occur in the way least expected.

It was intensely cold, so I closed the window. My hands were frozen and sore from holding onto the frame so tightly, and the latch was very stiff because it was rarely used. With great effort I got it to work, although it protested noisily, and amidst its screechings of rusted iron I heard a horrifying scream below. I turned the handle in the opposite direction, but even though I moved quickly, it took me a couple of seconds to make the latch work, and before the window was open I realized what the scream had been. Immediately I heard another cry and then a series of bellows and moans; I don't know why on cold nights cats in heat have to scream as if they had some terrible illness.

I closed the window again and went home. When I left, I'd asked them to have a fire going in the library and, as soon as I arrived, I made visible signs of needing to work late. Quitina didn't ask any questions. We ate almost in silence, but as we were finishing she suddenly asked me: "Why this sudden fury of work?"

"Oh, nothing. It's exactly what you said: I've been caught up in a fury."

She sat expectantly as if my explanation called for further development, so I continued.

"I have a lot of work, but there's nothing's pressuring me, and I don't have a deadline for finishing it. A few days ago I just started to work furiously so I could rest later. You know what I mean? The more tired you feel the more pleasurable it is to rest."

Quitina nodded in agreement, but her eyes registered disagreement and immediately she began to shake her head.

"I don't like either feeling tired or no longer feeling tired," she said.

"What do you like, then?"

"Not feeling tired."

She smiled with a childish, fake smile, as if to say: "See what a stupid thing I've said." It did not seem stupid to me, though. So many times I'd seen her run, swim, or ride a horse until she collapsed. She liked not feeling tired? I suspended my analysis, because I couldn't start one thing before I finished another.

"You like not feeling tired because you're tireless."

"Could be . . ."

There was another long silence, then I took her to her room and left her curled up under the comforter.

When I went downstairs, Rudy was waiting for me on the bottom step. "Let's go," I said to him, and I closed myself up in the library with him.

That same night I began to write in a notebook what would eventually be this tale, but I destroyed my first experiment several days later.

At that moment I hadn't made a clear decision about what plan I should follow for expressing most clearly what things suggest to me. For several hours, I filled a few pages with reflections, vague theories, until I came to the conclusion that I had to opt for telling my tale concisely: I ripped the pages from their metal spiral and threw them into the fire.

When I opened the door to let Rudy out into the garden, it was not yet light. There had been a frost in the garden, which seemed particularly white because the sky had cleared and was being watched by a waning moon still in its last quarter, high up. I didn't stop to contemplate the night because I thought, as I had in the Alvear: "No! Beauty, no; immersion in beauty relaxes the will."

As I was leaving Las Murtas early the next morning, my impatience to know and my need to repeat ritually things that I'd done in the past made me stop at the store and call Juncal. It was a few minutes after eight, so I thought the maid would have arrived, and in fact she did answer immediately. I asked her if there had been a telegram and she said no.

"Nothing new?" I added.

"No, sir," she said.

I didn't want to ask any more questions, but she would surely have told me if something had happened in the house. There was still time, though.

I got there still agitated from hurrying so much and from being overheated, because the clothing I'd put on was too heavy; when I was dressing, I remembered the frost from the night before but, as the sun rose, the temperature had started to rise. There was no wind and the street was quiet; as soon as I turned into Juncal I saw that great peace pervaded the entire block.

"It doesn't matter," I said. "It doesn't mean anything."

Javier's secretary was waiting for me in the office; he'd come to tell me about some possible modifications in the laws governing wages and layoffs. (Javier always kept his eyes open for me about things that concerned my holdings in Temis.) Attending to him was inevitable, which really annoyed me, both because attending to him totally was impossible for me and because this meant that the man was confirming my ineptitude: I didn't understand a word of his explanation.

But that wasn't only because of my inability—or unwillingness—to tear myself from the topic inside me; it was because at the same time I was listening to him, from the garden I could hear insistent, intermittent blows, which would stop periodically but then start in again right away. The sound was rising up through the window in the vestibule; I tried to identify it but could not, since we were talking. Suddenly I said: "Oh, yes!" It was not that I'd understood any the problems he was telling me about, and at that moment my exclamation was particularly irrelevant and inadmissible. I was about to say, "Oh, yes! They're splitting wood." But the second half of the sentence I could hold back. I justified the first half by explaining that I'd suddenly remembered something.

When I was showing him out, in the hall, he could not resign himself to leaving without repeating his explanations, which he'd seen fall into a void; but the sun was shining directly on the stained-glass panes and I was looking at the mauve, green, and rose panes that depicting some modernist water lilies in a lake, turned transparent by the radiant light in the garden, where you could hear the blows of the axe. That man, totally focused on his work and its procedures, saw me in the hall of my own house, looking at my stained glass as if I were a tourist in a museum, and he gave up trying to make me understand. He went off, thoroughly confused.

I opened the window.

The so-called garden was, in sum, a flowerbed less than three yards wide and a few plants. At the center there was a poinsettia, a very large plant covered with blossoms. Through its ragged leaves, I could see that the old man was sitting below, between the sun and the shade. And not only was he there, he was the very person chopping wood.

Without thinking any further, I went downstairs to the garden. I needed to see him close up, but I didn't stop to speak with him, because I couldn't hide my agitation. I said hello and walked on past to the water and gas meters at the back of the garden, pretending to be checking something. Then, when I had better control of myself, I walked over to him.

When I passed, he'd answered my hello with his light little voice, and when I stood close to him he raised a pair of clear blue eyes with healthy, clean lids.

"Mi scusa . . ." he started to say.

But at the same time I also began to give him a vague explanation of my make-believe chore at the meters, and he answered: "Sí, no e raro; these days everything breaks down."

I did my best to smile. His smile was so fresh that it won me over, and I didn't want my smile to be involuntary. Since it was so strange to see him outside, I asked him if he wasn't afraid to be sitting there in the open and he said no, it didn't do him any harm, and the only thing he suffered from was rheumatism. Once he'd gotten launched on his favorite subject, he kept expounding on it from different points of view, saying maybe he had rheumatism, maybe not. Everyone told him it was rheumatism, but he wasn't sure. Finally, as a conclusion: "Who knows what it is? Today, per esempio, I'm fine. Nothing hurts."

I wanted to make sure.

"Today you feel better than yesterday?" I asked him.

"I feel good, bene, benissimo. E la luna, señore, it's the moon. Didn't you see how it changed last night?"

6

The truth is, the obvious failure neither irritated nor overwhelmed me; rather, it released my tension. But not by reflecting, by understanding that things turned out better like this and would have been worse the other way. No, my release occurred through a natural biological process—forgetting. The drive within me for death and destruction died.

Even so, in my conscience I deliberately repeated several times that what the old man had experienced meant nothing, a thousand things could still happen, there had been nothing definitive, but this was merely an idea, cold and distant—outdated.

I set to work, making a few calculations about all the possible problems Javier's astonished secretary had raised for me, and soon it was quite late, so I grabbed a couple of sandwiches in a bar, considered them my lunch, and went home.

Feeling not at all uneasy, not deceiving myself one bit, throughout the day I frequently repeated to myself, "Something can still happen." But I saw early on that it was not going to: the only image alive in me was the life in those blue eyes, smiling beneath the plant, between the sun and the shade.

Much later, that night in the library, I began to feel rather spiteful, not because of my failure but because there had been a victory. "E la luna, señore, it's the moon."

What I wanted, even if it meant my undoing, was remote power, and a being far more remote than I was brimming with it. "E la luna," as everyone knows: it's the moon that manipulates the tides, influences seeds and pregnant women. The moon has that power and everyone acknowledges it. The little old man knew the moon was changing last night, and when his pains disappeared, he thought: "The moon carried them away." From his bed, with his eyes closed, he was probably recalling the face of Europe's moon, the face you can see only from this hemisphere by lying on the ground with your feet pointing toward the Southern Cross—as I discovered one night, stretched out on the grass, and my heart skipped a beat, the way it does when you run into a really old friend—; he was probably thinking about the moon, yielding to its influence with ancient docility. His thoughts were probably gravitating toward that mystery, like a vow thousands of years old obeyed by man since the first time he raised his head so he could see the moon's pale face shining in the sky. The moon's face, which is not a face, which is merely the moon, a mirror . . .

Then, is this what I had to understand? When man has that power, he's merely a moon?

Physical examples always turn out to be crude and limited; a person always finds it impossible to come to terms entirely with the supernatural event he's pondering, but that's just how myths are; besides, natural phenomena transmit revelations time after time. It's all a question of understanding those phenomena, and not because they should be considered rough examples; on the contrary, the first thing one must do is discard "a bit more or less"—because myths do hold a certain degree of accuracy.

Of course I know the moon is a body that travels through space, and it has its own mass and movements, which is the only reason it produces such strong effects. But at first people did not understand the moon this way; what they understood, and what must be understood here, is that with its pale face the moon watches over the secret work of seeds, fair weather at sea, or the growth of hair, and if a waning moon catches you, you must understand that a change in the moon's phases can carry off a storm, or a pain, or the flesh of a flounder.

That's what the little old man was talking about when he told me, "E la luna" with respect to the moon's face and light, so I would understand that he didn't really mean either its face or *its* light and that, even so, it's powerful from a distance.

The door opened silently, and Quitina came in. She shot me a glance that meant: "Wait a bit and you'll see." She went over to the fireplace, stirred the logs, drew a small armchair up to the fire, sat down on it; turning her torso toward me, and leaning on the arm of the chair, she made me wait a few moments to hear what she had prepared to tell me. In those moments I could see her smile, in which there was something innocently mischievous, capricious, or witty that struck me as light and playful. Maybe this was because, not far away, above her head, I could see the sylph at the same time, smiling over the fireplace.

Finally she spoke: "I bet you can't guess who I've been thinking about for two days . . . Señor Filippo."

Needless to say, I didn't answer. Quitina interpreted my silence as a question, and she added: "We have to find some way to eliminate him."

I was dismayed but managed to say: "Well, what's brought on such a sentence?"

"Oh, no crime he's committed; he's such a good man . . . That will just make things easier."

Quitina had started to tell me her plan, going straight to the point, but suddenly she felt overwhelmed by the colossal motive behind it all, and she could not help digressing: "You've got your head in the clouds! Don't you realize that things in Spain are about to end at any moment?"

"Why, yes, I know, but what difference does that make here?"

"It makes a difference here because if Herminia's husband comes out alive, he'll have to come here. Work, if he's able to work, will be hard for him to find, and the three of them can't be stuck in a rooming house indefinitely."

I took a deep breath.

"Uh-huh," I said, "now I'm beginning to understand."

Quitina recovered her smile.

"Besides," she said, "in any case, even if none of that were to happen . . . The other day Herminia told me how she loves to watch the rain in the garden, how there's nothing she finds more restful, and we can't live, we can't live the way we do while they're in that hole in the wall."

"No, of course not" I said, infinitely relieved.

Quitina laid out her plan. That first floor could be very comfortable once it had been renovated; the garden could become a real garden, even though not a very large one. As for señor Filippo's family, the children were getting older and they would soon need more space. There were new buildings going up all over the neighborhood, so it was only a question of finding them a good apartment and paying their moving expenses. Everything could be arranged amicably.

As soon as I managed to calm my spirits, I went over to sit on the carpet, at Quitina's feet, and we spent a long time planning, in great detail, what would have to be done. But even though I was paying attention very alertly to the things we were talking about, I didn't stop meditating—in another chamber of my brain—on the first few words Quitina had spoken: "I bet you can't guess who I've been thinking about for two days."

For two days, it turned out, the two of us had been thinking about the same thing, the same images had been passing through our minds: the long corridor running all the way to the back of the apartment and the series of rooms opening off from it; the path distributed among a few jasmines; the poinsettia with its bright red leaves, and the bougainvillea, almost always with a cage and a wet sweater hanging from its branches. That entire life, observed from our windows, had been turning up in our imaginations as something that had to be eliminated. Why? What was the reason that two goals with such different meanings converged right there? And why did they affect a similarity of expression? . . .

Quitina could have begun by telling me she was thinking about making some alterations in the house, she could have begun by speaking to me about Herminia's problems, but no, she began by planning to eliminate señor Filippo. I could not understand this at all.

Finally, while preparing a budget for a new kitchen, heating system, and refrigerator, I began to understand. When Quitina had tried to resolve Herminia's living situation, the first thing she'd thought of was that her solution would hurt the people who were already living in the apartment. Then, she'd reflected and understood that things could be arranged without hurting anyone; but the idea of doing some harm to señor Filippo muddied her real purpose of doing some good for Herminia. She didn't want to start by saying: "I want to give Herminia a present"; positively ashamed to put it in those words, she preferred to put it in these: "we're going to give señor Filippo a hard time."

Yes, that was it; I could see clearly into Quitina's soul and follow her thought processes, the way you can explain a law of biology without being afraid you're getting it wrong. Quitina, though, what did she know about my thoughts? Wouldn't she know something? Instead of shame because of her generosity, wouldn't there have been a desire to agree with me, even about evil?

No, that's not possible. I'd prefer a thousand times to have Quitina diverge from me than see her follow me to such an abyss. And above all, why does she have to follow me if I'm not there? I'm with her, I'm wherever she is. The other possibility is only something I've barely investigated, something that's trying to invade me, but something I have under control, because only in her am I whole.

That entire day and night, plus the days and nights following, I continued to ponder this, until two weeks later when the movers, along with the workers and deliverymen, arrived in full force. The pounding of pickaxes drove those ghosts out.

Negotiating it all turned out to be easier than I'd supposed at first, because several blocks from our house I immediately found something new and spacious smelling of fresh paint, and señor Filippo accepted it happily, observing that the large shop window would add something new and different to his business. There was nothing worth commenting on about the whole move.

Well, there was something, something childish and perverse, child-ishly perverse. It was, simply, that I myself took him there in my car. I insisted on placing the little old man in his new home. Señor Filip-po didn't want to accept, but his wife did, and the little old man got into the car, accompanied by his daughter-in-law, with a joy infrequent in younger, more robust people. Before starting the engine, I turned around to look at him sitting comfortably in the corner of the car. There was a certain nobility about his features, as if his head, which belonged to an age-old race, were a repository where the oldness of his stock com-bined with his own old age, and so much aging produced something indestructibly perennial.

Of course, "Could something still happen?" passed through my mind more than once during the ride, but I felt completely certain that noth-ing would.

Seeing death dead is a beautiful sight, even at the expense of accept-ing one's own impotence.

On Juncal the house was filled with pieces of green ceramic for the bathrooms, on the stairway you stepped in dust from the rubble, and in the car I carried samples of all the materials, taking them to Las Murtas for Quitina and Herminia to make their selections. Things continued like that until the month of September.

At first we'd thought about not saying anything to Herminia so we could surprise her, but this was impossible, partly because we wanted to take into account her taste, and partly because we wanted to keep her mind off things in Spain, where the Republicans were going under by the minute.

About Damián, there was no news; about my uncle, just an occasional word through the embassy that he was still fighting with the resistance in Madrid. Quitina's father was the only one from whom we received letters regularly, and through him we knew that everything would be over in a few months.

Herminia behaved with great fortitude, hiding her despondency so as not to depress Quitina—always treating her tremendous health as something very delicate—, but it's hard to weigh one's words, and silence is impossible.

One Saturday, Herminia and Miguel had come to Las Murtas; we were having lunch, spring had arrived for us, and there were upholsterer's samples on the tablecloth, along with a sketch made by an architect friend so we could build the study upstairs and that way finally get everything finished. Even Miguel had brought an ad for a fluorescent light that he wanted for his room more than anything else.

Doing, doing something, deciding that a particular thing has a particular form and then cutting it out, nailing, or gluing it together however you want . . . Matter itself feels so good in man's hands, all you have to do is pick things up, and use them for whatever occurs to you. Of course, before you can pick things up you have to purchase them, because everything must be purchased, everything must be paid for. That's the law, but actually there's also great beauty in commerce. It's almost as pleasant to acquire things by purchasing them as it is to make them, and sitting there after we'd finished eating, we were all filled with the highly satisfactory activity of selecting and building. Also, there was not much difference in our tastes—was this really the case or did everyone comply with mine?—and we'd point to a color or a detail and glance at each other approvingly.

But Herminia was too rigorous to leave things less than clear; her gaze and the smile that had been her contribution to our conversation did not carry the specific weight of truth, and she wanted to explain. Looking serious for a moment, she touched a piece of tussah, as if she were studying the weave.

"I don't know how I could possibly explain all this to you," she said finally. "It makes me so happy . . . everything matches my taste so well that not even in my dreams, but when I think about *why it is*, you understand? How can I be truly happy? Even so, I am. That's what's most appalling, because at the same time I feel despair."

It wasn't because Quitina's voice struck my ear immediately after Herminia's—Quitina's voice was also clear and smooth—that right then her voice sounded hoarse and dull.

"Among all the . . ." Quitina said, but she didn't say any more; she sat without speaking and held her breath, trying to get control of an irresistible emotion.

After a long silence, she spoke: "Of all the things that have happened to you, I think this would be the hardest to endure."

"Oh, no," Herminia said, "given the things that have happened to me, it would be impossible to know which is the worst, but in any case, this one is not more than I can stand; it just sours my happiness."

"Well, that, that's what horrifies me, that your happiness might be soured, which seems worse to me than if it were taken away from you."

"I don't know . . . ," Herminia said, puzzled. "If I had the choice . . ."

"You wouldn't choose to have it taken away entirely, I know that, and I might not either if I were in your situation, but those aren't things we get to choose. What I was meant was, sometimes I've seen people who can't be happy anymore, and I've seen others who've stopped being sad; but to feel happiness and despair at the same time about things that give rise equally to both emotions. If I were in your situation . . ."

Quitina was immersed in that situation, living a possible situation in which she found indistinguishable opposites; I couldn't imagine what hostile ghosts might be battling within her, but the battle made her turn pale and breathe with difficulty.

"When the situation arises, we all bear up better than we thought we would."

"Yes, I know, and I'm not saying I wouldn't bear up, but look, in the movies, for example, you always put yourself in the other person's place, because that's why you go, and only sometimes do you say, no, I can't put myself in this situation, not even for the time being. Things that make you afraid are also actually pleasant, and later you like to remember them, even if not all of them. I recall that when I was a little girl, when I saw something like that I would end up saying, 'Why should I have seen that? Why would I have needed to see that?'"

"I will never feel sorry enough that you heard this," Herminia said. Quitina had calmed down by now, and she answered her: "Why? If you can't avoid having it happen to you, I shouldn't be able to avoid knowing about it."

Then she smiled and tried to erase everything with a clever remark: "The two of you look so troubled! Don't worry; I won't have a miscarriage over some little thing like this. It's time for my nap."

She walked out of the dining room. As she started to move, spring once more filled the room. Quitina was spring, but not the prepubescent kore; she was an opulent spring blooming with conception, a maternal spring. She was a virgin mother, as Unamuno would say.

Because the mystery Unamuno referred to was occurring in Quitina; between her virginity and her maternity there was no space, and the space not there was not suffering because it did not exist. I realize this is unthinkable, but I'm not going to amend it.

Around Quitina's glorious maternity there was an intrusive spirit—Miss Ray, who was absolutely essential, given the prospect of a new baby. Her presence meant that the luxuriance of nature, the sensuality of an animal's den, of a newborn baby sticking to its mother's flesh, which are part of birth, were all sanitized, regulated, reduced to discrete proportions. Missing at that moment of transit was the chorus of compassionate crones who would have praised Quitina's youth, expounding the luxuriance of blood as only old village women know how.

This seems like a banal display of obscurantism, but it's not. Neither is it an excessive love of the bestial. Both in me and in the people I care about the bestial is something I would always want to see conquered; no; not conquered, overcome.

All this comes to mind because of Miss Ray, since I have the apprehension, as Quitina does, that our son's life is too orderly. I don't know if that's because he's too docile, or if he might be too healthy. His health scares me—although I'm grateful for it and I know it's a priceless gift, it still scares me because I see his vitality as a particular kind of confidence that goes right to its mark, and I'm afraid of the obstacles that sprout from the ground. He has my vitality and I know I deserve those obstacles. When I see the confidence and happiness in his gaze I wonder: which brilliantly colored flowers will be the ones stamped in his memory as a cipher of that luminous region? And where will the limits of that region begin?

But it's not yet time to pour any of this into the still.

At the beginning of October, the weather was warm, the windows were half open, and one day the doctor and his host of white robes took possession of the house. Quitina said it was not worth the trouble to go to a clinic, and so our son Jorge was born at Las Murtas. Another shoot from Quitina's body; impeccable and shiny, it moved in the hollow of her arm, seeming to sprout from her, strong as the buds on a chestnut tree.

Around the same time there was a change in our household routine that involved the questionable importance shared by everything recounted so far: in early October I began to sleep in the tiny garret-like room we continued to call Monington's room. The field had to be left open for Miss Ray, who needed to put the baby beside Quitina's breast at the right time and, watch in hand, after ten minutes, and not a second more, snatch him away with inexorable gentleness.

That tiny room had become almost like an attic; a stack of rejected books and a few suitcases had ended up there. More than a room, it's a tower reached by a flight of stairs in the upstairs hall, and because of the height it has a view the rest of the house doesn't. From the other rooms you can see the garden; from this one you can see the countryside.

I moved in there, temporarily, of course. My moving in, a sofa and a desk, the ones Monington had used, along with a pile of books and papers, is what I'm recording as important. Next I have to talk about the other things that happened—dramatic, tremendous things, events of incalculable dimension—but I'll mention them all quickly.

Summer arrived and Christmas passed, the way it does here—unnoticed. (I'm seized by a desire to lose myself in a long digression about Christmas in the New World, Christmas and asepsis, and Christmas and the Southern Hemisphere, but I have to get to the point.)

Toward the first of the year, the apartment on Juncal was finished as though made to order; rather, it was finished very promptly, something you have a hard time getting to happen when things are made to order.

No sooner was the garden finished than we had a real downpour. The only work done there had been at the very back, where they'd widened the border, which was now a bed of acanthus and philodendron; and at the foot of the wall they'd planted some climbers. As soon as the plants were in, the rain started to fall in droves. It's unusual for us to have heavy rain in January, but it rained for more than a week, with the sun coming out only very early each morning—a summer sun that had everything burning hot by nine o'clock. Soon, there would be multiple electrical storms forming on the horizon, and the storm cloud would remain for hours, covering everything with a fringe of water. The garden thrived on this diet of water and sun, and soon it looked like a grown-up garden. Everything was washed clean; the particles of lime left by the workers disappeared down the drain; in the new bed of shrubs the water formed its natural channels and the grass took hold, turning green everywhere.

They moved in over the holidays. Herminia didn't work fixed hours; she did translations for a publisher of scientific books, gave lessons in everything that came along, and still had time to publish book reviews in a magazine. It could all be put aside for a few days, freeing her to get the apartment set up.

Miguel had just taken his final exams, and he was hoping to finish high school the following year, at Salvador. Herminia had insisted that he go there because she wanted him to study humanities no matter what the effort.

In January, Herminia said spiritedly: "This year, with so many comforts, we're going to work without noticing the world's existence." But in February the world shouted so loudly we all had to pay attention.

The war's ending in Spain was a relief, but those final days were filled with such horror. Above all, since no army had been driven back, it took great effort to believe that all the internal whirlpools had suddenly grown calm.

We began to receive cables from both sides. At last, my uncle, who'd taken refuge in the embassy when Madrid fell, let us know he was alive, but there was no way to convince him to come; he said he would not leave Spain as long as he lived. Damián wrote from France, and we immediately took the steps necessary to bring him. That was no trouble; the only difficulty was coming to any understanding with him, because his answers made no sense and it was impossible to tell if he wanted to come or not. But Herminia said we shouldn't waste time thinking about whether or not he wanted to come; the only thing to do was bring him, and finally he arrived.

For Damián's arrival Quitina again had put bright-colored flowers on the table, and as I drove to the dock to pick him up, I was again expecting hair-raising tales about the retreat, but Damián didn't say even half a dozen words on the trip and, when we got home, he showed no sign of the agreement with which Herminia had responded to the scene prepared for her. She had accepted the restfulness, like one who's been aching to find it for a long time. Damián tried to accept it, courteously, but like one who can't rest and doesn't want to.

I would prefer to tell about all this very superficially, but there is a series of details I can't pass over: the visual facts, the way things and people looked—a kind of physiognomy of the event, in which people and things are mixed together.

While we were driving to the port to pick up Damián, I said to Herminia: "Maybe it would be better to take him directly to Juncal. He might prefer to rest a day at home and come to Las Murtas later; he'll probably want to be alone with the two of you."

Herminia nodded in agreement rather uncertainly, as if to say: "Yes, that's probable, but it's also probable that he won't."

Miguel, of course, didn't even move his head.

Once Damián was with us, I made the same suggestion to him, letting the choice be his.

"Whatever all of you want," he answered, "whatever you want. As far as luggage goes, as you see, all I have is this—a small suitcase that doesn't weigh anything—and I don't need to rest or bathe or anything. That's all I've been doing on the boat for three weeks."

"The best thing is to go to Las Murtas," Herminia then said decisively. "We'll stay there until Monday, and then we can start the week on Juncal."

That's what happened, and what I spent the whole day considering as if it were something that made sense, a sense that of course continued to escape me, was Damián's external appearance and the inside of his suitcase.

Damián was tall, broad-shouldered, erect; nothing about his attitude advised depression, but he was nearly fifty years old and his hair and moustache were completely white. It was impossible to tell if he'd been blond or dark-haired; his eyes were rather dark, but his eyebrows were white, like his hair. His skin seemed bronzed from the sun, except on his hands and in the whites of his eyes you could see a hint of jaundice. When he arrived, he was wearing a black suit, highly polished black shoes, black socks, an impeccably white shirt, and a black bow tie. The knot was narrow and it seemed to have been tied carelessly, because the bow drooped a little, giving him the air of a provincial poet; in contrast, his hair was parted on the left side and cut very short, military style.

Once we were at Las Murtas, Herminia told him it would be better if he changed into a suit more appropriate for the country, but he said that he didn't have another suit. He'd crossed the border in his uniform. In Paris, the refugees received some money from the Republican government to get them through the first days of exile and he had purchased only that one suit and a little underwear.

As he explained all this, we were in the bedroom and Quitina was saying: "These beds are for the two of you; Miguel will sleep on the couch in the library."

Damián agreed, automatically.

"Great, great," and as we were on our way down to the dining room, he stopped: "Wait a minute," he said, "I'm going to get some cigarettes from my suitcase." Then he added, as if he had finally found a few words he could say without effort: "I like French tobacco much more than American."

"So do I," I said, and I stood beside him, waiting while he got the cigarettes from his suitcase.

He put the suitcase on two chairs and opened it all the way, feeling around in one side and then other until he pulled six packs of Gauloise from beneath some shirts. When he'd taken the cigarettes out of the suitcase, everything that was left in it formed a contrast of black and white. On one side, there were a few white shirts, with rolls of black socks in the corners; on the other side, a few equally white items, on top of them a black oilskin notebook and a black leather toiletry kit.

My noticing all this is stupid, and trying to give it some meaning is even more stupid. Nevertheless, I noticed it and I'm writing it down here, because there was something at least distinctive about it all.

They spent four days with us, and since Damián showed not the slightest intention to tell us anything about the war, we all very much wanted him to tell about it. We didn't want to ask him outright, but we tried to steer the conversation in that direction. The first day we talked about some item or other in the paper on what was brewing in Europe—it was June of 1939—and I said, in order to say something: "It wouldn't surprise me at all, after what we've seen in Spain."

"What have you people seen?" Damián interjected. "Have you seen anything?"

No one answered and he continued: "Because for my part I've seen nothing. Nothing! I've seen less than a blind man."

Wanting to placate him, Quitina said, "Yes, I understand; the best thing you can do is forget it as if you'd never seen it."

He appeared not to have heard her.

"Ever since I've been able to think for myself," he continued, "I've grown accustomed to understanding what I see, and now I see things and understand nothing, absolutely nothing of what's going on. I do not call this seeing. But if there is someone who believes *he has seen* something, would he please explain it to me."

Damián's voice had not been strident, but it had been very hard for him; beneath his bridling discretion quivered a violence similar to delirium. I answered him forcefully so that my impulsive response would make him believe that his violent tone seemed natural to us.

"You've already explained it," I said. "What better definition? Those of us who watched from a distance thought we were seeing something—today this, tomorrow something else—but you've seen what it really is: something incomprehensible."

My answer did not placate him, it disconcerted him; I was making his discourse seem reasonable and that wasn't what he wanted. He'd blurted out those instances of incongruence in order not to let slip some sharp remark, such as: "Don't talk about things you know nothing about" or "You people have no right even to think about those things." That's what remained inside him, that and a tiredness, a skepticism when confronted with an answer, a desire to escape toward a kind of inner dementia where instead of repose there was disorder and the freedom it afforded. All this became clear to me in his faltering attempt to follow the conversation, when he really felt like telling me to go to hell, getting up, and leaving.

"It's curious," he said, "how that would have seemed like an explanation to you. Evidently, the world is divided between those who think they understand and those who know we don't understand."

"Well, so be it. That's why you explain it perfectly, because you know."

That was more or less the first anguished conversation, the day he came. It was a Thursday, on Friday nothing important happened. Herminia and Damián took a walk in the countryside; it was natural they would want to be by themselves. But I don't think there was even a minimum of harmony in their conversations. Miguel was as happy as if his father had come for a vacation. He took him to see the factory and gave him a better explanation of how everything worked than any technician could have provided. Then he took him to the henhouse and, finally, to the back of the garage to show him a top he'd made; it spun with an obsessing fixedness, seemingly nailed to one spot.

On Saturday afternoon, García telephoned. He hardly ever came to the factory now. We had a secretary who took care of anything pertaining to work, but when things in Spain reached the definitive stage, García appeared three or four times to find out what was happening, asking about everyone with great interest. The last time he'd said to

Herminia: "When your husband gets here, I'll come to offer him my services."

And he came on Saturday. Rather, they came, in their enormous car—Julieta, plumper, blonde, and smiling in folds of astrakhan, and García, immaculate and humble, as always.

"He's a total gentleman," García told me in an aside; "you can tell just by looking at him."

And there, as we were having tea with the Garcías, arose another of the conversations that weigh like storm clouds. Suddenly, Rudy came in from the garden and went over to Damián, who had petted him a few times, stood on his back paws and put his front paws, which were very muddy, on the black suit. Damián brushed himself off a little and said: "It doesn't matter."

"Of course not," Herminia added; "you can remove mud with a brush."

Then, as if she hoped that basing herself on a recent event would be persuasive, she said to Damián: "You're going to have to buy another suit right away."

"I don't think so," he said, "this one's fine."

"Not that there's anything wrong with it; it's just not appropriate for coming out to the country."

Herminia kept hoping to persuade him.

"I don't know why a person can't be in the country with this suit."

"I could tell you it's because it's not practical. Besides, though, you have to change sometime; no one wears black at all hours of the day."

"What do you mean no one?"

In the tone of that question, delirium already quivered. He received no answer, and in the midst of the overall silence he added, "Croupiers."

García burst out laughing.

"What a crazy idea, don Damián! What a crazy idea! To compare yourself with a croupier!"

"And why not?"

"Because . . . because, well . . ." García began to fear he wasn't sharp enough to answer such a clever joke: "Because I think there's some difference between a colonel and a croupier . . ."

"Well you're wrong, completely wrong"—great confusion in García's gaze, even greater violence in Damián's voice—; "you're wrong, because they are two things exactly alike."

We all tried to get García out of that hole; we smiled, to help him smile, and finally García smiled: "Well, you must mean . . ."

"They're the same; don't you see they're the same? What difference do you see between a command and a 'no more bets'? Eh? What difference do you see?"

"Caramba!"

That "caramba" could just as easily have indicated that there was a lot of difference as that the comparison was surprising. García took refuge in it.

"You've seen how a croupier spins the ball?"—affirmative nod from García—"well, what an artillery colonel does is exactly the same. That's what being a colonel is, you understand, nothing more than that—you spin the ball."

García was at a loss for words, precisely because he understood the full significance of the drama that moments before he'd thought a joke. He shrugged his shoulders and agreed by bending his head a little, as if it were weighed down by a massive piece of evidence. The rest of us jumped into the ring so as to put an end to that situation; we coughed and everyone talked at once, somehow or other breaking through the oppressive atmosphere in which we'd suddenly found ourselves.

Before sunset, they left, and until the last minute García wore the expression he'd assumed upon understanding. Even when he was in the car, while Julieta was repeating her last good-byes, I saw him with his head bent forward, as if he were carrying something enormous on his shoulders, and, what's remarkable, carrying it proudly; even more remarkable, you could tell he felt proud by the respectful way he was carrying it.

I'm getting off the subject by talking about García so much, but I can't help expressing my admiration for such a modest man. I have to make it clear that even though to me pride is second—or first—nature, I overestimate those beings who possess great humility: even though I consist totally in will and action, I can admire their passive integrity. What is García? A man who is only good for being there. But that *being there* he does better than anyone else. You can be sure that his *being there* will not desert.

Watching him as he grew distant in their magnificent car, I was thinking about the Cid: "God, what a good vassal . . ."

That Saturday night we slept peacefully, but you could say that our Saturday witches' sabbath had decisively closed one of the countless circles of the curse from overseas. The vortices of those whirlwinds in the heart of Spain, which we assumed could not be calmed, could form anywhere—no matter how far away—wherever the two currents met, wherever destiny brought them into confrontation unexpectedly. That night Quitina's father arrived at the Morón airport. He found no one waiting for him—the cable was received at Las Murtas the next day—and he went to the hotel. Since he did not want to phone until eight in the morning, when he called, Quitina, Herminia, and Miguel had gone to Mass. As they left, I saw Damián looking at them with the furious perplexity that was a sign of impending explosion, and I said quickly: "Come on, we'll get away from here. I'm going to show you . . ."

I have no idea what I showed him; I put him in the car and didn't stop until Cacharí. So when Quitina's father called, the maid told him none of us were home, and he left for Las Murtas without saying who had called, in order to surprise us.

It's impossible and unnecessary to describe step by step how things occurred. He arrived a little before we sat down to table; we saw a taxi coming through the gate and said: "Someone's coming, but who is it?"

We went out to the door and saw who it was.

The most disconcerting thing was the apparently natural course that the events took. Nothing happened at first, and the whole time we kept telling ourselves inside: "Nothing has happened yet."

Of course the effusiveness of the first moment, our happiness at seeing him back again, and his enthusiasm about the children prevented us from paying attention to anything else at first. The introductions were a little rushed and he responded with generous, nondiscriminating cordiality: they were our guests, our relatives, and for the moment they were nothing more. The others, especially Damián, received him properly: he was our father, for the moment.

Then lunch arrived, then coffee, and then the insurmountable silences.

Herminia knew that unless she wanted to bring that situation to an abrupt end, the only way she could lighten it up was to talk about her family's need to leave before too long, and she began to allude to their departure. She asked me when we would leave for Buenos Aires, and I said: "At four, if that seems all right to you."

We'd already agreed on this the day before; also we both knew, exactly, how long the trip would take, since we made it twice a week, but even so, we talked about the amount of time we needed to allot, about how the afternoons were beginning to grow shorter, about all the things that can keep themselves going for hours as you talk about them, although when you remember them you have no heart for writing down the banal words in which they were covered. But silence, which you would like to reproduce, you cannot. You cannot describe a smell or a melody, much less the silence in which we drift like floating islands, each of us burdened with his own thoughts, trying to avoid a collision, knowing that the least friction could cause a cataclysm.

When we could say nothing more about how long the trip was going to take or about how the suitcases would not take up too much room, it occurred to me to say to Miguel: "I assume you've left all your things straightened up in the garage. There's no way to stop someone from going in and misplacing one of your parts."

Quitina's father was interested in what Miguel was building, and between the two of them they carried on a dialogue that let the rest of us sit back for a few minutes. It was so reassuring to hear Miguel explain the mechanism in a top; as long their conversation lasted we could breathe.

"That's the best thing a boy your age can do," Quitina's father said. "Builders, inventors, technicians are what's needed in . . ."

We all would have liked to cover our ears, the way people do when a bomb's about to fall, but we managed not to shift our positions, and we heard with relief: " . . . in these times."

Did he correct himself? Did he veer gracefully at the last moment? I think so, because the sentence turned out to be so unsatisfactory that he perfected it right away.

"I mean they're needed if they have creative talent, because there are too many of the kind who don't."

It seemed to us that he'd avoided the obstacle, but the conversation continued: "And do you have much left before you graduate from high school?"

"No, I'll finish next year."

"And is the high school curriculum specialized here?"

"I don't know how it is in the public schools, but at my school we study humanities."

"Humanities! Humanities!" Damián let out, as if from another world. "That's what's happening; a person has lived in the belief that there was one humanity, and it turns out there are several humanities."

To redirect his ranting, bring him back to reality, make him return to his previous intention of containment, was already impossible. Even so, I tried: "That's why it's necessary to study them all, to try to understand them all."

"Understand them! Now it's a question of understanding. It would be better to demolish the humanities, before they finish by degrading them all."

Quitina's father, who always spoke vivaciously, who was almost always smiling, said solemnly: "It falls to some to finish what others started."

Here the dialogue was no longer a dialogue. The rest of us intervened in order to lessen the violence in their argument, but it was useless. In truth they were not arguing, they were giving vent to an avalanche of reproaches. They both wanted to revoke the other's charges with even stronger accusations, but the reasons behind their attacks did not respond to each other. Those of us who had not lived the drama day by day, those of us who did not know the faces that belonged to the names they mentioned nor knew exactly what it was like on a certain day when such and such a thing occurred, could not judge whether the answers made no sense because of a radical difference between the two men or because of an inevitable confusion, since they were dealing with issues that in the end implied something like death from discord.

One of them would talk about what the others did on a particular date, the other would answer with what people were afraid those on the opposing side were capable of doing to their side, and it almost always turned out that whatever needed to be done was the cause of whatever had been done initially. Then they began lamenting everything that should have been done and was not, insulting the accomplices who helped and cursing those who did not help.

The curious thing was that both of them were merciless when they condemned their enemies, but when they attacked the people who had refused to give any support they did seem to be in agreement, and they joined their insults, reinforcing them with shared disdain. To both, one's having belonged to the other side was despicable, but one's having been an indifferent spectator was vile beyond description. When either of the two referred to *them*—it was Damián who did this most often—the other remained respectfully silent, so the indisputable epithets could be heard clearly.

Four o'clock passed in this way, and then it was five.

Suddenly Quitina said: "It's gotten very late. Why don't you give up the idea of going now and get an early start in the morning?"

Damián's tone changed, as if the interruption had broken his momentum. He answered Quitina, directing his condescension at her markedly as he broke off the argument: "No, Quitina, we're going to retreat, we're in open retreat."

"About that you're wrong: *here* we are the ones in retreat," Quitina's father said, also without violence.

"The thing is that *here*," Damián said, tending again toward delirium, "you are not you, we are not us; *here*, quite simply, we're no one."

"About that, I must acknowledge that you are not wrong."

Taking advantage of such a deplorable armistice, we left.

7

I said at the beginning that these pages would not be memoirs because I did not want to give in to the voluptuousness of recalling; nevertheless, I'm gradually slipping into that.

When someone mentions memories, we always assume that amorous memories are meant, and this happens because in reality all memories are amorous. Even when you're recalling horror or disappointment, you wind up creating an amorous intimacy. Those of us who live by recalling—which is not living from one's memories, it's not living a preterit magnified by fantasy; it's living a present that faces up to memory and responds to it—, those of us who live by recalling so revitalize our memories that they can even offer us surprises. A memory that until yesterday was gray and vague, in the presence of current experience, sparkles and stands out in unsuspected relief. But I repeat, this is not what I set out to relate.

I began these pages in order to study a part of my life that without them would remain unexpressed—a series of inner events, the most dramatic and oppressive that I've ever lived, although I know full well that if I did not record them here, the day could come when not only would I not believe I'd lived them, I would not even admit to having thought them.

I'm recording those events before I judge them. I don't know if later I'll find them abominable, sublime, or idiotic, but I know that in a few years when I read these pages I won't be able to doubt that they filled my mind for the time it took to write them.

The decision to relate the events as a narrative is what led me to dwell too long on so many minor details. I could have written my narrative as an essay, I could have structured my experiences and reflections theoretically, but I believe I would still have wound up doubting. A day would come when it would seem to me that I'd invented them and, no, I've not invented them. I've lived them.

Here they're mixed with life, and, as life's lovers, we like to bear witness to life and every one of its pores. That sort of thought and that sort of passion are our Himalayas, but no beloved, no being, large or small, whom we've touched with our eyes can be forgotten. As passion or thought roared like distant thunder above our depths, someone pronounced a word, made a gesture, a movement of the hand that, along with the same inner spasm, will arise in our memories perpetually, and, sometimes it will even seem more credible. To narrate it, copying faithfully what we had before our eyes in an immediate way, is much more satisfying than precisely explaining the evasive phenomenon that evolved behind our retinas. That's what I must explain, curbing my desire to transcribe every word uttered, every change of light. So I won't insist on spelling out in detail how everything ended; I'll just note the indispensable.

The three of us stayed at Las Murtas and talked with complete freedom about what had happened. Quitina's father was happy, but he didn't seem intoxicated with the victory. He said winning the war had always been a sure thing; the hard part was only beginning now. But he didn't plan to get involved in politics. He was hoping his services would be repaid with a comfortable, peaceful post, and he would like it if they named him the commercial attaché for some embassy, which would allow him to cut back on his activities, now beginning to tire him, but he would continue to be useful in any way he could. We said this was a wonderful idea, thinking he could come to Buenos Aires; but he shook his head, telling us: "No, not here. You know I can't stand it here more than three days. Havana, though, would be a different story."

That time he stood it a little more than three days, but not as many as six; on the fifth day, he left. For him, Buenos Aires was the city he'd once left without warning, and as soon as he arrived, right from the start he felt the need to repeat that action. I'm sure that after he'd attended to his affairs, with the mechanical precision that ran by itself on the track of his experience, he would enter his true reality as the plane took off, thinking as he looked at Buenos Aires, "I'm going and you're staying . . ." Even though the woman who had inspired that revenge was now under the ground, it didn't matter, and each time he departed, the eternal nature of his revenge left her abandoned all over again.

There was a period of difficult adjustment between the house on Juncal and Las Murtas. The first weeks, Miguel came by himself to spend Saturday and Sunday, then all three of them started to come, and when I went to the office I would often stop by and visit them for a while.

Damián's mood never varied. Herminia and Quitina decided it was necessary to find him a job; the trouble was that not being employed depressed him and he felt inadequate when he was not contributing anything to the upkeep of the household. We tried to find him a job, but that was difficult. What work can you give to an artillery colonel? In the battle for life that's waged in the city, people weren't accustomed to using such noisy methods. Nevertheless, I managed to find him a vague but varied position in the editorial department of the magazine *Técnica*: he was to be in charge of the business side, which consisted primarily of the ads, but he would also be somewhat involved in layout and he would correct proofs. Since the magazine was bimonthly, this didn't amount to much work. The compensation was almost imperceptible, but the task kept him occupied, and I'm tempted to say that he didn't find it disagreeable.

The work didn't change his state of mind, but at least it allowed him to vary his life a bit. When they were preparing an issue, he would leave in the morning, or he would bring the proofs back to the house and spend hours going over them. Then, once the issue had been sent off, he had a few days of inactivity, and he spent most of the time sleeping, or at least he stayed in bed. Herminia and Miguel would go on with whatever they had to do, and he wouldn't move. When the cleaning woman entered and saw that his room was closed up, she would straighten everything without making a sound, and he'd lie there in the dark, asleep or awake, until it was time for lunch.

When Damián did not come to Las Murtas, Herminia would try, not to make excuses for him, because she knew we all excused him, but at least to explain his behavior. In fact, now that Damián was here, now that we knew him, she talked about him much more than before. It was as if before she hadn't wanted to judge him until she saw how things turned out, or as if she herself had not been able to explain him well until now. And when she tried to explain him to us, she was also explaining herself, because she'd never talked much about herself either.

Between them the only difference concerned their ideas about religion; this is the greatest difference possible, but one that is more a matter of individual nature than ideas. It seems ridiculous to believe there is one nature disposed to religious beliefs and another opposed to them. That's not what I mean; I'm saying that there are ideas and there are fundamental attitudes. This is where they differed. Damián *was* an atheist, a materialist, and an idealist. It's not that he thought that way, he *was* that way. Herminia *was* a believer, she *was* a Catholic and a realist. Not believing in God seemed insane to her; periodic doubt seemed a waste of time.

Why they married, what their early youth was like, are things I can't imagine; I always found them very distant from me, very old, but old only because they were marked by adversity. After all, the age difference is not so great, but their world is finished, and it even seems as if it had not existed. Yes, there is something unborn about them and their entire generation, something extracted as if by force and at the wrong moment and therefore something fundamentally failed. His carelessly knotted bow tie was really one you would see on a provincial poet, although he was not provincial, but his ideal collaboration of pen and sword was. Because for Damián, the militia was *the sword*—even though he was an artilleryman—, it was the sword, the physical arm of one's honor, the mainstay of moral values, the prow of freedom, and all the other clichés. The height of his career came at the end of the 1914 war, when he was twenty-eight. His campaign experiences amounted to nothing more than a brief stint in Morocco and a nice wound that earned him a promotion. When he returned to the Peninsula, the climate was that of a world in which a drop of blood would never be spilled again. Then he did battle in literary competitions and was inclined toward politics, literary politics, because Damián was a cultured soldier, a pacifistic, an anti-militaristic soldier.

Herminia, in contrast, was provincial, although she didn't seem to be. She'd been born in Segovia and received her doctorate in literature there. From Segovia she'd escaped to England, on a scholarship, and she'd made good use of the time; her culture and her demeanor were completely European. But her provincial core remained intact: in it was rooted her faith, free of vicissitudes, which she defended shrewdly when necessary, saying to herself: "You can all go your way, and I'll go mine."

They must not have married when they were very young. Herminia was already thirty when Miguel was born. About this I'll say nothing: her stubborn innocence is still mysterious to me.

Those are the most basic characteristics of the three beings that Providence placed in our city, and never could it be said more fairly than he who gives receives. I, in particular, took care of myself by taking care of them; in other words, the attention I paid to their affairs pulled me out of my ponderings, afforded me a vacation in the hot springs that soothe my affliction, in the springs of forgetting.

Quitina, for her part, was absorbing Herminia's experience; neither her physical appearance nor her behavior was changing, but you could see her maturing. I think the spectacle of those highly combated lives made her look reflective. Because I definitely cannot believe that she had any problem of her own, any change in her inner landscape. Life must have continued to be pleasant and easy for her; if it were not I would have no right to life.

Since my uncle persisted in his refusal to come over, it was not possible to convince him to leave clandestinely, so Quitina's father promised that when he returned to Spain he would take care of his legal situation. There had to have been some charge against him because he was a solid Republican, but since he never bore arms and since he only served as a medic, the charge could not be too serious, and with influence a person could get him released. I planned to go and bring him back as soon as we received word that everything was solved. But the negotiations dragged on, and then it was September.

What happened in Europe caused no less consternation because people expected it. At home, as everywhere else, we were glued to the radio, we would wake up and rush for the newspaper, hoping for something as absurd as a stone falling through the air, against all expectations, stopping before reaching the ground. But there's no need to say anything about this: we're in it.

When Damián would come to the estancia we hardly dared to make any comments because his comments were hair-raising. "Magnificent! Magnificent!" he said continually. "Now they'll see, all right."

Only once did I hear him say, with some lucidity, as if he were giving in and providing us with an explanation of what he was thinking about: "Now they'll have to do what they didn't do."

But when we were listening to the news or when someone would come with more information, he always had the same quip: "Magnificent! A splendid spectacle." And he would continue to stare into space, looking as if he were burying his eyes in some special, private estancia in hell.

During those same days we received a letter from Quitina's father, a long letter, which was unusual for him. Its size alarmed me; I immediately feared some difficulty, but it was something much worse; it was the worst thing possible. He began by giving me that news and then he explained everything that had happened. When he started the proceedings to secure my uncle's release, he had gone to see him at the embassy and had found him quite shattered; above all, he was totally indifferent to his release, and he even tried to dissuade Quitina's father from the endeavor. But he'd continued, and the day he was certain he would have the release, when he phoned in the morning to say he'd be there at the very end of the day with the papers signed, they'd told him my uncle had come down with a terrible case of the flu; it was diagnosed as pneumonia a few hours later, and when Quitina's father arrived with the papers and an ambulance to pick him up, all he could do was stay with him until it was all over.

It's so different to say, "I'm sorry for some sin I've committed, I recognize there was evil, and therefore error, which is naturally repugnant, in what I did, and now that I understand my guilt I am sorry," all that is so different from feeling that guilt has us choked with anguish and that we're trying to understand where our guilt lies but there is no way to tell. My uncle's death—still very recent—makes me approach a new abyss in my fallibility. Since I know I'm mortal, I must be ready to admit that my power failed, though it is vital for me that it not fail; but now I wonder: could there also be a flaw in my loving?

That's still unresolved; I don't see an answer to that question. I'm terrified of seeing it; I don't want to look, and I won't look, until I'm certain that when I do there will be no flaw.

The thing is, since my uncle's death, I have the feeling of not having paid a debt. But a debt for what? And how should I have paid it? I don't know, but eventually I hope to understand.

Damián's comment was: "What a pity! To leave just as the concert's beginning."

I too had the impression that my uncle had left like a once-hopeful person grown tired of waiting, like a person who understands that he can no longer expect anything and, perhaps deep down, I wanted to reproach him for not waiting a little longer, for having deprived me of the chance to pay. How can I know if, had he waited, I would have taken advantage of that chance?

8

I've stopped working on these pages many times during the last several days and then returned to them, picking up the thread of my memories where I'd left off. What happened was what had to happen; those memories were run over by the present.

Of course what happened yesterday or half an hour ago is now a memory, although it's not, it's still too external, it hasn't been decanted yet, which is why I stopped writing for the entire month of September. At first I wanted to keep this from being a memoir, now I'm afraid it will turn into a diary. But what I'm currently living, what I've been living for little more than a month, now demands to be included with things that have been developing for many years.

I began to write the night after that night I'd sat beside the fireplace until dawn. It was in June of '38. At that moment I thought I saw my life as a completed circuit and, in fact, that moment was completing a circuit. However, new circles get stitched into that circle, forming a web, and it's impossible to see their end.

When in my narrative I came to the night beside the fire, there had already been some new filaments that prevented me from putting a final period. Above all, the tale of reality was gaining on me, as if, just when I wanted to stop at one of the high points to build it to a conclusion, the small details of trivial events promised me something more conclusive a little further on. And so we reached 1939, we reached my uncle's death in the month of September, although of course, when I was writing about the things that surrounded his death, it was no longer September of '39 but June of '40, and that's where I left off again.

The memory of that day when I felt myself foundering in guilt silted down over six long months and, when I began to speak about it, I was still unsure whether or not to plunge into an analysis of the conflicts that had arisen recently. If I'd persisted along that path, I would certainly have plunged. But I stopped.

Now, in order to talk about the life I live today, I must keep on with what happened from September to June and continue up to the present.

That year hot weather arrived very early, and in order to have a change of scenery I thought of spending the summer in Uruguay. All of us together, of course; we couldn't think of leaving them alone, even less so since Christmas was coming. Herminia had told Quitina that she felt terrified as she watched that date approach. When times were good, she'd made their holiday celebrations the kind of family-centered fiestas that people have in Europe, with splendid meals and good wines, which meant the brunt of Damián's jokes would be things of this world, and things of this world could command respect because of their frequently exquisite smells and flavors. Now none of this was possible, now there could be words and even glances full of incurable anger.

Quitina was right, we had to avoid conflicts between the camps of the different humanities—the camp who didn't understand that the Nativity is celebrated in order to arrive at the Crucifixion or that it's necessary to weep for the Crucifixion if one is to reach the Resurrection, and the camp of those of us who understand everything and can't fix anything. At a time like the one we live in, the other camp seems to have the answer, and they don't, but how to prove it to them? . . . It's better to sidestep things, keep them from coming face to face with us too often, place other things in the way that can serve as screens. A trip in the middle of December, setting things up and getting our bearings in an unknown house where we felt uncomfortable for several days, especially since it was one of those houses you rent for the season, which have everything you need and lack for nothing, even though that's why they continue to seem unfamiliar for some time: this was the only way to have everything pass unnoticed. And it did.

Our summer holiday lasted a little over three months, and during that time Damián and I made several trips to Buenos Aires, in order not to abandon our work here completely. On those voyages, postponing the moment when we had to close ourselves up in our cabin, we'd stay on deck and sometimes we even spoke—words spaced far apart: mine, fearful questions hinted at cautiously; his, vague, condescending answers infused with a discouragement resonant in words aware of their futility.

From those conversations I remember only two or three specific situations. During one of the conversations, I talked about Miguel, wanting to talk about a subject that would steer our discussion toward something distant. Damián acknowledged that Miguel had great ability, I alluded to his character, saying I wasn't sure, I wouldn't dare to form any judgment about him, but I found him excessively focused. As I continued to present my opinion or, rather, the opinion I didn't have about Miguel, I inserted short questions, such as right? eh? don't you think so? to see if his opinion might be perceptible in some way. Finally he reacted to my siege, with effort.

"The truth is, I don't have an opinion either, because it happens that Miguel is not our son."

"What!"

"No; he's our grandson."

"Oh!"

"People should have children when they're very young, when they have some ideals."

"But children," I said, palliatively, "don't always inherit their parents' ideals."

"It doesn't matter, the important thing is that at some time they've seen their parents upright. Between us and Miguel there's a space our son should have occupied. He's a child who's seen nothing but rubble since he started opening his eyes."

"Well, there is some truth to that"—such a long paragraph was beginning to alarm me—"but the effect may be transitory. Who can tell how he'll react; he's a healthy boy."

"Healthy, healthy; his mother has given him an idiotic education."

We'd touched a sore spot, and from there on he was sure to get riled up. I couldn't keep my mouth closed: "It's the same education I received, you know . . ."

He braked. By chance I'd hit on just the right comment to reduce him to silence. First, because he had neither the energy nor the desire to tell me how idiotic he also found my education; second, because the respect owed to one's host prevented him from telling me openly what he thought. I believe the decisive factor was his not wanting to take the trouble to think about anything. We didn't say another word the entire night.

Through other observations about things in general I gradually confirmed that his moral devastation was enormous, precisely because his inner fortress was awfully meager. The war he'd lost was not like the war now occupying the area of Europe, its territory neither that of Spain nor Madrid; he'd lost a table at a club, a tertulia, where a few men with nineteenth-century ideas but from no century had believed that around their table they were forming a republic. Of all the things happening in the world, the only ones that interested him were those that might give him a way back to that scattered group.

And in Europe things were beginning to go poorly, very poorly. In March, when we returned to Buenos Aires, the news was bleak and became an obsession you could detect at the heart of any other thought, even though you kept on with the things you had to do.

As our yearly activities were getting under way, Javier arrived one day with a proposal for a new venture. He'd read one of those books you find on lists of best-sellers, ranging anywhere from novels to fashion, with the idea of our introducing the culture of poppies here. He thought that with the equipment I had at Las Murtas we could produce opium, laudanum. I liked the idea, besides it gave me great material for our after-dinner conversations on the weekends.

I tried to interest Damián, telling him his help could be very useful to me, and he agreed, almost smiling, saying that if he could be of some use, he'd be delighted to oblige. Then he added: "It's a great idea; maybe you can manufacture nepenthes. That wouldn't be more than a little bit of bottled sleep."

What other nepenthe could there be?

Books and magazines, every kind of American and British publication about the topic were soon informing us about the possibilities for undertaking our project. I gave Damián the job of looking through most of them and noting what he found most useful, in order to shorten my work. I also asked him to find out about the laws concerning this business and the procedures you had to follow.

He worked conscientiously, and in just a few days he'd selected the most important material from several hundred pages. The task was exhausting for him, although he didn't spend much time on it; I knew from the cleaning woman that he continued to stay in bed most days until lunch time.

I tried to load him with work, to keep him from paying attention to the rumors and news. The general opinion was that Germany would win, and that would erase any possibility of the light above a liberal gathering being lit again anywhere in Europe; but he seemed to take it all quite calmly and, as things got worse, he increasingly suppressed his sarcastic exclamations of Magnificent! Stupendous! He was always loaded down with books, which he filled with careful notes and, while were listening to the news, he'd have his head in a book, as if he didn't hear. Sunday the twenty-sixth, when devastating words announced the fall of Paris, I expected his anger to explode, but he didn't say a word. He let each of our comments, which were no more than weak expressions of discouragement, pass in silence; after a while, he closed his book.

"Great . . ."

He placed such definitive emphasis on that word it could have seemed like a sigh of relief. The hostile, fixed look also disappeared from his eyes, his expression of rage was erased, and he adopted an indifferent attitude, like someone who says: "Case closed."

Throughout that entire afternoon, in which there was nothing to talk about, he repeated that phrase several times. While each of us thought our own thoughts in silence, all of us, in one way or another, were thinking about the same thing; and he would change his position in the armchair, crossing the leg that had been underneath over the other one.

"Great." Nothing more.

In all of us, that "great" caused terror, but no one remarked on it.

The world's tragedy, which was breathed everywhere, which took over the city's conversations and even many people's activities, caused me to redouble my own activities. My uncle's death had awakened in me a feeling of indebtedness that I still have, but during those days it changed into a kind of urgency, an ambition to work, a desire to embrace everything a person can do and think in this world. Because I began to grasp the nature of my guilt. I was sure my good qualities did not fail to include generosity, compassion, and an understanding of other people; but I saw how I'd practiced them intensely, within a very small sphere, only in very direct human relations, where my generosity, although it existed, proved merely relative, because it always repaid me well. It repaid me well in the feelings or the simple presence of the other person; in other words, I moved exclusively in a sympathetic environment where everything was pure pleasure.

Clearly, I could do nothing to prevent any of the things that were happening—I found it repulsive to think of myself as one of the people who made sure others saw them administering half measures, but maybe it would be possible for me to immunize some part of whatever was not yet contaminated. My inner revolution flared with a spark: social man was born in me. Of course, he was born as a newborn—small, weak, and clumsy; these were his imperfections. But the important thing is, he was born, and the spark was a spark of life; this was his virtue.

I won't even outline the projects that avalanched from my head. For two days, I was totally intoxicated, with the lucid intoxication produced by mental calculation. Commercial man was also born in me: I took a look at our capital, an extensive look, which I'd never done. It's not that I have no interest in money; money always interested me a great deal, but only the money I have in my pocket when I want to buy something—the rest was pure abstraction. Also, at that moment abstraction became concrete.

I was sure Javier would respond enthusiastically to all my proposals, as he always does, although his enthusiasm doesn't usually last long; he's rather fickle. What took the greatest effort was inspiring a minimum of interest in Damián. In a way, I felt embarrassed that Damián would have met me when I was living in shameless, frivolous luxury; it was clear I hadn't known how to help him react.

We spent the first part of the week fixed on the news, which grew increasingly worse, and on Thursday, because of some holiday or other, Miguel had a long weekend at his school and they decided to spend four days at Las Murtas. Damián was preparing the new issue of his magazine and he said he'd come later. Since I planned to go to the office on Friday, I promised to take him to lunch somewhere.

I had the impression that Damián must have considered my idea of the poppy business a fantasy whose attractiveness tempted me, but that wasn't true. It was an important business opportunity; above all it meant industrial innovation, and I was sure I could convince him it was worthwhile.

When I arrived on Friday, the maid was leaving just at that moment and she told me that, as always, he hadn't gotten up. I was tempted to call him, but I let him sleep and when I was about to go downstairs, about one, I called him so he'd start to get dressed, but he didn't answer. Since he'd told me he had to work on the layout for the issue I decided to wait for him; half an hour later I called the magazine's editorial office, and they told me he hadn't been there. I began to feel alarmed and I went down without knowing exactly what would be the best decision. I saw the edge of a letter sticking out from under his door; the mailman had been there a few minutes after I arrived, so I was sure that he hadn't gone out.

I felt certain something was happening, but I felt certain because the signs were obvious; I thought about entering through the kitchen window, by breaking a pane of glass, but that seemed farcical, and I imagined how they'd laugh when I told them about it. Then, since I was downstairs, I crossed the street and went to buy cigarettes at the neighborhood grocery on the other side: I knew Damián bought cigarettes every day. I asked the old man if he'd seen Damián go out and he said he could almost guarantee that he hadn't gone out. But he couldn't guarantee it entirely, and I couldn't decide whether to break the glass. The woman who did the cleaning lived around the corner in one of those little houses with deep patios, and I thought I knew which one, but in any case I could ask. It was lunchtime and I found her right away. She said she'd been tidying up like always and hadn't noticed anything going on; I asked her for the key and started running toward the house. The woman came too, but I left her behind.

I opened hurriedly, but in the vestibule I was hounded again by the fear of doing something ridiculous and I said loudly, in a normal voice: "Damián!" No one answered. Without knocking on the door, I opened it and went in; it was dark and I turned on the light.

Damián was lying dressed on the bed, which had not been slept in; he was lying perfectly at the center, his arms at his sides, the right extended a little more than the left, as if it had fallen of its own weight, and the hand held a small black revolver.

I did not even try to see if he was still alive, because you could see that the event had occurred several hours before. I heard screams at the door of the room, from the woman who'd come in behind me; I got her out of there and closed the door. I could not hear her explanations, I could not think about either Damián or about what had happened; I thought only about the people at Las Murtas and how I was the one who had to tell them.

To pick up the phone and say in a serious voice: come right away, something serious has happened, was the easiest way, but how could I let them come on that highway, filled with uncertainty? How could I force them at a moment like this to endure the effort of driving for three hours? Herminia had driven the big car many times and Miguel could drive it as well, but I couldn't thrust them into that ordeal by themselves. To call Quitina and tell her would not solve anything either; I had to ask someone for help and I phoned García.

While he was on his way, and he didn't take even a quarter of an hour, I notified a doctor, asking him to come, and the officials who handle legal issues involved in such events. On the table there lay an envelope for the judge, so they didn't touch it; everything was left just as it was, and a grief-stricken García prepared to stand guard. I set out for the highway, once again, at top speed and almost unconscious.

What do I tell them? How do I begin to explain what has happened? How do I go in? Who do I talk to first? . . . The questions were hounding me when I left Juncal, but since there were no answers to them, I tried to erase them: erasing them was impossible, and I tried to suspend them. I decided not to prepare anything, to deal with things as they came up.

I went in through the gate and, when I reached the garden, I took the main driveway in order to stop right in front of the door; I drove slowly for fear of getting there.

Right after I entered the garden, I saw that Herminia and Quitina were coming out the door on their way to meet me. Francisco came out behind them and Quitina turned toward him, bent down to talk to him, made him go back to the house, and went into the vestibule with him. Herminia walked toward the car alone.

The natural thing would have been for her to ask me why I was coming back at that time, but I saw immediately that she was not asking, because she was upset about something.

"We're very sorry," she told me as soon as I leaped from the car, and I saw that in fact she was expressing deep sympathy, but I also saw that it wasn't about what had happened in Buenos Aires. Can she know? Could someone have been indiscreet and let them know before I got here? In my mind, I went over the people who could have done it. Julieta? No, that was impossible.

As I was thinking all this, Herminia was watching me, and she saw

I was more than upset. She said something unintelligible that I didn't understand.

"What?" I asked and she answered something I still didn't understand, because I saw Quitina running toward me, and she too looked very sad. Quitina assumed that Herminia had said what she was planning to say, and she only added: "What a shame, Santiago, what a shame!"

Herminia looked at her and gestured ambiguously.

"Miguel is devastated . . ."

No, it can't be, I thought. Although certainly it could have, because someone could have told them by phone, and the words of them both might correspond to an embarrassment like mine. But I saw that no, it was clearly not the same thing.

Finally, I began to hear Herminia explaining something about Rudy and a truck. I took them each by the arm and we went into the house.

If we're working like crazy to accomplish something that will benefit someone else; if we're racing toward something out there that's summoning us and on which our intention is so fixed at a particular moment that we're oblivious to everything else; if we've gotten up such momentum that we're surging ahead in a state of inertia with our thoughts focused exclusively on whatever we're after; and if an unexpected obstacle suddenly comes up and we crash into it, the blow brings us back to ourselves. For some time all we can do is collect our faculties, perform an examination, and make sure that we're still intact.

Damián's death irrupted into my plans in midstream, jamming their course, cutting them off, and I still haven't been able to recover from the contusion. Once again I'm examining myself, when what I wanted to do was forget myself; once more I'm probing my own enigma, when I was beginning to feel capable of understanding the people outside me.

During the first days we lived through the event—nothing else; we made specific efforts to consider the tragedy that way, specifically. Herminia neither held anything back, nor feigned serenity, nor feared she would weary us with her grieving; and we didn't try to console her or diminish the dimension the drama held for her. All we did was stay with her, talk with her for days and nights on end and, when she felt like crying, let her cry as much as she wanted; then we would talk again. As for Miguel, he was plunged ten fathoms deeper into thought than before.

But after those days had passed and precisely because all the emotion and thoughts had been expressed, the incident took on a descendant curve. In other words, we'd talked out everything that could be talked out and the current formed by the impressions we'd exchanged was pooling. Besides, Herminia and Miguel started to think about going back to work. They had been with us for over a month and they had to return to their life, exactly as it was before—unchanged except for what it now bore within.

All those days of interminable conversations about Damián—memories, details of his life Herminia recounted minutely, cogitations and conjectures about his final impressions, the ones responsible for his decision—are what I call the moment of the blow. Because all those days were one moment, in other words, the course of my projects and plans was flowing along rapidly and the event intersected that flow, causing the collision. Throughout all those days the event exerted exactly the same pressure; then the toll of my ecchymoses set in.

That expression seems too metaphorical, but I'll use it because there was a real mark, an obvious, material trace left on me by the effect of the shock. I neither changed direction nor altered the order of my ideas; in myself, in my own being, a phenomenon occurred that demanded my attention.

The phenomenon was a sort of taste. At times I seemed to find it in the air or in the water, but that's not where it was; it was life that had acquired—or lost—a taste. One taste was disappearing because another was absent, as when we try unsalted food and say it has no taste. All it lacks is salt, so we experience the authentic taste of the food, which lacks salt and to us seems devoid of any taste. Although, when we find taste in things, we don't think it's the taste of salt.

That taste—or lack of taste—was in my throat, making everything insipid. I tried to swallow it in order to pass it once and for all, but that did no good; I tried to take a deep breath and I still couldn't get rid of it: that taste was in the air too. But the strangest part was that if I looked at things—the color of objects, the light—everything seemed to have the same taste: no taste. And since I found no taste in any of my ideas, I couldn't finish any of them; I tried one after another, and they all gave me indigestion.

There was no doubt that my inner disorder was a response to that shock, but what I couldn't find was the way to get over it. I could do that by not thinking about the subject anymore, which I could do if I made a real effort, but I knew the consequence of mutilating my thoughts would be my finding the same insipid taste in everything else; thinking even more didn't fix things either, because that was nothing but a repetition of what had already been said—my own ideas or the things I knew from Herminia. No, neither thinking nor not thinking could fix anything.

In situations like this I always end up letting the horse choose the path; I surrender to my instinct, disconnect my head, let my feet go wherever they wish and let my hands do whatever occurs to them.

Obviously, I'm expressing it like this now, as I write it. To say that I'd let my hands do what they wanted, and that I was fully aware of letting them do so, would be an intolerable simulation. That's not how it was. What I mean is that one day, when I got to Juncal, in an absent-minded state—although what was absent may have been only my ability to connect—instead of going up to my office, I stopped at Herminia's door. After Damián's death I had a key. I opened and went in.

There was no connection between my mind and my actions at that moment, because I very well recall thinking: "It will probably be necessary to come and see how things were left, for when they return." I was thinking: "It will probably be necessary to come," but meanwhile I was going in. I was thinking: "It will be necessary to see how things were left," but I was already inside, and I wasn't looking at anything. The apartment was in semi-darkness; they'd drawn all the blinds; I walked as far as Damián's room, opened the door, turned on the light, as I had that other time, and stood in the middle of the room, maybe for a couple of minutes, maybe longer.

Then, I went up to my office, sat down at the desk and took out my papers, but I didn't do anything; I continued, mentally standing in the middle of Damián's room.

My feet had taken me that far; I had put two and two together, because that's where the taste was coming from, that was its source. After discovering it, I went on to something else and relived what had happened before: my arrival in mid-morning, my meeting with the maid who told me: "The señor didn't get up today either." Today *either*, because there were almost no days when he got up; so that day was like most days. I was totally immersed in activity, idyllically immersed in action; I was brimming with myself; I wanted to plant fifteen hectares of poppies . . . I wanted Damián to realize I could think of something that was useful for everyone, something worth supporting. I felt sure I could instill enthusiasm in him for my plans, that I could help him become revitalized by collaborating in an activity that would interest him the way an experiment would. Part of what I should have done at the very beginning and didn't; now I was going to do it.

I'd felt sure I could, because it was a splendid day, one of those brilliant autumn days when you want to make plans for the whole winter, to think, "We'll do such and such . . . We'll . . . "; and the light seemed be telling me, "Yes, you'll . . . ," the same light shining in the window of the room where Damián lay dead.

But up in my office, I wasn't the only one going about the day's business unaware of the event. In Damián's apartment, in his own kitchen, the maid was probably putting the pans on the shelf, carefully so as not to wake him; she was probably scrubbing the floor with a brush and not letting the vacuum cleaner groan too close to his door, because, right there, two steps away, the maid didn't have the feeling either that Damián lay dead in his room.

But how should I say it, in order to say it precisely? "We didn't have the feeling that *he was dead*?" Or "we didn't have the feeling that *he wasn't there*?"

When I turned on the light and saw him, what did I feel? I felt he wasn't there.

My grief was boundless, my compassion for the suffering evident in that act was infinite, but with respect to Damián, what was there was his form. He was not.

Then I recalled his letter for the judge: "I'm setting off, of my own free will. Damián Vallejo." That was all. Why would Damián have written "I'm setting off" if he didn't think he was going somewhere?

Could you set off voluntarily if you believed you were going, without fail, to the place people go because they look forward to it? Of course, if you don't believe, you have no fear about where you'll arrive. But if a person absolutely does not believe, he can't feel that *he's setting off.*

A nonbeliever would have to say instead, "Here's where I end," "Here's where I'll remain." Although you really can't say that he remains either.

What was certain was that Damián's posture as he lay there dead seemed more like staying than leaving. It was the posture of someone responding to "Attention!" and he was planted in the center of the bed as if he were rigidly facing the firing squad, with his arms stuck to his sides. Of course his right arm was extended, as if it had fallen obliquely; but that was the third arm. It was the arm that had executed the order while he was at attention, in the center of the bed. "There are moments when, no matter what position the body assumes, the soul is on its knees."

That's something I knew well from when I was very little, in the terrible winters of Geneva or Madrid, when I crawled between the icy sheets, thinking it wasn't necessary to pray on my knees beside the bed; under the covers, I'd be shivering with cold, but the blankets were pulled up to my head, and I prayed on my knees. I was lying on my right side, but my knees were bent, and I was in exactly the same position as I was when I knelt in church, and I felt certain that I was kneeling.

That's how it must have been for Damián; heels together, he was lying in the center of the bed, ready for "Attention!" with his arms glued to his sides, and when he commanded "Fire!" a third arm had been deployed and aimed at his temples with total justice.

Well, this part about the third arm, I don't know if it's some crazy idea or if it's the key to the question.

Remembering—but remembering isn't the word—, reproducing in my mind the image of Damián stretched out on the bed, I could read something in that image the way you can in a book, and it was obvious he had wanted to die at attention. Of course, when he lay down on the bed he was already holding the revolver in his right hand, but I'm certain he must have felt his two hands glued to his thighs as he brought his heels together; in that position there had to have been the man who was going to die. But, about the man who was going to say "Fire!" it's impossible to know what posture he would have assumed. That man, who was pure will, could be in any position.

Is this a gratuitous digression? Is there some indication that Damián experienced his suicide as an execution? Yes and no.

In his words, whether they were deliberate or casual, I'd never found anything that would make me suspect it—today I think about it until I'm worn out and, although I still don't find it, I'm afraid that's because of my own stupidity—but, the words he used when he was arguing with García about what a colonel is, those words do give me a clue.

A colonel is the one who spins the ball . . . Damián had come from Europe wearing his croupier's outfit because he'd left his uniform in shreds on the crags of the Pyrenees and, fixed between his eyebrows, he bore his having said "Fire!" so many times, so many and so many useless times. He bore the disappointment of retreat, which was what made him see everything as chance: his stepping back and spinning the ball and saying "Fire!" and never scoring for his own side. His delirious outbursts in which he would explode unexpectedly, almost without disturbing the correct posture, showed that the man who spoke the commands was the madman inside him; the man who was all will lived restlessly inside the material man, who seemed serene.

I had no more facts to reconstruct the drama, but I was sure this was how it had been. The more I looked at it, the more clearly I saw it. I saw his elegant black shoes, polished so highly they looked like patent leather, on top of the bedspread. I couldn't imagine what landscape might have filled his mind or if he felt beneath the soles of his elegant shoes the tiles of a barracks patio or the gravel of a highway; I saw only that stretched out there horizontally, he was at attention until the last instant, until he heard . . . until he spoke the word "Fire!"

And that's the problem: the man who was in command spoke the word "Fire!" in order to destroy the material man, but the arm that rose and aimed at the temple did not belong to the man who was giving the command: it was a material arm that left its position at attention in order to carry out the command, and in its place, next to the body, was substituted an arm of pure intention, which remained there, rigid, until the order had been carried out. The material arm, then, would have collapsed extended alongside his body beyond the attitude of attention, leaving room for the arm of pure will, which lay straight.

The one sure thing for sure is that I lacked a single piece of evidence for assuming that a similar process had occurred when Damián died; I did have the impression of being able to read something in his posture: nothing more. And what I'd glimpsed suggested to me an idea of splitting, which was leading me to deduce the process. I wasn't seeking the outcome of some psychological conflict, though, but the meaning of something general and absolute. It was this: Damián's was an image of total death; nevertheless, suicide is a type of death with a spiritual, indisputable cause. Will cannot be a thing of the body; if it were, a will to die would manifest itself as asthenia, and, on the contrary, its manifestation is a force exerted on an organism in perfectly normal condition. So, can we assume the suicide loses his soul by destroying it? Is that possible? Was I to imagine that Damián's anguished soul had gone in search of some greater tribulation, or, would it be that instead of going it had remained, had remained in nothingness? In that case, would the material arm be the one that had been raised to destroy the spiritual man? How could something that knows it's eternal possibly try to destroy itself? Damián did not believe in his eternity; but then, if his body was not attacked by any malady, if the body's tendency toward its own end had not been hastened, how had he been able to stop the machine? . . .

As I formulated that question to myself, I stood up abruptly, took a few steps around the room as if I were lost, as if I were in darkness—it was eleven in the morning—, feeling that I needed to look for something.

I haven't described the transformations that the house underwent when the first floor was renovated, and they're important, because some mental state links all my thoughts indissolubly with the shapes in front of my eyes. What I think in one room I could not have thought in another. And at times I leave where I am because I feel that something is missing and I can't have whatever thoughts I want to have. This is what happened that day, which explains why I have to talk about the alterations the house underwent.

My office, upstairs, was nothing but a large living room, with a big window that faced east. You went up by way of a staircase against the wall in the vestibule of my apartment; here we'd altered hardly a thing, only the staircase of dark wood, which seemed to have been there forever. I kept that refuge with its old furniture, with all the character of a familiar antique that had never changed. Upstairs, everything was white, spacious and luminous; with all that light you couldn't see anything. I went downstairs.

In the vestibule the light was soft, filtered by the pink and green panes. I opened the stained-glass window. There was no sign of fall in Herminia's garden: the large leaves, which simulated the précis of a grove, were as intact as if they'd been in a greenhouse. There, the alterations we'd made were so great it was impossible to recall how things had looked before. But one thing was still the same: the window, downstairs on the right, set at an angle to the high window where I peered out. There was the window I used to watch, knowing that the old man and the clock were there in the dark room like two throbbing machines, facing each other, alone—the window from which I had thrown the imaginary paperweight in order to destroy the life of that mechanism and had achieved nothing. I'd achieved nothing, because my material hand had not started to move. What use had come of all that tension, all my careful aiming; that concentration of my will, all those hours I'd spent that I was establishing contact, extending my power, and with that power, piercing windows and walls? None at all.

No, from my window I could exercise no power over the beings that inhabited the room below: no communication could exist, no contact. This was proven, because that exact room had later been Damián's, the one where the horrendous thing had occurred without radiating a bit of horror capable of reaching my window. Above all, how could I think that from such a distance there could have been the slightest possibility of action, if Damián himself, alone with himself, within himself—where there is no distance—had not been able to reach himself by means of his own pure intention, and had needed to use, for the purpose of killing himself, a hand he was going to put to death?

In order to continue using the simile of the contusion, I'll say that the day I clarified all this, it was as if I finally located the lesion after lengthy study. The recent blow had wounded me in my old illness, and, when I again confronted it, now, in a way even more intense and even more devoid of any visible object, the search was even more filled with longing, the lure of the vortex more powerful.

When Herminia and Miguel went home, life at Las Murtas returned to normal and I resumed my nocturnal work.

We had a very harsh winter, and several nights I stayed in the library until well after midnight and then ended up going to bed numb with cold, with no possibility of either reacting or sleeping for a long time: I decided to return to the little room upstairs. Besides, the library and the dining room fireplace became repellent to me, because as soon as I sat down beside the fire I'd think, "this was Rudy's place"; and I couldn't manage to revive his memory. It was impossible for me to recall the image of Rudy while he was alive, to envision his movements or his form curled up beside the hearth. I remembered only that the terrible day when I arrived, sentenced to give the news, I'd gone to search for Miguel at the back of the garden and found him looking at Rudy—I led him away from there with difficulty, in order to make him enter the true horror—and what he was looking at was a formless lump covered with blond fur. That wasn't Rudy, but it was all I could recall. Everything from before had been erased from my mind, as if it had never existed.

It was useless sitting beside the fire, trying to revive a memory that would not come—I mean, when all that came to mind was the idea that there was something I wanted to recall—, and I systematically constructed the remembrance of things rememberable: Rudy was a slender form moving beside me, something warm that I touched or that came to touch me, making a little growl or a whimper from time to time. Now there was nothing of that, nothing of what that was.

Through one of those mechanical processes, one of those automatisms that sometimes makes us hear phrases within our very selves that were lifted from the common herd, deliberations not bearing our mark but resounding within like echoes of other people's voices, I argued: "It seems that Damián might have taken him."

And immediately I saw the two of them, but not the way I wanted to see them: going off together; no, I saw them dead, stiff, distant, indifferent, nonexistent . . .

I tried to force my imagination, recalling how on the night of my digressions about dogs I'd already thought the dog's companionship is one appropriate to men engaged in the task of killing, and now I was seeing it as the only companionship a man could have, even at the moment of making the supreme decision; it was the only being that could be at a man's side, looking at him with the greatest tenderness, that, without becoming upset, would allow him to raise the revolver to his temple. That's why, I thought, Rudy's companionship belonged to Damián, and it was right that he'd taken him . . . I thought all this with effort, but I could only manage to see the two forms—dead, distant, indifferent. I abandoned the library.

My pretext was the inconvenience of moving to the bedroom in the wee hours of the morning. Upstairs, I could work in bed: I was translating a book about chemistry, which was tedious work, but I'd taken it on for the pure pleasure of giving me a lot more work to do. It seemed to me that if I felt the cold on my head in that room, if my feet were tucked under the guanaco blanket, I'd be able to think in a more orderly way, without losing myself in fantasies. But it was useless, because the fantasy relentlessly pursuing me was exactly the opposite of warmth. It was an insomnia, like a quietude in which even time was coming to a halt. That's how I spent July and August: sometimes, at night with it below zero in both my room and my head, I made zero progress.

Exhausting myself, if not my ideas because they're inexhaustible, in order to pursue my ideas about Damián's inner process during his last moments. Exchanging what I'd been contemplating about his third arm and its possible backdrop, I confined myself to thinking about the possibility that Damián might have been able to accomplish what he wanted without using any arm but his will.

This was a possibility I couldn't quite dismiss; what I couldn't know was whether the idea of accomplishing it that way would ever have entered his head.

After a real search—any attempt I might make to transcribe it would be futile—I managed to perceive a word, one that didn't give away the idea but did show me the phenomenon that might have fed it. The word was his "Great."

But I didn't find that word because of my search; on the contrary, I already considered the search useless when the word sprang up in me. I spoke it almost aloud, whispering it clearly enough that my ear could catch it, and the instant I heard it I understood: that word was death. Neither the idea of death nor the acceptance of death, it was not a rational process in the presence of death: it was the voice of death, as "ay" is the voice of pain. You don't say "ay!" *because something hurts*, pain breathes in your "ay!"

In fact, I'd repeated that "Great" many times since Damián's death, the way you repeat certain tunes that stick in your head. I'm sure I said it exactly the way he did, I'm absolutely sure I reproduced it exactly, but it was learned and misunderstood. I was probably repeating it in order to understand; that night I saw it clearly. Damián had said "Great" as the irrefutable arose in him. It seems that it would probably be the same to say, "when Damián heard the news about the fall of Paris, he understood that the triumph of fascism was certain, and he made the decision to commit suicide." That's how anyone would say it, but he would not be saying anything: the decision, if it came to that, had been made a long time before, but at that moment he became centered on it.

Once again the idea of a center, of a point beneath the arch . . . In other words, if Damián had known that emitting just the right note was enough, he would not have picked up the revolver. Nevertheless, in his tone there was just the right note. What more did he need for absolute justice? Perhaps only consciousness, only faith in his will. Discipline was habitual for him, and it forced him to think that an order must be followed by its execution; the command did not spring up in him as something conclusive in itself, as something that is *possibility* per se.

Although the fact is that from the moment he pronounced that word, Damián was dead. If he'd keeled over in front of us as he uttered it, what would the doctors have said? A heart attack, from the emotion caused by the news he'd just heard. No one would have been able to grasp that he'd died by uncoupling the continuity of his life. "Great"—this indicated that the knot was being untied. And when a knot is untied it means the knot *is not there*. "Great" . . . is a dissolution of continuity, a "this is as far as we go," a "no more."

My mental concentration on this word and its meaning, on the ontic process from which it sprang, was spreading out, overflowing my mind, and threatening to invade me totally. I slowed down and reflected on my resolve to understand the significance of that expression with my intellect; I wanted to put all my intellect into it, but not all my being. I didn't want to launch my will along that course, but my will to understand was so great I could feel it bolting. Every time I repeated the expression in order to think it, I felt I was living it in an increasingly intense or more centered way; I was afraid to utter it as an absolute, and afraid the knot would come undone. In that case, my intellect would not be able to register my experience and, unless it's a case of one going that far, there cannot be total understanding.

People have always said that after you pass away you attain the point of view where everything is understood: I thought, so now Damián understands everything? And I saw him again lying stiffly on his bed, with a position of his head and a lack of transcendence in his expression that made it impossible for me to accept that he'd passed through the moment of total understanding, of absolute vision. I wondered then how anyone could have seen the least mystery in a dead person. If you think about death, you see its mystery; but faced with a dead body like that one, not only do you not believe in survival, you don't even believe in life—you don't accept that the person has lived before.

This is what damnation must have been; what I had engraved in my memory was the image of eternal death. But *eternal death* and *total death* are two different things. By eternal death we understand living death eternally. But if that were the situation, I think the dying person, for the mere fact of seeing himself prevail, would revive, in other words, he would believe and he would be saved. Although I don't know if this isn't one of my own limitations, this not being able to comprehend consubstantiation with evil. Obviously, those who reached the circle where one loses all hope are there because they're totally bereft of grace and one assumes they can't feel contrite even in the very presence of good. But I say to myself, how can this sort of rebelliousness, this lack of malleability, when one is being punished, tested, be simultaneous with understanding? Of course the damned know they will not see God, but if knowing they are damned proves His existence to them, why is this not enough to make them worship Him? Undoubtedly, rebellion is something I don't understand. The only thing I would not tolerate from God is His not existing.

Because, if eternal death were total death, what would punishment consist of? Who would suffer it? Isn't it possible that in damnation there is no longer even punishment? That all punishment consists of is erasing the reprobate, letting him drop and shatter as if he were a jar that can't be used for anything?

The cavity of a jar is a cavity that belongs to the jar, but if the jar ends up in pieces, the cavity disappears, without leaving any pieces of itself.

Of course, the cavity could never break the jar; for the jar to break, there must be a force that attacks its matter, which once again shows the suicide's spiritual motivation. It would seem that the decision assumed would have to be obvious in those facial features that, subsequent to the evidence of that moment, can no longer be modified by anything of less magnitude, and that was not the case; in Damián's features there was nothing obvious. There was nothing but an annulment that spoke only of dissolution, which was obvious in that "Great."

If I experienced terror as I pronounced that word, it was intellectual terror, because the rest of my person was much won over by the word. My intellect was shouting at me, "You have to get out of here!" But I lacked the energy to get out because the aura of that word penetrated me. The cold, whose painfulness usually becomes unbearable, had invaded so deeply as to desensitize me. Maybe the cold is unbearable only because a person puts up resistance; at that moment, I gave in. Cold seemed to be that word's world, the word seemed to be the threshold of cold, and I remained motionless for a long time, neither entering nor leaving.

I have the feeling I spent hours in that state; it might have been only minutes, but I thought specifically that maybe now I was no longer in a state to be of any use in life again, that the material part of me more than my will had been invaded. My intellect, free by exception, began to look for complicity in something material and at last I thought: "Hot water! A long bath in really hot water . . ." That was definitely the only thing, but I didn't have the energy to get myself to it. I kept thinking: "A really hot bath, to be sitting in hot water and absorbing its warmth through my pores, like a sponge . . ."

The idea was reaching my body; my feet were like ice in spite of the vicuña blanket. I stood up, threw a poncho over my shoulders, over my thick wool robe, but the most serious thing was that next to my little room there was a small bathroom with a shower; to be in the bathtub I would have to go downstairs to our bedroom, and it was impossible to go into our room without making any noise. Since my feet were so cold, it wasn't hard for me to walk barefoot; I went down, holding my slippers in my hand, and entered the bathroom like a ghost. I closed the door before putting on the light, started to think what I would do to block the noise of the water, and finally wrapped the spigot in a towel that reached the back of the tub; the water ran down through the cloth almost in silence—only the water heater made a humming sound, and it wasn't very loud.

The warmth from the flame in the water heater and the steam from the water began to revive me; I stepped into the tub, sinking down into the water until it came up to my head. I left exposed only my nose and mouth, so I could feel the hot water on my eyelids, and I turned my head from side to side, lifting my ear out and then gradually putting it back in again, so that I could feel the warmth of the water penetrate my ear, and it seemed to reach all the way to my brain. In fact it did, not the water but its warmth. My circulation picked up, thanks to the liquid mass enveloping me, loaning me its vibration, and rousing me from the abandon into which I'd fallen.

Then my mind came to rest, words and questions were erased, my attention was devoted solely to my contact with the water, to the lightness that let me lie there afloat without resting anything but my heel on the bottom. There I also forgot about time passing, but feeling it pass.

Invaded by the activity coming from the warmth, I forgot my resolve not to make any noise and I stirred about in the water like a fish. When I turned toward the door, I saw that Quitina was peering in, looking at me.

If Quitina had entered the room and asked: "What are you doing?" I probably would have answered: "I'm cold, and I'm very sorry I woke you up." But we didn't say anything. I felt indescribably small and I started splashing around in the water as Quitina walked closer and looked at me from head to toe as if she'd never seen me.

The playful thing would have been to stretch out my arms to her and say, "Take me out of here." She would have said: "You're too heavy." We didn't say any of that either.

Quitina took down the bathrobe, and I got out of the tub. I put on the robe, dried my face on its sleeve, and sat down on the edge of the tub. Quitina drew up the stool, put a towel over her knees, and began to dry my feet.

It's not that we were silent the whole time, but we didn't say any of the things we were thinking. We certainly spoke a few words concerning what we were doing. When she'd dried and powdered one of my feet, Quitina said, "Come on now, the other one," because I was enveloped in a kind of stupor that had me forgetting movement, so much so that she had to repeat: "Come on now . . ."

When I put my second foot on her knees and she began to dry it, the delicacy of her hands, the tenderness and the compassion in her bearing made me think of saintly Queen Isabel curing lepers. When she looked at me, waiting for me to lift my foot, she'd said "The other one! . . ." with an imploring look, but in a way only the strong can implore. She'd said "Come on now! . . ." but she'd meant: "Let's continue, I can go with you anywhere . . ."

But exactly what did she know? Nothing specific; she was only stating that she could go, that she could dry or cure the foot she held between her hands, even if it had been attacked by an infernal disease.

Then she rolled up the sleeves of her robe and shook her hair; the steam in the room had made it curl and seem darker against the pink silk of her robe. She looked like a slave as much as a queen. I'd seen that look of oriental slave in her at other times. She shook the excess powder from my foot, adjusted my slipper, and extended the comb to me so I could wring out the little water left in my hair.

The pages about Damián's death and my immersion in my old obsessions I've written after that last day, during the first two weeks of September when, now that I'm in control of myself again, I can have a clear recollection of the things that happened.

I believe that my principal purpose—to understand—has not been achieved at all; when I began, I believed that things were going to take a different direction, and now I've come to this point and I don't know what direction that is.

It seems pointless to write any longer; I think what I need to do is forget, and forgetting always comes to my being when it's necessary, as naturally as one season comes after another.

Now spring has come, there are half-closed blinds, and the smell of chinaberries fills the house. Quitina takes long siestas, persisting in her sleep as if in painstaking work: her body is working now on our third child.

PART TWO

9

Cross out, cross out, that was the first thing I thought of when I un-earthed these notebooks after six years. Quite cunning, those two words: to cross out you have to pick up your pen again.

I'm rereading everything I wrote, and it seems awkward, inefficient, and positively useless for what I wanted: it clarifies nothing. So if it's useless, why not toss it into the fireplace? I don't know why, and I can't find any reason not to do that; but the thing is, neither do I find enough momentum in myself to do it. I can think I should burn it, but I know my hand won't move in the right direction; on the contrary, no sooner did the words "cross out" come craftily into my head than my fountain pen began to secrete its spidery web onto the page.

At first, I *did* cross out—a couple dozen words; within a few minutes I realized that what I'd begun to do was not destroy but continue. I must continue; I have no choice but to keep going until who knows where. Until the present moment would be easy, but if I start to establish even a slight connection between before and now, things will keep happen-ing as I write, and then who knows where we'll end up?

The most natural way would be to start with the event that made me remember this abandoned tale. The event's not important, I really don't believe it is. If it weren't closely related to the beginning of all this, I wouldn't grant it the least importance, but even if it is related, I still resist. Just to suggest that it might have some importance is to grant it

257

too much. It even seems that I'm trying to create a bit of suspense before stating what it was that made me start writing again. That would be stupid: I took out these notebooks—today . . . no, yesterday—at ten o'clock at night, and I've been reading them until four o'clock in the morning; right after that I crossed out a few things, and then I started to write, and it all happened because yesterday, at seven o'clock in the evening, I unexpectedly found myself with Elfriede.

Tom Drake, the new manager of CICSA, invited me to his home for cocktails so could introduce me to Mrs. Drake, he said, and Mrs. Drake proved to be Elfriede. He'd prepared that surprise for me, knowing about our friendship—one attributable, of course, to artistic affinities. It had already seemed odd to me, the first time I met this guy after he came to Buenos Aires as the manager of a firm that has so many dealings with ours, that he would suddenly ask me if I liked music. I said, yes, of course I did, and we went back to talking about lactose; five minutes later we were talking about painting. I assumed he wanted to show me how much he knew, suspecting the low esteem in which we Latins hold mere businessmen; but it was because Elfriede told him about my old predilections when she read the list of people to whom he brought letters of introduction. That explains why I was caught off guard when I went to see her make her Buenos Aires debut as the lady of the house.

Brilliant debut. I found her radiant, more beautiful than ever. Whatever seriousness the years might have bestowed on her is counteracted by American style, which is always somewhat frivolous. She was wearing a gauzy dress printed with bright colors; its numerous pleats flapped when she moved, and it contrasted sharply with the simple, almost masculine suits she'd worn in Berlin. The heels of her shoes were extremely high; not only were they just right for her digitigrade walk, they narrowed the base of her silhouette even further, making her hips look even more like an amphora. That describes her clothing. There was also the spacious, well-decorated apartment overflowing with gladiolas, the requisite glass-topped table and its reflections of the gleaming cocktail shaker, the cut glass bowl, and Elfriede's hand as she picked up her drink.

I applauded her mentally, shouting, "Bravo! Encore!" each time she circled about the room, watching her pass in front of the open balcony where the breeze fluttered the gauze of her dress, making it cling to her with its fan-like pleats. She moved profusely, with the same self-assurance as before—less pronounced now, more suitable for this climate.

We told each other about our lives. She's been married for some time. She has an eight-year-old daughter whom they've left in a school in Boston, until they find out if this country is habitable. She no longer even thinks about dance, remembering it as something that formed part of her education. Now she reads, preferably poetry, and Rilke is her favorite. Tom Drake listens to her and admires her.

We agreed they would come out to the house. Well, that's another matter. I will certainly have to reflect on what I should do and how, but not at the moment: there's time. I haven't said anything to Quitina, but not to hide it from her, which would be impossible even if I wanted to; besides, it's not necessary. I haven't told her about it, because when I got back I couldn't talk about it; that would have meant interrupting my thoughts, conferring validity on the event within the limits of its present, and when I got home I'd already exceeded those limits.

When I left Elfriede's house—the Drakes' house—I came walking down Leandro Alem, in the peculiar state where surprise always puts me: dissatisfaction when confronted with surface. Surprise is surface, a *painted veil*, and I don't accept this, I have to pierce the veil. I walked four or five blocks looking for a taxi—minor car trouble—, filled with highly intense animation. In situations like these I usually don't think about anything. I stood for a long time on the edge of the sidewalk, and the only thing I thought was: it's 9:15 . . . I repeated this to myself several times—9:15!—, meaning, it's very late, I have to find some way to get home. But I didn't feel the least impatient; I was contemplating the area of the street intensely, filled, entirely pregnant with things I did not understand and can now barely glimpse. Suddenly the present had a new, unexpected look, which was not comprehensible in itself. Maybe that's because all you see in any first viewing is the thing covered up; to see it naked you have to know the successive phases in which it's gradually developed.

For example, Elfriede represents a moment from my past, and at times, when a recollection of her has arisen in my memory, I've imagined her inserted as one element in the plot of that whole tale. I've never imagined that, naturally, she would have to be following her own course. Now she appears, and our present tangency is not a trivial event, because it's the convergence of two currents that come from a great distance. If this weren't the case, I would say, "I just met Mrs. Drake," and nothing more. What I said instead was, "How has she come to be here? How, and where has she come from?" And immediately I was overpowered by the desire to swim upstream.

Why does Elfriede arrive now? Is this a call to order? I find her transfigured, unrecognizable, because I'd forgotten her. I haven't followed her; her present surprises me, and the only part of it I understand are the changes one would already expect. If suddenly I confront myself, don't I find myself unrecognizable too? Haven't I forgotten myself lately? And when I haven't been able to forget myself even for a minute, did I not think it was my obligation to do so? Was this not my greatest ambition for many years? Why do I now feel this longing to return to the beginning? My having forgotten a few years weighs on me the way a tombstone on someone buried alive.

To resume the writing of these pages is to return to the light, but not because they clarify anything. I can't say they enable me to understand things better, but I can say that from them I look at things insatiably, seeing them differently each time. How can I bury what might still have something to show me? Let's run it by backwards. But let's do it quickly, rapidly recovering that submerged time.

Where to begin? Anywhere. During those years, between '40 and '45, everything was the same although, at times, there was the appearance of heterogeneity. The strange thing was, we often seemed to be ignoring important events and getting wrapped up in frivolous things. But in fact, we were simply taking those things as masks or, rather, as reductions *of the event*. We were being given horror in small doses, as if we were not quite adults—it was the weight of the world in easily assimilated form, in pocket editions. The movies were the best example of all that.

We went to the movies nearly every day, to forget what was going on. Our war cry was to go and see war pictures in order to keep the war in our mind. But that was false! False! We sought a tolerable image of the war. From time to time an image of something intolerable would appear on the screen but, since it was only an image, everyone tolerated it. That's where the falseness started.

Reasonable amounts of each anguish, death, and destruction, mixed well with a bit of infamy and heroism as the glue. Running time, ninety minutes. And then Bob Hope or Fred Astaire. During intermission, ice cream, of course, and the girl who walked along the aisles selling it; in the lobby, people would be making dates, planning parties and sharing dreams, unrealized and yet to be.

The shame of it all became clear during intermission. Obviously no one felt it as such, but they did feel it as a somewhat helpless impatience. The hellish vision would disappear; the houses reduced to rubble, the tears suspended from eyelashes, and the streams of blood running from the corners of lips would be erased; the rattle of machine guns, the groaning of motors, and the masterful scream of some actor or other would all fall silent, and the house lights would come up suddenly on people left there like little islands in the stretch of empty seats. Tentative couples, just embarking on relationships, or sedentary couples who'd left the cloth on the table and would go from the theater to their sheets, to their daily copulations, to the addition and subtraction of their shared finances. Some men would stay in their seats too, exhausted men who never stopped thinking about the work that awaited them the next day, or other, highly energetic ones who sat with their legs crossed, continually tapping one foot and saying to themselves: "What a way to waste time!" There would also be groups of mothers and aunts—bewildered and terrified mothers, or rather shallow and uninformed ones. Then darkness would return, and those same souls, having just sat with blood running over them, exposed their retinal mirrors to the rumps of superb young women and slow tropical kisses. This was our lie, and it was naked.

I'm a symbolist, and incurable! If I think about truth, I see her standing there, solid and stark naked, her beautiful belly uncovered, and her mirror held in one hand. If I think about falsehood in the same way, I try to see her naked, but falsehood cannot be made naked. To make a lie naked means undoing it, erasing it; and what I would like to do is see falsehood exactly as she is. Then I see her as filthy, vile, black, and slimy. But even as I see her like that I hear a bubbling deep inside her, something like a fountain or a weeping, something that's screaming for mercy. And if instead I see her gilded, as demanded by *le mot d'ordre*, I realize that she's starting to chip and that you can see her plaster interior, see her coming apart, limping and squinting. To make the story short, it's impossible to see her. Beyond our grasp and beyond words, as she is, movies are her mirror. Movies, precisely something that can be seen, but something we can't discern. We could say they're nothing because they happen and then vanish. Inevitable that we would bathe in those waters. Who could have denied himself, during that period? We certainly couldn't.

Before I go on, I'll explain that we went to the movies nearly every day because soon after Damián's death we came into Buenos Aires to live.

Things at Las Murtas looked very different. In the early years the house and the factory were perfectly compatible: they prospered independently of each other, like good neighbors. The garden was a veritable park, and people, some seventy-plus workers, truck traffic, and the materials and machinery that arrived periodically came and went on a side road. Everything was orderly and clean; the activity in the factory did not disturb the calm in the house. And in the surrounding countryside, with its silence and damp green I loved so much because it was so intimate and so close to my secret, the only inhabitants were a few cows that seemed to be there for decoration. Quitina would take the children to the milking yard when they went for walks, and sometimes I would meet them there, in order to inhale religiously the steam of life coming from the cows.

But that scenario changed completely, and at first I was afraid the job of running a farm was more than I could handle. Of course I'd hired some men who were experts in doing just that, but my inability to count on the capital of personal experiences scared me. When I saw the tractors pillaging those pastures made expressly for tender bovine muzzles, I began to tremble. I closed my eyes and forced myself to think: "Soon the poppies will bloom, soon evening will fall again over a field of white flowers . . . When they're all open, the whole expanse will have a narcotic paleness . . ." And I let my fantasy take flight that way so I'd forget my lack of skill.

On Juncal, two blocks from my old house, there was a new apartment building, and we took the apartment on the top floor. From our balcony we could see the trees in Palermo. And that simple modification in our material circumstances marked the starting point for numerous alterations.

The weekends with long family conversations around the table after dinner came to an end; Quitina and Herminia visited back and forth between the two homes at any hour of the day or they went out together while I was working. We renewed our old acquaintances, but of course Herminia and Miguel were still our closest friends. And it was precisely during this period that a strange tension between these two began to appear, although it didn't come to a head for a long time.

There were big changes in our living patterns. Work at Las Murtas was crazy; I'd be exhausted when I got to the city, but I never rested for a moment because I didn't want to deprive myself of city life—social life with its string of invitations that resembled a draft between two carelessly-closed doors disturbing the tranquillity of one's environment.

Javier, who some years before had married Clara Ezcurra—a pretty girl but one not the least bit interesting—proved to be a great help; I called on him in cases of minor difficulties, and of course we now see him—them—often. Laura also married, but she flew the nest and seems to be living happily in Canada. I have the impression that Mecha is steeling herself for unhappiness; Rafaela is cutting back a little, because of her health, so the niece will soon be promoted to aunt. Their house was the only family we had during the first years we were here, but now we found it half-closed, or at least in semi-darkness.

Besides all this, we were absorbed by the attention being paid to the course the war had taken, the confusion in Europe, and Spain's disappearance, because in effect Spain disappeared. Since that outcome pleased almost no one, everyone decided to be angry. If the topic came up in conversation, it was enough to wrinkle your nose a bit and talk about something else.

Fantastic! Years, days passed, one after the other (this is not just a manner of speaking: it's something important, because the reiteration of pain, even the smallest pain, of a continuous anguish, and therefore one without rhyme or reason but inhabited by a clock, a calendar, a newspaper sliding beneath the door, that kind of repetition is what slowly wears down a person's hope), days passed, and while they were passing, even though my attention was like a permanent insomnia, I didn't understand something I do understand now, something that explains the sentence I just wrote automatically. In the paragraph above, I mentioned "Spain's disappearance." That's how it was, seen from here and not from any opposition to what won out over there; no, Spain disappeared because of something more real. Many people loathe what won out in Russia, but it would not occur to anyone to say that Russia disappeared. Whereas Spain did disappear, like a bubble does when it bursts, when the conflict was resolved, because in Spain's case, no one was interested in the conflict because of the reality of life there in that one country, in that one spot on the globe, but only in the card they themselves had played in Spain, preparing themselves for their next move. Yet it's not fair to blame only the perverseness and selfishness of the spectators; no, a large part of the responsibility belongs to Spain, which did not send us testimonies of its conflict.

This seems absurd, but we were ignorant of one country's truth because that country refused to participate in the lie that prevailed by common agreement. But these remarks about *truth* and *falsehood* should not be seen as some childish game of good guys and bad guys; truth and falsehood are simply two categories that participate in the context of reality. After such a pedantic paragraph, it all comes down to this: Spain disappeared because Spain was no longer playing in the movie houses.

It's very simple. Everyone—maids or ticket takers on streetcars—if they hear people talk about what went on in France around 1940, if they retain the word "occupation" in their memories, they will also have preserved a few sufficiently eloquent images; that is, they will know what happened because they will have seen it. They will recall the huge boots marching along the Parisian pavements, the swastikas, the "Jawohls!"

With the same certainty they will know what happened to the Yanks, because they saw the machine-gun nests, the little Japanese faces hidden between the oak branches, the planes falling from the sky. But what can they recall if they hear talk about Spain? What can they know?

If they're educated, they will certainly recall what some writer said about one side or the other, but ordinary people recall nothing. How can they imagine a Spaniard, that conventional figure of an annoying shopkeeper light years away from what we could call the present, how can they imagine him living, suffering, forming some understanding of what's happening, and acting on the basis of that understanding? Impossible. Of course, educated people say, "But what about Picasso's *Guernica?*" No, that's not what you have to recall in order to know. You have to recall some unimportant citizen, some nondescript little man in his house, sitting in his armchair with its crocheted doilies; you have to see his glasses up close, his slightly balding crown, the fabric of his suit, and you have to see how they come in and seize him; you have to hear his voice when they've got him in their enormous hands. Or, to take a completely different example, you have to recall the perfect young men, the well-armed athletes advancing along the dusty road as the fatal object falls and explodes, leaving them smashed to pieces.

When you've seen all this through a people's genuine expression, when all this has been said as a single word through landscape, faces, and native language, then you know what happened to a people. And it doesn't matter if that word is largely a lie: I'm not saying that you need to know the truth but that you need to know reality, and it's reality that bleeds.

In short, we take stands about things we know—no one is going to start plotting some intrigue involving an Atlantis sunk in silence.

But I don't want to get lost in vague meditations; I'm only trying to bear witness to the sub-life that movies represented for all of us during that time, to the way people would bury themselves at movies in order to forget reality, in order to know reality and get facts that were artificial and altered, although they gave rise to other facts that were autonomous, if at times marginal and always contradictory. Those were the facts that proliferated, underground, the ones that caused the psychic states responsible for displacing people's usual feelings and worries. But such displacement was only relative, because those feelings and sentiments defended themselves and managed to keep the intrusive emotions at bay. Sometimes the two worked in a counterpoint, lending density to each other; sometimes they were both watered down by the mix.

This is common knowledge. All of us who supervise others notice when one of our workers is having a bad day. The better and more outstanding his work, the easier it is to see he's working poorly. Usually he's back to normal the next day and no one remembers the day before, but there are times when we get some illuminating piece of information: he was suffering the effects of a shock or a prolonged concern; he'd spent the night at the bedside of a dying person; he'd witnessed a catastrophe. The nervous mechanism that should produce a certain output in a certain number of hours becomes confused if any external element affects its personal economy. But that's called an accident, and a life ordered around those ups and downs would be untenable. Whereas the same machine, synchronized with another thousand or thousand plus machines settled in comfortable armchairs and united by darkness, loses only a slight amount of energy, which it recovers with a few hours of sleep. Naturally, no one's sleep will be disrupted by an emotion that cost him only a few dollars. This means that people's nerves are increasingly calm, and what's more, there are no surprises; everyone knows what they're going to see: "À la guerre comme à la guerre." They've received a lengthy, sound, predictable preparation since, during peace, things were already "comme à la guerre"; it was crime, misdemeanor, the pursuit of man by man.

Only a virile age, such as this one, has been able to create the game of persecution and possession through death that characterizes the detective film—our school, our ABC's.

The term "ABC" isn't fair, though, because the detective genre isn't the start of any understanding; rather, it involves performing an empty exercise, such as practicing penmanship, in other words, following a rigorous discipline, whether or not it has any meaning.

I could go on for hours about detective films—or novels—and it would seem like a digression; but it would not be. The only thing I want to talk about here is *what was happening in us*. My starting point is always selfish. But the limits of selfishness, if a person admits the vital truth, prove to be very vague. Maybe I should confess that I'm only interested in my own things, but where do my own things begin and where do they end? If I say "my own things," does this prove to be more selfish or less?

Is the detective film a fact of my private life? To follow good logic, I would have to say no. To tell the truth, the strict truth, I have to say yes. Because, the detective film—or novel—is first and foremost *an event*; as is the most trivial embodied thought. And if it's an event of my time, born in my time, how could my kinship with it be any greater? It's mine, legitimately mine, like "my king or my prison," to recall the words of that learned Mexican Sor Juana Inés de la Cruz. Consequently, I'm going to talk about myself, to talk about the detective film.

But first a parenthesis. Why not, if I just thought of it? Or, better, if it just thought me, experienced me? At this moment, what *has happened to me* is that an idea—arborescent, nourished by incalculable roots, and bursting with buds about to open on every branch—has been rustled inside me by some puff of wind's chancing to brush against it. This is an event. I don't know if any of my contemporaries will ever read what I'm writing, but I feel sure that if any of them ever does, he will say, "What a boring disquisition! Readers today are only interested in stories that contain action." People who say this usually don't have the least idea what action is. Above all, they are radically ignorant of both what controls the action they themselves are involved in and what controls that controlling action.

A bank teller, a court employee, an ordinary teacher, an upright, indolent woman all read novels about the lives of whalers or about men who mine coal or tap rubber. A resident of London or Stockholm reads about the adventures of the pioneers in equatorial Africa, and they all read with faith, they transport themselves completely to the milieu where the book takes place. Sometimes I see them on the bus, totally saturated with a world that will never have any direct bearing on their lives, although they sit there sipping the nectar of action with great pleasure, and I wonder what would happen if I were to touch one of those people on the shoulder and say, "The action yanking us back and forth, know where it's coming from? Do you know who's pulling the strings of this city? Do you know who's exploring the jungle of our times?" His stupefaction would be enough of an answer for me, and I would continue, "Two or three words, two or three ideas comprise the only motor, but if I were to say them to you right now, you would shrug your shoulders, and if I were to suggest that you read something about them, you would answer, 'Good heavens, no! They're just theories.'"

One of our contemporary philosophers has said that the intimate life of ideas should be novelized. That is definitely what's needed: the creation of a genre, a series of biographies of ideas, a thing very different from the novel of ideas. The biography of an idea would have to begin by being gravitational, prophetic, weighing on life like a pregnancy— exactly like a pregnancy, burdening and alleviating, giving hope—; then would come the delivery, the idea's incarnation in words, then its passion. But my using these terms doesn't mean I believe the idea should be made divine, because I don't; I'm only using them as signs of the idea's divine origin. Once in our hands, the hands of the man who receives the idea as a gift, man and idea fuse and become confused, jumbled, and here we find the crux of the novel. Incidents, chapters about love, adventure, sin, sacrifice, debauchery, death. That's what has to be revealed: the inner, ultra-inner, visceral, gut-level life of the man possessed by the idea, of the idea possessed by the man, until they've both been completely destroyed, until they're left in the grave, until their graves are covered with the ivy of memory.

But this can lead to confusion. If I say "man" I'm not referring to one of those men who've been the subject of so many biographies—wise old X, whose life was devoted to his idea. The life of a man does not have the same dimensions as the life of an idea. An idea consumes many men and the novel I'm talking about would have to recount the multiple romance, the incalculable agony, the plural drama of the idea with its men and women. Of course, thousands of times those men and women would end up beheaded, like marionettes, by the fury of the idea.

Probably further confusion. No barricades, no martyrs. The dramas I'm referring to would be primarily crossroads dramas. Some ordinary person, man or woman, is walking along *a road* when suddenly, like a Chinese wall, the idea blocks his path or, the opposite: the idea calls in such a seductive voice the person is made to turn back, or run ahead, or lose his way, because he cannot determine where the call is coming from. Someone, a man or a woman, puts down his drink, or begins to sob uncontrollably, or tears herself from the arms of her lover, because the idea has just jabbed her with a minuscule bit of proof—fine and sharp like a thorn. The idea, rudder of public life, insect found in libraries and lecture halls, flies over cradles, rips the mantle from lineages and traditions, and unravels enigmas. Its power is enormous, and something about it leaves man absolutely powerless; anyone who sees the idea cannot continue to be the same person he was a few minutes before he saw it.

Well, that's enough of a parenthesis. He who has ears, let him hear.

Back to my topic, to the detective novel, that is. People of my generation have been nourished on it as if it were some of grandma's home-canned food. Because grandma—the pragmatic age—put a series of primary forces in her jars, forces that could not be consumed right then but kept very well in broth and seasonings and could be fed to children a little at a time. Detective novels, which had arisen some while before, were characterized by their chasteness and were thus very appropriate for young people. Far removed from the romance novel, now fallen into mere senility and lust, detective novels devised their own labyrinths, risking in them intact pawns such as deduction, data coordination, theory of probability—a series of cold disciplines previously practiced in banks behind partitions or on laboratory tables that was suddenly organized in inner processes, resulting in the creation of fresh, unveiled, prepubescent erogenous zones. Swollen by a chord of anticipation, secrecy, and attainment, those vibrant, inflamed fantasies proliferated in the childish eroticism of my generation. And it was all waiting for something . . .

You could argue with me that combat always provided a stimulus for erotic impulses, that the ancient heroes, gladiators, medieval knights, and skilled swordsmen who are still so close to us were merely performing rites of a kind of super- or extra-sexual union. That's true, but it all occurred in the presence of spectators and in daylight, it was a combat between equals that took place at a given moment; it was an encounter. Whereas, in detective films there's a nocturnality and a sinuosity that tend to last, leaving a tension similar to desire. Suspense is the mainspring that sets the blood flowing to the heart and the sexual organs. In suspense, more than in the rage of combat, what prevails is the anxious eagerness of the hunt as shown by the detective film's images of pursued and pursuer stalking and ridiculing each other with skillful feints and dodges down the bends of unsavory alleys.

Irresistible backgrounds! What is literature, what can you do with words that would be as forceful as scenery that sweeps us along for a moment, on the fly, at the speed of an escaping automobile, scenery that nevertheless leaves us with an impression as detailed as if we'd turned it slowly in our hands—the shine on wet flagstones, a loose downspout, the corner in shadow, where whoever's being chased might be, where sometimes he is and sometimes he's not, but which being passed by, hurls its dark cavity into the depths of our eyes, promising as a tryst?

But it's not only a question of depths and backgrounds. In the chase itself there's an erotic force independent of the settings where it's often found: cabarets, red-light districts, and the interiors of bedrooms with unmade beds. Sometimes the chase lacks romantic intrigue and even a feminine figure, and that's when its impact is strongest. The chase that tries to seem stark is truly ruthless; a skillful combination of cruelty and cunning gives it a sense of something mental, as if there were no bodies involved, but in every chase there's an inevitable moment when we're confronted with the evidence of flesh. And it's not an image that gives us this evidence, it's something that stands out from the din of combat—the crash of overturned furniture and curses—as an appalling word, never written before now: the blow of a fist on the human body.

I won't describe it because there's no need; everyone's familiar with it. Eight-year-old boys, little girls, the most honorable of wives all know that word today. Adolescents who will become violinists or priests know it too, they've all heard it crash distinctly into the temple or jaw, hollow on the thorax, and dull on the abdomen, and they've all watched as the limb that's been hit falters momentarily, they've confirmed that it will bounce like rubber when it crashes into a wardrobe or against a counter and that the body, relaxed now by the succession of blows, will surrender, wholly persuaded.

Not only in detective films; it also crashes implacably in Westerns—the voice of the American epic—, except that in cowboy films the suspense always involves a horse race and everything ends in a shootout. The volley of their "bang, bang" and the "tac, tac, tac," repeated by the tin guns of neighborhood boys positioned on street corners, is more trivial. In a real tête-à-tête, the blows of a fist mark a virile, sustained tension rising and falling, perhaps it's most reminiscent of the blows of a fist you hear beating on drums in films with tribal dances. Those blows resound outside the flesh, but the masculine bodies seem to move toward them with tense, gleaming loins and taut legs, making the grass skirts shake spasmodically, while the feet keep time to the drums and their endless repetition of some phallic rhythm.

That reminds at the same time of something different; it has nothing to do with the movies and it's neither virile nor tribal, although it is very primitive, very close to the earth—the sound people make out in the country to attract a swarm of bees by banging on a cauldron.

It seems foolish, but making that sound must have some effect if you still find it done throughout Europe in our twentieth century of our age. I saw it as a boy, when I'd follow a group of peasants going after that swarm, which looked like a diffuse spot on some stubble in the field, but denser or wider. There would be a boy carrying a cauldron, beating on it with a stick and making a deafening sound, and two men with hats and veils would be walking behind him, carrying a bedspread, and when the bees would finally alight in one mass on a tree, all the men would throw the bedspread over them and wrap them up. Why did the bees alight? What is it that fascinated them or put them to sleep beneath the noonday sun, in the middle of a plain that for many kilometers seemed to offer not a single place different from the next? I ask myself this now, but then I saw it as the most natural thing in the world. The bees needed a cavity to nest in and the cauldron sounds like a cavity; nothing more. They're lost, God knows why, and they can't find anywhere to settle. Suddenly the cavernous sound starts to persuade them; they hear it and look for it, thinking they're the ones looking, when the sound is what's going after them, and this occurs time after time without the bees finding anything, but the sound continues, and since they hear it, since they're certain the hollow is somewhere close by, they finally land anywhere, hypnotized. With a similar fascination, the drumbeats in those African dances enthrall the horde of vibrating, trembling males controlled by the persistent rhythm, which seems to be coming from blows falling on the hollow in an immense uterus.

But what am I talking about? What's all this about bees and primitive tribes? Well, it's the same thing—I keep talking about the same thing, about what was happening. Of course during those war years, many people followed the war in detail, keeping themselves up to date about everything, responding to every development, whether it occurred here or somewhere else, and reacting appropriately. I wasn't one of them. I didn't want to be one of the well informed, because to me it seemed intolerable to be one of them and not be there. I was honest enough with myself to know I was one of the ones avoiding the test.

It's true I'm in my own country and I didn't come here in flight. Although it's also true that, instinctively, my mother had flight in mind when she pushed me in this direction. Just as Herminia took Miguel out of Spain, giving up everything. Women definitely accept that responsibility with great fortitude, and the man who doesn't rebel, who doesn't leave in order to grab a rifle, must have the courage to know he only declared solidarity with confusion.

That's the thing: that's where we're all equal. We're all attacked by the same disease, and we all toss and turn with the same fever, with similar nightmares, abscess bursts there, but not because of any lack of germs here. The experts will probably explain society's slowly stratified geographical formations and the volcanic convulsions that in one moment do away with everything; I stick to what's obvious on the surface because I belong to that superficial world—the world of people who did not enter the conflict. Besides, I want to express this in my own language, which I'm improvising at this moment, because then I never spoke about any of it, nor could I stand to hear other people talk about it in my presence. How many times I walked out of a house because I couldn't stand a conversation that had gotten started about the latest developments! And I could feel everyone's gaze following me, biting my heels, tearing me to shreds. "The aesthete's walking out; he doesn't want to hear us talk about disagreeable subjects!" When what I did not want to hear was how they were talking! If I'd intervened in their discussion all I could have done was shout: "It's not that! It's not that!"

"Then what is it?" they would ask.

"I don't know, but I swear, all I need is to hear your tone of voice and I know it's not that!"

It's stupid to keep on like this; I don't need to analyze or justify anything. I need to keep talking about the movies, if I want to talk about what *was happening*.

The movies were a chronicle and a letter, a confession and a mirror, a nightmare and a liberating dream. At the movies we saw what was going on, the horrendous things we didn't want to go on, but they were, and nothing could be done about it. At the same time, we saw cheerful things, things exactly as we wanted them, which, at the moment, were not really occurring anywhere. Besides, sometimes what we saw were flashbacks, and we could confirm that the horror we experienced as new didn't differ in essence from what we'd seen before: yesterday had incubated the nigh.

In passing, I'll point out something I observed around that time. All those people who made up the well informed, who were involved with the war at all hours and spoke of nothing else—I won't say they did nothing but talk, because they also did things, things that were surely useful—, all those people, on the personal level, weren't affected by the events. They didn't miss a step, life in Buenos Aires continued as always, nothing changed, nothing grew more porous; an ungraspable background submerged in indolence, a listlessness apparently serene but in fact unwilling to assume the risks and hazards of happiness, continued to exist in every house, just like always.

Whereas we had too much of Europe; people came to our house from over there to die or to live, and all we tried to do was shut our door to the din of the news, the stock exchange of apocryphal shares. The only thing we believed was the screen, which was like a spectrum in which war and peace were decomposing, showing us the rainbow of the human soul in its most seductive hues.

It's not inconceivable that someone would repudiate combat just because it's combat, on principle. And when combat is the means to despicable ends, it's repudiated more easily. But if every possible justification for combat is scrapped, if we can see every detail perfectly, distance doesn't cool off our vision, we feel the adversaries' breathing, and we can make out the beads of sweat forming as the shadow of ecchymosis appears, who among us could possibly tear himself away before seeing the finish? To the seduction of combat, to the fascination of physical pain captured in its most intimate moments—moans, blood-stained bandages, the throes of death filmed in the mud or in hospital backlighting—to all this, war movies added the spell of things suffering and dying. Things, especially machines, approached us, groaning until they splintered or were consumed in flames.

There was always, between landscape and the human face, a third order of things neither nature nor humanity but things created by man— houses, utensils, vehicles—; and from the beginning the movies elevated them to the category of characters, realizing them with expressive shots. In war movies, such realization was unnecessary, the mere fact of being threatened with death enveloped them in an aura. Exposed, just as they were, carrying out their simple functions, they were affecting enough on their own.

One night Miguel and I went to see one of those war pictures by ourselves. Quitina and Herminia hadn't wanted to go; they weren't in the mood for dramas. I don't remember either the title of the movie or the story, but it was about some espionage affair involving a naval battle. After the usual preamble of intrigues between a few grim-looking types, we were getting to the climax, which was the departure of a convoy. The fighting was shot from the air, so the boats looked very small as they moved into a sea smooth, dark, and polished. They proceeded in formation like a flock of cranes, as slow, as serene in that motionless sea as birds in space. Then the camera started to descend, to approach gradually, and the serenity began to waiver. From above, the battleships had seemed to slide firmly and impassively, but when seen up close, they pitched from stem to stern as if they were breathing, and they caused a murmuring that filled the entire expanse of the sea. The water was tearing like silk, but the rasping became louder and louder, the chasms opened by the boats as they passed came closer and closer, and the battleships dove into those chasms chest-first the way ducks dive into a pond.

Then there was a cabin with detection devices, where the arrival of the bombers was recorded and the activity on deck began. The battleships bristled with slender cannons coordinated in a way that made their movements appear to be guided by eyes, as if they were snails' horns, until a little white cross appeared in the sky, burst, and fell in pieces.

Tensed in my seat, I wondered, "What act of contrition will be able to purge us of this collusion with evil?" I wasn't referring to the actual event of the war, I wasn't worried about the agents of death that existed there at that moment, in the place I described. I was worried about my own guilt, which was my being there watching the beauty of all that. To formulate it this way—in line with my fundamental inability to lie to myself—, to use that sacred word to describe the sacrilege taking place before my eyes, seemed to me the first sin, the origin of everything I was watching. At that moment I definitely felt convicted and confessed of the original sin, like a new criminal who finds himself holding the object of his crime in his hand for the first time. Inside I was saying, "The event has been perpetrated; here it is, this is the corpus delicti: the greed of my senses soaking up this process of horror as if it were a symphony."

While I was trying to think of some stone to beat against my chest, I noticed that Miguel was fidgeting in his seat. He touched my arm lightly, telling me: "Look at those little faces, those snub noses."

At that moment the camera was focusing on the deck of an aircraft carrier; the deck was filled with tiny fighters with short fuselages and large heads, and they were all stopped there like flies. Their proportions and the stupid, stubborn fixed way they were waiting there made them look exactly like common flies. And one by one, they began to take off smoothly, accelerating immediately, executing swift turns. In the process, some of them splintered into a thousand pieces, others fell to the sea head-first, expelling tufts of flame.

Finally, it all ended in a victory of props, and we went out into the street.

We started up Nueve de Julio, engrossed in the movie without making any comment. Miguel was walking very slowly, as if he had no desire to get home; I asked him why he was walking at that pace. He stopped for a bit without making up his mind whether to speak, and finally he said: "Today I had a huge fight with my mother. I told her I absolutely would not study philosophy and you can't imagine how she got."

"I was aware of some misunderstanding lingering between you two," I said. "Why you didn't clarify things a long time ago is beyond me."

"But it was clear!" he said. "It couldn't have been any clearer. I'd told her fifty times and she'd never let me finish. Okay, okay, you have lots of time to make up your mind . . . then she would say to Quitina: 'It will pass; all boys like screws, wheels, things that turn.'"

"Of course," I said, "sooner or later you were bound to reach this point."

Miguel continued: "This afternoon was something else. She started shouting. 'How do you intend to convince me that's a vocation?'"

"Well, specifically what is your vocation?"

"Making things."

"What things?"

"Things."

"You mean technology, right?"

"Yes, electronics, if you want to call it by its official name. I say making things because it seems to my mother that things you make with your hands didn't come from your head. She believes you have to spend your whole life thinking and nothing else. Instead of thinking something and doing it."

"But that's what everyone does," I said. "The person who invents a theory thinks it first and then writes it down."

"No," Miguel said, with a really disgusted expression, "writing isn't doing. I'm talking about making things that seem and are new, different from those before. Look," he continued, "that's what I wanted to tell you when I pointed out those fighters; nothing like them had been seen before. There were all those little snub noses, with faces that seemed to be looking, and then they started to fly, and their flight was exactly the way it was had to be, and the noise they made. Huuuum . . . !"

Miguel traced their flight with a movement of his hand, imitating their pitiful little noise at the same time. I was looking at him, unable to say anything, too affected by seeing him approach my own stuff. He interpreted my silence as an unwillingness to understand, and he said: "But you have to understand it. Once I heard you say something exactly the same."

"When? What can I have said about this?"

"No, it wasn't about this," he agreed; "you were talking about something else, but it doesn't matter. It was one day when you were putting on some records. You made a comment, about *The Art of the Fugue*, I think, and you said that what you like about Bach is how when he moves from one theme to another the listener feels that the next theme had to come next, inevitably, as if he already knew it beforehand; and simultaneously he notices the newness, he sees that something has been said for the first time."

"Well, I do remember having said something like that," I said, waiting for the ending.

"Don't you realize? It's the same; that surprise of the thing that starts off and goes where it has to go. That day I didn't make any comment, but when you said what you did about Bach, it seemed very accurate to me, and immediately I thought about these things."

"The association is very curious and quite logical," I responded. "And I understand much better than you imagine. What surprises me is that it seems like an answer to what I've been thinking about for some time. Except I was thinking about original sin, and now I see we're dealing with the rebellion of the angels. You understand?"

"No, not at all," he said.

"Well, I don't understand the angels' rebellion either; that's something I never could understand. But the question now is not one of understanding; let's take that for granted. What's involved now are the effects, which could provide an explanation for many things. I'm in original sin, and you, who represent the next generation, are part of the angels' rebellion; because we're going toward the beginning."

"That I do seem to understand," Miguel said, and we sat down on a stone bench, since we were passing right beside it. We could have gone to a bar, and I think that's where we were headed—we were getting ready to cross the street at the del Plata market—, but just at that moment we came to the bench, beneath a ceibo tree, and we sat down. At three o'clock we were still there, and we'd clarified very few things.

The surprise Miguel's discovery had caused me made it hard for me to talk naturally; I wanted to probe his intelligence, but I didn't want to submit him to an interrogation. So I decided to probe his sense of humor, to see if he was able to take things as a joke without lowering the level, and I said to him: "I'm reminded now of a play by Lope de Vega . . . The doctor goes to see a sick man and says to him: 'If you have a fever, don't deny it . . .'"

Miguel laughed a little and then waited for an explanation of the enigma.

"You know, I thought you were dumb, what people call a moron?"

"Oh yes, yes, I knew that," he answered naturally.

"And now it turns out you don't seem to be. Of course I should have gone to the trouble to investigate, but instead I have the idea of asking you. So you're not as dumb as you seem? If you are, though, don't deny it. Okay?"

"No, I'm not hiding anything from you," he said with perfect innocence, without irony.

"In that case we can continue," and we continued.

However, it was very difficult to coordinate our differences and similarities. We'd been close for a moment when our minds grazed the idea of harmony, but "I was afraid, because I was naked and I hid." I was afraid of what I'd just learned, but he wasn't. I tried to explain to him that in his innocence there was a certain inhumanity.

"I think that in beings like you," I said, "evil is almost unthinkable, the way it is in angels, but there's something that can cause your downfall. The machine is your child and you're as pleased with it as if it were equal to the Creator's children."

"But don't you like machines?" he interrupted me, shocked.

"Yes, I like them a lot, but I'm aware at the same time that the machine holds me spellbound with its circles, with its groaning as seductive as a cat's purr, it's also murdering a number of citizens in a very amusing way. Wait, wait a minute," I said to him, refusing to be cut off. "If the camera takes me close to the murdered citizens, if I see them agonizing and vomiting blood, if I see them in the operating room, with their bellies open, I'm still enjoying myself a great deal. You said a moment ago that the precision and consequentiality in Bach's themes made you think of the consequentiality and function in machines; that in any process of destruction there's the same rigorous consistency."

"That's true. Have you noticed how fire consumes things?"

"Of course, I look my eyes out watching until every spine's left clean."

"And when there's an explosion on one of those huge boats, have you noticed how a dense, round flower forms? What happens is so different from magazine illustrations, for example—a bright-colored star all bristly with jagged points—, when in fact the star's contained in the atmosphere, where its development is regulated and occurs in spirals."

"Well, that beauty we find in destruction has an angelic origin. Except for certain insects that are drawn to the light, you won't see any animal attracted by a destructive element; whereas men, for all our worship of creation, find it fascinating to watch how the evil angels undo it."

"But machines aren't only used for undoing creation," Miguel said.

"They're for anything you want, but we like them for something that has nothing to do with their purpose."

We kept walking along Rivadavia that way, went in to have some empanadas at a bar on the corner of Libertad that stays open until after midnight, and finally took a taxi on the Avenida. When I left Miguel at the door of his apartment, he said by way of conclusion: "Of all the things we've talked about, the only one that's definite is the business about how we're going toward the beginning."

It's impossible, though, and it's not necessary to transcribe everything we talked about in those days. The truth is, for some time all we did was talk. Dreadful things were happening in the world, and we talked about them from our safe distance. Something was happening in our lives too; there were some important events during that period. The only truly important thing was what we said about those events and what we left unsaid.

To make the story short, the first planting of poppies was a failure and there was a considerable deficit, since for months that experiment had taken priority over everything else.

Back in the month of October, one of the workers had already advised me that someone—a Dutchman, I believe—had told him, "Don't expect a large harvest; good year for corn, bad for poppies." I'd taken it as one of those things you hear from people who live in the country. Of course before too long I could see that he came pretty close to the truth. In December, some of the plants did bloom; the rest died, and there was nothing we could do about it. But I refused to give everything up for lost, which would have been far more practical; I wanted to start producing the product, because I felt impatient to make it with my new equipment. I think that if I'd saved only one flower, I would have triumphantly carried its seed to the lab. Well, I saved more than one, but less than half of what would have been necessary to obtain a modest yield. And this is one of the things we did not talk about. So we reached the month of May and were still hiding the situation, until the moment arrived when we had to face it; we had to decide whether or not we would plant again the following month.

It frequently happens that men who had a really hard time finding a job recall their first paycheck. I've heard the most moving stories about this subject and always laughed at them. Immediately afterwards I've reflected on my circumstances, which were very special; everything was given to me at once, and a specific detail like that was lost in the host of impressions worrying me at the time. But then I've always added: in any case, no matter what the beginning of my life was like, I would never preserve that way—in an herbarium—the sweet memory of the first bit of money I earned. The memory of my first failure, I definitely would, and I admit it. That memory I will never forget.

I detest dry wind, the kind that whirls the dust around and throws it in your face; it was one of those days. I'd stayed at Las Murtas with Gálvez, the young man who works in the office, because the previous afternoon we'd started work on the books, and everything was turning out terribly. We wanted to believe there were mistakes, so we conscientiously went over everything again, but there weren't any. It got very late and I suggested to Gálvez that we stay there. I told him it was to avoid driving at night, one of the things I like most, but since he didn't know that my explanation seemed natural to him and we stayed. I wanted to think by myself, surrounded by the whole situation, and I was sure I'd spend the night wide awake, turning everything over in my mind; but as soon as I got into bed I realized I needed to stop, turn everything off, and wait for morning when I could look at things in the daylight. I slept like a log. And in the morning, daylight brought the worst light possible, to my taste. There was not a cloud in the sky, and a wild dust cloud was arising on the roads, coming in gusts to bang against the windowpanes.

I went to get out the car, shielding myself from the dust with my hand, but at the same time noticing everything as I passed, and everything wore a reproachful expression, a grief-stricken hostility, in the face of which I could find no excuses. The stubble remaining from the planting made the field look as though it were in tatters. I'd seen the pastures dry before, but this time it was different. What was there were ruins, rubble from a project.

We went as far as the gate at top speed; then, once on the road, I tried to slow the pace of both our trip and my agitation. I asked Gálvez if they would dock him for missing that morning, since I knew he had another job in Buenos Aires, and he said that no, he could miss sometimes and nothing much would happen. So I invited him to have lunch on Munich de Constitución in order to compensate him a little. He lived two blocks from there, and he left as soon as he finished eating, but I stayed, having a second cup of coffee and then a third. I was still in no condition to go home. What I needed was a dress rehearsal for my serenity; I had to talk with someone about what had happened. I'd talked a great deal with Gálvez, but in professional terms, and what I needed at that moment was to get used to saying, "This isn't anything very important. We'll do such and such right away. It will all be recouped in a few months." The only people I could talk with in that tone were the Garcías; I phoned and said I was going to stop by.

When I went in I felt sure I'd done the right thing by going, although I was afraid. I knew I would give them the news skillfully, but I was afraid of Julieta's reaction. I felt terrified, nauseated by the possibility their older son would be there; fortunately he was not and everything turned out well. I explained the situation, and they were the ones who hurried to tell me that there was no need to be upset, that those things always happen when one starts a new business, and that the second try was sure to produce better results. Everything went like a dream, but even so, in Julieta's living room I felt as though the wind from the pampa were rising.

García turned on the radio and Julieta exclaimed: "Ay! Tomás, you always put that blasted thing on too loud. You know very well I have a migraine today."

The look in García's eyes was so innocent I could tell he didn't know anything. He turned down the radio. Julieta picked up her sewing basket and began to knit rapidly. Afraid she might be revealing her nervousness, she smiled and said, running her hand across her forehead, "This way the music's enjoyable, and you don't have those trumpet blasts bouncing off the walls."

After a moment of embarrassment in which García didn't know how to broach the subject because he realized he was not a specialist but at the same time didn't want to let the subject pass without adding something of his own, without contributing at least a small declaration to that conjuring of danger, he decided to say: "About the poppies, there was something I didn't like from the first; or at least something that make me stop and think—the fact that you had to bring the stuff from China or from somewhere far away."

"But García," I said, "Europe is at war. It's not possible to deal with Germany or Hungary."

"Order them from Spain; it's safer."

"There are no poppy fields in Spain."

"Well, in my village there were always poppies."

"Really? And why did people plant them?"

"For decoration. The little garden at the hospital was full of them, and there was also a big clump at the station. Not that an opium poppy was such a rare thing. Royal poppies was what we called them there."

"Yes, García," I said, "for decoration that would be enough, but for what I plan to do . . ."

"I assure you they were used for everything. The pharmacist saved the husks and when someone had a toothache all he had to do was boil a few of them in milk and rinse out his mouth with it, so they must have had some effect."

"Of course, they were really poppies, but here we need to get material of the highest quality."

"And do you think the Chinese are going to send you the best they have? In my opinion, if you can raise poppies in La Mancha there's no reason they won't grow in Argentina."

"So you suspect the seeds they sent me were in bad condition?"

"It wouldn't surprise me a bit."

"Well, that's not how it was; no, we've made one mistake after another."

"You want to blame it all on yourself," García said, adding a triumphant smile: "The best thing that can happen is that both our reasons are accurate. I think poppies can grow well here, you say they were ruined because you didn't know how to raise them. Plant them again, and the second time you won't make the same mistakes; in other words they'll end up growing, that's how it seems to me."

"That's right," Julieta said, "listen to Tomás, he always knows what he's talking about." She smiled, agreeing with her husband's words, but in the corner of her eye or, rather, in a few sidelong glances cast into the corners of the room, she looked like a frightened little rabbit.

I left feeling somewhat calmer. It was getting dark, and I opened the door without making any noise, stepping softly on the hall carpet as I went in so they wouldn't hear me, because I sensed there were voices, and I wanted to know who it was; if there had been company, I would have turned back and gone in through the service entrance. But the person speaking was Herminia. I peered between the portieres that closed off the hall and saw Quitina and Francisco sitting on the floor, beside the fireplace. Quitina had Jorge in her lap, and the three of them were listening silently to a story Herminia was telling. Her resonant, professorial voice was saying, " . . . she was holding the child by the hand and it was very, very cold . . ."

I was just about to pull back the portieres and burst into the living room, but I thought: if I were to walk in upon a concert, the usher would stop me. Why break that confluence of emotions? If I go in, the children will pounce on me, and the story will be over; it's better to wait until the end. From my observation post I could watch them perfectly; both curtains had been left open a little more than a centimeter and, since I didn't turn on the light, they couldn't see me, whereas I didn't miss a detail.

I hadn't missed out on the plot of the story either; it was an old story that everyone knows.

"They got to the town," Herminia was saying, "and went knocking from house to house, and at every house people opened the door just a crack and said to them, 'May God help you, sister. May God help you, sister . . .' and they banged the door shut."

Francisco interrupted: "Was the woman real old?"

"No," Herminia answered, "the boy was very little."

Then, seeing that Francisco could not understand how one thing implied the other, she said: "Well, the thing is that the mothers in those small towns always look very old, but no, she wasn't."

Francisco nodded, convinced, and I was left not knowing if there had been some prior description or if what Herminia had taught him to interpret was the mother's magical presence.

The story was about a woman who boils stones so she can feed her son. Since she doesn't receive any alms in the form of real food, she pretends that she knows how to cook with stones, and the village women are tempted by their curiosity and provide her with all the necessary ingredients. The necessary ingredients are exactly what it takes to make garlic soup.

Told like this it all comes to nothing, though; whereas, when Herminia spoke, she was not following a story, she was casting a spell. It was all taking place there in the living room, as in the crystal ball, and what she conjured up was so powerful not because the story was perfect but because she knew exactly the right tone. Herminia was using her academic vocabulary to embody the most subtle nuances of the mother's humility and cunning, of a neighbor woman's greedy curiosity as she opened the door to her: "Come in, come in; here's the fire and the trivet . . ."

The village woman burst forth with those words. The mother asked gently: "If only I had a tiny bit of oil . . ."

The village woman shouted: "Girl, bring the oil."

Then, the mother said: "Ay! I have no salt . . ." and everyone, relatives and neighbors who had come to watch, moved aside to make way for the servant girl bringing the salt tin. Meanwhile the mother stirred the soup carefully so it wouldn't stick.

Herminia said: "It was so quiet in the kitchen you could hear the flies moving. Well, there weren't any flies because it was winter but, if there had been, you could have heard them while that soup was boiling. And nobody said anything because their nostrils were filled with the wonderful little smell, and they began to move closer . . ."

I was about to give myself away because I moved so close to the crack I hit my forehead on the drapes, but they were so heavy they barely parted. I could not help leaning forward because the crowd of people gathered in the kitchen was pressing on my shoulders. There was a concentric force in so much attention that swept me up with the others; and for the same reason, if the drapes had parted, Quitina and the children would not have noticed, since behind them also the neighbors were forming a chorus, and its pressure made them also lean forward without batting an eyelash, while the light of the flames danced on their faces.

Herminia's back was turned toward me, so for a couple of seconds while she remained silent, I couldn't see what she was doing. I had the impression she was lifting the lid off the soup so as to flood the room, all the way to my hiding place, with the marvelous steam and its message of fried garlic, that warm, secular, intimate smell laden with secrets.

"Finally," Herminia said, "the mother poured the soup into the child's bowl and tossed the stones into the yard."

"But, what about the stones?" asked the voice of a grumbling neighbor.

The mother answered, now with neither humility nor cunning, with the naturalness of the triumphant, because triumph is what's natural: "They've already given their nourishment. You can only use them once."

I drew open the drapes and exclaimed: "Bravo, Herminia! Not even an old sorceress could have told it better."

"Sorceress I'm not, but I am getting old," she said.

"No, no you aren't," I protested and went over to give her a hug. "You're something very ancient, from another time when the word 'youth' had a very different meaning than it does now . . ."

But my speech was lost in the shouting, as the boys leaped onto my neck, saying: "If only you'd been here, Papá! You missed a wonderful story!"

Quitina continued to sit on the floor, as if she were incapable of reacting.

"But I did hear it; I was there behind that curtain, and I heard the whole thing."

"Really, you heard the whole thing? How lucky!" Quitina said and reached out her arms to me.

I went over to kiss her and saw the sparkle in her eyes, which were almost wet, and they had that fixed look they take on when, like a sponge, she lets an emotion soak into her, meeting it halfway, in a kind of levitation that, far from resembling an abduction, is like a firm, decisive departure into space.

The boys went off to have dinner, and Herminia got ready to leave as well. We insisted that she stay but she refused. She wanted Miguel to eat early, because the next morning he had to get up at dawn. We made all kinds of suggestions, trying to show her the two possibilities were compatible, but there was no way to convince her. She spread herself thin in household details as if those things were highly important, although it was not as if she used them consciously, as a pretext; she felt truly driven by them, drowned in a glass of water. Within the limits of that glass, even if she were drowning, she felt more secure than if she were floating in the ocean where sometimes she got lost. Meanwhile, I had my arm around Quitina's waist and from time to time leaned my face against her cheek, bending down the way one does to kiss a child, as if I were playing—Herminia wasn't shocked by this game—, but I was doing it from feeling Quitina's tension as, in a state of total absence, she answered Herminia. Quitina could not come out of the previous moment, she could not come down out of it. My arm was around her waist, but it felt as though I could barely reach her, as if I were on a different plane, and I had to keep Quitina there by pulling on her. It will probably seem hyperbolic if I say there was a special taste on her skin, one I knew from other occasions: the intensity of her emotion was oozing through her cheek, as if all her blood were thinking.

When we were alone we sat in front of the fireplace again and, making an enormous effort, Quitina returned to reality and began to ask me what I'd done while I was gone for so long, what was happening at Las Murtas. She'd suspected something was wrong; I told her everything.

Quitina said that we'd done the wrong thing by leaving there. It was a sin to abandon all that and leave it reduced to nothing but a field for industrial cultivation; she'd felt this way from the beginning but hadn't said anything so as not to dampen the enthusiasm I was pouring into the new venture.

"You know what it seemed like to me? A betrayal, an infidelity; that's why I didn't say anything. I moved into your camp out of cowardice. If I'd started to reproach you, it would have been as if something from all that were getting to me, and I didn't have the courage."

It scared me that Quitina could formulate it all so clearly, and I protested: "No camps and no betrayals, everything you've just said is a novel, a very realistic one, but a novel you've invented with your imagination. The reality is we wanted to conduct the experiment, Las Murtas's tranquillity had to be sacrificed for a period; besides, there's no need for you to deny yourself city life, you don't have to stay cut off from the people you've known since you were a girl."

"Yes," she interrupted, "what you say is realistic too, but we have to try to make sure things there go back to how they were before."

"Naturally. I'm going to try again and as soon as I feel completely sure of the procedure, things will be in perfect order; that's not inconsistent."

Quitina shook her head: "No, no, no; what you have to do is move everything away from the house. A single strand of wire can separate the garden from the pastures where you enter the estancia, but not from an area where there are tractors driving around and gangs of workers showing up to take care of the plants."

"But, Quitina," I said, "we can't put the estancia next to the house and plant next to the dairy."

"No, of course not. What I'm telling you is everything should go back to the way it was before and, that if you want to plant, you should buy more land. The estancia is too small for both things. Below, near the hollow, there are lots; buy fifty, a hundred hectares, whatever you need . . ."

Too surprised for words, I let her speak. Finally I was able to say: "But don't you realize the most important thing about what I've just told you is that we've lost a heap of money?"

"Oh, well I'll ask Papá to send me some."

"No, please, don't say anything to him! There's something even more important," and I grabbed both of her hands forcefully. "Listen carefully," I told her, "you've never thought about any of this, it's like a lesson you haven't learned, but now the moment has come when you have to learn it."

Since there was nothing further from me, Quitina said: "I'm listening to you . . ."

"Well," I finally started, "your father has put all this in my hands; you must remember I had nothing, absolutely nothing."

Quitina looked up at the ceiling and shouted: "What nonsense! Is this what I have to listen to? I don't feel like it!" She was squirming, trying to get free.

"Well, listen to just one word, just to this. My responsibility is enormous, and you can take it as a joke if you like, but think about it carefully: Do you think Julieta would take it the same way?"

Quitina stopped struggling and grew serious: "No, Julieta no, of course not," she said.

"Julieta knows the value of money. More precisely, she's acquainted with the relation between money and suffering. Understand? Because there's a principle, and it's a lesson that's very easy to learn when you have enough experience." Quitina nodded silently, and I added, "Herminia knows this."

Quitina nodded her head again, but I noticed that she was moving away and did not hear me; she'd flown off after something. "The thing is," I said then, "the conditions are perfect for you to understand, I even think this could obsess you." She continued not to listen, and I squeezed her hands more tightly, shaking her a little; she nodded again, but without realizing. "I sense that this might be highly attractive to you, like an abyss," I continued, "I'm thinking that, deep down, sometimes you would like it if you had to boil stones for your sons."

She jolted out of her absence as violently as if I'd jerked her from a state of sleepwalking.

"But, how do you know I was thinking about that?"

"Well," I said, "I always know what you're thinking about, but this time it's been easier than ever. Don't you see that while Herminia was telling the story I was behind the curtains listening, and I could see everything that was going through your head as clearly as I can see it now."

"And do you understand it?" Quitina asked, enormously anxious.

"Not much better than you do."

"The thing is, I don't understand at all. Nevertheless, I know it's not anything false or seeming. I don't know what it is, but I know it's true."

"What is it that's true, what is it you felt while you were listening to the story?" Quitina looked at me questioningly and anxiously, as if to say, "Why are you asking me if you say you know?"

"Because," I added, "I want you to formulate it for yourself; if it's something true, say it."

"But I can't, I don't know . . . Look, I was there with the boys. Jorge was in my lap, I had my arms around him, and Francisco was sitting so close to me I could feel his breathing, and I was thinking: how different it would be if we were on that road, feeling so cold . . . You understand? Because that little child needed the warmth of his mother, whereas my children have the radiator, the fireplace . . ."

I smiled, although I was moved inside, and Quitina protested: "But this is serious. Not serious, tragic. I feel that there's something tragic in all this."

"I don't doubt that," I said seriously, and Quitina shook her head. "No, no; there's something tragic that's easy to see, but that's not what I'm not referring to. I see other things so different they seem the contrary but, if we look at what's tragic about them, they turn out to be identical."

My attention encouraged her to continue: "If a person says, it's tragic that some children have a fireplace and other children don't, anyone understands, but I was thinking about something else: it's tragic that some children *don't have* a fireplace and it's tragic that other children *do have* a fireplace."

Quitina took her head in her hands and buried her fingers in her hair, scratching her scalp hard, as if to activate her ideas.

"But don't you see all this seems crazy? Don't you see it's not like this, it's not like this?"

"I know how it is," I told her, "I've seen it from behind the curtains. So I want us to talk about it, to keep it from getting lost."

"That's reasonable, because the truth is, it seems to be trying to get away. I don't know," Quitina continued, "if that's because you can only feel these things as through a painting. Sometimes when I've been in a museum in New York, it's occurred to me to sit in front of a painting, and think things, which are happening inside it, which could only happen there inside it. You know what I mean? Herminia's story was like a painting; the way she told it was so wonderful."

"Yes," I said, "the way Herminia told it was wonderful, but in the story itself there's a perfection that doesn't consist in how the story is told. It's a very old story, it's tradition, and we can only use 'tradition' to describe things that, when we hear them, we say what you said before. I don't know what it is, but I know it's true."

"Yes, that's it, but why can't a person know what it is that's true?"

And she said, as if she were concentrating with great effort: "Look, while I was listening to her, while I was feeling a terrible pity for that little boy who was suffering from so much cold, at the same time I was feeling choked with pity for my own children because *they can't suffer that cold*. Do you understand? As if that cold were the most exquisite or the most beneficial thing, something so costly I can't give it to them."

It frightened me to realize that Quitina's voice was breaking and threatened by tears, and I regretted that I'd made her look into all this so deeply, but now I could not restrain her; now she was the one determined to keep bringing it into the open. She took a deep breath and continued firmly, although she was becoming more and more agitated.

"Because what can a person do with her children? Tell me. You devote your constant attention to them, you take care of them, you educate them, but nothing happens. Thank God nothing happens! That's the thing . . . If nothing happens, how can such a passionate love be proved?"

"But is it necessary to prove love?" I said, not able to restrain myself.

Quitina must have seen the anguish in my eyes, because her own anguish increased a hundredfold.

"No, it's not necessary to prove anything. Even so, one would like . . . I don't know what." And then, desperately: "Why is it necessary to want something if one has everything?"

I saw her grow absent again, look into space, and go back into the painting.

But at the same time she held fast to her resolution to tell me, and she started to speak, her voice rather neutral, as though afraid her voice might distract her attention from where it was fixed: "How could I explain to you what I felt as I listened to that? I felt it as though I were using an organ I'd carried around with me for a long time but never used . . . and now I remember that when I was very little, when I'd read the lives of the martyrs I'd feel something a bit similar."

I could see in her eyes that the painting was becoming more complicated, filling with very diverse horrors, and she continued: "How can a thing be horrifying but wonderful at the same time? How can suffering be not repugnant?"

She stopped looking at the painting and, looking at something very close, her own depths, she said desperately: "I think it's because a person is not good enough, a person is not good enough to be content with . . ." and she began to cry violently, racked with grief, like a child in a dark room.

All that is very distant, but I can make it out as if it were something climactic. And perhaps that flat, normal time, free of conflicts, was the high point of my life. I always thought so, my goal was always to reach a perfect equilibrium, and it turns out, when I recall that period, I can't help searching it for moments of anguish, unease, fear, the way one picks treasures from trash. This seems like an unhealthy inclination, and it also seems like cowardice, because I could certainly describe an entirely different perspective on our life; not everything was a failure.

Is this a question of my not daring to leave evidence of unsurpassed days of family life? Maybe it seems despicable to me, when the world was going through such terrible times? No, it has nothing to do with that. I was trying to live well, as were so many others, and I was managing to do that. Maybe I'm afraid that by telling about the family peace I've aspired to, I'll be describing a prosaic, rather embarrassing bourgeois scene? No, that's not it either. I often see those totally fulfilled couples, each with a pile of kids and a few hectares of land, and I stand spellbound, watching their most trivial activities. You could not find anything more harmonious; they're like colonnades or musical scales. Sometimes they have leggy Fords that can hold eight or ten, they ride bareback on their creole horses and wear baggy trousers and sandals like gauchos, but they're so composed they seem free of all limits. Such lives can be described: it's theater. Seeing them on their little plots of land, each with its willow and its ombu tree, you'd say they must feel confined, but they don't; time weighs lightly on them because they're full of future.

Well, those people who feel so certain, so satisfied, are generally small landowners with newly acquired property, and almost always from northern Europe. In the old families, it's something else entirely, because well-being doesn't make for peace among so many cousins, what with today's notion of refinement chock full of dumb vulgarity. Our situation's different: we neither follow the traffic lanes of family tradition nor are we simple, future-minded colonists, we're . . . It's evident we're not any one clear thing; above all, we aren't naive. There, I think I've hit it on the head: we aren't naive! And that's an extremely important condition. To work the land and raise children, a person has to be naive; to maintain at a level of nobility, without registering anything on the seismograph, a person has to be naive! When you come out of a trunk knocked about by great storms, when you've never taken root anywhere, you already look at yourself as a drifting seed, and you say: Good, let's get on with it!

Ordinarily, that kind of outlook on life leads people to confront great risks and tackle unusual, outlandish norms and styles. Extravagance was always repulsive to me; I was always drawn to normality as the highest goal. Because extravagance is easy, and normality is difficult.

I dared to place on love the burdens of a pile of children and a promise of eternal fidelity. It's well known love can't survive on such a regimen; even so I've imposed it on love, because that's the outrage I want to create. Maybe because it's the best proof? Quitina, in her absolutely pure, absolutely irrefutable love, Quitina wants to be scourged by proof; she feels anguished because nothing is happening, maybe because nothing happening makes her afraid, almost as afraid as the possibility that something might happen. We know that risk is an affirmation of life; nevertheless we don't want risk for the people we love, even though we fear the lack of risk will dim love. We're afraid of our comfortable, easy lives, but we'd be embarrassed to make them uncomfortable in order to find them more pleasurable. And above all, the die was cast a long time ago: we've decided together, and there could never be a more integral agreement. Only from time to time does some small character trait prompt us to notice that we each live in our own skin.

A few days after I met with the Garcías, when I was at Las Murtas one day in the afternoon, I was standing at the door of the factory talking with the foreman, when off in the distance, along the right bank of the stream on the land that used to be the Arcaya estancia, a car came bolting across the boggy ground where there's no road. It was bounding over the ridges and gullies like a goat, and it was a large car, a Packard. The foreman saw I was looking at it.

"Yes," he said, "it's the señora."

"What do you mean, the señora?"

"She came two or three days ago about the Arcaya deal," he said, "I met her on the road. Now she seems to be turning in here."

I started to run toward the gate, and in fact Quitina soon appeared driving the large car, which had escaped unharmed.

She stopped beside me, stuck her head out the window, and said, as if there were nothing else to say: "It's done."

"What's done?" I asked.

"What I was doing. I bought that lot below," she said, smiling.

"You bought it!"

"Well, I made a strong verbal commitment. Tomorrow you go, take care of the deed, and pay."

As she was saying this, Quitina opened the car door so I could get in; she moved over from the driver's side and settled herself in her seat as if she were ready to move to another topic. Before starting out, I asked: "But with what money?"

She raised her eyebrows, shrugged her shoulders, and didn't answer, looking at me as if to say, What a stupid question!

I began to get furious.

"I had made it perfectly clear to you, I had asked you to do me the favor of not saying a word!"

She cut me off: "Look, my father has been my accomplice for my entire life, and he's not going to stop now . . . Let's go, start driving. What are you waiting for?"

I started to drive, perplexed, silent so my anger wouldn't soften. Quitina leaned on my arm and, as if she were pushing the car with the pressure of her shoulder, and as if she were still driving wildly, she started to say: "You'll see how well those famous little plants produce on that slope. Now we don't have to worry about them! Of course, if you like another lot more you can exchange this one; nothing's been set in stone."

She was quiet for a moment and then she said: "We're at the end of April, it's bound to start raining a lot!" She curled her arm around mine and I shivered, as if for the first time I felt her breast pressing on my arm.

At that moment we'd gone nearly halfway up the road and were passing somewhere near the owl's post. It was a dry afternoon with a reddish sunset, but Quitina kept talking.

"When the pasture's grown in again, humid, on those short gray afternoons when there's no wind, when you can hear the tiniest sound the birds make . . . Look, I don't know . . ."

The dry afternoon with its ruddy sky had turned into the gray afternoon of my first day at Las Murtas as I heard her say, "I don't know . . ."; it turned into a night with a full moon when Quitina clutched my arm, saying as we passed through the gate: "I don't know what comes over me on this road with nothing special about it, but it's so beautiful."

I thought she was going to repeat those same words, but she said: "I don't know what I need to know here, but I always have the impression that soon I'm going to discover something."

I threw my seriousness out the window, the way you toss out a cigarette butt, and hugged her against me insanely, just as I had the first day that I brought her to Las Murtas.

Then we went back toward Buenos Aires, and then I don't know what else happened. What happened was happiness, passing like an eraser over the chalkmarks of anxiety. Constancy returned to spreading its flora.

There's a sort of vegetal, unforeseeable tenaciousness in fidelity. Where and when you least expect it, a seed appears in the air and a weed sprouts, eventually producing a new, intact blossom, but one absolutely identical to all the blossoms bound by the law of that weed. Does this mean within fidelity there's no freedom? No, that's not what it means, because I'm not referring to the natural, forced process but to the grace evident when you witness fidelity with your own eyes. Of course there is also the fidelity of the apprentice as he copies an illustration. But the fidelity that's worth something is the other one, the one that when you don't remember anything, a sudden appearance of spring can make everything burst into bloom, the same way it did the spring before.

I continue to use natural phenomena as examples, clinging to a mythic vision the educated man considers childish. Be that what it may, but I can't do without it. My intelligence needs the forms, expression, and gestures of matter as milestones; it's thanks to them that I can conduct my graphological study of God.

So we planted again in the lowlands. I found a very capable foreman—that Dutchman who predicted my failure. Now he's an old man in Argentina, and he has the advantage of knowing the land, without having forgotten the Asiatic secrets from his youth in the colonies. The traffic moved away from the house, but for a long time the cattle walked apprehensively on the hectares slashed up by the tractors. Since everything was calm, we went there some weekends, always saying that at any moment we would stay for good, but at that moment it was hard to leave Buenos Aires. Why? I don't know. News from Europe arrived simultaneously in all parts of the country. As I've said, we belonged to none of the groups involved in some activity related to the war; nevertheless, our social life was more intense than ever, and there was also another activity, one as useless as it was inevitable: making war on each other.

With each event, each rumor, no matter how patently false, you had to respond according to the ritual, say the word that meant *s'engager*;

and the courts that formed would don a dramatic and, at times, a comic nature.

It was indeed dramatic, and to such an extent that life's become tinged with drama, perhaps forever; it was dramatic to see the most mercenary, most wretched, most prostituted word worked marvelously as a picklock to force open the most honorable doors. It was dramatic to see how people who considered themselves proverbially noble would open their hearts to the most viscous vermin, just as long as someone just threw the ABRACADABRA in their faces.

It was comical, comical to the point of tears, to see how the poor little impostors, the imitators who copied some prestigious pattern, how they caricatured its style, thinking they were reproducing it. Nevertheless, the ritual continued. We could not separate ourselves, it was our way of watching over them; it was a magical simulacrum.

I say "simulacrum" because I'm not talking about the eighteenth-century-style gatherings that might form in certain cafés or in the homes of certain intellectuals—modest intellectuals, of course—where the bitter arguments could be justified by the rigor of their dialectic; I'm talking about the social get-togethers in which everything ran like clockwork. The gatherings of the well-to-do, the same gatherings as always, the ones that had arisen as a consequence of . . . but they seemed to be taking place beneath a bell jar of those consequences.

I won't talk about the dramatic gatherings in which many people were mortally wounded. That can't be helped! They're counted among the fallen. But one of the comical gatherings comes to mind, and it's worthy of being perpetuated. I recall it as something exemplary, vague, and violent, like a delirium.

Where was Quitina? I don't know, but we'd arrived a bit late at a cocktail party, which was in full swing, and we'd gotten separated by the current. I was by the fireplace when the thing started; my right foot was on the edge of the stone bench at the hearth, forming a small angle with my knee, letting me stand still without minding. I was comfortable; besides, I was drinking something I liked, something cold with a scent of gin that lightened the warm atmosphere of the living room.

I was talking with two women, two beautiful women; well, they were talking. I was absent, sailing in the cold of my aperitif, but I'd left them my smiling presence, which might have seemed attentive.

"What dahlias!" I heard suddenly. "Don't you like them?" And I realized that they were addressing me.

"Yes, very much," I said and looked at the dahlias, which were above the fireplace. In a vase, there were some large pink dahlias with long, irregular petals.

Unhappy with my answer, my interlocutor said: "Ay, no, it seems to me that you don't like them; you've said it without any conviction."

I didn't want to deprive her of the glory of having been right, did not want to miss my chance to talk about something comfortable, as comfortable as the position of my foot on the fireplace.

I felt slightly embarrassed; the conversation was descending too far. That kind of thing is tolerable only among sixteen-year-old kids. I smiled rather ambiguously, while I looked for a way to raise the level of our mockery. But my adversary beat me to it. To such an extent that I was startled; all of a sudden, she was talking about Aristotle. And she didn't stop there: before I could recover my senses, she was already on Saint Thomas, and two minutes later she was talking about Hegel.

Then I distanced myself conscientiously. Oh, no, I said to myself, I'm not following her along this course! My foot's nice and warm from the fireplace; my cocktail's gone, but any minute one of the servants will come by with his tray, and I'll get a refill. I'm comfortable and nothing makes me more uncomfortable than the inane.

While I was entrenching myself in this decision—what church fathers would she not attack? And all because of what? Because of what I'd said: a few anathematized words; I'd shown a preference for something rigorously aligned—a form of discipline, although a natural one. Who would be able to form an entente of elective affinities with me? That idea passed through my head, making clear to me how tricky a battle had just begun.

This is the important thing; we'd been standing beside the fireplace for fifteen minutes, apparently in peace, but a secret war had been unleashed two minutes after our conversation started. Suddenly, and without thinking, I'd said a few words about the most banal subject, about a flower—a flower that was not even in front of us—, a few words capable of suggesting remote concomitances with the spirit of the current war, and from that moment I could be considered an enemy. And therefore, the real war between us, the unmentionable war, could become more virulent.

But the worst thing was that I remained passive. Only the tedium was having an impact on me and, not finding the appropriate arms at hand, I was beating the most shameful retreat to unreality. She was talking now about Leon Chestov or maybe about Chiang Kai-shek, and I was soaring back to the first time I truly saw flowers. The incomparable smalt of Switzerland's flowers! Like a memory of love, the blue of its gentians perched before my eyes. Below, at ground level, that woman kept talking about Aristotle, and she obviously had a good body inside her designer dress, but . . . I was screaming at her, futilely: "No, my hands will not stray to that body because the pleasure it offers is insipid compared with this blue . . . ," and aloud: "You were saying? . . . Yes, of course."

I continued to see the lilies and the jonquils in their pure, strict forms, and those solemn, dark dahlias that seemed to be thinking—to themselves, "Which you, lady, apparently never could to do . . ."—, it appeared to me that they were thinking, because in their immobility they demonstrated the dynamism in their lines, their discipline that combined with the velvet of their surface to form a sort of double, contrastive smoothness.

"The Japanese have drawn that extreme softness . . ." I started to say.

"The Japanese!" my interlocutor exclaimed with dismay. "The Japanese!" she repeated in a rage. And she lashed out against the Japanese with angry, agitated words.

At first I didn't understand her rage. I remained enraptured in the memory of dahlias distinct or blurred in the mist of a Japanese gouache, until finally I realized that she was alluding to something different; she was alluding to the illuminated sign that now says Parque Retiro, where it used to say Parque Japonés.

Well, it's hardly necessary to say that my confidante did not mention the sign, even in passing; she was talking about the causes, the events that had occasioned the change, and from time to time I could put in "Of course, of course," "Naturally," "There's no doubt about it," while I was thinking of the tango "Garufa."

The cadence of the last line was wandering through my head like a lost soul: "En el Parque Japonés," "En el Parque Japonés" . . . and now where? Sparkling in the night sky, the sign was destroying my illusion of the park more than the actual sight had done. That ending of "Garufa" had an indescribably evocative force for me when I was still in Europe. The Parque Japonés was an Eden where I would meet my dates when I was eighteen years old. Beneath its almond trees in full bloom, beneath its kiosks, in the middle of its little vermillion bridges, I knew from then on that someone was waiting for me. And when I saw the real Parque Japonés, which was so different from what I'd imagined, the logical thing would have been for me to feel disappointed, but I definitely did not feel disappointed. Not even when I saw that in fact the meaning of the name was reduced to the decoration on the ticket booths at the entrance. I accepted its real form, and the marvels of its cardboard caves, which offered a tenebrist-style illustration of the tango's cadence. Whereas, when the name was missing, any evocation was shut out in the cold, as if it had been evicted and was desperately seeking asylum in my memory.

Meanwhile, I nodded my head in acquiescence, repeating: "Of course, of course." But the last cadence of "Garufa" was gradually enveloping me, and I probably ran my eyes over the body of my enemy with a certain languor, which she judged to be desire. Then she tensed up indignantly, as if to say, "Too late! Before, when we were talking about flowers, about nature, was the right moment, but you let it pass." Yes, she was certainly thinking all this as in her indignation she rambled on about imperialism, although it did not prevent her from simultaneously accentuating her charms with suggestive poses, thinking herself appreciated. And I, always enveloped by the ending of "Garufa," always saying aloud, "Obviously," I was sorry I had to be so implacable with her. A cruel stubbornness was leading me to continue by telling her, "There was only one moment when the tango called for a body as much as a bandonion. If one of these diplomats, writers, or landowners would suddenly have had a bandonion in his arms, I would have wrapped my arm around your waist, because your body is anti-Aristotelian but it's the one closest to me, and there, in the middle of the room before, all these respectable people, our steps would have locked in dance. Then I would have set you down on a chair, exactly the way one sets down a bandonion."

Insulted by this clarification, my opponent secured herself irreducibly in her convictions, classifying me as an Aristotelian, an imperialist, and an enemy of nature.

I've not wasted my time describing the folly of a social gathering like this one for the pleasure of caricaturing it, I've only tried to show that its fabric is reversible. On one side, a serious, continuous tone; on the other, a motley of colors. This lining is very appealing in an overcoat, but it's carefully concealed by the textile industry of high-society conversations; it's never mentioned in the ads, and you can't see it in the catalogs, which present only the outer side.

To be more precise: in social relations there's always a double background of unspoken words, of strangled intentions. The secret of this double plot is guarded jealously and reproduced in the underground workshops of opinion, where it's copied rigorously. Social relations endure, then, like paintings or wall tapestries, which constitute an everlasting testimony—of the skirmish, for example, between two people while they held cocktail glasses in never-wavering hands. (What a horribly snobbish paragraph! Well, that's how it seems, but it's a simple, realistic sketch. In its full scope, in the most elevated form it ever attained: "He who dippeth his hand with me in the dish"—there, you have the whole thing in a nutshell. But of course, customs have changed, so fashion demands different colors; although the saying's eternal popularity shows that always, before and after, life has been woven *à double face*).

The rules of this intricate labor are very complicated—on the outside, a constant smooth incandescence; on the inside, violent dissonances or correspondences, aversions or complicities. And the combinations are infinite: two people talk about a third, that is to say, one person talks to a second and tells him something. Usually what he tells him is true to life and straightforward but, on the reverse, the scratches, the wounds inflicted on him by that third person are indicated and the listener notes them and forms an allegiance—he weaves his reverse, agreeing or putting himself on guard.

I outlined this silly episode that occurred beside a vase of dahlias because the most dramatic aspect of those silenced battles usually occurs on sexual ground. Well, not the most dramatic, the most dramatic aspect occurs around money. I meant the most irreparable. When money's at the center, there's always the fear that things will change—for some people, they never change—; in any case, everyone knows they could. Whereas when it's sex at the center . . . in encounters where there's no flirtation, so that refusing or granting is not the issue, where gazes wrestle freestyle, kicking each other cruelly behind the mask of a conversation about social or literary topics . . . well, those encounters, they can set anyone on the path to ostracism.

Encounters that occur in the intellectual sphere are also dangerous; in those, rancor also flows like subterranean lava, devastatingly through their veins, while ambiguous adjectives, the definitions that cling to newly imposed clichés, tinge the outside with whatever color is appropriate to the season.

I repeat: the most dramatic encounters, the really bloody ones, occur on sexual ground, which does not prevent the outcome from usually being logical and foreseeable: the strong crushes the weak and that's it. But things are not always so simple; sometimes, in battles started by matters involving sex, unspeakable matters, the more skillful person—not always the stronger—trips up the other one financially or professionally, and the infinite combinations of rancor, the hidden wounds caused by the verification of one's own value or one's own impotence, spread their subtle web. Here's where slogans come in, to brand the one sentenced, tingeing him with the obligatory vilification.

IO

Finally the war ended, and many people felt happy. Those of us who weren't intoxicated with optimism were more or less considered war criminals. The inevitable comment came up at every turn: "They're not happy with the victory! That shows they were . . . ," and then the obscenity. An obscenity, nothing but a meaningless interjection. And it was true that we weren't happy. But why speak in the plural? I'm not making the same reference as when I usually say "we," because this wasn't something limited to our private world—mine and Quitina's. I say we weren't happy, because I don't think I'm the only one who felt this way. No, I can't possibly be; I know there are others, still watchful, still under arms, as I am. Also, I know this business of being ready for action is now beginning for us. Here, "we" means me and the others I sense at a distance, the ones with whom I think I communicate.

The phase just behind us had been bloody, without precedent; never was more blood spilled. But how stupid that sentence is, how pretty it sounds, how romantic! I meant that human matter was never more insulted, never mocked or dissected more exhaustively. Well, in spite of all that, I—we—sensed that the tumor had not been excised; it had been dissolved, its virulent progress had been halted, but we didn't see the disease right there before our eyes, dead, conquered like a wild beast dangling from a pole with its throat slit, or like an enemy lying flat under the conqueror's foot. The disease was a diffuse malady we all bore in our veins; and we bore the deaths on both sides. The winners' confident harangues about having killed "so as to give life to this or that idea" were useless. For the moment, nothing announced life; we were saturated with death. And this doesn't mean we were more affected or more inconsolable than others might have been on any other battlefield. No more tears have fallen on this field than fell on Troy: what we could not erase was the stench. What refused to subside was not the tribulation of our souls but the shivering of our flesh. It was as if death had taught us a new game, as if it had employed a new means of seduction and, of course, charms that neither painting nor poetry can capture. No blond wigs on skulls, nothing *sombre et pourtant lumineuse*. Death's artistic appearance, of course, can only be expressed in our genuine idiom, the cinema. Now courtesan Death has led us to her chamber and undressed before us, like the invisible man. And that's not the end of it: we've given into *that*, that which was in the process of opening, we've cast our seed into that definitive blindness.

My God, though, why does it all have to come out sounding so pretty? I want to talk about something nauseating and coarse, but if I say, "we're sunk in a filthy sewer," what I've said is gross but not very exact. A sewer's a conduit for the disposal of natural fertilizers. If someone falls into it, you can hardly assume he lost his soul; as for his body, it's added to material that can be used to manure a field. So the sewer can't serve as an example. You have to talk about the hole that remains where *She* undresses, the hole where we copulate.

This has to happen because, as I said before, we bear within us the deaths on both sides. Not the deplorable fact of their deaths, but the death they each bear within, the will to death, the contribution they made to death. Does this mean that we're equating the sides? Don't we point to one camp as more guilty? Yes, one of them is more guilty, but the other isn't innocent. And when it comes to questions of guilt, this business of *more* and *less* is so uncertain. We can say with assurance that, in terms of history, the ones who represent evil in this tragedy broke all records. But the ones who represent good! Write their biography, if you dare! In short, who contributes more to evil? Sin with its devastation, or indolent virtue?

The confluence of the two forms the whirlpool presently sucking up man's will. Both evils swim in that vortex: the two, or the countless, humanities pursue, drag each other, and they don't mix.

But enough generalizing. Everything's a question of humanities, everything is humanity's suffering, slashing, and this becomes clear when we look at it in individuals. Between individuals, military conflicts, outbreaks of hostilities occur every day in spite of a will to peace much greater and more authentic than can ever exist between peoples. When there are camps, the evils tend to be distributed, highlighted, and opposed; only in each person's humanity are they united, even though just as separate.

Each one . . . for example, she, Herminia, appeared one day with her eyes looking exactly the way they had the day she arrived. Her eyes don't get red when she cries, they seem drier, and they sparkle, as if they'd been bleached by her tears. He, Miguel, seemed to be in more of a huff than usual. Quitina was serving tea; there was no way to break the silence.

After drinking my tea, I said I had to work and went up to the little room above. Shortly afterward, I shouted down the stairs: "Miguel, would you bring me the encyclopedia that's on the table?" He came up, I closed the door and said to him: "What's going on?"

"Tonight's argument was really super," he answered, "really super."

"What for or what about?"

"The same as always. Well, expanded."

"Ah! Then there's something new."

"It's not new," Miguel said. "It's been going on for some time."

"But what is it?"

"I don't go to Mass."

"Ah! I didn't know," I said in astonishment. "You've become an atheist?"

"No, don't be absurd."

"Then?"

"I don't know how to say this, but I just can't stand it!"

"What can't you stand, Mass?"

"Well, what they do now in churches. The way in the middle of the Mass the priest starts to talk, and he doesn't stop saying stupid things for twenty minutes."

"He's explaining the Gospel!"

"Explaining it? He's breaking it into bite-sized pieces."

"Yes, in general that's true."

"But why explain the Gospel, can you tell me that?"

"Because people seem to be forgetting it."

"And have you noticed the Protestants recall the Gospel more effectively than we do, when they live by listening to sermons?"

"Not to judge by the results."

"Nevertheless, now we're copying them. I don't know when it started, but that's what people are doing to see if things improve. They don't realize! Nobody realizes what's happening."

"What is it that's happening? Do you know?"

"Yes, I know; God's fed up, that's what's happening."

"What nonsense!" I said, bursting into laughter.

"It's not nonsense at all. None of you wants to understand! No one wants to understand that all of that's useless now. I don't mean the Gospel, I mean the explanations. If the Gospel's useful for something, fine, and if it's not, fine. God doesn't want to go around making explanations any longer. Today God is something different."

"Finish."

"He wants to die," he said with great simplicity, as if it were the most natural thing in the world.

I paused for a little; surely traces of my laughter from before were still visible on my face, but my attention was redoubled. Miguel said: "Well, you can already see what's happened, and what can still happen. It's a new form of the Crucifixion."

I opened my eyes wider: ". . . !"

"Look, now I'm going to explain the Gospel to you. 'Each one take up his cross' . . . And then what? Did they do it? Did anyone take it up? No. Seeing that, God imposed it. Instead of parables he spoke to them as clear as crystal. Now each one has his own cross."

"I don't know," I ventured, "I think you're getting close to something, but the last thing you said is nonsense. The cross is something a person has to take up."

"I keep having to explain it to you. What about the hooded executioners, and the belt lashings? But no," he interrupted himself suddenly, as if he were afraid of getting lost. "Those aren't the correspondences we need to be looking for. Now things are done differently, now everything's done differently, now God incarnate expires differently. Understand?" he stammered, as if he couldn't go on. "In every way possible," he said finally. "Not just one way, like the other time, with people around, watching. Now it's with everyone and everywhere. It's not something as pretty as a cross."

"Really! In those days the cross was an artifact associated with infamy."

"Maybe it was, but its beauty was there within, it was a thing made to be looked at. We'll see if anyone sets out to explain the cross. You look at the cross and everything is already understood."

He stood for a minute wrapped in thought, making a very slight, involuntary movement of his head, and I realized was going to say something but then stopped. I pressed him. "Come on, what are you thinking about?"

He didn't want to answer, but since he knew that I wouldn't stop, he said: "No, I wasn't thinking . . . I was recalling that part about . . ."

"About what?"

"The part about . . . 'And You take leave, holy Shepherd . . .'"

"Ah! You were *recalling* that?"

"Yes, because the darkness wasn't as great. He left a sign. That's what the cross is: a sign. Whereas, now he's not even going to leave any traces. Now, the torture will consist precisely in the fact that nothing remains. Each person will depart, without leaving anything, and God will depart with each one."

"You mean that now destruction will replace the Crucifixion?"

"Yes, that's it. We'll see if that's how people understand it. Because already you see the things men have come up with, as proof of God's existence—useless things, absolutely useless."

After a silence, he continued, with the tone of a child about to confide a secret: "I'm sure that now they're going to find the proof that God doesn't exist. And it will be a scientific, irrefutable proof. When there's no longer a single person who doubts, the darkness will begin."

"Well," I said, "if that's the picture you paint for your mother, I can understand why she throws up her hands in horror."

"I'll tell you," he answered; "if it were presented to her in the form of a book about philosophy, that picture might not alarm her. My mother has studied a lot; she knows all the heresies, and when she meets up with one, she says, 'What an unfortunate error,' but she keeps on reading. It's not my theorizing she can't stand but my contributing to the destruction. To her it seems I'm playing the role of those hooded executioners."

"But remember you once told me that science is not only destruction."

"And it isn't only destruction. Rather, destruction is not *only* destruction. Who knows what sign or mind-set might be left after the Resurrection? Maybe something that seems degrading to us now."

"Well," I said, at that moment noting my own naïveté in the tone of voice, with which I began to ask, because, at that moment, the childish tone was mine. "But don't you think something can be done to avoid that destruction, that universal torture?"

"No, it neither can nor should be. Of course, if I were to find the way, I would avoid it, but knowing that I should not. Wouldn't you have prevented the Crucifixion, willingly?"

"Of course."

"And do you think you *ought to* have done it? This is something many people have already asked themselves. All that matters is that everything's not useless. We're not going to forget about redemption."

"No, that would be too much to leave out!"

"You know?" he continued, "I enjoy talking about these things in a dumb way like this. It makes them more current."

He changed his tone and continued: "But, what made everything get so bitter last night was something different. I want to go to the south, with Cecchini."

"Ah! I understand; your mother doesn't want you to go."

"She won't even talk about it. And you see, this is a great opportunity. Cecchini's uncle has a boat and he takes things to Chile, through the Magellan Straits. Then on the way back, they travel with the wolf hunters and bring back skins, so you can imagine . . . Great!"

"What reasons does she give to dissuade you?"

"All kinds of reasons, some of them clear, some of them obscure. The dangers of the trip, in the first place, then the dealings with the sailors who *have bad habits*. What bad habits? I ask her. Well . . . you know . . . they're very vulgar. It goes on like that, for hours."

"How were things decided?"

"Nothing was decided. After the tenth attempt, when we'd gone round and round about things a hundred times, I said quite categorically: 'Well, I want to go.' Then she exploded like a rocket. 'Go to hell!' and she went into her room, slamming the door."

"We'll have to convince her," I said, and we went downstairs.

I walked around the house a few times, sizing up the situation; I noticed that between Quitina and Herminia there was an agreement-filled silence. In their silence you could tell they'd talked a lot, or at least, enough. I glanced into the dining room and saw they were setting the table.

Quitina and Herminia were still in the living room, silent, almost in the dark; only a small table lamp was lit, in the corner. The two of them were sitting near a window, looking at the garden. I went up to them slowly, leaned on the back of Quitina's chair, looked out over her head at the avenue of agapanthus, and thought: "It's better not to talk now, because this silence is too serious in itself, and whatever falls into it will become dramatic; I'll let things wait until we're at the table. Or until we've finished eating; violent arguments in the middle of dinner annoy me, because I keep eating and everyone else is horrified that it doesn't take away my appetite. I'll definitely wait until we're having coffee."

Finally we sat down at the table. We remained silent. Miguel had been in the library during that whole interval; he didn't know if I'd managed to talk with them, and he shot me some questioning glances, which I tried to answer with smiling composure. Meanwhile I was devouring several things at top speed. I attacked the steak with such powerful blows that Quitina couldn't help saying: "But what a way you have of eating so fast. You know it's not at all good for you."

"Yes, I know," I said, "but I can't avoid it. When I eat in silence, I start to think about things and I eat at the speed of my thoughts. Well, not that fast; while I've eaten just one steak I've thought three hundred things."

"Well, you'll have to concentrate on just one; it's bad to eat fast, it's bad to eat fast."

"Don't say any more"—I cut her off—"that comment can accelerate to a dizzying speed."

"Just that?"

"Yes, that. Look, if you say, 'it's bad to eat fast,' and you stop, that comment gets used up. Immediately the reflections start: it's bad because of one thing or another, and God knows where the corollaries take you; in two minutes your head's filled with all kinds of different things. But if you want to stick with that one idea and you start to repeat, 'it's bad to eat fast, it's bad to eat fast,' that idea itself accelerates until it's speeding like an express train."

Quitina laughed. Miguel and Herminia smiled too.

"What nonsense," Quitina said, "you can repeat it slowly, syllable by syllable, a mouthful in each syllable, a grain of rice with each letter."

"Yes," I admitted, "that's possible at first, but then, everything after, contained, exerts pressure until they all make it accelerate, and the speed starts to pick up, the train starts shaking."

The sentence occasioned a couple of seconds of silence, which I spent struggling inside.

Now's the time, now's the moment to say: speaking of trains . . .

But no, it's better to wait a bit, when we're back in the living room. Although, this would be an opportune moment. I took the step, tossing everything aside the way a wet dog shakes the water from its fur.

"Don't forget that on Wednesday we're going to see the French."

Quitina said: "No, we hadn't forgotten."

And Herminia added: "I'm finally going to see *Phèdre*; I've wanted to see it for so long."

She'd hit on something that could spark enough interest for a ten-minute conversation. I said: "You've never seen it?"

"Never. In Madrid it's been given only a few times. I think one of them was many years ago, when I was in Palma."

"We'll see how it turns out. I think the scenery they're bringing is truly extraordinary and that there will be Cretan costumes, except for the usual chitons with their classical folds."

"How strange," Herminia said, "I'm not sure the verses won't prove to be inseparable from those classical folds. But it doesn't much matter; in any case we'll be able to hear those verses well."

"Will Javier and Clara be there?" Quitina asked.

"Yes, I've told them about it. There's room for six of us in the box," I added. "Although, of course there will be five of us, now that I think about it, because Miguel's going to Magellan, isn't he?"

Silence—deathly, boundless, invisible silence. Like someone charging a door with his shoulder, I pushed forward, looking at Herminia: "Miguel's leaving tomorrow morning, isn't he?"

But the door neither shattered nor yielded. After a couple of seconds, in which my effort was proved futile, it opened readily, if a bit too easily.

"For all I care, he can go to Cape Horn," Herminia said, calmly folding her napkin and getting up from the table.

We all got up and watched her walk toward a small table on which there was a box with cigarettes. She took one, lit it, and sank into the armchair beside the window in the living room. That's where she had her coffee, surrounded by clouds of smoke. Herminia smokes very little, but when she does, she produces huge storm clouds of smoke, as if to envelop herself in them.

Why go into further detail: after all that was said, came the action. Miguel went off to the south and Herminia stayed at Las Murtas, obeying Quitina's mandate, "You're not going home now, to be there all by yourself." And she did not go home.

Wednesday arrived and we met Javier and Clara at the Odeón for dinner. Two or three times during the meal, Herminia said how impatiently she was waiting to see the play.

"Don't be surprised," she told us rather ironically. "I'm from the boondocks and I've never seen *Phèdre*, even at my age."

"Really, you've never seen it?"

"Never, and I'm looking forward to it as excitedly as a schoolgirl."

They laughed at her naïveté, and finally we were in the box. The lights dimmed. We listened to the noble twin verses with their coupled meanings. Such sacrosanct pleasure can invade us as the rhymes clasp shut, such a feeling of culmination, of completion, as each pair of verses unites and succumbs, drifting off so as to make way for the ones to follow. An intensely vital chain was rousing things that before had been merely thought. The linked clues echoed throughout the hall, leaving a wake of moments so full I would almost dare to call them beings or worlds.

In the box next to ours someone was furiously chewing gum. A slight hissing sound came from the box beside it. Our neighbors laughed at their own rudeness, talking in low but annoying voices.

The act ended, and we went out into the corridor.

Feeling happy, we were willing to declare everything good. The Odeón has excellent acoustics, and not a single syllable was lost. The acting was correct, except in the case of Phèdre, who was not convincing, and one would have to say that the Cretan costumes were very novel. The men radiated nudity—good bodies, delicate bare feet walking across the stage, their ankle bracelets emphasizing the slenderness of their legs. The women, Phèdre, were enveloped in ineffective violet veils. (The color of the ancient world is what all artists usually interpret with the least success. Or maybe we all imagine that world in the color of our dreams, since we all carry it deep within.) Well, the women were good. Oenone was wearing her tight-fitting, flounced dress, but of course without the graceful details that give Cretan figurines all their expressiveness; you could see her breasts, the dark, prominent nipples that resembled eyes.

We talked about all these things during intermission, returned to the box, and heard the gum again. Again came the hissing, louder this time, emphasized with some emphatic phrase—the occupants of the protesting box were French—but our neighbors did not let up; they kept on with their little giggles, making comments and asides in low voices, oblivious to everything. Now I knew who the protagonists of the chewing gum were, at least the main characters—there was also an anonymous individual, whom I could not make out. In the darkness of the box I saw some blue eyes and said, Now I know who she is! I saw a rather British-looking head and identified him.

I was watching them from the shadows, and the only way I could find to describe them was a coddling, somewhat coded epithet that does refer to something, although the meaning is ineffable. It's that affected reproach we use here with respectable people: "They're uncouth!"

My attention was considerably dissipated as I watched the skirmishes between the two boxes and the way the faces of their inhabitants looked during the intermissions. In the third act, I was finally able to concentrate a little better, well enough to be unaware of what was happening in our box. There was nothing very obvious, but a few minutes before the final curtain, Quitina touched me on the arm and said: "Leave right away and get the car because Herminia's not feeling well."

Herminia was leaning on her, and when she saw that I was getting ready to leave, she tried to stop me: "It's nothing, it's nothing," she said. "I think something disagreed with me."

Right from the beginning it was my impression that this was not the problem, and we speculated, as we were saying good night to the Molinas, about what could have disagreed with her. Probably nothing.

Once we were in the car, Herminia said it probably had something to do with her liver, because she had a sharp pain in her right side. Besides, she felt chills, as if she were going to develop a fever. We decided to take her to Juncal so she could see the doctor first thing in the morning.

I called Las Murtas to say we would be spending the night in Buenos Aires. Everything there was fine. Miss Ray was watching over the house.

Since all the furniture in our apartment had been stored away, we put Herminia in her bed and prepared to spend the night there the best we could.

At two, Herminia was writhing in pain and running a very high fever. Half delirious, she kept saying she was thirsty, and we didn't know what to give her. Quitina found a package of linden blossom tea and brewed a lot of it; she cooled it in a glass pitcher and gave some to Herminia, who drank it eagerly. Soon after, she asked for more and drank another glass. Her thirst was irrational, like the thirst dogs get when they've been poisoned and can drink liters of water.

"Leave it here close by," she said.

We left her the pitcher where she could reach it easily.

Her fever remained just as high and she continued to moan and to lie curled on her left side, but she became less agitated and seemed to be resting a little, in a kind of drowsiness. We dimmed the light and went out of the room.

Quitina told me that whatever it was had been provoked by the end of the play. At a particular moment, when Theseus was about to start speaking, she saw Herminia covering her face with her hands. Immediately, she reached out one of them and pressed Quitina's hand, whispering in her ear: "This is something I didn't remember!"

But Quitina had deduced that she must have remembered it, because her gesture and her exclamation had made both of them miss the actor's sentence, which nevertheless had affected Herminia as if it had been an electric shock.

Then the end of the performance occurred in a veritable tumult of thoughts. The scene that Herminia said she'd forgotten unfolded implacably, unchecked by her memory's refusal, and Quitina, who did remember it and was free of any inhibition, stopped paying attention and tried to figure out the tragic comparison that might have been welling up in Herminia's soul.

We were speaking in low voices, so as not to disturb the sleeplike state into which Herminia had fallen, and we left the room in order to continue our conversation. We went to the small sitting room in the front, the small room that had been señor Filippo's workshop and was now so immaculate, so comfortable, with its small low armchairs beside the window that overlooked the garden, so you could watch it rain, which Herminia liked to do.

That night it was not raining; the night was very clear, although there was no moon, and we sat in the dark with the door ajar so we could hear Herminia if she called. We sat beside the window and Quitina soon left her armchair, put a cushion on the floor, beside my feet, and sat down, leaning against my knees.

There in the darkness, hand in hand, prepared to keep watch all night, away from our house, we were enveloped by such a strange mixture of happiness and fear. It was something like children's secret pleasure in disorder, even when that includes disaster: a pleasure of the moment, a voluptuousness, a savoring of a moment that's pure—a particular light, a particular place, a particular situation—independent of the cause. A sort of marriage between life and moment, which is why something imperishable remains, a fertile memory. Of course on that occasion we were far from our house but, between those walls, it was as if we were in the shell where every aspect of our story had germinated. Exactly above that room were my study and the living room; the window where we were sitting corresponded to the large polychrome window with the water lilies, and the big old chair was still nearby, next to the telephone.

So many things surrounded us there, weighed on us, made us press closer and closer together.

Quitina was telling me that when she realized Herminia connected everything on stage to Miguel's trip she'd felt distressed because she didn't know what could have happened between the two of them. Still, she believed she knew Herminia well enough to be sure that Herminia could not have perpetrated anything like that. What could have caused such apprehension, such sudden terror?

Quitina said: "I pressed her arm and spoke into her ear: 'Don't think such nonsense.' 'It's not nonsense,' she answered me. 'You don't know anything about it.' This frightened me, and then I didn't dare ask her anything more because I didn't know how; there was a word I could not utter. Later, when we got here, while you were making the phone call, I was helping her get undressed and she started to murmur something with her eyes closed and her head lowered. I saw she was about to explain it to me and, although I felt very impatient to find out, I began to tremble; but she murmured such an incongruous sentence that I thought she was delirious. Then I moved my hand across her forehead. 'Come and lie down,' I said, 'see if you can sleep a little.' She raised her head and looked at me; she was lucid. 'Didn't you understand what I said?' she asked. 'It's the same, exactly the same as the incident with Cape Horn.' Then I recalled what she said the other night when she got up from the table, and I reassured her, I started to tell her a joke but, at that moment, you came into the room to take her temperature, and I went to get the tea. When I walked over to her so I could hold the glass while she drank, she kept trying to tell me something. Finally I could make out something like, 'Cape Horn is hell . . . there's no difference . . .'"

I recalled the quarrel Miguel had described to me and how it had concluded with her saying "Go to hell" and slamming the door. I told Quitina about it and we agreed that it was a trivial phrase anyone could say in a fit of temper; the same for the one about Cape Horn.

"It seems strange to me," I said, "that Herminia has linked the two phrases that way, and even stranger that she's identified them with Theseus's invocation to Neptune."

Quitina spoke pensively, as if she were trying out that association: "I think that when she pressed my hand it was the moment when Theseus was saying, 'Fusses-tu par délà les collones d'Alcide.' The allusion to a geographical place—know what I mean?—made her forget she was in the theater. As she said, 'without the classical folds . . .' Theseus was there half-naked, like a man who's in his own house, in a bad mood. Because surely people said such things at the time, just like now any Italian will lie to the whole heavenly host, with no provocation at all."

Then, after she'd thought for a while in silence, Quitina continued: "But, I don't know if it might have been the opposite, if it might have been precisely the *tone* of the tragedy," and she stressed the word; "who knows if it didn't horrify Herminia to hear it said that way . . . you know what I mean? Saying something as if you were doing it. The business about Cape Horn might seem stupid to us, but she's the only one who knows how she said it."

Then I was the one overcome with emotion, as if someone had placed something ice cold or burning hot on my back. The hairs on my back were standing on end it hurt so much; I pressed Quitina's hands to my chest and started to speak. Where I started, though, how I managed to tell what I was sure I'd never told in my life, I don't remember. I mean, I don't remember the words, I could not transcribe the first sentences, because they were like groping in the dark, like a search for the emergency exit. Something, from deep down inside me, searched for its way out toward Quitina, and I told her everything, everything.

She listened silently, not interrupting me even once. In the darkness, which was not total, I could see her eyes opened toward me, but not in amazement, in persistent attention, an attention that could last as long as I needed to tell. She was listening to me, but listening so intently it was as if she were doing something for me. She was anxious but not curious, and I could see that she didn't have even one question.

When I had told her the whole long nightmare, I spoke to her of how the silence had overwhelmed me, how it had tormented me to live with my resolution never to tell her. Then Quitina shook her head and interrupted me, cutting me off, as if it were no longer necessary for me to continue.

"But how could you possibly not realize that I knew?"

"What did you know?"

"Everything."

"How could you know if I've never told a living soul?"

"No," she said, "I didn't know anything of what can be told, for instance about the fly and the details, but the rest . . . , well, the substance of it. But don't you see it happened the same in me?"

I let go of her hands and grasped her by the arms, touching her shoulders as if to convince her that I was still there. Suddenly the darkness made me feel anguished, I would have liked to see her face very clearly and convince myself that its features were still the same. They had always stayed the same, carrying all that inside!

I think I recall repeating vaguely, "I don't understand, I don't understand . . ." and then she began to tell me her nightmare.

"Imagine," Quitina said, "my state when I got to Havana—half unconscious. I had not spoken to my aunt and uncle during the entire trip. I went into the bar at the airport because the plane had a long layover there. All I thought about was telegraphing you again, and I asked a waiter where I could do that. Suddenly, although I didn't want to pay any attention to him, I saw my uncle walking toward me with a stranger, talking in a low voice. The two of them kept looking my way out of the corners of their eyes and I realized they were talking about me. I didn't want them to see me looking at them, but I looked furtively, and I saw my uncle stopping, turning his back, taking off his hat, and wiping his handkerchief across his face. It's the heat, I thought, but at the same time I saw he was making a very strange movement with his head and shoulders. Well, I said, what do I care what's wrong with him, I don't know why I'm worried. But at that same moment I heard something of what the other man was saying; I heard clearly, 'Señor Suárez said . . .' That was all I heard, but I don't know if that was because the man lowered his voice or because my heart gave a thump so hard it left me stunned. My father had said something, so then he knew what was going on; there was nothing else to talk about. I always had blind faith in my father; if he'd said something it could not be anything I would find upsetting. So I restrained myself from going to see what was happening. I felt saved and almost ashamed to show how wildly happy I was. Finally my uncle came over with a dreadful expression on his face, he was white as a sheet, and buckets of sweat were running down his fore-head. I could not help asking: 'What's wrong?'

"He moved his head and answered: 'Something has happened.'

"I interrupted him: 'But my father?'

"'Yes,' he said, 'your father will be here tomorrow.'

"'Good,' I thought, looking at him defiantly. 'The rest doesn't matter to me, whatever it is, all the rest doesn't worry me one bit.' But my uncle's expression panicked me, and I clung to my idea: 'It doesn't matter to me, nothing matters to me.'

"The man who had come over with him was Spanish; he was quite bald and he too was looking at me with a pathetic expression on his face. My uncle said: 'This man is the secretary of the consulate . . .'

"I nodded to him slightly but kept thinking: 'It's nothing, nothing; if my father is coming for me, I don't care about anything else.'

"'Let's go to the hotel,' my uncle said.

"I followed him, and when we walked by customs I saw that my aunt was sitting in a corner beside the suitcases, crying, with her face in her handkerchief."

Quitina stopped for a moment, as if to emphasize better the enormity of what she was about to say.

"I assure you," she continued, "I felt as though I'd been nailed to the floor. It was just a second, but my entire being refused to approach her. 'You can cry and writhe all you want to but I don't care.' My attitude must have been so provocative that I infuriated them. Then my uncle told me point-blank: 'Your mother has been killed in a car accident.'"

Quitina told me all this so violently she ended up on her knees on the cushion, with her arms crossed; her face was almost at the height of mine, and in the dark I could see her eyes opened inconceivably wide, the way you can only open your eyes in the dark.

"All the rest," she said, "that entire night, I don't know how I'll be able to tell you about it. Because you did a whole lot of things, going from one place to another, but I went into the hotel room and I was alone. Look," she added, trying to stress something specific, "I believe I had only one clear thought: 'Why wasn't I the first to know, why wasn't

I the first to know?' Of course, in any case, my mother's death meant my freedom, but if I'd known it before anything else, before throwing myself into that frenetic happiness, and—how can I explain it to you?— before walling myself up, withdrawing with the blind pride I'd begun to feel when I found out I would be with my father the next day and now I was invincible. I was struggling to flip all that around, struggling to feel it the way I would have felt it before. And I assure you, I'd felt it exactly the same way, I mean just as intensely as I would have felt it on any other occasion: I no longer felt happiness. But I recalled it the way a person recalls pain. Do you understand? The way, when you catch your finger in a door and then, even though it no longer hurts, you recall it perfectly, and you know if you catch it again it will hurt the same way. I knew I was going to feel that happiness again and all I did was tell myself: 'later, then there will be time for that.'"

As Quitina talked, I recalled that at certain times I'd felt how emotion would make her voice change, how she would be on the verge of ending up in tears; not now. She was speaking very softly, but with the momentum of a waterfall. In her, too, the sluice gate had been flung open, and something incalculable was coursing in her words.

"Do you know where I turned? To thinking about my father. 'My father found out suddenly,' I told myself, 'the news hit him straight on; for him it's something that no longer is. Now, when I talk to him about my situation, it take second place,' and this idea reassured me. Well, on the contrary, it upset me but, actually, that seemed right to me. 'This is how it has to be,' I told myself. Then I could start to think about seeing my father the next day and how with him I could feel what I truly felt. Being with my aunt and uncle nauseated me. They'd witnessed everything at the Plaza, they'd been present like judges; scandalized, they'd seen me turn on my mother like a wild beast. It nauseated me to go to them and have feelings get all muddled. No matter what their reaction might have been, it would have made me throw up. Because you can imagine how they would have reacted. They were in the room next door, and I couldn't hear the least noise, but I could see them in front of me reciting those stock phrases: 'You see your punishment! Now you know what it means to disobey one's mother . . .' Well, that's nothing; the most stupid, most ridiculous phrases came into my head. And not just the phrases, I saw the whole scene, I saw myself as well, grotesque, and I walked around the room, digging my nails into my scalp, without being able to cry. 'My God!' I said to myself. 'Won't I be able to cry? Won't I ever cry again in my life?' And I could see my aunt and uncle saying: 'Not a tear. What can you expect from a creature who's not even capable of shedding a tear for her own mother?'"

An expression flickered suddenly on Quitina's face, a kind of uncontrollable smile, and she passed her hands in front of her mouth as if to erase it.

"Can you believe," she said, "that there are some things I still blush to recall? Because at a moment like that, when I felt desperate, convinced I was going crazy, I couldn't get the grotesque part of those phrases out of my head: 'shed a tear.' And other phrases I can't even tell you; I'd die of shame." Quitina shook her head as if she were expelling the residue of those ideas. "When the comic aspect of it had grown so terrible I was afraid," she continued, "I threw myself on the bed, put my head under the pillow and began to say, 'My father! Oh God! Please let my father come!' I stayed that way until it began to get light and everything started to become more decent—you know what I mean?—those sarcastic things I'd said gradually faded and finally, before seven, my father arrived. I got him into my room and locked the door from inside. I pushed him toward the armchair, sat down on his lap, and put my arms around his neck, and the two of us sat there crying for a very long time."

Quitina sat down on the pillow again, and said more calmly: "Well, that whole night I didn't think of you even once, fortunately. First, in my moment of happiness it did not occur to me you could know anything, and all I thought about was making absolutely certain of every detail, about ensuring the outcome of things as soon as I had my father close at hand. Then, since that had only lasted a few minutes, when the horror started I didn't connect it with you either. Right in front of me, as an impediment, I had the presence of my aunt and uncle, which was making me so angry I couldn't see straight; and when things went back to normal, once my father was there, before I spoke to him about you, when I started to think I needed to do that, then it became clear to me you would know better than I myself, and you had known for much longer, what had happened."

Leaning against my knees, Quitina raised her face toward me, and in the darkness I saw her forehead, now indescribably serene; she was not smiling, but all her features seemed to have expanded, the way they do when a person has reached great peace.

"Everything you've just told me," she said, "you can't imagine how consoling I find it."

I must have made a gesture of surprise, but she refused to be interrupted.

"Whether earlier or later," she said, as if to cut me off, "it makes no difference. As soon as I thought about it specifically, I realized you had to have felt happy. I wouldn't have expected you to take it dispassionately, not at all; in short, I imagined the feeling of triumph had to be the dominant thing for you, this was clear. Your intention, as that girl from Berlin said . . . I don't know, I don't think it was that. However, if the news had caught you off guard, and you'd said 'I'm happy,' to me it would have seemed rather petty. The way you tell it, you paid so dearly! You see? That's what I didn't imagine—that there was something dramatic in you also, something that represented a great, complex suffering, something that would save you from simple satisfaction. Because of course I thought you would feel sorry about it for me, you would feel my suffering, but there was something I couldn't think about without horror, and it was precisely that 'I'm happy.' Right there I swore I would never ask you, I would always avoid any explanation. I only wanted to see you, to see if a trace of all this had remained in you. And I assure you, if it had I would have seen it."

I took her head and drew it toward my face, but Quitina stopped me.

"I think I hear her stirring," she said.

We went to the room on tiptoes. The pitcher of tea was almost empty.

When Herminia didn't see us, she probably thought we'd gone to bed and didn't want to call us.

The tranquilizer had been helping her stay asleep, although you could see from her face that the pain hadn't subsided. Quitina touched Herminia's forehead, which was burning, and suddenly she opened her eyes a little, letting us know she wanted to continue sleeping.

We went back to the living room and Quitina said: "Haven't you ever thought that there's something mysterious about my friendship with Herminia?"

"Yes, I always thought so," I said, "I think I even asked you about it more than once, and you always avoided the issue."

"Of course, since that's what it was. Herminia is the only person who knows all these things. Imagine what it was like for me when I had to come in contact with the people who knew what had happened during those days. I told myself that never, ever, even if I never had another friend in my whole life, would I consent to one of those questions, those indirect questions women ask. The Molina girls are very nice; I love Laura, and I always got along well with her, but Rafaela hated my mother. Well, she hated her for her beauty, and to what refinements won't an ugly woman's insinuations rise! I kept them at bay from the first moment; I walled myself up. If Herminia hadn't appeared, I don't think my relationship with humanity would ever have been reestablished."

Ashamed of my stupidity, I said, "I'd attributed it to something different."

"Yes, I already know that; and about that other incident, it was exactly the same way: I would never have put up with an indirect question. Because if things hadn't happened the way they did with my mother, then it would never have bothered me if my friends joked about the other incident. I would have told Laura about it myself. But this way, in the middle of the tragedy, you know what I mean? With the probability that they would dump all those stock phrases on me, ugh! Herminia, however—it seems impossible, but from the moment you started to talk to her on the phone I realized she was very beneficial for me. Then, as soon as I saw her—so virile, so different from other women. Talking about those things she told the first day! While I was listening to her, I was saying to myself, 'with a person who's gone through all that you can talk about anything.' In the end, though, the decisive thing was that she hadn't known my mother, she could only judge her through what I told her and from her I would not get the flattery I would from women wanting to emphasize my mother's defects in order to justify my behavior; nor would there be malicious distortions of her virtues if women wanted to wound me. Well, with Herminia I saw immediately that none of that could happen."

Around half past five it started to get light. Quitina looked tired, but she could not restrain her desire to talk. Seeing I was about to ask her to rest, she silenced me with a movement of her hand.

"I did everything systematically," she said, "according to a plan I drew up for myself. First I showed Herminia the portrait, which she found dazzling. 'She was wonderful,' Herminia said, and I: 'Yes, she was wonderful.' Herminia saw how she was there presiding over the library. I told her about the accident, told her she'd just turned forty, my father and I were away from Buenos Aires; in short, I let her picture the accident on her own. Then, after enough time had passed, I told her everything, exactly as I've told it to you now, without leaving out one detail, and she understood it the way I do myself."

"And I recall," Quitina continued, "a short time later you asked me suddenly, 'Tell me, how is it you've become such good friends with Herminia, why do you like her so much?' The only thing I could think of to answer was, 'Herminia is an admirable woman,' and you were left speechless."

Quitina yawned.

"We have to call the doctor before seven," she said.

"Yes, that's still a good ways off."

"Let's go see how she's doing."

Herminia seemed more awake at that point; her fever had gone down, but the pain hadn't subsided, and we didn't dare try any home remedies because we weren't sure of the cause. We tried to cheer her up with the thought that the doctor would come soon, and she began to apologize for the awful night she'd made us spend.

"Awful!" Quitina said, "if you knew how well we used it. We've done a spring cleaning."

I don't know if Herminia understood, but she smiled and Quitina added: "Now we're going to make tea, because I'm thirsty from having talked so much. We'll have it here in your room, to help the time pass until the doctor arrives. Come on, come help me," she told me.

We went to the kitchen, feeling worried because of the way Herminia looked; she was waxlike, almost green, and Quitina said: "It's been a nervous shock, I don't doubt that a bit. But she mustn't hear us talking about her. Here, cut the bread and then carry a little table into her room."

You could hardly see in the kitchen, but we didn't turn on the light because, as dawn enters, it reveals things, even things like a teapot or a porcelain pitcher, so gradually and with such transcendent slowness that it's an hour when electric lights seem unpleasant.

"Get out the butter so it won't be so hard," Quitina said, while she was working at the stove.

I got it out. I like to open the refrigerator and hear the insect-like murmuring inside the sanctuary. As I walked back and forth in the corridor carrying things to Herminia's room, I'd stop from time to time to look at the plants. It was six o'clock, and the sun was already up. What consequences would follow from that mishap? What might happen? I couldn't help asking what face to put on all that, couldn't help trying to read the oracle a person believes is present in inert things. And it's because one has placed so much love in them, or rather, one has placed them in moments of such love. "And as testimony, I set here this stone . . ." Of course, the natural thing is that later, when time passes, when one doubts or fears, one tries to extract a statement from the stone, and the stone says nothing. Nevertheless, it's hard to convince oneself that the stone, the inert thing, at times a group of things—a garden that one day was suddenly like a bouquet of flowers, even a limitless landscape that we believe we've made because we looked at it effusively just once—it's hard to admit that these things, which have been still while we struggled, which have witnessed everything, are not aware of higher designs. Because by seeing the group it would seem one should be able to understand. And of course, if a consciousness were to remain still at one point and look from there, maybe understanding would be possible. But it's stupid to ask this of things, and even so, we can't help it: suddenly we have that illusion and they seem to be making some gesture at us, a decipherable sign, and we ask.

In that apartment, especially, I suffered from such an illusion in a disastrous way. That apartment continued to be that apartment, despite a series of extensive and expensive renovations. We'd erased the trace of señor Filippo's people and, then, the trace of Damián. His room was now a workroom, with a typewriter and an aluminum screen. But everything was the same, everything was still there, and it was there that our communication had been purified. A secret that had lasted for years shattered as easily as a bubble bursts. It was all being reinforced by virtue of that change of course. The present was turning into a torrent because an accumulation of past was thawing and flowing toward it, becoming powerful and abundant, quantitatively, but also becoming . . . I'm about to say "exquisite." The savor of that moment seasoned by irregularity and danger was stimulating; I'll refrain from making a pun with savor and savvy.

"Twenty to seven," Quitina said.

"Yes, I'll call right now."

I called the doctor, who was just getting up, but he said he'd be there in twenty minutes. It took him twenty-five. Meanwhile we had breakfast, trying to cheer up Herminia.

The doctor, a good clinician, examined Herminia conscientiously and said there was nothing serious—a seepage of bile, for the most part. He prescribed the necessary medication and when Quitina saw him out, in the vestibule, she tried to explain the shock Herminia had suffered so he would understand how the problem had started.

"Look," the doctor said, "something like that doesn't occur in a minute. She'd been incubating that for a long time, and it happened to come to a head on that occasion."

"Why?"

"Who knows. The meal in the restaurant, some change in her usual diet; in short, it amounts to the same thing."

"Well, as long as it's nothing more," Quitina said, quite uncertainly.

"There's also something flu-like; that's probably what's causing the fever. I left those capsules for her."

"Yes, yes, but the way she looks."

"My dear, that's a respectable case of jaundice. It will fade, don't worry. I'll be back tomorrow."

The doctor left, and nothing worth mentioning happened that day. Herminia's illness took the usual course. The pain in her liver subsided a little both when she applied heat and took certain medicines, but it showed no signs of disappearing. The flu became more pronounced. Herminia said that while we were still in the theater she'd suddenly experienced a tremendous hot flash and then she'd felt cold and had sharp pains in her throat. We followed her treatment faithfully and the day and night passed normally. The next day the doctor said there was nothing new.

First thing in the morning sick people take illness on as a job, tackling the chore of the flu or whatever they have as if they were going to the office. It's annoying, but it has to be done, and they carry out all their tasks, potions, injections, and get washed with a certain lightness that lets the fever go down; later, the day gets more monotonous, they become passive, and then it's the illness that works on *them*.

There really was nothing new, the diagnosis was accurate, and the treatment was having its effect, but the second afternoon, a little past noon, Herminia did not succumb to passivity the same way she had the day before. In her features there was not the slackness of a patient who knows she's being well cared for. I remarked on this to Quitina, and she frowned and looked at the clock.

"Within two hours she'll be worse," she said, "within four worse than that, and so on successively."

"Why? What's wrong?"

"Nothing's wrong; the illness is running its course as it's supposed to, but there's nothing new."

Things turned out exactly as Quitina predicted, and the situation lasted eight days.

In the mornings, when the doctor came, he would find her exhausted from the effects of the night and he'd say: "You need to get her up a little; she's weak, very weak."

Then he would examine her and say: "Otherwise, things are going well. There's almost nothing left in her bronchial tubes. It's the gallbladder that won't listen to reason."

Sometimes he would add tranquilizers to the treatment he prescribed the first day and other times stimulants.

But the one who wouldn't listen to reason was Herminia. Suddenly when we'd go to see her she would have disappeared. She'd leap out of bed, close herself up in the bathroom and vomit up her insides. Shaking, coughing, and sneezing, she'd go back to bed; her fever would rise, she'd become delirious, and with some variation in the order things occurred, this was her repertoire.

I stayed at Juncal only at night, so Quitina could rest for a few hours, but she didn't rest; she was obsessed by Herminia's deliriums and, as soon as I arrived, she'd start to tell me about them. Herminia saw faces everywhere, tiny faces looking at her. But she didn't see them when she was asleep, she saw them when she was awake. She'd be taking a bite of sponge cake and, in the mark left by her teeth, she'd see a horrid, treacherous, or heartbreakingly pitiful face. Of course, we had to be careful not to leave any item of clothing draped over a chair and the folds had to lie flat when we drew back the curtains, so that any features would be impossible.

Sometimes, when I was able to get Quitina to go to bed, I'd keep watch on Herminia, and she'd be sleeping quite peacefully. If I saw she had her eyes open, I would ask her some question or other and she would answer me, totally serene: when I was the only one mounting guard there were no faces. With Quitina she allowed herself to play that game. Without being fully aware of it, perhaps in the same way Quitina had understood she could entrust her secrets to Herminia, only in Quitina's presence did Herminia reveal the part of her personality that gave in to weakness. I thought this came from reserve, from propriety, or from not wanting to make herself tedious that she transformed her profound anguish into those childish fears. When I expressed my opinion to Quitina, though, she answered, "No, it's not that, it's because she doesn't want to think about any extenuating circumstances. If she starts asking as, in fact, she does quite often, 'How many days has it been now? Is it past time for the mail? Could a telegram have arrived at Las Murtas?' we never answer yes or no, but start with 'It's not unusual,' or 'You have to understand that when a person travels with others,' or 'Communications are terrible.' This drives her crazy. I've realized and I don't use the tactic anymore."

"Well," I said, "what does that have to do with the faces?"

"It has to do with here no one's putting restrictions on her. The other day she said to me: 'Look at that piece of paper'—a piece of paper from the drugstore that had been left crumpled up on the table—'I'm seeing the head of a baboon with its mouth open, well, it's not open, the baboon's jaw is dislocated, and it's sagging so much the baboon can't close it. The baboon seems to be saying that if it could close its mouth it would talk.' I took the paper away, and a little while later, because she was drinking a cup of broth, she began to see a series of old men with little babylike bottoms in the napkin she had on the bed. Yes, wait a bit. The napkin was one of those damask ones with slightly embossed flower borders; well, in the border she saw some beings with the heads of old men and the tiny bodies of a babies, naked, of course, and they were combined so that the one in back was devouring the one in front, and all of them were like that, one after the other. Naturally, when she describes these things to me, becoming increasingly worked up as she tells them, because the details are so horrible, I never tell her it's not so bad, they're insignificant impressions. I tell her it seems horrible to me, because it does, really, and because most times I end up seeing it as clearly as she does."

"Well," I said, "you have to remember how wrought up Herminia's mind is. She's read a great deal and she's suffered too much; in a feverish state like this, everything gets mixed together and blown out of proportion."

But Quitina thought there was something more; according to her Herminia was undergoing a kind of crisis. In Herminia's periods of lucidity they'd talked about *Phèdre* again and Quitina had made an effort to erase Herminia's apprehensions, assuring her that the two verses weighing so heavily on her conscience were trivial and could in no way be called a kind of curse. Herminia denied and affirmed. She denied they were trivial; she knew they were loaded with anger. She affirmed, obviously, that they did not involve a design for disaster, for immediate punishment, and Quitina had thought she sensed that, in order to calm herself, Herminia was clinging to the idea that she'd told Miguel to go to hell, that it was a question of hell, exclusively, in both instances. As if hell were something more distant, less frightening. As if deep down she did not believe in hell—which, in Herminia, who was immune to all heterodoxies, would simply mean not believing—but she did believe in the material dangers directly provoked by a curse. And as if rather than believe in those dangers, rather than live fearing and waiting for them, she would prefer to believe in nothing—send hell to hell.

The seventh night I imposed my authority; I made Quitina go to bed in Miguel's room, and I prepared to stay in the little sitting room with a book. Before settling myself there so as to spend a few comfortable hours, I gave Herminia her nightly medications and put a glass of water where she could reach it. She'd draped a shawl over the table beside her bed, and one of the ends was sticking up on the table; smoothing the shawl out carefully, I made the end hang vertically, left the room in a gentle semi-darkness, and began to read.

Suddenly I remembered that I hadn't taken Herminia's temperature, and I went back, afraid I'd wake her up, but she hadn't fallen asleep yet. I gave her the thermometer, looked at the clock, and sat down at the foot of the bed. When I raised my head, I saw, not without amazement, that the end of the shawl I'd just smoothed out carefully was standing upright again and secured on the table with the glass of water.

"But! . . ." I couldn't help saying, "I thought you preferred not to have any folds or strange forms in here."

Even if she'd blushed I couldn't have seen her, but one discreet eyelid betrayed her embarrassment.

"Well, in general, I do," she said. "But that I always put like this."

"Why? Is it a ritual?"

"No, it's because it's so close to my head that I can't help seeing the flowers."

"Oh!" I burst out laughing. "And what do you see in the flowers?"

Herminia laughed too.

"They've gone to you with the story?" she said. "If you knew what I see! No one could understand it."

"Why? If you explain it to me I think I'll be able to see it too." I turned the headboard lamp, projecting the light on the shawl instead of the floor.

"Yes," Herminia said, "this is very easy to see; it forms a very clear figure. But what it says! My God! This you can't hear and I hear it even though I'm not looking at it."

"Let's see where it is. You have to confront ghosts, and answer if they say something."

"Oh, no! There's nothing to add to this. And don't expect me to tell you, I definitely can't do that, I don't have the strength. I couldn't tell you for anything in this world."

Herminia hid her face between the pillow and the top of the covers, as if to conceal a gesture of horror, and at the same time she let out a small guffaw.

"What nonsense, Lord, what nonsense!" she said.

"It's that risqué?"

"Not at all, there's nothing risqué about it."

"Then?"

"It's atrocious, atrocious! It's something ridiculous, bloody."

"Wait a bit; let's look at the thermometer. If your fever's up, I'm taking the shawl off and leaving the room as if this were a hospital."

But her temperature was only 37.2°C, and she set about showing me the ghost.

The figure was right in the center of one side of the shawl, where the two patterns on the corners joined, forming as they converged there a symmetrical composition made of little colored flowers and very fine black and red lines on the warm background of the cashmere shawl. Herminia pointed right to the center.

"Don't you see a face here?" she asked. "Look, it resembles the head of a king or an Indian god. See? It has a moustache and little horns sticking out of this sort of crown he's wearing."

"Yes," I said, "I see it perfectly. It looks like the head of an Incan god."

Herminia lay back on the pillow.

"Ah! That's it," she said, "that's it."

"Good," I said, "we agree that I see the head, but what about all the blood?"

Herminia neither sat up nor looked at the shawl.

"Don't you see it's being tortured?" she asked solemnly.

"Good heavens! That I don't see."

Propping herself up on her elbow, she began to show me, detail by detail.

If the ornamentation on those shawls from Kashmir doesn't come to mind, it will help to recall that the "little flowers" I described are some small concentric circles, similar to the floating water lilies people make with carrot curls. Below the head there were five of these flowers; two at shoulder height, two somewhat larger, a little below them, and between these two, one more, very tiny. Herminia explained to me that those circles were parts of arms, legs, and a sexual organ. I swear to God! That's what she saw. The arms were cut off, not far from where they originated, just like the thighs and the penis. Of course around the flowers it seemed that certain lines in the intricate oriental labyrinth were clearly outlining the torso and a type of throne supporting it; thus lending cohesion to the figure.

I looked at her silently, more alarmed than I would have liked, and said innocently: "But I don't see anything ridiculous."

Herminia took her head in her hands.

"Oh! Don't remind me of that. It's in what he's saying. You understand? That's where the ridiculous part is, and that's where all the magnificence of the thing lies."

"And what, by Jupiter, is he saying?"

"I can't, I can't say it; it's stronger than I am."

"Come on, Herminia, be reasonable; hide your face behind the edge of the covers and say it."

"It can't be said whether my face is hidden or showing; it simply can't be said."

I saw in her eyes that she was listening to it: her whole face was tense with attention as she listened.

"Realize that you must say it, that you *need* to say it," I told her seriously.

"Yes, that's possible," she agreed. "In any case, I don't know if I'll be able to make you grasp both sides of the thing. You're going to die laughing when I tell you, but I assure you that for me it borders on the sublime."

I threw up my arms, exasperated. Herminia sat up straighter, moved closer to the figure, and made me study it carefully: "See how it has the violent features of Indian carvings or masks—the slanted eyes, drooping moustache. But if you look carefully, you'll see that in the center of its mouth there's a tiny black circle, as if the mouth were open, in the form of an O."

I nodded, and she paused momentarily.

"See how petulant its expression is?"

"Yes, it does look a bit that way."

"Well, it's saying 'Oh, excellent, excellent!'"

There was a bottomless silence. I would have given anything to laugh, but I couldn't even smile. I tilted the lamp toward the floor again, stood up, took a few steps around the room, and with an enormous effort managed to say "Ha, ha," like a bad actor. Herminia was not expecting anything different, though; on the contrary, my silence bore witness to my understanding. I stood there at the foot of the bed, with my arms crossed, looking at her in the semi-darkness. She'd let her head fall sideways, with exaggerated slackness, as if relieved of a weight, but she was staring into space, looking disoriented and anxious.

"You're the most cultured person I've ever met," I said, as if speaking with myself. "I think you're the most cultured person that exists."

She turned her head a little on the pillow.

"Did you have to think very hard to come up with a remark more foolish than mine?" she asked.

"My remark was not foolish, Herminia, I said something I've been sensing vaguely for a long while and now see clearly for the first time."

"And how did you discover it?" she asked jokingly, sitting up a little.

"Well, I don't know how to tell you. You'll understand I've not set about measuring the amount of culture you possess; it's just suddenly I saw that culture . . . universal culture is right there with you, suffering your flu and your jaundice. I may put it rather stupidly; I meant I've never seen in anyone else as in you the drama of living culture played out."

"Well, you know I'm not vain," Herminia said, "so I'll confess to being confounded by what you say."

"Be as confounded as you like, but understand what I'm saying. You don't get angry like any normal person; when you get mad you're not content with anything less than an ecumenical fit, brandishing the traditions of both worlds left and right."

Herminia roared with laughter. I thought a good laugh would do her good, and I continued obstinately.

"You fly into a rage like Theseus, then you see yourself in a conflict worthy of the Mater Dolorosa, and you pick a quarrel with the masculine sphere. Yes you do, don't act dumb. You don't know what I'm talking about?"

"No," she said uncertainly.

"About the theory of aged children in the napkin."

She laughed again.

"You feel that although you're a doctor *ès lettres*, a person can say to you 'Woman, what have I to do with thee?' and leave you on the sidelines. Then you're assaulted by the vision of those graffiti, showing you in crude terms the masculine mystery."

"That's nonsense!" she said indignantly.

"I said 'you're assaulted by'; you can't prevent a vision like that from living in you. That's why you transform it into a saturnalian chain, in which along the way you let loose the drama of the generations, and since there's no solution to your conflict all you can do is arrive at an extreme stoicism. You look for a hero who can show you how to put a good face on things and there, in the Kashmir shawl, you find the Caupolicán, the heroic Mapuche leader, upon his throne."

This time when Herminia laughed, she covered her face with her hands and then rubbed her eyes with her fists, not so much to dry her tears as to stimulate them. Suddenly she looked at me with infinite anguish.

"What I wouldn't do to go crazy," she said. "It would be a liberation!"

"A liberation you'll never achieve. Your archivist's head is very well organized. All of a sudden your file cards get jumbled up by the sirocco provoked by your fever but, as soon as that wind dies down, you put them in order again."

"But I don't want order! I want to be insane!"

Herminia's voice took on the tone it had at culminating moments, and Quitina came in to find out what was happening.

"You heard: Herminia wants to go crazy, and I'm trying to convince her it's an unattainable ambition."

"That's not funny, it's not a bit funny that you've been talking with each other for two hours instead of letting her sleep. And you, waving your hands around, with your arms above the bed; you'll freeze."

She rushed over to Herminia and pulled the covers up to her chin, leaving her totally wrapped in the blankets. Herminia smiled, accepting the game of her weakness again; she lay motionless, as if bandaged in bedding, but her head was raised a little on the pillow and she looked so animated we could tell she wasn't ready to sleep.

Quitina sat down close to her.

"You're right," she said, "no matter how much you embellish it . . . your conscience is not very clear."

At first I couldn't imagine what she was insinuating, and I gave some vague answer or other.

Quitina explained things: "Look," she said, "I'm completely sure that all this woman's apprehensions are nonsense. Her fear of their anathemas, pure superstition; the faces, the old men, and the rest, the result of the agitation in her head, which never stops spinning. But at the same time I understand what's going on as well as she does herself; it seems natural to me, it seems necessary . . ." Then, looking at me admonishingly: "What should have been avoided is the cause."

"The cause?"

"You aren't going to deny you helped Miguel get what he wanted, I believe."

"No, of course I don't deny it. The boy was absolutely determined."

"Yes, the boy was very determined, but he was seriously upsetting his mother."

"But why should she be upset? He's almost twenty years old. She's not going to have him tied to her apron strings for his whole life."

"No, calm down," Herminia said, "he belongs to the masculine sphere. I cede my rights."

"Why do you have to cede them?" Quitina then asked energetically.

No one answered. Quitina had just entered the battle, full of innocence. That silence was her first blow. I saw she felt it in all its enormity, but she rallied, as if she were thinking: there must be something I don't know yet.

"I don't want to be the mother of Gracos, or a Spartan woman, or anything of the sort. I'm over the hill, you can throw me into the ditch right now."

As Herminia said this, her vitality belied her words. She hadn't moved so much as a finger; she remained as rigid as a mummy, wrapped in the bedclothes, but her head was detaching itself from the pillows and making little shaky movements, like a head speaking. She paused very briefly.

"You know," she continued, "you had good reason to say what you did a while ago. The two of you need to throw me in the ditch, along with universal culture in its entirety, all history, all human thought. Let it all end, because things can't keep on like this."

I ventured: "The change is already under way."

"What change!" Herminia said, shaking the locks of hair that were falling over her forehead. "If you call change the passage from living to dead . . . The relation between children and their parents can change—'shifts of the times'—, people say; but the other thing that's been called maternal love, let's see how the two of you change *it*."

"That's something no one's thought about changing."

"No one's even thought about what it is. Well, they *have* thought about it a great deal, but with very few exceptions all they've said is clichés. Self-denial, yes, I agree. But why self-denial? Why self-denial and nothing more? Why? *Because it goes in reverse*."

Quitina and I exchanged a quick glance of alarm. Quitina went to sit on the edge of the bed, at the head, and she wiped her handkerchief across Herminia's forehead, which had begun to glisten with small drops.

She sat down there, beside her, trying to tell from her eyes if she was losing her reason.

"Don't think I'm delirious," Herminia said, "it's just I've reached a truth on my own, an incontestable truth: the truth that maternal love goes in reverse. How can I explain it to you? Well, where is love going—any love—what's it going toward? From carnal love to the love of God, they're all going toward unity. Right? And isn't unity always difficult and always doubtful? Maternal love goes in the opposite direction: it starts from union, from an indisputable unity so easy no one took even one step to achieve it, it happened on its own. After this, what's left, will you tell me?"

Both of us would have liked to say something, but we couldn't and Herminia answered herself.

"Golgotha, that's what left. But that's what no one wants," and her head moved on the pillow as if it were free, floating. "Something that starts from union," she continued, "knows that it's on the road to disunity, toward total disunity. That's the sublime form of self-denial, the pinnacle. But it's better not to reach the summit, it's better to remain at a mediocre degree of self-denial."

"Sure," I said, "self-denial without climax is more self-denying."

"Of course, of course, and in any event it's preferable. But there's the masculine world demanding heroism."

"Demanding masculinity."

"Yes, yes, I realize that," Herminia said, "what's happened is, something has changed. Well, as I said before, something has changed from living to dead. But the living part of that is not what's changed; it's the dead part that has re-died, which is why we no longer have courage or confidence."

Herminia was verging on what Quitina had warned me about; something very fundamental to her was in crisis. But she saw she was letting it show too much, so she stopped. I realized immediately that Quitina knew about all this from her own observation and not because Herminia had confided in her, since Herminia had just slowed down precisely so as not to drag Quitina along with her. Then she continued without the impassioned tone, as if she'd only spoken after much thought.

"You would have to examine the primary, elemental feelings. You would have to see what part of them all can be left standing, what can be preserved in the middle of such complex times, by accepting life as it is. I think that could be a base."

But Quitina didn't let that task deceive her; she got up and immediately prepared a cup of Sedobrol.

"Well, this has come to an end," she said. And we had to obey.

The next day there was a telegram. "Everything wonderful. Heading home. Love, Miguel."

As soon as the doctor allowed Herminia to get up, she made us move her to Las Murtas so we didn't have to come here and take care of her. There, in two or three days more, she erased all traces of her illness, and when Miguel arrived the following week she forbade any mention of it.

Miguel came back happy. He didn't express this, but you could see it. Of course he didn't deny it either. He'd tell about the wonderful things he'd seen: the ice, the reefs, the canals . . . Everything was told as if it had happened to someone else, or as if it had happened to him for the hundredth time. In short, in his own way, exclusively his.

Herminia seemed very pleased as she listened to his tales; above all it seemed that she had always expected just such positive results. Not the least allusion to her previous opposition, no expression of happiness because her past fears were extinguished, no sign that between them there had been some type of reconciliation, some emotional compensation for the tension she'd sustained during more than three weeks. Nothing. Herminia remained valiantly at the degree of mediocre self-denial that she'd adopted, knowing she would never receive the least payment, because Miguel belonged to the generation of disunity. Of course, it would never occur to me to think that all young people of his age might be like him, but everyone knows that in each generation there are a few who seem to be the inventors of the glad—or sad—tidings.

Quitina did not accept this explanation.

"If at least he were little enough to spank," she said.

I reminded her that she herself had once defined him as an angel, and I told her that on another occasion I'd said his generation represented the rebellion of the angels. She found this very accurate and said her opinion of him had not changed; she still considered him an angel, but nevertheless . . .

"Nevertheless, what? You'd give him a bit of a spanking? You don't think that's how God probably settled the rebellion of the angels?"

"Why not? It's a great idea!"

I laughed loudly, but I suppose I looked frightened because Quitina perceived my alarm and assured me nothing in her was in crisis. She realized what she'd just said was more or less sacrilegious, but in essence it probably wasn't.

"Look," she said, "I've put it in rather absurd terms, but what I mean is, no matter what it takes, even if the blow leaves us wounded, what's needed is something that will eliminate evil. I know, I know that I'm still off, but I know what I'm saying: I'm saying that things can't keep on this way."

"Then you're saying the same thing as Herminia and Miguel, even though you're surprised. In fact, not long ago Miguel formulated, very explicitly, the same idea that God is going to deal us a definitive reversal at any minute."

"My being angry with him won't keep me from acknowledging he has talent," Quitina said. She thought for a bit and then proceeded, very pressingly: "Well, that's what Herminia, Miguel, and I say, and you, what do you say?"

I spent a long while asking myself inside: have I ever said anything, in my entire life? And, without finding an answer, I decided to respond to Quitina. I said something like I don't have the aptitude to discern whether that blow will be aimed or *should* be aimed at everyone, I only understand these things when they have to do with me myself. I also said I see evil clearly only in myself. I can pass judgment on some individuals and say with absolute certainty: So-and-so is an evil person. For myself, I know I'm not, but only by looking in myself can I *see* evil.

I don't know if I said anything else worth remembering, because for a considerable time I said nothing. And it may seem that what I did say means leading the life of a recluse, of a misanthrope or madman. Completely the opposite: it means leading the life of a normal man. In my case, when I live normally is when I say nothing. Nothing that can be written here, in these notebooks, which is why for years they lay in a drawer, dormant.

II

I've summarized briefly the time when I was silent. Now I have to face the things that continued to happen. A lot of things happened, as I feared, and they're still happening.

When I noted Elfriede's reappearance, I wrote, "I haven't said anything to Quitina, I need to think about what I should do." But I didn't think at all: I let things take their course.

That afternoon when I left the Drakes', things seemed to be pouring into my head in an avalanche, and I decided to read back through these pages, where I'd preserved the starting point. Right there on Leandro Alem, standing on the edge of the sidewalk, I thought: "Elfriede followed her own path all this time, she's not the motionless figure, completely defined by a few features I was storing in my memory. There's an angle of perspective I'm missing if I'm going to see her. The Elfriede currently visible is like a truncated cone: what I have here is its apex, the meager present encompassed by my gaze, then there's a large shadowy zone, then an extensive, basic memory." That night I read until well after midnight, and I wrote a few pages, but without being sure I'd continue. I wrote because I had to say just one meaningful utterance. "Why does Elfriede turn up now; is it a call to order?" Now I can say it: yes, it was. From that moment, the idea I'd intuited was becoming patently clear for all beings. In all of them I began to see the truncated cone, to realize there was a large shadowy zone in all of them.

342

Some time after that afternoon, one day when I had an endless number of things to take care of downtown, I left the house right after lunch, and twenty blocks from home my battery died. A compassionate citizen pushed me to a garage, and I was left on foot the whole afternoon. No hope of a taxi, because it was drizzling. I did catch one that agreed to wait for me at one of my stops, but then I had to go someplace where it wasn't possible to wait for me, so I found myself back on foot again, this time in a huge downpour. Then came the indescribable moment. Psychologically indescribable because, in fact, it can be described very well. What's remaining in the mist is what one becomes at such moments. The circumstances, quite simply: 6:20 p.m. on the Avenida de Mayo, beneath a torrential rain, among a couple dozen people trying to assault a colectivo.

After a while, watching amidst umbrellas and heads, I saw the colectivo coming; it stopped three meters beyond where people where waiting. En masse, the group rushed toward it. I was neither in the front nor the back of the crowd but in its most crowded part. The people ahead passed me a few jabs, which I sent on to the people behind, and they to the people after them. "Excuse me!" I said automatically, and heard behind me, like an echo, another "Excuse me!" from my victim to his.

That tone of voice, that rather guttural "Excuse me," stopped me in my attack. The colectivo took off, carrying a human cluster stuck to a running board like a colony of mollusks, and when I turned, there, among the people left behind, stood the little raven. That was the only name I could give him, because I never recalled his real one. He recognized me immediately, we greeted each other and tried to say or ask each other something—no use. With the hurricane hurling so much water you couldn't dodge it with an umbrella, at times the rain seemed to be coming down from under them.

"It's pointless to wait here, at this hour it's impossible," I managed to say.

"Impossible, impossible . . . ," he repeated. I induced him to go into the Tortoni.

And here's the thing: in my normal man's life, which has nothing to do with the present incident, I execute this same action—go into a café with someone or other—three or four times a week. I never wrote it down in these notebooks nor even mentioned the numerous individuals who form my social or professional life. Only a few, special situations matter here. This was one of them.

When we went into the Tortoni, I *saw* how the little raven walked into a café. He'd resisted, but since I started to run so I could get in out of the rain, and he was in front of me, I made him run, pushing him into the café. Once inside, he agreed to go in, to continue going in. I lagged behind a bit, taking off my raincoat and shaking off my hat; he went ahead through the tables as if he'd been lassoed, dripping water. He was wearing a gabardine hat and a raincoat whose waterproofing was worn thin, and he had no intention of parting from them.

"Take this off so it dries a little," I told him.

"All right, all right," he said, taking it off shyly.

Leaving it on a chair, he sat down across from me. Oozing moisture and smelling of raincoat, as if he'd left the garment's skeleton in the chair and kept the waterproofing, which pervaded his entire being. I wiped my handkerchief across my forehead, although it was not wet, as a suggestion that he do the same, and he did. With rapid, assured receptiveness, he drew a handkerchief from his pocket; it was not only folded but all rolled up, and that's how he dried his forehead—with that little ball.

So I'd have no doubt that his action indicated assent, he said: "Yes, the water, it's quite something!" And he gave a long, sustained smile.

I smiled too and wanted to say something, but at that moment the waiter came over to take our order, and it was hard for me to answer him; there was such a host of impressions racing in my head. Finally I said: "How about a whiskey, to get our circulation going again?"

"Oh no! No, not for me!" he said, moving his head and hand energetically but gently.

"All right, if you don't want alcohol, maybe you'd rather have some nice hot coffee?"

"No, not coffee either."

"Then?"

"Well, I don't know . . . Well, soda water, a soda water."

"Soda water! Do you know how high the humidity is at this moment? And on top of that you want to drink water!"

He laughed, covering his mouth with his hand to stifle some rather convulsed laughter. The veins on his forehead began to bulge so much they seemed about to burst. The whole time, he kept nodding his head in agreement and repeating: "Soda water, soda water . . ."

"All right," I said to the waiter; "a whiskey for me. Excuse me if I don't join you, but one more drop of water would be impossible for me."

"Of course, of course . . ." and he could hardly restrain his laughter, which seemed to come against his will, from a very distant and cruel sarcastic source.

I asked him a couple of trivial questions, in order to erase all that— where he worked, where he was from, etc.—and he told me he had commissions from several Chilean companies. I kept asking questions, as a way to keep up the conversation, and he answered: "Wines, wines," and was about to go into his convulsive laughter again.

I asked him if he'd adjusted to that type of life, assuming that in Europe he'd probably done very different things, but he said he didn't see the difference, he did what the situation or the moment required. On the other hand, he'd never held a permanent job; as a boy he'd studied economics in Constantinople, in Budapest, in Paris, and then . . . Then his story began to get personal; until that point he'd only named a series of places where entirely ordinary periods of his life had unfolded; now he was going to tell me something in which his own decisions counted, something it was stupid to tell if the motives were omitted, and he found it very difficult to share his motives with me.

I was looking at him so attentively I was almost scrutinizing him, saying to myself: What a deep mystery there is in this person! And how obvious that mystery is to me! This isn't contradictory, I'm not saying that his mystery was not mysterious to me, I'm not saying that I understood it, but I do assert I saw it. I even believe it was the only thing about him I could see. What's more, I believe that his mystery was the only real, the only living thing about his whole being. I felt it grow, approach and withdraw, becoming inhibited and suddenly slipping away. At the same time I felt he was aware of my investigations, and they didn't bother him; on the contrary, he admired me for them. He noticed I understood more about him than he could have suspected before that moment, but, naturally, I didn't understand it totally—I could not understand it totally even if he explained it to me—and then he decided to give me an explanation in proportion to what I understood on my own. He told me that at a certain moment, the Sorbonne and an uncle of his who ran an antique business on the Rue Bonaparte had become unbearable. Family, profession, degrees . . . he'd chucked all of it. And he'd begun to wait for the moment when he would do something, spending the winters in the library and the summers in Provence, with the grape harvesters.

"You harvested grapes?"

"I did, why not? And now, wine. Don't you see? What's it matter?"

I wanted to keep him from laughing and offered him some of the things they'd brought me with the whiskey; he didn't want anything. Finally, I moved the plate of olives toward him and said: "Not even an olive?"

"Well, an olive . . ." He took it with his fingers and looked at it for a long time, smiling as if to tell it, "I'm going to eat you, because, after all, an olive . . ."

The rain was not letting up, and people kept coming in, sopping wet. I phoned the house to say that I'd be a little late. I was hungry, but how could I suggest to him we eat something? I limited myself to ordering another whiskey and, when they brought it, he poured the other half of the small bottle of Belgrano soda water, which he'd carefully kept covered. He drank it at the same time I was drinking and, without going so far as to make the motion of a toast, he acted as if that new libation had lifted his spirits. I won't say it made him seem drunk, but it did seem to have corrupted, perverted him a bit; he reached out his hand toward the metal dish and pecked at a peanut with two fingers— I moved it toward him. He shook his head as if to say: "It's too much, but since we've already slipped . . ." He finally took a small pile, peeling the peanuts slowly in the palm of his hand as he ate them. Meanwhile we talked about Europe, about my uncle's sad end, the vague panorama the world was offering. He formulated pessimistic opinions, but without lamenting them, as if they were replies from an irremovable reality, "at least for a long time . . ."

It had gotten very late and we decided to leave. There was nothing left of the rain but fat, infrequent drops that dripped from the trees, in cleansed air.

"I would invite you to dinner." I said, "only I don't know . . ."

He cut me off: "But this has been a whole meal . . ."

We said good-bye. I renewed my former offer.

"You already know, if you need anything."

"Thank you, thank you. Good-bye."

How different! I thought, how different he's seemed to me than the last time I saw him. Even so, would I correct my first impression? No, there's nothing to correct. That view was accurate and so is this one. I was missing the area in the middle.

I got home, where Quitina had waited for me; while we were eating, I told her about my encounter, described to her my two views of the figure and explained to her, more or less, my theory about the shadowy zone. Then I said: "Well, I'd been thinking about this for two days because, can you believe, on Wednesday I suddenly found myself with Elfriede, that girl from Berlin."

"You did?" Quitina said. "Why didn't you tell me?"

"I don't know, I think because I didn't have the theory well formulated yet."

"Oh, what you were telling me about the shadowy zone. It was in her you discovered it?"

"Yes, I sensed it."

"And of the two zones in the light," Quitina said, "which is the more . . . the more brilliant?"

"Socially, the current one, no doubt about it."

Was Quitina going to say, "No, that's not what I was asking?" Perhaps, but she didn't say it and I continued to tell her about Elfriede's marriage to Drake; I described their apartment, the gladiolas, and of course, I told her I'd promised to invite them one of these days.

"We didn't set a date," I added, "because my thought was to call them after next week when we'll be at Las Murtas."

Was Quitina going to ask, "Why at Las Murtas?" Perhaps, but she didn't and I explained: "We'll have more to talk about there. Besides, Drake has told her about the factory, the farm, the estancia, and she's very fond of nature."

"All right," Quitina said and nothing else, although there was no need for her to have said anything more.

Meanwhile, I began to feel discontented with my theory about the shadowy zone. Not that I found it wrong; I found it limited. I saw that the sections, with their spatiotemporal slices, were only the most simple form of darkness; there were others much more intricate. And watching Quitina as she attentively ate a bunch of grapes, I thought: can there be a shadowy zone in her? Once again the same old question! How to divide her? Can there be light and shadow in Quitina? Of course; since my view of her lacked nothing, whatever shadow there is, if there is any, must be proportionate to the light: equal and constant. Then I imagined the cone of my perspective made of a very thin sheet, light on the front and shadowy on the back and rolled around its axis all the way. That's how a secret shadowiness had subsisted in her right beside me; I was never unaware of even one fragment, but the back went unnoticed. Quitina raised her head and said: "What are you thinking?"

I answered: "I'm imagining all the shadowy sections possible in a cone."

"Oh, they're infinite."

A high school kid could have answered the same thing, and Quitina knew enough geometry to be sure of her response, but she'd answered so seriously it was clear she wasn't looking at the problem from the point of view of geometry but from that of the shadow. Then I began to suggest different sections to her that could represent the countless characters a person meets up with: the ones that show us how inside a cone that's bright on the outside there's another cone that's shadowy and impenetrable; the ones that reveal how what is transparent and defined gradually becomes more cloudy and confused; the ones that break apart and let us see small, unconnected nuclei of darkness distributed here and there like boils. And so on until I had totally exhausted the topic.

Not long afterward, one morning when we were already at Las Murtas, I called the Drakes' house and no one answered. I planned to call again at noon, but it occurred to me that he would be in his office at that hour and I called there. I told him we were expecting them for lunch on Saturday.

"Delighted," he answered, "but I'll be alone because Elfriede has gone to New York."

Elfriede had gone to get their daughter, because it was the end of May and school vacation began the following month.

What a Saturday that was! In order for things to exist you need to believe in them, in order to believe in things you need to have created them; in other words, you need to carry in your blood the faith that created them.

Tom Drake arrived a little before noon and immediately he wanted to see the children.

"Three boys!" he said; then, looking at Quitina with a certain veneration, he added: "You're clearly not a bit selfish."

We laughed a little and said nothing, because what Drake had said was irrefutable.

He started to play with them. Spying a bow and some arrows they'd left on a bench, he told Francisco to shoot so he could see how he did it. Francisco shot and hit the bull's-eye.

"Good, very good," Drake said, "but you didn't shoot properly; you waste energy, and it's better for you if from the beginning you get into the habit of making the correct motion."

He paced off a suitable distance to the bull's-eye, stood behind Francisco, and made him adopt a particular stance. Right foot here, left foot there, this arm tensed, at this height, hand holding the string like this.

As Drake was giving all these explanations, he was placing each of Francisco's limbs in the right positions, as if Francisco were a jointed mannequin. When Drake said shoot, Francisco shot and missed the mark.

"Do it again, it's a question of habit."

"But how can I do it again if I can't see it?" Francisco said.

"I already explained it to you, don't you remember?"

"Yes, I remember what you told me, but since you were behind me nothing really sank in."

Faced with that reasoning, Drake was the one left perplexed, but before he could react Francisco said: "Do you shoot the way you explained to me?"

"Of course I shoot that way."

Francisco gave him the bow: "Would you shoot one?"

Drake adopted the proper stance and tried to theorize about each angle formed by his arm or leg. Both Francisco and Jorge, who were watching him attentively, surreptitiously pawed the ground a little—there's no other way to express it—and, mentally, I bowed to Miss Ray who's made them capable of restraining a "Hurry up and get on with it!" Francisco could not hold it back entirely; he wrapped it in an innocent smile.

"All right, shoot," he said.

Drake shot and hit the mark. Francisco picked up the bow, shot and hit it.

As soon as he picked up the bow, he jumped into position in the exact spot where Drake had placed his feet and, without reflecting even a moment, he repeated Drake's movement precisely. He didn't assume that position piece by piece, as Drake had, in other words, stopping at each angle to make sure it offered the proper resistance; he executed the act of shooting in perfect form, understanding all at once, with his whole body, the discipline athletes acquire over a long period of time.

Jorge wouldn't shoot because he'd broken his bow, and the one they were using was too stiff for him, but he made the gestures, exaggerating them rather theatrically—the movement of exerting force against nothing is always theatrical—, sometimes aiming at the sky, other times at the horizon, while he said: "I already know, I already know what it involves."

That was the appetizer. We had lunch then, and at the table Quitina did the talking. She spoke with Drake about cities she knew in the United States and about places in New York she'd liked to visit as a girl; she remembered brands in different lines from some of the ads popular then, saying the songs were very old and dated back fifteen years.

Then, while we were having coffee, Drake saw some horses meditating near the wire fence and said that it would be nice to take a ride. We had the horses saddled and went riding.

We actually did that; on a Saturday afternoon we took a long horseback ride. But Tom Drake was with us, which is why it could happen. We seldom rode, and when we did it was very early in the morning or on nights when there was plenty of moonlight. That day we rode from four to seven, until the sun began to set, limpidly snuffing out that Saturday.

Drake left content, effusively thanking Quitina for the day and saying that as soon as his girls were back, they would come again.

They returned two weeks later. Drake called me one Wednesday and asked when we could plan something.

"This Saturday, if you like," I said. "Come out here."

Friday afternoon when I returned from Juncal, I brought Herminia and Miguel along with me. On the way I tried to tell Herminia, more or less, about the nature of my friendship with those people and Herminia said: "Yes, yes"—nothing more, but it let me know that Quitina had filled her in. Between Quitina and Herminia the communicating vessels (head and heart) were definitely still in perfect balance.

Saturday morning was splendid, a warm autumn day. At a quarter to twelve the Drakes' car passed through the gate.

Elfriede's outfit was not right. You could tell she'd meant to wear something very serious—a gray tailleur, with those checks you see on the Prince of Wales that look horrible on a woman. It seemed to me she'd lost the sporty style that warmly complemented her femininity;

now, when she wanted to make a flashy appearance, she wrapped herself in colored gauzes, and when she wanted to be discreet it was cool cashmere, in a mediocre cut. But the child was stunning. You could see her mother had wanted to present her like an exquisite piece of chocolate. She was wearing a little corduroy dress in light coral with an almond-green Angora sweater on top. The rose in her complexion was not the same shade as her dress, but the two harmonized; her blue eyes were a good match for the green in her sweater, and her hair, held back by a headband of blue ribbon, fell in a cascade of golden curls over the ensemble. The girl was a picture. I thought she was a much better picture than any of the ones decorating Elfriede's apartment that Elfriede had forced me to look at, putting me in the awkward position of having to conceal my horror. Francisco and Jorge gazed at her in amazement.

They greeted her in English, and she answered in a very refined way. Drake said: "Don't speak to her so politely; she's used to playing with boys." And he told his daughter, also in English, to go and play with them in the garden.

Francisco decided to ask her name and she answered: "Nix."

"Nix is the name for a cat," Francisco said in Spanish.

Quitina intervened in dismay: "Francisco! Thank goodness she probably didn't understand you."

The girl hesitated for a minute before taking sides, looked around at everyone to size things up, turned to Francisco, and said: "Miaow."

She made a little catlike face and stood there very seriously.

She was a hit. The boys rushed toward her shouting: "She understood! She understood!" They took her by one hand and dragged her off to the garden. The ice had been broken.

Someone said that children understand all languages, and Elfriede declared in her rudimentary Spanish: "Children and grown-ups; it's all in wanting to understand."

Saturday morning had been splendid, but not long after noon it began to grow overcast. As we were having lunch, it began to spit. This meant staying inside, playing music, drawing out the coffee and cognac, smoking a cigarette, playing music, having tea, playing records.

At first the conversation was unhurried, and we listened to music; then the boys burst into the drawing room and the library. They'd already had their tea, but they came looking for more things, wanting to stuff their little guest with sweets and chocolates. She resisted a bit and ended up devouring everything. Then, although we couldn't tell why, they pretended to be fighting. Even Fernando managed to escape from Miss Ray and get into the brawl. As they were chasing each other and rolling in a heap on the carpet, I noticed that Nix would always land on the very bottom. They were shouting, laughing, and making an infernal din and Drake kept putting on records.

At seven they left. The rain had become heavier, so the good-byes were short; they had to make a dash for their car.

We didn't comment much on the visit. One curious thing: Miguel, who never makes any comment, came out with a few opinions, like a person who says "At least this much should be made clear."

"They're great," he said; "solid people. The way they dress isn't the way we dress here; even so, they're well dressed. They look like they come from Andy Hardy's family, that's what I find amusing about them."

Since no one contradicted him, his remark was brief.

The next day Francisco and Jorge began to ask very mysteriously when did Miss Ray have her day off. Quitina told them it was Thursday, the fifteenth. They conferred a little and said that on Thursday they wanted to go to doña Gabriela's house by themselves.

"Why by yourselves?" Quitina asked.

"Because she's offered us something, and Miss Ray won't go."

"Well then?"

"Well, even though she won't go . . . we want to."

I intervened. Why not let them? Doña Gabriela and her husband were two very old puesteros—he'd worked on the estancia, where they've lived since Puig's time—wonderful people, in the old style. She was known for her baking and sometimes she'd brought the children rosquitos de anís, and the little pastry rings were really delicious. Why not let the children go?

The struggle, always in low voices and asides, with sidelong glances when Miss Ray was present, lasted until Thursday; on Thursday, no longer under surveillance, they shouted their request until Quitina gave in, and the two of them shot off.

Francisco was carrying something under his arm, but I couldn't see what. When I advised them not to be gone long, they answered: "We'll just go and come right back."

From the upstairs window I watched them take a narrow path through the pasture and run like fallow deer, until they were out of sight. In fact, half an hour later I began to hear their voices; they were back already. I looked out the window. They were still way in the distance, walking so slowly they could hardly make any progress. They were carrying something between them—the canvas bag Francisco had taken for that purpose. It didn't seem to weigh much, it seemed to be filled with something so delicate they didn't know how to carry it. Several times I heard them say: "Be careful! . . . Don't pull! . . . Don't uncover it! . . ."

It took them so long to arrive I'd almost forgotten them when I heard a tremendous clamor downstairs. I went down, and they were in the playroom. Quitina was holding Fernando and she could hardly control his kicking; he was the one shouting the loudest.

The three of them were repeating a single word, all three saying it at once, and it was ringing inarticulately like a shout. Finally I could make out what they were saying: "Nix! Nix!" they were shouting, and Francisco was holding a small gray Angora kitten by the skin on the back of its neck.

Francisco and Jorge were repeating the name so the kitten would learn it, and Fernando was shouting like a lunatic.

"Give her to me! I want to hold her!"

Quitina was trying to calm him: "Don't you see that she scratches? Look at her claws."

Fernando was shouting: "I want her. I want to hold her."

Quitina put him in my arms saying: "Take him. I'm at the end of my rope with him," and she sank into a chair, exhausted from the struggle. She looked pale.

I went over to the others with Fernando in my arms, explaining to him how to touch her so she wouldn't scratch, and I started to convince them they should leave her alone for a while. Quitina stood up.

"Give him to me," she said, and she took the baby. "Francisco, put her here, on the table." She sat down with Fernando on her lap and said: "Touch her here on her back. You'll have a chance to hold her for a little while, and that will be it."

There was silence for a couple of seconds. Fernando was smiling and moving his hand across the cat's back as she sat quietly, and as if it were the formula for everything that was happening, he began to tell her very softly: "Nix, Nix, Nix."

"Okay, that's enough now," Quitina said.

Jorge seized her. Fernando started to shout again. Francisco, resisting the temptation to take her back, was repeating: "Be careful! Be careful! You're going to hurt her!" And the cat, hanging from Jorge's hand, was going "Miii!" or rather "Niii! Niii!" showing her impeccable teeth and little tongue, winking, whether angrily or voluptuously it was impossible to tell. Sometimes she relaxed her claws and the tips of her little fingers were rose-colored coral, but then she would close her claws again and they would be soft, wrapped in gray velvet. On her belly, where the fur wasn't so thick, you could also see rose color, and when she opened her eyes their metallic green irises sparkled like two sequins.

Francisco looked at Quitina, hoping to find in his mother the same smile of satisfaction and delightful play that was making the three of them so animated, but he noticed something was wrong and assumed it was their stubbornness about disobeying Miss Ray. Then he began to explain.

"Several days ago," Francisco said, "we were taking a walk with Miss Ray near doña Gabriela's; she was at the door, she called to us and showed us four little kittens she had in a basket, with their mother; they still had their eyes closed. Doña Gabriela told us if we liked one of them she would give it to us as soon as it knew how to eat by itself. But Miss Ray said no. She said: 'Dogs, fine, but not cats.' I don't know why. We gave in, but now we want to have her. And we'll convince Miss Ray."

He tried to take her from Jorge, but Jorge wouldn't let go of her and the cat began to meow, spoiled, between the four hands that were fighting over her.

Francisco finished his explanation: "Now we want to have her so we can call her Nix."

Jorge nodded. Quitina was still silent. Fernando was shouting himself hoarse again.

"Let them fight it out on their own," Quitina said, "they're big now. I'll try to get her out of here."

"But what's going on?" Francisco asked with a genuinely inquisitive expression.

"Nothing; you're the one who's responsible," I said. "The three of you have had your whim; now it's up to you to make sure nothing unpleasant happens."

"But what can happen?"

"I don't know. . . the cat could scratch Fernando."

"What does it matter if she scratches him?"

I gave him a small cuff on the head and he stood there looking at me indulgently, shaking his head like a father who puts up with a child's peculiarities.

Taking Quitina to the library, I kept repeating: "The noise they make is overwhelming! It's unbearable!"

This was to give her the chance to complain about something, since I could see she needed it; she let herself sink into an armchair without complaining, though, and that's how she expressed her exhaustion, which of course was not caused by the children's noise. As if she hadn't heard it, attentive to nothing but her own reflections, she said: "The power of a word!"

At that very moment we heard Miss Ray come in, although she usually returned much later. Quitina went to fill her in about the insurrection. She came back immediately and dropped into the armchair again.

"What did she say?" I asked her.

"Oh, nothing," she answered. She didn't feel like talking about that, but I kept talking about the boys.

"We have to decide about Francisco's schooling so he can start high school; he can't keep on in this babyish way indefinitely," I said, and Quitina nodded her head, but she didn't say anything. "It seems to me that Miguel's filled his head with arguments against Salvador, so we'll have to send him to the Escuela Argentina Modelo. Don't you think?"

"How do I know," Quitina said. But she didn't mean she didn't see clearly whether or not it was a good idea; she meant, no doubt about it, "how do I know what I want."

Understanding it that way caused a sneaky pressure in the pit of my stomach, but I didn't stop to think about it; I came up with another topic. Actually, what I came up with was another question, and I brought up an idea I thought I'd suggesting to her for days, one that didn't require an urgent decision, but I felt an urgency to ask her about. So I raised the question of whether it would be a good idea, in a few months, once the weather improved, to stay in Las Murtas for a long period and either close up the apartment or sublet it. Quitina hadn't suspected such a thing could occur to me, and the repetition of her response didn't indicate she was postulating a position, but she said again in a perfectly spontaneous way: "How do I know . . ."

The sneaky pressure was rising; it reached my throat and finally my brain, until it had me sunk in an unbreathable confusion.

Quitina *does not know* . . . Now that she knows everything, she doesn't know what she wants. Now, a dark, hermetic response answers the oldest and most vital questions. "What would happen if I made a long confession to Quitina?" "What would our relationship be like as a result of that?" Many months after my confession, the underground tremor has begun to register. Now that I've told her everything about me and she's told me everything about herself, now those ambiguous phrases start to appear between us, phrases that can't be cleared up with a question, these telltale signs that must be interpreted.

"How do I know!" Quitina has said it twice: "How do I know!"

"Where to find the clue to the enigma?" I knew she'd never said that in her entire life. Of course this is a stupid affirmation, because Quitina has said "How do I know" many times, like everybody else, but never before in that voice. Her tone, her voice, was the unusual thing; this was what appeared for the first time at that moment. For the first time? No, the second. Minutes before, the same mystery had already appeared in her voice.

When she collapsed into the armchair as soon as she reached the library, and said "The power of a word!" I already felt stricken with fear, but at that moment Miss Ray arrived and it all seemed to be vanishing. Nevertheless, the explanation was in Quitina's sentence. She *did not know*, because her whole spirit, all the faculties of her intelligence were employed in considering *the power of a word*. But was she considering the power of a word, in the abstract, or of *that* word particularly? This was still not clear to me. I only saw that she was stopped, suspended before words, before enormous powers. I felt that other phrases of hers— "Saying something as if you were doing it," "Your intention, as that girl said"—, were assuming such huge proportions in her mind that they blocked out the sunlight.

I tried to explain to Quitina that the idea about the apartment had occurred to me simply as a means of reducing our expenses, but meanwhile I was thinking inside: "We're becoming enveloped in such stupid anguish! The apprehension we feel is so gratuitous! Why grant validity to a past that was already subjected to its just appraisal? Why not burst out laughing at this moment? Why not give her a hug and a little pat on the behind and say, 'I'm laughing at your worries?'"

But I ended up not doing any of those things. Even though I saw the colossal phantoms rising in Quitina's soul and knew that a gesture on my part could banish them, somehow I felt afraid of making a mistake; I suspected that such a gesture might not be necessary and that, if it weren't, an explanation would have to be made. I wavered because I was afraid of doing something ridiculous, like the day I was at the point of entering Herminia's apartment by breaking a windowpane. Because I was afraid of looking ridiculous, and, because I was afraid of finding a dead body inside, if I was right. In other words, in this case I was afraid of being wrong and seeing myself forced to give an explanation, and afraid of being right and finding damage too devastating to be erased with a hug.

The thing is, within me my oldest problems suddenly became current, filling the present, when every day more and more of my effort, my attention, was necessary if I was to handle practical matters in even a moderately successful way. For example, the industrial equipment started to act up again. I *knew* something was going to happen, and my time would have to be divided between very different tasks. Nevertheless, I decided not to divide it but invest *it all* in everything at the same time.

That night wound up half-smothered, like a bonfire on which someone threw a bucket of water, but not enough water to put the fire out completely. The embers remained, hidden, and its liveliest spark lay in the different amount of time certain ideas had been in Quitina's mind as compared to mine.

My confession, that long, meticulous tale in Herminia's drawing room, had been absolutely faithful to the truth. I neither lied, nor deformed, nor downplayed things as I told them, and Quitina accepted them naturally, without getting upset, because I didn't abbreviate them, no, I accelerated them, going straight to the point; because that's what they'd been reduced to. What I gave her then had once been as large as a huge tree branching all through my life in incalculable bifurcations, but that night it was something as concrete, as round as a seed you could hold in the palm of your hand. And that's how she took it, but now the tree is growing in her mind. And Quitina is deliberately trying to hide this. She knows that within me, through a natural process, the way a bean shrivels and hardens, all that had turned into something that couldn't be grasped in one hand; she doesn't want anyone to see that within her it's gathering new strength. Above all, she doesn't want my present even to approach germination.

We'd spent some time in that kind of *vita mínima* created by secrecy. When I was enduring my unconfessable things, the situation was not as depressing, because Quitina's life was normal and I clung to her. But after our mutual confession, the unconfessable was shared equally between us. What can't be confessed is that the past does not pass, that because of the past the present fears the future.

Soon, however, external things forced us to unite against the common enemy. Well, we hadn't been disunited for even a minute; we had to combine our attention and focus on reality, as if we were making sure we'd synchronized our watches.

It was already the middle of June; the sowing could not be postponed and not beyond that week. The task awaiting me was a lot of arithmetic, and when it comes to arithmetic I've never been lazy. I can do it easily and I can always do more, no matter how much is called for. The hard part comes when I have to convert that arithmetic into money.

One Sunday, about the middle of the month, as soon as lunch was over, everyone left for Azul in the big car. The American Circus was in town. And before they were through the gate someone came to tell me that Mr. García was on the phone. I went to the phone, and it was Mr. García junior! As soon as I recovered from the shock and realized he was calling to say he was coming over, I hurried to say how sorry I was that Quitina had gone out and tried to suggest that he postpone his visit until the following Sunday. But he said: "No, no, it's to talk about business, so if you're home that's enough. We'll be there before five."

I thought: they're coming to talk about business! But they'll get here before five, so I'll have to offer them something. I begged the cook to make tea and some really tempting delicacies, in hopes of using those to distract their imagination.

When they arrived, mother and son were in the car; he was at the wheel and she was beside him, this time wrapped in beaver. I asked about the senior García and they told me he had a slight cold. I saw it was a lie and felt alarmed, realizing that they left him at home, the way people leave a child at home when they go somewhere; and I foresaw that, thanks to business, we'd find ourselves in a dangerous climate within a few minutes. Which is what happened.

We began by remarking on the cold, which was somewhat extreme; I settled Julieta comfortably near the fireplace and placed both a chocolate and an almond cake within her reach, as well as several plates of colorful canapés. Meanwhile, García junior paced around the room with holding a cup of tea and telling me he'd decided to acquire the remaining Arcaya land—four lots.

We had only purchased two ourselves, three hectares each, which is what we were sowing, because we wanted the land on the estancia to remain exactly as it was before. Since I didn't know how he was going to use his piece, I refused to feel alarmed as yet and I asked him indifferently: "Do you plan to build?"

"No," he said, "I'm going to sow it," and he added smugly, "I'm not going to get involved in industrial things, I think it's better to follow tradition."

"Oh, yes, much better," I agreed. And I stood there thinking about the problems this would lead to. Making a quick mental calculation, I thought: about six hundred meters of new wire fencing for the adjacent land, two hundred posts, and a few thousand pesos for labor. Beautiful! Perfect timing!

Continuing to repress my alarm, I said: "Let me know in advance when you think you'll get under way. Agreeing on things beforehand, you avoid any hitches."

He didn't answer, but I assumed it was probably because he found what I think obvious.

At that moment I was about to cut a piece of chocolate cake to give to Julieta, and I said: "Right now, this month, I won't be able to attend to anything but the sowing."

As I said this, I raised my head and saw an exchange of glances going on between Julieta and her son. His glance was commanding, goading her to action. Hers was submissive, definitely submissive, but at the same time lazy, half-entangled in a different bliss, from which she tore it with effort. Accepting his orders, she answered him with something like "I'll get to that, I'll get to that," and before her first obedient observation could sound, she told me quickly: "Almond."

I put a slice of almond cake beside the slice of chocolate, offered the small plate to Julieta and waited for her words to free themselves from that delectable petitioning, like flies from honey.

"We've been thinking for some time," she said, and it was a while before she continued. With her teaspoon, she took a small piece of cake but did not dare to eat it, leaving it on the edge of the plate and dividing it in half, as if she found it too large. She was struggling, stroking it with the spoon.

"Well," she went on, "remember that not long before my poor uncle died, when we were with Zelaski, we were already thinking about getting out of this business. We were never interested in keeping it up."

She looked at me and saw that my expression was not overly tragic; then she decided to eat the small piece of cake, only so she could savor it while she rounded off her next sentence.

"Well," she concluded, "I never understood these things and Tomás even less. Now it's different: Luisito wants to push ahead harder."

Then, with another glance, she delegated things to her son. It was as if she were telling him, "I did my part, now you take over." With her eyes lowered, withdrawing modestly to the background, she began to eat a little bit at a time.

García junior moved toward the footlights. And he moved without budging from the armchair where he'd settled himself during his mother's speech.

"In short," he said, "you must understand that we're not interested in the profit we get here. It's money that neither grows nor decreases, and it's continually exposed to . . . In a word, you know very well there aren't great hopes for this enterprise."

Not wanting to maintain a gloomy silence, I said: "I don't know, 'hopes' is too nice a word, but I don't believe that things have fallen behind in the last two years."

"Oh! Who's going to run a business because it's not going in reverse. That would be a nice *réclame* for a make of automobiles: 'It doesn't go in reverse.'"

The monster was allowing himself to make jokes. I said: "Yes, that would be original, and it might even prove very effective, but it would have to be something of a lie, like all ads, because a car must be able to go in reverse."

"Well, a car, I admit, does go in reverse, but a business . . ."

"A business established on a branch of industry that's not yet been developed must start out by achieving stability, then pick up speed gradually."

"Oh, *then*! I don't see this 'then' very clearly. Let's go do some arithmetic instead of making suppositions."

"Okay, let's do some arithmetic."

I said to Julieta: "You'll have to excuse us, this will be a bit boring for you."

"Oh, the two of you mustn't worry on my account" she said. "I'm very comfortable," and she added, "here where it's nice and warm."

I led young García to the desk and made him sit in my armchair. I put a pad of paper in front of him, opened a drawer on one side, and said while continuing to fumble around: "I have a few notes here . . ." And suddenly, making it seem like a coincidence, I took out a box of cigars and set it in front of him.

"Do you like these?"

"Yes, of course," and he took one immediately.

I lit it for him with the large lighter that was sitting on top of the desk and gave off a spark like a pistol shot. Smoke began to rise from the cigar, young García sprawled in the armchair, and I stood there a while contemplating *ma dernière touche*.

I walked around the table and sat lightly on the edge, rather close to the corner, as if to roost for a moment; but I chose that perspective because from there I could see them both, could see them look at each other and lament my presence—the way I was perched there on the table looking like a misplaced object. No doubt the way I was sitting there detracted from the solemnity of the scene, but not for me—for me I was invisible—and they were waiting for me to change my position. I didn't; I recited entire series of figures that represented dates, hectares, daily wages, machines, packaging, transportation. I recited past figures, with their percentage of loss, present ones, which were more or less balanced, and future ones, which bubbled with possibilities.

Young García raised numerous objections: "Well, those figures are a bit optimistic" or "You're not taking into account contingencies, unusual atmospheric conditions, and all the rest."

"Yes," I said, "I've taken all that into account; if we were insured against those contingencies, the figures could be much more optimistic."

"Oh, perhaps, perhaps . . . In any case . . ."

There was silence for a couple of seconds, but a solemn one. And, of course, in those two seconds I traversed planets and millennia. Again I saw their very brief, categorical conversation. Julieta had pondered things studiously for a long while; she stopped. Her silent attention was so abrupt I seemed to hear it burst into our conversation the way you hear "Adentro!" as they strum the samba or you hear the bugle as it's blown in the bullring when it's time for the kill. But I would not consent to *settle*. I abandoned the spot they'd been waiting so long for me to abandon, becoming mobile, unstable, so they'd have a slippery customer to contend with, and I finally went over to sink into the armchair facing the desk.

Before young García could begin to speak, I said: "But, naturally, it makes no sense for you to continue with a business that no longer interests you. Things can all be settled as soon as you like. Come to the office some morning in the next couple of days and the balance sheet will be ready." I beamed a smile at Julieta and said, "There's no reason to worry."

She responded with another smile and a lively movement of her hand, which dared to grab a cookie. As she was gnawing on it, almost without moving her lips, she said: "Oh, I'm sorry, but now I'm telling you . . ."

Then I was the one who created silence so I could keep studying them. The matter was ended; they had achieved their objective and without a struggle, contrary to what they feared. They were pleased, but not just pleased—they were already setting sail on a new ambition. Maybe their fundamental, most deeply rooted ambition, it hadn't entered the sphere of the possible until they saw their first plan consolidated.

They both wanted to open fire. Of course Julieta was not the proper one to do that, so she continued to sit expectantly, evidencing some agitation beneath her silk blouse. She was looking at her son, certain he would soon attack audaciously. But at the same time they both wanted to experience that instant, to ache with its yearning as if they'd already carried things off; this would let them assault more forcefully. And he chose to begin by asking a question. He made an eloquent effort to conceal the fact that their aching had been affectionately nurtured along the way—perhaps for months—and he had prepared a series of questions that could have seemed to lead to the issue *in question.*

"You intend to sow anyway?"

"Yes, why not?"

"Of course; I understand. You're not an industrialist, you're a technician and technicians are very fond of their gadgets," he said with playful irony.

"That's it, that's it," I said and I laughed a little as a tribute to his good humor.

"But you have a small apartment on Juncal, and I believe you've made a laboratory there, haven't you?"

"Yes."

"It's not a large apartment, across the front, but it's very deep, it seems to me."

"Thirty-some meters."

"Yes, that's quite deep. You could do whatever you wanted there. And the location couldn't be better."

"Oh, yes," I said, "the neighborhood's delightful."

He didn't know how to respond, because my comment did and did not have anything to do with what he'd said. Changing direction slightly, he started off: "Well, some things turn out well and others turn out poorly."

He sat there waiting, but I didn't press him, I waited calmly.

"I say that," he added, "because, you know, the business, let's say, the factory, the plantation . . . What you could call the industry, has . . . not worked out for you. You yourself must recognize this, I think . . . You have a reputation for being intelligent."

"Is that possible?" I said, with a naive gesture. Julieta felt it was her duty to laugh loudly, threatening me a little with her hand.

He continued: "At the same time, you've greatly improved the house, the park, well, the residence. All of that is unrecognizable. And, if you add to this the amount things have appreciated in the last few years . . ."

I didn't want there to be a silence on the basis of this sentence and I said: "Oh, yes, the house is very nice."

He nodded his head at length and said: "I imagine you'll go to any expense to get this under way, but well, it's a suggestion, simply a suggestion. In case you got tired, or saw there was no other way out, in case it occurred to you to change course, I, well, you can count on us at any moment."

His *suggestion* had been stated in such a protective tone that all I did was smile and look at him, engrossed. He nodded violently, fearing I hadn't understood him completely. Or I was waiting until I saw how far his generosity would reach. Then he decided to round things off.

"I tell you now, this is only a suggestion, but you should give it a little thought."

He took another puff on his cigar, starting to speak as he expelled the smoke, as if it were a very difficult task: "Well, a profit . . . ," and between his teeth now, in a barely audible way: "a profit of about 200 percent . . ."

I remained impassive. Then he sent a column of smoke to the ceiling and said in a clear voice: "Don't doubt it one bit, this has appreciated a lot. You probably remember what you paid for it, and not too many years ago. Well, now it's worth three times that much. Yes, yes, three times, without any exaggeration. And, I tell you now, we would always be willing . . ."

The blow, to the heart, had been dealt. I continued to smile and they sat there a bit, their blood pressure still elevated. I was missing none of the spectacle. When she'd heard "three times," Julieta had shuddered, but at the same time she'd watched her son's daring gesture with pride and she'd been replaying it mentally, also amazed at herself for having the courage to agree. I did not want to prolong her anticipation any further.

"Yes, this would be a great business," I said, "it's worth thinking about. Above all, at the rate things are going, you can imagine how much it will have appreciated when I've gotten tired of it."

Julieta tensed up, from head to toe, and immediately succumbing to disappointment, deflating. Discouragement almost had her bursting into tears of anger. The monster paled slightly and I saw that he was thinking, "Well, hostilities have broken out."

The meeting didn't last much longer. When they were in control of themselves, they began to say good-bye, send their regards to Quitina, etc. They left, at last.

I don't know why I'd always felt a decided horror of that boy, without ever seeing him more than in passing. And it wasn't even a horror mixed with curiosity; I would have preferred to remain uninformed about him. But now I could say that I knew him well. The monster-like being was Julieta's son! Calculating that in '35 he was probably fifteen or sixteen, now, in '46, he would be twenty-six or twenty-seven. What a dreadful age in one of these monsters.

He's complete. He has his law degree and his twenty-six years. On his vest, his tie, his tight socks with their horizontal stripes, with his straw-colored, slicked-down hair, wherever you look at him, he wears it firmly stamped. He's the young lawyer, son of Julieta Puig. Of course he's also the son of Tomás García, no doubt about that, but this is something different. What's obvious here is that Julieta has placed this monster in the world as an affirmation of herself, as a way to endure. What would Herminia say about this? Union? Not exactly. A type of continuation, whose temporal effect falls on her, because she walks behind, filially, transforming herself according to his experiences. Fearful Julieta, who once had no idea how to set a table. Most certainly she doesn't know now either, but now it doesn't matter to her; her monster is there to defend her, to be what she was not. And she pours herself into his becoming, she supports and nourishes him, altering herself accordingly as he goes about being.

Is this the true meaning of maternity or, better, of paternity or, more precisely, of the family? If instead of being the monster he is, one could say, "Here's the son of Tomás García," then, yes, I would recognize that meaning. But no, Tomás García does not continue in him. Perhaps Tomás García cannot continue, cannot endure because he is not susceptible to change. Tomás García does not cease to be, but he's that good vassal without a lord. Or whose only Lord is the one who can't die. And the thing is, at one time, serving that Lord helped you to live and endure; not now. If He is the Truth and the Life, this means what we're fighting for is neither truth nor life. The explanation is too definitive, too simple. If one measurement, one contrast, one touchstone for truth and life is not love, what could be? And, if it's love, what right do I have to disqualify Julieta's love for the monster? And how can life be this battle between loves?

Let's imagine a spectator seated in the second row: the only thing he'll see in this whole story is a struggle between two landowners, fighting over a few hectares of ground, with differing plans for developing it. At bottom, the truth that gives the whole issue its life is entirely different.

It was never my ambition to develop this entire property, because my greatest return I received that first day, the day I first contemplated it, and because it veered into my hands precisely through an act of love. Too much security, too much confidence . . . the one thing that occurred to me was planting opium. Now they're trying to snatch the land away from me, and not really because they want to develop it. I can understand very well the ambition that Julieta's son has been nurturing, and I know how he's gotten his mother to acquiesce—through love. He was a boy when the Garcías sold us the estancia; I don't know if he was opposed or not, but in any case, I was the one that his parents were most determined to please at the time. But later, as the years passed, the college boy with his well-heeled friends and their leagues of land, which stretched so far you couldn't see where they ended, would go whining to his mother and also asking her what return she was getting from the capital she'd invested here. It's possible if we hadn't been tied down financially the situation would have been considered settled. But this way . . .

I'm remembering now that one day, a long time ago, Gálvez said to me: "Yesterday Mr. García's son was out here with some other kids. They walked around looking at everything, and they stayed in the garden for a long time."

I don't think I even answered him or that I answered as if he'd said, "It rained yesterday afternoon." But, now I see how it was. I hear—because the voice I endured for three and a half hours will not stop ringing in my ears—, I hear the monster undoubtedly telling them as they rode past in the car: "That estancia used to belong to my mother. My parents sold it, which was stupid. Want to go in and take a look around?" I hear him undoubtedly telling his mother later about the impression the stately park—this was before the poppies—, the drawing room, and the library had made on him; and of course these things were part of the house that used to be his mother's. And he undoubtedly continued to work on her this way, leading her to become what is now Julieta. Between them there must have been the affectionate agreement there was between the mother in Herminia's story and her hungry little boy shivering with cold. Now Julieta fills me with horror, and before I thought she was very nice; this is unfair. I have to understand that what's happening is, simply, that she's fighting to satisfy her son's hunger. She knows the happiness Quitina wanted is necessary, that at certain moments it can cause a desire as pressing, as painful as a pang of hunger, as a cramp from the cold.

Then why do I say Julieta's son is a type of monster? Because he is, I'm sure of it. He's a monster because he's an abominable social being. But it so happens that besides being Julieta's son he's the boy who spent three years at Don Bosco working with files and pliers and who, suddenly, one day could be sent by his mother out into the world. An abominable side of the world, although I can see this and Julieta cannot, much less her son. Nor can García perceive with full awareness that his action is abominable; all he sees here is struggle and movement, and it seems unnecessary to him. They already have enough of that, so why have any more? He doesn't even need what they have. But there are many people who can't distinguish what I abhor from what seems ideal to me.

For example, Strugo, the little raven, would not see any difference between Julieta's son and me. Javier, sure, he sees it or, rather, he notices a difference; in other words, he could not be friends with Julieta's son and he can with me, even though he's constantly telling me what a moron I am, as if it were an unspeakable conclusion. What does he mean? That I don't follow in the footsteps of Julieta's son. It annoys Javier that a social climber of the worst kind hopes to sneak in through society's backdoor and that a person he can get along with prefers to be something of a tramp. But I don't! I might end up like that, but it doesn't scare me. I'm tempted to say I feel strengthened by the notion that such a possibility exists. I've said this from the beginning: I desire triumph, I adore triumph, but I demand that Fortune come looking for me at the edge of the pit. What I detest is security.

Well, let's take it one step at a time. I'm theorizing, which would not be regrettable if things turned out well for me the first time; but I usually have to agonize over them. Security is odious when it's within you and it obstructs the mechanism of your will. This doesn't mean you don't need to dwell in security, to circulate in it. What's evil is when security settles in men who dare to desire . . . No, that doesn't seem clear to me.

Many men dare to desire, and they set out like colts after whatever it is they want; they're not the ones I'm talking about. I'm talking about the ones who dare to desire in God's presence, the ones who confront the metaphysical meaning of their desiring before they move toward its object; these men become emissaries of human desiring. If they fall asleep in security they're lost. These men must be guarded by danger. I find it quieting to think I might be erecting all this over an abyss of error. Which is not paradoxical, because I don't feel quieted in the sense of disquiet but in that of justice. If I appear before the judge with my ridiculous mistake the only task to my credit, and it's not valid, I'll fall into His void. I only ask that He give me time to say: Thy will be done.

Here, there is definitely material worth a bit of meditation. Why not develop it? Why not admit to myself that the vocation pent up in me for two generations will in the end prevail in me? I've demonstrated a lack of aptitude in other things so often I might as well give it one more try. But I won't; for the moment I won't construct theories that could never be supported by specific events.

"Events," in common parlance, means things like the ones that happen sometimes on sown fields or in management. Events are people's mortgages, even their gossip, but there are still other kinds of events. Even though I realize they're the most important ones, I lack something of what it takes to face up to them; I've had it at other times, but now it seems to have been extinguished. I will not call *that* by the only name you can. As it happens, though, when *that*'s missing from events, which is the case here, something bothers me a lot: their psychological nature. I wish they were useful in a public way, like Newton's apple, with the phenomenon recorded and the law immediately following. None of this is possible in the kind of events or phenomena I'm talking about: you have to descend to the most shameful things; you have to describe the trembling of flesh, the terror; laboriously, from the tons of slime squeezed out, you have to extract the infinitesimal amount of luminous material that can result, at least provisionally, in a thing of the spirit.

The Garcías, rather the Puigs, left—since only Julieta and her son had come—, and I stayed in the garden, thinking. It was lucky that Quitina hadn't been home, because this way I could fill her in, not making the situation seem less serious than it is but sparing her from suffering that degrading human contact. The Garcías had never represented deep feelings or affection for us, but there had been a friendly relationship, maintained over the years through a series of pleasant associations. Suddenly, all that would become a conflict of interests filled with cunning and cruelty.

There's a sense of fate about this clash of ambitions that's sprung up again between the Puigs and me. We're at a draw now, which makes things more uncertain. Who's got more now? Who's asking and who's refusing? I don't know. My spontaneous response is that I find refusing unpleasant, but now, up to what point can I—or do I want to—give in? Who's more powerful now? Those were my thoughts, as I wandered among the Australian pines; the real truth was that the horizon was totally dark for us; we had to choose between giving in or facing up to a battle in broad daylight. Both prospects were hateful to me; above all, I saw them as a string of evils. Nothing definitive and decent, a clean break, would come to mind; and as I walked and paced, I found myself on the road to the estancia's gate. I definitely did not go in that direction unawares: I went there to charge my batteries, to find myself with myself, with the person I was when I was capable of anything. The experience did not disappoint me. I reached the conclusion that I am capable of more. Because I have more? No, no . . .

I stood there a long while. It was the same time, more or less, as the first day; the light equally gray, but more clear. The atmosphere had also been vibrant, but less uncertain; and there was no presentiment of defeat. I could not see myself being slapped around by invincible contingencies, it did not occur to me to wonder what would happen. I knew what I wanted was what would happen. But what was it I wanted? To understand. That's all I ever wanted: to see, to understand. To see, as to drink; I'm always thirsting to see, and when I got there I was beside the fountain.

That road was very old, it undoubtedly existed when Puig bought the estancia, undoubtedly was how he went in and it was the first thing he saw. Maybe he stopped right there and had the idea to buy it; there could not have been any conflict within him, but there would definitely have been the fervor that gets a plan off the ground. His excitement would have been a calm excitement, which progressively turned into satisfaction as he made his calculations. From that spot he would have seen everything he could do, imagining how he would rebuild the estancia's main house and surrounding buildings, planning the factory, seeing not what was there but what was going to be there. When I arrived I saw that, but of that, only the basics, what you can't look at. I came along the road, in the car, feeling the green as it passed alongside me and the still gray that covered everything. Seeing that was enough. When I left in disappointment, that was what I rebelled against losing. Then I looked at it and, fully aware of what I was doing, told myself it was what I wanted—to look at that, a piece of wire and some posts where owls perch at dusk. But now he comes along, the monster—the son, Julieta's little boy—and he's burning with desire too. What is he looking at? What was there, what is there, what will be there? When he came the first time, right after Don Bosco, he said if the factory weren't there, the terrace would seem like a golf course. Well, that's his ideal. Since then, he's gradually seen that while we've lived here everything has been fixed up little by little, has come to look more cared for, and the enhancements have grown more dominant. The garden is very different now, and the drawing room is filled with nice things. This makes him imagine how much possibility there would be in the house, which could be turned into a luxurious residence. That definitely must be what he desires, and that I disdain; but his desire, can I disdain that?

I started to walk toward the house, and one thing felt evident to me: inspiration. I'd inhaled something: the force issuing from those pastures . . . Not really from them . . . The force issuing from everything, when you look at that force, when you converse with it. That mystic force was there and had been there for years, while I was growing duller and duller, because ownership is blindness, just as vision is possession.

When Quitina arrived with the children it had already gotten dark. We sat with them for a while as they ate, and I didn't say anything, but Quitina looked at me suddenly and said: "What's up?"

"Nothing," I answered, highly annoyed to see that Quitina had asked me that question with an optimistic smile, as if she imagined it had been something pleasant. So much so that she accentuated her smile and repeated her question.

"What do you mean, nothing? There's something."

"Nothing, nothing. Rather, nothing good," I decided to admit.

"Well, to look at your face a person would say it was something wonderful," Quitina said. "When we got back I thought I noticed you were feeling unusually animated."

Quitina was unwilling to abandon her optimism, and something more serious was happening too. Francisco now took part in our conversations. He wouldn't interrupt if, as then, there was a police officer beside him, but his eyes would escape any form of discipline, scouring us and jumping from one of us to the other. His expression was as quick to copy Quitina's mischievous smile as my affected tranquillity. He fluctuated, without knowing which of us to believe.

I noticed, and this was moving to me, that while he was watching us, he never stopped eating, completely engrossed, as children frequently are when they are stupefied; instead, he was making everything on his plate disappear quickly and automatically, and then, without taking his eyes from us, he was looking for crumbs on the tablecloth and nibbling on them tirelessly. At that point I burst out laughing, to make him believe that his mother had been right, and I started to talk about something else. Did I fool him? I don't think so. Quitina's expression changed, because she understood that I didn't want to talk right then. She kept her smile, but it lacked the confidence of a short while before. Like a mirror, Francisco reproduced her expression.

We closed ourselves up in the library then, and I filled her in on the events.

We talked for hours about the change that had taken place in those people and, even though that change annoyed us, we still found it logical and understandable.

"Well, we don't have to think about those people," Quitina said suddenly. "We have to solve the problem."

I didn't ask how, because there was obviously only one option, but I was quick to say: "This time it's my turn!" We struggled. Finally I said categorically: "You must understand that I'm the one who should face the responsibility, I'm the one who must write that letter."

"All right, all right."

I didn't believe her, not even when it seemed as if she'd given in; when it comes to her father she can't be counted on for anything. I made her give me a solemn promise: she would allow me forty-eight hours before intervening. She promised reluctantly but tried to convince me not to make any decision right then, to wait until the next day, because that would be better. I would not let myself be convinced.

We talked until after twelve; I made her go to bed, and I went up to my little room, prepared to have the letter written before I fell asleep. It was very difficult. Having to write a letter that called for a mixture of business and feelings has always been abominable to me; it involves the puzzle I don't know how to solve.

I started by speaking about how humiliated I felt to have let things wind up in such a situation, to have made so many mistakes that jeopardized the things I loved most and now find myself incapable of defending those things on my own. But that was being on several pages at once, and I told myself: what's needed now is definitely not a mea culpa, it's a report, a clear and detailed explanation of our financial situation. For that, the first thing was to recall how much information I'd given him at other times, and the only thing I could recall were some letters in an evasive, humorous, even literary tone—to put another label on something that's nothing but beating around the bush. I tore up the sheets of paper and began to think in an orderly fashion.

The conflict had a double nucleus, one was simple and immediate: the impossibility of proceeding with our planting at the very moment that the firm was crumbling and our capital was cut in half. This could be stated in a telegram: "Injection of funds urgent." The other was diffuse, anguished, vague . . . the monster's whole maneuver, the suggestion of his determination to recover the estancia and the threat of his closeness as a neighbor, which obviously concealed no purpose other than making life impossible for us. It was very hard to write about this last part. Hard to explain? No, hard to bear. In all my apprehensions and predictions about his offensive, I seemed to be considering it already under way. It was more practical to stick to the first part, hinting that, maybe, the second would follow later.

Once I'd made up my mind, I started to state the situation succinctly. It seems impossible that a person can't manage, without a pause, to write something as trivial as a letter, telling things as they are and nothing more. Nevertheless, every two or three paragraphs an empty space, a silence, in my head, a void.

There was total silence in the tower; you couldn't hear the eucalyptus trees rustling beside the window, or a single cry from the nocturnal insects, or any barking. Instead of concentrating on the idea I needed to present, sufficiently clear now, I escaped toward that silence, wandering around the void in the room, looking for something. It was at one of those moments when *the event* occurred.

The tower is very small: the couch wedged against the back wall in a kind of niche formed by the sink and the built-in closet that had provided sufficient amenities for Monington, even though he was a refined, elegant man. On the back of the closet door there's a mirror, perhaps the remainder of a large, broken looking glass, since it has only three beveled edges. I've gradually been accumulating things up in the tower myself, and they make it hard to walk around, but I have a need for them. There are bookshelves above the couch, at some height up the wall; below the shelves there's a photograph of the temple at Sunion, then two starfish underneath, then, inside a small glass-sided box, a butterfly from Brazil, fully illuminated by my work lamp, with one wing bluer than the other because each of them reflects light at a different angle. From time to time my gaze would rest, engrossed, on all these things.

I would return to reason, write a paragraph, stop . . . The conversation in the library was echoing in my head like sea echoes in a shell. Curiously, at times, what made me feel anguished to the point of nausea was only the murmur of that conversation. Not that the ideas, the words were not reproduced clearly in my memory, it was just the tone, the accentuation of each speaker: Julieta's voice, a bit gelatinous, and the monster's oratory, the voice of a scholar with the style of an insurance agent. That murmur had been firmly stamped on my acoustic memory, with evidence of its horror, devoid of any formal logic.

I gave my obsession a shake, stopped listening to that repugnant rustling compatible with perfect silence, and went back to my writing. But not for long. Barely formulated premonitions of the coming struggle were prompting me to think about the work that would start momentarily and, taking off from there, moving me toward bringing in the harvest, with all the stress on the plants, and the possible conflicts that might arise. And I would be going back and forth across the fields, listing the inevitabilities attendant on our being situated on the same hill . . . Suddenly, out in space, I started to see the almost imperceptible slope toward the stream that, when you look straight at it, becomes lost on the horizon and, as I looked straight ahead, there on the wall, before the horizon, was the blue butterfly.

My gaze engrossed in its metallic brilliance, the following thought illuminated the void of my mind: "If I so determine, it will flutter its wings."

This determination did not intimidate me. I didn't stop to refute the idea or to affirm it. As if I'd unburdened myself of one of my principal duties or as if I'd found a point of departure, I applied myself to drafting the report very precisely. It was written out immediately, and quite clearly, although it might not have seemed pressing enough; I was afraid that the emphasis needed to convey the drama's tension might be missing. I reread what I'd written, and it seemed fine to me; I saw no weak spots, I didn't find a way to strengthen it, but I kept looking for the missing emotion. It was didn't come from any flaw in the writing, it came from . . . I raised my head.

What I felt is comparable only to the discomfort one can feel in the presence of certain stares. I lowered my eyes because I couldn't stand it. What I couldn't stand, though, was not what I was seeing but the certainty that if I continued to look at the butterfly . . . And inside my head the clear, concrete thought: "If I want to, I can make it flutter its wings."

I put the cap on my fountain pen, set the pen to one side, wiped my hands across my forehead, closed my eyes, and told myself: "This, in clinical terms, is what's called paranoia. Definitely, that's exactly what it is, but so what? Call it whatever you like, the truth is that if I so determine . . ." I took my hands away from my face and looked at the butterfly but, just for a minute, because I felt the butterfly would move its wings if I kept looking at it. I jumped up from the couch and took a few steps around the room.

Well, let's admit that this is paranoia, I told myself, and that paranoia's the name for this wave of will that swells and rises to the brain, the fact is, there's something floating above that high tide. There's a small speck of unsinkable reason—small, because simple: *Do I* or *do I not want* it to flutter its wings?

Calmed by this conclusion, I leaned against the wall for a while, took ten deep breaths, felt in better control of myself and said, very firmly: "*I do not want* it to flutter its wings."

I picked up the pad of paper and the folder again and reached out my hand to the switch, but, before turning out the light, I looked at the butterfly. I looked at it intensely, repeating to myself: *I do not want* it to flutter its wings. Only for a couple of seconds, though, because the certainty (there are no words to define that certainty—it's something like the momentary contact of what *is*), the assurance that the high tide's force *could* make it flutter its wings, even though, by my reason, I might say I *do not want*, made me lower my eyes. Then I turned out the lights and went to the library.

There I finished the letter, which wound up being just a report; I did not darken the shadows. There were more details than necessary for someone known, as he was, to have eyes like a hawk. I felt sure the solution would not mean much waiting.

Waiting . . . I found that reasonable, and assumed it wouldn't be long. But immediately I wondered: can waiting not be long? I calculated how much time it takes a letter to get to Havana, and even if things were telegraphic, it was a question of five or six days. Didn't that seem long to me? No, during those days I could make so many preparations the time wouldn't be lost. But this wasn't the issue; what was happening was that *I could wait*. And in order to understand that I could, I had to go down into my cistern and search through all its dregs for the impatience that in former times was thrown into convulsions by the effort to succeed in doing something like what lightning achieves. I found impatience, which was neither dead nor asleep but supple and thin, like a small snake in the mud. That was the difference; people say lightning is like a tiny snake and that a snake is swift, like lightning, but that's just a saying. The speeds are not comparable.

It was my impatience, my old emotion, that had snaked a few moments before, as I looked at the butterfly. With what difference in voltage? No one could calculate that. Before, the force of that spark encountered no barriers; now, I had the same evidence, but my reason wasn't foundering from its thrust. And the threat weighing on me now was as powerful as the threats at other times, or more so. The threat was equally direct and explicit. My will, however, was not responding to it with the same furious enthusiasm. I know I'm going to have to face a war, and, of course, I want to win it, but I don't want to annihilate my enemy, even though I don't respect this enemy more than the ones I annihilated at other times; I respect this enemy less, the least possible amount, but I don't want to win by destroying. Can I be defeated? Perhaps. Although I don't think I will be. But in any case, *I do not want* to destroy. And *not to want* can be as obvious as *to want*. Is this *to be more able* or *to be less able*? There's no answer. No one could give me one, not even I myself, if I wanted to answer myself with a criterion for confirming proof. I can't give myself an answer, but I can *vouch for one*, since I'm the only witness. But witness to what? Only to my certainty, to the momentary contact that leaves no trace, but, once known, is more certain than any material reality. And above all, I can respond from my unsinkable reason: I know when *I want* and when *I do not want*.

The letter was written and I could go to bed. There was no guarantee I'd be able to fall asleep, because I had the kind of vibrant insomnia it seems impossible to soothe.

I resorted to a system I adopt on such occasions: concentrate on imagining the face of someone yawning. At first there are no results, because your nerves are too tense to relax rapidly, even when the suggestion produces a faint desire to yawn. If you keep trying you'll finally manage an incomplete yawn; the yawning face persists in your imagination, you're able to remember the long inhaling and violent exhaling, and so on until you come up with another, somewhat more satisfactory yawn, and then another that's a bit better, and, finally, one that's complete. If you yawn successfully ten or twelve times, there's a good probability that you'll slip into sleep straight away.

That night the system did not fail me, and with four hours of sleep I found myself fully prepared to face the day. At eight in the morning Quitina never asks for explanations, so all she said to me was: "Did you write?"

And I answered: "Yes, I'll tell you about it later."

I left, and as soon as I got to the capital, at the first post office I sent the letter certified.

When I got to my study I found a letter from Havana on my desk.

It was a long letter. For some time we'd been receiving nothing but snippets, and this letter contained nothing new—comments about his health, questions about the boys and a few affectionate sentences for each of us. Then there were three pages addressed especially to me. He wrote: "Santiago, if you're really busy right now, save this letter for sometime when you take a break; I want to consult with you about something that's very important to me." But he didn't get to the heart of the matter immediately; there were a few paragraphs telling me about his life, about how unaccustomed he was to having any leisure time, about how this business of leisure has the advantage of letting you really think about things. Then he said: "Do you remember that the day we went to the furniture storage I told you something about a portrait? Hortensia wanted to have her portrait painted by Zuloaga. Well, now that can't happen and, even so, I can't resign myself to not finding a solution. Of course a person can't go to a famous painter, one of those painters who think they're geniuses, and ask him to paint a portrait from a photograph, but how do I know? Maybe it would be possible to find one. I don't know if this will seem mad to you, but Dalí?" Then he gave me a meticulous description of each photograph in his possession. He had them from when she was a little girl, an adolescent, in an evening gown, with her hair loose. Those were from Havana, but he also had some from Europe—with a sable stole and muff, wearing a dress with a train and *aigrettes* on her head, in a riding outfit. For backgrounds, he preferred the ones from Havana; they all had backdrops that represented tropical gardens, they all had palm trees, lianas, gardenias, and even an occasional stuffed bird. His description was endless and then he said: "Dalí, I think is in the U.S. now. I can go there with all this material and suggest something totally out of the ordinary to him. But I want you to tell me, with complete honesty, if the idea is idiotic. I'm assuming that if I don't argue about the price, there's a chance he'll accept, and I can even invite him to Havana. I told you and Quitina that I'd bought a house, but I didn't give you any details; it's a colonial residence, somewhat outside the city, on the shore. The garden's enormous, although the house isn't very large, but it has a very spacious drawing room. You get the idea? It would be necessary for Dalí himself to see the light he's going to have here and for him to make the decisions about everything that should frame the portrait."

I recalled the small portrait still in its silver frame above the fireplace at Las Murtas. Yes, it could be, the idea was not idiotic; it was just a question of silver, in this case an enormous silver frame. And the timing wasn't good, just now when my letter was going to arrive, with its account of a more than average bankruptcy.

It's obvious that my stupidity, my lack of premeditation, my failure to adapt to reality are compromising the future of my sons, I thought. Well, the statement is relatively obvious, because no one knows what convulsions of society or my consciousness will affect that future when one least expects it. On the other hand, the living present in that letter, the present of a desire, of a dream woven slowly that's filling every hour of a person's thoughts . . . To drop such a gross weight on him makes me shudder. Is this reasonable? I neither know nor care. The idea of spoiling one moment of a game with some problem is repugnant to me. Even if it's the game of an extravagant player, according to many people's way of thinking. For example, according to Strugo's way of thinking, the game of a despicable bourgeois; according to that of Julieta's son, the game of a grand gentleman; according to Javier's, the game of a crazy Galician; according to Quitina's, the game of an adorable, omnipotent being; according to mine . . . , assuming I have a style of thinking, the game of a great will, of a splendid sensorial machine, capable of extracting pleasure from things. And his things, his most prized object was the one demanding a silver frame. And it happened that I was precisely the person who had broken that precious object. It was me? Yes, it probably was me, but, at the same time, who knows if I was not also the person who made it accessible? Now it's his, perhaps he now owns it for the first time, as he goes into his empty house, filling it with his soul. There in the drawing room will be the portrait, and in the garden, the palm trees, the gardenias, and the hummingbirds—the whole house will be filled with her and, for the first time, she will be filled with something—with what he gives her.

I heard Herminia coming in from the street and walked downstairs; I needed to talk with someone about that letter. We went into her room because she felt very tired and wanted to stretch out for a while. Leaning my back against the dresser, I read her the letter. Herminia smiled in a sad way and made no comment. I said: "This might seem childish to you, but I'd feel uncomfortable to go to him now with my problems and draw him away from all that."

"I understand why you'd feel uncomfortable," Herminia said, "but you're not going to draw him away from all *that*. He'll most probably lend you and Quitina a hand or give you some brilliant suggestion for resolving the conflict yourself, but from *that* . . . no, he won't leave there."

Herminia sat up on the edge of the bed, put on her slippers, and came over to where I was standing. She leaned an elbow on the dresser and, a bit preoccupied, continued to talk. At the same time, still wearing her sad smile, she opened a drawer halfway. It was full of gloves, scarves, and handkerchiefs, which she separated a little, uncovering something concealed underneath; it was Damián's revolver.

"Why do you have that?" I asked a bit uneasily.

"So I can see it from time to time."

"I assume at least it's unloaded."

"No, it's loaded."

The only thing that occurred to me was to seize it, but Herminia put her hand in the way: "Leave it," she said, "it's been there for some time and it's going to stay there."

She closed the drawer and leaned her back against the dresser.

"Don't you see, I'm not at risk?" She went on, "that's why I have it there, to look at it continually and realize *not me*. I don't know how to explain this to you. It represents something I never wanted to peek at, or to approach. You understand?"

I didn't say anything, but she saw that I understood.

"Damián was in *that*, he lived in *that*, and I remained very calm in my certainty. Well, by that I mean his skepticism, which of course I regretted, but I'd be saying, to myself: if he's determined not to come out of it, what can I do? I never looked to see what it was like where he was, I never thought it might have been hard to come out of it. And above all, what most obsesses me now is suspecting that he might have found my security irritating, provocative. Just imagine! It's an impossible move to carry out; I spend my life trying to see myself from his point of view, attempting to judge myself with his criteria. But of course without entering that. Do you think it's possible?"

"I don't know," I said, "but it's dangerous. More dangerous than having the revolver loaded."

"If you could see . . . I'm embarrassed by the lack of danger it poses for me. My security, my strength, I don't know if they warrant punishment."

"Don't go fabricating an exaggerated idea of your strength," I said, "I once saw it flag."

"Ah, yes, of course, that's the punishment. Look, right now what I'm seeing is something very difficult to say. This is the punishment, the proof that human strength is not total, but it is colossal. You understand? The punishment is to let you see a point at which your strength would fail, but a point so appallingly distant that it gives you an idea of how enormous your strength is."

Herminia made a movement with her head, as if to indicate the drawer behind her, and said: "I assure you, having that in there, while I can't tell you I find it a consolation, helps me think about the need to confine myself to my own time. Of course my time has passed almost entirely, and now I see that I did not live it well, I was determined to live Miguel's time, and it seems this can't be, it's not permitted. At least," she added, as if she were stuttering, "maybe it's not permitted to me, especially, and that's why, because you can't skip a chapter of the book. I lived my time poorly, I have no right to a sequel."

"What foolishness," I interrupted her, "someday I'll tell you what I've been thinking about that recently. In short, though, I don't think there's anyone who has more right to a sequel than you do."

"You're mistaken, you're mistaken. I should thank you, but I'd rather you had a better understanding of what I wanted to tell you."

Herminia was pensive for a moment, and then she said suddenly: "Let's see. Why do you think I married Damián?"

"Oh, I don't know. Sometimes I've wondered, and I've never come to any conclusion."

"Well, even though it might surprise you, I married Damián only and exclusively because he was what you people in Buenos Aires call 'un muy buen mozo.' Twenty-some years ago, Damián was very handsome; you can't imagine how dashing he was. Well, that's why I married him, for *nothing more* than that."

"The truth is, it hadn't occurred to me," I said, "but now that I hear you say it I'm not surprised."

"Yes, I know it might not surprise you, but notice that I've stressed 'for nothing more than that.' This means that when we got married I was already aware of all the differences there would be between us. From the beginning, from the first time I met him, I would say to myself when he spouted his freethinking ironies or expounded his ideals: 'I could kill him for that,' but nevertheless . . . No, it's not just what you think."

"How do you know what I think?" I said, laughing, because I saw that she did know.

"Because nowadays you people are used to putting the importance of sex before everything else. I won't deny that importance, but there's also something else very different that I don't know how to explain to you. Look, it's something like the business of *seeing and believing*."

"For example," she went on, "when I was a young girl, I was nothing sensational, but I was very successful with my professors, and they all courted me. I would always say to myself: 'How crazy! Why would I let myself get carried away by this man? He knows a lot, I admire him, you could even say I adore him, but . . .' As soon as Damián appeared, my thinking was exactly the opposite: 'He's abominable, he's a foggy heretic, he's an army club Voltaire . . .' Absolutely, but I didn't hesitate for a moment."

My only response was some gesture of assent, because I seemed to see it all with absolute clarity, but Herminia was not content with her explanation, and she kept insisting.

"I haven't succeeded in giving you a clear idea of what I find most important. There's a disastrous pride in all of this. My attitude was that of a person who says, 'What you say makes little difference to me; I know more about you than you do yourself.' And it was true, I did know. All of Damián's qualities, and there were a lot of them, were evident to me, they held no secrets, but I never took the trouble to make him understand them. Look," she concluded, "all this is so serious because it's a national malady. There's something of this in everything that's happening to us Spaniards: first a sane, sure instinct that makes us go straight to the heart of things; then our satisfaction with security turns to pride; then our pride spoils and turns into a conceit that won't stoop to prove anything, and this leaves the road open to the final corruption—laziness. Do you think this can go on?"

"I don't know, I don't know what to tell you," I answered, greatly perplexed and overwhelmed by the statement I'd come out with several days before: "Tomás García cannot endure." Then I told Herminia that when the Garcías went to meet Damián, García had said to me in an aside: "He's a total gentleman, *you can tell just by looking at him.*"

"A Spaniard, what was he going to say?" Herminia said, "but his mind's already made up: see, believe, and that's it."

"What is a Spaniard?" I asked, in a perfectly idiotic manner.

Finding my question infectious or disorienting, she answered: "God! What could I say?"

"Nothing, don't say a thing. Some questions you answer ten years later or maybe ten years before. In fact, I formulated the response to this question some time ago, the day I arrived as you were telling that story to Quitina and the boys. 'Tradition has something to do with what a person says: I don't know what it is, but I know it's true.' And I was alluding to that a moment ago: what is it that makes you both—a young woman from a noble family who's spent time at Oxford, and Tomás García, a simple villager who barely knows the four rules of arithmetic—say about things: 'You can tell just by looking at it.'"

"I don't believe it's in the big things," Herminia said, "where you'll find the bond you're looking for. We have the same religion as other Latin peoples and, well, the bases of society were laid for all of Europe at the same time. It has to do with an inner thread. Language, maybe, a few harsh consonants, a few interjections, a series of secrets you understand only after appropriating."

"Exactly," I said. "On that day I also thought about the secrets contained in the smell of garlic soup."

"Yes, you have to look into the most basic things."

Suddenly I was struck by an idea and I said, almost interrupting her: "Speaking of basic things, I'm going to devote myself to rereading Nietzsche, thoroughly."

And then Herminia interrupted me outright: "Wait a minute, my friend. You came down to read me the letter from your father-in-law, which is quite important; from there we've soared to the most ungraspable topics," and now you hand me the news that you're about to plunge yourself into the hotbed of Nietzsche. Who's going to solve the problem of the estancia, will you tell me that?"

"Me. Well, me, although even if I applied all my five senses to that problem, even if I shut myself up in a dark room to meditate on it, I'd solve it no better and no worse than my gift for solving it allow."

"Which is patently obvious."

"Not that bad."

Just then Miguel appeared; he'd probably heard his mother's previous statement from the hall.

"Always such lofty topics," he muttered, the way a person does without saying anything.

"We'd just landed," I told him; "in fact we were beginning to think about covering some ground, because if I don't show some signs of activity in that regard, they'll pull my own ground out from under me, all of it."

"But what are you worried about? Consider the lilies of the field."

Herminia slipped out the door. First she looked at each of us for an instant, fixedly, with those eyes that don't question but scrutinize, suggesting she can't hope for an answer and, immediately, she disappeared, quick as a lizard.

Miguel sat down on the edge of the bed. I continued to lean on the dresser and saw him rest his hands behind him on the mattress, moving his feet in a way that reminded me of the moment when Herminia was looking for her slippers so she could get up; but Miguel was moving his feet so he'd feel more comfortable and be able to give full rein to his imagination, establishing himself there, as if to supplant the owner and occupant of that spot.

"Doesn't that little sentence get on your nerves?" he asked.

"Well, I hadn't thought about it. To tell the truth, though, I'm not wild about it."

"To me, it smells of something so false, so fake it seems like a literary embellishment in bad taste."

"Good heavens! I didn't think you had literary tastes."

"I don't have tastes, but I do find certain things distasteful. Things that don't stand up logically seem bad to me. And you're not going to make me believe they seem good to you."

"No, no."

"Analyze the subject a little. Can you say that the lilies of the field are clothed? No, they're naked, that's what they are. You can't say that about even the brightest, most colorful bird because, if you skin the bird, it won't survive."

"Yes, that's true."

"You can't peel a lily. But what you can deduce from this is that a gown as pretty as a lily's, or as King Solomon's robes, is something really valuable. Tell this to an ordinary citizen and you encourage him to live as carefree as a lily, cherishing the vague hope of becoming as handsome as King Solomon. What do you think?"

"Indisputable," and I added: "We've already commented other times that the letter itself must die. There's a certain language that's become impossible for us today."

"So until another language is found . . . Of course, another language that says the same thing."

"Yes, you have to be careful about inventing new interpretations that might be heretical. It's merely a question of excluding certain terms, certain images."

"Look," he said by way of a conclusion, "I think that's everything. Exclude, exclude until you're down to nothing that's not indispensable. Decide to believe in one single thing, which must be so unitary, so unique you couldn't possibly place anything near it. And you mustn't say a word about it until something happens."

"But there's a different danger in that. It can lead to vague remarks about the business of the supreme being or something similar."

"No, no vague remarks, I'm talking about reducing yourself to the core. Specifically, deciding to believe in the Incarnate Word, and that's it."

"Well that's no small thing, but such abstention, just like that and nothing more . . . Of course you say, 'until something happens.' And what is it that might happen?"

"Oh, I don't know. Either the Last Judgment, or maybe a truce, a new form of Revelation, which would be, I imagine, something like 'give us a chance,' as the Americans say. You understand? I told you once, the Crucifixion would now reach all men; in the same way, the revelation I imagine would also mean a modification of humanity. A revelation that would redeem man by transposing him to another scale. Well, in short, Superman."

"Help!" I stood there so astonished I couldn't even burst out laughing. Although basically that mishmash filled with naïveté struck me as something really funny.

"I don't know what you find so alarming," Miguel said. "Haven't you said yourself, the imitation of Christ seems meaningless to you? Well, if instead of imitation we imagine a kind of assimilation or absorption, something that goes to the root of human nature, what resulted would be Superman."

"All right, wait until I recover from the shock. If we take things little by little we might be able to move forward without getting dizzy. According to Nietzsche . . ."

"What Nietzsche, what Nietzsche, or any of that rubbish! Do you think I've read Nietzsche?" he said, as if such an assumption were the most offensive thing he could think of.

"Who said anything about Nietzsche?"

"Well, not me, unless you did."

"Absolutely not; Nietzsche's yesterday's junk and doesn't interest me one bit."

"Come now, continue, don't get discouraged."

"No, don't worry. But I don't see any reason to mention Nietzsche just because he talks about Superman."

"So what superman are you talking about then?"

"Well, Superman. Haven't you ever heard of him? Haven't you seen him in kid's magazines or the movies?"

"Oh, that's what you're talking about?"

"Of course. What else? That's Superman, not the other one."

"I'm not going to defend the other one to you but, if you haven't read about him, how do you know he's worse?"

"Everyone knows what he's like, he's already gotten a lot of attention," he said, thinking a while before he spoke. "Some other time we'll talk about what that superman would be if the chance I referred to earlier meant that's where we ended up, which could also happen."

"Why not talk about it now?"

"Because what I want to tell you is what the other one would be, the real one. In the first place, he would never be like Nietzsche's—some really weird guy filled with hermetic ideas."

"Ah, so you haven't read Nietzsche?"

"No, I'm telling you I haven't. But who isn't fed up with hearing people gush over Zarathustra?"

"Are you sure what you say about gushing isn't something you read somewhere?"

He shrugged his shoulders and shook his head, more evasive than negative: "Anything mawkish makes me sick," he said.

"Me too!"

"Well then, the other one, the real one, must be the opposite of an exaggeration, he must be a synthetic concentration. Take the Ten Commandments as your base and start looking for harmonics, stretching to the limit, creating contrasts until you're bordering on paradox . . ."

"That, in any case, would turn out to be a superculture or a super-moral."

"No, you didn't let me finish. The most important thing is one you've surely noticed in movies and comic strips, because it's been conceived perfectly now: Superman must be an instrument for detecting evil and human suffering. You understand? That's the modification that has to occur in human nature."

His naïveté was starting to make me feel dazzled, but I suppressed any irony, for fear of clipping his wings, and urged him to continue, so I could see what he was getting at.

"Fine," I said, "that would be worth the effort, but how are you going to graft this detector onto him? What kind of antenna are you going to give him?"

He went right on.

"That's not clear yet," he said, totally serious, "they still don't know what it might consist of. At the same time, it's entirely possible to imagine how a being endowed with such a detector would react. Let me think. The first effect would be his complete lack of all conflicts, all doubts. Haven't you seen the way they make him look so aerodynamic? Well, then that means he'd be like a missile propelled by will."

My expression must have altered because Miguel stopped, seemed discouraged, and said: "What, you find it stupid?"

"Exactly the opposite, exactly the opposite," I insisted immediately. "It scares me that this time we agree more deeply than when you linked Bach with the bombardiers."

"Thank goodness. What do you think about this?"

"That's a long story. I'll tell you some other time for sure, but to give you at least a sense of how important it is to me, I'll tell you that this idea is the crux of my life. Everything I've done, whether good or evil, and I've done a lot, I've done taking this idea as my starting point."

"Wow! I don't see how you've been able to do anything evil starting from something like that."

"Because I'm not an angel like you."

"Go to hell."

"No, that's not a compliment; have you forgotten your thesis?"

"Oh, you're referring to the business about rebellion? But there's not the least sign of rebellion in what I just told you."

"No, there's not. But you won't deny in your Superman there's a certain angelic aspiration."

"That's why he's the other's opposite. Because, let's see: what are people trying to do with the other one? Induce man to surpass himself as if he were magnetized by irrational forces. Isn't that the case, more or less? Well, the real Superman must be exactly the opposite. He must be able to assume his spirit infallibly, like what I've told you about, like a detector. Register good, justice, in short, all those things. Everything that seems to remain outside man, that is barely within his reach, must be as natural to him as his gastric juices."

"Fine, and evil, what do you do with it?"

"Well, evil, we already know you can't abolish it, but at least you get it cornered."

"With a well-aimed blow to the jaw, the way Superman does in the movies, right?"

"With whatever it might be . . ." He was rather quiet, as if indecisive, and I thought he'd reached a dead end, but after a few seconds he said:

"The first thing you have to do in order to corner evil, before delivering it the punch, is see its face. Understand? Know clearly which evil it is that you want to attack."

"Yes, that's exactly right."

"Well, you're not going to start by saying: this is evil, and so is this, and this, this is more or less evil. It's preferable to aspire to good, to try and identify with the Good. Because until now, in the Christian sense, trying to identify with the Good has simply meant sacrifice. But do you believe there can't be another solution?"

I allowed some space for the anguish of both his question and my impossible answer and said, finally: "We're bordering on rebellion."

He interrupted me: "No. No rebellion at all. One feels rebelliousness. Why worry about your teeth aching when they don't ache?"

"You're right, I'm not aching from rebelliousness either, and I aspire to the same thing you do. I see now that they're the same, although mine may not be formulated as well. I don't know if insanity could be contagious."

"But why insanity? A utopia is not an insanity."

"No; it's a greasy pole higher than anyone's strong enough to shinny up."

"As long as it's *high*. As long as whoever's climbing isn't sliding down instead of mounting. Look, you can't dispense with those terms—*surmount*, *surpass*. Superman might be a utopia, if you like, but what a person needs is to know is what's on the top of the greased pole, to know that it's very clear from up there because it *is* very high, even if no one reaches it, or perhaps just a few."

"And those few will form an aristocracy."

"Which is nothing new, sacrifice is also for just a few. Besides, that term, 'aristocracy,' is so worn out . . . I'd rather use others that are more current. I prefer 'nobility,' 'virtue'—they're tougher."

"*Areté*. What do you do with those humanities of yours that you never bring up under any circumstance?"

"They were left behind in that smock we had to wear at school."

"Fewer of them than you think. It doesn't seem to me you wasted your time there. Now you'll be able to devote yourself to your worship of the machine, but deep down you have other things you'll never be able to expel."

"I had to swallow them whole or not pass. And I was fed up with all that stuff."

This was another sign of detachment that surprised me in Miguel, and I said to him: "Your memories of high school are that bad? There's no trace of something pleasant, something that's become part of your personal life."

"Well . . . no."

"That's strange! It seems impossible to me that out of so many people—priests, professors, students—not one would be worth remembering."

"Worth remembering . . . yes, there were some nice kids; from time to time I'd get together with them somewhere. And the priests, well, you know what priests are like."

"What are they like? They come in all kinds."

"Don't believe that; they're all pretty much the same."

He thought for a few seconds and added: "In high school there was one who had something. They said he was a sage, but he was very funny. Not that he was one of those guys who tell jokes. No, on the contrary, he was very serious, and he didn't have much contact with us because he was the librarian. He only came down for a while in the mornings to play ball and sometimes, when something happened among the boys, who used to be mean to each other or get into fights, and if it wasn't too awful, in other words, it wasn't necessary to go to the Father Superior automatically, Father Ugarte would always appear and there, by talking, as if they were having a general conversation, he would analyze the situation, making it as clear as a theorem, until he saw that the boys had been thoroughly convicted of their offense. Then he would start to reprimand them in a way that made me die laughing. And, you know, precisely then I realized he was an unusual priest."

Miguel thought for a while, but he was not sure that he'd suggested very well what had been so special about the priest's personality.

"Too bad I don't know how to imitate people, because you can't get an idea just from my telling about him. He would always say: 'Well, I'm telling you now, so you don't say you weren't warned.' 'Who knows what you might meet up with somewhere . . . suddenly . . . someday' 'Perhaps . . .' And he would say all those things in such an ambiguous way it was exactly what gave you a tremendous sense of security. Because he was a rough, huge man, a jai alai player, and he would say those short sentences gently, in a tone very different from what he'd just used to explain his reasoning. It was as if he said: besides what I've told you, there is still something very subtle and delicate, something it's almost impossible to talk about but something that might drop on your heads at any moment."

"Yes," I said, "I can imagine that mix of roughness and intelligence. A guy like that usually makes a good teacher. It's too bad you boys didn't visit him more often."

Miguel said: "That way, coming out with just a few words from time to time, it's possible to have an influence. Although, of course, you can only be influenced by things you have an affinity with. Something else I liked about him a lot was when he played jai alai he'd be as energetic as a bull, to the point where he'd be sweating buckets, and when it was over he'd wipe his forehead with his handkerchief and say to the players around him: 'I have to sweat, I have to sweat to get rid of all the books I put in my head.' As if books were something unpleasant or harmful."

"Well, in that respect you've really turned out to be his disciple."

"No, because he spent his whole life reading, there was always a light in his window until very late."

"And what is man but an incarnation of dissonance?" someone said.
"Who?"

"Nietzsche, I think."

"Oh; well, it's pretty good."

"That's the bad thing about Nietzsche, who said a great many things that are very good."

"And others very bad?"

"No, those things he never said; he was too intelligent and too pure.

Nietzsche was not inclined toward evil, but there was a dissonant shrillness in him that clashed with the Promethean spirit of his time."

"I don't like Prometheus at all, he's horrible."

"Why?"

"I don't know, I don't like him."

"Then who are your heroes?"

"I don't have a favorite hero, but the truth is I do like heroes. I like someone who gets right to work and starts doing something for other people."

"Then your hero is Don Quixote."

"Nonsense! I could never understand him. Go on, you're not going to tell me Don Quixote is a hero who can stand on his own two feet?"

"Depending on what plane you place him. On the plane of efficiency, no, of course he can't, but he can on the plane of intention."

"And what can we do with intention, will you tell me that? We can die of laughter, right? As for me, I assure you, I don't find it the least bit funny."

"Funny things aren't what's most important in the *Quixote*."

"I don't know if they're important, but they've enjoyed a great deal of importance," he declared with such certainty I realized he was entering on well-worn ground. Immediately he added: "Funny things are Don Quixote's sin, and look at the sinners he's engendered."

"Another quote! What haven't you read, my boy!"

"I don't have to read a damned thing. Movies have us fed up with funny, beat-up heroes."

"Well, the person who incarnated the Quixotic spirit was Chaplin."

"Exactly. And you see what a plague, what an old bore."

"Aha! You don't like Charlie either?"

"I think he's more disgusting than a fetus."

"More or less, he was the embryo of the movies you adore."

"I adore them because now they've hatched out of their shell. If we were to keep on with those mutterings, with that sentimentality, with those touching, funny incidents . . . My hero is exactly the opposite. For me, Superman is simply the knight without the knight's contingencies.

You understand? A hero who has more power than his contingencies—the power not to become corrupted."

I agreed effusively, but a vague memory made me concentrate for a minute. So he wouldn't think that I'd stopped listening to him, I said: "I'm trying to recollect something I read when I was a boy. Well, it's impossible to give you an idea, because I recollect the phrase, and I also remember the impression it made on me. I don't know, I don't think the disproportion will be incomprehensible."

"Why not? It's all a question of extending the angle."

"Yes, that's it."

Aware he would comprehend whatever it was, I continued.

"Well, something to do with the Cid, I don't know if it was a story or a historical account for children, but the thing is, later, over the years, I've read the best work written about the Cid and none of it has given me a more perfect feeling of how great he was. In that sentence, I assure you I grasped the pure idea of omnipotence."

Miguel was waiting expectantly for the answer. I said: "And the fact is, the sentence was no more than this: 'Nothing bothered him.'"

"That's wonderful," Miguel said, and then he remained silent, gazing into space, extending the angle.

From the hallway, Herminia shouted: "Food's on the table! Because I assume you'll stay for lunch . . ."

"Why, yes, I'd love to."

Herminia shouted as if she were a kilometer away from us, but it was only two and a half meters and that small simulation made me realize that her footsteps had not been audible in the hallway. Clearly, she'd been even closer and wanted to convince us that the distance was much greater, so we wouldn't suspect her of having come to eavesdrop on our conversation. What would she have learned from it? I was soon to find out.

We sat down at the table. Herminia's face and especially her voice, which is what always gives her away, seemed serene to me. We began to eat in silence. In order for her serenity to take hold further, I thought I'd tell her about an encounter I'd had that morning.

"Imagine, today when I got to Plaza Lezica," I said to them, "a moving van planted itself in front of me and prevented me from going anywhere. Usually this kind of thing irritates me, but today it didn't; I let myself stay in *tempo lento*, I forgot I had to go to my office, and I began to contemplate the grove of trees. The trees are thick now, and they provide a delightful shade, and I was walking there, mentally, when I saw a rather conspiratorial-looking gathering of people under the bushiest tree. I recalled having heard someone or other say that the stamp collectors meet there and suddenly I said, Of course! And who do you think I saw there, like a fish in the water? That little guy Strugo. Remember him? I think I once told you about him."

"Yes, yes," they both said.

"He saw me too, because he was looking toward the road, as if he were expecting someone. He waved at me from a distance, but I stopped beside the sidewalk and went over to him immediately. 'So you belong to this clan?'

"'Oh, yes, I've been collecting stamps for years.'

"'I can imagine, you began when you were a boy.'

"'A very young boy.'

"'Then you must have a large collection.'

"'Oh, not exactly a large, large collection. But rather noteworthy, rather noteworthy.'

"'What a shame,' I said. 'If I'd known, I would have given you heaps of stamps. Last month I received packages and letters from the Far East.'

"'How fortunate!' he said, totally devastated.

"'Well, from now on I'll save them for you, if they interest you.'

"'They interest me very much!'

"'Then, come by the house in a couple of weeks, and I'll have some put by for you.'

"'Oh, thank you, thank you very much! Yes, I'll come by, yes, I do believe I will.'

"It's the first time the little raven has accepted an invitation without having to be coaxed. You can't imagine how proud he is and how obsessed with abstinence. Immediately he took refuge in the skirts of the tree, with all the others there, like chicks, and I began to drive up Rivadavia. After a little while I asked myself: where am I going? Could it be there below the Plaza Once or have I left the Plaza behind? Have I kept going straight or have I turned around? Am I in Buenos Aires or in a city I've never seen? It doesn't matter, I'll keep going, and I'll arrive somewhere . . . I drove in the same direction as the other cars, but mentally I remained fixed in Strugo's room, in front of his collection."

Herminia said in amazement: "Oh, you visit him that often?"

"No, wait a minute. That's what's extraordinary. Strugo's room sprang up for me from that sentence, 'Rather noteworthy.' It's undoubtedly very valuable, because he has the intelligence and the persistence to have put together something good, over so many years. He told me that from modesty and also from his habit of not divulging the existence of his treasure. With that discrete adjective he probably tried to hide it, but for me it produced the opposite effect. Around that sentence the whole decor sprang up.

"I've never seen Strugo's room, Herminia, I assure you, and he's never given me the least description of it, so for quite a while I was seeing two possible rooms, without deciding to choose either one of them. Well, it wasn't a question of choosing. In order to select one or the other, I would have needed to base my choice on some specific fact, and I had nothing in the way of facts. Both rooms, with the same veracity and the same strength, imposed themselves on me. One was a dark place in an old house, possibly windowless, lost in a corridor, with some bowlegged pieces of furniture, moth-eaten blankets, and drapes dense with dust and soot. The other was a small ground-level room, with a window on the street, in one of those little houses in some outlying neighborhood; white, totally stripped, with an innerspring mattress made into a divan and beside it a fruit crate with a lamp on it. In those two rooms I saw Strugo with his treasure. Not like the miser who amasses real gold or the dreamer who collects something he thinks is gold but is not. No, he knew very well what he had: something that *has come* to be worth a lot. Sometimes I saw him in the dark room, leafing through it all beneath a dim lamp; sometimes he was in the stripped room, protecting himself with the window shutter so he would not be seen from the street, because, undoubtedly it was worth a lot. Of course to me it's worth nothing; I wouldn't be capable of running my eyes over it for more than two minutes."

"But there are people who would give thousands of pesos for something like that," Herminia said.

"Yes, I know. There are people captivated by that abstraction, devoid of any intrinsic value, that carefully arranged nothing. They feel as though they're the owners of something, without the embarrassment that material possessions *should* cause."

Miguel said: "There's a good topic: saintly poverty."

Herminia got up and began to clear the table. I prepared to help her, but she wouldn't let me.

"I'm only clearing away a few things," she said; "my girl comes tomorrow, and she'll take care of everything."

I followed her to the kitchen, though, and Miguel walked behind me with a basket of fruit. He kept muttering: "Saintly poverty . . ."

"Poverty is not saintly, but saintliness is poor," Herminia said, without any harshness.

"Yes, that's true," Miguel answered, "that's how it usually is, I don't know why."

"Well, because it takes a long time to be a saint."

Not allowing herself to be interrupted and as if she were preventing the topic from becoming too serious, Herminia spoke directly to me: "And to be *non sancto* as well."

We could feel that lunch had ended in perfect peace.

The answer came quickly—a more than sufficient bank draft and a cable that promised a long letter.

Since the monster gave no signs of life, I had Gálvez phone him, and he said he'd had so much to do . . . He left it that he'd come out one day soon, and he did. Because I myself had so much to do, I could spend only about fifteen minutes with him. During those minutes I realized he'd put off appearing at Las Murtas in order to find out if we were really planting. And when he saw that the work was in full swing, he was left feeling rather perplexed. The division was effected without incident.

Quitina said several times: "It's great, we were really lucky to be able to plant this month."

But the sight of it wasn't the least bit pleasing to her.

One day when I'd needed to go in to the city, I got home and saw that everything was in a mess. I looked for Quitina and found her emptying closets and drawers.

She said she'd given the apartment a lot of thought and it seemed like a very good idea to her. In order to put the thought into practice, we had to go there for a while, repay a few invitations, see a few people. Consequently, she set about striking camp at Las Murtas that very day. She took care only of the most important things herself and left the rest to the servants.

The next morning, just as we were leaving, Miss Ray appeared with the children; on her arm was the raffia purse where she usually kept her needlework, but this time there was something moving inside.

"But Miss Ray!" Quitina said.

And Miss Ray, with a categorical tone and a victimized expression, insisted: "Against my will, absolutely against my will."

"You don't have to do anything against your will, Miss Ray," Quitina said.

"Oh, it's already done," she said and got into the car with the boys, who smothered her with kisses.

There are times when you can do something unreasonable in full view of everyone, and it never occurs to anyone to ask why you're doing it. That day when we started out, I drove the car through the agapanthus plants as slowly as you peel off a decal. The garden passed alongside us, plant by plant, tree by tree, and then, on the road toward the gate, it was impossible to go faster. I didn't come to a complete standstill, because that would have meant confining myself to a single spot, and so advancing at a snail's pace, I had the sensation of standing still the entire trip—needless to say, at each and every moment of the trip.

And Quitina was beside me. Quitina as the immense silence we were carrying away from Las Murtas. Although, maybe I was the one being carried away by that silence. To disturb it was impossible, the silence had to be maintained because within it was everything that had been said.

Once on the highway, I ventured a few trivial sentences, which Quitina answered in the same tone. Then, as if to summarize everything she had thought, she began to explain to me that while I was busy with the planting—she never liked to be there during the heaviest part of the work—she would look into subletting the apartment. She intended only to try with people from the diplomatic corps, and that way we'd be sure they wouldn't want to stay a long time.

I approved her plan, assuring her it seemed very good to me and, nevertheless, at that moment I felt so terrible! Since I didn't know why, I said nothing. What I felt was precisely what you feel when things turn out very different from the way you'd imagined.

12

This had to happen: the recollections, the long commentaries on events that had begun to sediment came to an end. Now I either return to silence, throw these notebooks into the fire, or start putting in dates and have the notebooks turn into a diary.

I hate diaries. I don't know how some people manage to keep them successfully. To start commenting on something that's weighing on you, to speak with the person who has his hand over our mouths, who has us by the throat! But today I can't help it. Come this hour of night, the perfect hour of vigil for me, and it's impossible to follow the thread of the things I'd been relating. Something happened today—it may be nothing—and it's all I can think about. Does it interest me vitally? No, no, no—a hundred times no! All the same, I can't think about anything else.

The incident took place at the end of the evening, just a little over three hours ago. We'd had a hectic day, because Quitina managed to sublet the apartment, on excellent terms, and tomorrow we'll go back to Las Murtas, we're not sure for how long. Francisco and Jorge wanted to go to the movies, and since it was our last day in Buenos Aires, they wanted this passionately, and we had to take them. Fernando had a bit of a cold and Miss Ray stayed home with him. Quitina and I went to the Opera movie house with the two boys. Before the lights went down, they spotted Nix in another section. There were shouts and promises to meet after the show. And we did meet, but separation was imminent because I'd been forced to park on Diagonal. The crowd was indescribable, the traffic jam hopeless. Drake proposed driving us home in his car, which by some miracle was at the door of the theater, suggesting that later I come back alone for my car.

This all occurred on a noisy, suffocating Sunday afternoon. And because it happened, the other thing happened afterward.

When we got to our building, the boys' good-byes to Nix were interminable. I already had one foot on the ground when I saw a figure emerging from the doorway, trying to pass unnoticed, slipping away, walking close to the wall. I stopped him: "Hey! Strugo, where are you going?"

"Oh, how are you? Good evening," he answered hurriedly. "I'll come back another day."

"No, wait a little. Why do you have to run off?"

"It doesn't matter, I don't want to bother you."

"It's no bother at all," I told him somewhat sharply. "Wait five minutes."

I tossed a few good-byes into the car and said to Strugo: "Come, I want to introduce you to Quitina."

Quitina had also gotten out onto the sidewalk and was trying very hard to bring the farewell to a close. Strugo greeted her with his brief shyness, at the same time casting a glance over his shoulder at the occupants of the car. His face became transfigured, and not only his face, his whole being: I had the impression he was growing taller by several inches.

"Oh, *gnedige frau!*" He rushed over to greet Elfriede. She greeted him warmly too, and Drake was his good-natured self. Strugo granted him an imperceptible greeting. With Elfriede, he exchanged a few sentences in German, of which I could understand only that he was inquiring with great interest about her health. Elfriede assured him she was absolutely fine, and he squeezed her hand for the last time.

"That makes me very, very happy!" he said.

The Drakes pulled away, and I pushed Strugo toward the elevator, but he was unwilling to go up.

"But I can come back another day. I'm in no hurry. It's just that I was walking by here and it occurred to me . . ."

"Well, and now that you're here, why not come up?"

"But . . . I was just leaving. It's not a very convenient time for you."

"Who told you it's not very convenient?" He gave an ambiguous little laugh. "Besides," I said, "if you don't take advantage of this chance, tomorrow we're going to Las Murtas."

"Oh! In that case . . ."

Once in the elevator he decided to come in, shaking his head.

As soon as we were in the library, I started to talk to him about the stamps to put him at ease. He picked up on the topic right away, trying to show me how much he knew, and I listened without expressing so much as an opinion, because I'm as uninformed about the subject as I am uninterested in it, and I could just barely get by. Meanwhile, I was wandering, lost in mentally reconstructing the scene I'd just witnessed.

Of course the first question was: how and from where did Elfriede know Strugo? But there was something I found even more intriguing: what strange relationship exists between them? That's where my mind got lost, in reliving the small details that made me suspect there was a strange relationship between them. In the first place, I was analyzing the impression I'd gotten immediately that some deception was involved and that Strugo was the one deceived.

Quitina had gone in with the boys, to turn them over to Miss Ray, in the hope that she'd be able to bring their excitement down a notch. I said to Strugo: "I suppose it would be useless to suggest that you have something to drink."

He answered: "Thank you: of course."

And he stressed his refusal with a shrug of his shoulders that, without being impertinent, was meant to show how unnecessary the suggestion was. I added: "I'm sure not even a nice glass of water would tempt you."

He'd tried to listen to me with complete seriousness, but he couldn't help bursting into laughter, like someone who gives in, moving his head with a gesture as if to say: With you it's impossible!

"Then, have a seat here and take a look at all this to see if any of it's worth anything," I said, taking out a box with the pile of stamps I'd saved for him.

"Well, I should think so! There are some very interesting things," he said, and he immersed himself in an examination of the stamps, making comments about each one and giving me explanations to which I appeared to pay attention, although I continued to reconstruct the previous scene.

Strugo had grown when he saw Elfriede. He rushed over to greet her with his heart in his hand—that much was unquestionable. It was so evident I immediately thought: in that greeting there is no mystery. That is, what I know is that the mystery is his: at this moment he's shown himself naked. I've seen him naked before her; but for me he's continued to be mysterious. However, Elfriede, simple Elfriede, so candid, so open, what did she do when she saw Strugo? A flash of annoyance passed through her, that was the first thing, but it wasn't a flash of antipathy, quite the contrary. It was only as if she saw she was forced to transpose herself quickly to another key. I noticed this in the way she ran her hand over all her clothing, in a series of automatic movements. Pushing a lock of hair beneath her hat, she tightened her jacket a bit, and shook the lapels as if to remove any specks of dust that might have landed on them from the air. In a word, she recomposed herself, as if to present an impeccable appearance, and she greeted him immediately with gentle—one could say emotional—cordiality. After reviewing all these details, I repeated to myself: What's clear is that shrewd Strugo, the sharp, devious Oriental, at that moment gaze before the limpid, candid Elfriede was like a bird beneath the serpent's gaze. Why? In what sort of net might she have him caught?

Strugo, in the meantime, had expounded all his philatelic erudition without receiving any more from me than frequent gestures of agreement. I saw that he was about to make a final point and, determined to detain him in any way possible, I searched through the few books that were going to stay in the apartment, thinking of one filled with photographs of Viennese streets, and I handed it to him.

"Look at these marvelous photographs, surely you like photography."

"Oh, yes, you're right, I do."

"Besides, you'll find many things you know here, won't you?"

"All of them, all of them," he said, leafing through the book and making comments about the technical perfection of some of the photographs and about the memories evoked for him by others.

I felt myself bursting with questions and chose to broach the subject with apparent indifference.

"I never imagined that you would know the Drakes," I said.

"Oh, I've known Mrs. Drake for a long time," he answered, and although he didn't lift his head from the photographs, the noble, naked tone appeared in his voice.

"You know her from Berlin?" I ventured.

"No, I was never in Berlin."

He closed the book and left it on the table. Then, without any ambiguity, as if it were something that, once said, everything would be said, he added: "I met her in Madrid."

No interjection in our entire language would have been capable of expressing my amazement, so all I said was: "Good heavens, I didn't know."

And at that moment, left senseless by surprise, from the hallway I heard steps approaching the door. Lord, please don't let Quitina come in now! Cutting off the conversation, changing the subject was impossible. Lord, don't let her think of eavesdropping! I added some comment, some trivial question, as if to show that I was interested, but not too much, and at the same time I pricked up my ears. Not that Quitina's in the habit of eavesdropping, but she might have decided to see how our conversation was going. It was dinnertime by then; maybe she wanted to know if we were saying goodbye or if the conversation was going to continue. Strugo started to tell me something about a health mission that had gone to Spain from the United States, and he spoke of Elfriede, of her dedication, of her courage.

"I don't doubt it," I said, with an admiring, respectful tone, "she's a wonderful person."

"She's a wonderful, wonderful woman!" he said emphatically.

The footsteps approached the door again. Dear God, make her walk right by! She walked by.

Strugo said: "Unfortunately, her health suffered greatly. Yes, it was too much, it was too much. The doctors spoke of a vitamin deficiency, from the poor diet, but I don't believe that. It's because she was putting too much into it."

"I understand, I understand," I managed to say.

"Just as well that, since those Americans can do everything . . . They can do everything!"

And here his exclamation was quite sarcastic, made in a soft little voice.

"Her husband came by plane and carried her away, wrapped in attention. Just as well, just as well!" and there was a diabolic little laugh tossed toward Tom Drake.

I said, in order to keep answering normally: "I'm surprised they haven't told me. Although," I added, "we've never talked a great deal. In reality, my relationship with Drake . . ."

"Oh, naturally, I would assume." He cut me off, making it clear that from the beginning he'd taken it for granted that I could only have known her through my relationship with her husband. His statement was sincere, and I saw he knew nothing of my old relationship with Elfriede. This reassured me. Even so, I was left feeling uneasy; everything he'd told me was true, there was not the least dissimulation in his words, but beneath them the lie was still quite apparent.

There was a long silence. It surprised me that in my presence Strugo would abandon himself to his own thoughts like that, and I was grateful to him, because it was an act of confidence. I saw him grow lost in memories, delve into a past more alive for him than his current person, which he'd abandoned in that armchair. The intense light of the lamp I'd placed close to him so he could study the stamps, along with the library as background, provided the appropriate milieu for his intellectual head. His coarse, almost peasant-like suit adapted poorly to the soft chair, his buttoned-up jacket was wrinkling, you could see that his pockets were bulging with parcels. His quietude, the withdrawal indicated by his crossed hands, and the inclination of his forehead all exuded an aura of saintliness. Only his eyelids quivered, from time to time, as if he were seeing visions so violent they almost caused slight winks emphasized by imperceptible sarcastic smiles—satanic smiles, to be more precise.

For a while, all that complexity lay abandoned before me and I pretended to fall into abandon as well, but I watched him intensely, almost holding my breath so as not to wake him. His reverie didn't last long. Suddenly he raised his eyebrows and took a quick breath as if he were about to speak, but he checked himself; rather, he flagged, as if it seemed useless to give in to a desire to communicate something I would understand only slightly. I was not resigned to letting him keep it to himself.

"What were you going to say?" I asked him.

"Oh, nothing, nothing in particular, nothing important."

"Even if it's not important, say it." I continued to press him.

"Chance, chance . . . ," he said, modulating the word the way someone turns a polyhedron around in his hand, and all Satanism disappeared from his smile; it grew pure, childish.

"I took Mrs. Drake to Ciudad Lineal, I introduced her to your uncle. Yes, I did, don't be surprised. How was I to imagine that today, when I came to pick up the stamps, I was going to find in your house, well, at your door, a person who makes me recall all those things so far away? Although to say that they *are* far away is optimism."

He fell silent. I didn't know how to draw him out further; I was disturbed by what I was hearing, and I was afraid that I'd commit some indiscretion if I spoke too much, so I spoke, in order to keep the conversation from breaking off. "I'm more aware than you think of how vitally important all this is to you," I said. But I was afraid the conversation would take a different turn and I added: "Of course, Mrs. Drake has never spoken to me about these things because she surely doesn't think they could interest me in the least, she certainly has no idea that I'm the nephew of the man she met in circumstances so far from my life here."

Then Strugo lifted his head and looked at me, raising his eyebrows and opening his eyes with the innocence of a young child, an infant.

"She doesn't even suspect it," he said. "She doesn't even suspect it. They're different worlds. I myself can hardly understand. It's stupid to try to explain to you, but there one had a reason for living that . . ."

He reacted, a bit ashamed of his elegiac tone and said: "Well, many people still live for that same reason, losing doesn't mean you give up."

"Oh, of course not," I said with complete sincerity, since all my phobias focus on the words "give up." "The strong don't give up," I ended.

Although he'd just begun to speak normally, impelled by a sort of mystic veneration, Strugo said: "Yes, the strong . . . of course, the strong who rely on force, they keep marching, but others . . . others are just fire."

I nodded in deep agreement, and this allowed me to bow my head and gaze at the floor. Then I thought: "Now he's alluded specifically to what I want to know. I'm touching on what I'm after, but I have to break off the interrogation. I can't profane this man's faith. I want to get to the heart of the question, but not in his presence, not through him, not by violating his confidence."

I almost felt a desire to warn him about me, to say, "Get out, get out of here right away, because something unpleasant might happen to you!" And the nicest way I could find to make him leave in a hurry was to say: "Wouldn't you like to stay for supper?"

"Oh, no, certainly not," and he started as if I'd suggested something unseemly. Immediately he added: "Thank you very much just the same," and he stood up.

I didn't detain him. At the door I promised to keep saving stamps for him, and he left feeling very calm. He got into the elevator laden with every bit of his innocence.

A problem in higher mathematics stimulates the mind, which studies the problem so diligently that it finally finds a breakthrough; but an enigma that appears, lacking any logical access and devoid of any explanation, so there is only its enigmatizing, perceived as an ache, an aroma . . . that persists, impenetrable for a long time. What aches is the unknown, which springs up unsought and turns the most ordinary sentence into an enigma because, when it becomes clear, it stuns like a blow.

"Others are just fire." The sentence persisted, fixed in front of me, and I saw clearly everything was condensed in it. What that everything might be I couldn't manage to make out. I recalled Herminia's secret: peer into disbelief briefly without letting yourself be controlled by it. This difficult exercise is definitely the one I can't manage to perform very well. Now I saw clearly that Elfriede, at the period of her life that for me is surrounded in shadows, was all fire . . . but, what fire? Not the one that Strugo had thought he saw. So I, who's seen nothing but shadows, in other words, who's seen nothing, who's totally ignorant about that period of Elfriede's life, I believe I possess more of the truth than he does, even though he was present for all of it. I believe I possess a truth but I don't know what it is. I want to know what it is, but I'm afraid Elfriede won't let me see, because she knows I want to see it coldly. On the other hand, with Strugo she doesn't hold back, because he's approached her with *his* fire. I'd bet anything their fires aren't *identical*. But the two of them can understand each other, can agree, because they're *identical*; they're fire, and I'm not, I stay on the margins.

Juncal Street, 2 September

Last night I wrote until two o'clock, then I went to Las Heras, taking the number 10, which left me on Diagonal, where I picked up the car. At eight o'clock in the morning we left for Las Murtas. Everything fine, nothing worth noting.

Only, Quitina did not return to Las Murtas with the silence of the day when we left. Once again she was quiet throughout the whole trip, but inside her there was no silence; quite the opposite—great upheaval. Two or three times she remarked that she'd forgotten to do something or hadn't it done properly. In fact, though, everything had been arranged and taken care of impeccably. Nevertheless, Quitina was uneasy, as if something needed to be modified, corrected, as if the plan needed to be changed. And now that could not happen; the plan was under way.

The plan was for me to come back in the evening and sleep in the study, so I could give the painters their instructions when they came to the apartment in the morning.

When we were already close to home, Quitina said: "The thing is, Herminia could have taken care of the painters."

"You were the one who forbade that categorically," I said. "She offered to do it, and you said you couldn't agree to burden her with that concern."

"That's true."

Quitina said "That's true," and I was going to say "Why?" but I said nothing. I saw myself breaking the windowpane again. Quitina had said "That's true" in a horrible tone. *True*: what truth did that hold? What irrevocable prediction? I didn't dare go into it and I didn't; I didn't ask anything.

And so the day passed. At seven I was on my way back. Herminia came out on the balcony when she heard me arrive and asked if I would eat with them. I said yes and went up to the study. Soon afterward, though, I felt, as Quitina had, that something in the apartment might not have been arranged properly; maybe there was some paper or other among the books we were leaving there, or in the drawers of my desk.

I went and looked everything over.

As I was checking to see that the windows in the servants' quarters were closed, I poked my head into the ironing room for a minute; the view from there was almost unknown to me, and before I left I wanted to familiarize myself a little with everything that had lived behind my back, thinking something like "this is about to slip from my hands almost entirely."

The sun had already set, but the sky was very clear, and from there you could see the small, low houses of the entire block. There were three or four from the same period as mine—those small houses built in the first decade of the century, with a bit of yard and a certain elegance expressed in stained-glass windows and balustrades. Then, a labyrinth of tenements punctuated by large garage roofs. Impossible to imagine what twisting alleys you'd have to follow to get to the apartment buildings at the heart of the block.

Right in the center, where countless walls leaned against each other like cards, forming fortresses, two houses stood above the others. One had a whitewashed, flat, Moorish-looking roof; on the other there was a balcony running around the second floor, with three rooms opening onto it. At the corner of the balcony, an enormous pelargonium hung from the rusty railing. There were fig trees and trellised vines climbing up and jutting from all the patios. Some of the walls and facades seemed to be totally covered with velvet by a wall-hugging vine.

I stood there, watching how the doves were returning to blackened wood boxes attached to a wall, how a black and white cat walked gently along a ledge, how a woman appeared on the whitewashed roof and carried the canary's cage inside, and I was filled with the kind of ecstasy that comes over me when I contemplate life that is humble, poor, small. But suddenly I had a violent reaction, went inside, and closed up the balcony.

I went downstairs feeling nauseated and very out of sorts. Any dilettantism nauseates me, but—come on!—it would be too hypocritical if I went so far as to find poverty moving! When it's so easy to be poor! Instead of defending myself this way, like a cat on its back, why don't I get rid of everything, find myself a modest job, and live in one of those little houses I find so charming? I wouldn't be the first. Other people, with much more than I have, up and did just that one fine day. Why don't I do it?

Thinking seriously about the possibility of doing it, I got into the elevator. I walked out of the building like a sleepwalker and continued to walk along the same side of the street. In a minute I elaborated a brief plan for the sale of lands, payment of debts, and vague donations to unspecified beings, and I tried to imagine the synopsis of a modest life. Needless to say, I did not end up in the tenement. Even though I felt carried away by a desire for sacrifice, it never occurred to me to deprive Quitina and the boys of basic hygiene. And immediately the vision of a two-room apartment passed before my eyes, with an Indian-looking girl brewing coffee in a flannel filter and in the kitchen something boiling in a huge pot into which women toss what they call greens, and a miserable smell that wafts toward the desk where I'm poring over formulas. For a nature like mine, this would truly represent expiation. It would be a sacrifice that would benefit no one; it would be pure mortification for me, but inevitably it would also fall on the members of my family. As I studied this scene, the question "why don't I do it?" was never even outlined. What took shape instead was the wounding assertion that "this would be true sacrifice." But for the idea of sacrifice to prove efficient, it must exude an inebriating emanation. Blood and fire have their alcohol; mediocrity does not, which is why I was repeating to myself again, "This would be the true sacrifice, the sacrifice I will not make."

But my rational refusal left me yearning for the atmosphere of a few moments before. I could not say that my previous emotion was false, trivial, or hypocritical; no, I knew it well, and my gut feeling was that deep within me there was a genuine path toward that ecstasy of piety, although I didn't know how to gain access to it. I thought that because of my effort to search for it I was beginning to feel once again something like its proximity, like its aura around me. But, in fact, I'd reached the block that runs beside the latrines of the jail. There was total solitude in the street, a warm, spring silence. Outlined against the yellow-colored crenellation, the turquoise blue sky presented a greenish cast. I turned onto Arenales and forgot what I'd planned to do; once more I was sunk in emotion.

Next to the thick walls of the beer factory, several couples were taking a stroll, walking slowly, leaning against each other, as if to give darkness time to descend and time for the straight solitary, naked street, with no doors or windows, sheltered by high, gray walls, to become a shadowy bedroom.

On Arenales, the lights were beginning to come on in some of the bars and stores, but most of the street was dark under the branches of the trees. Nothing disturbed the restfulness of that hour except throngs of children playing noisily, dragging iron objects or fighting, rolling on the sidewalk in the delirious state of sensual violence common among young kids. From the doorway of a building stepped a freshly powdered, freshly groomed girl wearing a tight-fitting dress of thin fabric and, as she passed under the streetlamps or in front of the store windows, she walked as if she were refracting the light, aware that, like the flicker of fireflies, she was sparkling, brilliant, bursting with the call of exultant adolescence.

Standing under a tree, sheltered from the intense illumination coming from a doorway, there were two women. I began to watch them as I got closer and, when I passed next to them, I saw them in great detail. I have no idea why I looked at them so intently, much less why I remember them even more clearly than I saw them. They were two working class women, still young but already matronly, eating ice cream they'd just purchased in the brightly-lit store. Each held an ice-cream cone in her hand. One was speaking very confidentially, resting her free hand on the other's forearm, as if to pressing her interest; the other one was listening and eating her ice-cream cone. She was a rather fat woman with black hair and a pink face, undoubtedly Italian. Her cheeks were round, as fresh as those of a five-year-old girl, and she had a large mouth that was trying to smile as she licked the ice cream. Her tongue moved slowly around the cone in her effort to keep the ice cream from dripping. She was sculpting it delicately, and her entire attention was concentrated on this; all she granted the speaker was a mocking, sidelong gaze.

I would have stopped heaven and earth to contemplate that woman. In fact, I think I did stop them, because it is impossible to see and feel everything I noticed about that being in the actual time you need to walk two or three steps. Besides, I don't know why I saw the other woman as background, as an accompanist. The woman I observed was accompanied by someone, but that someone was like the tree shading them, or like the warmth of the atmosphere, or even like that hour. Of course the hour was something very important, you could say it retained a trace of the Angelus, because in it one inhaled inactivity, respite from work. And the woman was enjoying that moment of conversation, in no hurry at all, holding on her arm the net bag that contained her evening purchases, letting time pass slowly over her cheeks. I noticed that the skin on her cheeks was soft, like a child's, but the important thing is, I also felt how she was feeling the warmth of the air pass over her skin. I saw and felt how she smoothed the sides of the ice cream with her tongue and then settled her lips on it skillfully and tenderly, innocently and freely, because she was alone—although accompanied—, slowly savoring that pleasure, which would spread through her veins. Her entire being was slowly soaking up that sweetness, and who knows if within her body the outline of another being was not appearing—yes, it's very likely, because she certainly had a *bel pancione*—which at that moment was probably receiving a message about her pleasure, as if the rhythm of its pulsations were swelling.

I reached Santa Fe and sat down to have a beer at one of the tables outside a bar. Soon after delving into the mystery of that woman, I realized that the emotion that overcame me at the window was neither dilettantism nor hypocrisy. With the inner sense of touch that leads us toward our true vocations, I identified definitively the object of my piety, I found with absolute certainty what it is about man that I want to defend: the vines and fig trees bursting from the miserable hovels at the center of our block, in other words, man's desire for pleasure, luxury, superfluity, sweetness. I realized that if I'm still capable of assigning myself a mission, that must be it: to ask for clemency for our senses. But asking for clemency is something you can do only through prayer, tears, and laments, and the truth is I don't know whom to ask for it that way. It's also true that here lies my greatest desire, that's the impulse I felt as I looked out the window and the impulse that filled me with emotion as I walked under the trees along Arenales and suddenly contemplated a human face radiant like a star, illuminated by the light of a store window. This is definitely what I care about most, and care about most deeply, but emotion is useless; first, I have to make an allegation, for myself.

Now it's long past midnight; in fact it's after two, so I'm in tomorrow. No, I'm in tonight. I'd like to sleep. I came up from Herminia's as soon as we'd eaten, telling her I had to get up early in the morning. Even so, I have a feeling I won't sleep. I feel, like Quitina—besides, I feel that Quitina feels this—that something has been left out of place. I walk mentally through the apartment, and all the doors are closed. It's in the library where the image lingers of a forehead bent over a notebook of photographs. It's in the door of the elevator where someone says: So long, farewell . . . and goes off intact.

But what difference can all that make to me!

4 September, at Las Murtas

Two days of intense activity. Great, mindless activity: oversee the painters, make sure everything's impeccable, and give the keys to the apartment to the Dutch consultant who will live in it for eight or ten months.

Long conversations with Herminia and Miguel, a few purchases and . . . nothing else? Yes, something else: half an hour I don't know whether to describe as stolen from my activities or think of it as blown into them. If I were to say: "I stole half an hour from my chores," a person would understand I took a given fraction of time and invested it in something else; that's not what happened. What happened was: at a precise moment, I felt myself seized by an unpremeditated activity. I was driving along Diagonal, and suddenly I stopped beside the door of Drake's office. Without even saying to myself, "I'll go up and see if he's there, I'll do a little investigating"; nothing more, nothing; I braked and I was no longer my own master. A silent force grabbed hold of me—being external, it did not express itself by saying: "Do this," it took no chance of being contested—, it mechanized me, hurled me in the dark toward its object; putting me in the elevator, it carried out all my normal motions, such as knocking on the door, saying hello, proffering a useless pretext, smoking one cigarette after another. All the while, like a suction pump, trying to absorb new developments by guiding Tom's thoughts toward the afternoon we met them at the movies, arranging my suggestions in a way that would gradually lead him where I wanted. First, some allusion or other to the film, then a word about how hard it was to find a parking place, then a comment about the children's endless farewell, then a silence, or pressure.

Suddenly Drake said: "Elfriede was worried afterwards about what that curious figure might have told you."

"Why?" I asked indifferently.

"A demonic guy! Smart, eh?"

"Oh yes, very smart."

Seeing that he didn't come forward with anything else, I decided to tug a little.

"He spoke of Elfriede with very sincere admiration."

"For him, everything to do with those things is sacred."

"Yes, of course, he's a believer."

Silence again. But Drake's smile had not vanished entirely. Finally, with some embarrassment, he decided to say: "We never mentioned that adventure to you, because the first day you went to our house you told us your father-in-law had a diplomatic post with Franco's government and we assumed you'd be against the Republic."

"Oh, in my case, when I don't take the trouble to work actively in support of something, I don't allow myself to be against anything."

"I understand," he said, although he didn't look as if he understood very well, and he added, as if to conclude, "Well, Elfriede said it would hardly be tactful to mention the subject without knowing."

I gestured my appreciation for their tactfulness and abandoned my investigation. Then I said: "You and Elfriede know we're back at Las Murtas now. Any weekend . . ."

But he didn't let me finish and said: "Oh, not right now. Our plans have gotten quite complicated."

I waited, with some fear, for him to continue.

"Well," Drake said, "we didn't find a truly satisfactory school for Nix. I would have put her in the Colegio Inglés, but her mother felt something or other was wrong with it. So we'll take her to Boston again."

"Ah," I said, "my boys will be very sorry to hear that, because they adore her. But you come alone then."

"No, that's not possible. This time I'll take her. I have to make a report to the Board about things here, and I think certain explanations are better made in person."

"Of course," I said, and I remained silent.

Drake continued: "I'll take the little one to school and, in the meantime, Elfriede will go to the South with the Weningers, some friends of hers who own property there."

I nodded vaguely and found myself in the car again, turning onto Esmeralda.

I'm sure I said good-bye to Drake in the normal way, that my appearance in his office was nothing out of the ordinary; I'd already gone up there to see him other times when I was in the area. What I can't shake is the sensation of having been literally beside myself, because of some trivial curiosity. When I left there, without finding out anything, I recovered my senses and realized my curiosity was impertinent. The subject doesn't interest me. Well, there's no subject that doesn't interest me, but this one doesn't interest me in a special way. So, half an hour lost; in other, never more precise words, wasted.

5 September, Las Murtas

A diary, in my life, is decidedly pointless. What prompted me to keep one was the impression Strugo's confidence made on me. Those occasional releases of the past into the present are exhilarating to me. I feel, simply because I know something new about *yesterday*, *today*, everything will be richer and more vivid *tomorrow*. And I feel this because, in reality, that's how it is; it's a law. But clearly there are exceptions. On this occasion, surprise and curiosity didn't prevail very powerfully; the present continued to be invaded by painters and advisers in Buenos Aires and by agricultural and financial affairs at Las Murtas.

Today I have the whole night ahead of me and, as I reread the last few pages, I'm amazed that I allowed such banal events to predominate over things I always took time to study for as long as it took—matured, settled things.

It's true, even before I began to record dates, my impressions were able to rest for shorter and shorter periods. I noted our departure from

Las Murtas ten or twelve days after it occurred, and then I didn't write more, waiting for everything to calm down. The upheaval of the day before our departure from Juncal made me forget things incomparably more valuable.

Between the day we went to Juncal and Strugo's appearance almost two months passed, and in them there was one extremely important day.

Nothing happened that day, absolutely nothing, but it was very important. I affirm that—so as not to fall out of the habit of considering days when nothing happens important days.

It was the middle of the week; I was planning to go to Las Murtas in the evening, because I needed to be there early the next morning. I gathered up a few things I wanted to bring from the apartment, among them a lamp I planned to use in the tower. As I was carrying it from the library where it was placed I said: "I'm taking this lamp because the light from it's so pleasant, but there must be something wrong with it; it's blown a fuse twice. I have to check it."

Miguel was around right then, and he said, "I can fix it for you in a minute."

He examined it and immediately found where the short was.

"I don't have any tools here, but I can go with you this evening and I'll leave it installed for you."

"Great," I said. And that's what happened.

When we got there, it was already nearly dark. Miguel went off to the garage with the lamp; I walked around looking everything over and fifteen minutes later I saw him coming out with the lamp all repaired.

"Don't bother with that now," I said. "Let's eat first, and then while you put it where it belongs—I'll tell you exactly where I want it—I'll make coffee. Upstairs I have everything we need."

We ate; the foreman's wife prepared us a few things. To complete the meal, there was plenty of cheese and wine, the two elements that are enough to nourish anyone who knows the pleasure of eating.

We went up to the little room right away, and I showed Miguel where I wanted the lamp—attached to the bookshelf and focused directly at the head of the couch, so I could just reach up and change the position of the bell-shaped shade. He got to work and I put coffee in the round glass top and lit the burner. I began to pack a pipe and asked Miguel if he'd brought his.

"Yes, I always carry it," he said.

I'd given it to him, initiating him into that delightful habit, which he adopted immediately. The day I gave it to him, Herminia tried to protest. "But a pipe! He doesn't even smoke cigarettes."

I was about to begin a defense, but Miguel beat me to it: "Of course not," he said. "Cigarettes are what boys smoke when they want to act like grown-ups and what girls smoke when they want to make little gestures. That's what cigarettes are, a movement you make with your hands; pipes are a truth."

To such an irrefutable defense, no one added anything. Herminia made a motion of desperation, as if to say: "He's hopeless!"

But I saw she was smiling with satisfaction, as she always did when she found a truth in Miguel.

As I was making the coffee, I thought about all these things; Miguel was drilling into the bookcase so he could mount the lamp. Suddenly I stopped in the middle of the room, with the sugar bowl in my hand. I must have created such silence around me that Miguel turned in surprise: "What happened?" he asked.

"Nothing," I answered in an unfamiliar voice.

"All right! If it's a mystery," Miguel said, and I nodded in agreement until I could get my voice back.

"Yes, it's a mystery. But wait a little, because there was a time when I referred to a mystery as a *nonsense*."

"And was it?" Miguel asked with curiosity.

"Well . . . I don't know. The thing is, I called it nonsense, but I believed in it. Just now, though, I stood here frozen on the spot, waiting to get angry enough to call it nonsense. And nothing!"

"But who did you want to get angry with?"

"With . . . Well, let's drink our coffee before it gets cold."

"I'm coming, I just have to fasten this with a screw."

He put in the screw and I lay down on the couch a minute to see how the lamp had turned out. After moving it in several directions, I said: "Perfect; it turned out exactly like I wanted."

After that I was silent again, and Miguel couldn't guess what I was looking at, even though he saw me running my eyes over the walls.

I drew the little table with the coffee over to the couch and Miguel sat on a stool alongside the foot of the couch, but I didn't let him get seated.

"Don't sit there," I said to him, "come over here."

"Why?"

"You'll see. Well, you won't see anything, I don't think, but you'll understand better."

"You can understand better from that side?"

"No, you can't understand from any side."

I started to drink my coffee, and I was getting ready to speak; I was concentrating on my memory of the night I composed the letter to my father-in-law, to send him just a couple of words that would convey the full horror of *the event*. Well, what happened? Exactly what I'd foreseen, what I'd feared on another very distant occasion: before I could write the first word, I sensed a smile spreading across my face. Not only did I experience the horror of that memory but also the horror of sensing myself smile, yet the smile could not be erased, the muscles of my face remained tensed in that position. Then I accepted it; I decided to explain the horror and the smile together, to see what happened.

"See that butterfly?" I said. "One night I had to leave this room because I was sure that if I put my mind to it, I could make the butterfly move its wings, with nothing but my will."

"What a blast!" Miguel said.

Did my smile become more accentuated? I don't know; I felt it run jaggedly across my face, the way an electric spark cuts through a cloud.

"But you can't imagine how intensely that idea controlled me. It's not something you can explain, you either understand it or you don't."

"Yes, of course; I understand it."

"Ah, you understand it? And what do you think?"

"It's dumb."

My smile was no longer sarcastic, light; it became still, mindless and empty. Everything antithetical on the reverse of that smile, everything that gave the smile mobility by creating an unstable contrast, everything else disappeared and nothing was left but the dim-witted smile, suspended before a dumb idea.

"Nevertheless . . ." I said.

"Yes, although . . ." Miguel said.

After that, we continued, saying something like: "Want another cup?"

"Okay. What huge matches!"

"For my pipe I like these wooden ones better. The wax ones smell."

"So do these. You have to wait for the flame to subside. Do you hear the chaja?"

"It was a bird? I thought it was a cat."

That justified the silence. We waited a couple of minutes to see if cat or chaja would scream again, but it didn't. Our silence went walking through the countryside, in search of the screaming creature, and was returning purified by the night; having lost its ponderousness, no longer inept, it became light, breathable for the mind.

Miguel said: "I've found a very good definition of original sin."

"Where?"

"In one of Pascal's *pensées*. You're already familiar with my vast erudition."

"I am, because it's like love and money—something you can't hide."

"Come on, out with it," I added.

"*La raison a ses passions que le coeur ne connaît point.*"

"Fantastic!" I said. "I don't understand it very well yet, but I sense something definitive about it."

"What is it you don't understand? You only have to think for a minute to see that it's accurate."

"Yes, yes," I said, and I repeated mentally to myself, *La raison a ses passions que le coeur ne connaît point.* "Listen, though; Did Pascal ever say that?"

"I didn't tell you that Pascal said it. I told you I found it in one of his *pensées*—the most famous one."

"Ah, right! '*Le coeur* . . .' How does it go?" I looked toward the bookcase. "It seems to me that I don't have it up here; no, it's downstairs."

"There's no need to go and look for it. What Pascal said is this, '*Le coeur a ses raisons que la raison ne connaît point.*' Well, you turn it around and it serves perfectly for the use I'm assigning it."

"You know, I think you're right."

"Of course I am. And because I *am*, because we are . . .'"

"Yes, that's true; reason's passions are terrible."

"Look, reason has the same dual condition as passion. Reason suffers in the presence of unreason. And when reason lets loose, it's devastating; it demolishes everything that gets in its path."

"Yes, but who suffers, reason or reasoner?"

"Reason. Of course I've never seen a reason by itself. Reason doesn't exist outside of man. But if we say it's the reasoner who suffers, immediately we imagine the unhappy person suffering from the things he reasons—suffering with his heart, his liver . . . That's definitely not what it is. Reason's suffering is the conflict that breaks out when white looks black. And even worse, when reason finds something to be false, before it possesses the truth this something supplants, when reason begins to be certain this is false and then undertakes the task of verification. Understand? Reason suffers from that inversion of order."

I clasped my head with both hands.

"Now you're on my territory!"

"There's only one territory, that of reason. Anything outside this territory doesn't have its feet touching terra firma."

"Well, I don't know. Let's see: according to what people have always said, it's reason that leaves terra firma, into abstraction."

"So people have always said! I know that, but people have said every sort of foolish thing."

"Yes, they've said many foolish things, and you have to be careful not to add to the number. Who inverts order on reason? The heart?"

"No, no. Order gets inverted because reason becomes passionate, entranced by evidence with its brilliant facts. Understand? And in this, the heart does second reason. But then things must be put in order, and reason moves ahead, leaving the heart in the lurch."

"Yes, that division of being is a sin."

"Not only the division; what happens is that reason, which knows itself to be human reason, scorns its family, the heart and all the rest. Reason isn't finite and, because it's been placed among all those other things, reason knows it too will die. Reason can't forgive that."

"No, it can't forgive that. We can't forgive that."

"So, you see? Right now your heart consents to the passion felt by your reason, but before, when you wanted to get angry, and you didn't get angry . . ."

I couldn't answer, or smile; I shrugged my shoulders and raised my eyebrows, questioning, desolate.

"Well, you couldn't get angry, because when you wanted to tell about that fuss you created once, only reason prevailed. Everything else you put at stake that day . . ."

I interrupted him: "What I put at stake was *everything else* and *this*—that was being. Will literally is a matter of life."

"Yes, of course: that's why will's mortal."

"You admit it's mortal!"

"What good would it do me not to admit it? What isn't mortal is reason's telling you the cells of this dried insect, which has been in a box for ten years, are in no condition to obey you."

There was another, very arid silence; this time there was no way out, no escape hatch. Miguel stood up, walked around the room a few times, stopped in front of the butterfly and said: "It's pretty from a distance, but seen up close it's repulsive. Well, I'm going to bed. Are you going to stay here?"

"Yes . . . , I'm going to stay. See you tomorrow."

I hurried to answer affirmatively, but that *yes*, it seemed very long to me. Uttering that word, I thought: "I don't want him to think I'm afraid. But am I? It seems to me that I'm not . . . Is that because I'm not even able to hope I'll manage to *feel* a little afraid? I'll stay here to see if by persevering . . ." I thought all this in the time it took me to utter a monosyllable.

Miguel went downstairs, and I tried to concentrate. Useless! There was something all dried up inside me that was in no condition to obey me, something that, seen at close range, was repulsive.

11 September, at Las Murtas

Once again a date. I'm not putting it here so I can tell about what's happening today but so I'll bear in mind that six days have passed between the last date and this one. Six days, no more!

I'd like to know what one of those people who can keep a diary would have written on days like the ones just past. Short notes? Observations about the facts? What comments can you make about the course of an inevitable day? When you're submerged in such a day you offer no resistance, you let the current carry you along and resolve to sail again tomorrow.

Now that these six days are here before me, like something concrete, will I be able to write a journalistic account of each one of them? And why do that? What occurred during them is banal. It's banal if *I believe* it occurred during them, but no, it's not banal, because the past, with the fury of everything that could not occur . . . Banal or not, that I might be ashamed to tell about those days when I was not ashamed to live them is more hypocritical than I can stand.

The fourth day I went to Drake's office. Consciously or not, I went to investigate. I could very well have continued not to know, and that piece of history, that singular adventure of which I was both origin and object, would never have gotten inserted into my personal history. With all my might, I want to repudiate that piece of history. But is that possible? Not only did I live and prompt its beginning, but over the years, in these very pages, I've always had a clear conscience about the first chapter. In other words, I always looked complacently at the base of its luminous cone. Now I want to stint on my contribution to its shadowy zone. Now, when there's no longer anything to be done.

Of course, the only thing to do was treat it with a certain distraction, automatism, to relegate it to the drawer of insignificant things and turn again toward the old mysteries, in total comfort. There are no more mysteries. Or, perhaps quite the opposite, now I'm in a mystery I can't even talk about. But it will be related journalistically.

Three days after I went up to Drake's office, I was in the study, in the morning, when the telephone rang. I picked up the receiver and heard a strange and familiar "Hallo." "Who's calling?" I asked: "Who is this?" and the person answered in a mocking tone, "Who's calling?" It was Elfriede's voice, her unmistakable accent.

"Ah, Elfriede!" I said in the most cordial tone. "How are you? To what do I owe this surprise?"

"What a question! Why not ask what you really want to know?"

She used the familiar form of address, which stunned me because it was something she'd never done in Buenos Aires, but I thought it might have been because she was not truly fluent in Spanish and I answered without taking any risks, not addressing her directly until she'd spoken again: "I want to know so many things I'd never stop asking."

"Couldn't it be that you like to ask about what you already know?"

"Elfriede!"

Once my exclamation had escaped, it was not possible for me to tell what tone it might have had at the other end of the line. I only wanted to express surprise, perplexity, but my voice sounded too serious. Could what was only a slight insinuation have seemed like a cunning, pleading delay? Maybe, but the thing is, our conversation lost the frivolous tone with which it had started. Elfriede tried to keep things exactly as she'd intended, and she'd obviously rehearsed this role well, but her voice also took on a seriousness that contradicted her wordplay.

"If you want to know," she said, "if you really want to know . . ."

A silence, filled with anxious waiting for my affirmation, which me wasn't forthcoming.

"Don't expect me to tell you over the telephone," she concluded, her attitude striving to seem faked, although it was real.

"Oh, of course not! I didn't expect that. But how then?" And since she didn't answer, since I seemed to sense the silence was hurting her throat, I added—now conceding fully, lavishing the tone requested by her silence: "How, where, and when?"

"Well, you'll see," she answered, with a small laugh that seemed like an explosion of happiness; "this will seem a bit absurd to you, but there's nowhere else. Besides, you'll understand later. In El Tigre, at Tres Bocas."

"Perfect. When?"

"Tomorrow, first thing, very first thing in the morning."

"At dawn?"

"Oh, no. How foolish!" A youthful laugh, full of confidence. "At eight or nine. Eight thirty would be better."

"Eight."

"All right, eight. See you tomorrow then."

And at eight I was there. What happened until eight, what I did, how I slept that night, I can't remember. At eight sharp, I jumped to the pier where Elfriede was waiting for me, wearing a sky-blue linen dress and sandals. She was not holding a purse or anything that would suggest she'd just arrived. I realized she'd spent the night there, but not at Tres Bocas. She had me cut through the garden, avoiding the area around the restaurant. Behind, there was a rowboat in the reeds; we jumped in. Elfriede shoved off with the boathook; I took the oars and beheld her wielding the world with a vigorous push to steer us, until the shore was lost to view. It was a mythic shore, and the boat glided forward, rending the water; she propped up the pole in the stern and stood there gripping it, steady as a gondolier, watching me row. Then she took over, and we passed through a small channel, then we docked beside a wall overflowing with climbing plants and went into a house. There were no explanations.

Now I want, futilely, to explain why suddenly I lost all interest in what I'd found so intriguing. I went toward Elfriede—no longer the day of our meeting, but earlier, ever since the moment I felt intrigued, taking as my goal the mystery of those events that occurred during times unknown. Nevertheless, when I jumped to the pier, I jumped over that time, and I ended up further back: I landed in the place I'd tried to reach ten years before in Montevideo. That time our encounter failed, and I could never find out why. It was one of the unknowns I hoped to see revealed by the shadowy zone, and when I encountered myself in Elfriede's presence, on the pier, everything returned to that moment.

When I saw her . . . No, it was not when I saw her. Either say nothing or tell everything the way it was, minute by minute and then cube the minutes, show them to be solid, with front, back, lower, upper, and lateral sides. It's exhausting, but that's how it has to be.

I was riding in the prow, and I saw Elfriede from afar. As the boat pulled alongside the pier, we smiled at each other; but it took a while to dock, and I couldn't jump out because the water was very low and the pier was at the level of my head. That's why, as the boy was positioning the rowboat at the steps, all I could see of Elfriede from on board was her feet, which took two or three steps, following the boat, then walked down a step and a half, where one of them remained above and the other below, motionless.

The transformation occurred in those couple of minutes. A little while before, I'd been traveling in the boat, aware of what I was going to do. I was going to El Tigre to meet Elfriede. But the pier turned out to be at the level of my head, and Elfriede's feet took two or three steps right before my eyes, walked down the first step and, on the second, her right foot continued descending, but the left foot stopped with the heel raised, supported only on the toes, allowing me to see the arch. This probably lasted a couple of minutes, and now, if I want to make it all clear, I'll have to fill several pages that will seem false and artificial. Nevertheless, the feet were there and of course they passed through my thoughts, but at that moment my thinking was not precisely in my head. Literature, history, myth—the entire trail man has left in the world—can be manifest in one contemplated shape, can be sensed, like a perfume. This is the work of Eros, whose arrow pierces and confuses, turning you into such a mess inside that your feelings are exalted to the point of meditation, and your ideas seem as appetizing as your favorite fruits, which make your mouth water just to look at them. What I want to express is something like the emergence of a world, something, for example, like the way we hear mentioned a forgotten name and that person springs up as image but also as hate or fear or happiness or tenderness or rage. As opinion too and, usually, with a backdrop, a country, a social class . . . Well, Elfriede's feet were at the level of my head, and I looked at them for a couple of minutes, savoring them, absorbing them with the fury of a vampire, because suddenly I found myself in the world of my old desire.

Of course it would be simpler to say: Elfriede's feet were so beautiful, their rosy whiteness so dazzling, they made me desire her furiously, immediately. That would definitely be enough, except there was also a counterpoint that neither diminishes nor increases the real fact of desire, which neither detracts from nor adds anything to the actual event but is decisive with respect to time. It might be called a phenomenon of resurrection.

I still haven't explained exactly how things were. Her sandals, almost like monks' sandals, without heels, were nothing but soles secured by some thin little straps that hid no part of her feet. And, walking softly, those feet came to meet me naked, with medieval daring. Naked, as Princess Elisena went to the room of King Perión. Does this comparison seem merely rhetorical? Well, it's not. This is something that sprang up there like a ghost, much more charged with meaning than it seems. Right there I thought of Princess Elisena's naked body moving through the night in the midst of a fearful darkness, to place itself in the hands of the caballero. About the knight it must be said—or thought—because of what's involved here with respect to . . . because "caballero" exudes a flavor of purity, of confidence, and also because of what makes certain the very forceful nature of the caballero's acceptance, that he cannot be unworthy of the bold offering in any way.

This was the world that sprang from Elfriede's feet at the edge of the pier, and I entered it, scorning all curiosity.

I keep on writing, without saying anything. No matter how hard I try to disentangle and examine all the threads of that moment, I can't manage to define the essential quality of my consent. It's like hitting a key and hearing E-flat; even if I also know I heard a fixed number of vibrations, what I actually heard was, simply, E-flat. In the same way, when that incalculable electric discharge vibrated in my nerves, I recognized the note. Medieval impressions, images of ancient statuary feet, and a thousand, a thousand million more vibrations, but in the middle of my chest, in the middle of my being, the note of that moment when I peered over the ferryboat's railing and believed I could feel Elfriede's body pressed to mine, spinning in a fast, endless whirl. Now, that note, which had been sustained during an entire night and verged on climax but was snuffed out when Elfriede appeared at the door of my room, was again buzzing in my veins, leaving me deaf to anything else. In that state I leaped to the pier, grabbed the hand Elfriede held out to me, and ran with her through the garden to the rowboat.

Then, while I was rowing, I watched her at the rudder and the willows began to close over her head, since they were becoming increasingly dense. The channel was choked with aguapé plants, true floating meadows that were continuously torn apart by the boat, only to close again quickly. We were entering vegetal humidity, slime. The air was warm, almost summery, but the morning was gray and the atmosphere loaded with moisture—you breathed it in the way you do in the parks in Berlin.

When we docked beside the wall, I saw on the door a name in Gothic bronze letters—Karl Weninger—half-hidden in the honeysuckle.

Elfriede opened the door, and the honeysuckle that overflowed the wall formed a tunnel into the house. To me, it seemed a very long, eternal road. Eternal, above all because it exerted a sort of spell that prevented you from moving forward. It was like a game and like a torture. The honeysuckle branches were lashing us, splashing drops of water on our faces, enveloping us in bursts of perfume when we collided with the posts of the pergola, on the verge of tumbling to the ground.

This fit of madness I can recall serenely—I don't know if I'll be able to explain why—but what happened after is, simply, disproportionate. Everything, the first day, was justified by that fit. There came a moment when Elfriede tried to speak, and I wouldn't let her—which filled her with happiness. She interpreted it to mean that the contact of our bodies, our conversation so pure, so exhaustive, had explained everything. But it was because I was terrified of hearing. I vaguely remembered the existence of a zone in the shadows and I was afraid of it the way children fear a dark room. I saw very clearly that Elfriede was experiencing that ecstasy, that perfect, glorious pleasure as the maximum expression of her secret, and I, looking deep into her eyes, was mentally pleading with her, "Go back, don't stop there; we're further, much further!"

That day survived intact, perfect, and immaculate. That day was wholly for the triumph of the flesh and I did not permit the spirit to spoil it with a single word. But that was only the first day.

The next day I could devote only a couple of hours to Elfriede. I hurriedly made a quick getaway, and she resigned herself, because I told her that I'd arranged things so I could spend the night there the following day. And the following day I arrived in the early evening, probably close to six. I was counting on fifteen hours at least, and fifteen hours of love is a very reasonable amount of time: you can surrender calmly to the cessation of desire, because you know you have time to see it reborn soon. A whole night is very long. Toward the beginning, in a moment of respite, I saw the rectangle of the window in the half-light of the room, then, later, I no longer saw anything but darkness as a form of silence that I would never have wanted to break.

Near midnight Elfriede suggested making some tea. I welcomed the idea happily because tea was what we needed in order to feel that we were *far away*. Elfriede opened a wardrobe and took out a silk dressing gown.

"I'll put on Lily's robe," she said.

"Who's Lily?"

"Lily Weninger, meinen kleines Lily. Oh, you don't know what that means! Lily is what you people here call *muy gaucha*. Isn't that what you say about someone who's really helpful? She lets me have this house for as long as I want."

"Why?" it occurred to me to ask.

"Because Lily knows . . . everything. She's known everything for a long, long time."

Elfriede's voice took on a melancholy tone in which I saw something that pointed to evocation, confidence, and I pounced on Lily's ghost.

"Oh, let me imagine what Lily's like," I said. "The Lily who lives here is a girl who studies classical dance, who wanders through museums in the mornings, skates in the afternoons, and at night makes tea and cuts thin little slices of black bread."

"No, that girl does not exist," Elfriede said, moved.

"Yes, she exists," I asserted. "I can smell her, the whole house is filled with her."

"But this house isn't mine," she said, as if wanting to invalidate my game.

"I know," I conceded. "It's not yours officially, but everything—its furniture, its curtains, that tea cozy, the board for cutting bread on top of the dining room cupboard—everything belongs to your atmosphere. This house may not be yours, but here I'm in your house."

"Oh, you've already seen that my house now is very different. It's a modern house, totally lacking in style, but as easy to put together as it is to take apart. Lily, however, even though she has no children, truly lives for her home. She's married to a man with a very good position, a German who owns lands in the South, and they get along very well," she added with a certain irony. "They're very understanding with me. Perhaps because I didn't marry a German; they understand that I did the right thing."

I didn't understand this and I asked naively: "How did you do the right thing?"

"Because it was certain I'd deceive him."

I didn't say anything, I asked no further questions; I sat on the bed, hugging my knees in a pose more tense than the Thinker's. Elfriede was slowly tying the sash on the robe; she was standing in front of me, arranging the folds around her hips, gathering up her hair, which she wears long now, piled on top of her head, and giving her appearance the composure whose meaning in her case is similar to self-esteem, and I

432   *Dream of Reason*

thought: "Something atrocious is going to happen." As I thought this, I split in two, emerged from myself, and perhaps perched on the window shutter, perhaps on the lamp on the headboard. Some place where I could see the whole scene, because I was thinking, "In this room there is a naked man sitting on the bed and a woman dressing with slow gestures, although her heart is so agitated it could choke her; something terrible is going to happen in this room."

Since I didn't press her to continue by asking a new question, Elfriede said, partially picking up where her last sentence had left off: "I could have married a German, I could have, and you mustn't doubt that."

"But of course," I said, "that would have been most natural."

"Yes, very natural, because men in my country don't have certain prejudices."

"Elfriede, please!" I managed to say, "don't you think I've also thought the same thing sometimes?" and I said this quite effusively; the tone of my voice slid soothingly over the deep wound that was beginning to show, but at the same time I prayed inside, "Please don't let her spend too much time on this, don't let her analyze why I never thought and, above all, don't let her ask me about it!"

In order to indicate that she hadn't taken my protest totally to heart, Elfriede said a little ironically: "I know very well, and I knew then, what a Spaniard thinks."

"But I'm not Spanish, I've told you that a hundred times."

"Then I believed it. Anyway, even if you aren't Spanish, in the end you're Catholic."

"Ah, that I won't deny."

Elfriede shrugged her shoulders resignedly, as if she were faced with an inevitable calamity, and she said: "Very well, I'll make the tea."

I followed her. In the dining room cupboard there were exquisite things; I began to pick at the paté. Elfriede, I saw, was more in control of herself; maybe the danger had been averted and her ideas were about to take a different course. I tried to distract her with comments about the things she was putting on the table and which we began to devour. I also tried to revive her nerves with a caress that might force her dark ideas into the background, but my own nerves were not really willing. I felt atrociously hungry. And I was confident I'd snap out of it soon.

Elfriede looked me over from head to toe and said: "You're going to catch cold. Or does your God keep you from that as well?

"I don't think so," I said. "He's more likely to toss me a good one as punishment."

"Punishment! Now it's come out! It was bound to," she exclaimed, throwing up her arms with a loud, cold guffaw.

I'd never talked to her about this subject; actually, she didn't know how I thought, but I saw suddenly that she was adopting that notion decisively, as if at last she were finding an enemy that was not humiliating. From that moment on, my God would be guilty of everything and on that basis we could continue our conversation.

Elfriede disappeared for a minute and returned with a bathrobe.

"Here," she said, "avoid punishment; unless you like it."

"Oh, no, I don't like it, what I like is sin."

"Sin! You make me die laughing," she said emphatically, extremely serious.

Since that was not the time to discuss it thoroughly, I preferred to produce something of a fog and I said, "Don't laugh so hard. I'll correct the cliché I just used: it's not sin I like, what I like is *what's called* sin, which, obviously, usually has sin inside, but the delicious part is what's on the outside."

Elfriede looked at me tenderly and smiled, enraptured with so much non-comprehension. My wordplay took her way back, to the time when I spoke to her in a language she didn't know. In order to show me her gods, she said: "I always knew how you thought, but it made me happy, deep down inside. This way, I told myself, it will all just be something fleeting that won't tear me away from my art. Because I must not belong to anything but my art; I have to be free, free. And when you left Berlin, it suited me perfectly. You promised not to write and you kept your promise, which also suited me; that was our agreement. A short time later Tom appeared and asked me to marry him right after he met me. We went to the park one afternoon, he kissed me, and asked me to marry him. Tom, like you, was passing through Berlin, and I went out with him a few times, to the movies or dancing; then he would take me home, kiss me, and ask me to marry him. I'd laugh and think: 'You have to defend yourself from men, denial is very easy, very easy.'" She paused and then spoke again. "Imagine, I even had the impression that denial had always been my response, that between us everything was the way it was because that's the way I wanted it."

At that moment I raised my eyes. I was eating a slice of bread and jam as I listened to Elfriede, proving my attention by sitting completely still, with my eyes fixed on the dark jam—blackberry—in my hand, but I raised my eyes to see what I knew I would see. The muscles around her mouth were quivering, and small, uncontrollable tremors were taking over her lips, making them lose their usual creases. Elfriede's mouth is rather large, with sharp contours, and it moves with studied grace when she laughs or speaks; at that moment her lips seemed to have softened, her will seemed unable to govern them. There was even a bit of moisture flowing into them, and they could not hold it back.

I put down the slice of bread, ready to rush toward her, but I held back. Elfriede had probably believed her tenderness had touched my heart, she'd probably believed my desire, like her tears, was a word, something that expressed something, and it wasn't. It was not that her feelings moved me; her weeping awakened my appetite. The trembling of her lips denounced the commotion in all her founts. I don't know if the tears reached her eyes, but I felt them bubbling like a spring deep within her. And I held back, at the same time asking myself: why am I holding back? I don't want to deceive her. But would that be deceiving her? Isn't it the truth, the true word?

Elfriede was speaking serenely now. She was biting her lips a little, as if she were polishing them with the edge of her teeth to make them recover their customary firmness, and I tried to devote my attention to her again, but it was difficult. I was thinking: why did I let that moment pass? I should have dived into her without stopping to think about it.

One of Elfriede's words returned me to reality once more: she was speaking about Montevideo. My blood pressure altered quickly, losing its moist voluptuousness, making me vibrant, expectant.

"When I saw you in the foyer of the hotel," she said, "I thought: 'What's going to happen, will I fall on my face?'"

Elfriede wanted to tell, tell to the end, tell at any cost, and she counted on her sarcastic tone to keep her momentum from flagging. Then she told about her indecision, her gaffes at the rehearsal and how they'd alarmed the entire troupe, her absences. The whole day she'd clung to the idea of defending herself, of saving herself for her art; if "that" were to be repeated, it would again be a fleeting episode, because she had to remain free. But in every error she made, in her state of alienation, she saw clearly that her freedom was seriously threatened. And so the moment came for her to go on stage.

"It was a disaster," she said, "a calamity!"

I remembered it as something entirely different, I assured her that to me she'd seemed enchanting, perfect.

"Perfect! Be quiet, please! I didn't do a single thing right; the director wanted to kill me. Then, at night, what do you know!" she said in a highly ambiguous way.

That night arose before me, and I saw that in fact I did know nothing. I saw myself lower the pulley lamp and sit under it to read a French magazine. This caused me a bit of embarrassment and a sort of fear, like a cold sensation in my back. I thought: I was there, reading under the lamp, and elsewhere, in a different room, different things were happening. Now I'm going to find out what.

Elfriede needed me to be beg her to continue; her secret refused to be told for free. I took her hand and said: "What happened that night?"

"That night I realized I hadn't defended myself from you so I could give myself to my art, but that I'd barricaded myself behind my art so I could defend myself from you. Yes, I had, you understand? When I saw how bad a dancer I was, the *bad dancer* I was—because I knew my craft and my physical facility weren't lacking, but what they call the *soul of a dancer*—I didn't come close!—, when I saw all this clearly, it was as if

I'd been left defenseless. Of course, I was absolutely certain you would have realized this."

"Well, I did not realize it, not at all."

"How is that possible! How is it possible not to detect something so disgraceful? I thought the spectators in the last rows—I don't know!—the ushers, the doormen at the theater could have shouted it at me."

She paused briefly and, raising her eyebrows high, as if she were discovering an unnoticed perspective, she said: "If I'd known you didn't understand, maybe I would have taken the risk. Because I spent the night, the whole night, trembling at the idea of standing in front of you without my shell."

She considered for a moment and said: "Sometimes I was afraid of that and sometimes I wasn't. Well, it doesn't matter."

I saw she was holding something back.

"What is it that doesn't matter?"

"Oh, nothing, just nonsense. You know how at those hours of the night everyone's thoughts are senseless but, as soon as it was light, I made a decision. I took a folder out of my suitcase and looked through the papers, newspaper clippings, letters—all kinds of things—, searching for a card Tom had given me when he left. While I looked for it, I was telling myself: if I find the card, I'll call him. If I find the card, it's because I *must* call him. Tom had made me promise that if I ever needed him at any moment, I would call without hesitating, and I found it. At seven o'clock I was at the telephone exchange asking to place a long-distance call to New York. They gave me an appointment at one. You know the rest."

While Elfriede talked, I was thinking she didn't know what had happened in my room at the same time and, as I remembered that night, which to me had always seemed a vibrant, plethoric moment until it burst in a spark of anger, I saw that it amounted to a small, cold confidence after the one that I'd received. Elfriede deserved to be paid with another secret, but even if I'd embellished and enlarged mine, it would never have been so much of a drama as hers, which she didn't try to enlarge but to conceal. That was obvious.

Finally I managed to tell her that all I remembered was how beautiful she was that day; how she'd appeared at the door of my room looking magnificent, the exact opposite of a woman who'd spent a whole night without being able to sleep. And I had almost found the way to paint her a vivid picture of how well her aspect had deceived me, but Elfriede was dominated by the memory evoked by my words, and she said: "Yes, I put on my best outfit. I was sure you'd recognized my failure, and I was prepared to deny it to you. You understand? A person can't come up with an aspect like that unless everything's already been decided. I could have said to you: now you see, I'm not an artist, I'm only a woman, a girl just like any other; but a person has courage for things like this only before dawn, in the hour filled with nonsense. And at that hour so many things happened that I'd used it all up."

"But what is it that happened? You're thinking about things you aren't telling me."

"About things people *don't tell*."

"Why not? Don't I deserve them?"

"No."

After denying me those things curtly, Elfriede could not rest there, and she said, as if she weren't serious: "People who sleep soundly at those hours don't need to know anything."

"And how do you know I was sleeping soundly at those hours?"

"Oh! . . . I just know."

I pleaded with her in every way possible, because I saw it was the only thing I could do for her; she needed to free herself of that secret. Finally she started to tell me, with much hinting and insinuating, how at the party they gave in honor of the troupe, she'd slipped away, taken a taxi, and gone to the hotel, where she closed herself in her room. She'd stayed there for hours, stretched across the bed, crying and tossing, without taking off her dress or shoes. There she'd thought over and over about how she was a failure, disarmed and defenseless, until a small accident had made her snap out of that state. She was lying face down on the bed, wiping her tears with her hand, with the flap of the sheet, or by rubbing her face against the pillow case, incapable of getting up to look for a handkerchief. Finally, at a moment when she half-opened her eyes, she saw that her nose was bleeding and both the bed and her dress were soaked with blood.

"It seems impossible," Elfriede said. "Can you believe that just because I was forced to get up from the bed, wet my face with cold water and clean things up a bit, just because of that, my thinking changed entirely? Yes, everything looked very different. Of course, a small hemorrhage is very relaxing and, since my face was all smeared, I used some cleansing cream and took off the rest of my makeup. I took off my clothes—the blood had run down my chest—and got into the bathtub, and there everything seemed so easy to me."

She was silent for a moment, but I didn't interrupt her silence, because I wanted her to continue. A slight blush began to move up her neck until it reached her forehead, not from modesty but from emotion, and she said, her voice almost trembling: "There I had just one thought: 'The only thing to do is go to his room right now. Go immediately, just the way I am, exactly as I am.' It seemed by saying this I said everything. I would go up to your room, I would enter without explanation, I would get into your bed, and I would cry there, pressed against you, but it would be from happiness. You know how after you cry you have this feeling of pleasure, how it's like a memory of something really delightful? All I wanted was to cry again, but without anger—to hell with my failure. And I did exactly what I'd thought about: I leaped out of the water, wrapped myself in my bathrobe and started running upstairs. I didn't take the elevator, because there was always an operator inside. I didn't want to knock, I wanted to enter like a shadow, but I was afraid you might have locked the door from inside, and you would hear me fumbling in the hall, because then you would have come out to investigate and things would not have been the same, so I turned the door handle very carefully, and it was open. But at that moment someone abruptly came out of the room next door. I didn't see who it was, it seemed to be an old man, some ordinary man going to the toilet, and he coughed or muttered something as he walked by me. I think he coughed, but for me it had the effect of an insult, and everything changed again. I lost my nerve, closed the door, and started running downstairs."

Elfriede wanted to keep recounting, but this time I did not hold back: I smothered her with kisses. Carrying her from there, I turned out all the lights and gave myself with devotion, silently determined to experience what should have occurred that night.

Again that moment I thought I could split into two. I turned out the light in the room and flung myself on Elfriede, completely blind, but at the same time concentrating my entire will on restraining myself, so I would not lose my mental image, repeating to myself: "I'm in the dark, Elfriede enters like a shadow. She is naked, wrapped in her robe; the ends of her hair are wet, and she smells of her bath, her makeup creams. She's come through the dark hall, naked under her robe. She's come to my room naked." Even if I were to repeat it a hundred times, I could not reach the dimension I did by inexhaustibly pondering the idea. Minutely, in detail, systematically I was imagining that night, inserting it into my current pleasure. And at the same time, in this instance unintentionally, I was enclosed in an emotion that resembles the terror of a prophecy murmured from far away—from the beginning of my adolescence.

Ever since I was fourteen years old, when I was astounded by the first pages of *Amadís de Gaula*, each time the image had come to mind it had caused the same shock. From the beginning it had the force of a memory for me. I thought it was the memory of the paradise that sex reveals to us when we're young, but here there was more mystery; it was a memory of the future, a promise. And when, two days before, on the pier, as I looked at Elfriede's feet, the memory had passed through my mind, the way it does in that game where you hide a garment, I'd sensed I was getting close, that I was going to place my hands on the spot where the promise was hidden. And finally I did place my hands there, to learn that, more or less, I'd passed up the promise. In other words, it had been granted to me when I was sound asleep. At that moment I held in my hands a body sentient and corporeal, a skin pulsing with life; I sank my teeth into that skin and the entire experience was what, on a certain occasion, had incarnated the prophecy. How to describe the reality of a moment that lasted for years? As I gave myself over to it, I thought how the moment could just as possibly last for eternity as become *the end*. But only the ideas became disarticulate, turning into trivial dreams.

A night is so long! Sometimes it slips away without your realizing, other times insomnia makes continual visits, like a security guard who walks around shining his flashlight into the corners and, suddenly, one feels exposed. I remember dreaming something banal, prosaic, and amusing when I felt the light of dawn on my eyelids. I looked at Elfriede, although it was still too dark in the room to see; Elfriede was a shadow on the white sheet. I moved away from her gently, slid out of bed, and went to get a drink of water. I was not gone long at all, but in those few minutes the light had progressed, and Elfriede was still asleep, unaware of my absence. Then I leaned on the foot of the bed and watched her gradually appear.

How different she looked than she had at night. The Elfriede I'd loved for hours was the same young athlete as always; now, her body was lax, and sleep revealed that it had expanded horizontally. Not that she'd put on weight or that she'd aged; there was possibly a greater physical richness about her now, but instead of being hard and agile, as before, now she was restful and mellow. I recalled the transformation I'd observed in her lips when the flow of her tears made them soften, and the supposition had occurred to me that her body had matured through weeping. But it hadn't, which might suggest that I'm referring to the tears that wither a life by macerating it in sadness; nothing could be more contrary to Elfriede. I was thinking about her weeping as flux, as an emission of feminine humors that had flowed from her hidden founts: tears, blood, life's extravagances.

This may seem like one of those reflections on human slime that beset many people after pleasure. Of course it is such a reflection, but in a reverse sense, because I love the nymphs and the batrachians and all the tiny lives teeming in the mud. Looking at Elfriede's body sprawled on the bed expansively in her abandon to sleep, I liked to think of her wide pelvis with her belly resting inside, motionless as a lake, where phenomena of sedimentation, erosion, and germination were occurring, and to know that if I touched the sole of her foot with the tip of my finger, she would explode in shrieks and bursts of laughter, something that can't happen with a water lily.

The temperature had dropped a little, it was the moment when night seems to have used up its heat reserve and the morning's supply hasn't arrived yet. I picked up the bedspread and the sheet, which had fallen to the floor, and covered her a bit. The spread was made of a pliant, pale blue fabric whose weight made it cling to Elfriede's body. Color began to appear and, wrapped in blue and white, as relaxed as if she were encrusted in the flat surface of the bed, Elfriede resembled a della Robbia relief. I don't know whether the weight of the spread or of my observation woke her.

I'd woken almost laughing, from one of those comical, arbitrary dreams; Elfriede woke as if she hadn't stopped thinking about what she'd talked about before. She smiled good morning, immediately sat up in bed.

"What was it that my Charon told you?" she asked.

"He didn't actually tell me anything, he assumed I would have no interest in all that. But he did mention a few things, enough to leave me speechless."

Elfriede rubbed her eyes, stretched and said: "Our minds work in such a strange way when we're asleep. You know, I was half-asleep and I began to think: 'What will we have for breakfast now?' And immediately I told myself: 'Chocolate.' The need I felt to have some chocolate woke me up and I felt you covering me with the spread, but I didn't say anything, because I couldn't stop thinking about how I wanted some chocolate. Can you imagine where I might have had hot chocolate at this hour?"

"I can imagine," I said.

"I think it was . . . Yes, it was called Soria, a small city. We were in a palace, well, hardly a palace; they said it had been the home of the bishop, and in the morning a very thin, authoritarian little old woman would bring me a tray with hot chocolate. I'd want to get up and drink it at the table and she'd say: 'No, breakfast chocolate in bed.' She'd give me very long lectures. But I did manage to understand that, because the people who lived in the house before, the bad ones, drank their chocolate in bed, we, the good ones, also had the right to drink it there."

I had sat down beside Elfriede, engrossed in her story. I saw I was going hear exact, truthful information from her about those horrendous moments, that once again I was in the presence of a true witness of that dreadful event, and her words were awakening in me something that has nothing to do with curiosity. I did not want to interrupt her with questions, I needed her tale to keep unfolding before me, and Elfriede kept telling it in great detail, very justly and with perfect understanding. So much so that I could not help feeling surprised by how incisive her judgments were, and a question burst from me spontaneously: "And you, what were you doing there?"

Elfriede looked at me intensely; a slight smile tinged with irony passed over her lips, and she gave me an impenetrable stare, maintaining it for a couple of seconds.

"What was I doing there?" She leaped up from the bed and wrapped herself in the bathrobe. "Well, let's go see if Lily has any chocolate."

I tried to stop her and force her to tell me. I knew that what she was going to tell me was something very important, I also knew it was what I did not want to know and that my duty was to keep asking questions. But Elfriede struggled, slid from my hands, and started to rummage around in the dining room cupboard.

"We'll see, we'll see if I tell you," she said. "If the chocolate inspires me to."

Finally, she found a package of cocoa in the cupboard.

"Here it is, now everything's solved."

She unwrapped the cocoa, opened a can of condensed milk and poured almost all the cocoa into it.

"To thicken it," she said, "because that chocolate was thick."

The bitter cocoa, blended with the burning sweetness of the condensed milk, tasted delicious. Elfriede cut a few slices of pound cake, which she then divided into long pieces.

"You have to eat it moistened like this," she said. "You can't eat this without dunking it in the chocolate."

The best thing was to keep on playing the game. She hadn't given in to my questions, but one memory would probably lead to another.

"You know, the old woman was so domineering, that once when I broke off a little piece of cake and ate it dry, she grabbed the hand holding the other piece, dunked the cake in the cup, with my hand in hers, and raised it to my mouth. She was almost shouting at me: 'Open your mouth, open your mouth. That's how you eat it, that's how it's good.' Of course, since I hardly understood her, she thought she had to treat me like a little girl."

I waited silently for her to continue. That episode didn't seem to reveal any decisive event, but Elfriede took profound pleasure in telling about it, because the entire tale was charged with something more serious and vital than it seemed.

"How old would she have been? I don't know, but more than fifty"; she continued to think about the old woman. "And she was very strong and very active. If you could have seen her; sometimes she seemed like a man to me. I wore wool suits there, which was natural, with riding pants, but my lingerie was the same as always. Well, I assure you when the old woman saw me in my nightgown, she could not take her eyes off of me. And you know something?" Elfriede covered her mouth with her napkin to hold back a burst of laughter. "I used to flirt with the old woman. I knew she was there, standing beside the bed as I ate my breakfast, so she could see me; and I let her see. Once I put on a very transparent nightgown, with the whole yoke made of Valentian lace, and I walked around the room like that, pretending to be searching for something. You can't imagine how she looked at me. Isn't that odd?"

"Yes and no," I said; "you tell it so realistically I seem to be seeing it, and I understand it."

"One day she tried to explain something to me that I didn't comprehend completely. I had my luggage more or less unpacked, and there were silk garments strewn on top of the furniture, toiletries too—bottles of cologne and things like that. She started to look everything over with the approving gesture of an inspector who's satisfied with what he sees, and she said something to me like *the ones before*, the bad ones, had all those things, and it was acceptable for us to have them too. I think that when she looked at me she was looking at my breasts through the lace, looking me over from head to toe, and at the same time she was thinking that it was acceptable for me to have all those things. Although, I don't know whether what she was thinking was that it was acceptable for them to have me; as if I were an object they owned. Besides . . . , no, that you can't understand."

"What can't I understand? For what reason?"

"Because . . . because you were sound asleep."

"Oh, Elfriede, please, I'm wide awake now."

"So am I, and nevertheless I seem to get delirious when I recall all that. It was something as senseless as those early-morning things from before. And it was powerful in the same way."

A new silence and finally she began to tell, very systematically in order to temper things.

"I'd say to myself: This skinny woman dressed in black like a nun should be scandalized to see me like this, and she's not, she's definitely not scandalized. She looks at me, and it's not curiosity to see what I'm like, because she already saw that the first day and she keeps coming and staying here for the same purpose. Maybe she was a lesbian when she was young, I thought, and I came to the conclusion that she wasn't. There was no malice in the way she looked at me, none of the mischievousness immodesty usually elicits from country people; she looked at me the same way you look at something to judge its value. And I liked being judged by her. I found it more satisfying than looking at myself in the mirror. I would happily have asked her: how do you think I look? if that had been necessary. I knew she thought I looked very good and this consoled me, it gave me courage to keep on. Regardless of what judgment she made, the fact that she looked at me kept me fit, because she had such wonderful eyes. You may or may not believe this: they were just like yours."

That left me breathless, and I took my head in both hands. Elfriede smiled a little, as if she were thinking: "Well, now it's been said," and she prepared to soften it with a logical explanation.

"I don't know how to explain it to you, it must have something to do with race," she said, "something familial, apart from color and shape, something like style, like an intimate characteristic. That woman was like one of your relatives, like you yourself, converted into an old peasant woman. Do you understand? An apparition."

"I wish I could laugh," I said, "because there's something comical about it, but it's affected me too deeply."

"You think it's comical an old peasant woman caused me to think of you? I wonder what you'd say if I told you the things that have made me laugh sometimes!"

"Tell them, for heaven's sake!"

"Those are the hardest things to tell, because they were all very fleeting. If I told you a bird or some other creature had made me recall you, it wouldn't be anything unusual, because we all resemble some creature. But the thing is, sometimes I'd see your profile or your head from behind, the back of your neck or your ears, in an ordinary object. I don't know, it happened to me so many, many times it's impossible to recall, but one of those times lasted so long I've never forgotten it. Just imagine! One day when I was sharpening a pencil with a penknife, after I'd shaved off a little bit, I stopped, as if I were electrified; there was an enormous resemblance to you. I don't know what personal detail, I think it was more a question of your whole person. I don't know! The proportion, something indefinable. The fact is, I kept the pencil and never sharpened it again because, if I'd shaved off any more, I would have lost everything. That way, just the way it was, it was perfect and I had it in my desk drawer for years."

I tried to say something, but she refused to be interrupted.

"No, that was nothing," she said, "there was something else even more shocking: suddenly I was what looked like you. I'd use one of your movements as I moved my hand, I'd say something with your tone of voice, with your way of emphasizing the expressive intent of words, making it more charged. I think people they used to call possessed must have experienced something similar. Because my will played no role in this. Sometimes I tried to provoke it by making an effort to recall a particular detail or a particular gesture and attempting to repeat it; that was useless, and it lacked even the least bit of emotion. But when it happened on its own, there was a flash."

I think I've faithfully reproduced the way Elfriede was expressing her feelings at that moment; she was that precise and intense. Her command of Spanish and French was recent but perfect, partly because of natural aptitude, partly because of diligent study. The chief thing is, she could talk for hours without ever starting to run out of vocabulary. From time to time, she made small mistakes that seemed funny, but I don't note them here because they aren't important. But just as I remember in complete detail what Elfriede said, I feel absolutely lost if I try to say something about what I was saying or thinking during that same time. As for what I was saying and doing, I don't know; I suppose I acted like an imbecile. As for what I was thinking and feeling . . . Since I'm not vain, since I lack even the root of that organ called vanity, in other words, since I'm entirely deaf and dumb in this regard, the only thing that occurred to me to think was: "What a shame, all that wealth wasted!" But my gratitude was so profound I prayed to heaven to inspire some gesture, some phrase that would not seem a ridiculous payment. I chose not to pay with words, but caresses are brief when they spring from emotion, when the senses are supersaturated, and immediately they lead to words, once again. I think I began to tell her that the things she'd been telling me, although they may have been able to make her laugh and although I'd found them somewhat comical, were like phenomena of the poetic universe—linkings, secret liaisons between certain ideas and certain affections: pure mysticism. And I added: "I experience things more stupidly; I don't have as much imagination."

"You don't have as much imagination!" she exclaimed. "But I learned all that from you. I've not learned to feel it, that's just the way I am; but I've learned to understand it, to analyze it. Before I knew you none of it would ever have occurred to me."

She looked at me, moving her head a little, as if she were facing something hopeless, and she said: "You don't realize how much you can influence another person. No, you don't realize it at all."

"Come on!" I tried to refuse the flattery in her words. "Those impressions, those evocations of my personality or my accent, occurred to you when you got to Spain, because there you found a thousand real things that could suggest them."

Elfriede said nothing; she got up, took my face in both hands, moved her face toward mine until our noses were almost touching, and right there, half a centimeter from my mouth, she said, her voice soft but cracking: "Idiot!"

Then, she let go of my head as if it were something that would fall to the ground, walked toward the door, opened it, and started to run beneath the pergola.

I ran after her. The sun was already about to reach the tops of the willows, but under the pergola it was shady and cool, almost odorless; the honeysuckle was cold, it was not yet emitting its intense perfume, and you could hardly smell it, in the same way I could hardly taste the drops of water on Elfriede's cheeks.

After much pleading and a bit of struggle, I finally said to her: "I think you were right when you spoke to me on the phone: maybe I do like to ask what I already know."

"Ah! Now that's more reasonable."

"Well, it's not that I like to, it's that I need to ask to be sure that I know."

"Yes, I understand," Elfriede said. "But it takes you so long!"

"Then you talk, if you want us to move faster."

She thought for a minute, searching for the place to start, and said: "*Bitte, könnte ich mit Herrn Lara sprechen?* Do you recall that phrase?"

"Oh, yes! How could I not recall it?"

"For me that phrase was the 'Open sesame.' But I'll behave myself and start from the beginning. I left the ballet and married Tom. During the telephone conversation, he was marvelous; before letting me say, 'Hello, Tom,' he reminded me of his proposal of marriage, and I told him that was exactly what I'd called about. His check arrived by wire. I was afraid the director would refuse to cancel my contract, but when I got back to the hotel and saw that you'd disappeared, I had the courage to do anything. And of course, the director was ready to embrace me when he saw I was ready to leave the company. Then for years there was nothing worth telling. Tom, as you've seen, is wonderful."

"That's the worst thing about it," I said, feeling truly devastated.

"Yes, that's the worst thing about it," Elfriede repeated, somewhat pensively. "But what do you expect? It's life, it's destiny. Well, in those first years I tried to give him the happiness he hoped for. It was hard for me, I assure you. I thought that everything in the past, even if it didn't vanish, would remain discreetly in the realm of memory. Of course I knew I would find you, and my whole life was arranged for that. The happiness I devised I tended like a flower, so one day you would see it and interpret it as *my* happiness. Because it was not happiness, but . . . comfort, leisure, frivolous, monotonous entertainment, like stagnant water. Clean, but stagnant. Unbearably clean! I spent three years sunk in all that, until the war broke out in Spain."

"And?"

Elfriede couldn't answer for a long time. She looked at me with a different gaze, you could see she was thinking about something quite unusual. There was anguish and skepticism in that gaze, as if she longed to ask me something but feared my response. Such torture in those times of pregnant silence! Two pairs of eyes devouring each other . . . thinking they're devouring each other and don't touch. Well, they touch visually, but a human eye is not an optical instrument. Reflected in my retina were two limpid, light blue eyes with their pink lids in the shadow of their large superciliary arches and, deep in those eyes, my own hard, dark eyes were no doubt mirrored. But was what our eyes wanted to say comprehensible? There was such an abyss between them! There, on the opposite bank, stood Elfriede, waving and shouting at the top of her lungs, and I was here, on this bank, silent. The distance was immense, even though it measured little more than ten centimeters, and that bottomless abyss split the world into two halves.

What I'm saying here is proof of what I say, because while she stood there on the opposite bank, clinging to her anguish and, one could say, absorbing that anguish from my image or confronting it with her own, I was lost in this digression and, besides, I was consumed with impatience to learn the outcome of that situation, to hear in logical language what her eyes were trying to say.

"How could you not know what that means!" Elfriede finally exclaimed.

"What what means?"

"That: *the war broke out.*"

"Well, no, I don't know. And the truth is I don't regret it. I'm glad that the virus didn't reach my country, although my attitude may seem selfish."

"Oh, no!" she interrupted me. "I wasn't talking about that. I'm not sorry you didn't take part in the war, quite the contrary. I meant you don't know what its breaking out was like. Look, I don't know how to tell you, I think everyone wages his own war. Even if in the end everyone agrees, because the outbreak brings solidarity. No, there's no point; you need to have experienced it."

"Why don't you tell me how you experienced it?" I asked, sincerely interested.

"Because I don't know how. Nothing occurs to me but silly details that seem to come out of a newspaper report, so I discard them; to tell about that, I say to myself, leads to nowhere. But then I think: if I don't tell about it, things are entirely different."

"Tell everything: what you ate that day, what shoes you were wearing . . ."

"Yes, that's how it has to be told, because everything occurred in the most insignificant way. Imagine what it's like to go somewhere so you can hear the news on the radio, well, to have to go to a house where people know they can go to hear the news on the radio and talk about politics. And this happens in an infinitely boring Romanian painter's studio. Imagine what it's like to go because you've gotten into the habit of going, because you've picked up the commitment to go often—without any great friendship, without any kind of interest, simply because going there is the same as going anywhere else. And you arrive, and everything starts happening like always, a little more agitated, a little noisier than usual. And you start to think: 'Why should they be shouting so much? Why not talk about something more amusing?' And not even wanting to hear, hear that something's broken out—war or revolution . . . And, presto! All that idea has to do is pass through your head, and you're swept up in the current.

"I don't know, I don't know how to explain to you the transformation in my feelings," Elfriede continued, her breathing agitated from the effort of dredging up things buried so deeply. "When we got there, Frantz, the owner of the house, was commenting on what had happened, and I was seized with terror as if the lights had blacked out, because I felt sure you'd been inside. You'd told me in Montevideo you were there as a tourist, and I thought you'd probably wound up going back to Spain. I tried to act as if I weren't paying attention, because I was afraid of hearing something that would make me scream or faint, even though my emotional reaction couldn't have made Tom suspect I had cause to feel so upset, since I'd never spoken to him about you. Before we were married I told him I'd had some romantic experiences, and I told him about a few flirtations and flings with boys, boys I knew in school; he didn't attach the least importance to any of it. Sometimes my conscience would caution me that I should tell him, but I could never do that, not because I was afraid he wouldn't forgive me but because I saw that to tell him would be to reveal a world to him. A world to which he could never gain entry. More than a fear of making him suffer, what I felt was a sort of scruple about not fracturing his innocence. Yes, I was afraid of ruining him, afraid that afterward he wouldn't know how to continue being himself. So I'd chosen to remain silent, and that day, at Frantz's house, I was happy I had. If Tom had known something, he would have understood immediately, because he noticed how upset I was. He brought me a whiskey and said, 'You shouldn't take things so hard.' It was at that moment I felt the floodgates opening. Frantz was holding forth against the things that had happened twenty-four hours before on the other continent, the way an eyewitness would tell them, interspersing his tale with harangues and curses. 'The farce is over! Now all those covered mouths will start screaming!' And at that time, even things like that usually made me yawn, I felt he was talking about me, that I was one of those covered mouths, and I nodded at him so effusively he spent the rest of the evening with me."

She looked at me again so anxiously that it was almost as if she were lying in wait, as if she were hoping to surprise something that was denied her. Once again I felt pursued by her silence.

"Tell me, you've really never felt anything similar?" she finally asked.

"No, I worry instead that I shout too much."

"Of course, you live in a well-mannered world here, you don't know what it's like to see that everything can be burned and demolished, that everything can be turned upside down; that this is your one chance."

She was tempted to pause again, but she didn't; she shook her head a little and said: "Well, the details aren't important. At that very moment I made my decision. Frantz was an important organizer and I begged him to include me in one of the things he was organizing. Convincing Tom was a job. He was flatly opposed, which was natural, but little by little I convinced him. It seems impossible that I did, if you think about it very hard, but at that moment it was possible to do everything. There were lots of people operating just as arbitrarily as I was, some of them with more despicable goals—from snobbery, most of them. The fact is that one day I found myself on a plane, among reporters, nurses, and various other unclassifiable figures like myself."

That last sentence Elfriede underlined with an ironic smile, caricaturing her gesture a little, but her smile vanished immediately, turning into a distanced, perplexed expression.

"I don't know why I don't kill you," she said suddenly, absolutely serious.

I burst out laughing and she added: "That's what I should do."

"Why, would you tell me why?"

"Because I once killed myself for you. I stayed there, in Ciudad Lineal. I was one of those people who fell in the Madrid front. The person who got up later, in New York, was someone different."

I hid my bewilderment with a trivial joke, something like "nothing was lost in the change" and, without letting her protest against my frivolousness, I said energetically: "Keep telling, without melodramatic interruptions. Just the thing itself is more than sufficient."

She nodded.

"I *was* going to continue," she said, "precisely because I was going to follow the events in chronological order and, without my being able to help, it a memory of something from later on popped into my head, which is why I came to that ending, one that's not completely un-founded. Well, I was going to tell you how wonderful those first days were and I delved so deep into my memory I touched bottom. They were wonderful because hope is wonderful, but then came the crash, and I don't know how to recall them, I don't know how to tell you how much confidence there was at that moment. Well, I did tell you: it was won-derful. When the plane took off I felt I'd gone into action, I was going to look for you, fearlessly. I'd heard people talk about bombings, fighter planes, and about how crossing the Bay of Biscay could be dangerous if we flew over Spanish waters held by the rebels. None of it made any im-pression on me. All I felt was calm, the certainty of my situation. Then I think we spent two days in Paris, because we had to meet with the people who would arrange for us to get into Spain. Now, when I want to tell you what it was like, I can't recall anything, nothing about what we talked about, or what our plans were, or what we said to all those people, but I assure you I did just as well as anyone else. Right away I assimilated the slogans, the tricky little expressions you had to use, the obligatory ways of showing your support; it was like a language and I learned it right away. But don't think I did it feeling I was play-acting. No, I put my whole heart into it. I said all those things like a person walking along a road who asks everyone she meets: 'How do you get to such and such a place?' or 'How far is it 'til I get there, maybe I'm head-ing in the wrong direction?' I felt I was getting closer and closer, and I hoarded all those details as if they were jewels. I tell you, if I'd gone from the house of one famous designer to the next, assembling a lavish costume for myself, I wouldn't have felt more satisfaction than the satisfaction I derived from outfitting myself with those experiences. Only when we crossed the Pyrenees, with its magnificent landscape, did I have the feeling of crashing against some rocks. Not because the plane might crash, but because there might be a sort of impassable wall. That was the only time I suffered a bit of anxiety. Then, in Barcelona, everything seemed easy to me again.

"A person can't do anything more absurd than go to an unknown country that's in the middle of a war, to look for a person she can't ask about. I wouldn't have uttered your name for anything in the world, but I looked for it in the newspapers, in the dispatches, in people's conversations. I thought I might hear it at any moment, that I might meet you as I turned a corner, as I went into one of the places where we made contact with the committees, most of them made up of men your age and height, wearing odd uniforms, unshaven. I'd say to myself: Who knows what's underneath? Did I look closely enough? Maybe he walked by and I didn't notice? And that's how it was until we got to Soria. We stopped there because they were sending a bus from Madrid to pick us up, and it took ten days. In those days, the old woman was my solace. In those days all I did was study Spanish. Of course I'd made some attempts before, I had some idea of how to pronounce a few names, say a few words, but in those days I mastered it. I assimilated its spirit. Because Spanish has to be spoken the way that old woman spoke it, the way you speak is too refined, and that's not how it is, it's not like that."

"I must tell you again, I'm not Spanish; I'm not going to speak like an old woman from Soria."

"Yes, I understand, and the truth is I can't imagine you speaking like her, but I can imagine, for example, that your mother spoke that way."

"She did speak like that, exactly; you guessed right."

"Well, you see, I wasn't so far from the truth. Well, one day the bus arrived with the interpreter, who was Strugo. He had his claws out as soon as he saw me. He took one look at me and put me in quarantine. Everyone else he greeted with a more than helpful courtesy, offering them his cooperation, promising to concern himself with their comfort and all their affairs; and to me he said, in English, 'How do you do?' standing a meter away, looking at my feet. But as soon as I saw him, I realized who he was, and I resolved to conquer him. All I had to go on in my search was your uncle's name, which I'd not forgotten. When I met that person who, without the least doubt, spoke German, even though he refused to speak it, it seemed to me I later I'd be able to say *Bitte könnte ich mit Herrn Lara sprechen?* to him without needing to dial the number, and he would put me in touch with the person whose face I never saw, but who I spoke to so many times. Well, Strugo was not moved by my tender glances, he had a huge distrust of me. During one of the stops we made on the trip to Madrid, I went up to him, trying to look very naive, and asked him, '*Sprechen sie Deutsch?*' 'Yes,' he answered me, in English. I pretended not to notice and continued to ask him ordinary things in German, and he continued to answer me dryly in English. Then, when we got to Madrid, while he was getting us settled at the hotel, the next day, when he came to get us early in the morning, I adopted the system of speaking to him in both languages. I'd start a paragraph in English and in a little while, as if I didn't have enough vocabulary, I would continue in German and then, as if I realized I shouldn't continue, I'd return to English. My hope was that, once it had been suggested to him, he would fall into the mixture, but there was to be none of that because he would not let himself get caught. I was doing it to create a group somewhat apart from the others, to find a chance to talk about personal things. But all I managed to do was get him to interrogate me relentlessly. He resolved to find out why I was there, what connections I had with the leftist parties, what I knew about the matters being discussed in Spain, what my ideas were about social problems. I was marvelously clever, but I saw I wasn't going to be able to keep up the game. One day, when they took us to see some building or other that had been seized, I got him a little aside and prompted him to start up with his investigations. We were speaking in English, and he asked me one of those unexpected questions, to see where I was coming from, and then—I recall we were in the cloister, the other people in our group had gone ahead with a Spaniard who spoke English—, without answering him, I sat down on a bench and motioned for him to sit beside me and, for the first time, he let himself be influenced. He sat down beside me. I looked him squarely in the eyes and said to him in German, with a familiar, intimate tone: 'Don't tire yourself out, Strugo, don't tire yourself out. What is it you want to know about me? That I'm a bourgeois woman completely removed from all these things? Well yes, that's what I am. In Berlin, when I was a girl, I was a ballerina, and social problems interested me less than coin collecting. Then I married a more or less wealthy American, and I never felt any curiosity to find out what was going on in the world. One day, though, I heard people talking about the war that had broken out in Spain, and that's all there is.' I paused a little and thought intensely about what had happened to me that day. Thinking about that and, of course, with *that* written on my face, I said to him: 'Do you want me to tell you what happened to me that day? I can't. And I hope, precisely because of that you will understand.' Strugo was conquered. He nodded; he hadn't decided to speak yet, but he was conquered. Then I added, 'Believe me, for me, rather than say something, instead of visiting monuments, it would be much easier to suffer the deprivations the people around here are suffering even if we aren't, or to go where the shooting's taking place. This is something I may have a chance to prove to you.' He'd listened to me with a religious silence and finally he decided to look at me, although rather obliquely, and he smiled with a kind of sweetness, the first time he'd smiled, and he said to me in German, a refined, university German: 'Science proves to us that there is no God; life, that there are miracles.' Well, the group came over, and we didn't talk further, but from that moment his attitude softened and gradually he began to turn into *mon chevalier servant*. For my part, each day I showered him with questions, which I asked at random, to see what might come out in his answers. When the group talked about someone I made him explain who it was, when they talked about a battle site I asked him how many people were there, who they were, what their names were. He answered me condescendingly, thinking I just felt like talking, but I proved to him that he was wrong, repeating to him the next day each name he'd told me, along with the situation and the position associated with each person. 'What a memory!' he'd exclaim. And I would tell him, allowing my gaze to reveal the depth of my soul, 'It's not memory.' He was very intelligent but rather inexperienced in some things, so he would examine the evidence and say: 'I've never seen anything like it!' Finally, after a week, I decided to tell him that a friend in New York had asked me to find out, if I could, the whereabouts of a certain señor Lara. He stood thinking for a moment and I was concentrating with all my will, I assure you, like the people who get down on their knees to pray, and inside I was repeating: *Bitte, könnte ich mit Herrn Lara sprechen*! 'Well I don't know, but we'll ask. It's not a very common name,' Strugo said. Then I added, 'I think he owns some laboratories in . . .' He didn't let me finish. 'But of course! I know him well. Don Andrés Lara.'

"I thought I would fall over.

"'Yes, that's it,' I said to him. I don't have the paper here where I wrote down his name, but I'm sure that's it.'

"Strugo said: 'Since they usually call him don Andrés, the last name by itself didn't ring a bell. An excellent person! Very cooperative.'

"'How lucky' was all I could say, and I began looking for something in my purse, blew my nose, and pretended I was about to sneeze. I didn't know how to explain the change in my expression. Finally I managed to tell him I felt very happy to be able to take back such good news and I would like to speak with him so as to tell my friend.

"'Nothing could be easier,' he said. 'I'll be seeing him in a few days.'

"From that moment I had my idée fixe: 'I must remain calm.' I thought I'd be able to pull it off, but I wasn't entirely sure, and I thought the best thing was to lay the groundwork in case of failure. I redoubled my activity, encouraging and assisting everyone else with their work. If anyone proposed long excursions to dangerous places, I was the first to accept, and I'd set out walking ahead of all the others. I didn't have to pretend; all I did was let people see I was in a state of constant agitation, so no one would be surprised if at any minute I got worse. Meanwhile,

I had my eye on the calendar. We'd been in Spain for twenty days, and the expedition was to last for two months.

"'When are we going to see señor Lara?' I asked Strugo.

"'One of these days,' he told me.

"My impatience was driving me crazy, and in order to settle myself I started to think about how wonderful it was that I'd found the trail so easily. After all, the loss of twenty days was nothing, because I was prepared not to return to New York. I spoke with some members of the Red Cross and laid the groundwork for joining up there at any moment. Finally, Strugo arrived one morning saying that we could go to Ciudad Lineal. He'd managed to get a car, and we went. I couldn't speak one word on the whole trip, and I told Strugo I'd had a bad night. When we arrived, there were two trucks at the door and they were loading. We stopped a few meters away and Strugo said: 'There's don Andrés.'

"He got out of the car and waved at him, without going over. 'Hello, my friend,' your uncle shouted; 'I'll be right with you, as soon as I take care of these boys.'

"Peering from the car window, I saw him speak to the men loading the trucks, without looking in my direction. 'Can't he feel I'm here,' I said to myself, 'crazy with impatience to talk to him?' I thought about those times when the telephone rings, and we sense that a second before we knew it was going to ring, and I recalled the nights in Berlin when you'd decided not go to the hotel for dinner and I'd placed the call to your uncle for you.

"'Can he possibly not sense the ringing, not realize there's someone here shouting: *Bitte, Herr Lara*!?'

"To keep Strugo from noticing my enthusiasm, I said: 'He looks like a nice guy, like one of El Greco's knights.'

"'Oh, yes,' Strugo said, shrugging his shoulders a little as if to say: 'Here they almost all look like that.'

"I thought of saying the same thing, although I saw right away that it was a commonplace, because he wasn't wearing some war drag. Everyone in action wore overalls or bomber jackets; he had a dark navy-blue coat, and he was wearing a white handkerchief or little scarf around his neck, tucked inside. That kind of white ruff made me think of El Greco, aside from the actual resemblance. Well, when the trucks pulled off, I got out of the car and he came toward us, apologizing.

"'I didn't realize that you'd come with a lady,' he said to Strugo.

"Strugo introduced me, and I thought: 'What would he think if I threw my arms around his neck and covered him with kisses?' But I managed to say a few vague things about the mission I'd come on and, then, seeing that Strugo was expecting it, I told him that a Spanish friend in New York had asked me to say hello.

"'Ah, yes!' he said. 'Who is that?'

"I'd already thought of giving him the name of Pablillo Torres, a dancer I'd seen not long before in a nightclub.

"'Torres,' I told him, 'his name is Pablo Torres.'

"Your uncle thought for a moment. 'Well,' he said, 'I don't recall. Has he been in America for a long time?'

"'He's been there for many years,' and I took the risk of saying something I recalled hearing about him. 'He told me, if I'm not mistaken, that he had been a friend of yours in Segovia.'

"'Ah, then it's a friend from my youth,' your uncle said, 'a classmate from high school. It's strange I don't recall, it's comforting when people from so far away still think of you.'

"He turned to Strugo, as if to talk about something they'd already discussed at other times. 'Today has been a good day for me, I had news from the Americas. There was a letter from my nephew.'

"We were still at the door to the laboratory, and a car went by at top speed. I turned to look at it so I'd have my back to them. Take it easy! I thought, he could have another nephew. But he continued. 'Things are going well for him, he has a wonderful little boy and an estancia or something like that. He insists I should go there with them, but I wouldn't consider it. There's no one who could get me to leave here,' he paused, and I was going to turn toward him, thinking I'd calmed down, when he added: 'Santiago would never be able to understand it.'

"And there everything ended."

Elfriede was pale, her eyes had sunken in two bluish pits, but she wanted to continue.

"Have you ever seen in the movies," she said, "how sometimes those guys kill someone with a pistol with a silencer? It always made a horrible impression on me to see one guy aim and the other fall, even though you don't hear any sound. I felt something like that right then, I realized I'd died from a shot no one heard. They kept talking, but I don't know what about, and we went inside, where in one of the corridors a boy was picking up pieces of a glass bottle from the floor; the smell of ether was unbreathable. I said I felt sick and they made a thousand suggestions, but what I wanted was to be alone, and I said the smell of ether had nauseated me. They took me to a bathroom. Strugo was very worried and asked if I would be all right by myself; I barely answered him and closed the door. How long I spent in there I don't know; at some moment I heard them knocking on the door, but I didn't open it or answer them. I heard the knocks as if they were coming from a great distance, until I thought: I better open it, because if I wait any longer I won't be able to. Then I slid the bolt, and when they came in I fainted. I had no idea what happened next. I think I was delirious for hours, but not like people who start to recount their sufferings when they have really a high fever. Afterward I recalled the nightmares I'd had and they were so hellish no one would have understood them even if I'd talked about them.

"You know, it's really curious," Elfriede said, as though she were recalling something inexplicable, "the mind either has a terrific mechanism or it's really hypocritical! The next day I had a period of lucidity when my temperature went down, and I didn't spend the time thinking about my drama but predicting that the war was being lost. I saw this with absolute certainty. At that moment Strugo came to see me and I felt that all my anguish was because his cause would fail. I reached out one hand to him and started to cry. The poor man stood there at the head of my bed while I squeezed his hand compulsively, tears streaming down my face, and I thought: I have to tell him something so he goes away, so he gets out in a hurry, because what he's looking for isn't here.

How can he not realize it's not here? I don't know what happened. The nurse intervened, and I was more or less unconscious again until suddenly I saw Tom beside my bed. I felt them putting me in an ambulance and, when I really regained consciousness, I was in a hospital, in New York.

"People can be so unfair and so selfish! Can you imagine, when I found myself in my own home again, saddled with that failure, I began to hate Tom fiercely, as if it were all his fault. But I realized in time. Well, I realized that if I gave in to that hate, if I broke off my relationship with Tom, I would be alone in the world, and I think I would have thrown myself out the window. Then, looking for something that would bind me to him, I invented Nix."

"What! You invented her. She's not yours?"

"Oh, yes, completely mine, I mean, well, you understand."

"Ah! I understand."

I can't describe my emotional state, not to mention my dismay, after hearing Elfriede's tale. What could I say to her? Only something that was almost exactly the truth. We were still sitting on the bench, under the pergola; it had gotten hot because the sun was now very high. My arm around Elfriede's waist, I buried my face in her shoulder.

"It's too much!" I said. "It's totally disproportionate! I don't deserve all that!"

Elfriede threw back her head so I would move away.

"You don't deserve it?" she said. "What modesty! But the truth is, you don't."

She laughed a little and continued. "Whether it's too much or it's out of proportion, I couldn't say, because cause and effect don't always correspond. But what you said about not deserving it must be accurate, because you didn't have it. I didn't find you and you didn't find me. Maybe it's because the one you deserve is the other one, the one from New York."

Her tone was a little resentful and I didn't want to let her take revenge so easily.

"But this one fulfills all my ambitions!" I said.

She straightened her neck and, without turning her face toward me, looked at me obliquely.

"Oh, don't be so sure! You don't know her," she said.

It frightened me that this might be true, but I treated it as a joke.

"I don't want to know her," I said, trying to immobilize her in my arms. "Well, without using archaic language, what I want, to put it bluntly . . ."

She cut me off: "No, no, no. First I have to introduce you to her. There's still the epilogue."

I stood up from the bench, took her by the wrists, and dragged her into the house. She defended herself, and it was impossible for me to get her to go beyond the vestibule. We fought, and I tried to turn the heightened state of my nerves into a game. I can't say I wasn't moved; I was, tremendously, but not moved in the way Elfriede wanted. In my agitation, I was so carried away I'd lost all sense of my bodily actions— in fact, at that moment I would have been capable of any stupidity—; at the same time, I was conscious, superconscious, aware that the intensity of my feelings for her was not adequate.

But that slip lasted less than two seconds, because the weight of Elfriede in my arms brought me back to reality. As we struggled, the large oak chest was pushing into her curves, throwing her off balance. I experienced a moment of terror when I saw that if I were incapable of supporting her she would fall backwards against that piece of furniture. And my desire to fall on her was so great it prevented me from estimating my strength accurately. When we were both at a forty-five-degree angle, I cushioned her head with my hand so she wouldn't be struck on the back of the neck; my knuckles collided with the wood and my pain assured me I'd acted opportunely. But my pain didn't diminish the pleasure of our brutal collision. Her thoracic cavity yielded beneath my weight, and I thought: "I'll have the one I want. Not the one I might deserve; the one, the only one . . ." But at that moment something horrendous happened: the phone started to ring just half a meter from us.

Why describe such a deplorable situation? I can't help mentioning it because the day ended there. Elfriede started. She lowered her voice unnecessarily, and said: "There's no need to answer!"

I wanted to overcome the mishap.

"No need to listen," I said. But the phone kept ringing.

"We can't take it off the hook," Elfriede responded, "because there's no one in this house. Understand? I'm with Lily at her father-in-law's estancia."

I sat down on the chest beside Elfriede, and we stayed like that for while without speaking, looking at the beast-like black thing vibrating obstinately. "There's no one in this house," I kept telling myself. "Maybe it's true."

When the telephone stopped ringing, it took us a while to get used to the silence, to feel confident again that we were alone. Out of pure stubbornness, I tried to continue our game, but in the dining room another admonishing voice chimed out, one stroke and another and another . . .

"I think that was twelve," Elfriede said.

And it was twelve. Then I remembered that I should have been in the capital at eleven, and I realized I was on an island in the delta.

I wanted to leave immediately, but that would have meant swimming. We had to row to the wharf and Elfriede had to bring the boat back, so I had to wait until she got dressed, and it was impossible to convince her I could go back without eating; she made me wolf down a few of the things left on the table. Finally, I was in the boat and the trip seemed eternal to me. I got here as fast I could, but it was close to four when I reached my office.

I said the day had ended, but no, it hadn't ended. Certainly, the important events were over. I was now the owner of Elfriede's past and, whether I liked it or not, my own past was tinged with its hue. In the last twenty-four hours—I'd left Buenos Aires the day before at six o'clock—the deepest deposits of my history, the sediment of my superficial actions had been set churning, and I now held in my hand a concentrated residue not devoid of bitterness.

Well, even though the really affecting things ended in El Tigre, I can't help recalling an insignificant detail that occurred when I got home. *A detail that occurred?* Yes; if I don't say it *occurred* and it too was *an event*, I'll cease to be who I am.

On the trip back I finished my pack of cigarettes, and before coming inside the house I went into the small store across the street. The little old man was there as always, engrossed in his reading; I asked for Chesterfields. He responded without raising his head.

"There are none left."

But he must have recognized my voice because, after answering me automatically, he looked at me. "Wait, wait a minute," he said. "I think I have a carton of them I haven't opened."

He put down his book; it was hard to turn around in his tiny lean-to, and he moved his chair to the shelf at the back so he could stand on the chair. This was too much acrobatics for him, though, not because of his years, which were surely fewer than it seemed, but because he has a bad leg, maybe an artificial one. I saw him hesitate.

"Don't you get up there," I said; "I can reach them." I went in through the doorway the lean-to parasitizes and took down the carton.

While he unwrapped it and meticulously counted the change, because I'd given him a large bill, it occurred to me to browse through his library, which was not in public view but under the counter. He watched me out of the corner of his eye. "They're all risqué, novelas galantes," he said with a little smile that suggested an apology but also a confidence.

I leafed through a couple of them and smiled back at him as my only comment. He thanked me for my smile by redoubling his own and handed me the pack of Chesterfields with a little bow and a "ha, ha, ha," which made his smile spread, allowing me see a abyss whose boundaries were marked by three lone teeth, as, from that abyss, burst a puff of cigar smoke, his Italian tobacco black as coal.

I came up to the office. There were three people waiting for me. Fortunately, Gálvez already knew what they wanted, and I could say *yes* or *no*, according to his indications, sign something where Gálvez rested his finger, say good-bye to someone because Gálvez made me notice there was someone standing in front of me, and he wanted to leave. Meanwhile, within myself, I was developing the microfilm.

Its impact was repulsive at first, but later, under the lens of analysis, the phenomenon one very much worth contemplating.

I was definitely not in the little lean-to more than five minutes, and I definitely held in my hands no more than two novels, which I opened by chance, and I certainly looked at the old man only at the moment he handed me the cigarettes, just the time it took to say "thank you." But all the old-world erotica filling his library rose before me *inside the abyss*.

Is this clear? No.

The cave of oriental tales, the viscous walls, the blackness, and under the stone slab, the room filled with light and studded with rubies . . . Perhaps . . . But not if what smiles is the cave . . . No, that's not it.

What it is, to be precise, is the secret of the most intimate relation, the tightest clasp: the mind and the senses.

For years I've seen him in the tiny lean-to, his nose buried in a book. He's an emigrant, from Asturias perhaps, blond man and half-disabled, hurled over here by some change in his luck. I buy my cigarettes from him almost every day, and I've stopped in front of his hole on the most disparate occasions, sometimes taking him from his reading. I recall having spoken to him the day of Damián's death, I also recall that from time to time, when I haven't had the right change, he refused to let me leave without cigarettes. So, for me, he was important in the neighborhood; I knew he was there, but I didn't know that on winter days when I'd see him sitting inside, numb with cold, a greasy scarf around his neck, and his nose dripping over his yellow beard, I didn't know that at the very same moment he was finding comfort in the arms of courtesans. Because his novels were novelas *galantes*, in other words, they were not without a certain refinement. In the little bit I saw—as you'd guess, there were illustrations—I glimpsed women in lascivious positions on satin-covered couches, in rooms with mirrors on the walls and heavy curtains on the doors. The whole scenario of those cheap editions from fifty years ago. And the old man strolled there, caressing those breasts, breathing the heavy perfumes of those chambers.

But who was the old man strolling there? I mean, with what body did he stroll through those adventures? Certainly the body he had when he was twenty, the one now was nothing but the vibration of pleasure clamoring in the desert.

I know that many people would probably define the old man as an escapist who takes refuge in irreality so as not to confront the truth of his misery. And because I've stopped here to contemplate him, and I waste my time digressing about his case, they would also call *me* an escapist. But I'm definitely not, because I'm not escaping from reality but running after a reality that's trying to escape.

At such a serious moment of my life, when I'm making an attempt on the very axis of my soul, with the obstinacy of a man sawing at the branch he's sitting on, at such a moment I lose myself in the consideration of lustful daydreams warming the mind of a frozen old man. I'm not sorry, and I'm not going to leave this for a better time. It's appeared now, and now is when I must consider it. I won't retract the astrological importance that I've granted to the conjunctions that occur at certain moments. I believe in their constellations, and I try to decipher them, because when I see them sparkle I know positively that they're a sign.

When the old man smiled at me and let me see his viscous cavern, that was when I saw his pleasure gleaming deep inside there as he lifted the stone slab. I know that in oriental legend this room is the soul, but human language can only describe its beauty to us as light shining on pearls and rubies. It's definitely not very difficult to conceive of the soul, but this is about something different. What that something different is called, I don't know. I don't know what to call the units of life that don't age, to the will that never tires. Eternity, which knows that it's eternal, aspires to the liberating orgasm, which is its word, and pleasure sparkles like a stream of light in the cave blackened by death.

Well, that constellation accompanied me the whole evening, and I watched it sink behind the mountains, but I knew its influence would make itself felt more than once.

After writing all night until dawn, today I feel nauseated by everything, but onward! now that I've set out to capture the *vera efigie* of the everyday.

This afternoon a brief, very brief getaway to El Tigre. No more than two hours, no more than ten words: perfect. I know Elfriede would have preferred to continue exchanging confidences; she was probably hoping to hear mine or hoping to find in me an echo of hers. Even some comment that gave her an idea of how valuable I found her confidences might have been enough. And speaking was precisely what I did not want to do. But neither did I want to disappoint her. Did I succeed in telling her something of what she wanted, without speaking? Did I manage to infuse my actions with the *tone* of what I didn't say? I don't know; I think so. I think the pressure of one's arms can *speak* of a particular thing; I think that in the simple, common, age-old action of two bodies coming together an immense prosodic difference can exist between the moments of *before* and *after* something has been said. In short, that's how it was.

I arrived at Las Murtas after it had already gotten dark, and I regained consciousness as I drove into the garage and saw an unfamiliar car. At the same time I began to hear Francisco and Jorge shouting wildly, which gave me a premonition of what was going on; I couldn't believe it. I would have liked a cup of strong coffee or a whiff of ammonia to sober me up, but there was nothing in the garage except a few cans on a shelf. I picked up the can of turpentine and poured a stream of it onto the workbench; then I wet my hands and wiped them on the shoulders and lapels of my suit.

I made up my mind to go into the house, and before I reached the door I had proof of what I'd suspected: the boys were rejoicing over the arrival of their grandfather. I went in and embraced him.

"Good heavens, you really stink!" he exclaimed.

"Yes," I said, "the turpentine container fell on me. But what brings you here? What's been the change of plans?"

"We'll tell you later; well, they'll tell you, because it seems as though it's been a secret."

Quitina appeared in the hall. She wasn't wearing the mischievous expression she has when she's managed to pull off some feat; her smile was serene, perhaps confident, but not happy. I kissed her on the cheek.

"I have to shower before dinner," I said; "I can't touch anything in this condition. If you don't mind waiting just a moment."

Quitina noticed the smell and agreed without asking for any explanation.

I stood under the shower, enveloped myself in the suds of pine-scented soap, scrubbed myself with a stiff loofa, and managed to erase the smell of turpentine. After letting the water run over me for a while, I sniffed around the steam-filled room and again thought I could smell the scent, which could not be erased. I loaded my toothbrush with toothpaste, brushed hard, and the minty taste lasted for a few seconds, but when I sniffed insistently, despite the taste, I could perceive, it had stayed in my mind. When I got home, I'd imposed on myself an atonement through turpentine, I endured the destructive effect, and any trace of voluptuousness was wiped out. But after the shower, my senses were free of their torment, and they appealed to memory in order to expand again.

We sat down at the table. The questions from both sides were endless. There had been only one plan—the one that had been in my father-in-law's head before he came, although he hadn't divulged it until he'd been thoroughly informed about everything. Since I was the one who had to inform him, I was at least reassured by the idea that, if I had to speak, I'd have something to talk about. But for the moment I was not the one who had to speak: it was Quitina. And Quitina spoke at great length, albeit unenthusiastically. For the second time, she told her father's story, although he was the person who knew it. She told it so I would hear it, but she told it to her father. Would he have noticed this absurdity? I don't know? Could he have been blinded by the love he felt as he listened to her? That would surprise me; he's not one of those people who's blinded by love but one who's all eyes. And the strange thing is that when he listened to her, I didn't think he was able to detect a false bottom in her words, although he glanced at me a couple of times—two brief glances that seemed involuntary and seemed to acknowledge a faux pas on Quitina's part.

What had happened was that on the first of the month Quitina had taken the train for Azul at seven in the morning, as she usually does on the first of every month. She'd gone to do her shopping at Provisión, which was owned by a Spaniard, and to place the large monthly order, which they send her immediately; but when she looked in her purse for the paper where she had everything written down, she didn't find it in the place where she thought she'd put it. The purse was really old; since it was large and cavernous and full of compartments, she hadn't used that purse for ages, but by chance that morning she'd decided to use it. She looked on one side and then the other, put her hand into the countless little pockets and finally pulled out a piece of paper that wasn't the list: it was a thousand-peso bill that had lain in the purse for years.

"I left the storekeeper standing there and went out to the street," Quitina said. "I wanted to spend those pesos at that very moment. Imagine, spending a thousand pesos in Azul at seven in the morning. And the curious thing is I left the store feeling sure I was going to spend them; I had no idea on what, but I was sure. It was really silly; I remembered the story about Martina the little cockroach you used to tell me and how you'd repeat: 'She found a little penny . . .' Because I wanted to spend them all on *myself*, on something I really wished for but didn't have."

Had I heard that tone in Quitina's voice before? Never. It was something like the tone in her voice at the times that voice seemed about to burst as sobs, but now she couldn't be afraid it might diminish or give in to some uncontrolled emotion; now the tension was as great or greater than on those other occasions, but it seemed capable of growing indefinitely without coming to a head.

She continued: "There was a series of coincidences, because usually when I go to do these things I drive the small car and take the boys: Miss Ray almost always comes with us, but that day I didn't have the car because I'd loaned it to Miguel, and I went alone, so I had to wait more than two hours for the train back. That's what made me think I

wanted to spend them by myself, there *by myself,* on something for *me.*"
(Quitina used those three words with the rage and the cruelty of someone who's using rage and cruelty for the first time, someone who's trying them out and finds them fresh and untouched.) "And suddenly: my
brilliant idea! I ran to the central telephone exchange and, after waiting
for an hour and a half, which passed before I knew it, in another twenty
short minutes my pesos had flown."

And as if she were issuing the command for her feat to be met with
a chorus of laughter, Quitina gave a loud laugh; she took her father's
hand and kissed it. We all laughed obediently.

"But you hadn't mentioned anything?" my father-in-law asked.

"No," Quitina said, and she began to explain why, quite simply. "You
remember that at the last minute, precisely when I was about to hang
up, I told you not to come, that it was absurd for you to make that enormous trip just when you'd gotten your own affairs in order? And you
said to me 'I'll be there, I'll be there right away.' And I told you, 'No,
no, don't come. Good-bye.' That was the last thing I said to you and I
was left with the fear you might listen to me and not come. That's why I
didn't say anything: if I'd talked about it, the time until I knew whether
or not you were coming would have seemed much longer. I kept quiet
as though nothing had happened, and I had no reason to assume you
were going to come. But you came."

Having a sharp nose for such things, my father-in-law sensed it would
be better to bring these sentimental subjects to a close.

"Yes," he said, "since I came, let's get to the point," and he looked at
me.

At that moment Jorge yawned—when their grandfather's here, it's impossible to make them eat early—and Francisco looked at him furiously,
thinking: "Now they're going to put us to bed." I pretended not to notice, but Miss Ray appeared as if by magic and, after a brief struggle,
she carried them off.

I began to talk about the business, giving a short summary of things
since the first failure, but I assured him that my various mistakes had

taught me a great deal; they showed me that both extremes were detrimental.

"The first time," I said, "we planted too little, but the second time we planted too much. You understand? Well it isn't that we planted too little the first time; what happened was that the harvest was lousy because the month of October was terrible. Since I'd never seen a plantation in full operation, it seemed to me we could get something from 50 percent of the survivors. But when it came time for production, the result was ludicrous. And so much had been spent on the lab, the machinery, the containers. Well, I'm sure you remember. Then . . ."

I could not continue. Suddenly I recalled the afternoon that Quitina appeared along the slope of the stream, after having bought land the way you buy chocolate bars—easy come, easy go. I remembered our arrival, as we passed through the gate. I could not continue.

I made an ambiguous gesture, as if I were being chased by a silly, amusing memory.

"I don't know what's behind it," I said, "but even things other people find dry and depressing sometimes become delightfully entertaining for me."

My father-in-law smiled as if he understood *too well*.

"That has its advantages and its disadvantages," he said.

"Oh yes, but more of the latter," I said. "I'm aware of that. Just now I was remembering a morning I spent tending to affairs with Javier: *tending to affairs*, something that terrifies people, and it proved to be poetic for us."

Since Quitina already knew the story, I could devote myself exclusively to my father-in-law. I continued: "You know, these days it's a commonplace, almost an obligatory cliché to bad-mouth bureaucratic procedures, visits to ministries and official offices. Not only here, now that the climate's become unbreathable, but all over the world, it's something universal. Javier happened to remember that years ago he met a guy, an agronomic engineer, who was both decent and very competent, one of those people you can go to and ask for advice. He set about tracking the guy down, and it turned out he had an important position in the ministry. We were ready to give up, but we said, who knows? Maybe he doesn't have political ties, and besides, what we're going to ask him is something unrelated to politics. We went there prepared to fight our way through the red tape and, when we got to the department where he worked, our suspicion was confirmed: there were two thugs who spared our lives and let us pass. But as soon as we walked in, the decor changed. The engineering department was located in a stately old house in the Barrio Norte; it had a large front door and to the left of the door there was a sort of vestibule where two old men sat dozing. We asked where we could find an engineer named Conrad, and one of them said: 'Third floor.'

"That baroque architecture gave no hint of a way to get upstairs anywhere.

"The old man pointed: 'There's the elevator.'

"It was so small we didn't see it. We got into a little candy box with mirrors and carvings of rococo garlands. A terrible odor of cockroaches rose from the basement, but at the same time (I don't know if it was wood, which was very old and very fine), there was a scent of perfume, like there is in a brothel, a resemblance that grew stronger as we stepped out onto a large landing with a railing around a large oval opening in the center. Little doors all around, and every wall decorated with countless half louis d'or."

I began to feel bad I was talking about this. Such nonsense! Other times talk would have come naturally. I filled a wine glass to the brim, swallowed the wine in one gulp, like medicine, and continued my tale.

"The department was spread out among the bedrooms and the studies of the house; the pantry served as the office of a man who was something like a custodian and who was very nice to us and said that Conrad the engineer was probably in a meeting, or in the director's office, or maybe somewhere else. He asked another, smaller custodian to go and look for him and gave us a couple of chairs. I was delighted, and I could have sat there for three hours contemplating a coat stand with several jackets hanging on it that was in the center of the room. Implements for making maté and coffee amidst the bottles of seeds or mineral fertilizers and, above all, the most wonderful thing was the paint peeling on the window shutters. A greenish gray paint blistered from the heat and split in some places. The edges twisted outward, exposing the primer, which had definitely been red but now was pink. Well, it was pure Venice, Perugia, somewhere like that.

"Finally the engineer appeared. A great guy. A huge, splendid criollo, with a very well formed head and rather oriental features, despite his name. He greeted Javier very cordially and we started talking about the poppies. Javier asked him a few things about raising them, which were the things we wanted to find out, and he also told Javier that soon they're going to start legislating production and you won't be able to manufacture the stuff on your own. Well, it's important to know this. But what matters is that within five minutes we were talking about poppies. How can I put this? We were immersed in the biography of poppies. Conrad began to talk. Of course, there were a few explanations first, but suddenly he said: 'The tricky moment is when they start to bloom, because, you know?' he asked me, 'the señorita . . . You understand? First she's like a little girl and, as you know, young girls are like foals, they're as hard as boys, but then comes the blossom, and you have to be careful. The least little thing—a hard rain at night followed by sun in the morning—and it's all over.'

"I was listening to him open-mouthed, and he kept talking about the differences between the ones that produce seeds in large, rather flat tomato-shaped pods and the others.

"'The ones I planted are white,' I said, 'perfectly white, like the flowers on broad bean plants.'

"'Yes,' he said, 'exactly, but I'll tell you, I like the pink ones more, the ones with a rather bluish cast. Ah, all of them together in a great expanse, you can't imagine the shades.' Javier interrupted to drag us out of that bucolic ecstasy, but I wouldn't let him. Sprawled in my chair while he dotted the i's, I imagined that dark, paternal man—like one of those statues of the great rivers, stretched out in a field of poppies and surrounded by flower-señoritas."

Right at that moment I saw a maid standing beside me, holding a dish of strawberries. I served myself and, as I was about to pour some cream over them, the perfume blurred my ideas. On any other occasion the same thing would have happened to me. But instead of feeling an irresistible confusion, I would have started to talk about berries beneath snow, dissipating in an evocation of poetic traditions. The wave of voluptuousness that rendered me mute at that moment, was precisely what, at another moment, would have inspired enough silly remarks to keep me going for half an hour. Not only at home, with members of my family, but also in a meeting with four or five grandees, at a UNESCO banquet—supposing I had access to one of those gatherings—, in either one of those places I would have interrupted the conversation about important subjects to speak to the man seated next to me about forest dryads, for example. I would definitely have been capable of making this kind of foolish comment in the House of Lords, in a conclave of cardinals and—I'm certain!—it would have been well received. My success with these things never failed, I was always repaid with a smile of gratitude, like one of those surprises that make the people who receive it exclaim, "Well, well, I certainly never expected this!" Because that was *mine*, the thing that was typical of me, what I usually do and what I do well, because *that* is *me*. And now, there at the table, filled with uncontainable confusion and agitation, who was I? Does this mean that from now on I am not *that* which I was? *That* was a cheerful shamelessness, confident of its lineage, a conscious talent for associating and mixing opportunely—with surprising opportuneness—things that were purely play and sensuality with serious, practical, proper things. No, what was happening now was neither shame nor a feeling of guilt! That guilt feeling overwhelms me on different occasions, and I don't avoid it, I sink into it fully conscious, but never into ideas of this nature. The dreadful thing was the chain created, the inevitable discharge that a simple image or perfume could provoke; the supercharge, the excessive accumulation of suggestions that was surprising to me—not like before, when it was surprising to others—, and it was sending me into the trance of not being, for a moment, in control of myself, in other words, of not being *me myself*.

That entire, highly complicated reflection passed through my mind like a flash of lightning as well as, at the same time, another, conclusive reflection. At the same time I recalled cartoons where the parrot or the fish, in a moment of rage, pulls a machine gun out of the air and goes bang, bang, bang! I was looking at Quitina and her father, who were themselves. "They're *themselves*," I repeated to myself, "and if this salt shaker were a stick of dynamite, right now I'd come out with some blasphemy and set off the dynamite in the middle of the table."

But now I had to keep eating the strawberry, and I chose to talk about something. These incidents from the official world I'd been relating reminded me of an important detail. Mentally, I invoked the monster and the monster came. Then I expanded on his *ideology*, which he'd expounded for me on his last visit. I steered the conversation on this tack, but I could not manage to control my nerves completely. Still confused, and furious about feeling that way, I decided, as a last resort, to translate the confusion directly, to put it, in all its immediacy, in the language— the terms, the situation—of other beings, the way you do when you have in front of you a text in one language and you read it in another.

I don't know if I'm making myself clear; this was hard to do, but it's even harder to narrate it. I was eating and thinking: "Why, this time, am I hiding the pleasure I feel eating strawberries? Why not reveal it through my silly remarks, prompting others to share it?"

I said: "The guy is so greedy it's nauseating, although he's careful not to let it show."

I thought: "It seems as though the dryad's bleeding on the plate, and it's true, she is bleeding, but she's not the only one. Even so, she's delicious."

I said: "I think he's capable of running roughshod over his father; he's fully aware of what it would mean to us to lose the estancia."

I thought: "How can one amputate a desire? Why does it have to prove harmful, infamous to desire something furiously?"

I said: "He can get whatever he likes; he'll probably double his capital in the twinkling of an eye. But he wants this because this is his past; this is what he wanted when he was incapable of anything."

I thought: "This desire, at other times, was not infamous. When it began it was the most innocent thing: it was youth."

I said: "He wants to make up for his childhood, which surely was horrible. Deep down, I understand him."

I thought: "It was horrible then, exactly when the desire had reached its climax, when he was carried along in the inertia of that rapid spinning. Then came the impact, the impossibility."

I said: "I'm sure that even the most ordinary people are governed by such very subtle things, that they kill themselves because of some poetic prompting. Without knowing it, of course, without realizing they're acting because of something from another world, from another time."

I thought: "That's the thing; what I'm doing now is nothing but remove the frustration from that time as if it were a thorn, opening the floodgate against which the current had dashed, where the impact occurred."

The telephone rang. The maid spoke a name to me and asked me if I wanted her to tell him that I was eating; I stood up.

"No, I've finished, I'll go."

It was some worried fellow who said he needed to see me. On any other occasion I would have avoided the appointment, but I felt so liberated by the phone call, I was so grateful to him, that I made the most complicated arrangements in order to give him half an hour two days later.

When I went back to the table I saw that Quitina and her father had kept talking about the same subject.

"Look," he said categorically with a beneficent smile, "I'm going to deal with that young man in person, because you're capable of throwing yourself into his arms if he talks about his childhood."

Since I was feeling calm, I continued the joke: "Oh, there's not the least danger that I'll throw myself into his arms. But if you take him out of my way you'll make my happiness complete."

After I said that, I felt devastated. Why would I have uttered that word? Would they have heard it? In other words, I wondered if they'd heard in it what I was hearing. I didn't dare look at Quitina, but I sensed that her father was going to speak, I heard him take a breath in order to formulate a phrase and I couldn't help looking at him. He'd heard the word exactly the way I'd heard it myself; he was going to respond to it. And he spoke with a toneless voice, a voice that did not seem to be emitted from his mouth but oozed from his forehead.

"What could I want but to make the two of you completely happy! It's all I have left to do in this life."

As if she hadn't heard, Quitina stood up, put an arm around his neck.

"Time for bed," she told him; "you must be tired."

She tugged at him, and when she got him to stand up she was saying: "Let's see if the bed's been made up the way you like it. You've already seen we have a new maid and she's not familiar with your habits."

And so they proceeded to go upstairs.

13 September, at Las Murtas

He told me scornfully, I was capable of throwing myself into his arms, but the fact is, this afternoon the two of them went out together to look over the land, and they came back thoroughly enamored of each other. Good-byes were said with long handshakes and little pats on the back. My father-in-law patted him as if he were a Labrador until he put him into the car. He stood at the door watching him drive off.

"Poor devil," he said.

Was he also going to feel moved? I thought, but immediately he shrugged his shoulders, shook his head, and corrected himself. "The truth is, he's an animal. Fortunately."

Then he informed me: "Tomorrow you and I have lunch at his house. Julieta wants to fete us."

I was dismayed. Luckily, it wasn't necessary to hide my annoyance, because the arrangement wasn't pleasant, but what worried me was the impossibility of notifying Elfriede. She'll call at the office in the morning, and they'll tell her I'm not there, but I can't call her because she won't dare answer the phone; there is no one in that house.

The more I think about the last phrase, the more true it seems to me. And above all, it seems irrefutable when I go there. When I was in the house with Elfriede was when there was no one in it. The telephone resonated in a total void, every action was interrupted, every breath cut off; one became fully aware of being no one. If Tom had suddenly appeared at the door and shot each of us a couple of times, what would have been happening? Nothing: there was no one in that house. I could argue this before the court.

And couldn't the premonition that something like this is going to happen be what's making me certain that I'm no one? No, no. Yes, it can happen and, yes, I have a hunch it will. Sometimes I've felt that history can end with a click! like when you turn out the light. But aside from that, what I feel to the point of obsession is not a fear of dying in a flask of gunfire; if that were the case I wouldn't go. My obsession's not one of fear but terror. What I feel is that I'm living this not-being. I've grafted a piece of my past onto my life, and my time is forking into two branches, one that is and another that is not, although it was. Of course, as then, when it was, it had that hitch, that not coming to be, now . . . now the present is interrupting. But enough of that! The present will be decided tomorrow at Julieta's.

14 September, at Las Murtas

Without my commenting on it; rather, without my comprehending it—that's how it was.

We left around ten, so we had just enough time to arrive precisely on the dot. At one point, when I started to drive quite a bit faster, my father-in-law said to me: "Don't be in such a rush, we have more than enough time."

Since he never complained about people driving too fast, I said to him: "It's obvious you're not anxious to get there and, in fact, I'm not either."

"You could have spared yourself," he answered, "if you'd phoned with some excuse or other."

"Yes, that's true, but it never occurred to me to abandon you."

"I would have preferred that, to tell the truth."

He surprised me, and I looked at him stupefied. Somewhat jokingly, he said: "You clash with him. I can definitely get along with Luisito. I convince him of everything I want because he's sure he's made a great impression on me. But then you appear and you complicate things."

"If only you'd said that! I lost a great chance to desert!"

"Well, I didn't say anything so you wouldn't think I wanted to exclude you."

"But what more could I want!"

Whether with a certain hope or purely in jest, I'm not sure, I continued: "Exclude me, go ahead, exclude me! I'll leave you at the door and make a quick getaway."

"Fine, if that's what you prefer."

"If that's what I prefer? You can tell them I have the measles or I fell out of the car as we were driving along and you didn't notice."

I couldn't believe he was serious. Besides, I was afraid to show too much interest in escaping, because that's not my style, and I might give something away. What did he know about Quitina? That's a question on which I could not—and I cannot!—dwell, because it involves another question that has me confounded: What does Quitina know about me? Why did she call him? The story about the thousand-peso bill . . . I'm definitely sure that's how it happened, exactly how it happened, nevertheless, when he said, "What also could I want but to make the two of you completely happy," his voice was dreadful. I'm sure his voice wasn't innocent.

But I don't want to dwell on this; something different began to catch my attention.

When we were just about there, he said to me: "If you want to disappear, I can tell them you had to continue on to La Plata. Something unavoidable."

"Wonderful!" I said. "Do you think they'll fall for it?"

"What difference does it make?" he said, shrugging his shoulders.

"All right, everything's in your hands. What time should I come back to pick you up?"

"Don't pick me up, if you don't want to. Luisito will take me back," and he corrected himself. "I'll ask Luisito to take me back, he'll be proud as a peacock."

When I was alone in the car, I continued aimlessly along Córdoba for a while. I felt indecisive whether to seize the opportunity they'd offered me through ignorance. It's terrible to witness error, pure error, and not be able to warn the person who's about to err. Since it was evident I couldn't do that, I decided to accept the opportunity. I took the Bajo and was at El Tigre in a flash.

As I stepped into the boat, I told myself: I must keep in mind the idea that I don't have very much time, I must get back immediately. And I savored in advance the haste of our meeting. I decided to exaggerate a little, for fear of a situation's arising like the one I'd foreseen the day before. Things were about to change at any minute, because Tom would soon be back. This might be the last or next-to-the last meeting at Lily's house. A sentimental explanation would give rise to projects, promises. I definitely didn't want to let my stingy dose of words depress me. When I see that look of a hungry child in Elfriede's eyes, something like the following runs through my head, "You think it's too little? I think it's a mere pittance. It makes you mad? It makes me nauseated. But there's nothing I can do about it." And this made me so anxious I felt dizzy. Since we had so little time, I didn't want to spoil it with that kind of scene. A short, quick, intense encounter bestowed on us by chance, nothing more.

Elfriede wasn't expecting me, so I had to rent a boat. This would also make it easier for me on the trip back. Everything turned out just as I planned.

Also, siesta time is an impressive moment. Since it's a time I hate, rather, a time I avoid and try to spend in semi-darkness, it's as unfamiliar to me as dawn is to other people; but today I lived it in all its splendor! Blinding light can be truly mysterious! The atmosphere swarmed with insects, perfume, and sun filtered through the leaves, and I was holding fast, as if to a single speck of consciousness, to my determination to return immediately. Elfriede knew she couldn't prevent that; as soon as I arrived, I told her quickly about the chance occurrence that had let me get away. Even so, she tried to keep me; just as I'd expected, her spirits that day tended to be excessively sentimental. All the dangerous subjects sprang up insistently: "Tom will be back at any moment." "What will we do?" "Will it be possible to live and keep hiding things this way?" I had no answer for any of her questions. All I could do was cover her mouth. My refusal to speak obviously irritated her, but I overwhelmed her so forcefully she wasn't calm enough to think logically, and at least to some extent she could see my exuberance and see it was spontaneous.

I didn't let her keep me more than two hours. When I left, it was probably not much after three; the garden was still teeming and sultry. The tunnel of honeysuckle seemed endless. At one moment, we fell against a post in the pergola, and Elfriede tore her peignoir. It was a shame, that huge rip in the flowered blue silk, but when she walked her knee protruded, like in the tears in the archangels' slit tunics. Her hair had come loose, and she'd lost her belt on the path, so she was barely covered by the sheer blue silk. In the sultriness of that moment she was the very picture of the siesta, of abandon.

All that can be described. One more detail. Why not? But why? Then, came the indescribable.

We were beside the door now, the large oak door with solid hinges and a heavy latch, we said good-bye for the hundredth time. I stepped back from her a little so I could look at her, also for the hundredth time, the way you look at a painting.

Sometimes the movements of two people coincide completely, for example, when two people embrace, and other times one of them makes a gesture that slightly overpowers the other's gesture, although he hadn't foreseen this. It's also possible that when a person has begun to make a gesture, the other person's more forceful gesture cannot arrest it, and what occurs are two simultaneous, unmatched gestures. Two and more than two.

We were beside the door. I leaned back a little to look at her. At that moment Elfriede reached out her hand toward the latch, at that moment I put my arm around her waist again to give her a quick, rather brutal kiss. Elfriede could not stop the movement she'd initiated; the latch lifted easily and, as I pulled her toward me, she pulled on the door. Not only were our two discordant movements simultaneous; on the other side of the door, someone, at the same instant, reached out his hand toward the bell. Someone who stood there inanimately, as if petrified: Strugo.

What happened was the only thing that could have happened: all three of us, without exception, behaved with the greatest clumsiness imaginable. My instinctive reaction was to defend Elfriede, but to defend her by hiding her, denying her presence. I gave her a quick push and stood in front of her, ready to convince that pitiful man he'd been seeing visions. But she refused to be hidden; once again our movements were disparate. "How impertinent!" she shouted at him, consumed by a rush of anger, and then, immediately, there was some interjection in German that I didn't understand. Strugo dropped the hand he'd extended toward the bell, but he didn't blink. I saw that he wanted to leave, that mentally he'd started to run, but he couldn't move. Not a drop of blood was left beneath the skin on his face.

I tried to contain Elfriede's anger, encouraging her to go into the house.

"Please!" I began, but she didn't let me continue. She made me stop with a look that could only be described in romantic terms. The oppressiveness, the lightning flashes, and the darkness of Hades, all at one time. (The crux of this is in the *all at one time*, because I can't tell it all at one time, and when it's told at various times it's no longer what it was.) Elfriede's eyes had retreated deep into two inhumanly blue caves from which she hurled daggers at Strugo. (It's idiotic to write down all these things; they retard, cool the dramatics of the moment. But since I'm not writing with the intention of moving anyone, since the only thing

I want to do is record everything, *absolutely everything*, I can't modify the real event by reducing it to tolerable proportions. I lack a talent for synthesis, to the same degree that I have too much talent for analysis. It's horrible that written language is incapable of conveying the notion of pressure.) I thought, with a kind of ontic terror: How is it possible for the chemical makeup of the human animal to produce something blue? It was a simple surprise, a simple question posed by my blood. Inconceivable! That's something Rilke might have asked. Well, it was a *strangeness* that distanced me, cast me to one side, changed me from a protagonist to a spectator.

Then I saw that Elfriede was trying to make herself presentable, adjusting her robe with her customary gestures. She couldn't put her hair up, but she tossed it back, shaking her head as she moved all the while toward Strugo the specter, lashing him with her sharp words. He did not budge, did not even tremble. With an automatic voice he uttered a name: "Herrn Weninger."

Immediately he corrected himself: "Señor Weninger," he said.

But Elfriede did not stop talking. It was impossible for me to understand a single word but, even so, I believe I caught the gist of what she said. I saw—I'll put it like that, since I don't know with which organ I perceived this—that Elfriede was destroying the past, annihilating, assassinating the time of her relations with Strugo—the time of her impotence—, demolishing it, trampling it with her current triumph. But Strugo did not react, he let the barrage of words slide over him as if words were useless; he'd understood sufficiently without them. And without waiting for Elfriede to insert a period or a comma, he spoke again, his voice dead, but his Spanish pronunciation impeccable.

"Señor Weninger is one of my clients. I came to see señor Weninger."

Rigid, unblinking, he turned on his heels and started to walk along the path, at the edge of the water.

Elfriede's behavior was very strange; I've spent hours and hours analyzing the smallest details of everything that happened, and that's been the most difficult thing to understand. When Strugo veered halfway around and vanished, she began to run toward the house, went inside, and slammed the door shut, leaving me outside. I ran after her and got there in time to prevent her from locking the door from inside, as she'd intended. She threw herself on the bed in a fit of tears that was impossible to quench. I tried to caress her but she shouted, completely beside herself, "Leave me alone! Go!" I drew back the hand I'd extended toward her head, with an instinctive motion, as if I were afraid she might bite me. Her weeping was like the howling of a wounded animal that cringes in a corner and fails to recognize its master. There was no way a person could have any effect on such weeping. I decided to stretch out beside her on the bed and wait in silence.

After a while, a while that lasted more than an hour, she began to calm down, and I would have thought she'd fallen asleep if from time to time she hadn't emitted a long sigh. I tried again to caress her hair and once again she said, "Go!" but less angrily, and then she added, her voice almost serene, "Weren't you in a hurry?"

"Yes, I was," I said, "but can I leave you like this?"

"Yes, you can leave me, you can leave me," she said. "It's over now."

I didn't rush off, even so; I wanted to be sure that she'd returned to normal, I wanted to make her use Spanish, and in order to calm her completely I assured her she had nothing to fear with respect to that poor man's discretion. Then she sat up in bed.

"No, I realize that," she replied. "I've nothing to fear from that man."

She got to her feet, reached for her comb and began to pull herself together. She also tried, not to apologize for being angry but to justify her anger by finding some advantage in it.

"Well," she said, with a deep sigh of relief, "at least this way I'm sure he'll never dare come into my presence again."

"But he didn't, Elfriede," I said. "It was a coincidence no one could have predicted."

"I don't know what it was; it makes no difference to me," she said, shaking her head as to expel some remaining bits of what she'd seen.

"All that matters to me is that I never see him again, you understand? Never again have any of that in my presence . . ."

Elfriede's face is so expressive, her reactions so violent and emphatic, that even though she did not complete the sentence, I understood thoroughly. Her reaction had been one of fear, superstitious fear. When Strugo appeared, Elfriede felt overpowered by terror, as if she'd gone back in time. Her brutal behavior, so cruel as to be indescribable, was a case of insurmountable fear. It was as if to shout No! No! at the ghost from that time.

I left her lying down in the half-lit room, and as I went out and put my hand on the cursed latch, I thought: "The truth is, the time prevailing here is the former one. That time, all the way back to its most distant past, is the one I've exorcised, the one I've been living all these past days. That time and no other."

I came home, leaving all those things there. Well, no, I couldn't leave them, but I came home and, when I got here, I found that we have, among other things, an attorney. We have leagues of land, cultivated fields, plans for construction.

I asked to be excluded, and I was excluded, but only from the agreements and brilliant decisions made by my father-in-law. The effects of those decisions will fall upon me, in the form of a terrific load of responsibility and work. That's good. Better than good! Marvelous!

We have an attorney, because "he's an animal, fortunately," and since he hadn't formalized his acquisition of the Arcaya lots, my father-in-law suggested to him that he become our attorney, convincing him his collaboration was very valuable to us, whereas his mother's capital was something we didn't need at all. Then, he worked on convincing him to cede the parcels to us as a whole and, as soon as he had him slightly convinced, that very afternoon, my father-in-law effected the completely legal purchase of the lots. It was definitely a very profitable day.

Naturally, the monster now regrets he mentioned withdrawing the capital; he would like to continue to play a role in the business, but my father-in-law told him that, as our attorney . . .

All this my father-in-law related to us while we were eating, and I said that, in any case, it was unpleasant to be tied to him in even the least little way.

"Tied to him?" my father-in-law said. "I'll get rid of him as soon as I feel like it."

To that I had no objection.

We also have an almost-engineer, because despite our grandiose plans, we still have plenty of land, to the point where we seem to have a bit too much. So, after deciding "this goes here, that goes there," my father-in-law said before we know it Miguel will have finished his studies and then he'll be able to do what he wants. He also said, without attaching much importance to it, that it would be a good thing if Miguel were to take charge of our affairs, because you should have a technician you can trust completely.

Yes, everything's fine. I asked to be excluded and I don't think they'll really exclude me as much as they should. Because I'm neither inept nor unconcerned: everything that's going on at home interests me enormously, and I have no thought of not doing my full share. But deep down, in my heart of hearts, there are other things that interest me more.

This constellation formed by Quitina's father and the monster, our attorney, will work out very well. Yes, that's for certain, but what interests me more, intrigues me, fascinates me with the magnetic force that analysis exerts over me is the constellation itself, in and of itself. The eye never tires of seeing, and I'm nothing but an eye facing the world. Exclude me, disqualify me, but don't deprive me of my nourishment. Let me read, look painstakingly at everything.

Well, the constellation is much less important in my life than the affairs of the estancia, and the affairs of the estancia, as important as they are, aren't one iota as important as other affairs. My life itself, an affair that's become quite gloomy.

But one of my obsessions is increasingly pronounced, certain persons are coming to assume colossal proportions for me, and the relations being created between them strike me as exemplary of something, as if they were keys to understanding the world.

For example, I know how I feel about the monster, I know I've thought about him intensely, I've been careful not to harm him, and I find his ambitions touching. He detests me, and he'd be more than happy to do me in. My father-in-law, though, who despises him as much or more than I do, who doesn't call him "the monster" but "that animal"—Luisito, in public—exerts an authority over him, inspires in him limitless respect and admiration. It seems clear that the monster will never take me as a model, but my father-in-law he will. Does this mean he understands him? No, he knows him as little as he knows me. The only thing he knows about either one of us is that my father-in-law is a man who can make money, and I'm a guy who can lose it. Well, what I'd like to know is, if the monster could hear an explanation like this, would having a real understanding of our respective natures influence him? Even more, not just an understanding of our natures, but an understanding of our intentions with respect to him. What effect would that explanation produce on him? The impossibility of not conducting that test, of experimenting with the different mixtures in order to see what happens is driving me crazy.

Well, this is like trying to solve problems of infinitesimal calculus by counting on your fingers. Precisely, that's definitely my system—my ambition—, to concretize the infinite: to add, subtract, multiply and divide the concrete, infinitely, as if when I say "two and two, four" I use my right hand to grab two and then two more fingers of my left hand. And so on infinitely.

What happens is that sometimes accumulation is not addition; it's more like a discharging. I've said before that when I gaze at a single man, he blocks out the horizon, I'm prevented from seeing Man. Yes, a single man can block one's view of the world, but a single man can also become so large he turns into the world.

My esteem for Strugo hasn't become colossal, not at all, but the consternation I've felt because of his personal catastrophe has led me to consider betrayal on such a grand scale that it reaches beyond Strugo's small context.

This isn't a question of splitting hairs, it's just understanding things when you see them from an unfamiliar angle. Because we're all *accustomed* to knowing that in these matters involving men and women one can betray and be betrayed. And, of course, every man who has an extraordinary woman is *accustomed* to being afraid that someone will take her away from him. So when this happens, the fact that he foresaw it can function as a shock absorber, although shock absorbers can always malfunction. Custom, however, or what could be called prejudice poised to attack, does numb your awareness if you live life adventurously. Since life seems to be going well, your scruples are a sort of surgical skill—precision and asepsis, and nothing more. You think about your victim and believe that you won't harm him if you proceed cautiously and that because of your extreme caution you'll avoid infection, in other words, scandal. Of course, you also think about an accident and possible denunciation. A thousand times I'd imagined that suddenly Tom could turn up, with good reason, with every right, to terminate things by pulling the trigger or, at least, by knocking me around. I'd thought about this so much I was completely *accustomed* to the idea. Nevertheless, when the door opened and that poor man appeared, without any right, but also without any suspicion, having fallen there thanks to some chance task, when I saw how the color drained from him slowly, as the avalanche of words overwhelmed him until he was left without a drop of faith in humanity, then I realized what one human can do with another.

Sentimentalism? Not at all; pure speculation. I've thought for hours and hours about that deplorable situation, not because it had touched my heart but, on the contrary, because my mind can spend a long time weighing the situation, free from extraneous considerations and, above all, exempt from the usual extenuating circumstances. If the one who appeared had been Tom, everything would have been classified proverbially as a question of simple adultery, of an enraged husband and a pair of surprised lovers. But it wasn't like that at all. It was a man going about his business who's dealt a mortal blow as he turns a corner.

Precisely because he's a small man who interests me only slightly, much less than Tom, infinitely less than Elfriede, who was his assassin. That's why I don't tire of having him in my sight, in my thoughts, slit down the center like a guinea pig. That's why this afternoon at El Tigre, when I left, before untying the boat, I stood there for a while looking at the path along which the poor battered man had disappeared. A dark, humid little path between the willows, thick with climbing plants. The water was low, and the smell of mud alternated in gusts with the scent of honeysuckle. Along that path he'd left and, naturally, along that path he'd come. On the island there's a shop that sells beverages, a grocery store, and a few bourgeois houses no doubt kept well stocked with good wines. He had come along that path to visit his clients, on that simple task, as if he were peacefully out for a stroll. Free of memories? Who knows. In any case, if that distant time is alive in him, it will of course be alive on a basis I can't begin to imagine. But I know him well enough to know on what his life centers, so that the image of Elfriede, inserted in that time of struggle and failure, would surely have been an oasis in his thoughts. With all this, he was walking along the little path. Even if he wasn't thinking about it at that moment, he was the man who carried all this within him and the man who, just like me or any other man, walked along at that sultry hour, inhaling the odors from the delta. Would he have felt the enveloping voluptuousness of that place, the sense of germination you inhale all over El Tigre, or was he insulated in his shell of thoughts, having overcome any natural impulse?

I don't know how long I pondered this as I untied the boat and made my departure along the canal. I continue to think about it the way I think about something that can teach me a great deal, I continue to probe his small being, as if he were an open guinea pig, studying the little machine as it runs. I continue to compare him with what I could learn from a being with whom I had a profound relationship: the man I would have to define *as my lover's husband*, and there is no doubt this other being proves more instructive to me. From so much contemplation, that smallness, so foreign to me, ends up seeming enormous, immense, absolute, and I can think of only one thing to say: Behold the Man!

There is only one other man in the world I could study with such total equanimity, without any inclination toward a prior influence or definition, without the least circumstantial or sentimental consideration: me myself. But when I speculate about myself, I rarely see something general that's applicable to everyone; I almost always see the particular—completely naked. And the particular is one person in a given type of persons. A single one, who belongs to a group already distinguished by its very nature, and distinguished, without doubt, as the lowest of the low.

16 September, at Las Murtas

I don't usually deceive myself when I judge moral actions; I always know very well which actions are noble and which are base, even if the latter adjective corresponds only to one of my actions. But if always with complete certainty I know this, that's not always how I feel it. If I begin to reflect here and reach extreme conclusions, I will definitely not soften my judgment about my behavior, although even the harshest sentence might not affect me at all. However, an ordinary situation, perhaps even a trivial one . . . Even though it's just as secret. And that's not to say I remain calm in the face of my own judgments just because the guilt and the sentence stay close to home, and I save my embarrassment solely for times when I'm in the presence of other people. No, in situations no one else knows about, I can sink into devastating confusion. But that's not what's important to me at the moment. I'm talking about this because it's the only thing I can talk about, since it's the only thing I know. I can't even imagine what might have happened at El Tigre. I just hope it's not something serious!

Perhaps the embarrassing thing about the situation is how that forced passivity quashes the masculine being. Masculinity, the quality that involves the most subterranean and primary aspects of human makeup as well as those most elaborate and spiritual, is beyond question in only one way—its inability to be passive. And when one has to be passive!

Well, talking about it like this, in the abstract, leads nowhere. But it was absolutely necessary for me to point out that my shame arose in total solitude. Or almost total; I was not even visible to him, the cause of my embarrassment. To him! Could the use of that pronoun be inappropriate? Could I say to *what*? I don't think I could. The being was so alive!

What transpired is the following. Strugo's appearance occurred on Wednesday. When I left, after Elfriede had calmed down again, I begged her to call me for sure the next morning. I was very worried she might have to spend the night there alone, but what could I do. The next day she didn't call me. I waited until 1:30, in vain. I was getting ready to go out there and see what was happening when my father-in-law appeared in my office with his assistant. They were in the area and thought I might not have eaten lunch yet—which was, in fact, the case. They pulled me away and took me to the Lancaster—naturally, the monster can't eat in ordinary restaurants—and from there we went to Las Murtas. I tried to come up with some pretext so I could stay in Buenos Aires, but it was useless; besides, I suddenly remembered that Elfriede had told me: "If I don't call, don't come."

And I didn't go. But by this morning I'd forgotten that. Once again I waited until noon for her call, and since heard nothing from her, I went out there.

It was more or less the same time as Wednesday. I parked the car near the wharf. When I got to Tres Bocas, I ate something while standing at the bar and rented a boat; I think it was the same one as the day before yesterday. I rowed in the blistering heat, which turned to mist and murmur when I entered the shade of the willows. I arrived quickly, tied the boat to the same post, and leaped to the ground. All in a lighthearted and automatic way and, like always! with all my thoughts focused on the honeysuckle, on the mud rent by the oars. But no sooner did I set foot on the ground, four or five meters from the door, than I heard barking coming from behind it.

I woke up, in other words, I emerged from my contemplation and feared that I'd made some mistake. I looked at the door—without moving, without approaching it, rooted to the spot where I landed—and saw the name in Gothic letters beneath the tuft of climbing plants. The barking persisted. A hoarse bark, although clearly not from a large dog. It was Lily's Skye terrier—the house is filled with his pictures of him.

At times he would stop barking and growl, snorting and sniffing—sure I was still there even though I didn't budge. Underneath the door there was a crack of light and I saw the shadow of the dog's paws moving from one side to the other, I saw him put his nose against the crack from time to time, sniff hard and bark again, full of conviction.

Softly, without leaving the slightest trace on the ground or the branches, I leaped back into the boat, untied it, and glided into the shady canal. The barking grew louder and more indignant.

That was the whole story. I returned with a sense of dreadful impotence, as if I were caught in a lasso, and everything continued to be shameful. My shame turned into something atmospheric; it was everywhere. And here, now, at three in the morning, it's also in the tower. But here it's not a climate anymore; here it has eyes. Here, now, I produce, with my implacable conscience, the face and the name of *him* before whom I feel embarrassed. What judge could hold such authority over me that I wouldn't try to confuse him with specious arguments? Before what intelligence would my word not wield its usual power? Before Puck, none of this could happen. Puck was not judging me according to a code open to debate or mockery but according to an immediate sense of whether or not he smelled betrayal.

Here, now, I see his clochard-like face, and the gray, nearly white whiskers that make him look mature and wise. I know all the phases he's passed through since he was no bigger than a ball of wool. Lily has a photo album in her room, and she's arranged the pictures with all the love of a sterile woman, so through the door I could follow his movements and notice the changes in his expression. And I still see him now: he's here, in front of me, gazing at me with his brown eyes, imposing his presence with the seriousness of his heavy head. With something else too, because if I say that I feel accused by that snouty face and those serious eyes, I caricature his expression in a grotesque way. And that's definitely not what makes Puck an unappealable judge; it's the integrity with which he was living his moment of alarm. Glued to the crack under the door, snorting, and trying to absorb the truth he smelled.

Why is it, since I've never seen him and, therefore, much less touched him, that I seem to feel in my hands the hardness of his muscles and his short, tense paws and the slight quivering beneath his rough skin? I seem to be touching him, because touch, all that gives me a precise idea of his blind clairvoyance—it really *is* that unthinkable. I understand with my hands something that's also intrigued me at other times: the morality of a dog. I feel that agitated body, that heart, accelerating because his nose says there's danger, there's an enemy on the other side of the door, a man who's come stealthily to threaten his beloved beings. His hair stands on end, his muscles tremble, and he lifts his thick upper lip so his canines can go into action as soon as the moment arrives.

Is this talking just to talk? I don't know, but in any case I can't change the subject. I'm still paralyzed like a criminal, my feet immobilized in the muddy bank and my gaze fixed on the crack under the door where Puck's keeping his nose, knowing full well why that's necessary.

17 September, at Las Murtas

Two days without news of Elfriede, no, three, because the day before yesterday the only thing I managed to find out was that she's in Puck's company.

What might have occasioned the Weningers' appearance I can't imagine, but now that there's someone in the house, Elfriede could have used the telephone at any time.

Something else I managed to find out is that Drake hasn't returned yet. I had Gálvez call, and they told him Drake was still away. What can I do? I don't know, but I have to do something. Tomorrow I'll go to El Tigre and conduct a police investigation, far out of reach of Puck's nose.

Today has been a day of truce. Atmospheric lull, humidity; everyone complaining, but not me. Such lulls irritate me in the summer, although I like them when they appear suddenly, alternating with cool days. This is turning out to be a very varied month, and today we've had a lull, like silence on a stave. I say we, because Javier very generously shared the day with me.

When my father-in-law said I'd gone on to La Plata on the day we were invited to Julieta's house, there was some basis for his statement. That very morning, while we were having breakfast, he'd been making plans to update our machinery and all kinds of equipment—he was preparing to present his plans at lunch, which I felt was very opportune, although I told him we'd run into some difficulties when it came to important things.

"Oh, I already know there are problems," he said, "but they can be overcome."

I saw he was thinking: "And I'll be the one who has to overcome them." Then, so he'd see I was going to take action immediately, I telephoned Javier. Right there, at the table. They brought me the phone, and I explained the situation to him. Javier was puzzled.

"Come on, you know I can't do anything with the government."

"Yes, yes I know, but let's see, rack your brains until you come up with any name at all."

"It's impossible, impossible," he repeated, "I have absolutely nothing to do with those people."

I hounded him for a while, made him stretch his memory this way and that, but nothing happened, it didn't work. Left totally without resources, I saw that, in fact, it would have to be my father-in-law who solved the problem. But five minutes later, Javier called back.

"I've got the man! Definitely a good fellow who I met some time ago; I'll tell you how later. He lives in La Plata and I've been told that now he's right in the thick of things. We can go see him."

"Javi, you're a sweetheart!"

"And you're a . . ." This time he didn't say an idiot.

We decided to go and see the man as soon as Javier could get an appointment, and yesterday he called to say they'd agreed to meet in La Plata this afternoon.

Today, first thing in the morning, my father-in-law said to me: "You know, the two of us could go now, in the morning. We'll have lunch in Buenos Aires and then you go off with Javier, and I'll stay to do a little shopping."

"Fine," I said, and that's what we did.

He was clearly in a great hurry to leave, and once we were on the road he said to me: "If we get there before noon, you can call Javier and invite him to have lunch with us at some nice place, where we can talk."

I agreed, understanding the whole game. If at that very moment I hadn't been struck by the memory of last week, when I'd said to him, "Exclude me, go ahead, exclude me!" adopting the tone of a spoiled child, and then the day had ended with the things it did, if all this hadn't come into my head, I would have repeated the joke and told him: "Yes, it's much better if you grown-ups come to an agreement, while I play a little awhile." I can say things like that to my father-in-law, not just because I'm close enough to him, but because he's intelligent enough to enjoy that sort of joke. So for a while I was tempted, but a much more distant memory carried off my last bit of good humor.

I started thinking that my father-in-law had an extraordinary tolerance for my little quirks, that he was a man with a lot of experience in large commercial enterprises who'd spent his entire life transferring, increasing, and multiplying money, but felt neither antipathy nor alarm because I was too clumsy to keep even the money he'd entrusted to me healthy, and I came to the conclusion that he could not feel antipathy toward anything concerning Quitina.

Suddenly I recalled a sentence: "Pancha's a girl completely devoted to pretty things, to luxurious things," and I saw that their criteria coincided in this notion, as in a marital habit. They both considered me a tidbit or a toy for Quitina. For the cold, inhuman mother, I was a reprehensible toy. For the sensual, cheerful, and generous father, a sacred object— Quitina's whim, her pleasure, discovered by her, chosen from among the multiple treasures he always tried to give her . . . And a strange voice: my voice. I definitely can't say it any other way: my own voice, with its characteristic tone, speaking to me as someone else's voice, distant within me: "What are you talking about? Who are you talking about? About Quitina, the child who nearly died crying and ranting? The little girl who played with the tassels on the drapes?"

And the image of Quitina I've never seen, displayed clearly and distinctly before me; her parents' little Quitina. The voice, with my particular tone—sharp, concise, lord and master of the truth: "Who are you talking about? You're the toy of *that* Quitina? No, not that one. Who's the other one then? What's the other one like? A shadow, an undefinable shadow."

My voice, then, answering neither a voice distant nor belonging to someone else, simply my voice, anguished: "I don't know what Quitina's like. I never knew less about a human being. It's not a fragment, a shadowy zone of Quitina I don't know; she's all shadow, I don't know what Quitina's like."

My father-in-law talked animatedly until we reached Buenos Aires. I'm sure I responded to him appropriately, but I couldn't pull myself out of these thoughts until we were seated in the Pedemonte, prepared to wait for Javier. I called him at his office, and he said he'd be there in half an hour. My father-in-law ordered a Cinzano and I asked for a whiskey; with the second drink I managed to achieve some appearance of normality.

Javier arrived, and the grown-ups talked, just as I'd guessed. I took charge of the menu, and we ate very well. Then we went to La Plata in Javier's car and left my car with my father-in-law, agreeing to meet at Herminia's so we could return to Las Murtas at night.

Javier told me that the man in question was a veterinarian from Tucumán, whom he'd defended in a lawsuit the man had had with an estancia owner. The veterinarian had cured his livestock once when there was an epidemic of anthrax, and then the man refused to pay, arguing that the cattle had been saved by a curandero. Since Javier defended him successfully, he was always very appreciative, but they hadn't seen each other in the last few years, and then suddenly one day Javier had seen him turn up in one of those newsreels where important figures are receiving hearty embraces.

"It didn't surprise me," Javier said, "the man has that kind of mind, as you can already imagine, but I promise you, he's a good person. When I called him, he was very happy, and he made me all sorts of offers. He lives in La Plata now because he married a girl from a well-to-do family that I believe owns a lot of property there."

"Well," I said, "it's the best thing that could have happened. If you're on friendly terms with him you lay out the situation and . . ." I didn't continue because Javier shot me a sidelong look, as if to say: "I know where you're headed." I smiled innocently.

We got there at the time they'd agreed on; nevertheless Dr. Salgado wasn't there. The maid who opened the door said he wasn't home, and she was ready to let us leave without an explanation, but his wife came out immediately to offer his apologies. He'd received an urgent call from the zoo, and he had no choice but to go.

"It was something extremely urgent," she said. "My husband was very sorry and he asked me to tell you that you could wait for him if you liked, or you could go to the zoo, if you don't mind."

Javier was in a bit of a huff, and I saw he was going to come out with something unpleasant about minding very much and about dealing with *certain people*, etc. I hastened to speak: "We'll go there, it's no trouble at all for us."

She suggested again that we wait for him, we'd be more comfortable. But I told her we would go and I added: "If you don't think it's a bad time for us to interrupt him when he's working."

"No, no," she said, "my husband went . . . Well, I think it had to do with a delicate subject. So it may take quite a long time. That's why he said for you to wait."

There was no way to find out what the delicate subject was, but I managed to get the situation resolved, and we set out for the zoo.

Javier was not at all happy about going; he suspected we might find some infamous gathering or hateful conspiracy, but when we arrived, the guard at the door, who had already been advised there would be some men looking for Dr. Salgado, prepared to take us to the veterinarian. The guard was also rather mysterious, telling us he didn't know whether the veterinarian would be able to see us right away or if we'd have to wait a while. A long while, perhaps, since it could take a long time.

"But what is it that could take a long time?" Javier asked, feeling extremely uncomfortable.

"Well, it's the monkey, the large one, the orangutan. It seems she's about to give birth. They didn't expect it so soon, but today they noticed she wasn't feeling well, and they called Dr. Salgado immediately."

"Oh! That's great," I couldn't help exclaiming. "We're going to see the baby monkey! Will they let us see it?"

"Well, I don't know. That will be up to the doctor."

"Of course, of course," I answered, completely involved in the situation, and Javier forgot his aversion to the higher-ups in order to curse me for being so frivolous.

The truth was, the veterinarian was a nice fellow; he apologized profusely for not having been at home, and I hurried to tell him it didn't matter and the baby monkey was worth any lapse in formalities.

"Well, for today there is no baby monkey," he said. "No, it was a false alarm. What happened was the monkey caught cold, and she didn't feel well all day. The event won't occur until next week."

I was very disappointed.

"And the monkey," I said, "where is she? Can't we see her?"

"Yes, come over here."

They'd set up a sort of burlap screen so she wouldn't be in a draft and she'd be protected from spectators when the time came. We walked over, and there she was, leaning against the bars, looking for all the world like a pampered invalid. Salgado went up to the cage and took a small lettuce heart from the pocket of his overalls, offering it to her, telling her first she had to hold out her hand, and she did, with the same look of surrender that women have for their doctors. Then she ate the lettuce heart, leaf by leaf, scratched her anus and her vagina thoroughly with one hand while the other rested on her bulging stomach, and she gazed at all of us, happy to see such a crowd. Since she was deprived of her mobility, her android appearance was even more deplorable: she looked like a pregnant old woman.

When we left the orangutan, the director of the zoo, who was with Salgado, began to praise the veterinarian's skill and knowledge, which it wasn't inappropriate for him to do, but the terms, the jargon that's taken hold everywhere, is enough to turn what could be an expression of sympathy or admiration for a colleague into party propaganda. As soon as I heard something like: "These young people are going to give a fresh impetus . . . ," I said to myself: "Divide and conquer," and almost by force I caught the attention of the man about to hold forth, leaving Javier with his friend Salgado.

Divide definitely seemed like a shrewd scheme, but on this occasion, to divide was to save the units, the people. Once we'd formed two pairs of interlocutors, we were what we are. Javier and his former client, a good boy for whom justice had to be done. The director and I, two men who loved animals.

Meanwhile, it had turned dusk. A guard was hovering around us, waiting for the interview to be over.

"It must be closing time," I said. "Don't you think so?"

"They've probably closed already," the director answered, "but it doesn't matter; the guard will open for us."

"What a shame we didn't come a little earlier. I'd like to see the creatures."

"A this hour they're probably all sulking," the director said, and he didn't seem to be in much of a hurry to leave. Then I gradually drifted away from both groups, as if I wanted to be by myself.

It was after seven thirty, the temperature was over eighty degrees, and the garden was now in full bloom.

The ferret was in his little cage, curling up for the night. I went over to the grate; the creature, which is usually so fierce, looked at me and refused to come out even though I banged on the bars insistently. I stuck a little branch through the bars to see if he'd bite it, and the animal opened his jaws, but he lacked the energy to come over. Almost as if he were yawning, he let me see the inside of his little pink mouth, with its perfect set of fearful teeth.

"That one's already gone into a ball," the director said; "now he wants people to leave him in peace."

You could hear the peacock's twilight cries, and an arbor covered with climbing plants teemed with chirps as the swallows fought for a safe place to spend the night, although it was not yet dark: it was still quite easy to make out the colors. There were rosebushes loaded with blossoms, very pale roses, and the air was so still not a single leaf moved. The roses stood out in the darkness as if sleep couldn't touch them, as if they were going to spend the night wide awake, keeping a serene vigil.

The anteater was strolling in its pen, and it seemed stranger, more monstrous than usual. I went closer; the anteater looked so monstrous because she was carrying a little one on her back. The baby was quite large, and it was holding onto the mother's back as she walked with it from one side to the other, as if she were trotting off in retreat. Her small house with its bed of straw was beside her, but she was looking for the path to her old lair.

"That one's as dumb awake as asleep," the director said. And the animal touched the grate with her tube-shaped face, which held two black button-like eyes and widened gradually toward her body, but apparently had no space designated for brains. She stopped for a moment, alarmed, and immediately resumed her little trot.

The seals had already bedded down on the edge of the pool. These were a pair of sea lions stretched out on the rim, with their backs to the water. They weren't resting on their bellies, as all other mammals usually do, more or less curled into a ball, but lying stiffly on their sides, with their feet folded in a way only comparable to the way the bat hangs, cloaked in its wings. The male was perfectly horizontal, as was the female, right behind him on the stone rim, but she was resting her head on his haunch. When I went closer and leaned on the railing, the male opened one eye a little and lifted his upper lip the way a dog does when it's about to growl, but he didn't make any sound—just showed me his teeth—, which were not white and pointed like the ferret's, but yellowish and coarse. Immediately he fell into a stupor, as if his ability to move had been interrupted. The director said: "Your friend's calling us. We've lagged way behind."

"Yes," I said, "but it doesn't matter. Well, it doesn't matter to me, if you're not in a hurry."

"Oh, no; this is a time when I don't have anything to do."

I waved to Javier, who was looking at us from a distance with his saintly patience, and we walked toward them, our pace not breaking the stillness of the air. The good-byes were very friendly.

"Remember," Salgado repeated, "everything that depends on me . . . you can count on it completely."

When we got out to the road, Javier began to give me an account of the business they'd taken care of. He talked and I nodded in agreement, but I probably agreed when I should have disagreed and vice versa.

"Hey, what's wrong with you," Javier said, "are you asleep?"

"No, I was listening to you, but I was somewhere else," I said. "The thing is, I haven't been able to leave there."

"Where?"

"The zoo."

"Well, the only reason we came to the zoo was to speak with Salgado."

"You spoke, I saw."

"But you're not going to tell me it's the first time you've seen the La Plata zoo," Javier said. "And you've surely seen it much better before, because today, when it's past seven thirty, what can you have seen?"

"Well, you know, today I've seen it in a way I never did before. Tell me, have you read *Paradise Lost*?"

"Yes, well, no; only part of it when I was boy."

"Ah, that's too bad," I said. "Neither have I. You're aware that my English is only good enough for books about science, and I never like the translations of such classics. But you know the language well, and I would have liked you to tell me about certain details. You understand? I want to know how Milton *lived*."

"Well," Javier said, cloaking his annoyance in common sense, "I promise you to read it over the vacation and give you a detailed summary, but, for the time being, I think it would be more worthwhile if I told you what I've accomplished with Salgado."

"You're right, you're absolutely right, as always. I'm all ears."

"This man's in a very good position with the government," Javier said.

"I have the impression his wife's family has put him there, but it doesn't make any difference. The thing is, he told me to let him know as soon as we've completed the necessary formalities, so that in his department he . . ."

It was exactly the moment when we were passing through some birch trees. Birches on both sides of the highway. Barely visible now, they were almost submerged in the night, and I thought how it would no longer be possible to make out the roses at the zoo. The guard would have gone and not one human step, not one light would be left. The animals would be cloaked in darkness and in . . . their fear, in their love . . . At that moment the only thing I wanted to do was go back and *speak* with that seal. With the male that had looked at me with one eye. I wanted to go back, to see into the heart of the seal, to know why he was afraid; to watch again how the wave of sleep rose, stronger than fear itself, and conquered him. Because at the moment he looked at me and showed his teeth, the seal was extinguished; he fell into lethargy, as into death. I don't know if at that moment he was afraid of me or of his own surrender. At day's demise, the entire garden was filled with terror. The anteater was trotting around with her baby clinging to her back, running away before night could overtake her. And all this because Adam sinned. If he hadn't sinned, the peacock's cry there on the branch of the cedar tree would not be heartrending, and the arbor would not teem with the sparrows' chirping as they fought over the safe places. At that moment I understood that the seal had looked at me because I was full of guilt. Yes, all human guilt weighs on me, but I want to know the extent to which my guilt includes the seal. Why does the seal have to earn his living with the sweat of his brow? Somehow, this definitely must be stated. The fatigue that overtakes him at sunset is the effect of an unimaginable activity that's engaged him all day. There in a pool that measures eight by ten meters, he's done his job with an honesty man rarely sustains. Man, the guilty, manages to smoke a cigarette, lean against the wall for a little while, and pretend to size things up. For those few minutes, he can rest his muscles. But the seal, who doesn't need to do this, because every day the keeper puts his ration of live fish within reach, the seal rends the pool in all directions, like a torpedo, doing his duty. It's certainly stupid to say that about duty, because the seal doesn't know anything about duties, the seal doesn't know anything about anything. But if he's afraid, he must know something. What could he know? Well, he knows he's edible. That's definitely it! Now I understand why there's no safe, no pantry, and no cupboard where edible things can feel secure. And we're all edible. We all fall into the stupor, the fatigue that won't permit us to defend ourselves but lets us succumb to something stronger and something more vigilant. And the terror gripping that seal has an equally strong hold on the urban jungle. Because people can't be on their guard every minute, they have to succumb sometimes. The stupor I'd just witnessed was both horrible and kind, like a caress of death. Like a preview, but in a gentle dose that has an invigorating effect. In the morning, that little taste of death is nourishing. But it's frightening to enter there. The seal and the unsilenceable swallows, leaping from one side to the other.

Suddenly I realized we were in Barracas.

"Well, that was quick!" I exclaimed.

"Well, that was stupid!" Javier shot back, indignantly.

"I tell you, I had no idea."

"Of course, you had no idea of anything. That's the trouble! You've made me waste forty gallons of gas so you could see the anteater."

"No, don't believe that, the anteater wasn't the most important thing. It's just, I haven't been able to stop trying to imagine what dusk would have been like before sin." Javier didn't say anything, but he gave me a furtive look, one not completely devoid of consternation. "And you got us here in such a hurry you didn't give me time to work the idea out very well."

"Damn. Why didn't you let me know? I would have come a *passo d'uomo*."

"That would have been really super! We'd still be in the birches, and I would have begun the poem. Because I'm going to make a poem, no doubt about it."

Javier had charged through the city as fast as he'd driven on the highway, but suddenly a traffic jam forced him to put on the brakes and negotiate his way a little through the mass of cars, all honking like a flock of geese. Finally we shot into Juncal, and he braked in front of the house.

"Well, see you tomorrow."

"See you tomorrow. I'll be here in the evening. We can get together when you leave your office."

"Fine, at six."

I went into the vestibule and was about to ring Herminia's apartment bell, but I saw that Javier was still sitting there, without pulling away. It seemed he was even sticking his head out the window a little, as if to say something and I went over to see what he wanted. When he saw me walk over he said evasively: "Nothing, nothing."

I grabbed the door handle.

"Don't hold back," I said; "come out with it."

"Listen," he answered, "is that really true?"

"What?"

"About the poem."

"Of course it's true. Truth itself. That's what it's about."

He didn't blink, he stepped on the accelerator and started off slowly. Suddenly he began to pick up speed, and I stood on the edge of the sidewalk until I saw the two little red lights disappear at the end of the street.

On the road to Las Murtas I told my father-in-law about how successful our trip had been. And I told him clearly, without making anything up because, actually, I pay attention to all these things much more than it seems. What happens is that almost everyone who lives in that world of business, of official matters, banks, ministries and all the rest, grants the most trivial detail solemnity that noticeably inflates its importance. I'm quick to pick up their little tricks and make sure I forget them two seconds after I've used them. So I was able to give him an accurate summary in just a few words.

Meanwhile, I kept asking myself why I'd told Javier that I was going to make a poem. I was surprised I'd said that to him because I hadn't thought about it beforehand—I thought of it as I said it. Then, as I thought back on it, I saw, in fact, I was going to do it. But not in the way Javier had understood. I was sure I didn't say, I'm going to *write* but, rather, I'm going to *make* a poem. And probably because at that moment I felt the call to action, in the Dionysian way that overcomes me sometimes. When I left the zoo and we were on the way back, my emotion was so immense I was sure I would do something with it and I had the idea of calling that a poem. Which is its right name: whatever I make will be a poem, that is, if I actually make it. After all, if I felt the need to tell Javier what I was thinking, it was to communicate something in code: I don't want to do anything in my life—not even live—unless it's full of that emotion.

We'd been silent for a while, and we finally wound up commenting on the calm spreading over the countryside.

"Spring's quite far along," my father-in-law noted.

"Ah, yes," I said, "that's true, it's spring."

And I thought: "That's why the calm of the countryside spreads over the haste of business. That's why there was an invincible calm in the garden. Perhaps my emotion didn't come from the ideas inspired in me by the animals' twilight terror, but from spring's enveloping snare. Perhaps an entire poem can be reduced to this: a buried, generative urge vibrating like an alarm clock at the center of one's sleep. Yes, probably all poems come down to that. Or perhaps only the good ones, the very good ones, the ones that are like beings; because one thing you can say for sure is that all beings come down to that."

We got there and everyone was asleep, so we said we'd see each other tomorrow and I came up to the tower.

I wrote this far, as fast as my pen would go; when I got to the subject of spring I paused, because I remembered its different voices. Now, silence is perfect, but other times on Juncal, in the hours right after midnight, the very sounds of the city made me feel spring as a call. Maybe because after the winter they were the first nights spent with the balcony windows open, but the sound of the distant streetcars seemed gentle as a breeze to me. After so many years in the neighborhood, I knew the nuances of their sound, knew when they got to the section of Las Heras where the road levels out and they can really pick up speed, and at this time of night they go pitching along like sailboats. Sometimes there's a rhythmic shrillness in that pitching that sounds like the cry of the lapwing.

Curious how sometimes the sounds of the city transport us to the country, and other times the sounds of the country transport us to the city. Just now those springs on Juncal came to mind because I heard a lapwing off in the distance, and this makes me recall another night when, from this same spot, the cries of the country animals on their nocturnal raids made me witness an unforgettable drama.

Suddenly, in the midst of a great silence, I heard a small, choked cry. Although the henhouse is far from the house, I knew the cry had come from there. The dogs barked immediately. An undeterminable number of dogs ran by in pursuit of something. I heard them go off in the distance toward the gate, and the lapwings that frequent the marsh beside the road flew off from that direction, crying. It was a long time before the dogs calmed down; they went from one side to the other many times, barking and whimpering, until things were silent again, and not long afterward I heard familiar little steps on the roof. I know there's been an opossum nesting up under there for some time; the creature's ugly, repugnant, and harmful, but I never wanted to expose her and have her destroyed. In the morning I asked the foreman, and he said that in fact a pullet hen had disappeared, and they hadn't found any human footsteps, the door of the henhouse was shut tight. My stealthy neighbor was undoubtedly the culprit and I continued to protect her. After all, one hen more or less. And it's not because the opossum's a more agreeable animal than the hen, but because the hen's going to end up with her throat slit one way or the other. It doesn't matter whether some morning the foreman's wife comes in, knife in hand, and cuts off the hen's head or the opossum enters at midnight, slipping very softly through a loose section of the wire netting, jumps on top of the hen and severs its head with one bite. In the first instance, a known process occurs: a plucking of feathers, a ripping open, a separation into pieces, and a toss into the stewpot. In the second, it would be worth following the whole adventure. Because what's certain is that the opossum took the chick out of the henhouse. It's also certain that the dogs followed the opossum's tracks without catching her, because no one found her dead anywhere. She probably scrambled up to some safe place until the dogs grew tired of patrolling below and, when the dogs left, she managed to return to her nest. Did she return with the booty or did she have to abandon it? The only access to the roof is along the wisteria vines. She must have climbed them, dragging behind her a dead body as large as her own, and she must have pushed it underneath the eaves into the attic. Then would come the divvying up with her babies and, maybe, with her mate, in the event, of course, that she came back triumphant. Because what scene would unfold in the attic if she came back empty-handed? Would they reproach her? Would she make apologies? Would she find some way to justify her failure?

All these undeniably idiotic questions took hold of me so vividly that night that I had no need to answer them, I lived them for a long time. I was truly in the opossum's house, experiencing the domestic scene. But one that was neither a witty dialogue, à la La Fontaine, nor a comical pageantry, à la Walt Disney—what I tried to experience was the hint of that totality, outlined in the animal silence. That totality—the successful undertaking, the sated hunger, or its opposite, the disappointment, the feeling of injustice on the part of the pursued, the dispossessed . . . That totality might possibly be represented in nonrational beings, because it's not formulated. Who knows if through the brain of those beings pass symbolic images, which would probably have to be compared to dream images, or if there are only real images, repeated until they die out in the creatures' feeble memory? And regnant over it all, more blind and more formless, but more imperious, is the command: "You must earn your living," with no respite for fatigue, no shelter in the face of danger.

I could spend hours lost again in those ruminations, but there's a good bit of work waiting for me tomorrow, and I should get up early so I'll have a head start. Although it might be better to compress things in time, like the air inside a can.

19 September, at Las Murtas

Yesterday I couldn't find a way to go out to El Tigre and investigate. My father-in-law came with me to the city, and I think he had the intention of doing some investigating too, but I can't be sure.

His undertaking is much more difficult because we know each other too well. He knows the dimensions of my intelligence to a tee, and he knows I know the dimensions of his as well. Both of us are perceptive, astute, and sincere, although those last two terms may seem incompatible.

We're clever, because we're both masters of the art of guiding ideas along a winding, complex, and infallible path until we reach our preconceived point. There's no interlocutor who can resist us when we set out to lead him through our labyrinth. There is definitely no such interlocutor for him, not even when I'm the interlocutor, and there's none for me, not even when he's the interlocutor. We both know this.

We're sincere, because we could never deny blatant truth. If a word is uttered, if a specific question is formulated, we won't deny it. The face that says *no*, when it's *yes*, is something certain men cannot assume, and we both belong to that kind of man. Consequently, his investigation borders on the impossible. I've seen him draw back many times before the imminence of the question he wanted to ask me, but was afraid of the irreparable. He knew to ask the question was to get the truth, and he did not want the naked truth. So he would try to lead me through his labyrinth, as if I were that little ball rolling between sonorous nails, between timbres, skirting holes, until it reaches its goal, because that way, with his clever method, he could find out, without his success ever being established. With this same clever method, however, I'd let myself roll around a little and, when I got close to the area of danger, I'd swerve and go off in another direction.

I think he's choosing to wait, to lie patiently in ambush, because he's been here for six days and has no thought of leaving. I've already heard him say several times that one thing or another is something we could do next week or the week after. Well, in any case, I'm not afraid of him. Rather, I'm no more afraid of the truth than he is.

The person I'm terrified of is Herminia. We haven't spoken to each other for days, we avoid each other, and when we can't help meeting, I feel as if she's about to leap at my throat. I know that mentally she's spanking me.

Nevertheless, no one knows anything, I'm sure no one knows anything, not even me. Neither do I know what I need to know. This afternoon, I managed to run out to El Tigre. I got there, rented the boat and took the same canal as always but, at the first fork, I turned left, and at a sufficiently isolated spot, I tied up the boat and leaped ashore. The spot wasn't really isolated, but like a service exit and no estates fronted on the small canal, only the backs of some properties belonging to some modest homes. When I leaped—onto a place that was almost a wharf—I saw crates of empty bottles among the bushes. I surveyed the territory and, as you'd expect, in the house on the other side of the bushes there was a store. I went in to buy cigarettes and look it over. A smell of oil and salami made me think: "Elfriede definitely doesn't shop here."

I went back toward Tres Bocas: there they had those large black breads made by Strudel, the Viennese company. Of that store she was sure to be a client.

As I made my way there, planning some absurd story that would give me an opportunity to ask questions, I saw a large, dark-haired kid coming out with a basket. He looked slow and simple, like people up north. I leaped to shore. He was about to get into a boat tied close by, but I went up to him. I don't know how I did it, although I wasn't really worried about whether or not my first words would make sense, because I was sure he wouldn't understand them, and that's what happened. But I was very careful to make my voice soft, melodious, and listless, so he'd think he'd understood, and that's what happened.

The boy naturally thought I was looking for someone's address, and he started to pay attention to me in order to give me directions, but when he saw that it involved something more difficult he said he had to go deliver a bill for tea to someone's house. Once again he was ready to leap into the boat and I took a ten-peso bill out of my pocket. He stood still then and, after countless questions and explanations on my part, with attempts at answers on his, he wound up saying: "Miss Lily? Oh, yes, the lady with the dog."

"That's it!" I leaped, "the lady with the dog."

"Yes, I deliver bread to them when they come."

"Well," I said, "I think they came a few days ago."

"They came, but they're not here anymore."

"They're not here anymore? Are you sure?"

"And . . . of course I'm sure. The señora got very sick."

"When? You don't know what day she got sick?"

"How would I know. Maybe she was coming back from a trip."

"Ah, it was right after she returned?"

"The day after, I think. That launch from the hospital came. The ambulance, they call it."

Already I knew enough. I took the boat again and rowed aimlessly for a moment, but when I reached the fork I was tempted by the desire to go to the house. I went, leaped stealthily ashore, and went up to the door: silence. I knocked on the wood a few times, rubbing it softly: nothing. Puck was not there, that was certain.

I skirted the garden, which is not small, until I got to where the thick stone wall goes no farther and a fence separates the garden from the adjacent grounds. By ducking between the vines I made my way onto the grounds and peered over the posts into Lily's garden. From there you could see the silent house, half wrapped in climbing plants, its shutters closed.

"There's no one in this house," I repeated to myself, as clearly as if the wall of the house were a movie screen, and I saw myself sitting on the large chest brutally hugging Elfriede, with the heartless face of someone who's no one.

I came home and, for today, there's nothing else.

20 *September*

In Spanish we don't have an expression equivalent to the French *après vous*, because Spanish pride hasn't endowed the language with many explicit forms of courtesy—whether of tenderness or praise—, even though both the sentiment and the habit of courtesy run naturally and deeply in our veins. It's pride, as I said, that envelops Spaniards in the downcast sadness we call modesty. In any case, the motion of *après vous*, when we want to make way for someone who merits our esteem, is as clear to everyone as the other motion, which we would have to call *avant toi*, when we see that someone we love is about to step into a dangerous spot and we give him a quick shove aside so we can go first.

Well, at this moment I feel I'm facing the two instances simultaneously.

This evening, past six, as I was leaving the lab, I heard a horse passing behind the shed at full gallop. I looked and it was Francisco. He wouldn't have heard me, so I didn't even try to call to him. I saw him ride off over the hill and cross the stream; he was exploring our new acquisitions. Jorge was in the pasture, with don Ignacio, and he'd been out trotting too. The old man pointed to Francisco.

"That one's getting away from me," he said; "I can't hold him back. Today he's been out trotting since five."

Jorge intervened, not to make excuses for his brother but to justify him, explaining that this was no game.

"It's because he has a lot of things on his mind."

"What things?" I asked.

"Things!" Jorge said, making a gesture that indicated something infinite.

I stood for a while watching him. Although he was riding in the distance, I could see him well. He galloped to the nearest hill, and there he tightened the reins and came back to the pass, following the edge of the water. He was gesturing rapidly, as if he were talking with someone else riding beside him. When he spotted us, he crossed the stream and broke into a brisk trot. He got there in no time, leaped to the ground, and came running toward me, all sweaty. I was getting ready to tell him that his escapade had been a little excessive, but he didn't let me speak. He caught me by the arm and, when I opened my mouth, he cut me off.

"Wait a second! Listen." A slight hesitation and then immediately: "I already know what I'm going to be!"

"To be?"

"Yes, yes, well, to study. The same thing as that man you told grandpa about the other day."

"What man? I don't remember."

"That man who lived on the bank of a very large river."

"In Venice," Jorge prompted.

"In Venice? What do you mean Venice? In Buenos Aires," Francisco said.

"It wasn't Buenos Aires at all. Papá said: 'That was Venice.' Didn't you?"

"It *seemed like*, idiot, it *seemed like* is what he meant to say."

"Ah, yes, now I remember," I said when they let me speak. "Conrad the engineer."

"That's it. That man was an agronomic engineer, wasn't he? And he had a lot of daughters and a field full of flowers."

"Exactly. Well, almost exactly: the flowers were his daughters."

"Come on! That . . ." Francisco said incredulously.

"Well yes, in the same way that his office seemed like Venice to me, to him the flowers seemed like his daughters."

"Fine. But he must have been a wonderful man, isn't that so?"

"Wonderful. A great guy."

"Well, I've decided that I'm going to be agronomic engineer. Right, Jorge?"

Jorge nodded seriously, as if the agreement had been made some time ago and subjected to much discussion between them.

We were already on our way to the house when I said: "But, listen! When I told that story about Conrad the engineer you two had already gone to bed."

Francisco blushed a little and Jorge looked at him, asking: "What do we say?"

Then, Francisco said naively but without losing his composure: "Yes, we had gone to bed, but we came back. As soon as Miss Ray went into her room we came into the hall and we were there for a long time on the big sofa."

"Grandpa was the only one who could see us over its back and he was dying of laughter," Jorge said.

"Great!" I said, "I think it's just great."

And Francisco looked at me as if to say, "Why wouldn't you think that?"

I added: "You're constantly tricking poor Miss Ray."

"Oh, Miss Ray already has her hands full with Fernando," Francisco responded. Then, wanting to tease Jorge a little, he said, "Well, you still have a year of slavery left. A year in the dungeon!"

"Jorge only has a year! And what are you going to do? You plan to escape?" I asked.

"Of course! I'm getting out," Francisco answered, very naturally. Soon his face darkened and he said: "But didn't you know?"

"Not a word."

Francisco burst into a run and went into the house shouting: "Mamá! Mamá!"

When I got there, Quitina and he were in the midst of a heated argument. "You said! She said! You said. And then, why didn't you say anything to Papá?"

Finally, Quitina explained to me that a few days ago she'd been speaking with Herminia about how next year Francisco had to start high school. According to Miss Ray, he was at the level of second year, at least, and it was absurd for him to waste any more time at home.

"Well," I said, "we'd already talked about this at other times, but it's six months until March. I don't know why the two of you are in such a frenzy over it."

"No, it's not that," Francisco said. "We were talking about something different, weren't we?"

"Yes, I know," Quitina said, and she decided to explain. "Herminia was telling me that now, since the apartment's rented, it was going to be a nuisance for Francisco to have to commute all the time. And, of course, it occurred to her that he could eat at her house."

"That's a good idea," I said. "It will mean a bit of work for her, but she'll like it too."

Francisco interrupted me, pressing his mother.

"And what else? Because there's also something else."

"Well," Quitina said, "what's been driving this child crazy is the fact that it occurred to me to say he could stay there and sleep in your room, in the office. You only go now to work, and if by chance you had to stay overnight, the two of you could work it out somehow."

I was going to speak, but Francisco, in a torrent, fearing that his whim was about to be denied, hastened to explain it to me so at least the plan would exist as something real.

"You understand, Papá?" he said. "I go there and stay in your bachelor's quarters. I stay by myself. If I have an alarm clock, I'll get along fine. I won't bother Aunt Herminia at all. What do you think? Will you let me use your room, Papá?"

Francisco asked his question with great anxiety, but I knew Quitina was waiting for my answer even more anxiously. Without looking at her, as if I found the question unnecessary, I said: "But of course. Why wouldn't I let you use it, if you like it? Now we'll see how you . . ." I couldn't finish the sentence; I was going to say how you behave, but Francisco turned into a trumpet.

Quitina's father came running to see what all the shouting was about, Francisco threw himself on his grandfather, Jorge followed suit, and for a long time they wrestled on the carpet, as if all three of them were in their first decade of life.

How nice! What a healthy, decent, bourgeois family scene! I have no reason to complain: I always wanted a healthy, decent, bourgeois life. Well, those adjectives are horrible: I set out to live a normal life and that's what a normal life is. That would definitely be a normal life, if this life were what it seems.

There's nothing more childish than people who love mystery stories, incomprehensible tales set in gloomy places. They're intrigued by that! What I've just told is really a mystery story.

The impenetrability of souls and the penetrability of times. Could we come up with anything more mysterious? Armored souls, safe behind their heavy protection, which consists in simply *not saying such a thing*. And against that, there's nothing you can do. Who could force them? Then, the moment arrives when those things are said, and the mystery's over. No, it's not over. At that very point begins mystery's metamorphosis toward what mystery will look like in the future. Time, immortal, indestructible time outcropping through itself. Without repetition, rather, as rectification, as a retouching of things that didn't turn out well in the first round.

The armoring must break open, this mystery in Quitina's soul will come to a head at any moment. I don't know how. I can do nothing to slow it down or hurry it up, because the mystery about which I remain silent has not yet taken a form that's intelligible to me.

What I do understand, and in all its complexity, is the siege of the two requests assailing me in the case of Francisco.

Francisco wants my bachelor's quarters, and I give them to him. It's the future. Is there anything more respectable? I stand to one side and let him pass with the most acquiescent movement of *après vous*. But it's the future of *my son*, who wants to enter *my room*. And I know everything that's in *my room*. I can't let him enter, I have to go first, because the things aren't in order. I didn't disinfect that place adequately. I didn't get rid of the miasmas. Naturally, though, Francisco won't let himself be stopped, and if I cut him off, if I try to spare him the dangers, he'll think I'm trying to *take* the dangers from him. And he probably finds them as desirable as Quitina found the cold and misfortune she *could not* give him.

I have to let him pass. At ten years old, he's decided on his future, as I decided on mine at eight. He's just as determined—I don't think he'll abandon the idea—and the cause of his decision is more arbitrary than mine. He won't imitate my mistakes: he'll improvise his own.

22 September

I haven't been able to write for a long time, not because there's nothing to write about, but because I can't overcome my resistance to the physical act of picking up the pen. I thought I'd managed to distance the phenomenon preventing me from doing that, but since I don't want to forget it entirely, and since it's so worthy of continued existence, as soon as I try to talk about it, it breaks out again and renders me useless.

That phenomenon is the impossibility of doing any ordinary task with my right hand.

Lord! The honorable thing would be to tell this in reverse order. That way it's less spectacular. To say that I can't use my right hand—a farce! because I'm obviously using it—and then to tell the story that led me not to be able to—not to want to, because I don't have the least symptom of paralysis—adds a sparkle to the thing that makes it truly interesting. When the fact is merely a relic of a rather dramatic episode, and it seems banal to overestimate such a residue, although maybe it's not.

I'll start at the beginning.

Yesterday, the twenty-first, we didn't leave Las Murtas all day, and since there were no people at the factory, my father-in-law and I made a detailed inspection of all the equipment and materials. For him, it was the first time he'd gone into the lab for the purpose of investigating, usually he never went past the door. I explained the entire manufacturing process to him.

"But this is great," he said. "I don't understand what's not working here."

"Nothing, there's nothing that's not functioning. The factory ran better and better. Our things are very reputable, because *people know* that the control is perfect. Everything gets inspected by me, personally, or by my second-in-command, and he's totally trustworthy. What caused the deficit was the business of the poppies."

"I think you're right," he agreed. "That was getting yourself in one hell of a mess. Why didn't you let go of it in time?"

I looked at him with such amazement that he burst out laughing.

"Yes, you're too stubborn to turn back," he said.

"But how is a person to turn back when what he wants is in front of him?"

"Well, a person can't go running after everything that wanders in front of him."

Again I felt myself rolling between the sonorous nails, sensed the proximity of the hole, and made a half turn.

"I'm not going to let myself be defeated in this business," I said enthusiastically, "even if I have all the elements of nature against me. I assure you, I've had them against me each time I planted. Sometimes elements related to the weather and sometimes elements of human nature. In the beginning, elements of my own nature: my foolish goal of doing everything right, without knowing how. Then, once I had the Dutchman, who really does know how, elements of his nature. Peculiarities, a peasant's bad habits. Since the new lots were pastureland, until he had them ready, he fertilized them, planted potatoes."

"Potatoes?" my father-in-law said in amazement.

"Yes, it seems that's a good idea. So, in the end, a year was lost in preparation, a year that was marvelous. Then came some other hellish years. The entire harvest, or half of it, was lost. It was impossible to get this outfit to run. And then this year, to top it off, just when we're ready to plant, that nasty beast of a lawyer we now have turns up, determined to make life difficult for me. Imagine, if we hadn't been able to count on you, everything would have gone to hell."

"Yes, there is that side to agriculture," he said. "You have to take a lot of things into account."

And after a short pause: "Well, the two of you can count on me for that and for everything. If only everything were so easy! There can be . . ."

I interrupted him; he'd taken a deep breath as if he were about to begin a long paragraph, but I didn't let him continue.

"There can't be any more difficulties now, unless we have an unseasonable storm. October's the hardest month to get through."

We went on like that all afternoon, skirting the well. Ever since he'd arrived, we hadn't been by ourselves for so long and in such complete calm. It was very difficult. It was like walking a tightrope, but dinnertime came at last and I found myself on the other side of the precipice.

I don't know why, but last night I couldn't write. Because of my forced inaction about the mystery of Elfriede and the Weningers, I had the sensation I was waiting for something that could happen when I least expected it. The same as always when I feel uneasy inside, I was seized by a need to sleep, and I would not have sacrificed sleep.

What happened was, this morning I went down to breakfast and my father-in-law was already all dressed up, waiting for me to go to Buenos Aires. Nothing worth mentioning on the whole trip. I stayed on Juncal and told him to take the car, because I knew he'd be running around the whole morning, but he said he'd rather take taxis, because he was going to be downtown, and it was almost always impossible to find a place to park. We agreed that I'd pick him up at City Bank at twelve thirty, so we could have lunch at the Pedemonte.

Everything turned out fine, according to plan, until the next-to-the-last stage. The last stage was the Pedemonte: in the previous stage the unexpected occurred.

Nothing can be more unexpected than what comes after you've been expecting something for a long time. You'd have to say, then, that it was unsuspected, because we'd been waiting, waiting, but what appeared was very different from what had been supposed.

At twelve thirty sharp I arrived at City Bank. Why did I go in? I don't understand it. We'd agreed that my father-in-law would come out the door as soon as he finished, since we assumed I wouldn't be able to leave the car nearby and that I would rather drive around until I saw him on the corner. But I found a parking place a few meters away and went in to look for him. I got there maybe a few minutes early.

He was beside the tellers' window, in a small group of people who hadn't formed a line but were taking turns, and there were three or four people ahead of him. He was standing right behind an enormous back that I recognized immediately.

I thought: "Should I leave? No, I can't leave." And I took a few steps toward him the way one must step toward the scaffold.

"How did you get here so soon?" my father-in-law said. I made an ambiguous gesture, without answering. He continued: "I've been looking at stills, and I don't like them. What was the other brand they recommended to you?"

If I'd remembered it, I could have uttered just one word, under my breath, but I hadn't the least idea and I had to say: "I don't recall, but it doesn't matter, I have it written down." Tom Drake turned around immediately, at the sound of my voice.

"Why, how lucky," he said, "how lucky to run into you. I should have called you, but you have no idea!"

"Why, Drake," was all I could say. And I quickly introduced him to my father-in-law. A name in an introduction usually makes a vague impression, but that's not how it was for my father-in-law: he realized on the spot who this man was.

As for me, I was telling myself, inside: "I can't look at him, *but I absolutely must look at him*, I must scrutinize him, I must know what's going on."

It was very easy. The anxiety with which I looked at Drake did not make him uncomfortable. He interpreted it as interest in what he began to relate without having to be asked.

"Many contretemps," he said, "we've had some real contretemps."

We listened to him so avidly he felt he was being interrogated.

"Yes," he continued, "Elfriede's not as strong as she seems. I should not have left her alone. It's not the first time this has happened to her; she already had a serious breakdown some time ago."

"It's possible!" I managed to say, almost breathlessly, and my father-in-law said: "Oh!"

"Well, I believe I already told you that while I was in Boston with Nix, Elfriede would spend the whole time in San Martín de los Andes.

She went there with her friend the day before I left. Imagine, a wonderful climate, every comfort you could ask for, a magnificent estancia, with good friends and, nevertheless, very bad, very bad. An attack of melancholy, insomnia, hallucinations."

"How dreadful!" we said, this time both at once.

"She was very well cared for, no question about that. Her friends brought her immediately to the Hospital Alemán, and they didn't leave her for a minute. Good doctors, good treatment. Even so . . ."

Our silence encouraged him to continue.

"Elfriede is very accustomed to the American system. Her psychiatrist understands her very well. He knows how to recover her stability."

"How fortunate!" my father-in-law said, and I continued to be silent.

"Of course, it was a bit difficult for me to request another leave so soon, but I found an excellent, excellent nurse who accompanied her all the way to the clinic."

We both let out profuse exclamations: "Really? She went back? She could make such a long trip?"

"She's already there, perfectly settled," and he added, his tone reasonable and calm: "I have the impression that this breakdown is not as serious as the first. No, it's not as serious: she walked up the steps to the airplane on her own two feet, looking quite normal. Obviously, it's a more benign manifestation."

At that moment the teller called out Drake's number.

"Excuse me," he said and went up to the window. The two of us studied the mosaic until we felt dizzy.

When Drake finished, my father-in-law went, and Drake told me that now he was going to ask them to give him back his old job in Boston.

"The experience in the South hasn't been very positive," he said with a smile, as if he meant, "It's better not to take things too tragically."

We said good-bye, and I assured him I was deeply sorry to see him leave Buenos Aires and we all wished Elfriede a speedy recovery. When he was already walking away, I said, almost shouted to him: "Keep us posted, don't forget!"

"Oh, of course, of course," he said, and he went off.

From there we left for the Pedemonte. We ate almost in silence—a happy, light silence. My father-in-law's happiness was mixed with puzzlement, mine with relief—an almost ironic, sarcastic, and cynical relief—and with horror, repugnance, compassion, and shame. An undrinkable cocktail!

Later, once we were home, we discussed the meeting, and Quitina showed not the least sign of happiness. She felt intrigued and disconcerted, the way you feel when a movie stops in the middle. Her expression was that of a person who's suddenly been left in the dark without knowing.

Now it will be necessary to explain something. Everything? Impossible, but something, definitely, something that may seem adequate. What gimmick won't the human mind come up with using fragments of truths, or similar materials?

Whereas the truth that can be touched . . . I know that what I'm trying to do is stupid. I don't want to say I already know it's impossible, because that would be to disguise it as a great undertaking and it's not, it's definitely not a great undertaking: it's merely stupidity tempting me. Here I should no doubt say *bêtise* for sure, because what I would like to describe is the unchallengeable intellection I achieve sometimes when my consciousness *s'abêtit*.

What foolish pretension! Could I describe the silence separating these two lines? Is total darkness something I could *see well*? Nevertheless, *I know* that in the oppressive episode at City Bank the only part of my person that *lived* the moment with true decency was my right hand. My naked hand in the naked of hand of Tom Drake.

Contiguous, friendly, restrained words. Daringly direct gazes, because the eyes know that the eyes don't see. And a body lying to another body, confronting its contact, its strong, cordial handshake . . . The palm of the hand, the papillae, reading, turned to pure intelligence, and the blood pounding unceasingly in the veins, like a flagellant.

11 October, at Las Murtas

This daily journal has been abandoned for three weeks. I knew I'd never be able to keep it regularly. What's happened is the rhythm of things has changed again. In September, things were happening *daily*, and now the things that *don't happen* are becoming important again.

When I began to date the journal, I thought it would be it difficult to summarize events, and it was very easy; now what's difficult is bringing to light the underlying, diffuse incidents that fill my life and resist any definition, because their action is inhibiting . . . so much so that I leave off. Never was it more relevant to say, "That is what we proposed to demonstrate."

But the notebook lies open in front of me and, beside me, silence sits like an empty jug beneath a fountain that produces no water. I need to start pumping, but I'm not in the mood, and I don't have the energy. It was so easy to take notes from life! I can attempt a still life—or what's called a still life, because nothing in life is still—, I can copy things that are there, that make up the world I live in and don't pressure me the way silence does, because they're not the void: they're forms. Beloved, beneficent, generous, corroborative. The kind of things beyond good and evil, in aesthetics and even in decency. Here in the tower, I give shelter to all the things society *does not admit*. Things that are in *bad taste* but that, nevertheless, leave a delicious aftertaste. I would have to say an *adorable taste*, because that's their secret, they're mere forms, which give rise to affections. Maybe they're nothing more than links in an endless chain: there are objects that drag behind them towns, landscapes, epochs. I confess my weakness for modernist trinkets, for a small bronze frog dressed like a woman. Yes, it's here on my desk and I look at it constantly, with real friendship. I also have a predilection, among my rare pipes, for the one that looks like the "Le beau Jacob," the famous Zouave, and a secret devotion for a few stuffed animals—a small alligator, an owl. Should I confess this? Yes, an armadillo. It sits in a humble place, on the floor in the corner, as if it lived there. I like that *as if it lived*.

Suddenly I'm assailed by the memory of Rudy. There was a time when I said, "He's the only fitting company for me," because it seemed to me that my confused conscience felt comfortable next to his pure lack of conscience. Now I close myself up among these inert things and refuse to admit they have no life. It's obvious *for themselves* they don't, but they transmit the life of the people who created their lives. Someone made them and left them here like a written letter, which I try to answer.

It's possible I will never be able to make something that's worth as much as this small bronze frog, which presentable objects would never admit into their society. I must spare no lines to save it. Because someone made it, some obscure artist conceived this freak and cast it in bronze and left it here sixty-some years ago, with the hope that someday *I* would look at it. *I*—its creator thought about me particularly, in other words, about the person who can look as only I look. There are many things I'm sure I can do well, but none so well as this. I believe I'm capable of satisfying the highest hope of everyone who's made something for others to look at.

But what use is my answer to these letters? Does it have some goal, some reason for being? Isn't it stupid to answer someone who no longer exists? It's possible that the creator also knew it was stupid to leave the written letter, the answer would arrive too late, but that didn't keep him from wanting it.

What other superfluous way could I find to invest these hours of lucidity capping the night's vaulted sky? I've picked up the myopic's habit of spending half an hour obsessed with something right in front of my nose. The daily focus of this journal has corrupted my focus, made me lose my customary predilection for distant things.

The daily! Well, today's daily brought some disturbing news.

I think I've found a good topic. It would be impossible to find anything more useless to think about.

At this very moment, more than a hundred dolphins, which for some unknown reason have run aground, are dying on the beach at Mar del Plata. There are various hypotheses: pursued by their enemy, the swordfish; terrified by some underwater phenomenon. The only thing people know for certain is that the dolphins will die because they can't get back to the water. They can't get back to their element.

And the most horrible thing is that in some situations they can be out of their element for a certain length of time. Because they aren't ordinary fish—if they were, they would have died in about half an hour, but they're warm-blooded creatures, capable of a very long death. Of course, for fish, to leave the water is to enter death, but it's different for these large bodies that nurse their offspring—the paper says that they're all females—, bodies that so delight in sticking their heads out of the water and leaping high in the air—which we've all seen them do in the newsreels—, bodies beloved by sailors, and bodies that have prompted so many legends and whose form adorns the world beside the foot of Aphrodite Anadyomene in Renaissance ornamentation and on baroque fountains. They have certain roots in the earth, certain bonds with its spirit, so it's natural their first immersion in this burning climate—we have to imagine what the earth, its contact and its air, will mean for their moist natures—, the first surprise, probably struck them as a bearable dip, but then, when they wanted to go back.

That stupid pretension again! It must harbor some great truth when it pursues me so persistently. I'm comparing voluntary rectification, turning back (either mentally or by retracing one's steps, which is always possible—it's always possible?), spurred by the *intense force of one's own world*, of which one lacks a memory but which dictates the way back, with nothing but the *absolute need* to go back in order to breathe in that element again, and to die, without returning.

Well, in today's daily news there was something even more horrible: the police have had to intervene so people don't stab them, because some people have found it amusing to slash them. "Incredible!" you can say. And you might say, "Naturally! That's what happens to beings when they're outside their world, defenseless. Because *worlds* are full of other beings that delight in such things, in sticking a knife in a being of flesh and blood and watching the blood run out. I've said *worlds* because I mean all existing—all conceivable?—worlds, the spiritual world first of all. Yes, the worlds of culture, art, business (maybe the most blood-thirsty of all), and we won't even mention the world of leisure.

Of course, in irrational worlds, such as the aquatic deep in which dolphins move, the various natures, because of their very form . . . Because, let's think about it, why must the swordfish be the enemy of the dolphin? Simply because the dolphin is plump, a roll of flesh that's familiar with pleasure—Saint Anthony's sermon has not reached the cetaceans—and the swordfish is firm, pointed, *made* for piercing. Since it lives in the same world as the dolphin, of course they meet up with each other and the thing has to happen. Why was the swordfish made to pierce and the dolphin to be pierced? And if they weren't made that way, by royal decree, why does the spermatic cell, a tiny clot of will imperceptible to the human eye, bear this form? Why this unheard-of marriage of seed and geometry? For centuries, the narcissist has been drawing two opposing triangles and a circle between them. Why, subject to equally strict laws, do we humans have that bird tied by one foot with a very long cord: freedom?

It's four o'clock. Will I be able to sleep for five hours? That would be enough for me and maybe I can, because I have a certain feeling that I've done my duty. When I read the news in *Crítica*, my first impulse was to get in the car, rush over there and shove them one by one, like an ox. But, hell! They weigh tons: I couldn't even have budged them.

My thoughts in the middle of the night have tried to absorb part of their agony. Perhaps they've felt a moment of letup in their torture because I'm a also a good technician in that respect. I'm an agonist by nature, and I can fight tirelessly for the most useless cause.

12 October

October is turning out to be splendid: the plants have now reached their full growth and the flowers are starting to open. Within two weeks the countryside will be covered.

Former and futile musings about beauty: the flower is beautiful because it heralds the fruit, et cetera, et cetera. It's definitely possible:

this well-being, which allows you to feel confident you haven't wasted your time, this tranquillity alongside promise may have prompted aesthetic enjoyment. Because then, the harvest is constant hustle and bustle; what's good is this moment when you finally seem to have something and what you have is merely something fragile as a flower, which a gust of wind or a heavy downpour can carry off in five minutes. Danger is what beauty best produces.

What a great system for not talking about what you're thinking about! Because it goes without saying, I'm not thinking about any of the things I'm writing about. Perhaps the ironic conclusion in my last paragraph, crafted in the style of twenty years ago, is, nevertheless, the only positive thing, because that ironic, trivial sentence is the counterfigure of the following dramatic sentence: "There where beauty begins begins horror."

For the record: what I'm thinking about can't be expressed with either the dramatic sentence or the frivolous one. Maybe without any sentence, by narrating it succinctly. But that's a system made for recent, day-to-day, not-yet-decanted things, and now I've let many days pass, everything's become condensed or, rather, now everything's wound as tightly as a silkworm's cocoon; it's very difficult to find the thread. I'll pull on the first loose end.

The last day of September, my father-in-law took off. But he didn't go back to Havana, as I assumed he would; he went to Europe. He said even though he'd resolved not to get involved in business again, by chance he'd run into an old acquaintance who'd suggested something worth investigating.

He certainly presented this very reasonably, but I know the heart of the matter is different. Some days before, it occurred to me to ask him about the portrait he'd consulted me about in his letter, and he responded with a categorical gesture, the way you refuse alcohol or tobacco.

"Oh nothing, nothing; don't even talk about that."

"You've given up?" I asked, surprised.

"No, not at all, but . . . the dead can wait."

Then, after a brief pause, he continued: "Sometimes I tell myself I don't yet have the right to go and join the dead, but I think what really holds me back is my spirit; because other times I tell myself: I'm old, I'm tired . . . but it's not true, I'm not tired."

"Neither old nor tired," I said, laughing. "You've got energy to spare."

"Oh, I don't know if I have any to spare," he said, and he shrugged his shoulders as if he were thinking: "whether I have energy to spare or don't have enough, I'm going to continue." And at that moment I saw him make a gesture of dreadful weariness, I saw how much he had to deal with, and I realized he was embarking on some new venture. When he told us he was going to Europe on business, he justified his decisions with silly phrases: "It's a vice." "I can't be still." But there's something more, there's something more: I think he feels he needs to watch out for us.

And it happens that now, although he may be right, his vigilance is unnecessary, because peace reigns between us.

I've said *between* us! How could I say something so horrible! Sometimes clichéd forms of language, commonplaces produce a gesture so unusual you're terrified. It's as if one of the puppets you were about to manipulate started moving its arms on its own and let out an autonomous shriek. I said *between* us, and the preposition ran wild and started shrieking—shrieking at itself, I should have said, because there's only one voice. But a voice that in repeating shows both sides, all the facets assigned it by the dictionary: first, second, third meanings. "*Between!*" it insists, "*between!*" repeats back to me the voice I uttered, not thinking of a shared action or thing but of an object or subject in the middle, *put in the middle* of two objects or subjects. And is peace what's between the two of us? What's the difference? It's there, put in the middle, and it reigns! In other words, the zone it occupies has borders, possesses a territory and, in order for us to be united again, we have to pass through that territory.

In short, there are a few reasonable, and therefore narratable things, before we get to the unnarratable moment when we run up against a brick wall.

The day after her father left, Quitina tried to sustain his presence in the house by making continual allusions to his trip and to his stubbornness about returning to his activities, exaggerating the remorse she felt for having made him give up his retirement. It was dusk, and we were in the library where the two of us had taken tea together by ourselves, and Quitina had talked about her father the whole time.

"I don't think you should regret it so much," I said. "The trip did him good."

Suddenly, like someone diving off a springboard, I added: "Besides, it solved many mysteries: the encounter at City Bank restored his peace of mind."

I was watching her carefully, expecting the subject I'd broached would make her shudder, but it didn't; she only raised her brows as if to say, "That's exactly what I was thinking about." Once launched, I couldn't ascend through the air again; I entered the fluid mass of things silenced.

"And I imagine that it's also restored yours," I said, feigning a smile so clearly ironic it was comical.

"Restored?" Quitina said, without responding even slightly to my smile, without perceiving or wanting to realize it was either ironic or comical, with the fixed, attentive gaze of someone who's about to express something difficult but obvious, and she added, "Not *restored*, but *bestowed*, a peace of mind that's more or less provisional."

"I'll be damned!" In my consternation the only thing that occurred to me was to accentuate the comical. "So that . . . well . . . in view of your statements . . . in other words, let's see, it turns out that you never had any peace of mind."

"Never."

"Never? How grandiose!" I said, to say something. "And if one may know?"

"Why?"

"That's it. Why?"

"Because I know you."

"Ah, of course, you've spent so many years witnessing my dissipation."

"No, exactly the opposite. I've spent many years seeing that you . . . that you weren't dissipating, let's say, and thinking that any moment . . . Well, the moment came."

"But, what is it that came? Tell me."

Quitina shrugged her shoulders, as if to say: "No need to ask."

"All right," I said, abandoning the ironic tone. "If we must speak about it openly, the case is clear: it came and it left."

"Yes, it left, but it came."

"As you prefer."

"No, I would have preferred that it not come."

"So would I!" This I said so violently Quitina felt somewhat relieved. "I didn't attach the least importance to it, especially because," I continued, "I didn't think there would be an offensive initiated in the first place, or in the second, or in the third—I simply didn't suspect there would be an offensive. I definitely didn't suspect it!" Quitina's skeptical gesture was exasperating me, but I went on, "Besides, I was sure that if something were attempted I would end up resisting."

"And of course something was attempted."

"Do you think I should have told you right away?"

"Of, I don't know if *you should have*. You know I've never been much concerned with what people should do."

"I have, when it coincides with what I'd like, as on this occasion."

I should *not* have boasted, *should not* have let on about a situation that was so marvelous for my vanity. And I didn't because I don't like to do it.

"Of course, of course. That's why it turned out so well for you."

"What turned out so well for me?"

"Not letting on."

It took me a while to respond: I couldn't let myself make the wrong answer. But prolonging the silence was just as risky. How to know what

Quitina had meant? She was aware of my dissimulation, but how aware? And couldn't her own sentence have been a probe? In any case, the thing had to be cleared up. Clarifying it was impossible, the more time that passed the more difficulty I'd have destroying it with something that would lead her thoughts in a different direction.

"Then I've surpassed all the great actors, whose exits always turn out well," I said, going back to irony. "It's much harder not to stage things and have them turn out well than it is to walk off the stage."

"Is that amusing?"

"What?"

"What you said."

"Well, I don't know, you decide."

"I was asking because I couldn't see."

"I'll switch on the light," I said sarcastically, but I felt quite irritated. It had gotten totally dark. I got up and went to switch on the lamp that stood on a table, drawing up the small armchair until I was face-to-face with Quitina.

"Can you see clearly enough now?" I said. Quitina didn't answer; she gestured ambiguously. "I asked if you could see things clearly."

"Clearly? There are things that don't look any better when they're clear."

"Fine! Then, is it quite clear that those things vanished, without leaving a trace?"

"Yes, that appears to be perfectly true."

"My God! What pigheadedness!"

Quitina had one leg crossed over the other. I picked up the foot in the air and gave it a hard squeeze. Quitina tried to free her foot.

"Don't even think of tickling me!" she said with real terror.

"I hadn't thought of tickling you," I responded, squeezing the foot cruelly. This had to be hurting her a lot, but she didn't notice, because she was intent only on preventing the game from leading to tickling and the tickling from turning into something else.

It's at times like this when people usually say, "I felt something like an electric current." And the comparison isn't totally inaccurate, but it both exaggerates the phenomenon and impoverishes it. Today almost everyone knows what it's like to feel an electric current, whereas this other feeling, which I'm trying to describe for the umpteenth time, is much more ancient—the cavemen must already have known it. At the dawn of human consciousness, this feeling might have been more frequent and, above all, more powerful, it might possibly have been what points the way with its trembling, like the compass that pointed to the North of great truths. Because what's electric about it is the magnetic attraction *toward a point*. The current we feel when we touch a cable is like a hostility that has neither cause nor reason: we touch it, and we get jolted, nothing more. The compass, however, produces no shock; but if we move it, its needle pivots, trembles, and trembles again, until it settles in the direction of the magnetic pole. The compass knows what it wants. As does this inner trembling, absolutely imperceptible to human sight, this vacillation when two surfaces meet that produces material contact, wavering for an instant until it points to a truth in one's conscience, until it's fixed on a point. And the trembling is produced precisely when between two bodies that touch there's a lie.

Between, again! Between two hands there can be a palpable lie, between a hand and a foot a lie can struggle and turn like a trapped snake.

Now I remember that when I touched Drake's hand, in City Bank, I thought that marriage makes a man and a woman one flesh. I thought that? I would have to say, *I touched it*. How many minutes and how many words will I need to describe the trembling of that moment, the wavering of the needle that, before it became fixed, pointed in a quivering semicircle to all the neighboring ideas and, of all those ideas, gave primacy to that one? Clenched by that Herculean but soft hand, my hand was an intrusive substance, totally foreign to it. And that hand, clenched by mine, the muscles not covered with a gram of fat, was a fleshly, passive limb, something like a thigh. The contact occasioned a certain embarrassment for me, a certain repugnance. Well, everything went off without a hitch, because he has no more intelligence in his hand than in one of his thighs.

But when I grabbed Quitina's foot, the trembling of the compass was identical in us both. It was the contact of two epidermises enveloped in a single flesh that, when pressed together, suffered as acutely as if between them there were a sharp knife so honed that to squeeze it was to plunge it into one's soul. I squeezed with all my might.

In order for Quitina not to fear being tickled, I moved my hand from the front of her foot, where I'd grabbed it, to the ankle, clenching it, because the pressure was so violent that contact was erased. When I felt the inner wavering, I squeezed to abolish the limits, as if the blade were only on the skin, in our touching—touch is what understands—and as if squeezing would cause the skin to be pierced, knotted. But Quitina didn't tolerate the pressure. She didn't take her hands and yank my hand from her ankle. I don't know how she exerted force, perhaps with her eyes. She also moved her leg in a way so sudden she could have broken it, but what she forced me to release was her gaze. Neither sparks nor darkness in her eyes: a clear, explicit, hard, dialectical stare equal to the most persuasive explanation: "Let go of me, don't try anything; talk as much as you want, but don't touch me. Bodies can't lie." All this— and much more!—at a single blow. Convinced, I opened my hand, and Quitina's foot returned to its companion.

There was a silence. We both tried to collect ourselves, keeping within the boundaries of the enclosed area defined by the truce. Our words from a few minutes ago had established that truce, enthroned it above reasons. We had to remain distant, peering through the brambles, one facing the other, and we had to keep talking. Words swim well through the mud of lies, as long as they hold a bit of truth, at least a will to truth; it's bodies that demand absolute truth in order to relax and forget their boundaries.

While I was considering all this, almost as clearly as I've just explained it, another much more pure, more vital occurrence clamored for an explosion, for a crumbling of walls that would hurl us one against the other, have us rolling on the floor crying, embracing. But that was impossible; I saw clearly that it was impossible, although I didn't know why.

I still don't!

13

It's pointless to keep putting in dates. The last thing I noted, on 12 October, had happened on the first, and there have been a lot of other important things since, but I don't even recall when they occurred. I can't even say they were occurrences: just things thought or spoken, although they were dramatic enough to alter the sunlight. Meanwhile, October continues, and so far it's glorious.

While my father-in-law was in Buenos Aires, I saw little of Herminia and Miguel, partly because those days I was completely caught up in my activities—both public and private—, partly because, as I think I've said, Herminia and I were avoiding each other. I was about to ask Miguel: "What's your mother up to?" but I was afraid I'd find myself confiding in him, and I didn't want to implicate Miguel. I've always treated him like a child. But something occurred a few days ago, the other afternoon when I was in the lab, and Miguel appeared. It was Friday and the two of them had made the trip to Las Murtas on their own.

It came time to stop working, and we left together.

"Let's go look at our little flowers," Miguel said to me. "They seem to be coming up nicely."

We went out, sat down on a fallen tree trunk, and gazed for a long time at the field, now covered with subtle shades of bluish pink. The white ones are still my favorites—they look like huge motionless butterflies.

Suddenly, Miguel said to me: "I'm going to tell you a story that's rather . . . curious."

I don't know why but this gave me goose bumps.

"You know Quitina often lets me her use car," he went on, "and almost every time I've borrowed it, I've gone out with some friends, two or three kids I've hung around with since high school. As you can imagine, once they've ridden in a car several times, they know it inside out; they remember the license plate number and, in short, they can't mistake it. Well, one day last month, Ferrari says to me, 'Yesterday we were behind your car on the road to El Tigre. We thought you were driving, so we raced it to catch up with you. We were in a Ford, we caught up with your car, and we were going to call out to you when we saw that the person driving was your mother.' What do you make of that?"

"I'd say it explains something I suspected for some time," I said, thoroughly dismayed.

"I had the same feeling," Miguel said.

"You?"

"Yes, my mother's a sleuth, and she can intuit things even if they're happening at one of the poles. But you know," he went on, "I don't think you need to worry very much now, now that everything's taken this turn."

"What floors me," I said, "is, apparently you're also completely in the know."

"Come on! It's totally obvious."

"Totally?"

"Totally. Of course, I also asked my mother why she'd gone to El Tigre. I put the question just like that, point-blank, when we were eating, and it took her breath away. When she recovered, the whole time she was explaining, she was cautioning me repeatedly, 'Not a word to Quitina. Understand? Not a word to anyone.' Then, since she saw I was going to obey her to the letter, even though she hadn't specifically warned me to, she said, as if she were changing her mind a little, 'Well, you can tell Santiago, if you think of it. Yes, it doesn't matter a bit if you tell him.' 'We'll see' I said, and I tell you, she looked a little disappointed. I think she would have liked me to tell you right away. But you know me."

"I see I know you relatively, I didn't think you were so perceptive."

"But a person didn't need to be perceptive to notice that."

"Damn! That's the worst part. Because, let's see, your mother is perceptiveness personified, you too more or less, and Quitina, although she may be no match for your mother, I always considered her more perceptive than you, so if you're well informed, what does that say about Quitina?"

"Quitina is not informed," Miguel said, "that's the difference. Quitina knows everything, not as well as I do, or as well as you yourself, but she's not informed. No, she doesn't know about El Tigre."

"Ah!" I breathed. "Are you sure?"

"Completely sure. That was the comment my mother made when she found out about City Bank: 'It's just as well that those trips to that blasted marshland ended without Quitina finding out.'"

"Well," I said, "learning about it like this, with certainty, is a lot for me."

"Yes, of course," Miguel said. "That's why I told you. I've been wanting to tell you for days so you wouldn't put your foot in your mouth, but I couldn't find the right time."

I looked at my watch, but it was almost impossible to see anything.

"I think it's after eight," I said; "we won't eat until nine. Let's go up to the tower; I want to show you something."

We walked toward the garden and passed under the wire—in passing, I touched a white poppy, as I did every afternoon, it was a ritual—and, as we crossed the ditch, I tripped slightly and leaned on Miguel's arm. He tugged at me, thinking I was about to go down. I felt as small and protected as if he were holding me by the hand.

Once we were there, I uncovered the hiding place where I keep these notebooks, which no one else, absolutely no one, has known about before now.

I didn't uncover it myself for a long time, because it wasn't my own doing. From the beginning, when I took over Las Murtas, I'd liked this tower a lot; at that time I called it Monington's little room. I didn't change anything from the way he had it. The couch was still the same one and it's in the same spot—because there's no other spot for it—but the space now occupied by the bookcase was covered before by an old, yellowish map of the world that looked fine there, and I never thought of moving it.

It was a long time afterwards, after I began to use the room often, which is the same time I began to write these confessions—that's what I decided to call them—, that one day as I was stretched out on the couch, I noticed some little cords on the side of the map that you can pull to make the map roll up. I pulled, and in the wall I discovered a square cubbyhole, which didn't resemble a cupboard or a niche for a saint and was clearly the spot that had been occupied by a small safe—not whitewashed, exactly the way it had been when the safe was torn out. Monington had covered the space with the map, and the remains of his treasure were still there: a bottle of whiskey, empty.

That cube-shaped space, with the plaster all chipped, revealed a great deal about the house to me. It was certain that at first it had been Puig's room. Probably the part that corresponded to the tower was the only thing left standing of the old structure, and Puig installed himself there right after he bought it, while he was overseeing the reconstruction of the rest. Later, once he was settled in his lavish bedroom, he tore out the safe and had it placed beside his bed. Then I arrived and, in order to turn the bedroom into a library, I had the safe torn out and I stored it with a pile of other junk in the garage.

As soon as I saw the cubbyhole in the tower, I decided to install the safe again. I was about to tell Quitina about it, but I thought the safe would never hold anything but these notebooks, and, of all the things in the world, these notebooks are the thing I would least like to see in her hands. (Maybe they're my first betrayal. Maybe they're my *only* betrayal. I don't know.) But it happened that Quitina, and not only Quitina, knew the word that served as the combination to the safe. It's an old system and a simple one, but you have to know the word to open the safe. Naturally, the word was in Puig's will. The Garcías never used that little safe, for the same reason they never used the bedroom. When they handed me the keys, they gave me the key to the large safe in the office. "Write down the word for the little safe," they told me, "so you don't go and forget it." But I hadn't forgotten it: the word was "Llaura."

I made so many evil caricatures of Puig's Llaura! "It never fails, the man who names one of these little safes for a lover ends up having a huge safe, like a big fat wife." And other such remarks.

When I decided to return the safe to its original place, I put it in the car and went to an expert to have the combination changed. The name's no longer "Llaura," now it answers to "Factum."

I dropped my entire secret on Miguel, although he didn't seem overwhelmed by its weight.

"I don't want to leave this word in my will," I said, "but someone had to know it. Someone who would come after me and before my boys. You understand? You won't forget it?"

"Don't be absurd! That's something a person can't forget."

"Not the arrangement of the shelves on the bookcase that hides it either. I worked really hard to come up with that and build it. By myself, of course."

"What you came up with is really clever," Miguel said. "You saw that when I was installing the lamp, I didn't notice anything."

"No, it's not noticeable, the secret's perfect. That's why I uncovered the niche for you; because if I told you I don't want anyone to ever read these notebooks, I would be lying. It's obvious, since I write them, it's so someone will read them. But who? I don't know. As you see, up to now they are four notebooks, two hundred pages each, and they fill exactly half the safe: half of the *factum* is still nothing but empty space.

"Listen, though," I said suddenly. "How did your mother find out I was going to El Tigre all the time?"

"I don't know," Miguel said, somewhat puzzled. "I didn't think to ask her. Of course, it's natural you would ask, but to me what seemed natural was her finding out. If she hadn't found out, I would surely have asked her: How can you not find out! But don't wrack your brains, because she'll end up telling you. I'm sure she's dying to give you a real tongue-lashing."

"Well, it won't be hard for her to find the opportunity."

And it wasn't hard for her to find the opportunity, because I hastened to provide her with one.

On Sunday Miguel left with the Chevrolet, and I told him not to worry about coming back to pick up his mother. I would take her, because I was planning to spend the night in the study so that I wouldn't have to get up at the crack of dawn on Monday morning.

We ate early and were on our way to Buenos Aires about nine. When we got to the highway, I slowed down a bit.

"All right, get started," I said, as if we had an agreement.

Of course Herminia was already gearing up, and it irritated her a little that I'd taken the initiative.

"You're so cynical," she said.

"Quite cynical," I agreed. "But not at the moment."

"Oh no?"

"No, and you're aware of it. So don't waste inappropriate insults, because there are more applicable ones you can use very conveniently."

"The thing is, the ones that fit you are the kind that don't appear in the dictionary."

I didn't answer, I just nodded, indicating acquiescence. Herminia seemed to be looking for something really devastating to say. She maintained the judgmental tension for a moment but immediately gave in to anguish, exchanging her accusation for lament.

"You're so stupid. My God, so stupid!"

"Well, no," I said, "I'm not stupid either; this time you err from kindness. If I were stupid I'd be unaware of the exact dimension of my actions. And I am aware, I assure you."

"Then, can you explain to me?"

"No."

"Well, I don't think I really have the right to interrogate you."

"You do, though," I cut her off. "Not the right, the obligation. It's the only thing you can do for me. Interrogate me and I'll answer you, but when it comes to explaining . . ."

"Why explain, after all that's happened," Herminia said dispiritedly. "The explanation won't erase the deed."

"No, it won't erase the deed, and I'm not trying to deny it either, but if there's something I wish I had the power to explain, it's that the deed . . . well, obviously it can't be erased, but it can be transferred."

"Transferred?"

"Yes, it would never occur to me to deny that what happened, happened, but I don't know what I would give to make you understand it did not happen *now*."

"But what do you mean, you idiot?" Herminia said, with a mixture of curiosity and fear.

"Well, that all this happened many years ago. Let's see . . . yes, fourteen years ago."

"Frankly, I can't take something crazy like that seriously."

"Listen carefully, Herminia, because this isn't easy. Here, the only person who has a precise idea of what I've just told you is the victim."

"What victim?" Herminia said indignantly.

"The victim is Elfriede, that's obvious."

"I don't understand one word you've said, and I don't feel the least bit of compassion for the victim," she said rather harshly.

"You don't understand. Herminia, you don't understand. Listen carefully, and see if you don't get some of it. The story goes back many years. For me, it had ended in '32. Not for a single instant, I swear it, not for a single instant did I suspect it hadn't ended. But the victim lived this story that entire time, she put her whole life into it or, rather, she put it, over the years, into her whole life; she coupled them. Her life was entirely subordinated to a story, and the story—and here's the important thing—was becoming storified. You understand? For her, the story was not ancient history but the series of efforts, attempts, and failures she lived until she came here. And she came here and found that, in me, the story had not continued. She saw my life has passed without a single tie to that past, and she won't give in."

"A total lack of dignity!" Herminia interrupted me.

"Well, *she* calls it perseverance and perhaps self-confidence."

"Vanity, in a word."

"I'm trying to make you understand a story, a life, a mentality that's not mine."

"Yes, yes, I understand."

"All right, so she doesn't give in, she attacks, and all she accomplishes is the resurrection of that time. Neither present nor future. She doesn't manage to set the tiniest plan in motion, she's not able to incorporate herself into the present, by modifying it. Look," I continued, not without some qualms, "I would find it repugnant to censure her, and it would be shameful on my part, but you understand that one's observation is independent from one's will. I assure you, the impossibility of her intervening in my present, in other words, her inability to alter my life, to provoke an imbalance, occasion the threat of a scandal or crisis that would change the state of affairs, was driving her crazy. To endure absolute confinement in the secretiveness, the solitude of that house, to see the perfection of the plot I devised around my trips, which were about to come to an end at any minute, without leaving a trace. The whole situation must have made her suffer horribly. It was like crashing against a wall. No, worse, because a crash is a real event, whereas this was different, it was living an event that was automatically denied. Or, as I told you before, transferred. It was seeing that what was happening here and now, for me, was nothing but the last movement of what happened before."

Herminia assented in silence, resigning herself to understand. Feeling perplexed, she was looking for a way to tell me it was all idiotic, but her intelligence wouldn't let her. In order to relieve her of her confusion, I said: "Now it's my turn to ask a question: How in heaven's name did you find out?"

"Oh," Herminia replied, "I have the reputation for being a gundog, but the thing is, it's chance that almost always puts me on the scent. I'm not sure of the date, but one day in September, no, it was the morning of the day before your father-in-law arrived, I decided to go upstairs and ask Gálvez for a sheet of carbon paper. Gálvez was alone, he started to look for it in the cabinet, and I was waiting beside his desk. At that moment the telephone rang, I picked it up and heard 'Hallo, hallo.' I recognized her immediately. 'Just a moment,' I said, disguising my voice and speaking very softly. Then I handed the receiver to Gálvez. 'Doctor Hernández isn't here,' he said. 'He's expected in half an hour.' I went downstairs and waited. You came before the half hour was up, and you weren't in the study for even ten minutes; I heard you go downstairs immediately. I looked out the balcony, without drawing back the curtains and saw that you'd left your car right next to the Chevrolet, which had spent the night there, and a truck had parked in front of you, which meant the big car was boxed in. I thought: it's going to be hard for him to get out of there. And, as I was thinking this, I'd picked up the key for the Chevrolet, which Miguel had left for me—I was planning to use it to deliver the copies I was finishing, and it was because they were urgent that I'd gone upstairs for the carbon paper. That's how fine the web was. I won't tell you any more; before you got to the corner I was in the other car, and I followed you at a discreet distance until you took the boat. Then, once I saw you moving off toward the silt, there was nothing for me to do but go back."

"What would be appropriate for me to say now is, 'You're so cynical!' You tell me about your exploit without batting an eyelash, as if it were a spy movie."

"With a totally clear conscience," she said. "I really *needed* to know the truth, because Quitina knows it. I'm not sure how; in her it definitely has to do with her being able to sniff things out. Sometimes I've tried to dissuade her, convince her she was deceiving herself, even though I knew she was right; but my power of persuasion wasn't strong enough, because, deep down I wasn't sure. In order to lie well you have to know the truth. Of course, even after I found out the truth," she added, "I still haven't managed to lie well. With Quitina it's so hard to know which is better for her."

I put on the brakes, nearly coming to a dead stop.

"What's wrong?" Herminia asked.

"Nothing, nothing," I said, "only, what you just said made a great impression on me. I don't fully understand it, but it seems to me there's definitely something to it."

"You mean the part about not knowing which is better for her?"

"Yes, that."

"Well, I don't know exactly what I said, but it's true." She was silent for a moment. Then she said, "You know, if you hadn't remarked on it, it would have passed by me unnoticed once again, because this is not the first time I've said that, and certainly not the first time I've thought it. When I try to remember, it seems to me it's the first thing I thought about Quitina when I met her."

"But how could you think it then, if the circumstances didn't raise this dilemma?"

"True: I surely thought it in another form, but with the same meaning. What you said, precisely, a dilemma. I'm sure that around Quitina I always saw something of a dilemma. You see, a creature so whole, so pure, that, when I looked at her, I always said to myself: yes, she *is* like that, exactly as I see her, but she could also be totally different."

I'd started to drive again, at a snail's pace. All the cars were passing us and enveloping us in clouds of dust, but I couldn't keep my attention on the wheel. I stopped again.

"Quitina, Pancha, Francesca . . . ," I said. "Recall? Once, just after you came, you heard us talk about that."

"Yes, I think so. You see? It's the same thing I was telling you. Do you know what's best for her?"

"No, I don't. Look," I said, taking hold of the wheel again, "if I back up a bit on that narrow path, turn the car halfway around, and drive on the highway at full speed in the opposite direction, in a little over two hours we'll be in Las Murtas, but we can't return to being in the time when you arrived."

"No, of course not. Even so, it's as certain we came from then as that we came from Las Murtas."

"Yes, but we know that Las Murtas is back there, still, and now that the time when I arrived is nowhere."

We rode in silence for a long while, and when we reached the city, we were both still lost in our reflections. Suddenly Herminia spoke: "Everything we've just said is a perfectly trivial. Yes, all those conclusions are the clichés of modern philosophy, platitudes. Of course, they're also truths, don't think I'm about to refute them. They have as much right to exist as the clichés of the past did, and we're forced to use them, I know, otherwise we don't circulate. But what I meant was, even though our current truth may be this one, of continual becoming with no turning back, the memory of what remained behind—well, it didn't remain, I know that, but it was there. How can I explain it to you? The pledge, the fidelity to the project . . ."

"Yes, yes," I said, "I know exactly what you mean. What happens is that the project is a becoming, decided in the face of the dilemma: leave this one and take the other one."

"See? You see? You're a child of our century! The pledge is to take this one until death."

"That's exactly what I was telling you: the pledge is to take *this one*, until the death *of the other one*. Understand? You condemn to death everything you don't take, and then comes the question, what is better?"

"Oh!" Herminia said doubtfully, and she didn't say anything more because we were there.

Miguel was waiting for us on the balcony, eating a sandwich while holding a glass of beer.

"Come in for a while," he told me. "There are a couple of bottles from lunch in the refrigerator, and they're just right."

I went in, ate a large cheese sandwich in silence, drank two glasses of beer, and came up to the study. It was a very hot night; I undressed, fell onto the bed, and was asleep immediately, deeply, but not for very long.

Suddenly, I was awakened by a sort of explosion in my head or my chest, and I found myself saying, "No, it's not that!" almost out loud.

I recall Herminia's exclamation of doubt, and I think I sense there was disappointment, anguish, outrage in her. Maybe she didn't understand me? Because I'd told her everything one doesn't take one condemns to death, and then comes the question. Could Herminia have thought I doubted my choice, that now I'm wondering which is better for me? No, that couldn't possibly have been Herminia's understanding. But neither could she have understood what I meant if she'd only paid attention to what I said.

I looked at the clock: later than I thought. My impression was that I'd slept fifteen minutes, but it was already three, which meant that three hours had passed since I came up from Herminia's. Even so—it seemed highly unlikely I'd be able to go back to sleep, I went to the vestibule and opened the window, in the hope of seeing a bit of light below. Maybe, like me, one of those two was wide awake, and then I'd make a little hiss from up above and go down to the garden and we'd talk until dawn. I saw some wicker chairs, under the philodendrons, where we could exhaust the subject until there was not one bit of equivocation left.

But the windows downstairs were open on the normal sleep of two working people. It seemed to me I could feel them inhaling. Like two breathing pumps, their bodies were being nourished, repaired, in sleep, and they were calm, because their lairs are much safer than those of the animals in the countryside. Men have made this wonderful thing called a house, so perfect, so tailored to our needs, and once we're inside it we have nothing to fear. Because the attack of other men who have no respect for locks is foreseen and prevented 99 percent of the time. There is only one danger that neither locks nor doors can contain: man's own mind when he's in his house.

A huge star appeared above the hops edging the garden wall. I saw it blinking among the leaves first, and then I saw it silhouetted against the boundless sky. I don't think the light came from the star, but there was a brightness that made it impossible to see things clearly, and for the hundredth time I looked, as I always did when I peered out that window, at a small imperfection in the stained glass's leading that I kept forgetting to fix. There had been so many changes made in the house, so many workers of all kinds had been here, but I never recalled in time to have it fixed. And the thing was, the imperfection had hardly gotten any larger. I'd known it for sixteen years, because I saw it as soon as I arrived in the house, and it was still almost the same. Almost, but not quite. The strip of lead was pulling away between the pieces of green and mauve glass for about three centimeters. The first time I saw it, it was probably less than three and, although it had gotten a little bigger, it didn't amount to four, so the glass seemed very old. But if the process of its aging was so slow, in order to imagine that glass molten I would have to assign it a legendary age, something like BC, and, of course, the friction or collision that had caused the break in the lead could be placed, more or less, in the Middle Ages.

I spent a long time imagining the very slow progress of that imperfection, so long that the star rose a lot, continuing to stand out because of its singular size but now seemingly leaner; now it sparkled like a well-cut diamond, whereas at first it had a watery brilliance that made its outline imprecise. I watched it a long while.

Suddenly, the blow inside my chest again, like an echo of the word "No!" and, clearly, the dialogue with the bad ending: "No, Herminia, that's not what I meant." Those words, which I did not actually say, had awakened me and were once more interrupting my dreams, returning me to reality. I stood with my back to the garden and leaned on the windowsill. Reality was passing through that vestibule again, like a planet through its orbit. But not like a planet! The star was definitely in front of the window now, exactly as it probably had been for thousands of years BC—without the window—and the reality of my life was culminating there again, identical, but different.

What was it that was culminating? What was it, at a precise moment, I was calling the reality of my life? Something that ten years before, right there, in that two-by-three meter room, as it was snatched from me, plunged me into insanity. Right there, on that unforgettable night, I felt *they were going to take from me* what was *going to be* my future. What a clumsy way to express this! Well, on that occasion, two things could have been *going to be*. One of the two had to win and, naturally, I needed it to be the one that I'd chosen, decided with all my will. The idea that the other could win was like a death threat, because it was hurling me toward an unforseen future on which my conscience shed no light. And now, so long after the one I'd chosen had *come into being*, it was culminating in my examination, showing me that the new characteristics it exhibited were not caused by the erosion of time: they were the result of my decision.

No, Herminia, no, I kept repeating. What I meant was, when we take one thing we condemn to death the one we leave, but it's possible for something much more horrible to happen; it's possible for us to condemn to death the one we choose. Our very decision, which makes it come into being, can make it come apart . . . I'm avoiding the specific event! And it's pure cowardice because I'm not that clumsy: I know how to write well enough to call a spade a spade. If I decide to do that, it all reduces to saying: "What is it that between us, between Quitina and me, we've made of Francesca?"

This was what I'd meant to say, and this same thing was what made me think, the day I was driving in the car with my father-in-law to meet Javier, "I don't know what Quitina's like. I never knew less about a human being. And it's not a fragment, a shadowy zone of which I'm ignorant: Quitina is all shadow." Yes, all of her, all of Francesca has sunk into shadow. Because it was Francesca who had lived those wrenching hours with me ten years ago. At a distance, between tears and shouts, between improbable curses and spells, in a fit of insanity or childishness, because impotence does not long for force or reason but for omnipotence. In that vortex, Francesca was the one who wanted to come into being, and the one who did.

I repeat: the shadow that envelops her now is not the erosion of time. No! No!

I find myself face-to-face with a truth I hate, one that's making an attempt on the foundations of my outlook on life. I must not try to deny this, which would be to acknowledge that it's defeating me, and it's definitely not defeating me. I acknowledge it without accepting it; I record it (I enjoy using this word now, one that's abominable to some people but necessary when there's no proof to make confirmation possible and we can only record something by touching it). By analyzing the truth and describing it, I will show my aversion, because the more thoroughly one understands it, the more one hates it.

The revolting truth is this: my abandonment created Elfriede; my choice nullified Francesca.

I could have prevented Elfriede's entire story with a simple postcard. Her hope for that postcard—who knows how long it lasted?—was the first storage battery. One day and then the next on which the card did not come, but *still could come*, and Elfriede's consciousness gradually became riveted on an unattainable desire. If I had sent her a just a couple of words, some form of normal communication would have continued between the courses of our two lives, and her preposterous undertakings would not have occurred. This is the strict, detestable truth.

Did Elfriede have a feeling when we met in Montevideo that a heart-to-heart talk between us, a simple and frank rapprochement, would be able to erase the mirage that gave her the strength to travel across the world? At the moment she became aware she'd failed as a professional, hadn't she decided to raise me up as a substitute for glory? To keep fighting for artistic fame, which her intelligence made her recognize was impossible, was pointless. But you can fight pointlessly for an impossible love. An essential condition of such a fight is that it be pointless. And, of course, to place me in that category was to refuse to sever the last mooring of her hope: thinking to establish a strong, elastic bond, she hurled at me a harpoon of impossibility and frustration.

Would I have written Elfriede's name in these pages where I pour out all the most unblemished things in my life? Would I have made my memory of her the starting point of a history of my conscience if that thread of impossibility had not kept us joined? Her beauty, so beautifully framed by her wintry country, her seventeen years, her marvelous body were not engraved indelibly in my arms, but the inconclusive embrace in Montevideo, that embrace did continue, latent and tense, like a spring that, eventually, had to release.

She definitely knew this. Aphrodite guides women firmly through these mysteries. Elfriede knew she'd left a breach, a point of vulnerability in me, and she was certain to find it because she'd paid for it with drops of blood. Perhaps during the years of her crazy undertakings, she recalled those drops like the signs lost travelers leave in a woods.

This is the revolting truth: *no* as the driving force.

Now, though, will I dare to analyze the hair-raising truth: *yes* as woodworm, as paralysis, as drain.

The thing is much more difficult, because before it was a question of assigning specific events to specific causes. That allocation is not based on anything certain, but it does provide an accurate sense of the correspondences, it lets you come up with a balanced theory. This other way, though, requires the proof of an *absence*. And that's extremely difficult, since the presence of what we adore is palpable and we must register its *lack* of something. Something it could have only if we had not done *it*.

This is a totally nebulous tangle. I must get to the point.

That absence has *presented* itself many times, prompting us to utter the lamentations appropriate to each instance. Not explicit, but definitely just and intense.

I recall feeling once that Quitina was abdicating her own form in which she was Francesca, and I asked myself clearly: "Did Quitina feel nostalgic for the grandeur she attained when someone fought with her?" She never evidenced even a hint of such nostalgia. If she was abdicating in some way, she remained whole in her abdication. But the day Herminia told the story, Quitina dove into the swarm of antitheses it provoked: "the anxiety that there's nothing wrong, that thank God there's nothing wrong. And if there's nothing wrong, a love so great, how can one prove it?"

The abyss that Quitina was trying to probe was infinite, simply infinite. And, I recall this well, as she spoke, the entire grandeur of that abyss was within her. Not reflected, though; it was not that she gained grandeur from the abyss, but that she stood before the abyss with a grandeur capable of measuring it.

I don't know why, but in the two seconds I've been meditating on this, trying to come up with a more accurate expression of the phenomenon—because what I've said so far doesn't even get close—I've seen in my mind an image that says it all. In my memory? No, because I don't recall where I've seen it, or even if I've ever seen it. And as I see it now— because I continue to see it—, I can't see *what it's like*, or *what it is*. I don't know if it's the figure of a man or a woman; I don't know if it's a painting or if it's a scene from life, truly seen: it's a human facing the sea. Not on the shore, definitely not; maybe the figure's on a breakwater, facing a brackish sea, and the whole thing is tinged with those dark tones characteristic of Belgian or Dutch painters. The figure's advancing a little, it's not standing still; I see it move toward the sea, against the wind, slowly, reflectively; it does not advance like a Nike; *it stands* facing the sea.

And if I cover the sea with my hand, and I look only at the figure, I notice that *it stands facing the sea.*

Is this clear? Perhaps not, but it is for me, absolutely clear.

Well, seldom, very seldom does Quitina *stand facing the sea*, because I have her closed up at home, although, of course, after I've made that home a paradise for her. The thing is, however, she doesn't face the sea very often and, as soon as I see her heading in that direction, I stop her because the breakwater's dangerous. Then I prevent appearing in her the trace of her grandeur that, facing another grandeur, always appears, as if it had been summoned.

Once, many years ago, I told myself—I think I also wrote it down in these notebooks—that "If Quitina were not entirely happy, I would have no right to live." The happiness I would like to give her does not lack grandeur, I know that. I'm sure I've reached the height, the high tide of happiness with her. I don't know why a person can't conceive of high tide as something stable. But the abyss is different. When I was afraid Quitina knew the adventures of my mind, I had the sense that if she were to peer into it, she would fall into the pit and never emerge. That other night too, that other tremendous night! when I sneaked down from the bathroom, after being at the gates of the other world, and Quitina came in because she heard me moving about in the water, sat on the stool, and dried my feet on her lap. Then, too, I seemed to see a majestic mercy in her, a grandeur capable of accompanying me to damnation.

Magnificent, the word is "magnificent": at that moment she seemed magnificent to me. I was coming from my hellish world, I had just performed the most daring experiments, I had peered into nonbeing and pushed my will to the limit, to the point at which the knot becomes untied and, once I was in the hot bath, the circulation of my blood began to remake my life the way you mend frayed fabric. At that moment Quitina walked in and stood there, looking at me in the bathtub. And, yes! Now I see it clearly; as she stood there looking at me, Quitina *was facing the sea*, she was at the edge of the breakwater, facing the wind, facing its immensity. Of all her gestures or poses this is the one that coincides most closely with the indefinable figure facing the brackish sea. Quitina was reading in me the traces left by the squall in my conscience, and she was not afraid. No, Quitina is never afraid. Then, as she sat there, her lap covered with a towel, she urged me to put my feet on it, and I reacted slowly, drowsy from the bath. That was when she shook back her hair, moist from the steam in the room, and told me impatiently and decisively: "Come on, now."

But, God! I did not want to take her anywhere. I wanted exactly the opposite, to return to her, I wanted her to be on solid ground, in a calm, sheltered place. Should I be sorry about having had that purpose? Must I repent? Or could logic be what's weak here? Maybe there's some mistake in the main points of my argument?

I tried passionately to join my life to the life of a being who appeared to me as the purest of passions; you might say that my ambition was to achieve the confluence of two huge currents that will form a pool. No, no; that's a pessimistic comparison. The lake requires sluice gates, a drain. Well, in some way, carnal union is a bit like that: the confluence of our bloods has spilled over into new lives that flow through the spring of the future. But that's not what I was talking about!

I wanted passionately, insanely, to create a harmony from our two deliriums, and I was undoubtedly successful. In the positive aspect of my private life there's been no failure, no crack in our union, no sign of a point where cohesion has diminished cohesion. What's occurred suddenly is the syncope that paralyzes the fluidness of our correspondence, although not because one of the two currents has swerved or because any external element has interfered. No, the proof this hasn't happened is that Quitina *was never calm*. And she was never calm because *she knows me*, she says, which means she has always known about the existence of a seed of conflict that was something intrinsic to our union. Quitina's calm must have been like the melancholy that overcame me when I sensed she was abdicating. I noticed Quitina was abdicating Francesca, and this disturbed me; Quitina felt that I was not abdicating (what can I abdicate or not abdicate? It's not in my nature to come out with 'things could have been entirely different'), that I was not abdicating my inclination for risk (it also seems stupid and pretentious to say I'm inclined toward risk. I lead a comfortable, almost sedentary life, to such an extent that at times it makes me feel ashamed. I recall the time I said: "social man has been born in me," and I'm not going to say he died, but he's grown very little.) I don't know what risk I'm inclined toward, although I cause anything but calm, and that inhibited Quitina, because the danger was not clear, she could not contemplate it, You would have to say, "it was a danger that did not call her." Quitina was not calm, but she'd grown accustomed to living in the face of mystery, as believers do.

Sometimes you stop writing because nothing occurs to you, and sometimes what occurs to you is so dazzling it prevents you from reasoning even the minimal amount necessary to say something intelligible. When I wrote a few days ago that Quitina lived the way believers do, I couldn't continue because I realized the risk I'm inclined toward is the risk intrinsic to unbelievers, infidels.

"The idea of science would be to explain all the events of the universe with a single idea." I don't know why I recall this now, because I read it some time ago; it must be because every time I venture into the narrow alleys of psychic life, I expect Newton's apple to fall on me. Let's see: yes, here's the text, and I can copy the entire paragraph. A few lines below it says this idea "isolates and defines a radical event of which all the others are pure modifications and combinations. So that physics has endeavored to show that the infinite types of movement observed in the cosmos are individual cases of a single type of displacement: the fall of one body on another."

I'm searching for *something*, in the midst of a great darkness, and I don't know what it is or where it's found, but my nth sense detects its existence. I'm searching with such determination because I'm driven by an ambition for decency, and there's nothing I find more comforting and soothing than one of those scientific paragraphs in which the truth appears naked and radiant with modesty.

This clear and tidy conclusion from physics soars to the comets and nebulae, descends to the infusoria and even to the mud, from which it emerges without a stain and without abolishing the mud, leaving the slime and the humus their substance. Well, something like that is what I'm after, because, like Kierkegaard, I too want to make a universal theme from my personal story, but Job and his school don't satisfy me entirely. Nor do I find strictly rational formulas useful; what I need is to find the law of correspondences. "Dans une tenebreuse et profonde unité . . ." The answers can be definitely heard only in the shadows and the depths; to bring them into the light is to defile them. To defile them? Why?

As I wrote the sentence from the preceding page that made me pause, I sensed the tenebrous correspondence between my now tepid relationship with Quitina and the lukewarm or even weakened condition of my religious life. Those two things don't depend on each other; definitely not, they correspond in a kind of conflict that carries its system internally, in what you might call it a technical difficulty . . . in short, a practical one.

There's a point of departure that's the start of everything. Everything comes from an error. If you broadened the definition of that word, you would have to say *sin*. The thing is that, without this error, there would be no history, no story, and there never could have been any. I don't know if the story there was can justify the error. I don't know.

Far from justifying it, the story aggravated it, if I recognize the error was a superconscious one. A few years ago, I wrote in these notebooks that "When a human life becomes so delirious with grandeur it wants to attain categories that surpass the human, when it wants to make something absolute and eternal from the union of two finite beings . . ." During that period I concluded that when this happens, as that human life expands unchecked, it can find itself suddenly with the Divine. Then, it gets swept away by the new contact; in other words, it has a hunch this might happen, but the human does not give in; he defends his earthly possessions and, what is more audacious, the more he knows, intuits, or proves the absolute, the more avidly he wants to insufflate it into his own perishable human passion. The sin of this ambition is purged by sinning against the ambition, something that occurs in a fatal way, because only the sinner, the idolater, the infidel can conceive of that ambition and, of course, in the end his infidelity appears and destroys the idol it created.

No, no; anything equivocal spreads like weeds. Without generalizing, to be specific, I sinned specifically with Quitina, not with Elfriede. It was with Quitina that I conceived of a lasting passion whose tension would remain unchanged as long as we lived. With her and only with her did I feel this desire of the absolute. And I no longer feel it? I feel it just the same. But *I only feel it* if I ask myself that because, when I call it into question, the question begins to look threatening. What collapses in this ambition of mine—I don't want to say ours here—is not the created idol; that's the only thing that remains standing, it's the only thing that explains my ambition. The excellence of the object justifies the cult. But can the cult last in and for itself?

I'm hopelessly inept! There's not a sentence I don't have to repeat a hundred times, flip-flopping from one side to the other. The night of my unfinished conversation with Herminia I wrote that "I wanted passionately, insanely, to create a harmony from our two deliriums." Why, why in heaven's name do passion, insanity, and delirium simply mean the strong attraction of one human being toward another? Those disheveled terms become meaningless as soon as the attraction is satisfied. Once the apple hits the ground, it goes no farther; it just goes bad, dies, and is absorbed by the soil. But between human beings things are different. The attraction's the same, it's that one single movement: the fall of one body on another. And once it falls, once the happy, corroborating crash has occurred, what role is there for passion, insanity, and delirium?

The subtle distinctions, the fine-tunings of expressions are endless. Neither the exaggerated terms above nor the attraction—the reasonable and exact term that involves them—signifies carnal desire alone. When it's merely a question of attraction, you can speak of erosion: time wears away surfaces and dulls sensations. There must be a respite in which time remakes what it's destroyed so it will want to destroy itself again. But when the phenomenon is an accident that involves the entire being and when union is achieved, the estrangement that's necessary for attraction to be renewed cannot be prompted voluntarily. The body that falls on another body does not get up on its own; there must be an outside force that pulls on it—a threat, whether very slight, such as a simple question, or the most fearsome, the interference of another being, a body whose attraction is more powerful, a hulk placed right in its path.

But of course, speaking of bodies, neither delirium nor fury ever come to mind. In order to comprehend mentally the extent to which it's appropriate to use those words, you have to imagine what a man probably experiences when he feels the barrel of a gun in his back. Even if he's a hero or a giant, he automatically freezes, because suddenly he finds that living, precisely the stupid thing he was doing, is furiously, deliriously necessary.

That's it! That's it: Quitina has lived in that automatic frozen state, because *she was never calm*. And that motionlessness of hers, which to me always seemed like her abdication, was what helped her maintain her secret tension. The driving force of NO! Of course here the *no* was not categorical, that refusal of mystery so fascinating to the believer—the fear that makes live passion and delirium prevail in faith and ensures they never deteriorate to something as silly as simple living.

Well, this is what happens in the believer, but what happens in the infidel? In the first place, what is it to be an infidel? It's something very different from being unbelieving. The person who is not a believer does not believe, and that's all there is to it. The person who's an infidel is a believer—perhaps too much of a believer, although that may seem crazy. Too much, not as excess, but as plurality. Idolatry, superstition? These are certainly the common forms of the phenomenon, but there are more original patterns available to superior minds.

The infidel rummages in the secrets of the temple, not without love, definitely not, but without respect, without the least respect. Well, the infidel is not content with the temple; he thinks he can pillage heaven, force open doors, make off with the most precious objects and carry them back to adorn his own house. This is very important: the idolater employs the deity's treasures for domestic purposes and, at first, this works out very well: life shines and life takes on a magic sparkle. No, a sacred one; it's like living in a prayer. But daily life can't always rise to the realm of prayer, to its flame; it invariably ends up degenerating into an automatic ritual, a formulaic list of tiny requests. And the saintly intercessors are bombarded with trivialities, such as helping an old woman find her thimble or a young girl to have rosy cheeks. We superior minds don't hover at such an altitude; we leave the intercessors in peace, that's true, and without asking for a hearing we go straight to God himself, where we clamor at the top of our lungs. We start out by asking for some celestial gem, an ambitious request although a request worthy of the One who can grant it; but if it's given to us, we keep asking, and then what excesses, what trivialities wouldn't we be capable of? We superior minds would end up asking for flashy miracles just because it makes us proud to know they'll be given to us, and I think we'd even go so far as to ask for those miracles simply to escape from our boredom for a while.

What results from living in such close quarters with divine love is the dimming and gradual extinguishing of the flame. Because in human love the other is there, and the presence of that other can be asserted in protests of all sorts. But the deity protests by remaining silent.

What I'd like to do is analyze relentlessly the process my religious life has followed, but I don't know which point of view would best get at the intricacy of that process. The fact is, I've lost all religious *feeling*.

My estrangement is not chiefly rational. I could say I've lost all faith or that I've given in to doubt, because there is doubt in me: I've lived in doubt and I live doubt to its logical conclusion, but that's not what I find insurmountable. What I can't conquer is the climate of my soul. It's like a planet that's cooled off, something that's completed its life cycle. And this sensation of death is so clear I can't tolerate it. I don't want to say stand it, because it's not that I can't bear it, it's that I won't admit it, because I know it's something inflicted on me. I know that it's a punishment, and I'm rebelling in the only way possible, with the only weapon I have left. What do I have left? If I've lost my faith, it's obvious that *what I have left is doubt*. In doubt I must place, not my faith, which would be the height of paradox, but my confidence. I'm left with doubt, an active doubt, not a void—a doubt that has devoured my faith, like a termite. I need to stimulate doubt, not combat it, to whet its appetite, so when it's finished with all the reserves in my conscience, it will keep on gnawing until it's devoured itself.

This won't restore my faith, no, it's not the way to do that, as I'm well aware. When doubt devours faith, what remains is doubt; when doubt devours doubt, what remains is suspicion. And suspicion does not involve love. Can suspicion be compatible with hope and charity? To exchange faith for suspicion is to exchange the *fear of God* for the *fear* of God.

None of this is new. Descartes followed the same process. Descartes sweetened it, veiling it according to the style of his age; I strip it bare, scrape off its flesh, according to the style of mine. Knowing full well I face the greatest sin, because it's a far greater sin to doubt God's existence than to doubt His mercy. And suspicion differs from faith in that faith stands face-to-face, accompanied by love and hope, whereas suspicion goes its way alone, sensing God's steps behind its back, sensing that God can reach out a hand, grab it by the neck and smash it against the wall.

This is the style of my age. Our contemporary sages don't advocate with a calmly atheistic science, as they did in the last century, because what if God is hard on their heels?

I set great store in my doubt because my memory affirms that I had faith and that I cursed rebellion. It's the last remaining stronghold of my strength, and I enclose myself in it, I persist. God departs from my soul and without leaving me the breath necessary to cry out in despair. Neither does He leave me enough calm to say, "God does not exist, so let's go on to something else." The truth that lies deep in the well of my conscience can be expressed with the most provocative of sentences: "You don't have me fooled!"

14

Land! How radiantly the sun shines on our earth; how clearly it lets us see things are here! After floating night after night, adrift in the amorphous mass, when you jump ashore you touch paradise. There might be monsters and wild beasts on land, but if I had to be eaten by either a tiger or a shark, I'd choose the tiger. At least on land you can breathe until you've been eaten, but in a mass of liquid you're both eaten and drowned. That's much worse, no doubt about it.

The important thing is that suddenly land has appeared on the horizon, and I've been able to jump ashore. Earth is the world of others, where things happen and I pay attention to them, whether I intervene or not, and I'm free of myself. But I find earth's charm disarming in other ways as well. Because unforeseen things have been developing right beside us, and suddenly they're blossoming with an incalculable variety of possibilities. And best of all, we don't consider this a spectacle or a diversion, but immediately take a vital interest in making sure that everything lives.

Today we're at the end of October, and the weather is marvelous. It's so hot it feels as though we're in Africa, but for poppies this is marvelous weather. This morning I was in the study, and I heard Herminia and Miguel arguing in the garden; I looked out the window in the vestibule and saw that Herminia was leaving for the market. Miguel must have been in the shower, because you could hear the water running, but they had the window open, and they were arguing through the window. Herminia went off in a huff, and five minutes later Miguel whistled from below.

"Come down here if you want to see something good," he told me.

On Herminia's desk there was an envelope with photographs. Miguel pulled one out and handed it to me. It was the picture of a white rooster, actually of the rooster's head taken at very close range; the rooster was in someone's arms and you could see the hands holding it. He immediately gave me another picture: a Russian greyhound, also white, one of its front paws resting on a chair, on the chair a stack of books, and the greyhound had its paws placed on top of the books, in the pose of a heraldic lion. Of course, a young man was holding the greyhound by the collar so it would stay in the right position.

Miguel pointed to the boy.

"That's Fransil," he said.

"Brazil?" I said, because that's what I understood.

"No, Franc Sil."

"Oh! And who is Franc Sil?"

"A great artist, I think. The other one's Raúl Menéndez."

"What other one?"

"The one with the rooster. But you can't see him there. Look, here you can see him better," Miguel said, handing me another photo.

I saw a pale young man dressed in black who looked very Spanish; he'd probably never been in the country, because he was holding the rooster with horror, as if it were a basilisk.

"And what are those kids doing with the animals?"

"Well, they were going to make a collage, but it didn't turn out, I don't know why. Then Franc Sil made a drawing."

"Ah, he's a painter?"

"No, he's an actor."

Miguel put down the envelope and picked up a large roll of paper, moved back a little, and unrolled it.

"Look," he said.

The drawing, which was rather clumsy but expressive, showed the dog in the position of a rampant lion, although it was not leaning on the chair but holding in its paws a parchment with some lettering that had been erased—the drawing was done in charcoal—and the dog was doubtless the dog, but it had the rooster's head.

"Terrific!" I said, and at that moment we heard the key in the lock.

Miguel quickly left everything where it was.

"Come to my room, and I'll explain it to you," he said.

He was speaking softly and hurriedly so he could tell me before Herminia realized I was there.

"Those young guys are my mother's court of honor."

"Ah, they're the ones from that magazine?"

"No, those are different ones; she has a lot. But now, just lately, these are the most important. They're working on something that will make really make history."

Miguel was enjoying the suspense.

"Well," he said, "you already heard me arguing a while ago; it was because the Chevrolet still isn't fixed. They promised to have it ready for today, but they don't, and my mother wanted me to take her, along with two or three of her little friends, to some joint or other out in the sticks. So, if you want to see with your own eyes, all you have to do is offer her your services."

Herminia's footsteps approaching out in the hall made us realize she'd heard us whispering.

I opened the door. As Herminia said hello to me, she regaled me with a whole host of subtle allusions: "I can imagine you came downstairs because you heard us arguing. I'm in a bad mood, but I'm happy you came down. I don't want to ask you to resolve the conflict, because I don't want to let you in on the secret, but it irritates me that I can't resolve it."

"Don't worry about that business with the car," I hurried to tell her, "because they never have them ready when they promise; I can take you wherever you want."

"Oh no, what foolishness, you're not going to waste the morning on that."

"But why not? I don't have anything pressing to do."

"Well," she said, beginning to give in. "It's that, you know," she was sure I already knew, "a couple of kids are going to come over, and we have to go somewhere that's pretty far from here. It's so hot—the street-car leaves us three blocks away—and I don't want to take a taxi, because they insist on paying, and they're just kids who don't have a lot of money."

"But of course; we'll go wherever you want. It's no trouble for me at all. I promise not to give away the conspiracy," I added.

"Oh, the conspiracy! Today you won't see anything, and who knows if it will turn out. It's all very difficult. I don't know if I'm doing the right thing to get mixed up in something like this."

Herminia thought I knew about the whole thing and was waiting for me to encourage her—or the opposite—but she saw my innocent gesture and decided not to say any more. The whole affair made her feel a little embarrassed.

"They said they'd be here at ten and it's already twenty past," she said.

"Where are we going?" I asked.

"To Cangallo Street, I don't know how far up, way beyond Billing-hurst."

"Oh, ten minutes."

At that moment the doorbell rang and two young men appeared. One was Raúl Menéndez, whom I recognized immediately; the other looked like a little boy to me at first, because of his curly hair and plump, rosy cheeks, but when I went over to him I saw he was the size of a normal adult man and his face frankly expressed not innocence but something rather like devotion. They told me his name, but I didn't recall it.

The young men came in noisily. Menéndez hugged Herminia and gave her a couple of kisses, calling her beautiful, goddess, and queen of the Atreides. He greeted Miguel affectionately but respectfully, as if Miguel were a long-bearded gentleman, although he was probably four or five years younger. Me, he greeted with a friendly cordiality, as if he'd known me all his life. We got into the car. Miguel stayed at home. Herminia sat beside me, and the two young men rode in the back, holding the large packages they'd brought with them.

Herminia had the drawing, and Menéndez asked her how she'd liked it. I gathered he'd left it at the house when she wasn't there. Herminia said she'd liked it a lot.

"He erased the lettering," Menéndez said, "because Franc wants to use Gothic lettering, which looks professional, and he's going to copy it from somewhere. He didn't know how to draw it from memory. But I think the drawing has more style. It's sad, isn't it?"

Leaning over the back of the front seat, he directed the question at me, and I should have said: I haven't seen the drawing. But I was incapable of lying, and I nodded, smiling at him in the mirror. Herminia shook her head, as if to say: Just what I figured.

"Are you sure where this is, do you know the number?" I asked Menéndez.

"Of course."

"Franc Sil called this morning," the little one interjected, "and he said he'd be waiting for us at the door. Look, there he is."

We were approaching some small, low houses, there was a furniture shop in one of them and in the doorway stood Franc Sil, who came to greet Herminia as soon as he saw the car drive up. She introduced him to me; he was very young, tall, and very thin, with a dazed expression. He could definitely be an actor.

We went toward the house beside the furniture shop, a small one-story house with only two windows and a door in between. Franc Sil opened the door and stood back a little to let us pass. On the other side of the door there was nothing but space. The only part of the house left standing was the facade; inside, a clean, totally empty lot stretched for what seemed to be about three miles, although it was probably thirty or forty yards. There were a few trees at the back and some climbing plants on the walls.

Menéndez told Franc Sil that the drawing had been a big success. He turned toward us.

"Right?" he asked. Herminia and I nodded.

"Oh, it's just a sketch," Franc Sil said. "Now I have to polish it. The line's very important because it's going to be a silhouette. You understand?"

"Yes, Raúl explained it to me," Herminia said. "This is going to be the motto for the theater," she added, assuming I couldn't totally understand what they were talking about.

Menéndez interrupted her, with adolescent impatience and exuberance, because her explanation seemed rather flat to him.

"Hanging from a horizontal flagpole. You understand? Well, not on a piece of paper like that, since we'll get it cut from a sheet of iron; then it will be painted on both sides and hung up. Not on top of the flagpole, because it would look like a weather vane, but hanging, so it swings in the air, like one of those, one of those . . ."

"*Enseignes*," Franc Sil prompted at the same time Herminia was saying: "Banners."

"That's it," Menéndez said, "like one of those banners hanging along the streets of London you imagine in Dickens's novels. What do you think, eh?"

"Terrific, absolutely terrific," I said in all honesty.

"Now it needs the Gothic lettering, real dark on the parchment."

"And what's the lettering going to say?" I asked.

"The name of the theater! You don't know it?" Menéndez asked in amazement.

"No, I don't know the name."

"Well, I haven't told you because we're still not certain," Herminia said. "Let's see what you think. First we thought of a simple name that would be easy to remember: 'Teatro Cangallo,' for example. But we said there can be a pizza place two blocks away and a bit farther down a little market with a bar on the other side, all with the same name; we have to look for something more original. Then it occurred to me: 'Teatro del Can-Gallo' or 'Teatro del Perro-Gallo.' Which combination do you like more?"

"Well, I don't know, let me think about it. The idea seems very good to me, but I don't know which of the two is better."

"What I thought of—" Menéndez started to say, but Herminia didn't let him continue.

"No, Raúl, what you thought of would be a series of disastrous consequences. Imagine," she said to me, "this boy knows all the Spanish poets from the time of the Republic very well, also the classic ones; he knows classic theater by heart, something that's not usual. Well, when I said 'Teatro del Perro-Gallo,' it occurred to him that it could also be 'Teatro del Perrigallo.' Imagine! I let out a shriek: No, for Christ's sake! A clever name like that would be the end. It sounds really Spanish, and people can't stand such things here. But the one with Perro-Gallo seems quite Parisian, and I think it could make a very good mascot."

"It seems to me that you're absolutely right," I said. "Except you have to think about it very carefully: if you use 'perro,' a lot of people won't realize that's because of Cangallo Street, but if you use 'can' a lot of people won't understand that it means 'dog,' even though they'll associate 'gallo' with 'rooster.'"

Franc Sil had been fiddling with his drawing, which the one little kid was holding up on the wall.

"I think people who speak other languages will understand 'can' better," he said, "because it has the same root that refers to dog in many other languages."

"Yes, that's true," I said, and I asked him: "Do you speak a lot of languages?"

"A few," the boy answered, rather gloomily, and Herminia gestured at me in a way that let me know I shouldn't talk about that.

I changed the subject and asked how they planned to organize the thing. Menéndez, who was the director, builder, alma mater of the whole thing, tirelessly described his plan to me. The auditorium would hold about a hundred people and occupy the space where the rooms had been. The stage would be in what had been the servants' quarters and garden, which were connected to the garden of the furniture shop by a hole they'd made in the wall. This is how the actors would enter. Everything was going to be somewhat makeshift. They wanted to start at the beginning of March, and if things went well for them during the first two months, they'd make it more comfortable for winter.

"And what do you plan to start with?" I asked.

Herminia reached out her hand to Menéndez, as if to cover his mouth.

"It's a secret! It's a total secret until two weeks before the opening," she exclaimed.

Menéndez made a bow.

"Tyrant queen," he said, "your wishes are our commands."

She shrugged her shoulders as if to tell him to go to hell. Obviously, it wasn't in Herminia's nature to play that role nor accept those titles, but she knew to take them as childish games that made the boys feel comfortable with her, just as she felt comfortable with them.

We got ready to go back and Menéndez gave numerous orders to Cholo, the little one, so he would pass them on to the kids who came in the afternoon, prepared to work like Trojans. Cholo stayed behind to have lunch in the furniture shop with Franc Sil, who apologized to Herminia for his uncle as they said good-bye, because some business deal or other had prevented him from being at home to say hello to her, and Menéndez came with us. Herminia invited him to have lunch at her house, but he said he had an important engagement at twelve thirty sharp in a café on Nueve de Julio, so we left him at El Ateneo and came back to Juncal.

As soon as we were alone, Herminia started to explain something at length. I saw immediately that she was prepared to keep me from interrupting her, and I made a huge effort to guess what it was she didn't want me to ask her, but I couldn't guess. However, I felt certain that there was something more important than met the eye: I'd already suspected that Miguel wasn't completely confiding his secrets to me either. But Herminia was talking nonstop.

"I told you not to ask that boy questions," she began, "because he's a boy who's suffered a lot. He's starting to recover now; you can't imagine how he was when he got here."

"Did he just arrive?"

"Not too long ago, considering the extraordinary way he speaks the language. He's been here a couple of years."

"Yes," I said, "it is extraordinary. Where's he from?"

"From France; he lived through the entire occupation of Paris. Well, I think he was born there. His parents are actors. They say his father was a great actor and his mother too, but I don't know . . . something happened with her. You can imagine what happened with the father: his name is Silberman."

"Ah, of course!"

"He spent the whole time in hiding, but I don't know where. The thing is, they got shipped over here, because he has an uncle—the owner of the furniture shop—with quite a bit of money who's willing to give the boy a future."

She paused briefly but started again right away.

"It's curious how solutions come from where you least expect. Take Raúl, for example—him I've known for a long time—, he's a kid with talent and a will of iron; well, he was like a person who couldn't find a tree to hang himself, going from one person to another asking for help but not coming up with anything. He doesn't have a cent, as you can imagine, and he's surrounded by kids who have even less. Suddenly this starving creature appears—when he got here, you could see right through him—; they introduce me to him one night at an opening, and I think here's someone as a group we can take care of. But a few days later Raúl phones me to say he has to ask my help, and he tells me that Franc Sil—the abbreviation was Menéndez's idea, he says it makes the name resonant and mysterious—, well, he tells me that Franc Sil has a rich uncle. What? I ask. Yes, yes, he has a rich uncle who's willing to help us and give us a building for free, Raúl assures me and asks me to attend a meeting they're going to have in that café, El Ateneo, so that Franc Sil can introduce them to his uncle. Spotorno, the theater critic, was also going to be there, and a professor of literature from Tucumán, who was passing through, I don't recall his name. They wanted the uncle to see that this isn't kid stuff. I did the right thing by going, because neither the boys nor the intellectuals knew how to get along with the old man. You can imagine, a furniture dealer from the Jewish quarter. When I got there, the poor thing was lost in the middle of a high-flown discussion the rest of them had started. I sat down beside him and began to talk to him about his nephew. He saw his chance, took a deep breath, told me his whole story, much more than you want to hear, and confided that he feels it's his mission to see that this boy has a chance to realize his potential, to make sure that he doesn't die young, as his father did. In short, his father died in a concentration camp, but it seems as though that was the least of his ordeals, and he left this boy, whom his uncle considers a genius—I think he does have talent, no doubt about that— and to whom he wants to pay, it seems to me, some outstanding moral debt to his brother.

"Well, the hardest part," Herminia continued, "was getting him to talk about practical things. I didn't know how to pull him away from those bloody stories so I could ask him, 'And what about the building?' But finally we reached port. He told me he'd bought a small house next door to his that had just been sold at auction and, by joining the two lots, he planned to build a very nice apartment house. For some financial reasons or other, though, it would be a good year before he could start construction, and in the meantime the boys could use the lot however they liked."

We'd reached the house. I stopped at the door and waited for Herminia to come to a stopping point so I could get out of the car, but she didn't let me.

"Then the good part started," she said, holding me firmly by the arm. "The old man had just met me, I don't know what the boys might have told him about me, but the thing is, when I praised his generosity and told him he wouldn't have to regret it because something was going to come of this, he began to fidget about on his chair and lean toward me, as if he wanted to speak to me confidentially, almost turning his back to the others. 'My plan is bigger,' he said in a low voice. 'Really,' I said, smiling at him in amazement. 'Much bigger,' he repeated. 'I'm telling you in confidence something I haven't told anyone else, and I wouldn't want the boys to know, because, in short, it's nothing more than a plan, but I'd like to give our neighborhood a theater, a real theater. You understand? By joining the two lots you have nearly a hundred feet of frontage. The ground floor would make a very nice little auditorium.' I whispered a shower of praise. Raúl was dying of curiosity, but I promised to keep it a secret, and I haven't told him; I trumped up some fish story instead.

Herminia was ready to get out of the car now. Miguel was peering over the balcony, consumed with impatience because we hadn't stopped talking, and when we looked at him he pressed his fingers together Neapolitan style. Then I was the one who held Herminia.

"You're not going to start making something to eat now?" I said. "Let's go to the Munich de Palermo and we can leave for Las Murtas from there."

"Oh no," Herminia said, "I have everything ready."

She started to run, and I couldn't stop her. I followed her, trying to make her change her mind.

"But everything's here," she kept repeating, "everything's here . . ."

Then Miguel said, "There's probably something . . ."

That something wasn't much. The three of us left for the Munich.

But Herminia, who'd been so talkative when we arrived, began to seem quite restless and preoccupied after lunch.

"I can't go on to Las Murtas from here," she said. "There's something I have to do in the late afternoon. Won't the Chevrolet be ready this afternoon either?" she asked Miguel.

"Maybe, they said it might be," he answered.

"But what do you want the Chevrolet for if the three of us can all go together?"

"The thing is, we can't," she said. "You two can leave now, if you want to, but there's something I have to do. I'll go later."

"Well," I said, "two secrets in one day seems abusive to me."

"There aren't two, it's only one, because what happened this morning isn't a secret," she answered.

"Secrets," I said, "once they're revealed, seem never to have been secrets. Don't worry. When we leave here now, we'll go by the garage."

And in fact we went to the garage: the Chevrolet was still convalescing. Herminia flew into a rage.

"Let's go home," she said. "I have to change clothes, I have a thousand things to do."

When we got home she said: "All right, I have no choice but to go with the two of you, but you can wait here for me until five thirty or six. I'll be there and back in no time."

"As you like," I said. "We'll wait for you, but can't I take you where you're going?"

"No, you can't," she said, and went into her room. I asked Miguel in a low voice: "Do you know?" He gestured affirmatively, but it seemed to me that he didn't want to talk about the subject.

"Fine," I said, "I'll go upstairs and see if everything's in order up there."

I went up to the study and in a couple of minutes I heard the door slam behind Herminia as she rushed out.

But I had nothing to do upstairs and after a little while I went down, although I didn't plan to subject Miguel to an interrogation. It was too hot in the garden. I sat down in the small living room, and Miguel went to get two Cokes from the refrigerator. At that moment the phone rang; I answered, and it was Herminia. Her voice made an impression on me because it sounded strident and anguished.

"I'm desperate," she said, "I left my money at home when I changed purses and I can't pay for the taxi or for what I came to buy."

I felt an incredible temptation to laugh, but I said: "Well, there's nothing I can do but bring it to you. Tell me where you are and I promise to close my eyes when I get there."

"It's not something to joke about," she said. "Come as soon as you can. I'm on Vicente López and Junín."

She paused briefly.

"Tell Miguel," she added, "to get everything from my room that I left ready to take to Las Murtas; you two can put it in the car and we'll go on from here."

We followed her instructions and left immediately to rescue her from her predicament. I couldn't help asking Miguel if he knew what she was doing on Vicente López.

"Yes," he said, "she's buying flowers to take to the cemetery."

"Ah!"

Herminia was standing outside the florist's. I went to settle with the taxi driver, and Miguel went in to pay for the flowers. Herminia put a huge armful of laurel and a couple dozen roses into the car. When we got to the vault, I saw there was a vase with the remains of a completely identical bouquet. Herminia changed the flowers, and we set out for Las Murtas. She was out of sorts because she hadn't been able to keep her secret, and she needed to justify the secret in some way. I didn't say anything, because it was impossible to talk as long as that hadn't been talked about.

"It will seem foolish to you," Herminia said, "but I couldn't let hoards of people go by there tomorrow and see that dried-up bouquet."

"Why is that going to seem foolish to me?" I asked sincerely.

"I don't mean it might seem foolish that I placed the flowers, but that I placed them because of the people."

"Yes," I said, laughing a little, "the truth is, that is rather foolish, but even so I understand it. Although, in you, it surprises me."

"That's why I told you. Don't think I'm always driven by higher reasons. I'm not; I have these things too, like anybody else."

"Like anybody else, no," I said, "because anybody else has them unknowingly and you know what you're doing."

"Which is worse? Anybody else operates from these small motives and thinks they're responding to sacred reasons. I know I'm responding to trivialities, and I don't refuse them: I place them beside the loftiest things, deliberately."

"Well I don't know which is worse, but what difference does it make? In any case, you aren't going to operate any other way."

"No, no matter how much I think about it . . . I don't know what should make me do what I do, but if I leave those flowers there today I'll think about something else in peace. If I hadn't left them I would have spent the whole day feeling that someone, as he walked by, would see those dry branches and it would be as if he read: "Object forgotten." One person after the other walking by and reading "Object forgotten." You understand? Whereas this way, with that fresh green laurel, they'll walk by and see something that looks alive, and I can be thinking peacefully about something else."

"You do a good job of ridiculing your small motives, but I don't find them so small."

Herminia was about to protest, probably by insisting on their smallness, but Miguel chimed in with his opinion.

"At this rate, the two of you will spend your lives running laps around a street sign."

We looked at each other, crushed to silence. After a while, Herminia spoke.

"An onager's a rare kind of ass, but that doesn't make it any less of an ass."

"Being rare has nothing to do with it," Miguel said. "An onager's a wild ass, one that's not totally unconventional. That's why they say it's rare."

We kept on like that, trading clever remarks, gradually working ourselves into a better mood, until we reached the house.

The sky seemed to be resisting night, although it was past nine. Quitina was waiting for us at the door, a little impatiently because she'd assumed we'd get there earlier.

The table was set, and we sat down to dinner immediately.

"Anything new?" Quitina asked Herminia.

She almost mumbled this—her tone reminded me a little of her girlish secrets—, hoping that Herminia would answer her with some coded phrase. I realized immediately that Quitina was in on all the secrets. But Herminia said: "Not much new, although everything's going well," and she continued, as if she were showing her hand. "This morning we went to see the property. Santiago took me, so now there's nothing to hide."

"Oh!" Quitina said with a smile. "Nothing? Nothing?" And once again I saw in her another impish gesture, as if she couldn't believe there was absolutely nothing left of the secret.

This time Herminia's answer was ambiguous. Quitina had reached her arm over the table as she'd asked her question, and Herminia took her arm, squeezing it, as if this were a sign they'd agreed on.

"Well, let's say there's nothing left, at least nothing of what you can see," Herminia said, and with a wealth of detail she began to tell about our excursion to the little house next to the furniture shop. Then she described Franc Sil's drawing to Quitina, although she hadn't brought it because it still needed the lettering, and she explained our questions about the name of the theater. She told her what I said, what Franc Sil said, and what she said.

Quitina was listening to her with such absolute attention that I felt intoxicated with joy. Could the blackness in Quitina's soul possibly have been washed away, was it possible she could listen again, holding the mirror of her virginal attention to Herminia's words with that youthful smile? Yes, this was possible, this and more.

Quitina asked me: "But do you really believe there could be someone who doesn't know that 'can' means dog?" And as she asked me, she turned the mirror in my direction and looked at me, her limpid gaze intact and devoid of a single impure memory. Her soul peered from that direct, questioning gaze and from her half-open mouth with just the hint of a smile, as naked as it had been when she was seventeen, and I could touch it as I answered very simply, yes or no. It seemed to me that I was kissing her for the first time.

I never tire of blessing the world, the images, the words, a single form that can have two names and thus give rise to both a purifying question and a purifying answer.

Such superabundance! The secret continued to shed its veils, and there were a great many.

Yesterday, after a wonderful night (I wrote until a little after three, then I fell asleep with the window open and didn't wake up until the sun hit me in the face), I spent the whole day plaguing Herminia with questions about her activities. I can't say I knew absolutely nothing about them, but I never suspected they would come to interest me so much.

I'd always known that at the publishing house for which Herminia translated pedagogical and scientific books—she started to work there a couple of months after she arrived—she'd met a boy who collaborated with a few others on one of those literary magazines young people put together and that, although according to Herminia she was neither young nor literary, he'd asked her to write short book reviews. I read some of her reviews in the issues she brought home, and they seemed excellent to me, very well written, although they were extremely short because there wasn't much space in the magazine. When Damián came, Herminia stopped bringing the magazine home, and I think that once, when we asked her about it, she said they weren't publishing it anymore. Then in 1945, after all the horrors had passed, she told us one day that a new magazine had come out, more important than the first, and she was planning to submit some short pieces. She also brought home some issues of this magazine, I also read these pieces, and I also found them to be very good, although I didn't pay much attention to them either. Yesterday Herminia told me those pieces had been her sleeping pills.

Herminia said she felt her insomnia was like an infernal, impalpable presence and there was no use fighting it. The only way to combat it is to be crafty, to do voluntarily what the insomnia wants. You have to create a situation in which sleep is impossible, you have to prevent sleep, so that the enemy is left with no possibility for action. Once she'd conceived of her plan, she started to go to the movies and the theater systematically; this she almost always did with us, or at least with Quitina. When it came to the theater, not the movies, I let them go by themselves, because theater either bores or enrages me, unless it's really good. Other times she told us she'd gone with the kids from the magazine, who'd invited her to see some of the amateur groups that are beginning to arouse some interest—mine has yet to be aroused—but what she didn't tell us is that she would come home in the wee hours of the morning and, instead of going to bed, she'd start to write about the film or play she'd seen or, if it wasn't worth spending time on, she would write about something else. In short, she'd do anything she could to prevent herself from sleeping until five in the morning, and at seven the alarm would go off. After a couple of years on this schedule she began to sleep normally.

If she'd been buying a drug at the pharmacy it's unlikely that Herminia would have gone from being the pharmacist's client to becoming his friend, but she was looking for her drug in theater lobbies, where she always managed to strike up a conversation on her way out in order to postpone the moment of reaching her house, and her opinions were becoming highly respected. Young people live on their guard against the hostility and lack of understanding found in already powerful people, but they didn't distrust her because it was well known she stayed completely on the margins of all material and moral interests (using "moral" or "immoral" to refer to those interests linked to vanity); that's why, and Herminia says this is something incredible, on one or another exceptional occasion they even went so far as to listen to her advice. The thing is, as time went on this small-scale opinions trade led her to feel esteem and affection for a few select boys, whom Miguel called her court of honor.

Throughout the entire day, at breakfast, at lunch, when we ran into each other in the house or the garden, which we did constantly, we continued to talk about the same subject. And suddenly I realized that when Herminia was recovering from her jaundice—Miguel was still sailing in the south—two boys came to visit her one afternoon, and they stayed for a long time, chatting. Quitina was with her; she served them tea and cookies, witnessed the long discussion, and, when I arrived, she told me about it in great detail, as if it were something not without importance. Between the two of us we formulated a hypothesis that to us seemed rather obvious, but, once Herminia was better, she tried to erase the memory of those days and then our life changed so greatly I didn't go back and reflect on what Quitina and I had thought.

As I recall it now—I was taking my last sip of coffee, after lunch, when it occurred to me—I looked at Herminia, trying to guess, but it wasn't easy, since her expression is both complex and serene. I said to myself, everything is possible, and I sat there thinking about whether it would be better to ask or observe. In any case, that wasn't the right time. If I asked her, it would have to be at a calm moment—never at siesta—, an unhurried moment when Miguel wasn't present; the subject was too delicate to have it exposed to his outburst about the onager.

At dusk we'd had tea in the part of the garden facing east, where the shadow from the house offers protection from the sun. In one section of the garden, where there's nothing but grass and a willow tree on the side as you turn the corner, where the hives were until they were banished because the boys wouldn't let them alone, but where the rosemary bushes, the privets, and the myrtles that gave the estancia its name still are, in that area there are always bees that come back as if they were returning to their grandparents' ancestral home. I was sitting on the grass, watching them fly past; they were coming from the sunny side, like bright little sparks that disappeared when they entered the shadow. There was a long silence; the three of us were alone.

I turned my head, looked at Herminia, and said: "I think you like to be with the young boys from a kind of maternal Don Juanism."

Herminia started a little.

"Let's see," she responded. "What's your idea? Explain it."

"Well, I was remembering what you told us about love that goes in the wrong direction, and I was thinking that when one chooses maternity, when maternity isn't forced or isn't unplanned, love recovers its original meaning. Isn't that it?"

"Cold, cold!" Herminia said, as if we were playing hide the button. "I thought you were going to put your finger on the wound, but you didn't."

"I've tried to touch the wound you showed us that day."

"Yes, I understand."

Herminia offered a silence, which I didn't dare to break. I felt some remorse for having broached the subject so bluntly; she returned to it immediately, as if she'd mustered her courage in those couple of seconds.

"What you said made an impression on me, because that definition had never occurred to me. But be careful, because I've known some real cases! Of course, those cases involve the negation of maternal love: in maternal love neither adultery nor divorce is possible. How is Don Juanism going to be possible in a type of love that can't burst from the *coup de foudre*?" Herminia continued, undertaking the analysis methodically, in a way very different from the time that her intuitions burst like feverish outbursts.

"If maternal love is not conscious at every moment that it's forced, it's not maternal love. And being conscious of this means the child's behavior doesn't matter or matters very little, because if it's too abominable, there can be a rupture, although not a replacement. That's why the rupture occurs very seldom, because it means total loss."

"Yes," I said, "even so, you can't deny there are gradations, there are incentives. Deep relationships and perfectly reciprocated loves reach greater intensity than you usually find in an ordinary mother's natural feelings for her family."

"Yes, yes, yes, but no," Herminia said. "What you say is accurate; it does happen that way, in fact, because in the end maternal love is a form of human love. But those gradations affect it only with respect to love: the maternal instinct is absolutely ordinary.

"Remember the day of my fever? That day I was really inspired," she said a bit ironically, so as to make her highly perceptive comments seem less brilliant. "I told you two that part of the union moves inevitably toward disunion. Remember? I said, 'After that what's left? Golgotha.' Yes, that's it, what is perfectly common, absolute. What's divine about the Mother of God is what's common. It's not something personal. What becomes deified is not a particularly wonderful mother; it's *the mother* to whom the divine son can say, 'Woman, leave me in peace.' The dagger, the famous dagger of our religious image makers, is in that sentence. But, be careful! There's nothing personal in that sentence either. It's not a sentence that reveals to us the relationship between a specific son and his mother. It's the *sentence* the Son speaks to the Mother. And the stab wound is not the Son saying something so horrific but the law that *obliges her to leave him in peace.* That sentence (well, not exactly as I've quoted it, but the Gospel is full of sentences and actions that have the same meaning), that sentence means: 'Your mission is over.'"

"A moment ago I was remembering the story of the garlic soup," Quitina said, "and there the mother had a mission."

"Of course, against cold and hunger, against foreign elements the mother has a mission, but not against the son himself. Imagine the mother of Christ opposing the law of God, and the tremendous thing is that her entire *nature* opposes it. Of course, from the day we're born, we're used to understanding that in the drama at Golgotha the mother cannot oppose what's written. But neither in the human drama has the mother ever opposed what the son was about to write: history. She has even assented to the most deadly undertakings; because, of course, the material act of war, for example, may mean the son's death, his destruction, but to prevent the spiritual, creative act that led to war would have meant his frustration. And things continued that way until our time; now everything's different and we can no longer understand how what happened before happened."

Herminia stopped talking and, after a few seconds, Quitina spoke, with a very special kind of sarcasm: "We can't understand it? Seems to me that you understand it quite well."

"Me?" Herminia asked, her question exaggerated, evasive.

"Yes, you."

"Well, when I have a fever."

"Don't give me that," Quitina continued. "A moment ago you said you were going to explain everything point by point."

"And now I've explained it."

"Not all of it, there's something left to explain."

"Ah! what foolishness," she said, "you've interrupted a very funny story I was going to tell you." Quitina shook her head, and Herminia repeated: "Very funny, very stupid, and very dramatic," trying to pique our interest.

Part Two 577

"All right, but you can't get off the hook so easily; I'll trap you one way or another."

"Quiet!" Herminia shouted, with the voice a teacher uses as she slaps her ruler against the desk. Quitina crossed her arms and looked at me with a smile, as if to say "I'll attack again later."

In that smile, Quitina was promising me Herminia's secret. At that moment she was with me, against her, rather, she was taking me into their circle, where there could be no disagreement; she was admitting me.

The sun had just set, and the bees were no longer sparkling, but there were two or three stars above the willow, and I accepted all of it— tree, stars, and smile—as a single house, separating that whole from the world, and I swore to spend centuries guarding it. Perhaps I recalled the strange curse that Job uttered against the day and night he was conceived: "Let that day be darkness; let no God regard it from above, let that night be solitary and let no joyful voice come from therein." Of course we all know the book of Job is the height of the absurd; it's impossible to go further, because the desire for a day that *was* to keep *being* is an absurdity too great for the mind to grasp. Although, in the eternity of desperation, to say: "let that day *be*" . . . might possibly be the equivalent of saying "now I see that that day *was*." And wouldn't it be equally absurd in the eternity of happiness, of joy, for a person to swear that he's going to spend centuries guarding a moment? Who knows how those centuries yet to come already *are*? But they aren't, they aren't. They will be however I want them to be if I'm capable of guarding them.

In that fantasy I spent several centuries. Meanwhile, Herminia went on with her funny story.

"There were always things like this everywhere," she said. "Mothers have a universal way of talking to their small children, one I always rejected, simply because I found it disagreeable, although I didn't understand it. Until one day a few years ago, after I was here, I had to put up with a mother and her brat for a long bus ride. She was a young woman, very attractive, made up, and perfumed, not upper class, but a refined little thing, and the child was a two-year-old athlete three times as strong as his mother. I was sitting beside the window; they got on and sat next to me. You can't imagine what it was like. All the way to Constitution! The little boy's kicks, his bawling, his mother's struggle to keep him from pawing the hat of the man in front of us or from sucking on the back of the seat, and above all her struggle to remain clothed, because the kid kept grabbing at the neck of her blouse and pulling it down as far as he could.

"Well, there's nothing special about any of this; what struck me—there, while the situation lasted, I was so irritated that I would have gotten off the bus if I hadn't been in such a hurry, and then I couldn't get it out of my head for hours—, what obsessed me was the leitmotif the mother used as a last resort. She had a melodious, indulgent little voice, and she never shut up, trying to amuse him with one thing after another, but the child paid no attention because the things were so stupid: 'doggy, ducky, bunny . . .' When the little monster was ripping at the neck of her blouse, though, she kept telling him, "No, darling, no. Don't you see you're tearing mommy's blouse?" When he was kicking my skirt or lunging at the man in front, she'd say: 'No, darling, if you bother the lady, Mommy won't give you any treats.' And when he was shouting like a lunatic, it would be: 'No, darling, don't shout that way. What does Mommy do when you shout? Eh? What does Mommy do? Smack, smack.' She went on like that, Mommy, Mommy, Mommy, two hundred fifty thousand times for the whole trip. At one point she opened her purse to get out her handkerchief, the little boy grabbed hold of the compact and opened it, and the brush all covered with powder went rolling off. She picked it up quickly, took the compact from him, and put it back in her purse. He got mad as a tiger, let out a shriek, and gave his mother a good slap. The mother grabbed him by the arm and shook him a little. 'Mommy! Mommy?! You slapped Mommy?!' she told him in a feline voice, her tone equally interrogative and exclamatory. Then what do you think happened? The chorus, the voice of the people—not as catlike as the mother's, but just as melodious. An old country woman who was sitting in the seat behind us, corroborated the reprimand: 'Where did you ever see such a thing, a little boy hitting his mommy?!'

"I stood up and pushed my way toward the front. We still had a good piece left to go, but I moved close to the door, because the scene had me beside myself."

Herminia smiled a little.

"Have you ever felt that excessive stupidity is obscene?" she asked. "I was embarrassed to have witnessed all that, but I couldn't think of anything else, as if I'd seen something obscene."

The two of us laughed, and Quitina was ready then to insist that Herminia go back to what she'd been talking about before, but Herminia raised her hand, as if she were trying to keep us from speaking, in case we wanted to interrupt her.

"Up to there was the funny part," she said. "But then came the long hours of meditating on the subject. I reconstructed it in my memory, studied it, and contemplated it. I heard that tone of voice physically, I saw the struggle of those two bodies, which were so unequal, boxed into a space of less than a meter—the little boy's clumsy movements, the mother's stupid ideas. Well, I reached the conclusion that there was some great wisdom in all that. Universal wisdom was definitely at work there, in an infallibly effective way."

"What makes you say that about being infallibly effective?" I asked. "Maybe the little boy will end up being a famous criminal. And they'll never be able to identify him. You should have asked him to show you his enlistment card."

"That's true," Herminia said, "it would be really interesting to see that little boy in ten or fifteen years. This might seem absurd to you, but I think I'd recognize him.

"About being effective," she continued, "it has nothing do with whether or not he's a criminal. What was under way there was work that precedes the rationalization of moral values. Because even though I say the boy was a little beast, he was very affectionate with his mother, and he kept giving her loud kisses, squeezing her, and mussing her curls. But he was also capable of giving her a swat—his affection didn't prevent that. What the mother had to get through his head was that *this was something you can't do.*

"It's so strange!" Herminia continued, concentrating on her problem. "The situation is absolutely universal, what's important about the whole thing is how common it is, how invariable, but nevertheless, in order for the two of you to understand it, you would have to see what they were like. As I reflected on my memory of them, I understood things I'd meditated on for years, but without getting anywhere. Then, as I thought about that image, as I saw that small, thin, very strong woman—she spoke like a criollo, but she had Spanish blood, 100 percent—and the enormous little boy who made her feel so proud—because his Mommy, Mommy also flaunted her being the one to bring those kilos of live matter into the world—, as I watched her manage the imprinting of the chief rules of behavior. Because when a little boy learns the Ten Commandments, he must then be prepared to some extent. How to refer to the furrow where you sow the seed of reasoning? Matter must be prepared if it's to receive profound impressions, traces like the ones probably left by that 'Mommy?! Mommy?!'—prepared by questions and surprises, by all manner of insinuations. Seeing all that, I wondered: would it have been the same if she'd said 'You can't hit me'? The little boy was probably saying inside, 'I feel like it,' because at that moment he was furious with her. Could she have said to him, 'Don't tear *my* blouse?' 'I can give you treats, and I can give you a smack, smack, but you can't *hit me?*' No, she couldn't speak to him like that; she wouldn't have the courage, she couldn't confront the little boy as one person to another. She had to speak in the name of Mommy, of something larger than herself, because it was a question of making him understand she was that larger something, the largest something. Here, the role of the chorus was very important.

"That's why I spoke of effectiveness, because I saw with my own eyes how at that moment the little boy had acquired a clear idea of what's referred to as *the world*. How can you tell the extent to which language is comprehensible to a little boy who speaks only a few words? It occurred to the old, half-Indian woman full of tradition to say 'Who ever saw?' If she didn't *know* the little boy understood, she wouldn't have said it. And I saw he'd understood. Until that moment, the little boy's rosy, chubby-cheeked face, with its huge, sparkling, calf-like eyes had expressed only desire or displeasure; he wanted something, and he was lunging after it; they were taking it away from him, and he was bawling his head off. But when his mother shook him by the arm and said that to him in a scandalized voice . . . That, that was what added complexity to the sentence. Because there was feeling in her tone as well: she was saying it as if she were hurt because he had said that to *her*, but she was even more scandalized that he had done it to *Mommy*. And the old woman behind, saying: 'Who ever saw . . .!' When the situation had reached that point, the little boy didn't bawl, he reflected. I don't know what the little boy will be when he's old enough for military service but, I assure you, that day on the bus was fundamental in his life."

Quitina had listened engrossed, but she hadn't forgotten her purpose, and she spoke as soon as Herminia paused: "Now the boomerang's back in your hand."

"What do you mean?" Herminia said, although she'd understood perfectly.

"It's returned," Quitina said, "in other words, you've finished your funny story and now . . ."

"Oh, you're impossible!"

Herminia was defending something furiously, but Quitina kept attacking.

Herminia decided to say: "All this seems totally unrelated to what we were talking about before, but the two are very closely related. My friendship with those boys of course arose from a series of circumstances, but on my part it's a kind of experiment, or research."

Quitina looked at me as if to say, finally, we're getting to the heart of the matter.

"The education I gave Miguel was completely absurd," Herminia said. "It's taken me a long time to realize that."

I recalled with emotion the trip from Montevideo with Damián and how he said, "His mother's given him an idiotic education," but I didn't say anything.

"He's very happy to be a dunce who knows nothing of conventionalities, but he's simply the product of a conventionalism I adopted, against all aspects of the established order. Especially its preponderance of the personal, raised to the highest degree. My generation made so many mistakes! When I was twenty, if I'd heard that 'Mommy, Mommy' it would have nauseated me. My plans for motherhood were Spartan, genuine, rational: from one equal to another: *You* and *me*. Let's experiment and see what happens."

"You can't complain," I said. "The experiment turned out quite well for you."

"I'm not complaining, I'm marveling, because the truth is, it didn't turn out poorly for me, but the results were totally unexpected. You see, that's what I'm studying in the boys—the results yielded by the different combinations in a given era. The very large changes that were planned with B in mind but produced C or P or X. Highly different effects sometimes, have a common cause."

"Such as, for example . . . ," Quitina said, beginning to lose patience.

"Oh, now I'm recalling a very amusing scene at Sarita Helguera's house."

"Herminia," Quitina shrieked.

"It was tremendous," Herminia continued unperturbed. "I've never felt more certain of having said something profound and exact, but it seems as though anyone at all can be socially excommunicated for much less."

Quitina gestured as if she were throwing a boomerang.

"Imagine," Herminia continued, "a lot of people had gotten together there in order to organize a new amateur theater company, with very high expectations. And it wasn't poorly thought out. No, I wasn't trying to criticize anything, but I started to discuss some general issues and wound up saying this enthusiasm for theater among members of the upper class always occurs in a decaying society."

Quitina and I burst out laughing.

"Yes, that's how I said it, I spelled it as bald as that, because I believe it and because it's true. I gave a few examples: in the first place, that of Spain, right before the revolution, but of course they didn't understand. I tried to analyze the phenomenon, exactly as it's happening now: the dissolution of social *forms* through corruption and the confusion of any sense of society, resulting—among other things, of course—in this anxiety to save hollow forms, the theatrical element to society, which lives in theaters . . . and there was a deathly silence. Raúl Menéndez was looking at me from a corner; he was pale, and he walked out with me, and told me he thought I'd been overcome by a fit of madness."

"Why didn't you tell us about it?" I asked.

"Well, because, deep down, sometimes I think everything I say and do here is madness. How can I explain it? It's not, I think of something, and then it seems wrong to me; no, it's as I walk around everywhere I experience a sensation of irreality, I see everything as foggily as a person who emerges from a dark room, because it's only in the dark room where I see clearly."

"Then tell us what you see in the dark room," Quitina said, and Herminia remained silent.

"Well, I think you have a secret forbidden to my curiosity in particular," I said.

"No, no," Herminia answered and, suddenly, she changed her mind: "Well, yes, it is secret from you, in particular."

"Why?"

"Because she's afraid of your judgment," Quitina said. "It's not enough for her that we less important judges assure her she'll be successful."

"But successful in what?" I asked, and as I said this I understood. I recalled how Herminia had prevented Menéndez from talking when I asked what work they were using to open. "A total secret!" she'd said.

I pounced on Herminia and tried to persuade her as violently as I possibly could, begging her, threatening her, cajoling her.

"I'm weak," she said, "the work we're doing is the result of a scene like this one. I don't know how to say no."

I saw she was going to tell us, and I sat down at her feet.

"I had a few notes," she said, "and I was planning to write an essay, a sort of social commentary. I'd thought at different times that if someday I ever wrote my memoirs I could include it, as well as many other things that have happened to me. But one evening the two boys turned up at the house—Raúl Menéndez and Rossi, the one who edits the magazine and who wanted to give me a book of his poetry, which had just been published. They brought little Franc Sil with them and, although he spoke poorly—this was about a year ago now—, he understood perfectly. We talked, as always, about current life, about today's young people—I always try to get them to talk about their things—and it occurred to me to tell them something about what I had in mind. But the worst part was, their obsession with theater was contagious, and I had the bright idea of saying, 'This is a definitely a drama! You could turn it into a great play.' And they went crazy. They begged me to do it. Raúl and Rossi lavished me with compliments, trying to tempt me with extravagant praise of my talent. But the other boy, without any emotion in his voice, almost in tears, took one of my hands and said: 'Do it *for* me . . . just for *me*.' He wavered anxiously between the two, but he was much more persuasive than the others. 'It's work I *can* do,' he finally said. 'You can count on it, you can count on it.' So to get them off my back, I promised I would do it, I would consider it. I also decided absolutely not to work on it anymore. And every time they asked me, I said, 'I'm letting it ripen.' Until a few months ago, when they began to have some hope of getting the place, they demanded I keep my promise and I was weak enough to give in."

It had gotten dark by now, and I saw some headlights crossing the garden. I guessed that Miguel had finally rescued the Chevrolet. But Herminia's back was turned and she didn't see. I hurried to make her tell us the play's subject very briefly, before we were interrupted.

"In short, you did it," I said. "And what is it? What's it about?"

"I haven't finished it," she said. "The second act won't come. The first and last are finished, and they've turned out well. But the second act doesn't work; I've already written it a hundred times, and I'm not satisfied with it. No, I'm definitely not satisfied, the play's stuck there."

I saw Miguel's shadow appear behind the house, but his footsteps weren't visible on the lawn.

"Well, stuck or not, what's the play?"

"Orestes."

"Nothing less!"

"Nothing less."

Quitina heaved a sigh of relief. From the shadow where he'd been hiding, we heard Miguel's voice: "I've just seen some steaming noodles, and I don't think they look unfriendly."

The maid appeared in the doorway, and we went in to dinner.

I thought I'd be able to convince Herminia to read it to us. If she had agreed, Miguel and I would have made the round trip that night to get the manuscript, but she wouldn't let herself be talked into it. She said she didn't want to read the play before she'd finished it, and she still had another week's work. Then I forced her to tell us about it, at least.

"I'll tell you the premise," she said, "how the idea occurred to me, and what I want to do with it. Quitina already knows. I'm not really sure about how to dramatize it. So when you read it, Santiago, you'll see if I've achieved what I was after."

She was thinking about it, but she was reluctant to speak.

"Cut it out!" Miguel said. "You're dying to tell about it. I don't know why there have to be all these preliminaries."

"You know too?" I asked, and Miguel made a motion that suggested he was fed up to the gills with it.

"He means he's sick of it," Herminia explained.

"Of course I'm sick of all these doubts, these worries, these mysteries. The thing's good, they ask you about it, you tell them, and that's all there is to it."

"So you think it's good?" I asked.

"It's not what I think, it *is* good."

"Fine! What are you waiting for, then?"

"Do you think unity of time's an important issue?" Herminia asked, unsure of her métier. "The action takes place over many years, twenty years or so. It's something like a dramatized novel. As much as I thought about putting a flashback in the first act, I cut it out because it was much too long, and it would have meant including another twenty years from the past, because the story is really the story of the first forty years of the century."

"Ah, so it's set entirely in the present day?"

"Entirely."

"In that case, don't worry: modern tragedy's quite free."

"That's another question!" Herminia said. "I don't know if I can call it a tragedy."

"But isn't it about Orestes?"

Herminia nodded.

"If it is there's no question."

"Just the same," she said. "It's precisely the drama of Orestes, but no swords, no axes, and no implements for cutting. So I don't know if it's a tragedy, technically speaking. Although it's infinitely cruel. Perhaps more cruel."

"More cruel!"

"Well, it's impossible to find anything more cruel than the tragedy of Orestes, but in this tragedy everything remains unpunished. And since there are neither blows nor blood, the victims have no reason to scream. They have no *right* to scream."

"Yes, now I understand."

"You can't understand completely. No one murders anyone, because it's not about murder but *mater*. You understand? Clytemnestra checkmates the King, Orestes checkmates the Queen, without the least qualm, without disrupting law and order, simply by making use of the freedoms our culture gives us."

"That's not bad!" I said. "It seems to me it's not bad at all. Although I still don't have a clear vision of the whole thing."

"When I was a young girl—which means in a distant age—," Herminia said, "well, I was a very feminist young girl, but there was no cause that prompted me to act like one because my generation found everything already accomplished. Nevertheless, that spirit always stayed with me. Maybe my two years in England, certain readings—but the important thing is I never lost the feelings involved in that struggle. After I was here, years ago, as I was reading the *Oresteia*, in a Spanish translation, I was struck by a sentence, in the way I find it most suggestive to be struck by something. Not the way you're struck when you understand something through illumination and suddenly everything is explained, but in a way that you suspect something.

"There's a sentence of Casandra's in *Agamemnon*:

To think that woman will stop at nothing,
To kill the male!

"If you can imagine, I was struck by that sentence in exactly the same way as I was by the incident with 'Mommy, Mommy.' The character disappeared, she was no longer Clytemnestra, killing Agamemnon, but Woman killing Man . . . something that can't be, that never was. This obsessed me for a long time; I compared them with the biblical heroines, who were such manslayers—Deborah, Judith, Delilah—and no, no, no; there was something else. The writers of our psychoanalytic century— well, Hebbel is from the last century, and he was already poking around in this—, hoping to spice up history a little, can now find that these women had individual motives; the truth is, these women killed colossal, fearful men luck placed within reach of their wiles, but they killed those men on behalf of their people, knowing that they were doing their duty and that they would be revered and glorified for it. Whereas with Clytemnestra it's quite the opposite: Clytemnestra performs an act that will be sanctioned terribly. And why? What act does she avenge with her own deed? The sacrifice of Iphigenia, which was entirely legal."

Herminia was silent for a while. I'd been listening attentively to her impassioned approach to those characters, but I was following without knowing where she was going to end up and I couldn't contain my curiosity.

"Well," I said, "how do you relate all this to the present day?"

"It *is* the present day," she answered, with exemplary naïveté and stubbornness.

She didn't refuse to give me explanations, but first she wanted to make it clear that the fact is incontestable. In this I recognized the intellectual, the creator. I saw she was involved in and identified with this vocation for life, and I waited patiently for her to explain herself in her own way. It was necessary to let her reach the end step-by-step.

"It is the present day," she answered. "Woman has avenged, not her daughter but her sacrificed grandmother, believing that for her there could be triumph without sacrifice, but no, that's not possible. And the error is comprehensible, because you'd think that leaving behind the realm of the natural—a struggle between male and female is anti-natural—the laws would be different. But they're the same! This means that not even the anti-natural manages to be extra-natural."

"Well, yes, I agree, it seems to me that I thoroughly agree with your thesis. But what about your play?"

"Ah, the play is this same thing, novelized more than dramatized. The play . . . what happens with the play, is that I never should have thought of writing it. That's what happens."

"For God's sake!" I shouted.

"But don't you realize it's absurd to try to convert slow impossibility, the infinite variations of the immutable, into dramatis personae? The spectator has no patience. People go to the theater to see attitudes, staged blows—not to witness the drama of characters who die without a blow being struck. If the public puts up with this, I'll write another play that will be called 'The Moth,' because everything has *its* moth."

"No, please! Don't tell me about the second play, tell me about the first."

"Oh, you're a true spectator; all you need to do is stamp your feet. Well, the play starts . . . You'll see, I'm going to have you pass judgment on something that can and cannot be. If I take it out, the work doesn't lose anything. It occurred to me on one of those days when a person's infected by *modernity* in the worst sense of the word. Something like a temptation of demagoguery."

"Very precise; I understand very well what you're saying, so put it in! . . ."

"It would be a sort of prologue that, although very short, would test the spectator's patience. Imagine a completely dark stage, a black curtain, but off to one side, beneath a spotlight, a man and a woman—young—seated across from one another playing chess at a small table. The game must last several minutes, in total silence, but all the moves must be clearly visible. Imagine what this would be like in a film! There it would be worth doing, but in the theater . . . Well, the whole scene depends completely on the actors, who make or break it. His game must alternate between timidity and temerity, and he must always be losing, while she advances steadily. Surely, calmly, in absolute silence, until at the end she says, Checkmate the King. She bursts out laughing—something very dangerous and very difficult—, overturns the pawns, stands up and pounces on him, repeating, Checkmate the King! The King is dead! She ruffles his hair and shakes him vigorously. 'But darling!' is all he says. 'Come on, come on, not so hard! Not so hard, darling!' And the lights go out.

"If this is done well it's bound to achieve a particular effect. The light goes out as she's strangling him; his last words must be spoken in the dark and they must truly sound tragic, suggesting Agamemnon as he dies. After a few seconds of silence and total darkness, the spotlight shines on the other side of the stage, where at the same table the same woman, although this time she looks somewhat older, is playing chess with a seventeen- or eighteen-year-old boy. Everything is repeated exactly as before, but now it looks like the boy will win, and he does, screaming: 'Checkmate the Queen! The Queen is dead!' He grabs her with both hands, forces her to stand up and spin around very fast a couple of times, the way children pretend to be windmills, and he keeps repeating: The Queen is dead! 'Come on, Orestes!' she'll say over and over. 'Come on, not so hard! Enough, Orestes! It's too hard, son! And just like the last time, the lights go out before the struggle ends. Their footsteps and their fighting can be heard in the dark. After a couple of seconds the light goes on, and the three actors bow as if the play were over. If there's a little applause—there's always applause—, when it dies down, the actor who plays the father steps forward: 'Ladies and gentlemen,' he says, 'if anyone is dissatisfied, he should recognize that the play didn't last very long; you've seen all you came to see. If anyone is pleased and not bored, prepare to watch the repetition of this perennial drama.' Curtain. What do you think?"

"I think there might be applause."

"Oh yes, but it makes me nauseated. I mentioned it to the kids because, as I told you, I was going through a bout of depression, but a few days later I told them I'd eliminated it, and they protested furiously: they found it very theatrical. Raúl was shouting himself hoarse trying to convince me, and I said to him, 'I'll only allow it to be performed in a theater where there's good fire equipment.'

"'Why?' he said with dismay.

"'Because if there's applause, I'll grab the hose and clear the theater.'

"'I think she'd be capable of doing it, I think she'd be capable!' Raúl was saying, imagining the scene. And Franc Sil smiled a very complex smile and kissed my hands. Is this success?"

"It could be," I said. "I understand that you find such comedy repugnant, but maybe it's important to bear in mind one small detail: theater is comedy."

"No, no! It's tragedy. If it's not tragedy, it's disgusting."

"It's not disgusting; it's theater, because theater is not only tragedy. The thing is, you don't like theater, nor do I."

"That might be it. In any case, tragedy is like a natural phenomenon: you forget it was fabricated. To achieve one of those great syntheses, which are merely like gestures or like statues placed right in the center, in sight, that kind of thing is definitely worth doing. But in our day there are no grand gestures: it's the only synthetic material we lack. And I won't stoop to some ready-made *concoction*, I'd rather devote myself to construction. I've constructed this piece by piece, with the patience of a watchmaker. I've looked in Greek tragedies for everything that could support my thesis. They're so rich! And I've fabricated equivalent characters and situations."

"And?"

"And, well, Agamemnon is a man who has more courage for war than for life. He sacrifices Iphigenia because he's incapable of confronting the other kings. And today you find men plenty of men with that kind of personality.

"The piece begins with a conflict that's social and financial in nature. The protagonist is a powerful man, he owns large companies and he's morally sedentary . . . See! See the limitation, the one-way street? In order to talk about war and peace, I have to make the protagonist a guy who manufactures weapons, because if he harvested crops or made ice cream, I'd have to get involved in so many detours he wouldn't fit in the play, and if he didn't manufacture something, if he were a lawyer or a writer everything would become much more difficult, when in truth each of them is as much a *protagonist* as the others."

"Come back to earth!"

"Well, the first scene is the departure, when he goes off to resolve the conflict, and the second is the return, with the conflict resolved, but it's a false resolution. Finally, she's waiting for him, all ready, and she crushes him.

"That's it in nutshell, but as you can imagine it's constructed with very vivid, lifelike scenes. I'm not giving you any details, because everything depends on the dialogue. What's important is not that one character is conquered by another but that one idea of the world is destroyed and replaced by another. Up to here's the first act. And now comes the hard part: the second act won't come for me, because it corresponds to a phase of transition.

"If this were a question of an essay—as it should have been, instead of an idiotic pantomime!—the thing wouldn't present such difficulty, because it would consist of a thorough analysis of the transformation of certain values: the values of the male par excellence: heroism, the feeling of power, the risk of conquest, etc. All that's been modified. Because of woman's influence? I wouldn't dare to defend that assertion. But I would assert that all these things have yielded to the *feminine world*. Rather, the *feminine element of the world* has asserted itself over all of them. That's how Nietzsche described it, although of course in the form of an insult, because Nietzsche—these are things that happen to us geniuses," Herminia said, making a joke of it because she felt a little embarrassed about holding forth for so long—"Nietzsche forgot one small detail: half the world—not of humanity, of nature—is feminine. Well, I don't know if he forgot this or if he simply considered one half of the world inferior. And he might have. In that case, if the world now rests on its feminine half, it's a sign that the world's running on its feet, not with its head.

"But don't think that all this is free of tendentiousness. To advocate feminism today would be ridiculous. There's only one interpretation of certain events that, it will make Santiago happy to know, has a rather glorious source: Goethe. Goethe's *Iphigenia in Tauris* acquainted the barbarians with the idea of peace and forgiveness and the abolition of their bloodthirsty customs, and all of it as moral progress. Who told Goethe this tale about Iphigenia? I don't know, I don't know where he might have gotten it, it's not in the Greek tragedies. But I think Goethe got it from his own time, not from history but from his eighteenth century, which was pure future."

Herminia stopped for a moment to take a breath and, in the silence, three bells sounded. Sometimes the wind carries the bell from the clock at Las Flores church.

Miguel said to Herminia: "What if instead of this you and I were to recite a duet of some classical Spanish poetry?"

The three of us looked at him, waiting for the solution to the mystery. Miguel continued: "You recite López de Vega's 'Sonnet to Violante' and I'll recite the one about 'You should know, Inés my sister' . . ."

"Yes, that's best," Herminia said. "'Leave it for tomorrow.'"

"Ah, no! Definitely not that!" I said and held Herminia tightly by the shoulders, preventing her from getting up. "You're not moving from here until you've explained everything to us clearly, all the way to the end."

But Herminia didn't try to get up, just the contrary. I'd placed both my hands on her shoulders, quite forcefully, and I felt her yield and give in as she sat in the armchair, with the relaxation that indicates a mental concentration similar to absence or sleep.

"It's really enormous!" she said finally. "A really enormous idea just occurred to me! No, it seems tonight I won't be able to tell you the end, because suddenly I've seen something that makes me change my plan."

"We're done for! What have you seen, may one inquire?" I asked, feeling truly annoyed.

"I've seen who told Goethe the story."

"Who?"

"Apollo."

Quitina and I exchanged a look of panic, the same we exchanged that day near her bed, although we knew she had no fever.

"Do you feel all right?" I asked, trying to take her pulse.

"Wonderfully well. So well that all this talking has made me hungry."

Quitina and Miguel were off to the refrigerator in a flash.

"And now, may one inquire?" I began to say, but Herminia restrained me with a gesture.

"Goethe is Apollonian, isn't he? I don't think there's any question about that."

"Of course."

"All right, then that's all. Goethe had to find the Apollonian solution to the matter."

"I don't doubt it, but what's the solution?"

"The sister! That's it! It's wonderful!"

Beyond that I could get nothing out of her. We ate, drank, and went to bed. This afternoon I managed to extract a very brief and less cabalistic outline than last night's fragments, and I'll have to content myself with that for two weeks, because she says the new Apollonian plan makes it impossible to finish in eight days.

It's curious to watch the spectacle presented by the process this play has followed in Herminia's mind. There's a form of obsession in which the subject sticks obstinately to his idea, always referring it to his own case and scratching at its particular characteristics until he turns it into a sort of pain, a rash. And there's another form of obsession that involves the opposite, that involves pursuing the obsession to the ends of the earth, scouring the world for anything that might refer to it in even the slightest way, and making no distinction or hierarchy. Whether the voice that *speaks of the idea* is the voice of Aeschylus or of some banal woman riding a bus in Buenos Aires makes no difference. The second of those systems is the one Herminia is following in her obsession. I don't know how she'll solve the transition phase, I'm afraid she's going to find herself in a bind. But the third act definitely does have dramatic elements.

It seems the third act will be a faithful portrait of young men today. The telephone conversations, the combinations for snaring or substituting a girl. No mercenary relationships: you dial X's number, and if X doesn't work out you call Z, and if Z doesn't work out, P, C, or N. Of course, two girls are ordered for two boys and three for three. Other men don't order any. Homosexual relationships occur, just as they have always have, because of physical or psychic irregularity, because of industrialized depravity, neither more nor less than any other industry or any other depravity and, because of a predominance of an exaltation of the *masculine mode*, the same as there's been in certain periods. A principal coefficient of the sporting life.

"They're winning, they're winning! But what can be done about it?" Herminia asked, as if she were watching a boxing match between males and females. "When men and women walk around outdoors stark naked, men always win."

"Well, I don't see it so clearly. People have always said . . ."

"What counts isn't what people have said"—she cut me off—"but what they've done. You only have to think in universal terms about the plastic arts. When women won, it was always because of clothing. And here's the important thing. The contest has been repeated ever since the world was a world, and this is always the law: naked bodies exposed to view—men win. Elegant attire, silks, jewels in the salons—women win. For the first time in history—it's important to recognize this—*for the first time in history*, men are winning, even in clothes. The fashion of this century is masculine. I know, not entirely and not at every moment, but it's definitely the case in certain things that never existed until now.

When would women have worn their hair, not long and curly but boy-ishly bobbed the way they did in the 1920s, the way they do now—these puny postwar girls shorn like orphans, as if they had mange? People say they look very naughty like that, and indeed they do. They look a lot like riffraff, although most of them are just unfortunate, wretched. That's what motivates riffraff: they degrade themselves in order to incite the pederasty that might be latent in every man."

Herminia fell silent, shaking her head in a negative way. I thought she was going to retract one or another of her opinions, but she said: "All this is accurate, indisputable, except that there's much more: there's all the reverse, with the same evidence. And it's not even that the coin has two sides. No, it's the same side, the same sign that's ambivalent, polyvalent. Vixens and snakes know this . . . Feminine cunning knows it can stoop that low, in order to rise.

"What I said about the vixen is ambivalent too. There's a cunning that serves vanity, such as people attribute to that hen in the story. I'm not sure if it's one of Andersen's or not. 'Even if you pluck out all my feathers I'll still be beautiful.' And there's another kind of cunning that serves more noble aspirations. Something like saying, 'If I have to go through this to reach my goal, I'll go through it, I'll bend, I'll swallow the pill.' Because what's obvious is that with today's fashions woman has invigorated her beauty and given it a certain nobility. There's not so much *bluff* anymore. Now women see men as Jacob's staffs, useful for giving birth to slender, sinewy daughters, free of superfluities; let's hope they'll be the true female of man the animal.

"But I don't want to get sidetracked," she said, slowing down. "The thing is this: our age gradually became feminized—no, not effeminate, because the two are completely different, which is what Nietzsche did not understand—in the sense of pacification, mercy, respect for life. It seems contradictory, since we've experienced so many wars and killings. But that's not important, for at same time we're *living* the idea of peace, as never before. It's possible there will still be more wars, but deflated ones. The idea of war no longer has any moral credibility. And it did! Trying to establish the ideal of peace in man by slandering the old ideal of war is a mistake. No, it's a lie—the worst disease that can enter the human soul. War *was* a lofty, truly lofty, sacred ideal and *it no longer is.* You understand? *It was, and it no longer is.* Clytemnestra killed Agamemnon, which means, first he was alive, and then he was dead. But things couldn't stay that way: you can't kill the male, the inventor of war, and get away with it; Apollo and Pallas Athena protect the avenger in order to uphold masculine values.

"And we entered the era of Orestes. The *moment* of revenge, something as brief as a stab wound, blankets our entire age: that's where we are now. Now what prevails is the fatal adolescent. He cannot bring his father back to life, definitely not. In other words, there will be no more wartime ventures, with their tempting booty, but taking risk, conquest—whatever it might be, whether science, space, or fame in any field—is reaching heights never before imagined. The male tends to kill less, but increasingly he's in danger of killing himself. And even though the female beat her father at the game, she cannot beat her son. She must let him kill himself, which means killing her. She must let him assassinate her, by devaluing her. Devoid of any splendor, she must witness this age, which to some degree is the way it is because she won. To a large degree."

When Herminia reached this point in her explanation (of course with many more nuances and facets than I can transcribe), she said: "Here's where I thought to stop, this was the original plan for my tragedy. I wanted to carry the mother's bloodless death in abnegation or annulment to its final consequence, to the furthest possible point. I wanted to make a temporal impossibility. I don't know if that's clear. Clytemnestra's death is not the fact that a sword pierces her neck and severs her jugular. No, her real death is the *moment* when she *sees* that her son is going to kill her, that he is killing her, that he is killing her inevitably. This moment is what I've wanted to turn into an era; I've wanted to make of it a *mystery*. I don't plan to formulate it this way in public, but for me this is called the mystery of the free woman."

"I think you'll be able to do it," I said spontaneously, because I saw her so firmly in control of her purpose I had no doubt she would succeed. She spoke with the certainty of someone who intends to do nothing but copy faithfully, to bear witness to a reality right before his eyes. And I remembered that yesterday, when Quitina said to her, "Tell us what you see in the dark room," the idea of the shadowy zone passed through my head, but naturally I didn't want to mention it. And I saw then that for twenty years Herminia had lived alongside us, with her shadowy zone carefully veiled. If we were unaware of it—perhaps only me, and not Quitina—it was not because I lacked information about the events with which I was familiar. That zone, Herminia's life, was not unreality. Her unreality I knew completely, but I didn't know the shadow.

For a few seconds I was lost in thought about this, but Herminia brought me back.

"And there's been so much talk in our era about the Oedipus complex! Now it's out of date, since it corresponds to the period when Baudelaire buried his nose in perfumed chinchillas and sables. The accursed came out of that period, because Oedipus himself sanctions his own guilt: knowing it and expiating it are one and the same thing. If Oedipus had worn the harsh face of today's psychoanalysts and told himself, 'Bah, this happens to all kids,' his name would not be eternal. Oedipus sins on a grand scale, but his atonement is grandiose. On the other hand, Orestes, the official avenger, works justly. Of course the Furies still pursue him.

"The dissatisfaction kids feel today, their fear of being alone . . . because they're not a bit afraid of a machine gun or a time trial or a climb to some peak or a place where there aren't peaks anymore, but of conscience, silence, solitude . . . That's what the loud speakers are for, to scare off the Furies. They expel the Furies from your thoughts by stealing their space, uninterruptedly reviving pleasant associations that expel the Furies. Their sinister presence leaves you limp as a rag, but the loudspeaker has a gentle, very effective rhythm, like monkeys copulating, that's capable of bringing back the dead, so everyone's all worked up until the curtain falls.

"Of course I was thinking that the curtain would fall on this kind of scene, and I'm not sure I would have shown what I wanted to—this way of ending life, giving the slip to your conscience, to the Furies.

"Since the ancient world won't be mentioned even once in my tragedy—well, the name Orestes is the clue—, and there won't be a single allusion or evocation, everything has to consist in the exactness of the comparison. And the circle could close there, without anyone's noticing that Apollo and Pallas Athena's acquiescence was incomprehensible. But I noted it.

"Obviously, in Euripides' Iphigenia Goethe saw the sacrificed maiden who accepts her sacrifice willingly and therefore becomes *worthy of Achilles*, to whom her father has been foolish enough to promise her in marriage. In other words, Iphigenia, in Aulis, identifies with the hero, equates herself with the male, enters the Apollonian sphere. What might Goethe have been thinking of? What redemption could he imagine for Orestes? The god orders him to go and rescue his sister. And Orestes goes to Tauris with the intention of stealing the statue of Artemis, because he doesn't understand that his sister is involved in this, since she was saved by Artemis and kept in her service to work at the shrine. And the Iphigenia in Tauris is the one we saw in Aulis, *worthy of Achilles*. The one who says to the Scythian king, 'I was born no less than any man,' and who imposes her benevolent ways on Tauris while she's at the shrine. Goethe's is more modern, and he goes much further: he adds the rest of the eighteenth-century's futurity, when the king asks Iphigenia if she thinks that a Scythian will be moved by the voice of truth, which went unheeded by a Greek, and she answers him:

"Anyone,
Born under any sky can hear it
If the source of life flows
Pure and free from his breast."

"Well, this is the sister Orestes must return to her homeland.

"And here a small question of words arises. I've always hated the way we say *the* sister, *the* mother in Spanish. For example, 'Yesterday I saw so-

and-so with *the* mother,' as if we were talking about a cow. Who would use such a vulgar form if he were speaking in French? On this occasion, however, that form is necessary because, although Iphigenia is the sister of Orestes, my redeemed Orestes does not go in search of *his* sister but of *the Sister*, the fraternal female, the equal.

"As you can see, the thesis is brilliant," Herminia said, intoxicated with her discovery. "It's the only form of hope possible: Apollonian perfection. But how do I put that ending in the play? My plan was exactly the opposite: it was the curtain beheading the present at the exact moment of devastation. Now I see that perspective, and I can't act as though I don't. What happens is I see it in another color . . . made from a different material. With the difference that exists between the real and the ideal."

She smiled, with a naive, nostalgia smile.

"That ending," she said, "I can only imagine as one of those finales."

Listening to her evocation I felt the same smile arise within me.

"J'ai vu parfois au fond d'un théâtre banal
Qu'enflammait l'orchestre sonore,
Une fée allumer dans un ciel infernal
Une miraculeuse aurore . . ."

I spoke, and Herminia cried out, throwing her hands to her head.

"That's it, that's it! That's exactly what I was thinking. It can't be said any other way. And it truly never ceases to amaze me that a man could say it so perfectly. That's the miracle! Because what the ideal yearns for is the miracle, the miracle is what it cries out for.

I continued:

"Un être que n'était que lumière, or et gaze,
Terrasser l'énorme Satan."

"'Terrasser l'énorme Satan'! Would it be possible to say anything better about the future? I don't know, I don't know how to introduce that stream of light into the play. Because I don't want hope to be simultaneous with despair. No, I want to portray a moment devoid of hope. So how can I present that image of a reality that hasn't yet come into being?"

Beyond this point, more or less, we went no further. They left at dusk, and what remained here was the aura of the radiant vision that had dawned because of those lines. It truly never ceases to amaze me that a man could say something so perfect.

15

The poppies are losing their petals. Impeccable weather—not one bad day, and there are more flowers than we ever hoped for. In a week or so the harvest will be over, and we'll have an unprecedented quantity to work with. Everything's ready, and the new cauldrons await their food, like circus animals at feeding time.

We've been receiving cheerful letters from Italy. Our father is traveling around Tuscany these days, in the middle of winter, but you'd think he was taking the sun. His business activities—something to do with engines, I think—aren't worrisome to him and don't weigh on his thoughts, because he tells us about countless plans for tourist trips that have nothing to do with his work. In short, he's happy he went there. I must write to him, but the letter will be very brief, because "Everything's going well" can be said quickly. Whereas you really have to beat around the bush when everything's not going well! When everything's going well, the quietude that falls is indescribable. The blossoms open little by little, until they fill the entire field; then they begin to wilt, the sun devouring the colors and scorching the white flowers until they look like old paper. Then the petals fall off, and what's left are little stripped heads, dripping from their wounds. Nothing more, there's nothing more to say when things go well.

Of course I could say, "We've harvested X amount. After production we'll have X. The current market price is at X. Packaging, transportation, and labor costs come to X. In total, a profit of X." But I only lay all these rough calculations out in a letter when I'm up to my neck in problems. If there's prosperity, I gaze at the flowers, oversee the work automatically—without becoming informed and without making mistakes—and I never talk about the subject.

And to speak about private, personal, family things . . . That would be natural, but I don't know. I don't know why it's so hard for me to speak about simple things. I think it's because as soon as I look at them everything stops being simple. Especially the things I try to experience most simply.

Herminia's speculations prove that there's nothing simple about those things. You bring a few children into the world and try to raise them simply. Useless. Our intimate drama, the drama of our culture, and the drama of our society will influence them—everything we try to keep from touching them, even in passing. And we actually manage to believe we do. So where and how does such contact occur? In what form do they inhale the atmosphere that we believe we've kept far away from their bedrooms? Impossible to know.

I remember now the day Francisco went wild over the idea of living by himself in my bachelor's room during the next semester. It was Quitina who suggested that plan. Quitina, who at the time felt enslaved by her suffering—in other words, not emancipated—tried to have her son defend her. Of course he didn't know this. He didn't? The result was the same. At that moment Francisco was pushed by his mother toward a manly act, one that was almost excessive for his age, but for that very reason it will become an act of prevailing. March will come, Francisco will move into my room, and he'll set his alarm every night. Quitina no longer needs to have him there standing guard, and she may deplore this situation, she may have some bad nights knowing he's so far away, she may try to talk him out of the plan. Francisco's already there. Ever since that day, it's the day that he'll be there. At that moment he absorbed the climate of the tragedy that forced him to surpass himself. His mother was tormented, she asked him to undertake that feat for her, and he'll undertake it, whether it's necessary or not.

For some time now I've been looking for a crest, but I still haven't found one, or an acronym either. My things can never be defined in four words and expressed with a letter from each one. The whole alphabet would not be enough for me. Of course, when I told myself 'you need a crest' I didn't mean a motto but a motif, an object outside me, outside my subjective world, and I might be close to finding it.

The peace that reigns *between* Quitina and me might stop being horrible. It began as a huge insulating block of glass, and now I have hopes of melting it, by achieving a high temperature. Life, things, people can provide the warmth necessary for the mass to liquefy.

Now, Quitina's not inside me anymore, she's facing me. If I leap toward her with my old overwhelming voracity, I won't be able to get through the glass. Whatever's between us must come to a rolling boil, producing currents and whirlpools that in sweeping us along reunite us. But it's moreover necessary—reality corresponds to necessity—that this warmth and this activity must not be fabricated or provoked simply for the purpose of winning Quitina back. And they aren't: they have their own life, they've sprung up on their own. I have faith in them.

A question and an answer, exchanged when I returned on Tuesday: "What's Herminia doing? What's happening on Juncal?"

It's working. There's a creative silence coming from her department. Spoken that way, half in jest, her question and answer are something very serious. As serious as ascertaining the world's not polluted, a gentle breeze has purified the atmosphere: forgetting.

Something very silly occurs to me, and I don't want to reject it. How to make the allegory of forgetting? Can you represent forgetting with a very beautiful, very pure, intact image? No, no one would understand it. Besides, forgetting has many faces, because there is also an impious, sterile forgetting, and another form that's stupid and inept. Definitely, forgetting can't be represented by an image, not even in my case, and my imagination is always inclined toward symbolism.

Nevertheless, in the first meaning I mentioned, forgetting produces beauty. Yesterday, Friday, when I got to the office, I recalled a thousand things, and I recalled them without feeling afraid, because forgetting had restored their original color. What happens is that forgetting is a re-storative for recollection. This must obey a more hermetic law of physics than the one advising the field be left fallow, because I think even an ax, which gets used every day, will cut better if you give it a bit of rest. And the material of the soul loosens up delightfully as it roams through its clean dwelling. It goes from one room to the next, checking: Nothing! nothing! Here nothing and here neither.

About four Miguel came up with the Chevrolet argument, which gets repeated frequently. Herminia didn't want to leave for Las Murtas in the middle of the afternoon; she was having a flash of inspiration, and she wanted Miguel and me to go then, and she'd arrive the next day. I tried to negotiate a friendly settlement. The moon comes out tonight at ten, I told her, and at midnight it's high in the sky. It's now five o'clock, and we'll give you seven hours of total solitude; at twelve I'll come back to pick you up, the two of us will leave, and Miguel can have the Chevro-let. Naturally she agreed.

The still, humid heat took us to a place I never went. We decided to go to the Comega and to get there early so we could find a table outside, which we did. We ate there and talked there, or from there. I mean we talked about things suggested by the place.

"What do you understand by 'revolution from above'?" I asked sud-denly.

"First, I understand what everyone understands, and then a lot of other things. I assume those other things are the ones that interest you."

"Of course, they're the ones that always interested me, things way above the ones alluded to by that stock phrase. Specifically, though, I mentioned it right now because I started to think about other things that remain submerged but are what give the ones above their real mean-ing. Understand? You don't, do you? Well, the things alluded to in that stock phrase are the ones in the middle."

"I don't understand that either."

"It's very simple. Revolution from above refers to revolution made by the upper classes, but I wasn't thinking now about either upper or lower classes, I was thinking about the physical fact of revolution, which takes place below, in the street.

"In this city there will be a revolution some day. That's certain; today every city can expect it, but in this city you can sense it, have a presentiment of it. Where it will come from, I don't know. But now, as I looked at the streets, the port, the roads, the train station, it occurred to me that revolution might come on one of those paths."

"Of course."

I realized that Miguel couldn't guess why this seemed so urgent, and I explained to him, briefly, that this phrase had been very important in my life and that the mere fact of looking from above had brought it to mind.

"There's still another association of ideas that arose with this one and it's even more confused," I said. "This host of tiny lights reminded me of something I thought not long ago about infinitesimal calculus. But now we're talking about the things that are farthest above. You have to start with the things beneath."

"Yeah, now I'm catching on."

"I don't know how I started to think about this, but when I realized it, I was *seeing* the revolution, here, in this labyrinth that's the city, and I thought: how different a revolution is from a war, and how dreadful it is that they have to take a similar form. Because imagine what it will be like here below, fighting beside some people but without knowing exactly where the other people are. I know when things like this break out, groups and fronts form, but only up to a certain point. Some of them can come down that street and others from the street over there, and the shooting can occur here on the corner, but there's a block that ends up in the middle. What's inside it?

"That enigma is the city, and revolution is a thing of the city, even though there are uprisings staged by peasants and others. You can see that enigma, that crossroads in a café, in a train station, anywhere you find a large number of people. In those faces, those gazes, you see factions and firearms, but you don't see well-defined fronts. In a few faces there's a bit of one faction and a bit of its opposite. Of course some of them are whole, pure, that's obvious, but so many of them are right in the middle that you don't know whether to grieve because they're going to get trampled on or because they'll not only be dead weight for people who want to be involved in the combat but also a nuisance underfoot for the people who want to run away."

"Well, what you're talking about now has to do with the subsoil."

"Exactly: you've understood it perfectly. That subsoil of consciousness is what demands a revolution from above, but from *way above*. Of course what will come will be a revolution between classes, which is what comes between. Our present classes, the products of a *way below* and a *way above* that produced them, are defined explicitly, and there's an urgent need for them to settle their scores, because man can't live by ideas alone. I don't know if it will be the first, the second, or the third time, but I'm sure that sometime freedom and justice will be distributed fairly. Yes, I already know what you're going to say—that these are only ideas—right? They are, up to a certain point. They were, but today they're things that people eat, people live, that other people want to snatch out of their hands. And they have good reason. Well, I don't want to say all of them have equally good reason, but all of them, or almost all, have *their* reasons, and even that all of them have some reason. That's the labyrinth. The obvious things get resolved quickly, with a few shots, but the subsoil . . ."

"Yes, I don't know: that's incalculable. And, by the way, what about that business of infinitesimal calculus? Where does it come in?"

"Here, right here. It's a much-studied topic, evolution and revolution. Revolution is quick and imperfect, evolution slow and infallible. Can you believe one day, when I was thinking about other things, I found myself conceiving the idea of achieving a universal revolution by changing the name of every man, one by one. Stupid, isn't it? Well, I'm not going to back down from it."

"I understand, and it won't necessarily always be stupid."

"Precisely! Where do we start?"

"We can't start yet. Although, maybe it already started a while back."

"Yes, it has definitely started already. I don't care a bit if my idea's not original, I prefer to confirm that what I perceived is a slow existence or, rather, a slow, infallible action."

"That's what you perceived: man's march toward immortality step-by-step."

" . . . ! No one can hear us, can they?"

I looked around us and saw that both the terrace and the dining room inside were so crowded there wasn't a single table empty; with a quick glance I scrutinized all the diners one by one, and I found a few, quite a few, who were some of the wholes, but the rest belonged to the dead weight. They were dead people, eating.

"Do you believe they're all on their way to immortality?" I said.

"You're touching the crux of the problem. No, those people aren't on their way there, and neither are we. Well, we're on our way, but we won't get there. Because man won't achieve immortality until all the conditions he's created and assimilated are appropriate for immortality."

"That goes without saying."

"Nothing goes like that; because I'm not talking about biological conditions. That would be like saying man will achieve immortality when he's immortal. I could have said to you man will achieve immortality when he's worthy of it. But that would make it seem to be a question of privilege, and it's not. What I meant was when man has created an order of things so firm the appearance of immortality won't make it totter."

"But the attainment of immortality, can it affect the order of things?"

"Our current order of things? Obviously. It would be cataclysmic. Remember, the Greeks believed in the immortality of a few, of the best, because their entire order moved in that direction. But now, you can imagine the row that would ensue if a small group of people started becoming immortal. And every one of them at one fell swoop, just by divine intervention."

"Of course, all of them at one fell swoop would change nothing, at least not for some years, when people saw those who were seventy at the time of that divine intervention were still just like new. What would be serious is if immortality arose as a possibility everyone could hope for, an attainable goal. Many would die to attain it."

"Right. And many would kill. But that wouldn't be the only disaster. The conflict among people is obvious. Total sterility would amount to a repugnant and partial stagnation. Well! There's only one solution to all these problems: immortality means people's mobility must be limited."

"Exactly! Besides, that would offer the only form of aristocracy imaginable. Nobility would consist in cosmic courtesy. Because the spirit of conquest and domination would prove ridiculous once space and time were available to everyone. I think the noblest people would be those who went farthest, the ones who made the greatest effort not to get in the way. Wherever things began to seem a bit constricted, wherever a bit of envy sprang up, one person would take flight, leave the field clear, and go off on his own, at his own risk, farther, so much farther that no one, or almost no one, would dare follow him. That would be a noble person."

"Yes, such people would be nobles. You set it up in jest, but it's far more serious than it seems, because that paraphrase shows only that man *will be* immortal when the *sense* of immortality, *in everyone*, has the *dimensions* of immortality."

"Yes, now I see that what you say is not entirely foolish, but you have to be very optimistic in order to take it seriously."

"You're wrong there. Scientific progress can lead to an unsatisfactory immortality."

"Good heavens! I can't imagine where so much demand would come from."

"Well, it's very simple: what man wants is an absolute immortality, like the immortality of the spirit, and what's achieved *first* might be merely the immortality of matter, which is not free of chance, of destructive accidents."

"Ah! You're right. That would result in something most ignoble—the furious avoidance of danger. All enterprises, all risk, all distancing would disappear. Men would end up living carefully crated, like earthenware jugs, so as not to break."

The waiter came over for the hundredth time, with his insinuations. After several rounds of diners, the dining room had practically emptied. We'd ordered three coffees each and a bottle of French brandy since we'd finished eating, so they'd let us stay on there in peace, but finally we stood up.

It wasn't even eleven. We wandered along Alvear, then turned at Belgrano and sat for a while in a bar having another coffee. At twelve o'clock sharp we were back home.

Herminia got into the car as if she were sleepwalking, but she woke up for a minute to ask Miguel: "What time will you come tomorrow? Will you be there for lunch?"

"No," he said, "we'll get there first thing in the afternoon; because I'll be with a few kids." He looked at me and said, "Will there be four horses available?"

"Yes, of course," I answered, and we started off.

It was a perfect night. You couldn't see the moon because it was right over the roof of the car, a little to the left, but the light was crystal clear, like the silence.

"You won't fall asleep?" Herminia asked.

"Oh, don't worry. I was silent so I wouldn't scare off your ideas."

"It turned out I didn't work as much as I'd expected," she said. "Not that I totally wasted the time, but it occurred to me to read Racine's *Iphigenia*, which I didn't know, and I spent the evening doing that. The worst thing is it didn't give me anything new."

"It's set in Aulis, isn't it?"

"Yes, in Aulis, almost a detective movie, with a happy ending where the bad guy gets punished. Well, I can't say I got nothing out of it, I got a curious observation, if nothing else. In the prologue, Racine explains that he worked up his invention of how Tesseus and Elena's mysterious daughter—apparently there's a mention of her in some ancient texts— served as a substitute in the sacrifice, because in Racine's day it would have seemed bizarre, almost comical if the goddess had kidnapped Iphigenia and replaced her with a deer. Imagine, Racine considered that an affront to reason, and a century later Goethe adopted it with all seriousness."

"Yes, it is curious."

"Not only curious. It supports my thesis conclusively. Goethe has no qualms about adopting the substitution because his Iphigenia is a symbol, an allegory of the *Sister*. She's the *Sister* given by Apollo."

I let go of the steering wheel and grabbed at my head.

"Be careful!" Herminia shouted.

"It's useless for you to be careful," I said. "You're lost!"

"But why? What nonsense it that?"

"You're lost because you've developed a sectarian mentality. All you think of is bettering your own breed. You'll end up getting involved in politics."

"Oh! I'm in no danger of that. I already underwent that test and came out unscathed."

So we talked about these things and reached home about three. We went in quietly and said goodnight, and I came up to the tower. If I make sure to step right beside the wall, the stairs don't creak.

I went to the classics shelf and put Aeschylus, Euripides, and Sophocles beside the couch, planning to look through them so I wouldn't seem so ignorant, but within ten minutes I was sleeping like a log.

This morning I walked through the lab, even though it's Saturday, putting a finishing touch on things. I like to check over the lab when there's no one there, so my inspection doesn't make people feel pressured while they're working.

We ate lunch, feeling stifled by an unbearable heat, and I came up for siesta, but before falling asleep I heard Miguel arrive. He was with another boy and two girls, and they were all wearing jodhpurs. In a little while I heard them ride off in the hot sun.

I slept for a couple of hours and then I read for a while—*Prometheus*, which is very short. I went downstairs, and we had some cold tea; nothing really quenches your thirst right now. We hardly spoke, we were too exhausted.

Suddenly I recalled that several nights I'd wanted to open the upstairs window all the way and the wisteria made it impossible to move one of the sections in the shutter. I went to the shed where we keep the gardening tools to get something to cut the wisteria branches. The riders had already returned the horses to the pasture and were roaming about the garden.

The branches were too thick to cut with scissors, so I went to get some pruning shears and busied myself for a while sharpening them. As I was doing that, I heard a truly cryptic conversation beside the shed. I recognized the voices immediately: it was Miguel with his *partenaire*, an attractive girl—I think both girls who'd come with him were students— along the lines of Veronica Lake, who might have a pretty face beneath her abundant golden hair.

The first thing I heard was an "Ay!" from the girl and a protest: "You're mean! Not so hard." "It has to be like that," Miguel said. "Stick out your tongue." The girl let out another shriek. "Ay! Yes, it's delicious." I left the shed in a hurry before I burst out laughing. But my curiosity is irrepressible, and as I left the shed I gave a furtive little glance. I didn't want to watch, but I couldn't resist one quick glance, and the scene I saw was so decent and so worthy of being observed!

There's a eucalyptus trunk lying beside the shed, and the two of them were sitting on it. The girl, with her elbows on her knees, letting her beautiful hair fall forward perpendicularly, and Miguel was combing it with hard, fast strokes, using one of those clear plastic combs. Suddenly he would say: "Now! Now!" The girl would lift her head and stick out her tongue; Miguel would move the comb to within a centimeter of her mouth, and she'd give a little shriek because the comb would send a couple of sparks to her tongue.

Of course I didn't need to watch the whole time it took for this routine. One glance and I understood right away, because Miguel had explained the phenomenon to me, and he'd told me while the electrified comb lets off sparks when it gets close to any other body, only the tongue can feel them and, what's more, the sparks have a taste.

I took the pruning shears and went to free the shutter. Then I saw that all the kids were in the drawing room and Quitina was giving them sandwiches and cold drinks. I was about to go downstairs, but I started to laugh so hard when I recalled the scene I didn't want to risk seeming unpleasant. They left before eight.

We had dinner immediately, and I came up to write, because yesterday I couldn't fight off sleep. Today the moon came out very late, and it's very much on the wane. I don't know why this would be, but the waning moon is not as clear as the *croissant*. Even so, it's a very beautiful night and a person can begin to breathe. I'm sure to sleep well because, besides having the shutter open all the way, I have a sense of well-being, of the special sort of relief you feel after laughing by yourself.

The whole time I've been writing this episode about Miguel and the girl I've been laughing like an idiot. Sometimes I had to stop writing because I burst out laughing, and as soon as I think about it I'm overcome with laughter again. Laughing like this, when you're alone, is like laughing in your sleep. When you wake up laughing, sometimes you don't recall what you were dreaming about or you recall and it doesn't seem funny to you, but the laughter is authentic, and it's made you so happy you don't need to justify it with any cause. Maybe it's just the joy that comes from confirming that man is capable of joy.

16

Today I must put the exact date, and I don't think I should put anything else. What am I going to write here, the tale of a fact? I can't be afraid of forgetting it.

Nevertheless, I'll write about it so that it's recorded here with the appropriate tone. Tomorrow it's not likely to seem weaker or worse. Enlarging it would be neither possible nor necessary. I'll try to recount it here exactly as it was on this day.

The morning passed normally, we talked about various things I can't recall. Well, I do recall that Miguel came close to noon and, during lunch, we discussed everything that happened yesterday. He left immediately, because there were races in Azul. We had coffee in the drawing room, like always. Quitina got up to look for a magazine, I believe, and the telephone rang just as she was passing beside it; she answered.

My chair was facing her and, when I heard her speak English, I looked up at her; her expression had altered dramatically. She said something like, "Oh, it doesn't matter a bit, but we'd be delighted, just the same; we'll be here all afternoon. See you in a little while."

Herminia and I waited for Quitina to break the silence.

"It was Drake," she said. "He'll be here at five, to say good-bye and return a record album you loaned him."

614

"Yes," I said, "that's true, but I'd forgotten."

"So had he; he gave me a million apologies."

I shrugged my shoulders as if to say it made no difference, and we began to wait valiantly until it was five. I thought: well, a good-bye is the corroboration of absence, but it would have been better if there'd been no need to recall anything.

At five on the dot Drake arrived, and we welcomed him very cordially, managing to imitate his own warmth discreetly. Herminia took upon herself something she knew was too difficult for us.

"And what news do you have of Mrs. Drake?" she asked. "I imagine she's recovered completely?"

"Oh yes, completely," he answered. "It was a false alarm. Well, I saw from the beginning that it wasn't anything serious, it was something very different from the time before."

"Ah, that's wonderful," Herminia said. "I'm very happy to hear it." We agreed, smiling like puppets.

"It *makes me happy* too," Drake repeated, placing a specific intent in his words and adding, when he realized that we didn't understand: "A nervous woman is a real source of fear. A person feels frightened by the least occurrence, even when it's a happy occurrence."

Did one of us say something? I can't remember. All I know is that he continued: "Of course, it's disconcerting not to feel well during the early stages, and she was scared, because she was very apprehensive, but as soon as the symptoms were confirmed, everything passed."

"Ah!" we said, and Drake smiled.

I think Herminia was able to speak: "Congratulations."

And I was strong enough to get up and put on a record. Something thunderous and horrible, something weird, fractured, and despicable like a curse, like a latrine.

"Hey, that's terrific!" I told him. "That's super!"

He agreed, enraptured, and when the time was up he left.

I don't know what else happened until now, a few minutes after twelve.

Tuesday, the 11th

Yesterday alone together, in silence.

The resolve not to speak, like an idée fixe. "Don't speak, don't speak. Can all this be dispelled eventually? Not speaking doesn't necessarily mean anger or suspicion. In any case, don't speak . . ."

I was very active during the morning, and I multiplied the demands on me a hundred times beyond what was necessary, so at lunchtime I was worn out and this justified my silence.

By the time it was night, the nature of our silence was so stable it was a cause for fear, the fear caused by anything gigantic. Nevertheless, the night managed to pass under its weight, with a sleep at times empty, at times riddled with stupid, dull, ugly images—a sleep broken by sudden thuds in my heart, like pits, but resumed when the arid feeling of insomnia turned into a sort of abdication or swoon.

Today, breakfast in silence.

We were about to get up from the table when the maid came in and told Quitina she had put water in the vases and left the scissors on the table in the hall.

"Good, I'll be right there," Quitina said.

It was Quitina's job: to put flowers and greens in all the vases, and she began to perform it as usual. I sat there a few minutes leafing through the newspaper, and by the time I left she had already placed a large bouquet in the hall and was cutting flowers in the clump of bushes near the door.

I already had my foot in the doorway when I remembered that yesterday morning I met the mailman as I was coming into the house; he gave me a couple of letters, which I read in the library and left there in the desk drawer. One of those letters definitely had to be answered today, and I went to get it so I could give it to Gálvez.

Going back like that made me feel very uneasy.

When I got to the door, I saw Quitina cutting flowers; she didn't raise her head, although she saw me because I noticed her quick, oblique glance. At that moment I went inside. It was senseless to suspect she might have thought I'd gone back to escape from her, but even so I felt very upset, very annoyed. So much so that, when I reached the library, I couldn't remember what I'd gone there to do.

By making a great effort I finally recalled and sat down at the desk. I opened the drawer; the letter wasn't visible, or maybe it was and I didn't see it. I looked through all the papers and, in fact, it was there. Just as I found it, Quitina came into the library. I was incapable of getting up and walking out with the letter, which is what I would have done on any other occasion. I kept looking through the papers and thinking at the same time about how absurd my behavior was, how impossible it is for a person to perform some natural act when you're choked by poisonous, insane silence. At the same time, I was watching Quitina, who was pretending to go about her task quite naturally.

Carrying a bunch of wallflowers, she walked across the library and went to put them in the earthenware vase that's always on the table where we put the magazines.

As she walked into the library determinedly, I kept acting as though I were searching through papers, but I was looking at her, assuming she couldn't tell because at that moment I was sitting against the light. In the library there are two facing windows; beside one of them, in the corner, there's the desk; in front of the other one there's a long antique table, like a table from a convent, and that's where we put magazines. The earthenware vase always sits at an angle; it's a huge beer mug, without a lid, which I found in an antique shop.

Quitina went toward the table and gently set the flowers on a magazine, and I realized that the cat was asleep on the far edge of the table where there were no magazines. Quitina walked around the table so that she was in front of me. Did she know I was watching her? I thought then she didn't. She went slowly toward the cat so as not to wake her, and she stood there looking at her. I no longer had a good view of Quitina's face, because she was bending over the cat, but I could see she was saying something almost imperceptibly: "She's sleeping so soundly!" Then, without changing her position, she reached out her hand, picked up the mug by its handle, and raised it over the cat's head.

I was going to shout "Quitina!" but I didn't because she looked at me at that very moment. For her, I was completely in shadow and she couldn't see my face, but she looked at me in such a way I found it impossible to speak; besides, I saw she was smiling. Yes, there's no other way to say it; a very slight grimace that stretched her bloodless lips can only be called a smile, so I saw she was smiling, and I saw that she was going to speak. I remained silent.

"It would be delightful," she said, "it would be wonderful to smash her."

I was able to say "Quitina!" but my voice was like a puff of air. Her voice was horrible, like her smile, something like a grimace made with her throat. And she remained motionless in that same position, as if petrified. The mug was full of water, and it was probably very heavy, but her hand didn't tremble. She was holding it fifteen centimeters above the cat's head, but the cat didn't move, because she's an animal so accustomed to swipes and shouts she lacks an alarm system. She was stretched out there to take advantage of the breeze, with her little head on the top of the table: she'd be smashed if the mug were dropped. But Quitina didn't plan to drop it; she was holding it tightly by the handle, and she raised it, as if to gather momentum and deliver a real blow.

Once again I was ready to shout but kept silent. The whole scene lasted a couple of seconds. I thought, I shouted inside myself: "Smash her, destroy her, if you'll make yourself feel better that way, but you won't. You're about to do something useless, harmful to yourself. I would like to prevent you, but I won't, you won't see me defend her."

Quitina lowered the mug quickly, but she stopped when it was four inches from the cat's head; then she diverted it and dropped it to the edge of the table. The cat woke up from the thud, but she didn't run off; she raised her head and straightened up her ears. Quitina gave her a shove that sent her flying to the middle of the room.

"That little head is not the one I'd like to smash," she said.

I continued to say nothing, begging her silently: Don't explain anything! It's already clear enough! Don't speak in that voice; it has to be painful for you!

Quitina picked up the wallflowers and put them in the vase, but not all of them at once; she placed them carefully, as she usually did, so the stems would bend slightly and the flowers would be nicely spaced and, at the same time, without looking at me, as if she were paying attention to what she was doing, even though she was addressing me openly, she was saying: "How could you think I would do something like that? How could I destroy something if that *something* belongs to my children?"

I could not remain silent, because I needed to silence that voice. And when my voice came out, I thought it seemed even more horrible: it made me feel even more frightened. I recognized neither my voice nor my words, because I said something uncharacteristic or, rather, something I had never mixed with horror.

"Light of my life, you're going to drive yourself crazy," I said.

Quitina looked at me again and sent another penetrating glance toward the shadow of my silhouette.

"You spat out that insult spontaneously."

"Quitina!"

"Have you ever seen anything more revolting than life?" she asked; she bent over to pick up a few leaves that had fallen to the floor, held them in her hand, and left.

Could a person lose so much weight in one night that it would be noticeable in her body, even in her feet? Because a face can become haggard in a few hours, but as Quitina went out of the room—there may have been a slight draft that made her dress cling to her body—I saw that her entire skeleton stood out in the fabric, as in a shroud. And I saw something even more shocking, more astonishing, because it was *the same thing as always*: once again I saw Quitina's virginity. But at other times her virginity had appeared as something active, fertile, like a perennial strength. Now it was manifest as despair . . . secular despair. Secular, because it didn't seem to be a state caused by accident, but something that had *always* had been that way.

This takes a long time to explain, but seeing it was as quick as noticing the difference between a virgin, a young woman, a "real girl" and *une vieille fille.* That's how Quitina struck me as she left the library, like a child who'd been waiting century after century, but who was no longer waiting—a being saturated with hate, like a sponge, who had never, ever known love.

Thursday, the 13th

Yesterday, first thing in the morning, when I went downstairs I heard Quitina talking on the phone. From her tone I realized she was speaking with Herminia; she said something like "I'll call you tonight," and she hung up.

She'd eaten breakfast before I came down, and she walked past me in the hall as if she didn't see me; I heard her walking around giving orders, and there was a certain commotion noticeable in the house. I drank a cup of tea without sitting down and went into the lab.

Somehow the morning went by. At lunchtime there was only one place set at the table. Miss Ray told me that Quitina had called a taxi and gone to Azul, to buy some things she wanted to take with her. I was about to ask where, but I could see she thought I already knew and I didn't want to confuse her.

I ate, barely, and left immediately for Buenos Aires. Herminia said: "It's very serious. It's the worst thing that could have happened."

"Yes, the worst," I said, and we sat in silence for a long while, speechless. Then, Herminia told me that Quitina had decided to go to Quequén, with the children. They would leave right away if she could get tickets.

I begged her to go with them. This meant disrupting all her plans, but she didn't hesitate.

"Yes, you're right," she said, "she can't be allowed to go alone." Her suitcase was packed in a minute, and we came back to Las Murtas. Miguel came too because I suggested they take the big car, which meant they wouldn't have to worry about trying to get tickets. Miguel could go with them, because it was too many hours for them to drive, and he could take a train or bus back.

As soon as we got to the house, I went up to the tower. I told them I wouldn't be down for dinner, and Miguel came up very late to tell me that Herminia had arranged everything so they would leave early in the morning. Quitina had come back very annoyed because they couldn't promise her tickets for six days, and she agreed to everything that Herminia had planned.

Today, at seven, they left for Quequén.

I was awake from five on, but I didn't go down until I saw Miguel putting the suitcases in the trunk. The children were in and out of the car, happy to be going to the ocean. I told them that I would have liked to go with them, but with so much work . . . This is something they were familiar with, and they found it natural. We said good-bye.

Union! What is the famous union? Is it a farce, a fantasy, an exorbitant aspiration, a conventional legend, or is it a real, autonomous phenomenon that prevails even when we think it's impossible? It may be that certain senses, like touch, hearing, smell cannot be closed off to the outside. Contact occurs, whether you want to touch or you touch without wanting to. So when two wills that always tended to unite struggle to separate, their habitual contact turns into a tugging every bit as horrible as the tugging of fish on the line.

If I doubted the reality of everything I perceived this morning, I would have to doubt everything that I've believed in my whole life.

Quitina was possessed of a great serenity, and she employed the most clever reasoning to keep the children from finding it strange that she would be in a bad mood: she was tired from packing so many suitcases, they had gotten up very early . . . it all seemed perfectly logical.

When they were about to leave, I held Fernando for a moment, and I kissed Jorge; Quitina turned her back, looked at the sky, and made some prediction about the weather. Francisco, who was helping to tie the bicycles on the car, came to say good-bye to me when he'd finished; to do this he had to run past Quitina, and I saw her hesitate, on the point of turning to look at him and stop him as he ran, but she checked herself, and Francisco came over like a torrent to give me a hug. He put his arms around my neck, gave me a kiss, and said a few affectionate words to me with his customary haste.

In the middle of his effusive good-bye, we heard Quitina's voice: "Francisco!" He made an unconcerned gesture that's also customary for him, as if to say, "I don't think it's anything urgent," gave me another kiss, and went to see what they wanted. Quitina didn't turn around, but she was vibrating like a high-voltage cable.

"Francisco!" she said, "seems to me this is too loose . . ."

When Francisco reached her she continued to express concerns, which he brushed off, assuring her everything was fine, and they got into the car.

They took off and went through the gate.

I stood there, frozen in the middle of the road, feeling the brutal tug with which Quitina's voice had tried to tear Francisco from me, at the very moment he was hugging me. I was some four or five meters from the car, and she was beside the car door, waiting for Miss Ray to settle herself with the younger children and pretending to check everything over with her gaze. But I knew, I *felt* that she was not really involved in that. She was *seeing*—although she'd turned her back—that her children were coming to kiss me and, when it was the younger ones, she tolerated it, overcoming her nerves, but when Francisco came—at that moment, I saw Quitina's preference for him, which perhaps I share—then she could not contain herself, and she shouted "Francisco!" as she would have shouted if she'd seen him approach something harmful.

She shouted with the same violence as on the day I took hold of her ankle, and she was afraid I was going to caress it. An embrace wrapped around a lie is deadly to her, like a strangulation. She shouted, not when Francisco came toward me, but at the precise moment he was putting his arms around my neck, so her voice would erase the contact Francisco was going to feel, without knowing the truth.

I've worked the whole day, unconscious; I've wandered around the house and the garden, with a persistent memory fixed in my head. One of those memories that instead of being something you observe is the presence of someone who's looking at you. And keeps looking.

I started to write, to scare it away, but as soon as I stop I find it's still there. I'll face up to it; maybe it wants to say something.

It is—or it *is?*—on the right bank of the Quequén River. The sun hasn't set completely, but it has disappeared now behind a mountain of eucalyptus trees. First half of January, a calm, warm day. Quitina and I are looking at the river from a small hill. (Did I say something in these notebooks about our summer vacations in Quequén in 1940 and '42? I don't remember and I don't feel like looking back through them.) Quitina and I are watching the river. A man emerges from the Club Náutico in a canoe and starts rowing upstream. He rows with academic perfection, his rhythm so sure and deliberate it seems impossible he'll ever get tired. He's blond and perfectly proportioned, and he's wearing nearly invisible swimming trunks the same color as his sunburned skin.

"He's so golden and gleaming," Quitina says. "He looks like a soul."

"Yes, he looks every bit like a soul making it way upstream, tirelessly."

There's something that corroborates the idea that he's on his way to heaven; less than a hundred meters above the water, the gulls are passing on their way back to spend the night on the sea. This same brief migration takes place every day at the two twilights; the gulls arrive at dawn and spread out in search of earthworms along the river and the sown fields nearby. And they return, unwaveringly following the river's meanderings, so a river of gulls—hundreds and thousands passing, passing for more than an hour—is silhouetted against the sky, identical to the river of water, and you can imagine them converging in infinity, or rather, rising from a single source.

Quitina and I watch the river and the lone navigator sailing up that water; we say a thousand things suggested to us by the now minuscule, distant oarsman. He looks small to us, but we continue to feel the rhythm of his stokes.

Suddenly I say: "Oh, to sail on the río Quequén!"

Quitina asks: "What's that, a poem?"

"Yes, a poem."

"It's pretty. What comes next?"

"Nothing. That's all there is."

"Oh, I had the impression it would be very long."

"And it is very long. It's just like the river: three triads of infinitely flowing syllables. Listen, you have to say it like this:

> *Oh, to sail*
>> *On the rí*
> > > *o Quequén . . .*"

The oarsman had disappeared, but we repeated the poem's lone line many times there on the bank of the river.

When you tell a dream, it analyzes itself. So that recounting this memory has revealed its meaning.

Quitina's on her way to Quequén and, someday, she's sure to cross the hanging bridge and, by herself, she'll take the road on the right bank, the Necochea side; she'll go toward the port and, perhaps, after she passes the Club Náutico, she'll stop for a moment at the edge of the slope. I know that all this will happen; I've known since this morning, and I can't think about anything else. But I don't know what I think . . . I don't think anything: I see the scene. I know that Quitina will meet me there. Do I know what I feel or what I want? Less. Quitina is going toward me: this time I can't be afraid that the past will contain seeds of infidelity, because the past she is going to recover is filled with me. Anything in the past I can fear? Can't I feel jealous that she's going to relive *her* love there, leaving me here, my only nourishment the image of her white lips stretched in a mortal expression, her hand raised with the enormous mace, her suddenly thin body walking out the door, against the draft?

Friday, the 14th

The whole day I've received nothing but a few distrustful, disdainful glances.

It's natural. I demanded so much activity, I promised so much: improvements, profits, benefits for everyone. Today they've seen my discouragement, and they suspect my promises will come to nothing.

And I'd had started out to be so exemplary! Around the year 1940, I wrote: "The social man has been born in me"; now I wrote nothing, but I didn't follow that impulse and, this time, things became rather public in the small world under my management. If my efforts are aborted, no one will understand how serious the situation is.

No one will understand how serious the situation is for *me*, because everyone's going about his own business. That's how it has to be, and above all, that's how it is. What's happening, what happened—it occurred as a consequence of this. Everyone's going about his own business.

And my greatest ambition was to *look after everyone and each and every one*!

Justice is something you can eat; I have a small handful of justice I must dole out like wheat to a brood of chickens. Each person will stave off his personal hunger with a portion of the grain that falls to him. That's how the metamorphosis takes place: justice becomes incarnate in that grain, dispersed freely. This is so clear that failing to achieve it seems impossible. Nevertheless, they don't trust me. They see that now, at this critical time, I'm looking out for my own personal hunger. They neither suspect nor find interesting the possibility that I might hunger to fulfill my ambition; all they see is I've dissociated myself from the common interest.

Which isn't accurate, because I have definitely not dissociated myself, although now it's not possible for my portion to turn into something that might mean freedom for me. My life has fallen into the trap of a different freedom, because it's so difficult to reconcile the question of *everyone and each and every one*, even in cases where everyone is reduced to *two*!

If I explained to them the only possible solution to this situation, they would not understand and they'd even feel maltreated. Because the solution is this: I'll give them a little less than what I was thinking and they'll all be happy. Less! they'd shout. Yes, less; I'll take from them something that in truth, strictly speaking, they don't need one damned bit: my cheerful and enthusiastic cooperation.

When I proposed melting down the insulating block by using an extremely high temperature, this was one of the elements I planned to ignite. "Things, people," I told myself. Here, with this huge space, if the factory were productive, we could do something exceptional, exemplary. And, of course, not merely with the goal of getting Quitina back. No! At that time I formulated it very clearly. I placed my entire trust in things being true; it entailed setting in *precise* motion a chain of authentic, efficient, fertile acts, which would propagate, gradually invade the area involved until they filled it with a present, real and clean. All that has collapsed; for me there is no longer the least possibility of a clean present. But I won't cloud the present of others.

They're distrustful, because they can't imagine that what they expected from my smile, from my project and my outgoing optimism, which, because it was recent, they attributed to the abundant harvest, is something they would get just the same from my self-absorption, or my indifference, or my bitterness. The bit of—what we'll call—the bonanza that time has placed in my hands will be administered in the form I planned. When everyone employs his life in whatever action he finds possible for him, no one will stop to think.

Four o'clock, or later

It was so hot that I couldn't keep writing. I stood under the shower, but when I left the bathroom the atmosphere in the bedroom seemed even hotter. I went down to the garden in shorts and without a shirt; not even the hint a of breeze. The trees and shrubbery seemed to be blocking the airflow and I started to walk quickly toward the countryside; it felt exactly the same. All I managed was to interrupt my rumination of a few moments before. I wasn't thinking about anything, just walking and confirming the absence of any wind; I kept walking, in hopes of finding some.

I don't know why, but suddenly I felt I was not alone, in other words, I felt I'd not been alone for some time. And at that moment—maybe I shortened my step, as if I were about to turn around, although I didn't quite—at that moment something moist touched my hand.

I haven't wanted a dog of my own again, but there are several dogs on the estancia. I recognized the one that belonged to the foreman, a hound of some indefinite breed; the foreman says it's a real good dog. It definitely struck me as a *real dog*. When I turned sharply, it backed away a little, intimidated, and I saw it silhouetted against the light beside the shed. It's a young dog with rather long, silky black hair; it looked very genuine to me. It was not a mastiff, or a setter, or a poodle; it was a dog. I shooed it away, because I didn't want any evocations, but the dog didn't take me seriously; it moved back a few steps, thinking I wanted to play. I kept threatening it, and finally it went off.

I walked as far as the factory; several lampposts there mark the exit toward the road. I walked over to the land in cultivation; I observed what was left of the plants, which had died as they fulfilled their purpose, and suddenly, next to the ditch, not far from the ground I spotted a crooked white poppy. A late plant, from a seed that may have fallen at the wrong time, outside the fence. It looks like the flower opened today. I cut it and put it here on the table, in a glass.

It's starting to get light.

Saturday, the 15th

Only One could say with perfect right: "My God! Why have you forsaken me?" He was sure He was abandoning him, even though He had never abandoned him for even an instant. But when *one* feels like crying out that same thing, suddenly he begins to doubt who's abandoned whom.

Before the court I'll assume the guilt without the least hesitation. I will dare to affirm: I was the one who abandoned him. But I want to know when. I want to go back, return to the crossroads, and see clearly where I took the wrong path. I want to *see* a path different from the one I followed. I want to see clearly how and when I *could* take it, instead of this one, the only one I know.

What's irreparably shattering my future is a single event. Even with everything else, I wouldn't find myself so fenced in now. Of course, the earlier storm was serious and more extensive than the single, decisive event. But it had begun to pass, it was already conquered. If this dreadful thing hadn't happened, it wouldn't be impossible for me to remake my peace.

And if it had happened and we'd not received any news of it? Let's see: the knot's tied way too tight; I can't find the end, but I won't stop trying.

In the first place, what is the end? The end is the total, absolute meaning. Of course it's my own part that's of vital interest to me, but a single part has no meaning. Even if the decisive action originates, in this case, in a single part. It's obvious that, without the piece of news that put some of the parts in communication with others, the action would not have been felt.

I'm making no headway, none of this is what I'm looking for. The dialogue of intentions is like a messed-up puzzle; in order to understand it you have to look for the question that corresponds to a certain answer.

Quitina said something almost blasphemous, which was like pointing violently, as if to accuse: "There's goes the guilty party!" There he goes, because the key word was present in something I said as if in passing. "Light of my life," I said, amidst the vertigo in my mind, and she didn't let it escape. She didn't hear the affectionate words a person speaks in an ordinary situation, without thinking what he's saying; she heard the phrase and sounded the alarm. Her terrifying smile at that moment, her voice, her gaze weren't accusing me; I would almost dare to say they were merely reproaching me: "Why do you refer to something that's turned into an insult, something revolting? Why do you mention the thing that's betrayed me?"

Those are definitely the pieces that fit: Quitina said that to me because one day I said—to no one, to myself—: "In order to conquer, Quitina has aligned herself with life." And this is so accurate that when she heard me refer to life, she swore, infuriated. Beneath her sarcasm was unfolding a clear reasoning: "How dare you mention that when Elfriede has aligned herself with it in order to triumph?"

And the messenger putting the parts in contact! Because, if we hadn't known! I say it again.

You're pushing me to this, Lord, to shout: "Take out this thorn! Let this cup pass from me! Free me, even if it's through ignorance or any other denial, free me from this unbearable pain . . . or explain its meaning to me!" But I know the last thing is something You won't do. I know perfectly well that "To You, all things are possible" as well as that You could do it, but You don't want to, and now I have no strength to fight with You.

Can it do any good to ask like this, without any strength, without struggling? Then if I know that struggle alone is effective, why don't I have any strength? This can only be because You've taken it from me. And maybe the only thing *You cannot take from me* is this knowing, which You gave me, and even though it's far from boundless, You gave it and that means it's true. Therefore it's *knowing*.

How different from the battle between faith and reason! I imagine the simple path walked by those who loved You when they were young and then decided not to love You, because their reason told them You were only a mirage. My reason, on the other hand, is Your mirror. A mirror in which now You clearly aren't looking at Yourself, but which would reflect You if it came to be placed in front of You. What I lack is the ability to *place myself* in front of You.

I know there's a place where You can be seen. I know there's a *point*, but I can't reach it. "I cannot make the motion of faith." If I could, that butterfly would flutter its wings. Definitely, Miguel! An idiocy like this is a touchstone, a small thing that lets one dare and, on that basis, go on or not go on to larger things, and if one does not go on it's because *one cannot*, because one doesn't have the strength. When *one can*, capability swells like a powerful tide and reaches everything, it reaches the All, and when it does not, it's only like a minor upheaval. Like a brief excitement, similar to desire, but desire that does not sustain its tension until the generative act, desire that detaches not a single speck of eternity from our being.

That's how it was the night I sat down to write the letter. The butterfly tempted me, with a wave of horrible voluptuousness. My whole being awakened, inclining toward the absolute act, but I resisted temptation. Why I resisted is a separate issue, but the thing is, nothing happened. I know it could have happened. Definitely, Miguel. Even with the most colossal effort, man's will cannot give life to the dried cells of that insect, and I'm well aware of that. But the thing is, that's not what man's will ever attempts. What it attempts, in one of those moments of desire (I'm speaking specifically about desire of the flesh, because I find nothing more similar to pure volition), what it attempts is to touch the will of God. His heart was touched, they say, when someone takes pity. The heart of God is pure will. The famous energy, which you assume can be transformed into matter, is the will of God. The will that says "Let there be light," four syllables in our language, is in God's language a point that moves three million kilometers per second, well, a point for which there are neither seconds nor kilometers. And with this instrument, or *word*, God *can* flutter the wings of a dead butterfly or move a mountain, or make not to have been something that was.

Well, I know that this is one of the things God *cannot* do, but He can do something that will have same result. Yes, it's certain He can do this, so certain we can't guarantee that He hasn't done it.

We know that the history of those miraculous events doesn't record the one about God restoring the arm to the man who lost it, as Kierkegaard proposes, but if God were to remove some common event from human memory and from the annals filling the archives, the way you squeeze water from a sponge, no one would have proof of that miracle, and if God has the hairs of our heads and the channels in a sponge numbered, He *can* very well remove all traces of any event. Who knows if some grace-filled soul hasn't asked for this and had it granted? Since the world has existed as world, has there not been a single man with sufficient strength to move a mountain—to ask that it be moved?

I remember with absolute clarity that at times I've experienced cold, hunger, and sleepiness, and I remember with the same certainty that I've experienced faith and, when I did, I could move mountains. If I didn't continue to move them, it's because I didn't pay the necessary price. And that's why, because I knew the price, that's why I resisted the temptation of the butterfly.

Price comes up in the following way: if I had lived in one of those periods when my country was threatened by the invasion of a foreign army, if at that moment I had been in possession of my faith, I would have asked God to move Aconcagua to the valley through which my enemy was advancing. If I had seen that God was listening to me and, like a shovel of energy, His will was lifting the mountain and placing it in the valley, if I had seen God's will slice into the rock the way a silver serving spatula slices into a flan, but a hundred trillion times shinier and thinner than the spatula, one made from the same matter as a flash of lightning, which severed it with one cut and carried it through the air, I wouldn't have been amazed. Definitely not, because that's not where the mystery lies, that's not where the absurd lies.

I want no part of individuals who say, "I believe, because it's absurd." No, I believe because it's logical, because there's good reason. If this colossal event had occurred before my eyes, my relationship with God would be perfectly in order; I would have paid the fair price, without bargaining. I would not have let escape an amazed Oh! I would have beamed with happiness, with triumph, with glory, and I would have fallen on my knees for life. In other words, I would have *fallen* to save my country. Something that's natural: others would fall in the fray, and I would fall in a felicitous transaction, paying with the smallness of my being for colossal good fortune.

But if the mountain obstructs the path toward my own happiness . . . Here the mountain no longer serves the purpose, because a mountain is surrounded. If I insert something into life's continuity, something of the same kind, it appears and it remains; and if, as a result, the atmosphere I breathe changes totally, from the moment that something manifests itself, I'm left uprooted from my element, with no possibility of returning to it. Like dolphins on the beach, exactly; in that insurmountable alteration of my environment. A line: on one side, water, the fluid region where movement is possible, where contact is gentle, homogeneous, appropriate to their way of being; on the other, sand, dryness, immobility, death. That's the way my world has been severed, with a division that clear. A line—a moment: on one side, happiness, pleasure, desire moving freely, and on the other, bitterness, self-accusation, every impulse constrained. Well, then, if in the face of all this I ask for the miracle and it's granted to me . . .

Now, of course, the miracle cannot consist, as it did for me in the past, in the destruction of an obstacle. If some catastrophe were to eliminate the being—the beings—that weigh on my future, my sense of relief would be only very relative, because that would not allow me to experience the fluid element of joy and confidence. Therefore, the miracle would have to consist in making *not to have been something that was.*

Impossible? For God there are no impossibles. I know that! It would be very easy for Him to perform this miracle, and I could ask Him to do it with a very logical, very clear explanation. "Father," I would say, "for You everything is possible; take the past in Your hand, like a sponge saturated with events, and pull at the radical point, which diverges in millions of threads harmful to my happiness. Yank them all out—just the harmful ones, of course—and leave the past as before—clean, joyful, and breathable.

God could do this and, if He were to do it, what would be so extraordinary? Nothing; that's not where the mystery lies. If He doesn't do it, it's not because He would find it difficult. Maybe then it's because my request is impudent? Because His mercy isn't vast enough for Him to pardon such an unworthy soul? That's not it either. At times I've dared to doubt His mercy; I've definitely gone even that far! But not really. I know His mercy is infinitely greater than what it takes to pardon a shameless sinner. I know He could pardon me; I know it would be easy for Him to perform that delicate task, but I'm not asking Him to; no, I'm not asking Him to. The mystery of man's relationship with God lies in something subsequent to the miracle.

If God had taken pity on the dolphins and sent a huge tide to gather them up, they would have gone back to swimming, eating, procreating, and to being beautiful, mobile forms instead of poor, inert rolls of flesh. They weren't obligated to do anything more. But if the miracle were granted to me, how would I pay for it?

When I say that "the miracle is feasible for God," that there would be nothing strange about His performing it, I'm referring only to its execution (if there's any meaning in the phrases "God made the world," "Not a leaf on the tree moves unless He wills," and "He sees to it that the swallows have food," there's just as much meaning as in the nonsense I come out with. A meaning, of course, strictly of *possibility*); however, the fact of the understanding between God and man, the concession of a reply, is something so formidable for human reason that reason is led to lose the sense of its dimensions. In addition to this hypertrophy—man's aspiration to continue the dialogue up to the last question—, in addition to this, man experiences rapture—a mixture of gratitude (the logical effect of a cause) and contemplation (the *sainte volupté* I mentioned before)—which makes worldly interests pale by comparison. Man feels *chosen*, and he responds, he surrenders. This, although it may seem absurd, destroys the effectiveness of the miracle.

When Moses makes water burst from a rock, it's so the thirsty can drink. Of course, falling to your knees in adoration and drinking water are compatible things. But living the joyful life of the body, the fury of human love, sating one's senses and falling to your knees, are not.

If God answers us, knowing as He did that it was this, *this and nothing else*, that we were asking, why is His condescending response a gift that He takes from us? Why does He give the thing and snatch it away from us?

Could it be because our request seems paltry to us in comparison to the immensity of His gift? That might be why, but then why make an immense gift of something paltry?

I resisted the butterfly's temptation because I didn't want to pay that price. Now I would pay it. Just as every man accepts any risk in order to save his country when it's in danger, I would accept any destructive risk, any transaction, to save Quitina from unhappiness. But suppose that did happen, suppose my past were cleared of all guilt, if in fact it were erased from my memory, I would go back to being what I was before and, probably, end up, step by step, in the same place. But if everything were erased from other people's memory, and not only from their memory, if the books that record dates, trips, and job transfers were modified, if it turned out that Pan American had never issued certain tickets, if a certain car never passed through the gate and so there was never a Sunday with children's games on the carpet, nor, later, a cat miaowing around the house, nor all the rest . . . and if I preserved the memory of the events, exactly as they were, as well as the vision of their destruction by God's hands, if I contemplated the harm I did as if it were a plant ripped from the earth with its thousands of little roots exposed to the air, would I be any good when it came to making Quitina happy?

Maybe only by taking her with me in my rapture. Of course, I couldn't explain the cause of the rapture to her, I couldn't reveal something that would disturb her innocence, her happiness. But in some way I would definitely be able to enrapture her; I could suggest to her a detachment from all earthly things, a different valuation. But, Lord, this was not what we wanted!

A new concern: did Quitina and I want the same thing? In that simple question there is more mystery than in the most fantastic reversal of the laws of nature. Because Quitina wanted, she always wanted me to be what I am. She *wanted me* as I am and not some other way, although the way I am was inevitably going to cause her misfortune and although knowing this prevented her from having any peace. I, too, always wanted to be the way I am, without really knowing how I am. What I wanted was to try to see how I was at every moment. So that, yes, we did both want the same thing, that I would be the thing capable of causing the most fear, the thing that was bound to destroy our lives. This enigma alone is already quite serious, but there was something else. There was someone else who wanted the same thing, and here's where agreeing on something can cause immense discord.

Elfriede wanted the same thing as Quitina and, in order to achieve it, she employed the same means: she initiated a life that is now here, one that nothing and no one can deny. It doesn't matter that one of the two achieved public sanction, and the other must live without revealing the secret: the purpose is identical. Faced with the threat of frustration, Quitina provoked the event that is pure future, permanence. She affirmed herself, strengthening her forces, duplicating herself. It was the first time she had asked her son to come to her defense when she saw herself in danger. Her preference for Francisco is definitely her thanks for the speedy assistance he lent her.

Faced with the sentence of destruction, which seemed inexorable to her, Elfriede affirmed herself by following the same procedure. This way she cannot be totally erased and, above all, she cannot be considered part of the past. That was her wound: she felt I was embracing her *in the preterit* and she was determined to be part of the future. To weigh on my future, simply, with the news of a probable existence that is going to be and that, at a distance, will continue being.

And what role do I play in all this?

I could say: I, with my sensuality, my lack of premeditation . . . But no, that's not enough. If I must judge myself, I have to analyze my behavior thoroughly and rigorously. And I must press even further, I have to define my masculine personality as a whole. All that I've done here is consider the deepest, most intimate areas of my conscience and my feelings, but maybe there's still subsoil in the area that to me seems deepest: the part of my personality and my behavior in which conscience and feelings operate obliquely, almost seem not to be operating at all but, nevertheless, obey an identical law.

This isn't easy, but I'll try to reduce it to the simplest of questions: what have *I* given until now?

A man's generosity cannot be proved by a list of everything he gave to his beloved, because people will ask, What about the others, society, the world? Obviously, there are men who will dispossess everyone else in order to give to a single being they love. But there are others, and I count myself among them, who cannot give more than one thing, whether to a single being or to the world. We have only a single thing for everyone and every one. Is this thing really a thing? No, because we can't. (I'll speak only about myself, although this exception is not so unique.) I can give only one thing, which is not a thing, because it is *I myself.* I can give myself to everyone and to every one in such a way that they seem to have, through me, all things. I believe if I proposed it to myself, I could be a *leader.* But I won't try, because the *leader* guides people toward the attainment of things, and my goal is to give them things suddenly, to create them from nothing.

Well, the things a man can create from nothing aren't things people can eat. Or are they? Maybe some of them, but up until now I haven't created them; it hasn't gone beyond being one of my goals. However, I have managed to give a few things, by uncovering them. I can't give what people eat as much as I'd like to, but I can always reveal what it is people want to eat. Then my role in the world is this: to be an explorer of human desire, to make lack of appetite impossible.

Could this be how, according to Elfriede, I influence others without realizing it? That's possible. So where does this condition lead? Is it something positive? Does it really mean giving something?

Up until now, my influence has centered on two lives, and I've guided them toward an insoluble conflict. The brief upheavals I experienced as a social man caused no one any harm, but neither were they of much benefit. Would I be able, in some way, to guide a great many people toward the extreme tension to which I've guided the two of them? Undoubtedly, only a *leader* can do this . . . well, so can a poet, and I don't believe I'm either of those.

I wouldn't want to be the first, although I would the second. Of course, that's because the second is the *first.*

The famous poem I saw among the birches in La Plata! That day I intuited something very true. "I don't want to do anything—not even live—that's not filled with this emotion," I told myself. And my emotion had welled up in the zoo, in the presence of the animals' terror at dusk. Then, later that night, I relived the scene in *the opossum's house,* and what I was hoping to achieve with all that was to reach the limit of reason, "the reason of unreason." Because the greatest "unreason my reason is subjected to" is that this limit exists and that beyond it lie the sources of all the things reason is dying to attain.

Contemplating the terror and love of beings that know they are vulnerable, edible, I felt that I could write a poem, in other words, something—an action, a word—that would create a sort of tent of mercy for them, I felt called to protect them.

Back after a three-hour break. I stopped in the middle of the last paragraph because the sun began to enter the room. I hadn't noticed it had been getting light for some time, because the sun comes up at five. I closed the shutters halfway and didn't have the energy to start writing again. Hearing the bell from Las Flores, I realized it was already Sunday. At least it was guaranteeing me twenty-four hours of solitude.

No question of sleeping. The smell of coffee in the room and on my hands made me feel terribly nauseated. I washed the machine, the filters, and the cup six or seven times, but the smell won't go away, no matter how much I scrub myself with the brush. Thinking that a glass of lemon water might do me some good, I decided to go down and get one, although the thought of it made me feel even more nauseated. But I went to the garden instead of the kitchen. I pulled off a few lemons and smelled them; the smell erased my feeling of nausea a little and, without thinking, I started following a path beside a row of thorny shrubs. While I walked, I kept scratching at the lemon with my fingernail; little by little I started to feel better. I heard a clucking in the shrubs, and some childish habit or other, which leads me to investigate anytime I hear an animal, made me change course, and I went toward the shrubs where I heard the clucking; a spotted brown hen rushed out indignantly from between the branches and ran off between my feet. My hunting instinct made me bend down to look for the nest, and there it was. I saw three eggs, reached out my hand, and picked up one of them. Its incomparable warmth engrossed me for some time. Can you contemplate warmth, *a warmth*, with its uniqueness differentiated? Absurd! Warmth is a certain degree of heat. Well, all right, then, that's not what it was, because I held the egg in my hand, put it against my cheek, my lips, my eyelids, and it ended up losing its uniqueness, ended up being a thing with the same temperature as my hand. So much so that I picked up another egg and found in it once again the same *fresh* warmth, in other words, a warmth not faded but intact. I didn't want to take the third egg from her; I looked at the eggs against the light; they were perfectly transparent.

Even at moments when I'm most oblivious, my manual dexterity and my facility for getting anything to work with improvised tools never fail. Someone said that "a person who can't drive nails with a saw and saw with a hammer is not an experimenter," and I'm an experimenter. Without stopping to think about it, on the buckle of my wristwatch I found the sharp point I needed to puncture the eggs. I sucked on them; it had been more than twenty-four hours since I'd had anything to eat, and I didn't plan to have lunch. The maid would insist on bringing me something, but I'd tell her to leave me in peace; I wouldn't let anything disturb my remaining twenty-four hours of solitude.

I came back up to the tower, sat down in front of the notebook, and tried to continue with what I'd left hanging. Impossible. I reread a little of it, because I seemed to have lost the thread, and as I read the sentence, "The beings that know they're vulnerable, edible," I tried to remember the famous line from Whitman, but it was useless; I never knew it well. Why does man have to live from the flesh of the ox? I thought about this for a long time, I thought about our tremendous enslavement to need. But suddenly I said, it's not only that! I got up and walked from one side of the room to the other, living everything *that is*, everything *that had just finished being*.

In order to continue what I was writing before I stopped, I had to tell about what happened in between. Now I can pick up the thread in the paragraph I left unfinished.

I who "feel called to protect them" have just crouched down in the thorny thicket, like a fox, after I sensed there was a nest. Of course I'm a carnivorous animal, subject to the need to live on another's flesh. But also a rational animal accustomed to having my needs satisfied. What will never, never ever be satisfied is my longing for pleasure.

I went down to the garden because I felt like I was dying of nausea, of vertigo; it seemed to me I was totally drunk on coffee and cigars, which I smoke endlessly. This physical discomfort distracted me a little from my inner cataclysm, but all it took was the clucking, with its betrayal, and an irresistible instinct led me to surprise that nearby life, and then the ecstasy of contact made me feel a sort of thirst for that taste. And I found it impossible to define the ineffable warmth with a specific number of degrees of heat because I would have wanted to find an epithet for it that would indicate something recently emerged from living innards. That smooth, immaculate thing, formed in the moist membranes of a womb, had been deposited in the nest, sheltered and cared for until the moment when my steps made the chicken run off, letting out a few trills that sounded like swearing.

And all that, the chicken's fright as she was surprised in her illicit nest where she had her secret, where she would go one tiny step at a time, slipping between the little thorns and fluffing up her feathers, settling herself in the site of her pleasure, all that, the three warm, defenseless eggs, each of them contemplating within a chick coiled around itself, condensing itself, preparing to chirp and scamper, all that had come to a couple of shells tossed in the ditch because I'd punctured them and sucked on them. All that was what I'd found delicious because it was something so authentically alive, so close to the generative female, because its warmth was like a dialogue between two lives, a warmth given, loaned. Like the warmth left in the necklace's pearls! But the pearls' warmth did not engender life, it could only seep out in the abstract vibration of a pact. The vibrations from this other warmth were words of love between two creatures' bloods, and I had broken them, violated them.

Sentimentalism? What foolishness! I assume there's no one stupid enough to think I'm talking about a brown, speckled hen. No, I'm talking about a hen as large as the universal womb, which beats and radiates warmth, produces and incubates gentle, smooth, and appetizing things—everything in which contact with the hand is followed by the impulse to apply one's lips and suck.

The matron sucking on an ice cream at the hour of the Angelus, leaning against a tree on Arenales! I recall saying she was eating freely, as if she were alone, because it was the movement of her mouth that made the biggest impression on me. If her face had been at rest as I passed, I would surely have noticed that she was pretty, but I wouldn't have turned to look at her. What happened as I took a couple of steps was that her mouth, which at first was spread open in a wide smile, puckered a little without actually closing, advanced toward the ice cream, and nibbled at it with a slow pressure. The movement of her mouth held such an appealingly free expression of desire that my own desire was awakened. Because my emotion was obviously nothing more than desire, although a curious, passive desire. I didn't want to throw myself violently on that woman, I wanted to find myself between her hands and, from the ice cream's vantage, watch her mouth change suddenly and advance toward mine.

The atmosphere in that dusk had been highly charged with eroticism, it had encompassed everything. It began disclosing itself as I leaned out the ironing-room window: then the couples in the depth of the beer factory, the girl gleaming brightly as she walked beside the lighted shop windows, the boys rolling around on the sidewalk, panting in an intertwining of arms and legs that turned them into a living knot, and, finally, the woman with her inviting ice cream.

This whole theory of love had led me to think, a little while later as I was sitting outside a café: "Now I know what my mission is: to ask for clemency for human pleasure, for the desire for luxury, sweetness, superfluity." In other words, from here I can now see those two moments of dusk as identical: the one at the zoo, when it seemed night was coming in order to devour "all flesh," and the one on Arenales, when the hunger for human flesh was on the loose.

I decided to formulate my allegation! What allegation can I formulate? I belong to the party of hunger, of desire, and being from that species, I receive a tribute of love of which I'm not worthy. But it's obvious I receive it *because I am that way*. Just as I am I present myself before Quitina, haloed by my peacock's tail.

Should I clarify this or not? I can't clarify something that's clear as day to me. I can't clarify it! I don't even know how to talk about it, I don't know what will have to happen for me to understand it rationally, but the thing is, I know what the peacock's tail represents. I know what's written on it, I know it offers graphic proof, that its purpose is inscribed like a text. In short, I know it's a system of praise like any other, which is an apology, a dithyramb of the act of love. It's like the man who says to his beloved: "I will give you a kingdom." It's an excessive promise that fascinates, terrifies, and immobilizes, as if to say: "I will breathe the explosion of a million stars into your body, I will inject you with gold and emeralds."

Luxury! Always luxury and pleasure! But enough talk about chickens! I want to talk about eros, I want to talk about love and good. I don't know why I'm incapable of seeking them on some other path.

I don't know where the path I'm following might take me, but even so, I don't have the least doubt about its origin: I know it starts from love. The part about good is what's doubtful. How can this be? If I call my inclination a path, and I know this inclination shoots off from love, can it possibly lead toward anything but good? It's the part about love I need to analyze.

In the first place, what right do I have to use this word "love" so recklessly? Am I alluding to something concrete and demonstrable or to a beautifully colored nebula? So far I've given no factual proof of my love of humankind, but I can definitely affirm my not being inhabited by the vermin that are mankind's natural enemies—greed, envy, falsehood. If I notice the existence of something in the place I know to be indisputably free of those emotions, there's no cause to doubt that it's love. But is there cause to believe it is?

There might be a sign. I've been so daring with respect to taking on my humanity, or more precisely, so much humanity has polarized in me, I feel a solidarity with all human beings. I believe that until now this solidarity has been useless, but another sign is my wanting it to be of some use. Will I dare to employ it in some practical way? Can any good come of my action?

I'll return to the context of transactions. Let's suppose that now I set out to do good. What I can do isn't much; I can, as I've said, organize a system of justice that governs the life of a small group of people. Do I have the right to believe that with the moderate well-being I give to a few—fifty, a hundred—I pay off the license and luxury of my previous life?

Of course I can give something more, in addition to that small material well-being, and of course if I alluded to luxury in my life I wasn't alluding to material luxury; mine was never extraordinary in any way, and I never lost any sleep worrying about increasing it. The luxury of my life was my mind's freedom and my unbridled ambition for plenitude. If now I set myself the goal of giving other people some inner good, what do I give them? The lesson I've learned? Will I, who can influence them, everyone and every one, lead them along a path of moderation, continence, and restraint? In other words, will I give them what I don't want for myself, what I never desired nor ever will be able to desire; what they never desired, when my movement toward them, my love never doubted, because it was the verification of our brotherhood—was inspired by the climate of their longings? When I promised at a moment of true communion to be their attorney, to plead for mercy for their senses, to pour all my strength into a superhuman struggle and to save for them—also for myself, of course—what everyone and every one desired: *that and not something else?*

I know *now* that license leads to a bad end, and I want sincerely to prevent others from rushing off in that direction; I can start shouting, Be careful, don't take that path, don't go near it! But if they ask me, What is that, that path, where does it lead? then I must describe the danger to them, and I'm afraid my description will present them with such a radiant image that they'll race toward it. Because I can influence others. Definitely. I can influence, and I want to influence. Their souls also tempt me; on them I can also exercise my longing for contact.

What rubbish! Inertia is so blind! I've been capable of writing *I want to* and *I can*. For a moment I felt perfectly willing to turn a cartwheel before their souls, without recalling that I can no longer *promise*.

What a person has to give is his wealth, not his poverty, and I have to get used to the idea that I've lost everything. Now, the very year we have a good harvest. Now that all my material goods are guaranteed, I have enough to give and to take. I will give, there's no doubt about that, but the poem . . .

Had it not been for the decisive event, I would have created the poem. In what form, I don't know; it might have been reduced to a couple of words spoken to someone whose path just happened to cross mine, it might have been an entire work. All I know is that the happiness I would have placed in it would have been fertile. Of course, had it not been for that event, my happiness would be advancing by riding roughshod over a misfortune, it would be moving forward toward the present by trampling and erasing, the way a foot erases something in the sand, a past from which I pressed the best juice and then threw away the empty skin. With that I would have worked some good. With my hard experience and my current lack of trust, can I do it? It seems impossible to me. Nevertheless, I can't help seeing my entire past as an apprenticeship. Perhaps a useless apprenticeship, because it could only be of some use to me, and I don't want that use! No. If that's the gain my past has to offer me, I'll throw it away, I'll vomit it! Because what bit of virtue there might be in me is less than a blade of grass, less than a hair, but that blade of grass is a certain color, and it's made of a certain matter of which there's more, but it's less authentic. The only good to be found in me is a spontaneous, natural, and total sympathy for the good of others. Even so, it's obvious I didn't make much of an effort to contribute to that good. It's obvious? From a practical point of view, no doubt it is, but from a point of view that's. . . blind, subterranean . . .

I always had *true* sympathy for the good of others and a true longing for my own—the difference is merely quantitative. After having lived my own life to the full, I find myself in the most excellent of conditions to concern myself with the condition of my fellow man. Because I'm fed up? No! Because I know it's impossible to have enough. I don't run the risk of feeling too contented after giving them a moderate bit of something or other; I know they can't be sated. I know I can help a few to climb this first rung, the justice I've been given to administer, but don't let anyone get too close to me, don't let anyone see what I'm looking at or what I'm pointing out with my finger, because whoever makes that mistake will feel he's been launched like a hound, fatally after the quarry, until he's totally done for!

This longing for repose is like the gadfly that pursued Jupiter's beloved maiden. I can hear now the voices of the Oceanides around Prometheus: "May the irresistible stare of a powerful god never be fixed on me!"

Seven o'clock

The sun's beginning to set, soon the swallows will be on their way back. I wonder who Quitina's with. Maybe she's in the hotel with the boys, maybe she's taking a walk with Herminia or by herself along the breakwater, maybe she's crossing the bridge, toward the right bank of the river. Wherever she might really be, I know she's there, on that hillock, because there are places where something reaches a climax: an unsurpassable moment was lived in those places and remains in them inevitably. But what will Quitina do with that moment now? Because the eternity of that twilight is there, Quitina and I are there, watching the lone navigator row off into the distance. *We* are there and now Quitina arrives alone and doesn't find us.

I once thought Quitina would be capable of following me to damnation, but that was an illogical assumption. At that time she would certainly have followed me, but to save me. Now, however, she's the one who condemns me and condemns herself. She's the one who can raise her hand above life and give herself totally—a virgin, as always—to a hatred for the woman who has betrayed her. I know at this moment her hatred is not fed by jealousy, even less by rancor toward a woman she knows is completely unhappy, but by the deception of what she thought to be the most loyal, most pure, most *hers*—by the horror of the similarity, as in a crazy, topsy-turvy universe.

No, Quitina can't forgive. She would have forgiven me and, when she heard Drake's voice on the phone, her reaction was only sadness, because of the inevitable reminder, but there was no hate in her, and I saw she could also forgive the absent, unhappy woman. But the thing that happened, exactly like what she lived as a daring, triumphant bet—exactly!— now turned into an inevitable, persistent defeat, because it's impossible for this to heal, because everyone knows, if you begin to relive peace in benign oblivion, the unexpected, the news, even the presence will appear at any moment. Every phone call, every letter, every traveler can bring a message. Someday, news of a new existence will arrive by some means or other, and with it the fear of actually seeing. And at the same time there will be a certain desire to know about what you don't want to see. If the chance arises, the experience will provoke a feeling of aversion mixed with respect; it will be like something at once cursed and sacred.

That's the climate in which Quitina can't breathe. When—so many years ago!—Herminia tried to explain to us the contradictory feelings that hampered her happiness, Quitina said it was an experience she didn't want to endure. There is no happiness hampered here, but there is the two-facedness of an impossible hope.

I, too, was once horrified by the fused duplicity revealed in insanity. Our whole lives are filled with reprimands . . . no, it's something more unthinkable. To speak of repetition, of eternal return, is to give ungraspable phenomena forms our minds can grapple with. Because what really happens is that everything's simultaneous, everything's made once and for all, and we see it only little by little. But question and answer reply to each other at their point of origin, then they follow their course, unaware of each other, and when they meet they're mortified. This is the trap laid for us so we won't understand.

It's requiring an enormous effort to continue, but I can summon the energy. I'm out of tobacco, and I don't want to go down to the library for another tin until I see they've turned out the lights. I'll go in the dark; I know where the tobacco is, and I'll find it immediately: I don't want to see that desk.

I'm in the trough of the wave now; coffee disgusts me, but I need it. I'll brew some later, when I can smoke. If it weren't such an effort to guide my pen across the paper, I'd let flow a few lukewarm ideas that are watching me from a distance as if they weren't mine, but this is hard work. It's curious, I'm waiting to be able to lubricate the machine, and I regret not describing the slackness I feel while waiting. Later, my pipe will prompt a very efficient flow; you can feel the nicotine all the way to your hands. Your veins become quite swollen and your pulse speeds up, rather, it gets stronger; mine is usually slow, but it can turn into a fulling mill. That's the best moment to write: you don't feel either the effort or the passing of time.

It's ten o'clock. The light is marvelous, and it's a perfect night! Now I can see clearly. My exhaustion a while ago was really saturation. This morning I stopped writing a little after nine, because I felt I'd come to a dead end; I had the impression that things were all muddled because of my awkwardness. I needed to go back and check, and I reread the last two notebooks. My awkwardness is not in the telling; on the contrary, these notebooks are the skillful telling of some awkward events.

If I'd been given an average intelligence, there would be nothing strange about my not understanding, but the rules of the game were to give me enough strength to follow after truth as if it were a queen bee, to rise quite high, to get very close to it, but not have enough strength to reach it.

As early as the first notebooks, I said I was undertaking this task so someday I would understand my life. I understand increasingly less. Well, no, that statement's not accurate. I would have to say: the more I understand or, rather, now that I understand everything, I don't understand the why of anything.

I understand everything, because I see clearly how to weigh the effects of it all, but I don't understand why my first inclinations, my causes, never attained the priority they deserved.

Vanity? No. Pride? Yes, of course. Because it may be only from pride that I understand anything. I understand what I want, and I continue to want it in order to understand it. My story isn't that of the ordinary ambitious person who sees himself punished by his downfall; on the contrary, my personality has met with nothing but success. But the thing is, this success is not the superiority I believe I deserve. I believe my causes deserved to have been exempted from harmful effects. And it turns out their effects were always harmful to others. I know I don't deserve this. But it's also in the rules that the lash must fall on a healthy part of the body.

It seems like error, obstinacy, blindness, to believe my virtue lies in my aversion to the evil worked by others when, at the beginning of my life, I would have been capable of condemning and destroying. Nevertheless, it's not obstinacy: that beginning privilege *was my due*. Because if what drove me was misguided (assuming God knew, as He did, the faith I had in it), the obstacles placed in my path should have been respectable, superior enemies that gave me some clear indication of the path toward humility. But, no, what opposed my ever-increasing drive were despicable puppets on the ascent. Naturally, I rode roughshod over them.

That was in the days when I was moving mountains. One thing is certain, because it's in my own law: even an instance of high morality, such as moving a patriotic mountain, had things depended on me, I would have dawdled a long time before deciding to lay a finger on the mountain; I would have gazed at it for hours before losing respect for it, before opposing its will to be there where it had settled. Why, when I wanted to fight my personal battle, wasn't I faced with an Aconcagua?

Maybe it's because I was supposed to feel my smallness in the face of God's greatness? Perfectly, but then why make me feel my own greatness by putting me beside pygmies who don't believe in God, large or small?

I'm getting nothing out of this struggle, this review of my past, but a destructive fatigue. I read for seven or eight hours straight. I might have dozed off a little, although I don't think it was real sleep, because I don't feel rested. I must have experienced the type of absence that eradicates one's idea of time. The only thing I did with complete lucidity was assign headings to the two parts of my life I've written about. It's been something like finding the crest.

The first part of my life was totally paralyzed by *wanting* and *being able*, by *power*. The second, slacker, easier, has led me into the labyrinth from which the only exit is *understanding*.

And I don't understand! It's useless to ask for that grace, it's useless to implore them to give you the reason for things—that's never given. Yes, I know that some people have attained beatitude and understood everything. But they kept the secret well. I'm not too sure that those contemplatives comprehended anything. The Word of God is the only gift of obvious clarity we've received, and it's shrouded in so many shadows! Clearly, however, even with the shadows, from the moment the Word speaks to us, speaks to our carnal ears, to our perishable reason, from that moment we believe in clarity. Because clarity is edible, like the Word that Christ "once gave to creatures of a day."

I don't use that phrase from Aeschylus because I identify Christ with Prometheus, definitely not. But it did occur to me that in *Prometheus* there's an early echo of the prophecy (that's what the prophecy is, a resonance, very faint at first but growing stronger, then clearer and more precise, until the Voice arrives). It's Hermes who tells Prometheus he will only be freed by a god who descends to the region of the dead, and Christ descended to hell. With His word, given to men here on earth, he unbound Prometheus, because, nourished on that word, man became titanic and demanded a greater portion of it every day.

"I don't find Prometheus at all sympathetic," Miguel told me once. Yes, that's true, rebelliousness is unpleasant, but no one can keep it from breaking loose. I don't want to rebel courteously, the way a person demands his rights; I prefer to shout my longing for reason at the top of my lungs, because, deserved or not, I want more.

How can it be, out of all that reason, you can only attain just a tiny part? This is the unreason "so enfeebling to my reason." Halting, weak, and confused, you say: "Let's take it bit by bit," and you start to count on your fingers: "Let's see, I have one, two, three, four . . . , a thousand

..., a million ..., a hundred billion truths." But I definitely lack the truths of greatest beauty.

Father, I have sinned—I use these words, the saints did too, but the strict truth is, this is one of the truths we don't possess. Why, Lord, do you allow men to surround you with this concept? Pearls and rubies beneath the stone slab, and what will we say about the Beloved who passed through these meadows? Is it because all this gives us a slight idea of Your essence? If that's the case, what's strange about us desiring like hungry wolves? And if it's not, why don't You give us a different language, a different way to refer to You?

You changed the Word into bread and wine so that you could speak to our flesh, and flesh has no other code of intellection than the senses. With the best things they see, touch, hear; with incense and exquisite ox flesh roasting over the charcoal they call You. Why don't You allow beauty's sparkle to be always and totally, near and far, the exact equation of good for everyone and for every one?

I know You will never allow my reason to attain that sparkle, and I know my reason will remain fixed on a hunch. If beauty, pleasure, the pearls beneath the stone slab, the peacock's tail, the roses, the dusk, the street-turned-bedroom, if in everything that touches me as it passes I sniff the divine, and if I must pay dearly for so wanting to touch it, then I can justly say that "with reason I complain about Your beauty."

It's twelve o'clock, and I'm sure that from the hotel you can hear the sea beating against the breakwater. Quitina is probably tossing in bed, maybe she gets up and peers out the window. I don't think she'll take a walk, because the place is too scary. One night we went out together to the end of that breakwater: the sea is always terrible at night, but there it's worse, because there are tiny iron horns peering from the sunken boats under the water, which seems to get caught on them, and they cast a sort of spell. It's sad, that coast, although it's very beautiful, and the dunes are magnificent.

Quitina is probably tossing in bed, not far from those drowned souls. She's probably poking her head out the window, and I think she's even capable of taking a walk at midnight—I hope Herminia's keeping an eye on her. Quitina was never afraid. Before, it seemed to me that this resulted from her having led such a safe life, and if she's not afraid now, it's probably because now she disdains safety. But could Quitina possibility not be afraid of herself? That very sad coast, with its sunken boats, is less scary than Quitina; the dead souls beneath the water cast less of a spell than the dead she carries in her breast.

I don't know which causes me greater anguish—those nights in the hotel, facing the sea and dunes, or the afternoons on the riverbank. Because now, if she's peering out the window—I seem to sense that she is—there's something homogeneous in it all. Now Quitina is not facing the sea, she's as fearful as the sea, and the sea continues in her; the waves reach wherever she stands.

Instead, both of us stand on the right bank of the river, and what will our ghosts do if she arrives, laden with death up to her throat? Will they be able to take her in their arms, rock her with the rhythm of that verse of poetry, get her soul flowing again until the blood tints her lips? No, ghosts can't do that when their enemy is not a ghost. Ghosts can't lift an earthenware pot and smash a head. Quitina could do it, and she refrained. Now, when she finds herself among them, far away, with reality abolished, maybe she'll deal them the blow with the mace she suppressed in the library; maybe she'll destroy them, ripping them roots and all from the past, maybe she'll succeed in making them *not have been*.

Lord! Why do you grant evil such strength? Why, if I ask You, won't You rip the error out of my past when, instead, You allowed error, evil free rein to wreak havoc? I'm asking You to turn the laws of the universe inside out, to give me back my happiness, my purity, and confidence, concepts I don't have to look up in the dictionary. But as I say to You, "Give them back to me!" I think: then I had them. And I look at my past, I review the places where I thought they were, and they aren't there. They're not even there. I take one fragment, highlight an instant I called *happiness* and see it in a different hue. *I feel* that I never experienced happiness, and *I know* this is false: *I know* I experienced it, *I know* it's been ripped from me.

It's not yet one, I could take the car and drive into the city. That would be the most sensible thing. At three there are plenty of places to eat. If I ate and drank a lot, maybe I'd recover my common sense. Why not do it? Why not accept being the normal man I've always tried to be?

I'll be there in less than three hours, walk along Callao, go into El Tropezón, and have a sumptuous meal. Around me, bourgeois men like myself will be eating with their lovers, or with their wives, or by themselves. They're all—we're all—industrialists, technicians, they all—we all—have cars parked outside and a lot of work waiting for tomorrow. All the others, just like me, have some drama in their lives, they're all fighting for loves, money, or ambition, or they're suffering from slander or failure. The city's made up of men like these, I'm one like the rest. My pride leads me to distance myself from them. The most sensible thing would be to go right now and get together with my fellow men, cutting out this nonsense fast. Nevertheless, I won't go. Maybe I'll go tomorrow, today I have something different planned.

Or maybe today I'm someone different. If I were to go—I'm still not sure I won't—I know what would happen: ten pairs of eyes would turn to look at me. Because even if I agreed to be among them, I would have this air about me, and people notice it. Women, especially, see it right away. But not only women. "The feminine half of the world," Herminia would say, because when this happens—when a certain person appears among ordinary people—the world divides; the feminine half waits expectantly as the meteor passes and all masculinity is polarized in it.

The proverbial attraction wielded by dangerous men, as well as by men who live in danger, is also true about the dangerously minded man. And the nature of this attraction is markedly erotic, because it's only the bravest and freest mind that strives for being and for *being able, powerful,* and its action is always copulative: every being knows it can be penetrated by that action and becomes paralyzed, like the female peacock facing the male.

If you can arrive at humility by imagining that in El Tropezón, in the midst of the fattest, most bourgeois public given to comfort and ignorance and drowsing before an open newspaper, you might find that certain person inside any raincoat, walking across the room, the person so unique, so powerful, so extraordinary—if humility lies in understanding this, then humility also has its charm, humility also proves man's greatness. To refuse to be one of those people is small-minded; it's more elegant to lose yourself among them and go about your daily chores, just like anybody else. Definitely, I should go and get the car right now. But if I did, I would lose these forty-eight hours of tension I'm determined to maintain. The city's there, with its restaurants and bourgeois people; I can go whenever I want. The more solitude I store up here, the more I charge my batteries, the more I'll be able to offer the anonymous person I meet later among my fellow men.

It's about to strike three, I don't know how the time passed. I stopped writing and, for the hundredth time, I made coffee, cleaned my pipe, left it all ready beside the couch and went to stand under the shower, because tonight's turning out to be even hotter than last night. Then, I opened the wardrobe to look for matches in the pocket of one of my jackets.

That was more than forty minutes ago, and what I want to describe lasted a couple of seconds. Now there's a whole throng of ideas after me, pressing on me from behind this one; until I get free of it I won't be able to make way for the others.

What happened was I opened the closet and saw a bottle of cologne on the upper shelf; I took off the stopper and splashed a lot of cologne on my head, so much it ran down my shoulders and chest. I left the bottle on the shelf and began to rub myself with the cologne.

Oh, it's easy to say someone's riding in a colectivo and, because of some small ordinary incident, a passenger or you yourself ceases to be who he is and turns into Man, into Humanity. It definitely doesn't frighten anyone to hear that, but what I want to say is truly outrageous. Nevertheless, I'll say it.

There, facing the open closet, I stood absorbed for quite a while, looking into the mirror and finding the beauty of man.

The actual sight holds no novelty for me. In the summer I see myself naked in this mirror every day. But every day I'm me; half an hour ago I was *the form that's been given to man.*

Why did Quitina say that about the rower resembling a soul? I don't know, I never asked myself. When I heard her say it, it seemed obvious to me, and now it's the only likeness I can find for my body. That's it! The only thing a body can resemble is a soul. And who do body and soul resemble? Ah! . . . And if they resemble Him, why don't they resemble each other a little more?

The thing is, the more I think about the similarity, the greater it seems. They do resemble each other! We resemble each other! What I saw in the mirror was His beauty reflected in me. That beauty was something like the hand from which Adam becomes detached. Definitely, as he sleeps, Adam falls like a fruit from the hand of God. And then . . . Then, having been stripped of the beauty of the gods, we were finally allowed to see our God naked . . . but dead.

What I've seen now, Beauty, being reflected in a living man, is one of the things forbidden to us. Nevertheless, I've seen it.

The clock just struck three, within an hour it will start to get light. Might one be able to stop the sun while it's still moving through the other hemisphere? Why not? If you're *able* to do one thing, you're able to do anything.

I wish this hour of deep night left to me were immense. I'm terrified of seeing the dawn, even though I love it so much. I never understood how anyone could feel anguish as he saw dawn come; for me it was the moment when night was elevated to memory. Now, everything has changed.

My watch, which I took off so it wouldn't get wet, is leaning against the bronze frog, and it doesn't seem to be obeying me much; it's advancing faster than I'd like, because from time to time my imagination goes after something that's hard to grasp—I have the feeling it's an instant, but I look at my watch, and it has advanced. I should stop writing: what I'm trying to do is unattainable. I've reached the point of high tension where the activity of thought bolts out of control, and I'm trying to narrate the death agony of my reason in a reasonable way.

Until now I haven't said a word that would give any indication of that agony. It's definitely impossible to be the boxer and, at the same time, the referee, as well as the speaker who refers to the agony.

Besides, when I define something and I'm just about to say it, it always turns out to be something I've already said a long time before. I've spent an infinite amount of time, a hundred lives, wanting to say the same thing, wanting to do the same thing, and the alternatives are always: *to want, to be able, to understand.*

Now, this fear of dawn is something new: it's a fear of *not wanting.*

The loftiest points I've reached in my explanations have been the aspiration to be able—the aspiration to power—, the petition that would make the butterfly's wings move. This means, strictly speaking, *the answer.* This would mean *seeing* God; and it's common knowledge you can't see Him without dying. The fighter's most audacious blow is to want to see Him just the same.

The other point is lofty in its depth: it's the sounding of the abyss, and it was formulated completely in that word: *Great!* At that time I approached the answer without being afraid, because it seemed to me that *not wanting was impossible* in me. I was sure I was clever enough to loosen the knot—the way you study a knot on a rope until you know exactly how it's made—, to loosen it, follow the string in all its loops without untying, without undoing it. These are my two peaks.

I know very well there are simple, categorical human laws, which I've broken. I've broken the Ten Commandments to my heart's content. To say "I have sinned, I have sinned!" may be a virtue in others; in me it's a simple conclusion: it's obvious that I've sinned.

Does this mean I'm incapable of contrition? No, in me there is deep contrition. *Deep*: above it floats my unsinkable reason, wanting to know why I sinned. No, not that: it wants to know why, when I carried the opposite of sin inside me (because, if there are opposites, these are incontestably: sin, in other words, evil, and love, in other words, good), why I've been able to sin.

Simple and categorical human laws I could have obeyed, simply doing my duty in the world, being one of those men in whom the citizen's personality trots along peacefully and healthily, with no more than a slightly troubled conscience, for which there are always analgesics. But if I've found it impossible to be one of those men, it's been from an excess of . . .

I see huge excesses in myself, huge excesses of Your generosity. And I don't lack gratitude, but as I consider Your generosity, gauge the value of Your gifts to see how much gratitude they merit, I see they're enormous: the greatest of them, this reason, which I use to gauge their value and which, stunned by such greatness, wonders: why not a little more?

I'm repeating, I'm always repeating. Before, when I saw Your image and likeness in the mirror, I stated without embarrassment that I'd seen Your reflection in my body, because, after all, it's the form You gave to Your Son so You could crucify Him. And man is satisfied with this: man conceives of no more beauty than the beauty You gave him. But more reason! Why do You crucify reason in "the sons of Your beauty"?

My watch definitely will not obey me, but the sky remains dark. The cocks have crowed many times, but day is still distant. Chores, discontent, gossip are all distant. Gossip! What could I care about gossip? About God they said . . .

Yes, definitely, they also said things about You. Not only about Your Son, embodied in human form, but about You, Father, they also said things about You. They said that you're opium. How stupid! Saying You're opium when You could keep a stone from sleeping!

Who pays any attention to gossip? You know very well who You are, and I know too. I know You're insomnia, restlessness, vigil, vigilante.

About opium: well, I would also say You put opium in nature, You store it as that flower, in the seed. But the white corolla, alert, its white so total it holds the whole spectrum—a secret manifesto . . . The corolla is right there, looking at me with its eye and its thick lashes, pure and inexorable as it hears my confession.

By the time Father Ugarte read the last page there was enough light to see clearly on the patio. He poked his head out the window and stood there for a while wondering if that faint light was dawn or dusk, but he realized immediately that it was morning. He remembered that the bells had already chimed and that he had heard them as far off in the distance, the way he used to hear the village's church bell from his room when he was a little boy, even though the church was half a league away.

He guessed that he'd been reading for about fourteen or fifteen hours, counting the short breaks demanded by the routine at the school. The day before, Miguel Vallejo, a former student, had appeared in the morning and entrusted him with four notebooks and a small package, containing a box that held a dried butterfly.

The boy had begged him to read the notebooks, telling him that his cousin, a man whom he had loved dearly and who was rather . . . strange, although . . . an excellent person, had died very suddenly and mysteriously. Miguel had found him when he went to his house, with the notebook beside him, open to the last page.

"Read the last word, please, Father," Miguel had said.

"Well, yes," the priest agreed after reading it; "you might have good reason for saying that. Leave the notebooks here. And that bundle?"

"That too, keep it."

Father Ugarte unwrapped the butterfly, and saw that one of its wings had broken off.

"It's broken," he said.

"I don't know, maybe you'll be able to tell when you read the notebooks."

Father Ugarte read without stopping, without taking a breath, and when he had finished he said nothing. He poked his head out of the window, dried his forehead with his handkerchief, because it was already quite warm although the sun had still not risen, or perhaps he was sweating from reading, as if he had exercised vigorously, and he merely muttered under his breath.

"Who knows?"

656   *Dream of Reason*

In the European Women Writers series

The Human Family
By Lou Andreas-Salomé
Translated and with an introduction by Raleigh Whitinger

Artemisia
By Anna Banti
Translated by
Shirley D'Ardia Caracciolo

The Edge of Europe
By Angela Bianchini
Translated by Angela M. Jeannet
and David Castronuovo

Bitter Healing
German Women Writers, 1700–1830
An Anthology
Edited by Jeannine Blackwell
and Susanne Zantop

Tomboy
By Nina Bouraoui
Translated by Marjorie Attignol
Salvodon and Jehanne-Marie
Gavarini

Dream of Reason
By Rosa Chacel
Translated by Carol Maier

The Maravillas District
By Rosa Chacel
Translated by d. a. démers

Memoirs of Leticia Valle
By Rosa Chacel
Translated by Carol Maier

There Are No Letters Like Yours
The Correspondence of Isabelle
de Charrière and Constant
d'Hermenches
By Isabelle de Charrière
Translated and with an introduction and annotations by Janet
Whatley and Malcolm Whatley

The Book of Promethea
By Hélène Cixous
Translated by Betsy Wing

The Terrible but Unfinished Story
of Norodom Sihanouk, King of
Cambodia
By Hélène Cixous
Translated by Juliet Flower
MacCannell, Judith Pike, and
Lollie Groth

The Governor's Daughter
By Paule Constant
Translated by Betsy Wing

Trading Secrets
By Paule Constant
Translated by Betsy Wing
With an introduction by
Margot Miller

White Spirit
By Paule Constant
Translated by Betsy Wing

Maria Zef
By Paola Drigo
Translated by Blossom
Steinberg Kirschenbaum

To order or obtain more information on these or other University
of Nebraska Press titles, visit
www.nebraskapress.unl.edu.